Praise for
HARRY TURTLEDOVE

THE COLONIZATION SERIES

"The whole saga . . . certainly ranks as something few other writers would have attempted and even fewer would have brought off so well."

—*Booklist*

"Hugo winner Turtledove lives up to his billing as the grand master of alternative history."

—*Publishers Weekly* (starred review)

"[A] tour de force of speculative historical fiction. Highly recommended."

—*Library Journal*

THE WORLDWAR SERIES

"Readers will have a perfectly delightful time. . . . Turtledove's storytelling and historiography now march in perfect step. World War II buffs will have a particular romp."

—*Chicago Sun-Times*

"Totally fascinating . . . triumphant . . . possibly the most ambitious in the subgenre's history and definitely the work of one of alternate history's authentic modern masters."

—*Booklist*

BOOKS BY HARRY TURTLEDOVE

The Guns of the South

THE WORLDWAR SAGA
Worldwar: In the Balance
Worldwar: Tilting the Balance
Worldwar: Upsetting the Balance
Worldwar: Striking the Balance

COLONIZATION
Colonization: Second Contact
Colonization: Down to Earth
Colonization: Aftershocks

Homeward Bound

THE VIDESSOS CYCLE
The Misplaced Legion
An Emperor for the Legion
The Legion of Videssos
Swords of the Legion

THE TALE OF KRISPOS
Krispos Rising
Krispos of Videssos
Krispos the Emperor

THE TIME OF TROUBLES SERIES
The Stolen Throne
Hammer and Anvil
The Thousand Cities
Videssos Besieged

A World of Difference
Departures
Counting Up, Counting Down

How Few Remain

THE GREAT WAR
The Great War: American Front
The Great War: Walk in Hell
The Great War: Breakthroughs

AMERICAN EMPIRE
American Empire: Blood and Iron
American Empire: The Center Cannot Hold
American Empire: The Victorious Opposition

SETTLING ACCOUNTS
Return Engagement
Drive to the East
The Grapple (forthcoming)

HOMEWARD BOUND

HARRY TURTLEDOVE

BALLANTINE BOOKS • NEW YORK

Homeward Bound is a work of fiction. Names, places, and incidents either are products of the author's imagination or are used fictitiously.

2006 Del Rey Mass Market Edition

Copyright © 2004 by Harry Turtledove

All rights reserved.

Published in the United States by Del Rey Books, an imprint of The Random House Publishing Group, a division of Random House, Inc., New York.

DEL REY is a registered trademark and the Del Rey colophon is a trademark of Random House, Inc.

Originally published in hardcover in the United States by Del Rey Books, an imprint of The Random House Publishing Group, a division of Random House, Inc., in 2004.

ISBN 0-345-45847-8

Printed in the United States of America

www.delreybooks.com

OPM 9 8 7 6 5 4 3 2 1

☆ **I** ☆

Fleetlord Atvar pressed his fingerclaw into the opening for a control. *There is a last time for everything,* he thought with dignity as a holographic image sprang into being above his desk. He'd studied the image of that armed and armored Big Ugly a great many times indeed in the sixty years—thirty of this planet's slow revolutions around its star—since coming to Tosev 3.

The Tosevite rode a beast with a mane and a long, flowing tail. He wore chainmail that needed a good scouring to get rid of the rust. His chief weapon was an iron-tipped spear. The spearhead also showed tiny flecks of rust, and some not so tiny. To protect himself against similarly armed enemies, the Tosevite carried a shield with a red cross painted on it.

Another poke of the fingerclaw made the hologram disappear. Atvar's mouth fell open in an ironic laugh. The Race had expected to face that kind of opposition when it sent its conquest fleet from Home to Tosev 3. Why not? It had all seemed so reasonable. The probe had shown no high technology anywhere on the planet, and the conquest fleet was only sixteen hundred years behind—eight hundred years here. How much could technology change in eight hundred years?

Back on Home, not much. Here . . . Here, when the conquest fleet arrived, the Big Uglies had been fighting an immense war among themselves, fighting not with spears and beasts and chainmail but with machine guns, with cannon-carrying landcruisers, with killercraft that spat death from the air, with radio and telephones. They'd been working on guided missiles and on nuclear weapons.

And so, despite battles bigger and fiercer than anyone back on Home could have imagined, the conquest fleet hadn't quite

1

conquered. More than half the land area of Tosev 3 had come under its control, but several not-empires—a notion of government that still seemed strange to Atvar—full of Big Uglies (and, not coincidentally, full of nuclear weapons) remained independent. Atvar couldn't afford to wreck the planet to beat the Tosevites into submission, not with the colonization fleet on the way and only twenty local years behind the fleet he commanded. The colonists had to have somewhere to settle.

He'd never expected to need to learn to be a diplomat. Being diplomatic with the obstreperous Big Uglies wasn't easy. Being diplomatic with the males and females of the conquest fleet had often proved even harder. They'd expected everything to be waiting for them and in good order when they arrived. They'd expected a conquered planet full of submissive primitives. They'd been loudly and unhappily surprised when they didn't get one. Here ten local years after their arrival, a lot of them still were.

Atvar's unhappy musings—and had he had any other kind since coming to Tosev 3?—cut off when his adjutant walked into the room. Pshing's body paint, like that of any adjutant, was highly distinctive. On one side, it showed his own not particularly high rank. On the other, it matched the body paint of his principal—and Atvar's pattern, as befit his rank, was the most ornate and elaborate on Tosev 3.

Pshing bent into the posture of respect. Even his tailstump twitched to one side. "I greet you, Exalted Fleetlord," he said in the hissing, popping language of the Race.

"And I greet you," Atvar replied.

Straightening, Pshing said, "They are waiting for you."

"Of course they are," Atvar said bitterly. "Eaters of carrion always gather to feast at a juicy corpse." His tailstump quivered in anger.

"I am sorry, Exalted Fleetlord." Pshing had the courtesy to sound as if he meant it. "But when the recall order came from Home, what could you do?"

"I could obey, or I could rebel," Atvar answered. His adjutant hissed in horror at the very idea. Among the Race, even saying such things was shocking. There had been mutinies and rebellions here on Tosev 3. Perhaps more than anything else, that told what sort of place this was. Atvar held up a placating hand. "I obey. I will go into cold sleep. I will return to Home. Maybe by the time I get there, those who will sit in judgment on me will have learned more. Our signals, after all, travel twice as fast as our starships."

"Truth, Exalted Fleetlord," Pshing said. "Meanwhile, though, as I told you, those who wish to say farewell await you."

"I know they do." Atvar waggled his lower jaw back and forth as he laughed, to show he was not altogether amused. "Some few, perhaps, will be glad to see me. The rest will be glad to see me—go." He got to his feet and sardonically made as if to assume the posture of respect before Pshing. "Lead on. I follow. Why not? It is a pleasant day."

The fleetlord even meant that. Few places on Tosev 3 fully suited the Race; most of this world was cold and damp compared to Home. But the city called Cairo was perfectly temperate, especially in summertime. Pshing held the door open for Atvar. Only the great size of that door, like the height of the ceiling, reminded Atvar that Big Uglies had built the place once called Shepheard's Hotel. As the heart of the Race's rule on Tosev 3, it had been extensively modified year after year. It would not have made a first-class establishment back on Home, perhaps, but it would have been a decent enough second-class place.

When Atvar strode into the meeting hall, the males and females gathered there all assumed the posture of respect—all save Fleetlord Reffet, the commander of the colonization fleet, the only male in the room whose body paint matched Atvar's in complexity. Reffet confined himself to a civil nod. Civility was as much as Atvar had ever got from him. He'd usually had worse, for Reffet had never stopped blaming him for not presenting Tosev 3 to the colonists neatly wrapped up and decorated.

To Atvar's surprise, a handful of tall, erect Tosevites towered over the males and females of the Race. Because they did not slope forward from the hips and because they had no tailstumps, their version of the posture of respect was a clumsy makeshift. Their pale, soft skins and the cloth wrappings they wore stood out against the clean simplicity of green-brown scales and body paint.

"Did we have to have Big Uglies here?" Atvar asked. "If it

were not for the trouble the Big Uglies caused us, I would not be going Home now." *I would be Atvar the Conqueror, remembered in history forever. I will be remembered in history, all right, but not the way I had in mind before I set out with the conquest fleet.*

"When some of them asked to attend, Exalted Fleetlord, it was difficult to say no," Pshing replied. "That one there, for instance—the one with the khaki wrappings and the white fur on his head—is Sam Yeager."

"Ah." Atvar used the affirmative hand gesture. "Well, you are right. If he wanted to be here, you could not very well have excluded him. Despite his looks, he might as well be a member of the Race himself. He has done more for us than most of the males and females in this room. Without him, we probably would have fought the war that annihilated the planet."

He strode through the crowd toward the Big Ugly, ignoring his own kind. No doubt they would talk about his bad manners later. Since this was his last appearance on Tosev 3, he didn't care. He would do as he pleased, not as convention dictated. "I greet you, Sam Yeager," he said.

"And I greet you, Exalted Fleetlord," Yeager replied in the language of the Race. His accent was mushy, as a Big Ugly's had to be. But the rhythms of his speech could almost have come from Home. More than any other Tosevite, he thought like a male of the Race. "I wish you good fortune in your return. And I also want you to know how jealous I am of you."

"Of me? By the Emperor, why?" When Atvar spoke of his sovereign, he swung his eye turrets so he looked down to the ground as a token of respect and reverence. He hardly even knew he did it; such habits had been ingrained in him since hatchlinghood.

"Why? Because you are going Home, and I wish I could see your world."

Atvar laughed. "Believe me, Sam Yeager, some things are better wished for than actually obtained." Would he have said that to one of his own species? Probably not. It somehow seemed less a betrayal and more a simple truth when told to a Tosevite.

Yeager made the affirmative gesture, though it was not one

Big Uglies used among themselves. "That is often true. I am jealous even so," he said. "Exalted Fleetlord, may I present to you my hatchling, Jonathan Yeager, and his mate, Karen Yeager?"

"I am pleased to meet you," Atvar said politely.

Both of the other Big Uglies assumed the posture of respect. "We greet you, Exalted Fleetlord," they said together in the Race's language. The female's voice was higher and shriller than the male's. Her head fur was a coppery color. Jonathan Yeager cut off all the fur on his head except for the two strips above his small, immobile eyes; Big Uglies used those as signaling devices. Many younger Tosevites removed their head fur in an effort to seem more like members of the Race. Little by little, assimilation progressed.

On Tosev 3, though, assimilation was a two-way street. In colder parts of the planet, males and females of the Race wore Tosevite-style cloth wrappings to protect themselves from the ghastly weather. And, thanks to the unfortunate effects of the herb called ginger, the Race's patterns of sexuality here had to some degree begun to resemble the Big Uglies' constant and revolting randiness. Atvar sighed. Without ginger, his life would have been simpler. *Without Tosev 3, my life would have been simpler,* he thought glumly.

"Please excuse me," he told the Yeagers, and went off to greet another Tosevite, the foreign minister—foreign commissar was the term the not-empire preferred—of the SSSR. The male called Gromyko had features almost as immobile as if he belonged to the Race.

He spoke in his own language. A Tosevite interpreter said, "He wishes you good fortune on your return to your native world."

"I thank you," Atvar said, directly to the Tosevite diplomat. Gromyko understood the language of the Race, even if he seldom chose to use it. His head bobbed up and down, his equivalent of the affirmative gesture.

Shiplord Kirel came up to Atvar. Kirel had commanded the *127th Emperor Hetto,* the bannership of the conquest fleet. "I am glad you are able to go Home, Exalted Fleetlord," he said, "but this recall is undeserved. You have done everything in your power to bring this world into the Empire."

"We both know that," Atvar replied. "Back on Home, what do they know? Signals take eleven local years to get there, and another eleven to get back. And yet they think they can manage events here from there. Absurd!"

"They do it on the other two conquered planets," Kirel said.

"Of course they do." Atvar scornfully wiggled an eye turret. "With the Rabotevs and the Hallessi, nothing ever happens."

Seeing that Ttomalss, the Race's leading expert on Big Uglies, was at the reception, Atvar went over to him. "I greet you, Exalted Fleetlord," the senior psychologist said. "It is a pleasure to find Sam Yeager at your reception."

"He is your corresponding fingerclaw on the other hand, is he not?" Atvar said, and Ttomalss made the affirmative gesture. The fleetlord asked, "And how is Kassquit these days?"

"She is well. Thank you for inquiring," Ttomalss answered. "She still presents a fascinating study on the interaction of genetic and cultural inheritances."

"Indeed," Atvar said. "I wonder what she would make of Home. A pity no one has yet developed cold-sleep techniques for the Tosevite metabolism. As for me, I almost welcome the oblivion cold sleep will bring. The only pity is that I will have to awaken to face the uncomprehending fools I am bound to meet on my return."

Sam Yeager looked at the doctor across the desk from him. Jerry Kleinfeldt, who couldn't have been above half his age, looked back with the cocksure certainty medical men all seemed to wear these days. *It wasn't like that when I was a kid,* Yeager thought. It wasn't just that he'd almost died as an eleven-year-old in the influenza epidemic of 1918. Back then, you could die of any number of things that were casually treatable now. Doctors had known it, too, and shown a little humility. Humility, though, had gone out of style with the shingle bob and the Charleston.

Kleinfeldt condescended to glance down at the papers on his desk. "Well, Colonel Yeager, I have to tell you, you're in damn good shape for a man of seventy. Your blood pressure's no higher than mine, no sign of malignancy, nothing that would obviously keep you from trying this, if you're bound and determined to do it."

"Oh, I am, all right," Sam Yeager said. "Being who you are, being what you are, you'll understand why, too, won't you?"

"Who, me?" When Dr. Kleinfeldt grinned, it made him look even more like a kid than he did already—which, to Yeager's jaundiced eye, was quite a bit. The fluorescent lights overhead gleamed off his shaven scalp. Given what he specialized in, was it surprising he'd ape the Lizards as much as a mere human being could?

But suddenly, Sam had no patience for joking questions or grins. "Cut the crap," he said, his voice harsh. "We both know that if the government gave a good goddamn about me, they wouldn't let me be a guinea pig. But they're glad to let me give it a try, and they halfway hope it doesn't work. More than halfway, or I miss my guess."

Kleinfeldt steepled his fingers. Now he looked steadily back at Sam. The older man realized that, despite his youth, despite the foolishness he affected, the doctor was highly capable. He wouldn't have been involved with this project if he weren't. Picking his words with care, he said, "You exaggerate."

"Do I?" Yeager said. "How much?"

"Some," Kleinfeldt answered judiciously. "You're the man who knows as much about the Race as any human living. And you're the man who can think like a Lizard, which isn't the same thing at all. Having you along when this mission eventually gets off the ground—and *eventually* is the operative word here—would be an asset."

"And there are a lot of people in high places who think having me dead would be an asset, too," Sam said.

"Not to the point of doing anything drastic—or that's my reading of it, anyhow," Dr. Kleinfeldt said. "Besides, even if everything works just the way it's supposed to, you'd be, ah, effectively dead, you might say."

"On ice, I'd call it," Yeager said, and Dr. Kleinfeldt nodded. With a wry chuckle, Sam added, "Four or five years ago, at Fleetlord Atvar's farewell reception, I told him I was jealous that he was going back to Home and I couldn't. I didn't realize we'd come as far as we have on cold sleep."

"If you see him there, maybe you can tell him so." Kleinfeldt looked down at the papers on his desk again, then back to Sam. "You mean we own a secret or two you haven't managed to dig up?"

"Fuck you, Doc," Sam said evenly. Kleinfeldt blinked. How many years had it been since somebody came right out and said that to him? Too many, by all the signs. Yeager went on, "See, this is the kind of stuff I get from just about everybody."

After another pause for thought, Dr. Kleinfeldt said, "I'm going to level with you, Colonel: a lot of people think you've earned it."

Sam nodded. He knew that. He couldn't help knowing it. Because of what he'd done, Indianapolis had gone up in radioactive fire and a president of the United States had killed himself. The hardest part was, he couldn't make himself feel guilty about it. Bad, yes. Guilty? No. There was a difference. He wondered if he could make Kleinfeldt understand. Worth a try, maybe: "What we did to the colonization fleet was as bad as what the Japs did to us at Pearl Harbor. Worse, I'd say, because we blew up innocent civilians, not soldiers and sailors. If I'd found out the Nazis or the Reds did it and told the Lizards that, I'd be a goddamn hero. Instead, I might as well be Typhoid Mary."

"All things considered, you can't expect it would have turned out any different," the doctor said. "As far as most people are concerned, the Lizards aren't quite—people, I mean. And it's only natural we think of America first and everybody else afterwards."

"Truth—it is only natural," Sam said in the language of the Race. He wasn't surprised Kleinfeldt understood. Anyone who worked on cold sleep for humans would have to know about what the Lizards did so they could fly between the stars without getting old on the way. He went on, "It is only natural, yes. But is it right?"

"That is an argument for another time," Kleinfeldt answered, also in the Lizards' tongue. He returned to English: "Right or wrong, though, it's the attitude people have. I don't know what you can do about it."

"Not much, I'm afraid." Yeager knew that too well. He also knew the main reason he remained alive after what he'd done was that the Race had bluntly warned the United States nothing had better happen to him—or else. He asked, "What are the odds of something going wrong with this procedure?"

"Well, we think they're pretty slim, or we wouldn't be trying it on people," the doctor said. "I'll tell you something else, though: if you ever want to have even a chance of seeing Home, Colonel, this is your only way to get it."

"Yeah," Sam said tightly. "I already figured that out for myself, thanks." One of these days, people—with luck, people from the USA—would have a spaceship that could fly from the Sun to Tau Ceti, Home's star. By the time people did, though, one Sam Yeager, ex-minor-league ballplayer and science-fiction reader, current expert on the Race, would be pushing up a lily unless he went in for cold sleep pretty damn quick. "All right, Doc. I'm game—and the powers that be won't worry about me so much if I'm either on ice or light-years from Earth. Call me Rip van Winkle."

Dr. Kleinfeldt wrote a note on the chart. "This is what I thought you'd decide. When do you want to undergo the procedure?"

"Let me have a couple of weeks," Yeager answered; he'd been thinking about the same thing. "I've got to finish putting my affairs in order. It's like dying, after all. It's just like dying, except with a little luck it isn't permanent."

"Yes, with a little luck," Kleinfeldt said; he might almost have been Montresor in "The Cask of Amontillado" intoning, *Yes, for the love of God.* He looked at the calendar. "Then I'll see you here on . . . the twenty-seventh, at eight in the morning. Nothing by mouth for twelve hours before that. I'll prescribe a purgative to clean out your intestinal tract, too. It won't be much fun, but it's necessary. Any questions?"

"Just one." Sam tapped his top front teeth. "I've got full upper and lower plates—I've had 'em since my teeth rotted out after the Spanish flu. What shall I do about those? If this does work, I don't want to go to Home without my choppers. That wouldn't do me or the country much good."

"Take them out before the procedure," Dr. Kleinfeldt told him. "We'll put them in your storage receptacle. You won't go anywhere they don't."

"Okay." Yeager nodded. "Fair enough. I wanted to make

sure." He did his best not to dwell on what Kleinfeldt called a
storage receptacle. If that wasn't a fancy name for a coffin,
he'd never heard one. His wife had always insisted on looking
for the meaning behind what people said. He muttered to
himself as he got up to leave. He and Barbara had had more
than thirty good years together. If he hadn't lost her, he wondered if he would have been willing to face cold sleep. He
doubted it. He doubted it like anything, as a matter of fact.

After reclaiming his car from the parking lot, he drove
south on the freeway from downtown Los Angeles to his
home in Gardena, one of the endless suburbs ringing the city
on all sides but the sea. The sky was clearer and the air cleaner
than he remembered them being when he first moved to
Southern California. Most cars on the road these days, like
his, used clean-burning hydrogen, a technology borrowed—
well, stolen—from the Lizards. Only a few gasoline-burners
still spewed hydrocarbons into the air.

He would have rattled around his house if he'd lived there
alone. But Mickey and Donald were plenty to keep him hop-
ping instead of rattling. He'd raised the two Lizards from eggs
obtained God only knew how, raised them to be as human as
they could. They weren't humans, of course, but they came
closer to it than any other Lizards on this or any other world.

The Race had done the same thing with a human baby, and
had had a twenty-year start on the project. He'd met Kassquit,
the result of their experiment. She was very bright and very
strange. He was sure the Lizards would have said exactly the
same thing about Mickey and Donald.

"Hey, Pop!" Donald shouted when Sam came in the door.
He'd always been the more boisterous of the pair. He spoke
English as well as his mouth could shape it. Why not? It was
as much his native tongue as Sam's. "What's up?"

"Well, you know how I told you I might be going away for
a while?" Yeager said. Both Lizards nodded. They were physically full grown, which meant their heads came up to past the
pit of Sam's stomach, but they weren't grownups, or anything
close to it. He went on, "Looks like that's going to happen.
You'll be living with Jonathan and Karen when it does."

Mickey and Donald got excited enough to skitter around
the front room, their tailstumps quivering. They didn't realize

they wouldn't be seeing him again. He didn't intend to explain, either. His son and daughter-in-law could do that a little bit at a time. The Lizards had taken Barbara's death harder than he had; for all practical purposes, she'd been their mother. Among their own kind, Lizards didn't have families the way people did. That didn't mean they couldn't get attached to those near and dear to them, though. These two had proved as much.

One of these days before too long, the Race would find out what the United States and the Yeagers had done with the hatchlings. *Or to them,* Sam thought: they were as unnatural as Kassquit. But, since they'd meddled in her clay, how could they complain if humanity returned the compliment? They couldn't, or not too loudly. So Sam—so everybody—hoped, anyhow.

He did put his affairs in order. That had a certain grim finality to it. *At least I get to do it, and not Jonathan,* he thought. He took the Lizards over to Jonathan and Karen's house. He said his good-byes. Everybody kissed him, even if Donald and Mickey didn't have proper lips. *I may be the only guy ever kissed by a Lizard,* was what went through his mind as he walked out to the car.

Next morning, bright and early—why *didn't* doctors keep more civilized hours?—he went back to Dr. Kleinfeldt's. "Nothing by mouth the past twelve hours?" Kleinfeldt asked. Sam shook his head. "You used the purgative?" the doctor inquired.

"Oh, yeah. After I got home yesterday." Sam grimaced. That hadn't been any fun.

"All right. Take off your clothes and lie down here."

Sam obeyed. Kleinfeldt hooked him up to an IV and started giving him shots. He wondered if he would simply blank out, the way he had during a hernia-repair operation. It didn't work out like that. He felt himself slowing down. Dr. Kleinfeldt seemed to talk faster and faster, though his speech rhythm probably wasn't changing. Sam's thoughts stretched out and out and out. The last thing that occurred to him before he stopped thinking altogether was, *Funny, I don't feel cold.*

* * *

Kassquit bent herself into the posture of respect before Ttomalss in his office in a starship orbiting Tosev 3. Since she didn't have a tailstump, it wasn't quite perfect, but she did it as well as anyone of Tosevite blood could. Why not? She'd learned the ways of the Race, of the Empire, since the days of her hatchlinghood. She knew them much better than she did those of what was biologically her own kind.

"I greet you, superior sir," she said.

"And I greet you, Researcher," Ttomalss replied, an odd formality in his voice. He was the male who'd raised her. He was also the male who'd tried, for the most part unintentionally, to keep her dependent on him even after she grew to adulthood. That he'd failed, that she'd carved out her own place for herself, went a long way towards accounting for his constraint.

"By now, superior sir, you will, I am sure, have read my message," Kassquit said. She couldn't resist tacking on an interrogative cough at the end of the sentence, even if she claimed to be sure.

Ttomalss noticed that, as she'd intended. The way he waggled his eye turrets said he wasn't too happy about it, either. But he held his voice steady as he answered, "Yes, I have read it. How did you learn that the Big Uglies are experimenting with the technology of cold sleep?"

"That is not the question, superior sir," Kassquit said. "The question is, why was I not informed of this as soon as we discovered it? Am I not correct in believing the wild Big Uglies have been developing their techniques for more than ten local years now?"

"Well . . . yes," the male who'd raised her admitted uncomfortably.

"And is it not also true that the Tosevite male named Sam Yeager availed himself of these techniques five local years ago, and in fact did not die, as was publicly reported, and as I was led to believe?"

Ttomalss sounded even more uncomfortable. "I believe that to be the case, but I am not altogether sure of it," he replied. "The American Big Uglies are a great deal less forthcoming about their experiments, this for reasons that should be obvious to you. What we think we know is pieced together from intelligence sources and penetrations of their computer networks. They are, unfortunately, a good deal better at detecting, preventing, and confusing such penetrations than they were even a few years ago."

"And why did you prevent me from gaining access to this important—indeed, vital—information?" Kassquit demanded.

"That should also be obvious to you," Ttomalss said.

"What is obvious to me, superior sir, is that these techniques offer me something I never had before: a chance of visiting Home, of seeing the world that is the source of my . . . my being," Kassquit said. That wasn't biologically true, of course. Biologically, she was and would always be a Big Ugly. After years of shaving her entire body to try to look more like a female of the Race—forlorn hope!—she'd acknowledged that and let her hair grow. If some reactionary scholars here didn't care for the way she looked, too bad. Culturally, she was as much a part of the Empire as they were. Even Ttomalss sometimes had trouble remembering that. Kassquit continued, "Now that I have this opportunity, I *will* not be deprived of it."

After a long sigh, Ttomalss said, "I feared this would be your attitude. But do you not see how likely it is that you do not in fact have the opportunity at all, that it is in fact a snare and a delusion?"

"No." Kassquit used the negative gesture. "I do not see that at all, superior sir. If the technique is effective, why should I not use it?"

"If the technique were proved effective, I would not mind if you did use it," Ttomalss replied. "But the Big Uglies are not like us. They do not experiment and test for year after year, decade after decade, perfecting their methods before putting them into general use. They rashly forge ahead, trying out ideas still only half hatched. If they are mad enough to risk their lives on such foolishness, that is one thing. For you to risk yours is something else. For us to let you risk yours is a third thing altogether. We kept these data from you as long as we could precisely because we feared you would importune us in this fashion."

"Superior sir, my research indicates that I have probably already lived more than half my span," Kassquit said. "Must I live out all my days in exile? If I wait for certain perfection of these methods, I will wait until all my days are done. For a species, waiting and testing may be wisdom. For an individual, how can they be anything but disaster?" Tears stung her eyes. She hated them. They were a Tosevite instinctive response over which she had imperfect control.

"If the Big Uglies' methods fail, you could give up your entire remaining span of days," Ttomalss pointed out. "Have you considered that?"

Now Kassquit used the affirmative gesture. "I have indeed," she answered. "First, the risk is in my opinion worth it. Second, even if I should die, what better way to do so than completely unconscious and unaware? From all I gather, dying is no more pleasant for Tosevites than for members of the Race."

"Truth. At any rate, I believe it to be truth," Ttomalss said. "But you have not considered one other possibility. Suppose you are revived, but find yourself . . . diminished upon awakening? This too can happen."

He was right. Kassquit hadn't thought about that. She prided herself on her fierce, prickly intelligence. How would she, how could she, cope with the new world of Home if she did not have every bit of that? "I am willing to take the chance," she declared.

"Whether we are willing for you to take it may be another question," Ttomalss said.

"Oh, yes. I know." Kassquit did not bother to hide her bitterness. By the way Ttomalss' eye turrets twitched uncomfortably, he understood what she felt. She went on, "Even so, I am going to try. And you are going to do everything you can to support me." She used an emphatic cough to stress her words.

The male who'd raised her jerked in surprise. "I am? Why do you say that?"

"Why? Because you owe it to me," Kassquit answered fiercely. "You have made me into something neither scale nor bone. You treated me as an experimental animal—an interesting experimental animal, but an experimental animal even so—for all the first half of my life. Thanks to you, I think of myself at least as much as a female of the Race as I do of myself as a Tosevite."

"You *are* a citizen of the Empire," Ttomalss said. "Does that not please you?"

"By the Emperor, it does," Kassquit said, and used another emphatic cough. Ttomalss automatically cast his eye turrets down toward the metal floor at the mention of the sovereign. Kassquit had to move her whole head to make the ritual gesture of respect. She did it. She'd been trained to do it. As she usually wasn't, she was consciously aware she'd been trained to do it. She continued, "It pleases me so much, I want to see the real Empire of which I am supposed to be a part. And there is one other thing you do not seem to have considered."

"What is that?" Ttomalss asked cautiously—or perhaps *fearfully* was the better word.

"If the Big Uglies are working on cold sleep, what are they likely to do with it?" Kassquit asked. Her facial features stayed immobile. She had never learned the expressions most Big Uglies used to show emotion. Those cues required echoes during early hatchlinghood, echoes Ttomalss had been unable to give her. If she could have, though, she would have smiled a nasty smile. "What else but try to fly from star to star? If they reach Home, would it not be well to have someone there with at least some understanding and firsthand experience of them?"

She waited. Ttomalss made small, unhappy hissing noises. "I *had* not considered that," he admitted at last. "I do not believe anyone on Tosev 3 has considered it—not in that context, at any rate. You may well be right. If the Big Uglies do reach Home, we would be better off having individuals there who are familiar with them from something other than data transmissions across light-years of space. The males and females back on Home at present plainly do not qualify."

"Then you agree to support my petition to travel to Home?" Kassquit asked, eagerness in her voice if not on her face.

"If—I repeat, *if*—the Big Uglies' techniques for cold sleep prove both effective and safe, then perhaps this may be a justifiable risk." Ttomalss did not sound as if he wanted to commit himself to anything.

Kassquit knew she had to pin him down if she possibly

could. "You will support my petition?" she asked again, more
sharply this time. "Please come straight out and tell me what
you will do, superior sir."

That was plainly the last thing Ttomalss wanted to do. At
last, with obvious reluctance, he made the affirmative gesture. "Very well. I will do this. But you must see that I do it
much more for the sake of the Race and for Home than for
your personal, petty—I might even say selfish—reasons."

"Of course, superior sir." Kassquit didn't care why Ttomalss was doing as she wanted. She only cared that he was doing
it. "Whatever your reasons, I thank you."

"Make your petition. It will have my full endorsement,"
Ttomalss said. "Is there anything else?"

"No, superior sir." Kassquit knew a dismissal when she
heard one. She hurried out of Ttomalss' office. Inside, her
liver was singing. The Big Uglies spoke of the heart as the
center of emotion, but she was too much under the influence
of the Race's language—the only one she spoke—to worry
about that foolish conceit.

Even after she submitted her petition, wheels turned slowly.
More than a year of the Race went by before it was finally approved. She watched Tosev 3 from orbit. She had never visited the planet on which she'd been hatched. She did not think
she ever would. Because she'd been exposed to so few Tosevite illnesses when young, her body had inadequate defenses
against them. What would have been a trivial illness or no illness at all for the average wild Big Ugly might have killed
her.

Another snag developed when the American Big Uglies
proved reluctant to send a physician up to her starship to give
her the treatment she needed. At last, though, they were persuaded. Kassquit didn't know what went into the process of
persuasion, but it finally worked.

"So you will be going to Home, will you?" the Tosevite
asked. Even in the warmth of the starship—the Race naturally heated the interior to their standards of comfort, which
were hotter than most Tosevites cared for—he wore white
cloth wrappings. He also wore a cloth mask, to keep from in-
fecting her with microorganisms. He spoke the language of

the Race reasonably well. These days, most educated Tose-vites did.

"I hope so, yes," she answered.

"All right." He bobbed his head up and down, the Big Uglies' equivalent of the affirmative gesture. "Our treatment is based on the one the Race uses. I will leave detailed in-structions with the Race on how to care for you, what in-jections to give you when you are revived, the proper temperature at which to store you, and so on. And I will wish you luck. I hope this works. We are still learning, you know."

"Yes, I understand that," Kassquit said. "To see Home, I would take almost any risk. I am not afraid. Do what you need to do." She lay down on the sleeping mat.

The Race gave injections with a high-pressure spray that painlessly penetrated scaly hides. Big Uglies used hollow needles. They stung. Kassquit started to tell the physician as much, but the world around her slowed down and it no longer seemed important. The fluorescent lights overhead blurred and then went dark.

Glen Johnson and Mickey Flynn floated in the *Lewis and Clark*'s control room. The glass in the broad view windows had been treated to kill reflections, leaving them with a splen-did view of the local asteroids—quite a few of which now sported American installations, or at least motors adequate to swing them out of orbit—and of far more stars than they would have seen from beneath Earth's thick mantle of air. The sky was black—not just blue-black, but sable absolute.

"We've spent a hell of a lot of time out here," Johnson re-marked, apropos of nothing in particular. He was a lean man of not quite sixty; because he'd spent the past twenty years weightless, his skin hadn't wrinkled and sagged the way it would have in a gravity field. Of course, everything came at a price. If he had to endure much in the way of gravity now, it would kill him in short order.

"We volunteered," Flynn replied. He'd been round under gravity; he was rounder now, but he also did not sag so much. With dignity, he corrected himself: "I volunteered, anyhow. You stowed away."

"I was shanghaied." Johnson had been saying that ever

since he boarded the *Lewis and Clark*. The ship had still been in Earth orbit then, and he'd faked a malfunction in his orbital patrol craft to give himself a plausible excuse for finding out what was going on with it. The only trouble was, the commandant had thought he was a spy, had kept him aboard to make sure he couldn't possibly report to anyone, and hadn't trusted him from that day to this.

Flynn sent him a bland, Buddhalike stare—except the Buddha had surely had a lot less original sin dancing in his eyes than Mickey Flynn did. "And what would you have done if you hadn't been?" he inquired. "Something honest, perhaps? Give me leave to doubt."

Before Johnson could muster the high dudgeon such a remark demanded, the intercom in the ceiling blared out, "Colonel Johnson, report to the commandant's office immediately! Colonel Glen Johnson, report to the commandant's office immediately!"

"There, you see?" Flynn said. "He's finally caught you with your hand in the cookie jar. Out the air lock you go, without benefit of spacesuit or scooter. It's been nice knowing you. Can I have that pint of bourbon you've got stashed away?"

"Ha! Don't I wish!" Johnson exclaimed. Ships from Earth were few and far between. He couldn't remember the last time he'd tasted whiskey. Every so often, someone did cook up some unofficial alcohol—highly against regulations—aboard the *Lewis and Clark*. It was good, but it wasn't the same.

"Colonel Johnson, report to Lieutenant General Healey's office immediately!" The intercom wasn't going to let up. "Colonel Glen Johnson, report to Lieutenant General Healey's office immediately!"

"Well, I'm off," Johnson said resignedly.

"I knew that," Flynn replied, imperturbable as usual.

With a snort, Johnson glided out of the control room and toward the commandant's lair near the heart of the ship. The corridors had handholds to let crewfolk brachiate along them. The *Lewis and Clark* had never carried bananas, which struck Johnson as a shame. Mirrors where corridors intersected helped stop collisions, a good thing—you could swing along at quite a clip, fast enough to make running into somebody else also going at top speed no joke at all.

"Colonel Johnson, report to . . ." The intercom kept right on bellowing till Johnson zoomed into the commandant's office. He'd slowed down by then, enough so that he didn't sprain his wrists when he stopped by grabbing the far edge of Lieutenant General Healey's desk.

He saluted. The commandant remained a stickler for military courtesy out here in space, where it didn't matter a dime's worth to anybody else. "Reporting as ordered, sir," Johnson said sweetly.

"Yes." Lieutenant General Charles Healey returned the salute. Johnson hadn't liked him at first sight, and familiarity hadn't made the commandant any more lovable. Healey had a face only a snapping turtle could love: round, pugnacious, and wattled. He had a snapping turtle's attitude, too. He bit often, he bit hard, and he didn't like to let go. Glaring at Johnson, he demanded, "When an American starship flies, how would you like to be one of the pilots aboard her?"

Johnson stared back. Healey wasn't joking. He never joked. As far as Johnson could tell, he'd had his sense of humor surgically removed at birth, and the operation had been a smashing success. Logically, that meant he wasn't joking now. Considering all the trouble he and Johnson had had, the pilot still had trouble believing his ears. "My God, sir," he blurted, "who do I have to kill to get the job?"

"Yourself," Healey answered, still in the hard, flat, take-it-or-leave-it voice he usually used. By all the signs, he wasn't kidding about that, either.

"Sir?" That was as much of a question as Johnson was going to ask, no matter how badly he wanted to know more.

"Yourself—maybe." Healey sounded as if he didn't want to unbend even that much. More grudgingly still, he explained, "Cold sleep. If you're not going to be too old by the time the ship finally flies, you'd better go under now. It's still a new technique—nobody's *quite* sure you'll wake up by the time you get to where you're needed." He spoke with a certain somber relish.

"Why me, sir?" Johnson asked. "Why not Flynn or Stone? They're both senior to me." Nobody had intended the *Lewis and Clark* to have three pilots. If he hadn't involuntarily joined the crew, the ship wouldn't have.

"This would be in addition to them, not instead of," Healey said. "Two reasons for having you along at all. First one is, you're the best at fine maneuvering we've got. All that time in orbital missions and trundling back and forth on the scooter means you have to be. Do you say otherwise?" He scowled a challenge.

"No, sir." Johnson didn't point out that piloting a starship was different from anything he'd done before. Piloting a starship was different from anything anybody had done before.

Healey went on, "Second reason is, you'll be on ice and out of everybody's hair from the time you go under till you wake up again—if you wake up again. And then you'll be a good many light-years from home—too many for even you to get yourself into much trouble." The scowl got deeper. "I hope."

"Sir, the only place I've ever made trouble is inside your mind." Johnson had been insisting on that ever since he came aboard the *Lewis and Clark*. While it wasn't strictly true, it was his ticket to keep on breathing.

By the way Lieutenant General Healey eyed him, he wondered how much that ticket was worth. "You are a lying son of a bitch," Healey said crisply. "Do you think I believe your capsule had a genuine electrical failure? Do you think I don't know you were talking with Sam Yeager before you poked your snoot into our business here?"

Ice that had nothing to do with cold sleep walked up Johnson's back. "Why shouldn't I have talked with him?" he asked, since denying it was plainly pointless. "He's only the best expert on the Lizards we've got. When I was doing orbital patrol, I needed that kind of information."

"He was such an expert on the goddamn Lizards, he turned Judas for them," Healey said savagely. "For all I know, you would have done the same. Indianapolis' blood is on his hands."

How much of the Lizards' blood is on our hands? Johnson wondered to himself. *We pulled a Jap on them, attacked without warning—and we attacked colonists in cold sleep, not a naval base.* He started to point that out to Healey, then saved his breath. What point? The commandant wouldn't listen to him. Healey never listened to anybody.

After a deep, angry breath, the three-star general went on, "And I'll tell you something else, Johnson. Your precious Yeager is on ice these days, too."

"On ice? As in cold sleep?" Glen Johnson knew the question was foolish as soon as the words were out of his mouth.

"Yes, as in cold sleep." Healey nodded. "If he hadn't decided to do that, he might have ended up on ice some other way." His eyes were cold as ice themselves—or maybe a little colder.

He didn't say anything more than that. He just waited. *What's he waiting for?* Johnson wondered. He didn't have to wonder long. *He's waiting to make sure I know exactly what he's talking about.* Figuring that out didn't take long, either. Slowly, Johnson asked, "Sir, are you saying *I'm* liable to end up on ice some other way if I don't go into cold sleep?"

"I didn't say that," Healey answered. "I wouldn't say that. You said that. But now that you have said it, you'd better think about it. You'd better not think about it very long, either."

Lots of ways to have an unfortunate accident back on Earth. Even more ways to have one out here in space. *Would people on the crew be willing to help me have an unfortunate accident?* Johnson didn't even need to wonder about that. Lieutenant General Healey had plenty of people aboard who would obey orders just because they *were* orders. Johnson was damn good at what he did and he had some friends, but he couldn't stay awake twenty-four hours a day, seven days a week. He couldn't keep an eye on all the equipment he might have to use all the time. If Healey wanted him dead, dead he would be, and in short order.

Which meant . . . "You talked me into it," he said. "You're persuasive as hell, sir, you know that?"

"So glad you're pleased," Healey said with a nasty grin. "And just think of all the interesting things you'll see eleven light-years from here."

"I'm thinking of all the things I'll never see again," Johnson answered. Healey smirked, an expression particularly revolting on his hard, suspicious face. Johnson went on, "The one I'll be gladdest never to see again, I think, is you. Sir." He pushed off and glided out of the commandant's office. If they were going to hang him tomorrow anyway, what difference did what he said today make?

It turned out not to be tomorrow. A doctor came out from Earth to do the dirty work. Calculating the cost of that, Johnson realized just how badly they wanted him on ice and on his way to Tau Ceti. All that sprang to mind was, *If it weren't for the honor of the thing, I'd rather walk.*

"Are you ready?" asked the doctor, an attractive woman named Blanchard.

"If I say no, will you turn around and go back?" Johnson asked.

She shook her head. "Not me. I'll just hold you down and give you the treatment anyhow." She could do it, too. All the work in the ship's gymnasium and on the exercise bike couldn't make up for Johnson's being out of a gravity field the past twenty years. Dr. Blanchard was undoubtedly stronger than he was.

He rolled up a sleeve and bared his arm. "Do your worst."

She did. He felt hot first, then nauseated, then dizzy. His heart slowed in his chest; his thoughts slowed in his head. *This must be what dying is like,* he realized. Had something gone wrong—or right? He stopped thinking altogether before he could finish shaping the question.

Jonathan Yeager had started shaving his head when he was a teenager. It made him look more like a Lizard, and he'd wanted nothing so much as to be as much like a male of the Race as he could. He still shaved his head here in 1994, though he wasn't a teenager any more; he'd had his fiftieth birthday the December before. The Race still fascinated him, too. He'd built a good career out of that fascination.

His father had gone into cold sleep seventeen years earlier. Most people thought Sam Yeager was dead. Even now, cold sleep wasn't much talked about. Back in 1977, it had been one notch higher than top secret. Of the few aware of it nowadays, fewer still knew it had existed that long.

As Jonathan checked the incoming electronic messages on his computer, he muttered under his breath. The mutter wasn't particularly happy. To this day, people seldom thought of him as Jonathan Yeager, expert on the Race. They thought of him as Sam Yeager's kid. Even to males and females of the Race, for whom family was much more tenuous than it was for humans, he was Sam Yeager's hatchling as often as not.

"Not fair," he said quietly. He was as good with Lizards as anybody breathing. No one had ever complained about his ability. The trouble was, his father had had something more than ability. His father had had precisely the right instincts to think like a male of the Race, instincts that amounted to genius of a highly specialized sort. Even the Lizards admitted as much.

For whatever reasons of background and character and temperament, Jonathan didn't quite have those same instincts. He *was* an expert. He was damned good at what he did. It wasn't the same. It left him stuck being Sam Yeager's kid. He'd be Sam Yeager's kid till the day he died.

"What's not fair?" Karen said from behind him.

He spun in his chair. "Oh, hi, hon," he said to his wife. "Nothing, really. Just woolgathering. I didn't know you were around."

Karen Yeager shook her head. Her coppery hair flipped back and forth. She was almost his own age; these days, she had help keeping her hair red. "Don't talk nonsense," she said briskly. "We've known each other since high school. We've been married almost thirty years. Do you think I can't tell when something's eating you?" She ended the sentence with an interrogative cough, tacked on almost automatically; she was as much an expert on the Lizards as he was.

Jonathan sighed. "Well, you're not wrong." He didn't say anything more.

He didn't have to. Karen pounced. "You're letting your dad get you down again, aren't you?"

More than a little shamefaced, he nodded. "Yeah, I guess I am."

"Dumb." She didn't hesitate about giving her verdict. "Dumb, dumb, dumb, with a capital D." This time, she added an emphatic cough. "You're here. He's not. He was good. So are you." Another emphatic cough followed that.

"He was better than good, and you know it." Jonathan waited to see if she'd have the nerve to tell him he was wrong.

She didn't. He wished she would have. She said, "You're as good as anyone in the business nowadays. I'm not lying to you, Jonathan. If anybody ought to know, it's me."

She was probably right about that. It made Jonathan feel very little better. "I'm not a spring chicken any more," he said. "I'm not a spring chicken, and I'm still in my father's shadow. I don't know that I'll ever get out of it, either."

"I'm in his shadow, too," Karen said. "Anybody who has anything to do with the Race nowadays is in his shadow. I don't see what we can do about that."

Jonathan hadn't looked at it that way. He'd always imagined Sam Yeager's shadow over himself alone. What son of an illustrious father—especially a son in the same line of work—doesn't? Grudgingly, he said, "Maybe."

"Maybe, nothing. It's truth." Karen put the last word in the Lizards' language, and added another emphatic cough. She went on, "And Mickey and Donald think you're pretty hot stuff."

He couldn't deny that, because it was obviously true. The two Lizards raised as human beings took him as seriously as they'd ever taken his father. That they were adults now astonished Jonathan as much as having one son in graduate school at Stanford and the other a junior at UCLA. The boys were both studying the Race; that passion had passed on to the third generation. *Will they ever think of me the way I think of my old man?* Jonathan wondered.

He didn't try to answer the question. Just posing it was hard enough. To keep from having to think about it, he said, "Mickey and Donald didn't turn out *too* bad. Of course, we couldn't isolate them from other Lizards as much as the Race isolated the human they raised Lizard-style."

"Right," Karen said tightly. Jonathan knew he'd goofed by referring to Kassquit, even if he hadn't named her. Thirty years earlier, he'd been her introduction to humanity, and to a lot of the things humans did. That had almost cost him Karen, though he still didn't think it was all his fault. He hadn't planned to go up and visit Kassquit just at the time when war broke out between the Race and the *Reich*. That had kept him up there with her a lot longer than he'd expected, and had let things between Kassquit and him get more complicated and more intimate than he'd thought they would.

Karen looked as if she was about to say something more, too. She hadn't let him completely off the hook for Kassquit, not after all this time. That Kassquit herself had been in cold sleep for years and was probably on her way back to Home by now had nothing to do with anything, not as far as Karen was concerned.

Before the squabble could really flare up, the telephone on Jonathan's desk rang. *Saved by the bell,* he thought, and almost said it aloud. Instead, though, he just picked up the phone. "Jonathan Yeager speaking."

"Hello, Yeager." The voice on the other end of the line didn't identify itself. It carried so much authority, it didn't really need to. "Are you by any chance familiar with the *Admiral Peary?*"

Ice and fire chased themselves through Jonathan. Not a whole lot of people knew about the *Admiral Peary.* Officially, he wasn't one of them. Unofficially . . . Unofficially, everybody in the first rank of American experts on the Race had been salivating ever since that name leaked out. "Yes, sir," Jonathan said. "I have heard of it." He didn't say how or when or where, or what the *Admiral Peary* might be; no telling how secure the telephone line was.

The authoritative voice on the other end of the line said what he'd most wanted to hear ever since that name began being bandied about: "How would you like to be aboard, then?"

And Jonathan said what he'd long since made up his mind he would say: "You are inviting Karen and me both, right?"

For close to half a minute, he got no answer. Then the voice, suddenly sounding not quite so authoritative, said, "I'll get back to you on that." *Click.* The line went dead.

"What was that all about?" Karen asked. "Inviting us where?"

"Aboard the *Admiral Peary,*" Jonathan answered, and her eyes got big. Then he said something he wished he didn't have to: "So far, the call is just for me."

"Oh." He watched her deflate, hating what he saw. She said, "That's why you asked whether it was for both of us."

"Yeah." He nodded, then took a deep breath. They'd never talked about this, probably because it cut too close to the bone. It had been in Jonathan's mind a lot the past few years. It had to have been in Karen's, too. He said, "If they say it's just me, I'm not going. I don't need to see Home bad enough to get a divorce to do it, and you deserve the trip as much as I do."

"*They* don't think so," Karen said bitterly. She gave him a kiss, then asked, "Are you sure about this? If you say no now, you'll never get another chance."

"I'm sure," he said, and so he was—almost. "Some things aren't worth the price, you know what I mean?"

"I know you're sweet, is what I know," Karen said. "What did the man say when you told him that?"

"He said, 'I'll get back to you,' and then he hung up on me."

"That doesn't tell us much, does it?"

"Doesn't tell us a damn thing," Jonathan answered. "If he calls back with good news, he does. And if he calls back with bad news or he doesn't call back—well, close but no cigar. This is the way I want it to be, hon. I like being married to you."

"You must," Karen said, and then looked out the window and across the street so she wouldn't have to say anything more. For a moment, Jonathan didn't understand that at all. Then he did, and didn't know whether to laugh or get mad. Yes, Kassquit probably was Homeward bound right now. Karen meant he was throwing over a chance to see her along with a chance to see the Race's world.

He wanted to remind her it had been thirty years since anything beyond electronic messages lay between Kassquit and him, ten years since Kassquit herself had gone into cold sleep. He wanted to, but after no more than a moment he decided he'd be better off if he didn't. Even now, the less he said about Kassquit, the better.

"Did this man say how long it would be before he got back to you?" Karen asked.

"Nope." Jonathan shook his head. "Nothing to do but wait."

"Any which way, there'll be—" Karen broke off, just in time to rouse Jonathan's curiosity.

"Be what?" he asked. She didn't answer. When she still

didn't answer, he used an interrogative cough all by itself. The Lizards thought that was a barbarism, but people did it all the time these days, whether using the Race's language, English, or—so Jonathan had heard—Russian. But Karen just kept standing there. Jonathan clucked reproachfully, a human noise. "Come on. Out with it."

Reluctantly, she said, "Any which way, there'll be a Yeager on the *Admiral Peary.*"

"Oh. Yeah. Right." That had occurred to Jonathan before, but not for a long time. His laugh wasn't altogether comfortable. "Dad's been on ice for a while now. We're a lot closer in age than we used to be. I wonder how that will play out. I don't know whether it's a reason to want to go or a reason to stay right where I am."

"You won't say no if they give you what you want," Karen said. "You'd better not, because I want to go, too."

"We have to wait and see, that's all," Jonathan said again.

Mr. Authoritative didn't call back for the next three days. Jonathan jumped every time the phone rang. Whenever it turned out to be a salesman or a friend or even one of his sons, he felt cheated. Each time he answered it, he felt tempted to say, *Jonathan Yeager. Will you for God's sake drop the other shoe?*

Then he started believing the other shoe wouldn't drop. Maybe Mr. Authoritative couldn't be bothered with him any more. Plenty of other people wouldn't have set any conditions. Plenty of other people would have killed—in the most literal sense of the word—to get a call like that.

Jonathan had almost abandoned hope when the man with the authoritative voice did call back. "All right, Yeager. You've got a deal—both of you." He hung up again.

"We're in!" Jonathan shouted. Karen whooped.

We're in. Karen Yeager hadn't dreamt two little words could lead to so many complications. But they did. Going into cold sleep was a lot like dying. From a good many perspectives, it was exactly like dying. She had to wind up her affairs, and her husband's, as if they weren't coming back. She knew they might, one day. If they did, though, the world to which they returned would be as different from the one they knew as today's world was from that lost and vanished time before the Lizards came.

The Yeagers' sons took the news with a strange blend of mourning and jealousy. "We'll never see you again," said Bruce, their older boy, who'd come down from Palo Alto when he got word of what was going on.

"Never say never," Karen answered, though she feared very much that he was right. "You can't tell what'll happen."

"I wish I were going, too," said Richard, their younger son. "The *Admiral Peary*! Wow!" He looked up at the ceiling as if he could see stars right through it. Bruce nodded. His face was full of stars, too.

"One of these days, you may find a reason to go into cold sleep," Karen told them. "If you do, it had better be a good one. If you go under when you're young, you stay young while you're going, you do whatever you do when you get there, you go back into cold sleep—and everybody who was young with you when you left will be old by the time you're back. Everybody but you."

"And if you're not young?" Richard asked incautiously.

Karen had been thinking about that, too. "If you're not young when you start out," she said, "you can still do what you need to do and come back again. But most of what you left behind will be gone when you do."

She sometimes—often—wished she hadn't done such figuring. The Race had been flying between the stars for thousands of years. The *Admiral Peary* would be a first try for mankind. It wasn't as fast as the Lizards' starships. A round trip to Home and back would swallow at least sixty-five years of real time.

She looked at her sons. Bruce was a redhead like her. Richard's hair was dark blond, like Jonathan's. Hardly anybody in their generation shaved his head; to them, that was something old people did. But if she and Jonathan came back to Earth after sixty-five years, the two of them wouldn't have aged much despite all their travel, and their boys would be old, old men if they stayed alive at all.

Karen hugged them fiercely, each in turn. "Oh, Mom!" Richard said. "It'll be all right. Everything will be all right."

He was at an age where he could still believe that—not only believe it but take it for granted.

I wish I could, Karen thought.

She not only had to break the news to the children of her flesh, she also had to tell Donald and Mickey. She'd been there when the two Lizards hatched from their eggs, even though Jonathan's dad hadn't really approved of that. She'd helped Jonathan take care of them when they were tiny, and she and Jonathan had raised them ever since Sam Yeager went into cold sleep. They were almost as dear to her as Bruce and Richard.

They were older in calendar years than her human sons. She wasn't a hundred percent sure how much that meant. Lizards grew very rapidly as hatchlings, but after that they aged more slowly than people did. Some of the important males who'd come with the conquest fleet were still prominent today, more than fifty years later. That wasn't true of any human leader who'd been around in 1942. Even Vyacheslav Molotov, who'd seemed ready to go on forever, was eight years dead now. He'd hoped for a hundred, but had got to only ninety-six.

The two Lizards raised as people listened without a word as she explained what would happen. When she'd finished, they turned their eye turrets towards each other, as if wondering which of them should say something. As usual, Donald was the one who did: "Are we going to go out there and live on our own, then?"

"Not right away," Karen answered. "Maybe later. You'll have to wait and see. For now, there will be other people to take you in."

She didn't like not telling them the whole truth, but she didn't have the heart for it. The whole truth was that somebody would keep an eye on them for the rest of their lives, however long those turned out to be. The Race knew about them by now. By the very nature of things, some secrets couldn't last forever. The Lizards' protests had been muted. Considering Kassquit, their protests couldn't very well have been anything but muted.

Karen didn't care to consider Kassquit. To keep from thinking about the Lizard-raised Chinese woman, she gave her attention back to the two American-raised Lizards. "What do you guys think? Are you ready to try living on your own?"

"Hell, yes." To her surprise, that wasn't Donald. It was Mickey, the smaller and most of the time the more diffident of the pair. He went on, "We can do it, as long as we have money."

"We can work, if we have to," Donald said. "We aren't stupid or lazy. We're good Americans."

"Nobody ever said you were stupid or lazy. Nobody ever thought so," Karen answered. Some Lizards *were* stupid. Others didn't do any more than they had to, and sometimes not all of that. But her scaly foster children had always been plenty sharp and plenty active.

"What about being good Americans?" Mickey's mouth gave his English a slightly hissing flavor. Other than that, it was pure California. "We are, aren't we?" He sounded anxious.

"Sure you are," Karen said, and meant it. "That's part of the reason why somebody will help take care of you—because you've been so good."

Mickey seemed reassured. Donald didn't. "Aren't Americans supposed to take care of themselves?" he asked. "That's what we learned when you and Grandpa Sam taught us."

"Well . . . yes." Karen couldn't very well deny that. "But you're not just Americans, you know. You're, uh, special."

"Why?" Donald asked. "Because we're short?"

He laughed out loud, which showed how completely American he was: the Race didn't do that when it was amused. Karen laughed, too. The question had come from out of the blue and hit her right in the funny bone.

She had to answer him, though. "No, not because you're short. Because you're you."

"It might be interesting to see Home," Mickey said. "Maybe we could go there, too, one of these days."

Did he sound wistful? Karen thought so. She didn't suppose she could blame him. Kassquit had sometimes shown a longing to come down to Earth and see what it was like. Karen wasn't sorry Kassquit hadn't got to indulge that longing. Worry about diseases for which she had no immunity had kept her up on an orbiting starship till she went into cold sleep. Those same worries might well apply in reverse to Mickey and Donald.

No sooner had that thought crossed Karen's mind than Donald said, "I bet the Lizards could immunize us if we ever wanted to go."

"Maybe they could," Karen said, amused he called the Race that instead of its proper name. She doubted the U.S. government would ever let him and Mickey leave even if they wanted to. That wasn't fair, but it likely was how things worked. She went on, "For now, though, till everything gets sorted out, do you think you can stay here with Bruce and Richard?" Stanford had promised her older son graduate credit for at least a year's worth of Lizard-sitting. Where could he get better experience dealing with the Race than this?

"Sure!" Mickey said, and Donald nodded. Mickey added, "It'll be the hottest bachelor pad in town."

That set Karen helplessly giggling again. Until Mickey met a female of the Race in heat and giving off pheromones, his interest in the opposite sex was purely theoretical. But, because he'd been raised as a human, he didn't think it ought to be. And Bruce and Richard would love a hot bachelor pad. Their interest in females of their species was anything but theoretical.

Doubt tore at Karen. Was this worth it, going off as if dying (and perhaps dying in truth—neither cold sleep nor the *Admiral Peary* could be called perfected even by human standards, let alone the sterner ones the Race used) and leaving all the people who mattered to her (in which she included both humans and Lizards) to fend for themselves? Was it?

The doubt didn't last long. If she hadn't wanted, hadn't hungered, to learn as much about the Race as she could, would she have started studying it all those years ago? She shook her head. She knew she wouldn't have, any more than Jonathan would.

No, she wanted to go aboard the *Admiral Peary* more than anything else. She wished she could go and come back in a matter of weeks, not in a stretch of time that ran closer to the length of a man's life. She wished that, yes, but she also understood she couldn't have what she wished. Being unable to have it made her sad, made her wish things were different, but wouldn't stop her.

The day finally came when all the arrangements were made, when nothing was left to do. Richard drove Karen and Jonathan from their home in Torrance up to the heart of Los Angeles. Bruce rode along, too. Richard would, of course, drive the Buick back. Why not? He could use it. Even if everything went perfectly and Karen did come back to Earth and Southern California one day, the Buick would be long, long gone.

Richard and Bruce might be gone, too. Karen didn't care to think about that. It made her start to puddle up, and she didn't want to do that in front of her sons. She squeezed them and kissed them. So did Jonathan, who was usually more stand-offish. But this was a last day. Her husband knew that as well as she did. Not death, not quite—they had to hope not, anyhow—but close enough for government work. Karen laughed. It *was* government work.

After last farewells, her sons left. If they were going to puddle up, they probably didn't want Jonathan and her to see it. She reached for her husband's hand. He was reaching for hers at the same time. His fingers felt chilly, not from the onset of cold sleep but from nerves. She was sure hers did, too. Her heart pounded a mile a minute.

A man wearing a white coat over khaki uniform trousers came out from behind a closed door. "Last chance to change your mind, folks," he said.

Karen and Jonathan looked at each other. The temptation was there. But she said, "No." Her husband shook his head.

"Okay," the Army doctor said. "First thing you need to do, then, is sign about a million forms. Once you're done with those, we can get down to the real business."

He exaggerated. There couldn't have been more than half a million forms. Karen and Jonathan signed and signed and signed. After a while, the signatures hardly looked like theirs, the way they would have at the end of a big stack of traveler's checks.

"Now what?" Karen asked after the doctor took away the last piece of paper with a horizontal line on it.

"Now I get to poke holes in you," he said, and he did. Karen hung on to Jonathan's hand while they both felt the drugs take hold.

"I love you," Jonathan muttered drowsily. Karen tried to answer him. She was never quite sure if she succeeded.

☆ 2 ☆

A Big Ugly walked into the office at the Race's headquarters in Cairo that Ttomalss was using. "I greet you, Senior Physician," the psychologist said. "It was good of you to come here to talk to me."

"And I greet you, Senior Researcher." Dr. Reuven Russie spoke the Race's language about as well as a Tosevite could. The hair had receded from the top of his head, as often happened with aging male Big Uglies, and what he had left was gray.

"Please—take a seat." Ttomalss waved to the Tosevite-style chair he'd had brought into the office.

"I thank you." Russie sat. "You are, I gather, interested in the American Tosevites' progress on cold sleep."

Ttomalss used the affirmative gesture. "That is correct. You will, I trust, understand why the issue is of considerable concern to us."

"Oh, yes." Reuven Russie's head went up and down. The way he nodded was a subtle compliment to Ttomalss. An ignorant Big Ugly would have used his own gesture because he did not know what the Race did. A Tosevite who knew more would have imitated the Race's gesture. Russie, who knew more still, knew Ttomalss was an expert on Big Uglies and so of course would understand a nod even where some other member of the Race might not. The physician went on, "I think they know enough to fly between the stars. That is what concerns you, is it not?"

"Truth." Ttomalss' tailstump twitched in agitation. "But how can this be so? It is only a little more than fifty local years since we came to Tosev 3. Before then, neither the Americans nor any other Tosevites would have had the least

34

interest in cold sleep. And they have had to adapt our techniques to their biochemistry, which is far from identical to ours."

"Every word you say is true," Reuven Russie replied. "I do not know the details of their techniques. They keep them secret. But I can infer what they know by what they do not talk about. Lately, they do not talk about a great many things, enough so the silence is likely to cover all they need to know of this art."

"I had arrived at a similar conclusion," Ttomalss said unhappily. "I was hoping you would tell me I was wrong. When trying to figure out what Tosevites are capable of, the worst conclusion a male of the Race can draw is usually not bad enough."

"I do not know what to do about that," the Big Ugly said. "But I can tell you where some of the differences arise. How long has the Race known cold sleep?"

"More than thirty-two thousand of our years—half as many of yours," Ttomalss answered. "We developed it when we knew we would send out our first conquest fleet, the one that brought Rabotev 2 into the Empire. That was twenty-eight thousand years ago."

"You started working on it . . . four thousand of your years before you needed it." Russie let out a soft, shrill whistle. Ttomalss had heard that sound before; it meant bemusement. Gathering himself, the Big Ugly said, "That is even longer than I had thought. And now, of course, you take it completely for granted."

"Yes, of course," Ttomalss said, wondering where Russie was going with this. "Why should we not? We had it largely perfected for the first conquest fleet, and have made small improvements in the process from time to time ever since. We want things to work as well as they possibly can."

"And there is the difference between you and the Americans," Reuven Russie said. "All they care about is that things work *well enough*. Also, they reach out with both hands—with every fingerclaw, you would say—in a way the Race never seems to have done. Add those things together with their strong motivation to learn to fly from one star to another, and I am not so very surprised they have learned enough to attempt this."

"Will they—can they—succeed?" Ttomalss said.

"This, you understand, is only a matter of my opinion," the Big Ugly replied. "I would not, however, care to bet against them."

Ttomalss did not care to bet against the Big Uglies, either, however much he wished he could. "But suppose they visit Home? Suppose they fill their ship up with ginger?"

Russie's shrug was uncannily like one a male of the Race would have used. "Suppose they do," he said. "What can you do about it? Destroying their ship would surely start a war here. Are you certain the Race would win it?"

Thirty local years earlier, at the time of the last great crisis between the Race and Big Uglies, the answer to that would undoubtedly have been yes. The victory might have left Tosev 3 largely uninhabitable, but it would have been a victory. Since then, though, the Americans—and the Russkis, and the Nipponese, and even the Deutsche, whom the Race *had* defeated—had learned a great deal. Who would beat whom today was anyone's guess. Ttomalss' miserable hiss said he knew as much.

Not wanting to dwell on that, the male changed the subject. "I hope your sire is well?" he said, such matters being part of polite conversation among Tosevites.

"I thank you for asking. He is as well as he can be, considering that he is nearly eighty years old," Reuven Russie replied.

Even doubling the number to make the years match those of Home left Ttomalss unimpressed. His own folk wore out more slowly than Big Uglies. He wondered whether the frenetic pace with which one generation replaced another on Tosev 3 had something to do with the equally frenetic pace of progress here. He knew he was not the Race's first researcher to have that thought.

"I am glad to hear it," he said, perhaps a heartbeat more slowly than he might have. He swung one eye turret to the computer screen for a moment. "You have also a kinsmale who now lives in the not-empire of the United States, is that not a truth?"

"David Goldfarb lives in Canada," Russie answered. "The two not-empires are similar to each other in many ways. He is also well enough. He is younger than my sire, but not by much."

"I thank you for the correction," Ttomalss said. The record stated Goldfarb was living in North America, the local name for the northern part of the lesser continental mass. He'd assumed that meant the United States. The not-empire of Canada often got lost in the shadow cast by its more populous, more powerful neighbor. He wondered what the Canadians thought of that.

"Is there anything else, Senior Researcher?" Russie asked. "I have told you what I know, and what I have guessed. You will be aware that I am not formally affiliated with the Moishe Russie Medical College, nor have I been for many years. If you need technical details, someone who completed the full course there or one of your own experts could do a better job of furnishing them."

"I was not seeking technical details. I wanted a feel for the data," Ttomalss said. "You have given me that, and I thank you for it."

"You are welcome." The Tosevite physician rose, towering over Ttomalss once more and demonstrating why the rooms in the Race's headquarters were the size they were: they had originally been built for Big Uglies. Reuven Russie nodded stiffly and walked out of the interview chamber.

Ttomalss began drafting his report. He suspected no one would pay much attention to it. It would not be optimistic, not from the Race's point of view. The powers that be favored optimism. They pointed to the successful colonies on Tosev 3, and to the way animals and plants from Home were spreading across the warmer regions of this planet. They did not like turning an eye turret toward the Tosevites' continued technical progress, any more than they cared to remember the rebellions that still simmered in China and elsewhere. But colonists here were trained as soldiers. This world had what bid fair to become a permanent Soldiers' Time, something unprecedented in the Empire. The authorities did to some degree recognize reality, even if they wished they didn't have to.

Tosev 3 imposed haste even on the Race. Ttomalss finished

and submitted his report at what would have been a break-neck pace back on Home. But he was astonished when, three days later, his computer screen lit up to show the features of Fleetlord Reffet, who was in charge of the colonists. "I greet you, Exalted Fleetlord," the psychologist said, assuming the seated version of the posture of respect.

"And I greet you, Senior Researcher," Reffet replied.

"To what do I owe the honor of this call?" Ttomalss asked.

"The American Big Uglies have launched what can only be a starship," Reffet said bluntly. "Its course is in the general direction of Home, though not precisely aimed toward our sun."

"Oh," Ttomalss said. "Well, we did think this day would eventually come."

"Yes, but not so soon," Reffet said. "You understand that this means the folk of Home, folk with no experience of Big Uglies, will now have to learn to deal with them and try to understand them."

"They will have a lively time of it, then, as did we of the conquest fleet—and as did you of the colonization fleet," Ttomalss said. "It may even be good for them. They have not begun to understand us when we talk of what things are like on Tosev 3. Now they will gain the experience they need to form a more accurate opinion." He did not say, *Serves them right,* but the thought was prominent in his mind.

But Reffet said, "That attitude will not do, Senior Researcher. We have to assume that ship is heavily armed. For the first time since the Empire was unified, Home may be in danger. They need to have someone there with some real knowledge of Tosevites."

"Fleetlord Atvar is there," Ttomalss said.

Reffet hissed angrily. "Fleetlord Atvar is a disaster waiting to happen. He proved that often enough here on Tosev 3. We need someone there with real expertise, not just wide-mouthed bombast. We need someone like you there, Senior Researcher."

"Me?" Ttomalss hissed, too, in horrified dismay. "But my research program here is progressing so well!"

"Nevertheless, I am ordering you back to Home," Reffet said. "Which counts for more, the individual or the Race as a

whole? Have you yourself been infected by the rampant ego-
tism of the Big Uglies you study?"

At first, Ttomalss reckoned the question horribly unfair.
The more he turned his eye turrets towards it, though, the more
reasonable it seemed. In any case, Reffet had the authority to
do as he said he would. Ttomalss assumed the posture of respect again. "You may command me, Exalted Fleetlord."

"Yes, I may," Reffet said complacently. "I may, and I shall.
Settle your affairs as quickly as you can. I want you in cold
sleep on the next Homeward-bound ship. I do not know when
the Tosevite starship will get there. I hope you will arrive first.
I believe you will; the Big Uglies' acceleration was relatively
low. Remember—you may directly serve the Emperor himself." He cast down his eye turrets.

So did Ttomalss. He would have reckoned the honor
greater before years of studying Tosevite superstitions, none
of which took seriously the cult of spirits of Emperors past or
the reverence given the living Emperor. The Big Uglies' ignorance had sown the seeds of doubt in him. But excitement
soon cast out doubt and hesitation. After so long dealing with
this barbarous world, he was going Home again at last! And
if he did gain the privilege of seeing the Emperor—well, so
much the better.

For a long time after Atvar woke up on Home once more,
he'd thought the sun looked strange in the sky. He'd got used
to the star Tosev, which was hotter and bluer. Only Tosev 3's
much greater distance from its primary left it with such a
chilly climate.

Now, though, the sun seemed normal to him once more.
Life on Home had also seemed strange to him when he came
out of cold sleep. That dislocation had lasted longer. In fact,
it hadn't disappeared to this day. He had changed, changed irrevocably, during his tenure on Tosev 3.

The change wasn't just one of holding a prominent command, either. He would have been glad enough to lay that
aside. But he had lived with danger and intrigue and the unexpected for year after year. On Home, such things scarcely
existed. They had been obsolete here for so very long, most
people forgot they had ever existed. Atvar had long since

given up trying to explain them. He knew it was hopeless. He might as well have tried explaining the effects of ginger to a female who had never tasted it.

His mouth fell open in a sardonic laugh. As he'd known they would, smugglers had brought ginger back to Home. The herb was fabulously expensive here, which only seemed to make males and females want it more. It had already produced its first scandals. More, no doubt, would come.

Even the look of things had changed here. That had truly rocked him back on his tailstump, for it was almost unprecedented on Home. But young males and females seemed to enjoy acting and looking as much like Big Uglies as they could. They wore false hair, often in colors no Tosevite could have grown naturally. And some of them even wore cloth wrappings over their body paint, which seemed a ploy deliberately designed to cause confusion. Atvar had expected the Big Uglies to imitate the Race; that was how things were supposed to work. For the process to go into reverse struck him as altogether unnatural.

The fleetlord had never been found guilty of anything. Males and females here had endlessly questioned his judgment, but no one came close to showing criminal intent. That struck many other members of the Race as altogether unnatural. Atvar lived in half disgrace: the first fleetlord of a conquest fleet who wasn't a conqueror.

He'd published his memoirs. They hadn't made him rich. Along with his pension—which, thanks to the Emperor's generosity, no underling had cut off—what they'd earned did keep him comfortable. He hadn't won any new friends in the government with their title—he'd called them *I Told You So*.

Males and females here needed telling. As far as those who didn't pretend to be Big Uglies were concerned, Tosev 3 was just a world a long way off, light-years and light-years. They knew the conquest hadn't gone the way it should, but they didn't know why, or what that meant. Despite Atvar's memoirs, most of them seemed inclined to blame him.

These days, one needed special skill with computers to coax his telephone code out of the data-retrieval system. Too many males and females had that expertise; he got a lot of crank calls. Because he got so many, he didn't rush to the

phone when it hissed for attention. Instead, he went at more of
a resigned amble. "This is Atvar. I greet you," he said, while
his fingerclaw was poised to end the conversation on the instant.

The male on the other end of the line said, "And I greet you,
Exalted Fleetlord. This is Senior Planner Facaros, in the Ministry of Transportation."

Facaros' body paint confirmed his title. "What can I do for
you, Senior Planner?" Atvar asked, intrigued in spite of himself. Home did not have a Soldiers' Time now. There was no
Ministry of Conquest. The Ministry of Transportation, which
oversaw ordinary spaceflight, came as close as any other body
to taking charge of matters military.

"We have just received word from Tosev 3," Facaros said.
"The Big Uglies from the not-empire known as the United
States"—he did not pronounce the Tosevite words very well—
"have launched a starship. Its apparent destination is Home."

"Have they?" Atvar's hiss was phlegmatic, not astonished.
"Well, it was only a matter of time, though this was a bit
sooner than I expected it of them." He paused to think. The
radio message from Tosev 3 had had to cross interstellar space,
of course. While it was crossing the light-years, so was the
Big Uglies' ship, at some respectable fraction of the speed of
light. "How long do we have until they get here?" he asked.

"About forty years, or a bit more," Facaros replied. "We fly
at about half of light speed, so—"

"Tell me something I do not know," Atvar snapped. "I have
done it. Have you?"

"Well . . . no, Exalted Fleetlord," Facaros admitted. "As for
what you do not know, the Tosevite ship seems to average
about one third of light speed. Its total travel time between
Tosev 3 and Home will be over sixty years."

"More than forty years from now," Atvar said musingly. "I
may be here to see it, but I probably will not. I have lived a
long time already. Forty more years would be beating the
odds."

"That is one of the reasons I have called you today," Facaros said. "I wondered if you would consider going into cold
sleep once more, so that you could be revived when the Big

Uglies' arrival is imminent. You are one of the Race's experts on them, and—"

"You admit this now, do you?" Atvar broke in. "Do my critics in the government—which means just about everyone but the Emperor—admit it as well?"

"Formally, no," Facaros said. "Informally . . . This request would not have been made in the absence of a consensus about your value to the Race."

That, Atvar knew, was bound to be true. Even so, he said, "I am not a bowl of leftovers, you know, to go from the freezer to the microwave again and again and again."

"Certainly not, and we will richly reward you for the service you perform," Facaros said. "Never doubt it."

Atvar had lived among Big Uglies too long. Whenever someone told him not to doubt something, he doubted it all the more. He said, "I care very little for money. I do care for my reputation. If you promise your principals will leave off all attacks on me while I am not conscious to defend myself, I will do this. If not, they can take their chances with the Big Uglies. Why should they worry? They already know everything, do they not?"

Facaros hissed reproachfully. "This is not the proper attitude for a male to take."

"I do not care," Atvar replied. "In my opinion, the attitude a good many in the government have shown is improper. If they do not wish to change it, I do not wish to cooperate with them."

"Would a personal request from the Emperor himself change your mind?" asked the male from the Transportation Ministry. "It can be arranged."

"I am honored," Atvar murmured, and cast down his eye turrets. "I am honored indeed." But he made the negative gesture. "However honored I am, though, the answer remains no. I have my terms. I have stated them for you. If your principals care to meet them, well and good. If they do not . . . If they do not, Senior Planner, I must conclude they are not serious about wanting my assistance."

"They are," Facaros declared.

"Then let them show it." Atvar had every intention of being as stubborn and unreasonable as he could. Why not? Those who had mocked him—those who now decided they needed him—had been anything but reasonable themselves.

Facaros let out a long, unhappy sigh. But he made the affirmative gesture. "Let it be as you say, Exalted Fleetlord. Let everything be exactly as you say. My principals shall offer no opinions on you while you are in cold sleep. They are convinced the Race needs you."

"I am not convinced the Race needs them," Atvar said.

Facaros sighed again. "One of them, in fact, predicted you would say something along those lines. Your reputation for cynicism precedes you. Is that how you care to be remembered?"

Atvar shrugged. "I expect that I will be remembered. I also expect that most of the Emperor's ministers will be forgotten."

Facaros stirred in annoyance. "You are unfair and exasperating."

"Now, now." Atvar wagged a fingerclaw at him. "No insults, mind you."

"You are not in cold sleep yet, except possibly from the neck up," Facaros said.

Instead of getting angrier, Atvar let his mouth drop open in a wide laugh. "Not bad," he said. "Not bad at all. And yes, Senior Planner, I am unfair and exasperating. If I were not, we would not have enjoyed—if that is the word I want—even such success on Tosev 3 as we did. Until you have dealt with Big Uglies, you do not know what unfair and exasperating are."

"I am only a hatchling in these matters," Facaros said. "I am sure you can instruct me."

He intended that for sarcasm. Deliberately ignoring his tone, Atvar made the affirmative gesture. "I am sure I can, too. And if I do not, Senior Planner, the Tosevites will when they get here. You may rely on that."

"That is what concerns my principals," Facaros said. "For the sake of the Race, Exalted Fleetlord, I am glad we have reached this agreement." He said nothing about being glad for any reason besides the sake of the Race. That also amused Atvar more than it annoyed him. He was laughing again as he broke the connection with Facaros.

Here, unlike on Tosev 3, he could take his time about preparing for cold sleep. One of the preparations he made was for a software search on his name during the time when he would lie unconscious. He intended to check that after he was revived. If the results weren't to his satisfaction, he was perfectly willing to let the government deal with the Big Uglies without him.

He sent Facaros an electronic message, letting the other male—and those behind him—know what he'd done. *This does not surprise me,* Facaros wrote back. *Why should you trust those of your own kind, those who are on your side?*

I do trust, Atvar wrote. *But trust must be verified. This too is a lesson of Tosev 3.* He got no reply to that. He hadn't really expected one.

When he went into a hospital for the cold-sleep treatment, the physician there asked him, "Have you undergone this procedure before?"

"Twice," he answered.

"Oh," the physician said. "You will have traveled between the stars, then?"

"Not at all," Atvar told her. "I did not care for what was being televised, and so I thought I would store myself away, hoping for an improvement some years down the line. No luck the first time, so I tried a second. I am sure this third time will prove a success."

The physician gave him a severe look. "I do not believe you are being serious," she said, and used an emphatic cough to let him know how much she did not believe it.

"Believe what you please," Atvar told her. She did not seem to have the slightest idea who he was. In a way, that was annoying. In another way, it was a relief. In spite of everything televisors and pundits could do, he managed to escape into anonymity every now and again. Even his fancy body paint meant less here than it had on Tosev 3.

"Give me your arm, please," the physician said. Atvar obeyed. In all his time on Tosev 3, he hadn't had to obey anyone, not till he got the summons to return to Home. He'd given orders. He hadn't taken them. Now he did. He hissed as the jet of air blasted drugs under his scales. The physician sighed at his squeamishness. "You cannot tell me that really hurt."

"Oh? Why not?" he said.

His reward was another injection, and another. Presently, the physician said, "You are tolerating the procedure very well."

"Good." Atvar's mouth fell open not in a laugh but in an enormous yawn. Whatever else the physician did to him, he never knew it.

When Glen Johnson woke, he needed some little while to realize he was awake and to remember he'd gone into cold sleep. Something here was emphatically different from the way things had been on the *Lewis and Clark,* though. He had weight. He didn't have much—only a couple of pounds' worth—but it was the first time he'd had any since the *Lewis and Clark* got out to the asteroid belt. The *Admiral Peary* stayed under acceleration all the time.

"Here," a woman said. "Drink this." *Dr. Blanchard,* he thought as his wits slowly trickled back into his head. *Her name is Dr. Blanchard.* She handed him a plastic squeeze bulb. The liquid in the bulb had weight, too, but not enough to keep it from madly sloshing around in there.

It tasted like chicken soup—hot and salty and fatty and restorative. And he needed restoring. He had trouble finishing the bulb, even though it wasn't very big. Sucking and swallowing all but drained him of strength. "Thanks," he said. "That was good. What was it?"

"Chicken broth," she answered, and he would have laughed if he'd had the energy. Little by little, he noticed he was hooked up to a lot of electronic monitors. Dr. Blanchard checked the readouts. "Sleep if you want to," she told him. "That seems normal enough."

"Seems?" he said around a yawn. He did want to sleep. Why not? The habit of a lot of years was hard to break.

"Well," she answered, "we haven't thawed out a whole lot of people yet. We're still learning."

He yawned again. "Why am I one of your guinea pigs?" he asked. If she answered, he didn't hear her. Sleep reclaimed him.

When he woke again, he felt stronger. Dr. Blanchard gave him more chicken soup, even if she primly insisted on calling it chicken broth. He found out her first name was Melanie, right out of *Gone with the Wind*. She disconnected him from the monitors. He looked at his hands. His nails seemed no longer than they had when he went under. He felt his chin. His face was still smooth. "This beats the heck out of Rip van Winkle," he said.

"I thought so, too." There was a familiar voice. "Then I found out what I'd have for company."

"Well, well. Look what the cat drug in." Johnson yawned again. Talking still took an effort. Getting his mind to work straight took a bigger one.

"I was thinking the same thing about you," Mickey Flynn replied with dignity. "I have better reason, too, I daresay."

"I wouldn't be surprised," Johnson said. Another yawn came out. He wondered if he would ever feel awake again. He looked around. The chamber where they'd revived him wasn't big enough to swing the cat he and Flynn had been talking about. "Where the devil are we, anyway?"

"The middle of nowhere," Flynn replied. "And I mean that more literally than anyone has in all the history of humanity. We're more than five light-years from the Sun, and we're more than five light-years from Tau Ceti, too."

Even in Johnson's decrepit state, that sent awe prickling through him. But then he asked, "Why wake me up for this? I don't know anything about flying the *Admiral Peary* out here. I'm the in-system pilot."

"Two reasons," Flynn said. "One is, I wanted to see if you were still alive. Present results appear ambiguous."

"And the horse you rode in on," Johnson said sweetly. The fog was beginning to lift—a little.

"Thank you so much," the other pilot replied. "As I was saying before I was so rudely interrupted, I wanted to see if you were alive. If by some mischance you weren't, that would make *me* in-system pilot and change the revival schedule. So I needed to know. You went into cold sleep earlier than I did. The techniques have been improved since."

"That's 'cause you're the teacher's pet," Johnson said. "Healey couldn't wait to put me on ice, the son of a bitch." He didn't much care what he said. That was probably an effect of coming out from under the drugs, too.

"I could call that a slander on the whole of the Hibernian race," Flynn said. "On the other hand, seeing that it's Healey, I could just nod my head wisely and say, 'You're right.' All things considered, I have to go with the second approach. However Irish the man may be, a son of a bitch he is, and that without a doubt."

Back on the *Lewis and Clark,* he never would have admitted such a thing. Of course, back on the *Lewis and Clark* he had to deal with Lieutenant General Healey. Now he must have been sure the bad-tempered officer was as far behind them as the rest of the Solar System. More than five light-years . . .

"You said there was more than one reason to wake me up now," Johnson observed. He remembered. He was proud of himself for remembering. That said something about how fuzzy his wits had been before.

Mickey Flynn nodded. "That's true. I did."

"What's the other one?" Johnson asked.

"In my ignorance, I thought you might be interested in seeing what the sky looks like out here as we turn the ship," Flynn said. "No matter how good we get at flying between the stars, this isn't something a whole lot of people will ever get to do."

"I should say not!" Johnson exclaimed, eagerness blazing through him no matter how weak and woozy he felt. "Most of the passengers will stay frozen from start to finish." He turned to Dr. Blanchard. "Can I go up?"

"I don't know," she answered. "Can you?"

"We'll find out." He tried to lever himself off the table where he lay, only to discover he was strapped on. Melanie Blanchard made no move to set him free. *It's a test,* he realized. *If I can't undo the straps, I don't deserve to do anything else.* His fingers were clumsy and stupid. They took longer than they should have to figure out how the latches worked, but they did it. He sat up, torn between triumph and worry. "My brains *will* come back?" he asked her.

"They're supposed to," she said, which struck him as imperfectly reassuring.

The *Admiral Peary*'s acceleration produced barely enough weight to keep him on the table. When he slid off, he glided ever so slowly to the metal floor. He would have had to go off a cliff like Wile E. Coyote to do himself any serious damage. He bounced from the floor toward Flynn. "Lead on, Macduff."

"That's, 'Lay on, Macduff.' " Flynn looked pained. "Don't tamper with the Bard."

"At this late date and this distance, I doubt he'll complain," Johnson said.

"Oh, so do I," the other pilot said. "That's why I'm doing it for him."

"Helpful," Johnson observed, and Flynn nodded blandly. Johnson went on, "Well, anyway, show me. Show me around, too. This is the first time I've been conscious—as conscious as I am—on the *Admiral Peary.* Would be nice to know what I'm flying."

"You don't ask for much, do you?" Flynn brachiated up the hatchway. The starship's tiny acceleration wasn't enough to worry about, not as far as motion was concerned. Feeling like a chimpanzee himself—an elderly, arthritic, downright spavined chimpanzee—Johnson followed.

The *Lewis and Clark* had had observation windows fronted by antireflection-coated glass. The *Admiral Peary* had an observation dome, also made from glass that might as well not have been there. Coming up into it was like getting a look at space itself. Johnson stared out. Slowly, his jaw dropped. "Jesus," he whispered.

Mickey Flynn nodded again, this time in perfect understanding. "You've noticed, have you? It does hit home."

"Yeah," Johnson said, and said nothing else for the next several minutes.

There was no sun in the sky.

That hit home, sure as hell, like a left to the jaw. Johnson understood exactly what it meant. It wasn't that the Sun was hiding, as it hid behind the Earth during the night. When it did that, you knew where it was, even if you couldn't see it. Not here. Not now. There was nothing but blackness with stars scattered through it. And the closest of those stars was light-years away.

"And I thought the asteroid belt was a long way from home," Johnson murmured at last. "I hadn't even gone into the next room."

"Does make you wonder why we thought we were the lords of creation, doesn't it?" Flynn said. Johnson hadn't thought of it that way, but he couldn't help nodding. Flynn continued, "Look a little longer. Tell me what else you see, besides the big nothing."

"Okay," Johnson said, and he did. He knew how the stars were supposed to look from space. Not many humans—probably not many Lizards, either—knew better. As Flynn had said he would, he needed a while to see anything else by the absence of a sun. But he did, and his jaw fell again.

The outlines of the constellations were wrong.

Oh, not all of them. Orion looked the same as it always had. So did the Southern Cross. He knew why, too: their main stars were a long, long way from the Sun, too far for a mere five or six light-years to change their apparent position. But both the Dogs that accompanied Orion through the skies of Earth had lost their principal stars. Sirius and Procyon were bright because they lay close to the Sun. Going halfway to Tau Ceti rudely shoved them across the sky. Johnson spotted them at last because they were conspicuous and didn't belong where they were.

He also spotted another bright star that didn't belong where it was, and couldn't for the life of him figure out from where it had been displaced. He finally gave up and pointed towards it. "What's that one there, not far from Arcturus?"

Flynn didn't need to ask which one he meant, and smiled a most peculiar smile. "Interesting you should wonder. I had to ask Walter Stone about that one myself."

"Well, what is it?" Johnson said, a little irritably. Mickey Flynn's smile got wider. Johnson's annoyance grew with it. Then, all at once, that annoyance collapsed. He took another look at that unfamiliar yellow star. The hair stood up on his arms and the back of his neck. In a very small voice, he said, "Oh."

"That's right," Flynn said. "That's the Sun."

"Lord." Johnson sounded more reverent than he'd thought he could. "That's . . . quite something, isn't it?"

"You might say so," the other pilot answered. "Yes, you just might say so."

Tau Ceti, of course, remained in the same place in the sky as it had before. It was brighter now, but still seemed nothing special; it was an intrinsically dimmer star than the Sun. Before the Lizards came, no one had ever paid any attention to it or to Epsilon Eridani or to Epsilon Indi, the three stars whose inhabited planets the Race had ruled since men were still hunters and gatherers. Now everyone knew the first two; Epsilon Indi, deep in the southern sky and faintest of the three, remained obscure.

"When we wake up again . . ." Johnson said. "When we wake up again, we'll be there."

"Oh, yes." Flynn nodded. "Pity we won't be able to go down to Home."

"Well, yeah. Too much time with no gravity," Johnson said, and Mickey Flynn nodded again. Johnson pointed back toward the Sun. "But we saw *this*." At the moment, it seemed a fair trade.

Kassquit swam up toward consciousness from the black depths of a sleep that might as well have been death. When she looked around, she thought at first that her eyes weren't working the way they should. She'd lived her whole life aboard starships. Metal walls and floors and ceilings seemed normal to her. She knew stone and wood and plaster could be used for the same purposes, but the knowledge was purely theoretical.

Focusing on the—technician?—tending her was easier. "I greet you," Kassquit said faintly. Her voice didn't want to obey her will.

Even her faint croak was enough to make the female of the Race jerk in surprise. "Oh! You *do* speak our language," the technician said. "They told me you did, but I was not sure whether to believe them."

"Of course I do. I am a citizen of the Empire." Kassquit hoped she sounded indignant and not just terribly, terribly tired. "What do I look like?"

To her, it was a rhetorical question. To the technician, it was anything but. "One of those horrible Big Uglies from that far-off star," she said. "How can you be a citizen of the Empire if you look like them?"

I must be on Home, Kassquit realized. *Males and females on Tosev 3 know who and what I am.* "Never mind how I can be. I am, that is all," she said. She looked around again. The white-painted chamber was probably part of a hospital; it looked more like a ship's infirmary than anything else. *Home,* she thought again, and awe filled her. "I made it," she whispered.

"So you did." The technician seemed none too pleased about admitting it. "How do you feel?"

"Worn," Kassquit answered honestly. "Am I supposed to be this weary?"

"I do not know. I have no experience with Big Uglies." The female of the Race never stopped to wonder if that name might bother Kassquit. She went on, "Males and females of the Race often show such symptoms upon revival, though."

"That is some relief," Kassquit said.

"Here." The technician gave her a beaker filled with a warm, yellowish liquid. "I was told you were to drink this when you were awake enough to do so."

"It shall be done," Kassquit said obediently. The stuff was salty and a little greasy and tasted very good. "I thank you." She returned the empty beaker. "Very nice. What was it?"

She'd succeeded in surprising the female again. "Do you not know? It must have been something from your world. It has nothing to do with ours. Wait." She looked inside what had to be Kassquit's medical chart. "It is something called *chicknzup.* Is that a word in the Big Ugly language?"

"I do not know," Kassquit answered. "I speak only the language of the Race."

"How very peculiar," the technician said. "Well, instructions are that you are to rest. Will you rest?"

"I will try," Kassquit said. The sleeping mat on which she lay was identical to the one she'd had in the starship. Why not? A sleeping mat was a sleeping mat. She closed her eyes and wiggled and fell asleep.

When she woke, it was dark. She lay quietly. The small sounds of this place were different from the ones she'd known all her life. Along with the noises of the starship's ventilation and plumbing, there had been lots of tapes of random sounds of Home. But she knew all the noises on those by now. Here, her ears were hearing things they'd never met before.

Something buzzed at the window. When she looked that way, she saw a small black shape silhouetted against the lighter sky. It moved, and the buzzing noise moved with it. She realized it was alive. Awe washed through her again. Except for males and females of the Race and a few Big Uglies, it was the first living thing she'd ever seen in person.

She got to her feet. Slowly, carefully, she walked toward the window. Her legs were uncertain beneath her, but held her up. She peered at the creature. It sensed she was near and stopped buzzing; it clung quietly to the window glass. As she peered at it, she realized she knew what it was: some kind of ffissach. They had eight legs. Many of them—this one obviously included—had wings. Like most of them, it was smaller than the last joint of her middle finger. Home had millions of different species of them. They ate plants and one another. Bigger life-forms devoured them by the billions every day. Without them, the ecosystem would collapse.

Kassquit knew all about that from her reading. She hadn't expected to find any ffissachi inside buildings. She especially hadn't expected to find one inside a hospital. Didn't the Race value hygiene and cleanliness? She knew it did. Her experience on the starships orbiting Tosev 3 had taught her as much. So what was this one doing here?

As she stood there watching it, it began to fly and buzz again. Its wings beat against the window glass. She didn't suppose it understood about glass. Everything in front of it looked clear. Why couldn't it just fly through? It kept trying and trying and trying. . . .

Kassquit was so fascinated, she thought she could have watched the little creature all night. She thought so, anyhow, till her legs wobbled so badly she almost sat down, hard, on the floor. She also found herself yawning again. Whatever went into cold sleep, it hadn't all worn off yet. She made her way back to the sleeping mat and lay down again. For a little while, the ffissach's buzzing kept her from going back to sleep, but only for a little while.

When she woke again, it was light. Sunlight streamed in

through the window. The ffissach was still there, but silent and motionless now. Before Kassquit could look at it in the better light, the technician came in. "I greet you," she said. "How do you feel this morning?"

"I thank you—I am better." Kassquit pointed to the window. "What is that ffissach doing there?"

The technician walked over, squashed it against the palm of her hand, and then cleaned herself with a moist wipe. "They are nuisances," she said. "They do get in every once in a while, though."

"You killed it!" Kassquit felt a pang of dismay at the little death, not least because it took her by surprise.

"Well, what did you expect me to do? Take it outside and let it go?" The technician sounded altogether indifferent to the ffissach's fate. There was a stain on the inside of the window.

"I do not know what your custom is," Kassquit answered unhappily.

"Do you know whether you want breakfast?" the technician asked, plainly doubting whether Kassquit could make up her mind about anything.

"Yes, please," she answered.

"All right. Some of your foods came with you on the starship, and I also have a list of foods from Home you have proved you can safely eat. Which would you prefer?"

"Foods from Home are fine," Kassquit said. "I am on Home, after all."

"All right. Wait here. Do not go anywhere." Yes, the technician was convinced Kassquit had no brains at all. "I will bring you food. Do not go away." With a last warning hiss, the technician left.

She soon returned, carrying a tray like the ones in the starship refectory. It held the same sorts of food Kassquit had been eating there, too. She used her eating tongs as automatically and as well as a female of the Race would have. When she finished, the technician took away the tray.

"What do I do now?" Kassquit called after the female.

"Wait," was the only answer she got.

Wait she did. She went to the window and looked out at the landscape spread out before her. She had never seen such a thing in person before, but the vista seemed familiar to her thanks to countless videos. Those were buildings and streets there, streets with cars and buses in them. The irregular projections off in the distance were mountains. And yes, the sky was supposed to be that odd shade of dusty greenish blue, not black.

Kassquit also looked down at herself. Her body paint was in sad disarray—hardly surprising, after so many years of cold sleep. As she'd thought she would, she found a little case of paints in the room and began touching herself up.

She'd almost finished when a male spoke from the doorway: "I greet you, ah, Researcher."

Reading his body paint at a glance, she assumed the posture of respect. "And I greet you, Senior Researcher. What can I do for you, superior sir?"

"I am called Stinoff," the male said. "You must understand, you are the first Tosevite I have met in person, though I have been studying your species through data relayed from Tosev 3. Fascinating! Astonishing!" His eye turrets traveled her from head to feet.

"What do you wish of me, superior sir?" Kassquit asked again.

"You must also understand, it is later than you think," Senior Researcher Stinoff said. "When you came to Home, you were kept in cold sleep until it became evident the starship full of wild Tosevites would soon arrive. We did not wish to expend undue amounts of your lifespan without good reason. That starship is now nearly here, which accounts for your revival at this time."

"I . . . see," Kassquit said slowly. "I thought that, as a citizen of the Empire, I might have had some say in the timing of my awakening. I made it clear I wished to become familiar with Home as soon as possible."

"Under normal circumstances, you would have," Stinoff said. "In your case, however, how can circumstances be normal? And I thought that, as a citizen of the Empire, you would recognize that the needs of society take precedence over those of any one individual."

He had a point, and a good one. Aggressive individualism was a trait more common and more esteemed among the bar-

barous Big Uglies than in the Race. Kassquit used the affirmative gesture. "That is a truth, superior sir. I cannot deny it.
How may I be of the greatest use to the Empire?"

"You have direct experience with Tosevites." Stinoff was
kind enough or clever enough to keep from reminding her
again that she *was* a Tosevite. He went on, "Negotiations with
these foreigners"—an archaic word in the language of the
Race—"will not be easy or simple. You will work on our side
along with Fleetlord Atvar and Senior Researcher Ttomalss."

"Oh?" Kassquit said. "Ttomalss is here, then?"

"Yes," Stinoff said. "He was recalled while you were on the
journey between Tosev 3 and Home. He has spent the time
since his revival preparing for the coming of the Tosevite starship."

Ttomalss had more time to spend than Kassquit. That hadn't
seemed to matter when she was younger. Her own time had
stretched out before her in what seemed an endless orbit. But
it was not endless; it was spiraling down toward decay, burn-
out, and extinguishment—and it spiraled more quickly than
that of a male or female of the Race. Nothing to be done
about it.

"I was told this would be a starship from the not-empire of
the United States," Kassquit said. Stinoff made the affirmative gesture. Kassquit asked, "Do we know the identities of
the Tosevites on the ship?"

"No, not yet," the male from Home replied. "They will still
be in cold sleep. The ship is not yet in our solar system,
though it is close."

"I see," Kassquit said. "Well, it may be interesting to find
out."

When Sam Yeager returned to consciousness, his first clear
thought was that he was dreaming. He knew just what kind of
dream it was, too: a dream out of some science-fiction story
or other. He'd read them and enjoyed them since the first
science-fiction pulps came out when he was a young man.
The elasticity that reading science fiction gave his mind was
no small part of how he'd got involved in dealing with the
Lizards to begin with.

This dream certainly had a science-fictional quality to it: he didn't weigh anything at all. He was, he discovered, strapped down on a table. If he hadn't been, he could have floated away. That was interesting. Less enjoyably, his stomach was doing its best to crawl up his throat hand over hand. He gulped, trying to hold it down.

I'm on my way to the Moon, he thought. He'd been to the Moon once before, and he'd been weightless all the way. So maybe this wasn't a dream after all.

He opened his eyes. It wasn't easy; he felt as if each one had a millstone on it. When he succeeded, he wondered why he'd bothered. The room in which he found himself told him very little. It was bare, matte-finished metal, with fluorescent tubes on the ceiling giving off light. Someone—a woman—in a white smock hung over him. Yes, he was weightless, and so was she.

"Do you hear me, Colonel Yeager?" she asked. "Do you understand me?" By the way she said it, she was repeating herself.

Sam nodded. That was even harder than opening his eyes had been. He paused, gathered strength, and tried to talk. "Where am I?" The traditional question. He wondered if the woman heard him. His throat felt full of glue and cotton balls.

But her nod told him she'd got it. "You're in orbit around Home, in the Tau Ceti system," she answered. "Do you understand?"

He nodded again, and croaked, "I'll be a son of a bitch." He wouldn't usually have said that in front of a woman, especially one he didn't know. He still had drugs scrambling his brains; he could tell how slow and dopey he was. Had he offended her? No—she was laughing. Bit by bit, things got clearer. "So the cold sleep worked."

"It sure did," she said, and handed him a plastic drinking bulb. "Here. Have some of this."

Clumsily, Sam reached out and took it. It was warm, which made him realize how cold his hands were, how cold all of him was. He drank. It tasted like chicken broth—and tasting it made him realize the inside of his mouth had tasted like a slit trench before. He couldn't empty the bulb, but he drank more than half. When he tried to speak again, it came easier: "What year is this?"

"It's 2031, Colonel Yeager," the woman answered.

"Christ!" Sam said violently. His shiver had nothing to do with the chill the broth had started to dispel. He was 124 years old. *Older than Moses, by God,* he thought. True, he remembered only seventy of those years. But he had, without a doubt, been born in 1907. "The starship took off in . . . ?"

"In 1995, Colonel. It's called the *Admiral Peary.*"

"Christ," Sam said once more, this time in a calmer tone. He'd been two years old when Admiral Peary made it to the North Pole—or, as some people claimed later, didn't make it but said he did. He wondered what the old geezer would have thought of this trip. *He'd have been jealous as hell,* was what occurred to him.

More slowly than it should have, another thought crossed his mind. He'd gone into cold sleep in 1977. They'd kept him on ice for eighteen years before they took him aboard the starship. It wasn't just because he was an expert on the Race, either. He knew better than that. They'd wanted to make sure he stayed out of the way, too.

And they'd got what they wanted. He was more than ten light-years out of the way. If he ever saw Earth again, it would be at least two-thirds of the way through the twenty-first century. *To heck with Moses. Look out, Methuselah.*

"I'm Dr. Melanie Blanchard, by the way," the woman said.

"Uh—pleased to meet you." Sam held out a hand.

She gave it a brisk pump, and then said, "You won't know this, of course, but your son and daughter-in-law are aboard this ship. They haven't been revived yet, but everything on the instrument panels looks good."

"That's good. That's wonderful, in fact." Sam still wasn't thinking as fast as he should. He needed close to half a minute to find the next question he needed to ask: "When did they go under?"

"Not long before the ship left. Biologically, your son is fifty." Dr. Blanchard talked about Jonathan's age. With a woman's discretion, she didn't mention Karen's.

"Fifty? Lord!" Sam said. His son had been a young man when he went into cold sleep himself. Jonathan wasn't young any more—and neither was Karen, dammit. Sam realized he had to catch up with a third of their lives. He also realized something else: how mushily he was talking. Dr. Blanchard had been too discreet to mention that, too. He asked, "Could I have my choppers, please?"

"You sure can." She gave them to him.

He popped them into his mouth. He hadn't worn them in more than fifty years . . . or since yesterday, depending on how you looked at things. "That's better," he said, and so it was. "I can hardly talk like a human being without 'em, let alone like a Lizard."

"I understood you before," she said. "And there were other things to worry about."

Like what? he wondered. Answers weren't hard to find. Like making sure he was alive. Like making sure he still had two working brain cells to rub against each other. If they'd hauled him more than ten light-years and ended up with nothing but a rutabaga . . . *Some of them wouldn't have been too disappointed.*

Before he could get too bitter about that, a man's voice called from a hatchway leading out of the room: "Anybody home?" Without waiting for an answer, the man came gliding down into the chamber. He was about sixty, very lean, with a long face and graying sandy hair cropped close to his head. He wore a T-shirt and shorts; the shirt had a colonel's eagles pinned to the shoulders. "You're Yeager, eh?"

"Last time I looked—but that was a while ago," Sam replied. The other man grinned. Sam added, "You're one up on me."

"Sorry about that. I'm Glen Johnson."

"Are you? I'm damned glad to meet you in person, Colonel!" As he had for Dr. Blanchard, Yeager stuck out his hand. The other man took it. He didn't have much of a grip. Even at seventy, even coming out of cold sleep, Sam could have squashed his hand without half trying. Maybe his surprise showed on his face, for Johnson said, "I spent more than twenty years weightless out in the asteroid belt before they decided to refrigerate me."

"Oh. You were on the *Lewis and Clark*?" Yeager asked, and Johnson nodded. Sam went on, "I wondered why I never heard from you again after we talked when you were flying orbital patrol. Now I understand better." He paused for more thought. "So they put you away in . . . 1984?" His wits were clearer, but still slow.

"That's right." Johnson nodded again. "How about you?"

"Me? It was 1977."

They looked at each other. Neither said anything. Neither needed to say anything. They'd both gone into cold sleep—been urged, almost forced, to go into cold sleep—years before the *Admiral Peary* was ready to fly. The reasons behind that seemed altogether too obvious.

"Isn't it great to be politically reliable?" Sam murmured.

"Who, me?" Glen Johnson said, deadpan. They both laughed. Johnson went on, "Actually, depending on how you look at things, it's not that bad. They were so eager to send us far, far away, they gave us the chance to see Home." He said the name in English and then in the Lizards' language.

"Well, that's true," Sam said. "They can get some use out of us here, and we're too far away to get into a whole lot of trouble."

"That's how I figure it, too," Johnson agreed. "And speaking of seeing Home, how would you like to *see* Home?"

"Can I?" Sam forgot about the straps and tried to zoom off the table. That didn't work. He looked at Dr. Blanchard. "May I?"

"If you've got enough coordination to undo those straps, you've got enough to go up to the control room," she told him.

He fumbled at them. Glen Johnson laughed—not mockingly, but sympathetically. He said, "I've done that twice now."

"Twice?" Sam tried to make his fingers obey him. There! A buckle loosened.

"Yeah, twice," Johnson said. "They woke me halfway through so I could help in the turn-ship maneuver. Everybody here will get a good look at Home pretty soon. I saw the sky with no sun anywhere." A certain somber pride—and more than a little awe—filled his voice.

Yeager tried to imagine how empty that sky would seem—tried and felt himself failing. But his hands seemed smarter when he wasn't telling them what to do. Two more latches came loose. He flipped back the belts that held him to the table.

That was when he realized he was naked. Melanie Blanchard took it in stride. So did Johnson. Sam decided he would, too. She tossed him underpants and shorts and a T-shirt like the pilot's. "Here," she said. "Put these on, if you want to." He did. He thought the underpants were the ones he'd been wearing when he went downtown to go into cold sleep. The shirt, like Johnson's, had eagles pinned to the shoulders.

"Come on," Johnson said, and went up the hatchway.

Slowly, creakily, Sam followed. Johnson was smooth in weightlessness. He would be, of course. Yeager was anything but. A splash of sunlight brightened the top of the corridor. He paused there to rest for a moment before going up into the control room. "Oh," he said softly. Here he was, resting like a cat in the sunlight of another star.

Tau Ceti was a little cooler, a little redder, than the Sun. Sam stared at the light. Was there a difference? Maybe a little. The Lizards, who'd evolved here, saw a bit further into the infrared than people could, but violet was ultraviolet to them.

"Come on," Glen Johnson said again.

"I'm coming." Sam thrust himself up into the control room. Then he said, "Oh," once more, for there was Home filling the sky below him. With it there, *below* suddenly had a meaning again. He had to remind himself he wouldn't, he couldn't, fall.

He'd seen Earth from orbit, naturally. The cloud-banded blue, mingled here and there with green and brown and gold, would stay in his memory forever. His first thought of Home was, *There's a lot less blue.* On Earth, land was islands in a great, all-touching sea. Here, seas dotted what was primarily a landscape. The first Lizards who'd gone around their world had done it on foot.

And the greens he saw were subtly different from those of Earth. He couldn't have said how, but they were. Something down in his bones knew. What looked like desert stretched for untold miles between the seas. He knew it wasn't so barren as it seemed. Life had spent as long adapting to the conditions here as it had back on Earth.

"I'm jealous of you," Johnson said.

"Of me? How come?"

"You'll be able to go down there and take a good close look at things," the pilot answered. "I'm stuck here in the ship. After so long aboard the *Lewis and Clark,* gravity would kill me pretty damn quick."

"Oh." Sam felt foolish. "I should have thought of that. I'm sorry. You must feel like Moses looking at the Promised Land."

"A little bit—but there is one difference." Johnson paused. Sam waved for him to go on. He did: "All Moses could do was look. Me, I can blow this place to hell and gone. The *Admiral Peary* came loaded for bear."

Ttomalss looked up into the night sky of Home. Some of the bright stars there moved. The Race had had orbital vehicles for as long as they'd been a unified species—a hundred thousand years, more or less. But one of these moving stars, the first one ever, didn't belong to the Race. It was full of wild Big Uglies.

Which one? Ttomalss couldn't pick it out, not at a glance. For all he knew, it could have been on the other side of the world. That hardly mattered. It was there. No—it was *here.* The Tosevites were forcefully reminding the Race they weren't quiet subjects, weren't quiet colleagues, like the Rabotevs or Hallessi.

It wasn't as if he hadn't known this day was coming. He wouldn't have been recalled to Home if it hadn't been. But he'd been revived for years now, and nobody seemed to have any better idea of what to do about the Big Uglies than males and females had had before he went into cold sleep. That not only worried him, it also annoyed him.

Quite a few things about Home annoyed him these days, from the ridiculous appearance of the young to the way males and females here seemed unable to make up their minds. Nobody decided anything in a hurry. It often looked as if nobody decided anything at all. His time on Tosev 3 had changed him more than he'd imagined while he was there.

The psychologist's mouth fell open in a laugh, though it really wasn't funny. If you couldn't make up your mind on

Tosev 3, you'd end up dead—either that or hornswoggled by the Big Uglies, depending. You had to be able to decide. You had to be able to act. Here . . . This place felt like the back side of a sand dune. The wind blew past overhead, but nothing here really changed.

Ttomalss laughed again. Strange how living among barbarians could be so much more vivid, so much more urgent, than living among his own kind. The Race didn't hurry. Till he went to Tosev 3, he'd thought of that as a virtue. Now, perversely, it seemed a vice, and a dangerous one.

His telephone hissed. He took it off his belt. "Senior Researcher Ttomalss speaking," he said. "I greet you."

"And I greet you, superior sir," Kassquit replied. Here on Home, her mushy Tosevite accent was unique, unmistakable. "Activity aboard the Tosevite starship appears to be increasing."

"Ah?" Ttomalss said. Even here, the Big Uglies on the starship were enterprising. "Is that so?"

"It is, superior sir," his former ward replied. "Reconnaissance video now shows Tosevites coming up into the ship's observation dome. And our speculations back on Tosev 3 appear to have been correct." Her voice rose in excitement.

"Ah?" Ttomalss said again. "To which speculations do you refer?"

"I have viewed magnified images from the video footage, superior sir, and one of the wild Big Uglies appears to be Sam Yeager."

"Really? Are you certain?" Ttomalss asked.

"I am." To show how certain she was, Kassquit used an emphatic cough.

"Well, well." Ttomalss had to believe her. Like any male or female of the Race, he had a hard time telling Big Uglies apart, especially when facial features were all he had to go on. He hadn't evolved to detect subtle differences between one of those alien faces and another. Kassquit had. She did it without thinking, and she was usually right.

It worked both ways, of course. She'd once told him she recognized members of the Race more by their body paint than by differences in the way they looked. And wild Big Uglies even had trouble telling males and females apart from one another. To Ttomalss, differences in scale patterns, eye-turret size, snout shape, and so on were glaringly obvious. He and his kind had evolved to notice those, not whatever different cues Big Uglies used.

Kassquit said, "I wonder whether Sam Yeager's hatchling is also aboard the Tosevite starship."

"Time will tell," Ttomalss answered.

"So it will." Kassquit sounded eager, hopeful, enthusiastic. Years before, Jonathan Yeager had introduced her to Tosevite mating practices. Ttomalss was aware he understood those, and the emotional drives that went with them, only intellectually. Kassquit sounded not the least bit intellectual.

"Perhaps I should remind you that, as of the time when I went into cold sleep, Jonathan Yeager remained in an exclusive mating contract with a Tosevite female," Ttomalss said. "In fact, they both appear to have entered cold sleep not long before I did, though I do not know for what purpose. This being so, if he is aboard the starship, his mate is likely to be aboard as well."

"Truth." Now Kassquit might have hated him.

Ttomalss silently sighed. He had once more underestimated the power of mating urges to shape Tosevite behavior. Those and the bonds existing between parents and hatchlings were the strongest forces that drove Big Uglies. Even Kassquit, with the finest civilized upbringing possible on Tosev 3, was not immune to them.

The other thing Ttomalss had to remember was that, if he underestimated those forces despite his extensive experience, other alleged experts on the Big Uglies, "experts" who had never been within light-years of Tosev 3, would do far worse. It was, no doubt, fortunate that he'd been recalled to Home. However important it was that he continue his work on Tosev 3, this took priority.

"May I ask you something, superior sir?" Kassquit spoke with cold formality.

"You may always ask," Ttomalss replied. "If the answer is one that I possess, you shall have it."

"Very well. Was it at your instruction that I was left in cold sleep for so long after reaching Home? I do not appreciate being used as nothing more than a tool against the Big Uglies.

I have the same rights and privileges as any other citizen of the Empire."

"Of course you do," Ttomalss said soothingly. "But how could I have done such a thing? You left Tosev 3 for Home years before I did."

Silence followed—but not for long. Angrily, Kassquit said, "How could you have done such a thing, superior sir? Nothing simpler. As soon as I went into cold sleep, you could have arranged to have the order sent by radio from Tosev 3 to here. Radio waves travel twice as fast as our ships. The order not to revive me at once could easily have been waiting when I arrived. The question I am asking is, did you send such an order?"

In many ways, she was indeed a citizen of the Empire. She could figure out the implications of interstellar travel and communication as readily as any member of the Race. Somehow, in spite of everything, Ttomalss had not expected that.

When he did not answer right away, Kassquit said, "I might have known. And yet I am supposed to work with you. By the spirits of Emperors past, superior sir, why should I?"

For that, Ttomalss did have an answer ready: "For the sake of the Race. For the sake of the Empire."

"What about *my* sake?" Kassquit demanded. Despite her upbringing, parts of her were Tosevite through and through. By the standards of the Race, she was a pronounced individualist, putting her own needs above those of the community.

"In the larger scheme of things, which carries the greater weight?" Ttomalss asked.

"If the larger scheme of things is built on lies, what difference does it make?" Kassquit retorted.

That charge had fangs—or it would have, had it held truth. "I never told you I would not send such a request to Home," Ttomalss said. "While you may put your own interests first, I am obliged to give precedence to the Race as a whole. So are the males and females here who concurred in my judgment."

Now Kassquit was the one who needed some time to think about how she would reply. At last, she said, "Had you asked if I would accept the delay in revival, I probably would have said yes. I recognize the needs of the Empire, too, superior sir, regardless of what you may think. But it was presumptuous of you to believe you could decide this matter for me without consulting me. That is what gets under my scales."

She had no scales, of course, but that was the Race's idiom. She did have a point . . . of sorts. Remembering that he would have to try to work with her, Ttomalss yielded to the degree he could: "I apologize for my presumption. I should have asked you, as you say. I will not make such an error again. I will also try to keep any other member of the Race from doing so."

Another pause from Kassquit. At the end of it, she said, "Thank you, superior sir. That is better than nothing. It is also better than anything I expected to hear you say."

Ttomalss sighed. "You are not fully happy among us."

"That is a truth, superior sir." Kassquit used another emphatic cough.

"Do you believe you would be happier among the wild Big Uglies?" he asked. "That can in large measure be arranged if you so desire, now that they have come to Home."

But Kassquit said, "No," with yet another emphatic cough. "I am betwixt and between, one thing biologically, something very different culturally. This is your doing. There have been times when I was grateful to you. There have been times when I loathed you beyond all measure. There have been times when I felt both those things at once, which was very confusing."

"I believe you," Ttomalss said. "What do you feel now?"

"Are you still working on your research, superior sir?" Kassquit gibed.

"Of course I am. I always will be, till my dying day," the male answered. He said nothing about Kassquit's dying day, which was liable to occur first. "But I also want to know for my own sake—and for yours. Your welfare matters to me. It matters very much." Now he let out an emphatic cough of his own.

Maybe his sentiment helped disarm Kassquit. Maybe that emphatic cough convinced her he was sincere. Slowly, she said, "These days, what I feel is that what I feel does not matter so much. You did what you did. Neither of us can change it these days. Far too much time has passed for that to be possible. I have to make the best of things as they are."

"That strikes me as a sensible attitude," Ttomalss said.

"It strikes me as a sensible attitude, too," Kassquit said. "That is why I strive to hold on to it, but holding on to it is not always easy."

Just before he asked why not, Ttomalss checked himself. Males and females of the Race were full of irrational behavior. The Big Uglies, from all he'd seen, were even fuller. Their hormonal drives operated all the time, not only during mating season. He sighed again. At bottom, the Race and the Big Uglies were both evolved animals. That they behaved like animals was no wonder. That they sometimes *didn't* behave like animals might have been.

And now the Big Uglies were here. Ttomalss looked up into the night sky again. No, he couldn't tell which moving star was in fact their spaceship. Which it was didn't matter, anyhow. That they were here at all meant one thing and one thing only: trouble. And when had dealing with Tosevites ever meant anything else?

☆ **3** ☆

"Hey, son. Do you hear me?"

Jonathan Yeager heard the words, sure enough, the words and the familiar voice. At first, in the confusion of returning consciousness, the voice mattered for more. A slow smile stretched across his face, though his eyes hadn't opened yet. "Dad," he whispered. "Hi, Dad."

"You made it, Jonathan," his father said. "*We* made it. We're in orbit around Home. When you wake up a little more, you can look out and see the Lizards' planet."

With an effort, Jonathan opened his eyes. There was his father, floating at an improbable angle. A woman in a white smock floated nearby, at an even more improbable one. "Made it," Jonathan echoed. Then, as his wits slowly and creakily began to work, he smiled again. "Haven't seen you in a hell of a long time, Dad."

"Only seems like a little while to me," his father answered. "You drove me downtown, and I woke up here."

"Yeah," Jonathan said, his voice still dreamy. "But I had to drive the goddamn car back, too." He looked around. His neck worked, anyhow. "Where's Karen?"

The woman spoke up: "She's next on the revival schedule, Mr. Yeager. All the signs on the diagnostic monitors look optimal."

"Good." Jonathan discovered he could nod as well as crane his neck. "That's good." Tears stung his eyes. He nodded again.

"Here, have some of this." The woman held a drinking bulb to his mouth. He sucked like a baby. It wasn't milk, though. It was . . . Before he could find what that taste was, she told him: "Chicken broth goes down easy."

It didn't go down that easily. Swallowing took effort.

Everything took effort. Of course, he'd been on ice for . . . how long? He didn't need to ask, *Where am I?*—they'd told him that. But, "What year is this?" seemed a perfectly reasonable question, and so he asked it.

"It's 2031," his father answered. "If you look at it one way, you're going to be eighty-eight toward the end of the year. Of course, if you look at it that way, I'm older than the hills, so I'd rather not."

His father had seemed pretty old to Jonathan when he went into cold sleep. From thirty-three, which Jonathan had been then, seventy would do that. From fifty, where Jonathan was now, seventy still seemed a good age, but it wasn't as one with the Pyramids of Egypt. *I've done a lot of catching up with him,* he realized. *That's pretty strange.*

"Can I get up and have that look around?" he asked.

"If you can, you may," the woman in the white smock answered, as precise with her grammar as Jonathan's mother had always been.

"It's a test," his father added. "If you're coordinated enough to get off the table, you're coordinated enough to move around."

It proved harder than Jonathan thought it would. What was that line from the Bible? *If I forget thee, O Jerusalem, let my right hand forget her cunning*—that was it. Both his right hand and his left seemed to have forgotten their cunning. Hell, they seemed to have forgotten what they were for.

Finally, he did manage to escape. "Whew!" he said. He hadn't imagined a few buckles and straps could be so tough. The woman in white gave him shorts and a T-shirt to match what his father had on. He hadn't noticed he was naked till then.

"Come on," Sam Yeager said. "Control room is up through that hatchway." He pushed off toward the hatchway with the accuracy of someone who'd been in space before. Come to that, Jonathan had, too. His own push wasn't so good, but he could blame that on muscles that still didn't want to do what they were supposed to. He not only could, he did.

Jonathan pulled himself up the handholds and into the control room. Along with his father, two officers were already in there. The leaner one eyed Jonathan, turned to the rounder one, and said, "Looks like his old man, doesn't he?"

"Poor devil," the rounder man . . . agreed?

"These refugees from a bad comedy show are Glen Johnson and Mickey Flynn," Sam Yeager said, pointing to show who was who. "They're the glorified bus drivers who got us here."

"Two of the glorified bus drivers," Flynn corrected. "Our most glorified driver is presently asleep. He does that every once in a while, whether he needs to or not."

"Stone'd be happier if he didn't," Johnson said. "He'd be happier if nobody did."

He and Flynn did sound like a team. Jonathan Yeager would have been more inclined to sass them about it if he hadn't started staring at Home. He'd seen it in videos from the Race, of course, but the difference between a video on a screen and a real world out there seeming close enough to touch was about the same as the difference between a picture of a kiss and the kiss itself.

"Wow," Jonathan said softly.

"You took the words out of my mouth, son," his father said.

"We're really here," Jonathan whispered. Hearing about it in the room where he'd revived was one thing. Seeing a living planet that wasn't Earth, seeing it in person and up close . . . "Wow," he said again.

"Yes, we're really here," Flynn said. "And so the Lizards have laid out the red carpet for us, because they're so thrilled to see us at their front door."

"Excuse me," Johnson said, and looked down at his wrist, as if at a watch. "I think my irony detector just went off."

"Can't imagine why." Flynn cocked a hand behind one ear. "Don't you hear the brass band? I'm just glad the Race never thought of cheerleaders."

How long had the two of them been sniping at each other? They might almost have been married. A light went on in Jonathan's head. "You two are off the *Lewis and Clark,* aren't you?"

"Who, us?" Flynn said. "I resemble that remark."

Johnson said, "It's the stench of Healey, that's what it is. It clings to us wherever we go."

"Healey?" Jonathan wondered how hard his leg was being pulled.

"Our commandant," Mickey Flynn replied. "Renowned throughout the Solar System—and now here, too—for the sweetness of his song and the beauty of his plumage."

"Plumage, my ass," Johnson muttered. "We thought we'd gone light-years to get away from him—worth it, too. But turns out he came along in cold sleep, so now he's running this ship, dammit."

"Healey's a martinet—one of those people who give military discipline a bad name. There are more of them than there ought to be, I'm afraid," Sam Yeager said.

Johnson looked as if he wanted to say even more than he had, but held back. That struck Jonathan as sensible. If this Healey was as nasty as all that, he made little lists and checked them a lot more than twice. "I wonder who's president these days," he remarked.

"As of last radio signal, it was a woman named Joyce Peterman," Johnson replied, with a shrug that meant the news surprised him, too. "Of course, last radio signal left more than two terms ago, so it's somebody else by now—or if it's not, things have really gone to hell back there."

"As long as the radio signals keep coming, I'm happy," Jonathan's father said. "They could elect Mortimer Snerd, and I wouldn't care."

Jonathan, who'd grown up as television ousted radio, barely knew who Mortimer Snerd was. He understood what his father was talking about just the same. Radio signals from Earth to Tau Ceti meant the Lizards and the Americans— or the Russians, or the Japanese, or (since the last Nazi-Lizard war was almost seventy years past by now) even the Germans—hadn't thrown enough missiles at one another to blast the home planet back to the Stone Age.

My kids are as old as I am now, Jonathan thought, and then he shook his head. That was wrong. If it was 2031, his kids were older than he was. In any sane universe, that should have been impossible. But then, nobody had ever shown this was a sane universe.

He looked up—or was it down?—at Home. The universe might not be sane, but it was beautiful.

"Radio signals are useful things," Flynn said. "We let the Lizards know we were coming, so they could bake us a cake. And we let them know that if the signals from the *Admiral Peary* stopped coming while she was in the Tau Ceti system, we'd bake them a planet." He paused for a precisely timed beat, and then finished, "I love subtle hints."

"Subtle. Right." But Jonathan knew the Lizards would be pitching a fit down there. This had been their imperial center for tens of thousands of years, the place from which they'd set out on their conquests. Now they had uninvited guests. No wonder they were jumpy.

"We've got one ship here," Glen Johnson said. "One ship, against everything the Race has in space. They came at us with their goddamn conquest fleet when we were flying prop jobs. I don't waste a lot of grief on them."

"They didn't even expect us to have those," Jonathan's father said. "They were looking for knights in shining armor. Hell, if you've ever seen that photo their probe took, they were looking for knights in rusty armor. If they'd found them, they might not have lost a male."

The Race always took a long time to get ready before doing anything. That had saved mankind once. Jonathan dared hope it would work for the *Admiral Peary,* too. But the Lizards back home had seen they couldn't sit around and dawdle when dealing with Big Uglies. Did the ones here also realize that? *We'll find out,* he thought.

Something else occurred to him. As casually as he could, he asked his father, "Have we heard from Kassquit? Did she make it through cold sleep all right?"

"Well, yes, as a matter of fact," Sam Yeager answered with a rather sheepish grin. "Difference is, you know she went into cold sleep. I didn't, because she went in after me. I got a jolt when I heard what had to be a human speaking the Lizards' language and asking for Regeya."

Jonathan laughed. The two American pilots looked blank. "Regeya?" Flynn said plaintively, while Johnson asked, "Just who is this Kassquit person, anyway? A traitor? You never did exactly explain that, Sam."

"Regeya's the name I used on the Lizards' electronic network back home," Jonathan's father said. "And no, Kassquit's not a traitor, not the way you mean. She's got a right to be loyal to the other side. She was raised by the Lizards ever since she was a tiny baby."

"You've met her?" Glen Johnson asked. Jonathan and his father both nodded.

"Raised by Lizards, was she?" Flynn said. The Yeagers nodded again. The pilot asked, "And how crazy is she?"

Sam Yeager looked to Jonathan, who knew her better. "Some," Jonathan said. "Maybe more than some. But less than you'd expect. She's very smart. I think that helped." *We did the same thing to Mickey and Donald, too,* he thought. *They at least had each other. Kassquit didn't have anybody.*

His father was still looking at him. He knew all the reasons Jonathan had asked about Kassquit. Oh, yes. He knew. And so would Karen.

Consciousness came back to Karen Yeager very slowly. She couldn't tell when dreams stopped and mundane reality returned. She'd been dreaming about Jonathan and his father. Next thing she knew, she saw them. She would have accepted that as part of the dream, for they were both floating in space in front of her, and dreams were the only place where you could fly. But then she realized they weren't flying, or not exactly, and that she was weightless, too.

"We made it," she whispered. Her tongue felt like a bolt of flannel. It didn't want to shape the words.

"We sure did, honey." Jonathan had no trouble talking. For a moment, Karen resented that. Then, on hands and knees, a thought crawled through her head. *Oh. He's been awake for a while.*

"How are you, Mrs. Yeager?" That brisk female voice hadn't been part of her dream. The woman in a white smock also floated above her head.

Answer. I have to answer. "Sleepy," Karen managed.

"Well, I'm not surprised. All your vital signs are good, though," the woman said. "Once the drugs wear off and you get used to being normal body temperature again, you'll do fine. I'm Dr. Blanchard, by the way."

"That's nice," Karen said vaguely. She turned toward Sam Yeager. "Hello. It's been a while." She laughed. She felt more than a little drunk, and more than a little confused, too. "How long *has* it been, anyway?"

"Everybody asks that once the fog starts to clear," Dr. Blanchard said. "It's 2031." She gave Karen a moment to digest that. It was going to take more than a moment. *I'm almost ninety years old,* Karen thought. But she didn't feel any different from the way she had when she went into cold sleep. She looked at her father-in-law again. *How old is Sam?* She had trouble with the subtraction.

The woman in the smock gave her chicken soup. Swallowing proved at least as hard as talking, but she managed. She felt better with the warm broth inside. It seemed to help anchor her to the here and now.

"Can I get up?" she asked.

Jonathan and his father both started to laugh. "We both had to figure out how, and now you do, too," Jonathan said. After some fumbling—her hands still didn't feel as if they belonged to her—Karen managed to undo the fasteners that held her to the revival bed. Only a towel covered her. Dr. Blanchard chased the male Yeagers out of the revival room and gave her shorts and a shirt like the ones they had on. Then they were suffered to return. She pushed off toward them.

When she came up to Jonathan, he gave her a quick kiss. Then he let her go. He'd known her a long time. Had he tried for anything more than a quick kiss just then, she would have done her feeble best to disembowel him.

She saw her father-in-law watching her in a peculiar way. Sam Yeager had always noticed her as a woman. He'd never once been obnoxious about it, but he had. Now, for no reason at all, she found herself blushing. Then she shook her head, realizing it wasn't for no reason at all. "I've just aged seventeen years right before your eyes, haven't I?" she said.

"Not a bit," he said. "You've aged maybe five of them."

Karen laughed. "Did they bring the Blarney Stone along so you could kiss it while I was asleep?" She was a child—a great-grandchild, actually—of the Old Sod, even if her maiden name, Culpepper, was English.

Then Jonathan said, "Dad's right, hon."

She tried to poke her husband in the ribs. "You of all people really ought to know better. It's very sweet and everything, but you ought to."

"Nope." He could be stubborn—now, maybe, endearingly stubborn. "Here on the *Admiral Peary,* he really is right. We're weightless. Nothing sags the way it would under gravity." He patted his own stomach by way of illustration.

"Hmm." Karen thought that over. She didn't have a mirror—which, right after cold sleep, was bound to be a mercy—but she could look at Jonathan and Sam. "Maybe." That was as much as she was going to admit.

Jonathan pointed to the passageway where he and his father had gone while she dressed. "Home's out there waiting, if you want to have a look."

Sam Yeager added, "It's out there waiting even if you don't want to have a look."

Jonathan grunted. "You've been listening to that Mickey Flynn too much, Dad."

"Who's Mickey Flynn?" Karen asked.

"One of the pilots," her husband answered darkly.

"He's a bad influence," her father-in-law added. "He's a professional bad influence, you might say. He's proud of it. He has a dry wit."

"Any drier and it'd make Home look like the Amazon jungle," Jonathan said.

"Okay," Karen said. "Now I'm intrigued. Would I rather meet him or the Lizards' planet?" She pushed off toward the passageway.

But Mickey Flynn wasn't in the control room. The pilot who was, a sober-looking fellow named Walter Stone, said, "Pleased to meet you, ma'am," when Jonathan introduced her to him, then went back to studying his radar screen. Karen saw how many blips were on it. That still left her slightly miffed. Stone seemed to care more for machines than he did for people.

Then Karen stopped worrying about the pilot, because the sight of Home made her forget him and everything else. She knew the map of Tau Ceti 2 as well as she knew the map of Earth. Knowing and seeing were two different things. Someone softly said, "Ohh." After a moment, she realized that was her own voice.

"That's what I said, too, hon," Jonathan said.

Stone looked over his shoulder. "We'll deal with whatever they throw at us," he said. "And if they start throwing things at us, we'll make 'em sorry they tried."

Karen believed the last part. The *Admiral Peary* was armed. A ship that went to strange places had to be. If the Lizards attacked it, it could hurt them. Deal with whatever they threw at it? Maybe Brigadier General Stone was an optimist. Maybe he thought he was reassuring her.

She didn't feel reassured. That was what she got for knowing too much. She stared down at the golds and greens and blues—more golds, fewer greens and blues than Earth—spread out below her. "They're the only ones who've ever flown into or out of this system till now," she said. "We hadn't even started farming when they conquered the Rabotevs."

"And they were in space inside this system for God only knows how many thousand years before that," Sam Yeager said. "They've got reasons to be antsy about strangers."

"We've got reasons for coming here," Karen said. "They gave us most of them."

"Don't I know it!" her father-in-law said. "I was on a train from Madison down to Decatur when they came to Earth. They shot it up. Only dumb luck they didn't blow my head off."

"I'm glad they didn't," Jonathan said. "If they had, I wouldn't be here. And I sure wouldn't be *here*." He pointed out toward Home.

Would I be here? Karen wondered. The Race had fascinated her ever since she was little. Even if she'd never met Jonathan, she probably would have done something involving them. Would it have been enough to get her aboard the *Admiral Peary*? How could she know? She couldn't.

An enormous yawn tried to split her face in two. "That happened to me after I'd been awake for a little while," Jonathan said. "They've given us a cabin for two, if you want to sleep for a bit."

"That sounds wonderful," Karen said.

"It's right next to mine," her father-in-law added. "If you leave the TV on too loud, I'll bang my shoe against the wall."

Brigadier General Stone looked pained. "It's not a wall. It's a bulkhead." He and Sam Yeager wrangled about it, not quite seriously, as Jonathan led Karen out of the control room and back to the fluorescent-lit painted metal that was the starship's interior.

The cabin didn't seem big enough for one person, let alone two. When Karen saw the sleeping arrangements, she started to giggle. "Bunk beds!"

"Don't let Stone hear you say that," Jonathan warned. "He'll probably tell you they're supposed to be bulkbunks, or something."

"I don't care." Karen was still giggling. "When I was a little kid, my best friend had a sister who was only a year younger than she was, and they had bunk beds. I was so jealous. You can't believe how jealous I was."

"They've got the same sort of straps on them that the revival bed did," Jonathan said. "We won't go floating all over the cabin."

"I wish they'd spin the ship and give us some gravity," Karen said. "But it would kill the guys from the *Lewis and Clark,* wouldn't it?"

"Like that." Her husband snapped his fingers. "It would screw up fire control, too. We're stuck with being weightless till the Lizards let us go down to Home."

Karen grimaced at the thought of fire control: a euphemism for *this is how we shoot things up.* The grimace turned into yet another yawn. "Dibs on the top bunk," she said, and got into it. As she fastened herself in, a question bubbled up to the top of her mind: "Have we . . . lost anybody?"

"A couple of people," Jonathan answered. "It was a little riskier than they said it would be. I suppose that figures. I'm damn glad you're here, sweetie. And I'm glad Dad is. They really didn't know what they were doing when they put him under."

"I'm glad you're here, too," Karen said. The chill that ran through her had nothing to do with cold sleep. How sorry would certain people back on Earth have been if Sam Yeager hadn't revived? Not very, she suspected. She also suspected she was falling asleep no matter what she could do about it. Moments later, that suspicion was confirmed.

When she woke up, she felt better. She realized how groggy she'd been before. The buckles on the bunk were just like the ones on the revival bed. Those had almost baffled her. She opened these without even thinking about it. When she pushed out of the bunk toward a handhold on the far—not very far—wall, she saw Jonathan reading in the bottom bunk. He looked up from the papers and said, "Hi, there."

"Hi, there yourself," Karen said. "How long was I out?"

"Just a couple of hours." He waved papers at her. "This is stuff you'll need to see—reports on what's been going on back on Earth since we went under. We've got to be as up-to-date as the Lizards are, anyhow."

"I'll look at it." Karen laughed. "It still feels like too much work."

"Okay. I know what you mean," Jonathan said. "I'm a day and a little bit ahead of you, and I'm still not a hundred per-cent, either—not even close. Still, one of these days before we go down to Home, it might be fun to try it weightless. What do you think?"

If Jonathan was chipper enough to contemplate sex, he was further ahead of Karen than he knew. What she said was, "Not tonight, Josephine." What she thought was, *Maybe not for the next six months, or at least not till all the drugs wear off.*

She also almost reminded him that he'd already fooled around in space. At the last minute, she didn't. It wasn't so much that he would point out he hadn't been weightless then; the Lizards' ship had spun to give it artificial gravity. But she didn't want him thinking about Kassquit, and about the days when he'd been young and horny all the time, any more than he had to. Yes, keeping quiet seemed a very good idea.

Sam Yeager spent as much time as he could in the *Admiral Peary*'s control room. Part of that was because he couldn't get enough of looking at Home. Part of it was because the control room wasn't far from the revival room. He got the chance to say hello to some people he hadn't seen for more than fifty years. That was what the calendar insisted, anyway. To him, it seemed like days or weeks. It was a matter of years to them, but not anything like fifty.

And he enjoyed the company of Glen Johnson and Mickey Flynn—and, to a lesser degree, that of Walter Stone. Stone was too much the regulation officer for Sam to feel completely comfortable around him. Such men were often necessary. Yeager knew as much. But he wasn't one of them himself, and, as far as he was concerned, they were also often annoying. He gave no hint of that opinion any place where Stone could overhear him.

Johnson, now, Johnson was as much of a troublemaker as Sam was himself. The authorities had known as much, too. Yeager asked him, "Did you get the subtle hints that it would be a good idea for you to go into cold sleep if you wanted to have a chance to keep breathing?"

"Subtle hints?" The pilot considered. "Well, that depends on what you mean. Healey didn't quite say, 'You have been ordered to volunteer for this procedure.' He didn't quite say it, but he sure meant it. You, too, eh?"

"Oh, yes." Sam nodded. "They looked at me and they thought, *Indianapolis*. I'm not sorry I'm a long way away."

"I've been in Indianapolis," Flynn said. "They should have given you a medal."

Sam scowled and shook his head. Johnson said, "Not funny, Mickey."

"They were people there. Everybody back in the States thought I forgot about that or didn't care," Sam said. "What they wouldn't see was that the Lizards we blew up were people, too."

"That's it," Johnson agreed. "I was up there on patrol when we did that. I figured it was the Reds or the Nazis, but it wasn't. The Lizards would have got their own back against them. They had to against us, too."

"We spent so much time and so much blood making the Race believe we were people, and deserved to be treated like people," Yeager said. "Then we didn't believe it about them. If that's not a two-way street, it doesn't work at all."

Before either of the pilots could say anything, alarms blared. They both forgot about Sam and swung back to the instrument panels. Equipment failure? Lizard attack? No and no. The urgent voice on the intercom said what it was: "Code blue! Code blue! Dr. Kaplan to the revival room! Dr. Garvey to the revival room! Dr. Kaplan! Dr. Garvey! Code blue! Code blue!"

"Damn," Glen Johnson said softly.

"Yeah." Yeager nodded. When the Lizards went into cold sleep, they were all but guaranteed to come out again when revival time rolled around. As often happened when humans adopted and adapted the Race's techniques, they made them work, but less efficiently. Sam often wondered how very lucky he was to have awakened here in orbit around Tau Ceti 2.

"Who's getting revived now?" the pilot asked.

"I haven't looked at the schedule for today," Sam answered. "Do you have a copy handy?"

"I ought to, somewhere." Johnson flipped through papers clipped together and held on a console by large rubber bands so they wouldn't float all over the place. He found the one he wanted and went down it with his finger. Suddenly, he stopped. "Oh, shit," he muttered.

"Who, for God's sake?" Sam asked.

"It's the Doctor," Johnson said.

"Christ!" Sam exclaimed. People had been calling the diplomat the Doctor for years. He was a lucky Jew: his parents had got him out of Nazi Germany in 1938, when he was fifteen. He'd been at Harvard when the Lizards came, and spent a hitch in the Army afterwards. When the fighting ended, he'd gone back to school and earned his doctorate in nineteenth-century international relations.

He'd moved back and forth between universities and the government from that time on. Ever since Henry Cabot Lodge retired in the early 1970s, he'd been the U.S. ambassador to the Race. With his formidably intelligent face and his slow, ponderous, Germanic way of speaking, he was one of the most recognizable men on Earth. He would have been a natural to head up the first American mission to Home.

Sam wondered when the Doctor had gone into cold sleep. Probably not till just before the *Admiral Peary* took off. The two of them had met several times before Sam went under, and the Doctor had consulted him about the Race by telephone fairly regularly. Sam had looked forward to working with the diplomat here ever since spotting his name on the list.

He had, yes. Now . . . Hoping against hope, he asked, "Have

they ever managed to revive anybody they've called a code blue on?"

Glen Johnson shook his head. "Not that I remember."

"I didn't think so. I was hoping you'd tell me I was wrong."

He wondered if he ought to pull himself down the hatchway and see what was going on in the revival room. Regretfully, he decided that wasn't a good idea. Everybody in there would be desperately trying to resuscitate the Doctor. As soon as anyone noticed him rubbernecking, they'd all scream at him to get the hell out of there.

"If the Doctor doesn't make it," Johnson said slowly, "who the hell dickers with the Lizards?"

"I haven't studied the whole passenger list," Sam said. "Besides, who knows how many people got important between the time when I went under and when the *Admiral Peary* took off?"

"Yeah, same goes for me," the pilot said. "They put me in cold sleep after you, but before that I was as far away from everything that was happening on Earth as you could be if you weren't on a starship."

The only human—well, sort of human—on a starship before us was Kassquit, Sam thought. He hadn't been surprised to find out she was here. It made sense for the Race to have their best experts on Big Uglies help deal with the wild ones. And who knew more about humans than somebody who biologically was one?

Dr. Blanchard came floating up into the control room. One look at her face told Sam all he needed to know. Back when he was a minor-league baseball player, he'd worn that same expression after grounding into a game-ending double play with the tying run at third. "I'm sorry," he said quietly.

"We did everything we knew how to do." Dr. Blanchard might have been trying to convince herself as well as Yeager. "We did everything we knew how to do, but his heart just wouldn't get going. Hard to revive a man if you can't give him a heartbeat."

"Cool him down again, then?" Sam asked. "Maybe they'll have better techniques when we get back to Earth." *If we ever get back to Earth.*

"Kaplan and Garvey are doing that," Blanchard said. "I

wouldn't bet the farm on it, though. If we can't revive him, he's probably been dead—dead in slow motion, but dead—for a long time."

"Dead in slow motion. There's a hell of a phrase," Glen Johnson said. "Reminds me of my ex-wife." By the way Dr. Blanchard laughed, she might have had an ex-husband to be reminded of. But then Johnson's face clouded. "She's dead for real now. Everybody I knew back on Earth is probably dead now."

"I've got two grandsons," Sam said. "They were little boys when I went under. They're middle-aged now—hell, if you're not talking about clock time, they're older than their dad and mom. I wonder if they remember me at all. Maybe a little."

"Most of the people here don't have a lot of ties back home," Blanchard said. "I've got cousins and nieces and nephews there, but nobody I was real close to. Some of them are bound to be around now. But when we get back again?" She spread her hands and shook her head. "Cold sleep's a funny business."

"The Lizards have a whole little subsociety, I guess you'd call it, of males and females who spend a lot of time in cold sleep," Sam said. "They keep one another company, because they're the only ones who know what it's like being cut off that way from the time they were hatched in. And they live longer than we do, and they've got faster starships, and their culture doesn't change as fast as ours."

"So you think we'll do the same?" Johnson asked.

"You bet I do," Sam said. "You ever see Joe DiMaggio play?"

"Sure." The pilot nodded. "In Cleveland. I may even have seen *you* once or twice. I used to go to bush-league games now and then."

"Thanks a lot," Yeager said without rancor. "Forget about me. Remember DiMaggio. Suppose we come back in 2070-something and you start going on about Joltin' Joe. Who's going to know what you're talking about, or if you're talking through your hat? Nobody except a guy who's spent a lot of years on ice."

"*I* never saw DiMaggio play," said Melanie Blanchard, who looked to be in her mid-forties. "He retired about the time I was born."

"You at least know about him, though," Sam said. "By the time we get home, he'll be ancient history." They went on talking about it, none of them getting too excited. It hurt less than talking about losing the Doctor would have.

The next three revivals went well, which helped make people feel better about things. Then Sam got summoned to the commandant's quarters. He hadn't had much to do with Lieutenant General Healey, and hadn't wanted much to do with him, either. Healey was Army through and through, even more so than Stone. Sam wasn't, and doubted very much whether the commandant approved of him.

Approve or not, General Healey was polite enough, waving Sam to a chair and waiting till he'd buckled himself in. He owned a round bulldog face and eyebrows that seemed to have a life of their own. They twitched now: twitched unhappily, if Sam was any judge. The commandant said, "We have communicated our unfortunate failure to revive the Doctor to the Race."

"Yes, sir." Sam nodded. "Unfortunate is right, but you had to do it."

"Their response was . . . unexpected." Healey looked unhappier yet.

"Yes, sir," Sam repeated; that was always safe. "Do you need my advice about whatever it was they said?"

"In a manner of speaking, but only in a manner of speaking," Healey replied. "They were disturbed to learn they would not be negotiating with the Doctor. Everything they had heard about him from Earth was favorable."

"I can see how it would have been," Sam said.

"There is one other person aboard this ship about whom they said the same thing," Healey went on, each word seeming to taste worse than the one before. "In the Doctor's absence, they insist that we negotiate through *you,* Colonel."

"Me?" Sam yelped. "I'm no striped-pants diplomat. I'm a behind-the-scenes kind of guy."

"Not any more, you're not," Lieutenant General Healey said grimly. "They don't want anything to do with anybody else. We're in no position to make demands here, unfortunately. They are. As of now, Colonel, the fate of mankind may well ride on *your* shoulders. Congratulations, if that's the word I want."

"Jesus Christ!" Sam said. And that wasn't half of what they'd say back in the USA more than ten years from now when speed-of-light radio told them what had happened. *The fate of mankind on* my *shoulders?* He wished he'd never heard of science fiction in his life.

"Is this the Tosevite ship *Admiral Peary*? Do you read me, *Admiral Peary*?" The shuttlecraft pilot on the other end of the line made a mess of the U.S. starship's name. Glen Johnson didn't suppose he could have expected anything different.

"That is correct, Shuttlecraft Pilot," he answered in the language of the Race. "I have you on radar. Your trajectory matches the course reported to me. You may proceed to docking. Our docking collar is produced to match those manufactured by the Race."

"Of course it is," Mickey Flynn interjected in English. "We stole the design from them."

"Hush," Johnson said, also in English. "It's useful to have parts that fit together no matter who made 'em. That's why most railroads have the same gauge."

"I am proceeding." The shuttlecraft pilot sounded dubious. "I hope you have the same high standards as the Race."

Humanity didn't. Johnson knew it. He was damned if he'd admit as much here. He said, "We crossed the space between the star Tosev and your sun. We have arrived safely. That must say something about our capabilities."

"Something, yes," the shuttlecraft pilot replied. "It may well also say something about your foolhardiness."

So there, Johnson thought. *Had* he been crazy to come aboard the *Admiral Peary*? Maybe not, but it sure hadn't hurt. He watched the shuttlecraft's approach, first on the radar screen and then with the Mark One eyeball. After a little while, he keyed the radio again. "You can fly that thing, I will say. I have flown in-atmosphere aircraft and craft not too different from that one. I know what I am talking about."

"I thank you for the compliment," the shuttlecraft pilot replied. "If I were not capable, would they have chosen me for this mission?"

"I don't know. You never can tell," Johnson said, but in English and without transmitting the words. Flynn let out what sounded suspiciously like a snort.

The pilot docked with the shuttlecraft. To Johnson's relief, the docking collar worked exactly the way it was supposed to. He went down to the corridor outside the air lock to say goodbye to the Yeagers and the others who were going down to the surface of Home.

"I'm jealous," he told Sam Yeager once more. "If I could take one gee's worth of gravity after going without for so long . . ."

"A likely story," Yeager said. "No girls to chase down there, and the weather's always hot. You'd do better staying here."

Lights on the wall showed that the outer airlock door was opening and the shuttlecraft pilot was moving his ship into the lock. The Race had wanted to inspect people's baggage before they went down to the surface of Home. Sam Yeager had said no. The Lizards didn't seem worried about weapons, at least not in the usual sense of the word. They were worried about ginger.

Just how worried they were, Johnson discovered when Karen Yeager, who was looking through the window set into the inner airlock door, squeaked in surprise. "It's not a Lizard!" she exclaimed. "It's a Rabotev."

That set everybody pushing off toward the window, trying to get a first look at one of the other two races in the Empire. Johnson's weightlessness-weakened muscles were at a disadvantage there, but he eventually got a turn. The Rabotev— what amazing news!—looked like the pictures the Lizards had brought to Earth.

It was a little taller, a little skinnier, a little straighter than a Lizard. Its scales were bigger and looked thicker than a Lizard's. They were a gray close to black, not a greenish brown. On its chest, the Rabotev wore a shuttlecraft pilot's body paint. Its hands were strange. They had four digits each; the outer two were both set at an angle from the middle two, and could both work as thumbs. Two digits on its feet pointed forward, two to the rear.

The Rabotev's head was a little more erect on its neck than a Lizard's, less so than a man's. It had its eyes mounted atop short, muscular stalks, not in eye turrets. They moved all the time; sometimes, it seemed, independently of each other. Johnson wondered if the shuttlecraft pilot had a snail somewhere way up his—her?—family tree. The Rabotev's snout was shorter than a Lizard's. When the alien opened its—that did seem the safest pronoun, in the absence of visible evidence one way or the other—mouth, it displayed a lot of sharp, yellow-orange teeth.

Sam Yeager said what Johnson had already thought: "They probably don't have to worry about getting this one high on ginger. Odds are it doesn't do anything for him."

"Would you let him in, Colonel Johnson?" Karen Yeager asked. "This is a first contact, in a way."

"Okay," Johnson said, and opened the inner airlock door. "I greet you," he called to the Rabotev in the language of the Race. "I am the pilot with whom you were speaking on the radio." He gave his name.

"I am Raatiil," the Rabotev said, pronouncing each vowel separately. "And I greet you." He sounded like a Lizard; try as Johnson would, he couldn't detect any distinctive accent, the way he could when a human spoke the Lizards' language. "You are the first Tosevites I have ever seen." His eyestalks wiggled. They weren't long enough to tie in knots, which was probably a good thing.

"You are the first Rabotev any Tosevite has ever seen in person," Sam Yeager said. "We recognize you, of course, from pictures, but none of your kind has come to Tosev 3."

"Some are on the way now, I believe, in cold sleep," Raatiil said.

Johnson wondered if the Race hadn't used Rabotevs and Hallessi in the conquest fleet because it feared they might be unreliable. He doubted he would get a straight answer if he asked the question that way. Instead, he inquired, "What do you think of the Race?"

"They took us out of barbarism," the shuttlecraft pilot said simply. "They gave us the freedom of the stars. They cured diseases on our home planet. We are never hungry any more, the way we used to be. And the spirits of Emperors past watch over those of our folk, the same as they watch over those of the Race." The Rabotev's eyestalks set its large green eyes staring at its own feet for a moment.

Raatiil sounded altogether sincere. If it was, there went any chance of even thinking about raising rebellions in the subject species. Johnson had always figured that chance was pretty slim. The Lizards had held the Empire together for a *long* time.

Jonathan Yeager asked, "What did your people used to reverence before the Race came to your planet?"

Raatiil opened and closed both hands. That must have been the Rabotev's equivalent of a shrug, for the alien answered, "These days, only scholars know. What difference does it make? Those other things could not have been as strong as the spirits of Emperors past, or we would have learned to fly between the stars and brought the Race into our empire instead of the other way round."

Was that what the Lizards had been teaching ever since they conquered what humans called Epsilon Eridani 2? Or had the Rabotevs come up with it themselves, to explain why they'd lost and the Lizards had won? After all these thousands of years, did anyone still remember how the story had got started?

"May I ask a question without causing offense?" Sam Yeager said. "As I told you, I am ignorant of your kind."

Raatiil made the affirmative gesture. With the Rabotev's two-thumbed hand, it looked odd, but it was understandable. "Ask," the shuttlecraft pilot said.

"I thank you," Yeager replied. "Are you male or female?"

"They predicted you would ask me this," Raatiil said. "As it happens, I am a male. The sand in which my egg was incubated was warm. But, except during mating season, it matters not at all to us. I am told it is different with you Tosevites, and I see this is so."

In English, Johnson said, "They've been studying up on us."

"Well, good," Jonathan Yeager replied in the same language. "I hope that means they take us seriously."

"Oh, they take us seriously, all right," Sam Yeager said. "We're here, so they have to take us seriously. Whether we can get anywhere when we talk to them—well, that's liable to be a different story."

The Rabotev's eyestalks kept swinging toward whoever was talking. *Does he understand English?* Johnson wondered. *Or is he just surprised to hear any language that isn't the Race's?* The Race was nothing if not thoroughgoing. Signals from Earth had been coming Home for almost eighty years now. *Could* the Lizards have taught some of the folk of the Empire the human tongue? No doubt about it.

Easiest way to find out might be to grab the bull by the horns. "Do you speak English, Shuttlecraft Pilot?" Johnson asked, in that language.

Raatiil froze for a moment. Surprise? Evidently, for after that freeze he made the affirmative gesture again. "I have learned it," he answered, also in English. "Do you understand when I speak?"

"Yes. You speak well," Johnson said. That Raatiil could be understood at all meant he spoke well, but Johnson had known plenty of Lizards who were worse. Still in an experimental mood, he told that to the Rabotev.

He got back another shrug-equivalent. "Some males and females are better than others at learning strange things," Raatiil said.

So much for that, Johnson thought. He'd been curious to see whether Raatiil enjoyed getting praise for doing something better than members of the Race. If he did, he didn't show it. Maybe that meant there really wasn't any friction among the different species in the Empire. Maybe it only meant Raatiil was too well trained to show much.

Sam Yeager caught Johnson's eye and nodded slightly. Johnson nodded back. Sure as hell, Sam had known what he was up to. No flies on him, no indeed. Everybody on the ship had been gloomy because the Doctor didn't make it. Johnson was sorry they couldn't revive the Doctor, too. He didn't think the diplomacy would suffer on that account, though. It might even go better. The Doctor was clever, but he'd always liked to show off just how clever he was. Sam Yeager was more likely to do what needed doing and not make any kind of fuss about it.

Raatiil said, "Those Tosevites going down to the surface of Home, please accompany me to the shuttlecraft. It has been fitted with pads that will accommodate your physiques."

One by one, the humans boarded the shuttlecraft. Sam Yeager was the last. "Wish us luck," he told Johnson.

"Break a leg," Johnson said solemnly. Yeager grinned and pushed himself into the air lock.

Johnson closed the inner door. Yeager went through the outer door and into the shuttlecraft. Johnson pressed the button that closed the outer door. He waited by the air lock to make sure the shuttlecraft's docking collar disengaged as smoothly as it had caught. It did. He headed back to the control room. From now on, most of the action would be down on the planet.

Deceleration pressed Jonathan Yeager into the foam pad that did duty for a seat on the Lizards' shuttlecraft. Rationally, he knew it wasn't that bad, but it felt as if he were at the bottom of a pileup on a football field.

He looked over his shoulder at his father, who was older and had been weightless longer. "How you doing, Dad?" he asked.

"I'll be fine as soon as they take the locomotive off my chest," Sam Yeager answered.

"Landing soon," Raatiil said—in English. He'd never seen a human before in his life, but he spoke fairly well. Would he have admitted it if the pilot hadn't asked? There was an interesting question.

The shuttlecraft touched down. The landing jets fell silent. It was already hot inside the craft. The Lizards liked it that way; they were comfortable at temperatures like those of a hot summer day in Los Angeles. They found Arabia and the Sahara delightful. They also found them temperate, an alarming thought. Jonathan asked, "What season of the year is it here?"

"Spring," Raatiil answered. "But do not worry. It will be warmer soon." That spoke volumes about the kind of weather Rabotevs preferred.

It also drew several involuntary groans from the humans on the shuttlecraft. Karen Yeager said, "Our world is cooler than Home. I hope you will arrange to cool our quarters."

"I do not know anything about this," Raatiil said. "Now that you remind me, I remember in my briefing that Tosevites prefer weather we would find unpleasantly cold. But I have no control over your quarters."

It's not my job. That was what he meant, all right. Some things didn't change across species lines. Jonathan had seen that back on Earth with the Lizards. It obviously applied here, too. Then Raatiil opened the hatchway, and Jonathan forgot about everything but that he'd momentarily be stepping out onto the ground of a planet that spun round another sun.

"You Tosevites may go down," Raatiil said. "The descent ladder is deployed. Go with some caution, if you please. The ladder is not made for your species."

"Many of us have flown in the Race's shuttlecraft on Tosev 3," Jonathan said. "We know these ladders."

The air inside the shuttlecraft had had the same sterile feel to it as it did aboard human spacecraft. It had smelled very faintly of lubricants and other less decipherable things. Now Jonathan got a whiff of dust and spicy scents that could only have come from plants of some sort. That was a *world* out there waiting for him, not the inside of a spacecraft.

For a moment, none of the half dozen humans moved. Raatiil's eyestalks swung from one to the other. He plainly wondered why they held back. Then Karen reached out and touched Jonathan's father on the shoulder. "Go ahead," she told him. "You've got the right. You've been dealing with the Race longer than anybody."

The other three humans—another husband-and-wife team, Tom and Linda de la Rosa, and a military man, Major Frank Coffey—were all younger than Jonathan and Karen. Nobody aboard except Sam Yeager (and maybe Raatiil: who could say how long Rabotevs lived?) had been around when the Race came to Earth.

"Yes, go ahead, Colonel Yeager," Linda de la Rosa said. She was blond and a little plump; her husband had a beak of a nose and a fierce black mustache. He nodded. So did Major Coffey, who was the color of coffee with not too much cream.

"Thank you all," Jonathan's father said. "You don't know what this means to me." His voice was husky. He hadn't sounded like that since Jonathan's mother died. He awkwardly climbed over Frank Coffey, who lay closest to the hatch, and started down. Then he paused and started to laugh.

"I only get half credit for this," he observed. "Kassquit's been here before me."

"You do get that, though, because she's only half human," Karen said. She was right. If anything, Kassquit might have been less than half human. But Jonathan wished his wife wouldn't have had that edge in her voice.

Out went Jonathan's father. The others followed. Jonathan went after Major Coffey. He'd just stuck his head out of the hatch when his father stepped down onto the flame-scarred concrete of the shuttlecraft field. In English, Sam Yeager said, "This is for everyone who saw it coming before it happened."

How long would people remember that? Jonathan liked it better than something on the order of, *I claim this land in the names of the King and Queen of Spain.* And it included not only all the scientists and engineers who'd built the *Admiral Peary,* but also his father's science-fiction writers, who'd imagined travel between the stars before the Lizards came.

If it weren't for them, I wouldn't be here, Jonathan thought. *Here* wasn't just Home. As his father had said, if he hadn't got involved with Lizard POWs, he never would have met his mom. Jonathan shied away from that thought. He didn't like contemplating the strings of chance that held everyday life together.

Somebody swatted him on the fanny. "Don't stay there gawking," Karen said from behind him. "The rest of us want to come out, too."

"Sorry," Jonathan said. He hadn't been gawking, only woolgathering. He didn't think his wife would care about the difference. The descent ladder was narrow, the rungs too close together and oddly sloped for human feet. He went down slowly, then descended next to his father and Coffey.

"Looks like an airport back home," the major remarked. "All this wide open space in the middle of a city."

"I'd want plenty of wide open space around me, too, in case one of those shuttlecraft came down where it didn't belong," Sam Yeager said.

"That doesn't happen to the Lizards very often," Jonathan said. "They engineer better than we do. Of course, just once would ruin your whole day."

Off in the distance, beyond the concrete, buildings rose.

Most of them were utilitarian boxes. Jonathan wondered how many different styles of architecture this city held. How old were the oldest buildings? Older than the Pyramids? He wouldn't have been surprised.

Across the concrete came a flat, open vehicle crowded with Lizards. It stopped about twenty feet away from the humans. Two of the Lizards descended from it and strode toward the shuttlecraft. "Which of you Tosevites is Sam Yeager?" asked the one with the more ornate body paint. Jonathan's eyes widened as he recognized a fleetlord's markings. Was that . . . ?

His father stepped forward. "I am. I greet you, Fleetlord. You are Atvar, is it not so?"

"You are to call him Exalted Fleetlord," Raatiil said.

"Yes, I am Atvar." The male who had commanded the conquest fleet sent the negative hand gesture toward the Rabotev shuttlecraft pilot. "The Tosevite is correct to address me as he does. As an ambassador, he outranks a fleetlord." He turned back to Jonathan's father. "In the name of the Emperor, superior Tosevite, I greet you." He and the male with him bent into the posture of respect.

After moving down at the mention of the Emperor's name, Raatiil's eyestalks swung toward Sam Yeager. Jonathan had first met the Rabotev only a little while before, but he knew astonishment when he saw it. He was all but reading Raatiil's mind. *They're making this much fuss over a Big Ugly?*

Atvar went on, "My associate here is Senior Researcher Ttomalss. Some of you Tosevites will have made his acquaintance on your planet."

"Oh, yes," Jonathan's father said. He introduced Jonathan and Karen, Frank Coffey, and the de la Rosas.

"One of you Tosevites, at least, will be easy to discriminate from the others," Atvar remarked, his eye turrets on the black man.

"Truth," Coffey said. "No one on Tosev 3 ever had any trouble with that." He owned a dangerously good deadpan. Jonathan had all he could do not to laugh out loud. Beside him, Karen let out a strangled snort.

"Indeed, I believe I have met all of you Tosevites at one

time or another," Ttomalss said. "And you Yeagers performed
an experiment that is an outrage to the Race."

"You would be in a better position to complain about it if
you had not performed the same experiment with a Tosevite
hatchling," Jonathan answered. "And how is Kassquit these
days?"

"She is well. She is still as stubbornly opinionated as ever,"
the Lizard psychologist answered. "You will see her shortly.
Since you have come to Home, we thought this first greeting
would appropriately come from the Race alone."

Jonathan wondered how Kassquit had taken that. Not well,
if he had to guess. She'd never quite learned how to be a
human, and she'd never quite been accepted by the Race, either. *Neither fish nor fowl,* Jonathan thought. All things considered, it was a miracle she wasn't crazier than she was.

His father said, "Would it be possible for us to get in out of
the sun?"

That plainly surprised the Lizards. For them, the weather
was no doubt springlike. For Jonathan, the only place that had
springtime like this was hell. Ttomalss said something in a
low voice to Atvar. The fleetlord made the affirmative gesture,
saying, "As we were always cold on Tosev 3, so you may find
yourselves warm here. I should warn you, though, that you
will not find it any cooler within."

"We understand that," Sam Yeager said. "At least we will be
out of this bright sunlight, though."

"I hope so," Karen murmured in English. "Otherwise,
they'll see a red human along with a black one." With her fair
redhead's skin, she burned with the greatest of ease.

She did on Earth, anyhow. "Tau Ceti's redder than the sun,"
Jonathan reminded her. "It puts out less ultraviolet. The
Lizards can't even see violet—it looks black to them."

"I know, I know," his wife answered. "But any ultraviolet at
all is enough to do me in right now. I forgot to put on sun-
screen before we came down."

Atvar gestured toward the vehicle. "Join us, then, and we
will take you to the terminal, where we will inspect your baggage."

"I have already had this discussion with the Race," Sam
Yeager said. "The answer is still no."

"You confuse me," Atvar said. "First you want to go in, and then you do not."

"Going in is fine," Jonathan's father said. "Inspecting baggage is not. We are a diplomatic party. We have the same rights as if we were back in our own not-empire. You must know this, Fleetlord."

"And if I do?" Atvar said. "If I do not like it?"

"You can expel us," Sam Yeager said. "You can send us back to the *Admiral Peary*. I think that would be foolish, but you can do it."

"How do I know your cases of possessions are not full of the herb that causes so much trouble for us?" Atvar demanded.

"You do not know that. But you do know your own folk must smuggle more of the herb than a few Big Uglies could. And I tell you that we have none of it with us here. Will you trust me, or will you not?"

"You I will trust," Atvar said heavily. "I would not trust any other Tosevite who made this assertion, not even the Doctor. Come, then, and we shall see what we have to say to one another."

Kassquit waited inside the terminal at the shuttlecraft port, along with a small swarm of middle-ranking functionaries from the Race. When she looked out the window, she could see the shuttlecraft that had descended from the Tosevite starship. She could even see the wild Big Uglies who had come down from it.

As wild Big Uglies were in the habit of doing, these wore cloth wrappings and foot coverings. The wrappings were minimal, leaving arms and legs mostly bare, but she wondered why the Tosevites wore anything in this climate. She looked down at her own body, nude except for her body paint and the foot coverings she too used. Her soles were softer than those of the Race, and often needed protection.

Which Tosevite out there was Jonathan Yeager? She saw only one who shaved his hair, but that didn't necessarily prove anything. He might have stopped shaving, as she had done, and some other Tosevite might follow the practice. At this distance, it was hard to be sure.

And which wild Big Ugly was Jonathan Yeager's permanent mate? There, Kassquit had no trouble finding an answer. That female had copper-colored hair, and only one of the Tosevites fit the bill. Kassquit's nearly motionless face would have scowled if only it could. She knew her resentment was irrational, but that made it no less real.

The Big Uglies outside boarded the passenger-mover that normally ferried elderly and disabled males and females around the shuttleport. It had been adapted to Tosevite needs with special seats. Kassquit had been the model on which those were formed. What fit her back and fundament, so different from those of the Race, should also accommodate other Big Uglies.

The passenger-mover came back to the terminal building. A door opened. A male with a cart went out to take charge of the Big Uglies' baggage. The cases he brought back were larger than those members of the Race would have used. Of course, members of the Race didn't take extra sets of wrappings with them wherever they went.

In came the baggage handler. In came Ttomalss and Fleetlord Atvar. And in came the wild Big Uglies. As soon as they got inside the building, someone aimed televisor lights at them. Half a dozen reporters thrust microphones at them and shouted questions. Some of the questions were idiotic. The rest were a great deal stupider than that.

"How do you like Home?" a female yelled, over and over.

"Fine, so far. A little warm," said the Big Ugly with the shaved head. That *was* Jonathan Yeager; Kassquit recognized his voice. He caught her eye and nodded, a very Tosevite style of greeting.

"Do you understand me?" another reporter shouted, as if doubting that a Big Ugly could speak the Race's language.

"No, of course not," the white-haired Tosevite replied. "If I understood you, I would answer your question, and I am obviously not doing that."

Kassquit recognized not only Sam Yeager's voice but also his offbeat slant on things. The reporter, by contrast, seemed to have no idea what to make of the answer. "Back to you in the studio," the female said, looking for help wherever she could find it.

Another reporter asked, "Will it be peace or war?"

Had someone asked that of Sam Yeager in private, he would have said something like, *Probably.* But, while it was a foolish question, it wasn't one where a joke was fitting in public. He said, "We always hope for peace. We have lived in peace with the Race on Tosev 3 for most of the time since you first came there. Now that we too can fly between the stars, that seems to me to be one more reason for each side to treat the other as an equal."

"You sound so . . . so civilized," the reporter said.

"I thank you. So do you," Sam Yeager said.

That reporter went off in confusion. Kassquit's mouth fell open in the silent laugh the Race used. One of the noisier kind Tosevites favored almost escaped her. If Sam Yeager kept this up, he would clear the terminal building of fools in short order. And if his methods could be more widely applied, that might have a salutary effect on the Race, or at least on how it did business.

None of the reporters or cameramales and -females wore false hair and wrappings. Those had jolted Kassquit when she first saw them. They seemed as strange to her as the first shaven-headed Big Uglies with body paint must have seemed to the Race back on Tosev 3.

Ttomalss beckoned and called out something. In the noisy chaos inside the terminal, Kassquit couldn't make out what he said, but she thought he was beckoning to her. She pointed to herself. He made the affirmative gesture. She pushed forward through the crowd.

Males and females grumbled as she went by them, then got out of the way in a hurry when they saw who and what she was. That even applied to a female in the body paint of a police officer who was holding back the crowd. As she stepped inside, the female asked, "Why are you not already with them?"

"Because I am a citizen of the Empire, not a wild Big Ugly," Kassquit answered proudly. She went on up to Ttomalss. "I greet you, superior sir." To Atvar, she added, "And I greet you, Exalted Fleetlord."

"I greet you," the two males said together. Ttomalss went on to present her to the wild Big Uglies.

"I greet you," Sam Yeager said. "It is good to see you again. We have both spent a lot of time on ice."

"Truth," Kassquit said after a moment's pause to figure out the idiom, which did not belong naturally to the Race's language. "Yes, indeed. Truth." She glanced toward Ttomalss. The Race had kept her on ice till it needed her here.

"And I greet you," the male named Frank Coffey said. "I have heard much about you. It is a pleasure to make your acquaintance."

"I thank you. The pleasure is mine," Kassquit said. She studied him with interest. She had never met a member of the black race of Big Uglies in person till now. Coffey spoke the Race's language well enough, if less fluently than Sam Yeager.

Back in the days when the conquest fleet was still trying to bring all of Tosev 3 into the Empire, the Race had tried to use black Big Uglies in the not-empire of the United States against the pinkish Big Uglies who often oppressed them. The strategy had failed, for too many of the dark Tosevites had feigned loyalty to the Race only to betray it. Coffey would not have been hatched at that time, but he was plainly loyal to the regime of the United States. Were he not, he never would have been chosen for this mission.

Thinking about him helped keep Kassquit from thinking about Jonathan Yeager, who was standing beside him. "I greet you," Jonathan said. "I hope you have been well, and I hope you have been happy."

"I have been well," Kassquit said. Happy? She didn't want to think about that. She doubted she could be happy, caught as she was between her biology and her culture. She did not know how to be a Tosevite, and she could never be the female of the Race she wished she were.

Jonathan Yeager said, "I present to you my mate, Karen Yeager."

"I greet you," Kassquit said, as politely as she could. She was as jealous of the copper-haired Big Ugly as she was of females of the Race. Karen Yeager could live a life normal for her species. That was something Kassquit would never know.

"And I greet you," Karen Yeager said. "Forgive me, but it is customary for Tosevites to wear some form of wrapping."

"This is Home," Kassquit said sharply. "Here, the customs of the Race prevail. If you want to wrap yourself, that is your business. If you expect me to do so, you ask too much."

Several of the wild Big Uglies spoke to Karen Yeager in their own language. Kassquit had learned to read Tosevite facial expressions, even if she did not form them herself. Jonathan Yeager's mate did not look happy. Jonathan Yeager himself did not take part in the discussion in English.

In a low voice, Ttomalss said, "Remember, being without wrappings is often a sexual cue among the wild Big Uglies. The other female thinks you are making a mating display in front of her nominally exclusive mate."

"Ah." Kassquit bent into the posture of respect, which was itself derived from the Race's mating posture. "I believe you are right, superior sir."

Greetings from the de la Rosas followed. The female of that mated pair made no comments about what Kassquit was or wasn't wearing. Kassquit thought that wise on her part.

Ttomalss said, "And is the female named Karen Yeager correct in having such concerns?"

Kassquit didn't answer right away. She had to look inside herself for the truth. "Perhaps, from her point of view," she admitted unhappily.

"We do not want to provoke the Tosevites," Ttomalss said. "Any matings or attempts at matings leading to such provocation are discouraged in the strongest possible terms. Do you understand that?"

"Yes, superior sir. I understand it very well," Kassquit said. She did her best to keep her voice impassive, but her best wasn't good enough. Ttomalss, after all, had known her since she was a hatchling. He asked, "Do you not only understand but agree to it?"

"Yes, superior sir," she said again. She knew she sounded sulky, but she couldn't help it.

"This is important, Kassquit." Ttomalss used a soft emphatic cough.

"I said I understood and agreed," Kassquit answered. "If you do not believe me, remove me from the diplomatic team."

Challenged, Ttomalss retreated. "I do not wish to do that.

Nor does Fleetlord Atvar. Your insights will be invaluable—
provided you do not let emotional involvement color them."

"I would have thought my insights would be valuable precisely *because* I am capable of emotional as well as intellectual involvement with Big Uglies," Kassquit said.

Ttomalss waved that away, which could only mean he had
no good answer for it. Fleetlord Atvar was saying, "We will
convey you Tosevites to a residence that has been set aside for
you. We have made efforts to ensure that it is as comfortable
as possible for your species."

"I thank you," Sam Yeager replied. "Will our rooms have
air coolers? It must be around forty hundredths here, and we
prefer a temperature closer to twenty-five."

"I am not familiar with all the details," Atvar said. "Believe
me, though—I know Tosev 3 is a cooler world than Home."

"Yes, Fleetlord, I am sure you do," the white-haired American Big Ugly said. "But does the same also hold true for the
males and females here who have never visited our world?"

Kassquit was sure that was a good question. The Race had
been traveling between the stars for thousands upon thousands of years. In some ways, though, it was more parochial
than Big Uglies were. They'd had to deal with differences
much more than it had. She sighed. She was a difference, and
the Race had trouble dealing with her.

☆ 4 ☆

Back when the Race first came to Earth, people would have had trouble making a Lizard happy in a Hilton. Karen Yeager supposed she shouldn't be too critical of the rooms the Race had arranged for people here in the town of Sitneff. On the other hand, she had a hard time being delighted with them, either.

In 1942, people hadn't known anything about Lizards. They'd had no idea the Race even existed. She'd heard her father-in-law and her own parents go on and on about how astonished everyone was when the conquest fleet went into action. Her folks had thought the Lizards were Martians when the conquest fleet arrived. The idea that the Race could have come from beyond the Solar System hadn't crossed anyone's mind.

The Lizards here, by contrast, had been getting data back from Earth ever since the early 1950s. For some considerable while, they hadn't wanted to believe what they were getting, but finally they hadn't had any choice. So why couldn't they have done a better job adapting rooms to fit human tastes?

They had remembered air conditioners. Those cooled the air only to the mid-eighties, but even that was better than nothing. Sleeping mats were less comfortable than mattresses, but Karen knew she could tolerate them. The odd lumps of foam rubber that were intended for chairs were harder to put up with. So were low ceilings and doorways.

And, when it came to plumbing arrangements, the Lizards showed they were indeed alien. Water came out of the tap at one temperature: a little warmer than lukewarm. She didn't think much of that. The showerhead was set into the wall at a level between her chest and her navel. It had only one setting:

abrasively strong. She didn't have scales, and felt half flayed every time she came out of the stall.

But the sanitary fixtures were the worst. Lizards excreted only solid wastes. Their plumbing was not adapted for any other sort. Cleaning up the mess that resulted from those differences was not something that endeared the Race to her.

"Fine thing for an alleged diplomat to do," she grumbled, using a towel for a purpose it hadn't been intended to serve.

"All right, leave it for the chambermaids, then, or whatever the Lizards call them," Jonathan answered.

Karen made a horrible face. "That's worse. And who says they'd clean it up? They might think we do it all the time, or we like it this way."

"There's a cheery idea," her husband said. "We can always piss down the shower. Then it would be good for something, anyhow."

"That's disgusting, too," Karen said. Finally, the job was done. She washed her hands. What the Lizards used for soap was also industrial strength. It would probably wear raw places in her skin before too long.

She laughed, though it wasn't particularly funny: the soap didn't seem to have done Kassquit any harm, and she'd put every square inch of skin she had on display. Karen didn't think Kassquit had deliberately appeared naked to titillate. Kassquit did follow the Race's customs and not mankind's. But what she'd intended and what she got were liable to be two different things.

Kassquit looked to be somewhere around forty. Karen knew the Race's counterpart to Mickey and Donald had gone into cold sleep years before she herself and Jonathan had. The Lizards' starships were a good deal faster than the *Admiral Peary*, too, which meant . . . what?

That the Lizards had kept Kassquit on ice for a long time after she got to Home. Why would they do that? Only one answer occurred to Karen: so their pet human could deal with the Americans when they arrived and still probably stay in good health. In a cold-blooded way, it made sense. If something went wrong, Karen wouldn't have wanted to entrust herself to a Lizard doctor who'd never seen a human being in his life. It would be like going to a vet, only worse. Dogs and cats—even turtles and goldfish—were related to people. Lizards weren't. Nothing on Home was.

Karen almost mentioned her conclusions to her husband— almost, but not quite. She wanted him thinking of Kassquit as little as possible. She'd noticed him looking at her not quite enough out of the corner of his eye. Of course, she'd also noticed all the other men in the landing party (even her father-in-law, who should have been too old for such things) doing the same. But unlike the rest of them, Jonathan had memories.

Memories and a naked woman were a bad combination. Karen was convinced of that.

Jonathan was fiddling with electronics. A light on the display went from green to yellow-red. "Ha!" he said, and nodded to himself. "They *are* bugging this room."

"Are you surprised?" Karen asked.

"Surprised? No," he answered. "But it's something we can give them a hard time about later on, if we have to. You're not supposed to do that to an embassy."

"Those are our rules," Karen said. "The Russians and the Germans break them all the time, and I wouldn't be surprised if we do, too. So why shouldn't the Lizards, when they don't play by our rules to begin with?"

"When it comes to diplomacy, they pretty much do play by our rules—at least on Earth they do," Jonathan said. "They've been unified so long, they've almost forgotten the rules they used to have. How they'll act here is anybody's guess. Except for the ones who've come back from Earth, the Lizards we'll be dealing with here haven't had anything to do with people up till now."

"Yes, and you know what that means," Karen said. "It means we'll have to waste a lot of time convincing them they really need to talk to us."

"Well, we're here, and we got here under our own power," Jonathan said. "That puts us ahead of the Rabotevs and the Hallessi." Wonder spread over his face. "We've finally met a Rabotev."

"We sure have," Karen echoed, amazement in her voice as well.

"We'll probably meet Hallessi, too," Jonathan said. "That

will be something pretty special." As he had a way of doing, he went back to what he'd been talking about before: "The Lizards didn't need to remember much about diplomacy when they brought the Rabotevs and Hallessi into the Empire. They just walked over them, and that was that."

"And if they'd come right after they sent their probes to Earth, they would have done the same thing to us." Karen's shiver had nothing to do with the air in the room, which wouldn't cool down till doomsday.

Jonathan nodded. "That's true. But they waited, and they paid for it." He looked down at the bug spotter again. "Some of these are pretty easy to find. Most, in fact."

"Do you think you're missing any?" Karen asked.

"Well, I don't know for sure, obviously," he answered. "Judging from the ones I'm finding, though, I'd be surprised. The technology on these just isn't that good."

"We wouldn't have said *that* when we were kids," Karen remarked. Her husband nodded. When the Lizards came to Earth, they'd had a considerable lead in technology on people. Humanity had been playing catchup ever since. The Race's technology was highly sophisticated, highly effective—and highly static. If it had changed at all since the Lizards bumped into humanity, no one merely human had been able to notice those changes.

Human technology, on the other hand . . . Human technology had been in ferment even before the Lizards came. When Karen's father-in-law was a little boy, the Wright brothers had just got off the ground and radio was telegraphy without wires. Nobody had ever heard of computers or jets or missiles or fission or fusion. It was only a little better than even money whether going to a doctor would make you better.

The arrival of the Race only threw gasoline on the fire. People had had to adapt, had to learn, or go under. And learn they had, both pushing their own technology forward and begging, borrowing, and stealing everything they could from the Lizards. The result was a crazy hodgepodge of techniques that had originated at home and on Home, but some of it made the Lizards on Earth swing their eye turrets towards it in surprise.

Jonathan said, "When the Lizards get something to the

point where it does what they want it to, they standardize it and then they forget about it. We aren't like that. We keep tinkering—and we manage to do things the Race never thought of." He patted the bug sniffer.

"They'll be listening to us," Karen said. "They'll know we'll know they're listening to us."

"For a while," Jonathan said, and said no more about that. Before long, the Lizards would be hearing either nothing or what people wanted them to hear.

They would know human electronics had caught up with and even surpassed theirs. In fact, they would know more about human technology than Karen and Jonathan did. They'd been getting continuous reports that were more than twenty-five years more recent than anything the newly revived humans knew first hand.

"They're starting to borrow from us by now," Karen said.

"They sure are. Did you see the green wig on that one Lizard on the way here from the shuttlecraft port? Scary," Jonathan said. "But you meant gadgets. Well, when they borrow from us, they'll check things out before they use them, right? Have to make sure everything works the way it's supposed to—and have to make sure whatever they introduce doesn't destabilize what they've already got."

He spoke with the odd mixture of scorn, amusement, and admiration people often used when they talked about the way the Race used technology. If people had had the same attitude, the *Admiral Peary* wouldn't have flown for another hundred years, or maybe another five hundred. When it did leave the Solar System, though, everything would have worked perfectly.

As things were, the starship orbited Tau Ceti 2 now, not some unknown number of generations in the future. That was the good news. The bad news was that the Doctor and some other people who'd started the journey weren't here to appreciate its success. People took chances. Sometimes they paid for it. Sometimes it paid off. Most often, as had proved true here, both happened at once.

Karen went to the window and looked out. Sitneff reminded her of an overgrown version of the towns the Race had planted in the deserts of Arabia and North Africa and

Australia. The streets were laid out in a sensible grid, with some diagonals to make traffic flow more smoothly. Most of the buildings were businesslike boxes. The tall ones housed Lizards. Males and females had offices in the medium-sized ones. The low, spread-out ones were where they made things.

Cars and trucks glided along the streets. From up high, they didn't look much different from their Earthly counterparts. They burned hydrogen; their exhaust was water vapor. These days—or at least back in the 1990s—most human-made motor vehicles did the same. Karen wondered if any gasoline-burners were left in 2031. She'd grown up with Los Angeles smog, even if Gardena, her suburb, did get sea breezes. She didn't miss air pollution a bit.

Plants halfway between trees and bushes lined some of the boulevards. They had several skinny trunks sprouting from a thicker lump of woody stuff that didn't come very far out of the ground. Their leaves were thin and greenish gray, and put her in mind of nothing so much as the leaves of olive trees.

Something with batlike wings, a long nose, and a tail with a leaf-shaped flap of flesh on the end glided past the window, close enough to give Karen a good look at its turreted, Lizard-like eyes. "My God!" she said. "A pterodactyl just flew by!"

"I wouldn't be surprised," Jonathan said. "They don't have birds here. You knew that."

"Well, yes. But knowing it and seeing one are two different things," Karen said. "If they weren't, why would we have come here in the first place?" Jonathan had no answer for that.

Ttomalss sat across a park table and bench from Sam Yeager. The psychologist would sooner have done business inside a building. This setting struck him as unfortunately informal. For the third time, he asked, "Would you not be more comfortable indoors?"

For the third time, the Big Ugly's thick, fleshy fingers shaped the negative gesture. "I am just fine right where I am," Sam Yeager said. He had an accent—no Big Ugly who used the Race's language could help having one—but his speech was almost perfectly idiomatic.

"How can you say that?" Ttomalss inquired. "It must be too

warm for your comfort, and this furniture is surely too small for your fundament."

"The weather is not bad," the Tosevite replied. "It is early morning, so it has not got too hot to be unpleasant for me. And we are in the shade of that kesserem tree—it is a kesserem tree, is it not? I have only seen photos up till now."

"Yes, it is," Ttomalss said. "That is well done, to recognize it from photos alone."

"I thank you." Sam Yeager made as if to assume the posture of respect, then checked the motion the instant it became recognizable. A male of the Race would have done exactly the same thing. Yeager stretched out his long, long legs and continued, "Anyway, as I was saying, the shade keeps the hot glare of your sun off my head." He laughed a noisy Tosevite laugh, no doubt on purpose. "How strange for me to say *your* sun and not *the* sun. To me, this is not *the* sun."

"So it is not. When I first came to your solar system, I had the same thought about the star Tosev," Ttomalss said. "Before long, though, it faded. A star is a star, and Tosev is not a star much different from the sun." His mouth dropped open in the laughter of his kind. "From your sun, you would say."

"I would now. Maybe not in a little while, though." Sam Yeager shrugged. "And this bench is all right, since I am not trying to get my legs under it."

"You would still find it more congenial in an office," Ttomalss said.

But the Big Ugly used the negative gesture again. "That is not a truth, Senior Researcher. I know what the Race's offices are like. I have seen plenty of them back on Tosev 3. I have never seen one of your parks. I spent lots of years in cold sleep to see new things, and that is what I want to do."

"You Tosevites are incurably addicted to novelty," Ttomalss said.

"No doubt you are right," Sam Yeager said placidly. "But we have fun."

A stray beffel that was ambling along suddenly stopped in its tracks when the Big Ugly's unfamiliar odor reached its scent receptors. It stared at him. Every line of its low-slung body said nothing that smelled like that had any business existing. It let out an indignant beep and scurried away, its short legs twinkling over the sandy ground.

"Those creatures were becoming first-class nuisances back on Tosev 3 long before I went into cold sleep," Sam Yeager said. "They were, and so were a good many other plants and animals of yours."

Ttomalss shrugged. "This continued after you went into cold sleep, too. But you cannot expect us to settle and not bring bits of our own ecosystem with us. We want to make Tosev 3 a world where we can truly *live,* not just dwell."

"When your animals and plants displace the ones that were living there, you cannot expect us to be very happy about it," the Big Ugly said.

With another shrug, Ttomalss said, "These things happen. Past that, I do not know what to tell you. Had you come to Home, you would have brought your creatures and your food crops with you. Do you doubt it?"

He waited. How would Sam Yeager respond to that? He laughed another noisy Tosevite laugh. "No, I do not doubt it, Senior Researcher. I think it is a truth. We have spread our own beasts when we colonized new land masses—including the one where I was hatched. And there are some that could easily make themselves at home here. But you will understand that we like it less when it is done to us."

Was that irony in his voice? Or was he simply stating a fact? With a male of the Race, Ttomalss would have had no trouble telling the difference. With the Tosevite, he wasn't quite sure. He decided to take it as seriously meant. "No doubt," he said. "But you will understand that any group looks to its own advantage first and to the situation of others only later."

"I wish I could say we needed the Race to teach us that," Sam Yeager answered. "I cannot, however, and I will not attempt it. We have quite thoroughly taught ourselves that lesson."

He was, Ttomalss judged, fundamentally honest. Was that an advantage in diplomacy or the reverse? The psychologist had trouble being sure. Had the Big Uglies' chief negotiator been the male known as the Doctor, Ttomalss would have known what to expect. That male was notorious for doing and saying anything to advance the cause of his not-empire. Sam Yeager probably would not go to the same extremes—which did not mean he was incompetent, only that his methods were different.

A female out walking a tsiongi suddenly noticed Yeager. Both her eye turrets swiveled toward him, as if she could not believe what she was seeing. "Spirits of Emperors past!" she exclaimed. "It is one of those horrible Big Ugly things!"

"Yes, I am a Big Ugly," Sam Yeager agreed. "On my planet, we have nicknames for the Race, too. How are you this morning?" His interrogative cough was a small masterpiece of understatement.

"It talks!" the female said, perhaps to Ttomalss, perhaps—more probably—to the tsiongi. "No matter what they said on the news, I did not really believe those things could talk."

Sam Yeager turned to Ttomalss. The psychologist wanted to sink down into the ground. "Are you certain there is intelligent life on this planet?" the Tosevite asked.

"What does it mean?" the female squawked. "Is it being rude and crude? Come on, you with the fancy body paint! Speak up!"

"This is the ambassador from the not-empire of the United States to the Empire," Ttomalss told her. "He is, I will note, behaving in a much more civilized fashion than you are."

"Well!" the female said with a noisy sniff. "Some males think they are high and mighty. If you would rather take the side of a nasty thing from who knows where than a hardworking, tax-paying citizen, I hope you come down with the purple itch. Come along, Swifty." She twitched the leash and led the tsiongi away.

"I apologize on behalf of my entire species," Ttomalss said.

To his astonishment, Sam Yeager was laughing again. "Do not let it worry you, Senior Researcher. We have plenty of males and females like that ourselves. It is interesting to learn that you have them, too."

"I wish we did not," Ttomalss said. "They contribute nothing."

The Big Ugly used the negative gesture once more. "You cannot even say that. For all you know, she may be an excellent worker."

"I doubt it." Ttomalss was not inclined to feel charitable toward the female, who showed the Race at its worst. "She is bound to be incompetent at everything she does."

"Do not worry," Sam Yeager said again. "We were talking about ecosystems. You will know we do not seek to damage yours when we bring *rats* down from the *Admiral Peary.*" The name of the animals, necessarily, was in English.

"I know of rats from your planet," Ttomalss answered cautiously. "I know they are pests there. Why did you bring them here, if not with the intent of taking a sort of vengeance on us?"

"Because this is your planet and not ours, and because some of the things on it are different from those on Tosev 3," the Big Ugly said. "We will use the *rats* to test foods here, so that we do not make ourselves ill by accident."

"There are few differences between Tosevites' biochemistry and the Race's," Ttomalss said. "We did not have many problems with food and drink on your world."

"What about ginger?" Sam Yeager returned. "We do not want to get that kind of surprise, either."

Ginger had been a surprise, all right, and a singularly nasty one. Ttomalss made the negative gesture to himself. Ginger had been a plurally nasty surprise. It had complicated the lives of the males of the conquest fleet. But it had complicated the lives of both males and females from the colonization fleet, especially those of the females. When they tasted ginger, they not only got the pleasure the males did, they also went into their mating season regardless of whether it was the right time of year. And the pheromones females released sent males into a breeding frenzy of their own.

Big Uglies had evolved to deal with continuous sexuality. The Race hadn't. Repercussions on Tosev 3 were still sorting themselves out. Some of the males and females there had even gone so far as to seek Big Ugly–style permanent mating alliances. The first ones had been expelled for perversion from the areas of the planet the Race controlled, to live out their days in exile in the not-empire of the United States. There, no one seemed to care what anyone else did so long as it didn't involve mayhem or murder.

But, from what Ttomalss had gathered since his awakening

on Home, the colonists had begun to relent. They'd had to. Too many males and females had sought such alliances. Losing them all to the Big Uglies would have been a disaster, especially since Tosevite technology was already advancing so alarmingly fast.

"Well?" Sam Yeager scuffed his feet in the sand. Was he trying to get comfortable or just fooling around? Members of the Race liked to feel sand between their toes. But the Big Uglies covered their soft feet. How much enjoyment could you get out of playing in sand with covered feet? Yeager went on, "You do understand why we need the animals?"

Ttomalss sighed. "Yes, I suppose so. Very well. Have your way there. I will inform my superiors of the circumstances."

"I thank you," Sam Yeager said.

"You are welcome." Ttomalss realized he had better clarify that: "For now, you are welcome. If these *rats* escape from captivity, you will be blamed. You will be severely blamed. We have no furry little animals here on Home. If they suddenly start appearing, we will know where they have come from, and we will take appropriate steps against you. Do I make myself clear enough?"

"You do indeed." The Big Ugly's mobile lips drew back from his teeth. One corner of his mouth turned up. The other didn't. Ttomalss, who had made a particular study of Tosevite facial cues, thought that one showed wry amusement. He was pleased to be proved right, for Sam Yeager went on, "You do see the irony in your words, I hope? You will blame us for doing on a small scale what you are doing on a large scale on Tosev 3."

"Irony? I suppose you could call it that," Ttomalss said. "What I see is power. We are strong enough to ensure that what we desire is what occurs. Had it been otherwise, you would have discovered us, not the other way around."

"You are frank," Sam Yeager said.

"I want no misunderstanding," Ttomalss replied. "Misunderstandings—especially now—can prove expensive to both sides."

"Especially now, yes," the Big Ugly agreed. "Before, you could reach us and we could not reach you. But things are different these days. How many starships are they building back on Tosev 3?" Ttomalss hadn't liked thinking about one starship full of wild Tosevites. Several of them? Several of them were several orders of magnitude worse.

Atvar was a frustrated male. That was nothing new for him. He'd spent much of his time on Tosev 3 frustrated. But he'd dared hope such conditions would get better when he returned to Home. There, he'd proved optimistic.

The Race had known for years that a Tosevite starship was on its way. It had adapted spacecraft for use in combat, should that become necessary: the first time since Home was unified that military spacecraft operated within this solar system rather than going out to conquer others.

But no one seemed in charge of the spacecraft. The Emperor had not declared a new Soldiers' Time. There was no formal military authority for defending Home. No one had ever imagined such a thing would be necessary. Along with the Ministry of Transportation, those of Police, Trade, and even Science claimed jurisdiction over the armed spaceships. Where everybody was in charge, nobody was in charge.

When Atvar tried to point that out, no one wanted to listen to him. That didn't astonish him. It did irk him, though. He'd come back to Home under a cloud because he hadn't completely conquered Tosev 3. Then they'd called him out of retirement on the grounds that he was an expert on the Big Uglies and on matters military—the greatest expert on matters military on Home, in fact. Having praised him to the skies when they decided they needed him, they then decided they didn't need him badly enough to take his advice.

He'd petitioned for an audience with the Emperor to try to get a rescript to make the various ministers pay attention to him. When he submitted the request (written by hand, as tradition required), the subassistant junior steward who took it from him warned, "While many petitions are offered, only a handful are selected for imperial action. Do not be disappointed if yours is not heard."

"I understand," Atvar replied. "I am of the opinion, however, that my petition is more important than most."

"As who is not?" the subassistant junior steward sniffed.

Atvar wanted to claw him. The only thing restraining the

fleetlord was the certainty that that would get his petition rejected. Instead, he said, "The Emperor will know my name." The subassistant junior steward plainly didn't. He, no doubt, had been hatched long after the conquest fleet left for Tosev 3, and after the fighting stopped there as well. To him, the fleetlord was ancient history. "See that your superiors read my words," Atvar told him. They, with luck, would have some notion of what he was talking about.

He got on better with Sam Yeager than he did with most of the males and females allegedly on his side. He and the Big Ugly had more common experience than he did with the comfortable bureaucrats who'd never gone beyond the atmosphere of Home. Even though Yeager had been in cold sleep for many years, he still understood the uneasy balance of the relationship between the Race and the Tosevites back on Tosev 3.

And Yeager had done the Race the enormous service of pointing out who had attacked the colonization fleet just after it reached his home planet. He had, not surprisingly, got into trouble for that with his own authorities. Atvar asked him, "Things being as they are, why did the not-empire of the United States send you on such an important mission?"

The two of them sat alone at a refectory table in the hotel the wild Big Uglies were using as an embassy. The other Tosevites who had come to Home were on a tour of the more distant regions of Home. This was not a formal negotiating session, only a talk. Yeager used a set of Tosevite eating utensils to cut up smoked zisuili meat. He'd eaten that on Tosev 3, and knew it was safe for his kind. After chewing and swallowing a bite, he answered, "Maybe my superiors thought I would not wake up again. Maybe they thought that, as a junior member of the expedition, I would not be in a position to decide anything important. And maybe—most likely, I think—they just wanted me as far from the United States as I could go."

"And yet, plainly, you remain loyal to your not-empire." If Atvar sounded wistful, that was only because he was.

"I do." Sam Yeager used an emphatic cough. "I am."

"What do you expect these talks to yield?" Atvar asked.

"Fleetlord, the Race has never yet treated us as equals," the Big Ugly answered, adding another emphatic cough. "You have dealt with us. We showed you you had to. But you keep on looking down your snouts at us. And that is on Tosev 3, where you have got to know us. Here on Home, things are a lot worse. I have already seen as much. Will you tell me it is not a truth?"

"No. I would not insult your intelligence," Atvar said.

Sam Yeager made as if to go into the posture of respect, checking himself at just the right moment. "I thank you. But it is time that the United States got its due. We have also traveled between the stars now. Do I understand correctly that the Soviet Union is also going to launch a starship?"

"So I have been told. It will be called the *Molotov,* after the longtime ruler of that not-empire. Having met Molotov the Tosevite, I hope the ship proves less unpleasant." Atvar vividly recalled his first dreadful encounter with the Big Ugly, who at that time did not yet rule the SSSR. Molotov had explained—had been proud to explain—how his political faction came to power by murdering the emperor who formerly ruled their land. Back then, the mere idea that an emperor (even a Big Ugly) could be murdered was enough to shake Atvar's mental world. He'd had no idea how many more unpleasant lessons the Tosevites would teach him.

"And the Nipponese and the Deutsche are also working on them?" Sam Yeager persisted.

Reluctantly, Atvar made the affirmative gesture. "I believe this to be the case, yes." He let out an angry hiss. "How it could be, however, I confess I do not completely understand. We defeated the Deutsche. We *smashed* the Deutsche. We put strict limits on what they could do. How they could return to space even around Tosev 3, let alone contemplate an interstellar spacecraft . . ."

"We called the war we were fighting when the Race arrived the Second World War," Sam Yeager said. "Until you came, we did not know what a world war really was, but we thought we did. A generation earlier, we had fought the First World War. The Deutsche were on the losing side there, too. The winners disarmed them and tried to make sure they stayed weak. It did not work."

"You are Tosevites. You are slipshod. You forget things. You might as well be hatchlings," Atvar said. "We are the Race."

"So you are," Sam Yeager replied. "And, evidently, you were slipshod. You forgot things. This puts you in a poor position to mock us."

"I was not mocking you." Atvar checked himself. "Well, yes, perhaps I was. But I was mocking Fleetlord Reffet and Shiplord Kirel much more. For you are correct, of course. They let the advantage we held over the Deutsche slip away. They should not have done so. That they did so is mortifying."

"If it makes you feel any better, Fleetlord, the Deutsche have more experience getting around such restrictions than the Race has imposing them."

"This may make me feel microscopically better," Atvar replied. "On the other hand, it may not." His tailstump quivered with anger. "For remember, Ambassador, I was recalled for incompetence. Those who came after me were going to do a far better job. They were sure of it. And look what they accomplished!"

"It does show your people that you were not to blame," Sam Yeager said.

"I already knew as much," Atvar said acidly. "That others also do is a matter of some gratification, but not much. I know I could have done better. I doubt I could have kept your not-empire from launching a starship. But the Deutsche, by the spirits of Emperors past, would not be a problem now if I still headed administration on Tosev 3."

He cast down his eye turrets. Any citizen of the Empire, whether belonging to the Race, the Rabotevs, or the Hallessi, would have looked down at the ground at the mention of Emperors past or present. Sam Yeager did not. However well he behaved, however well he understood the Race, he was an alien and would always remain one.

Yeager said, "What we wanted with this mission, Fleetlord, was respect."

"Well, you have that. I do not know precisely what you will do with it, but you have it," Atvar said. "Along with it, you also have hatched a considerable amount of fear. Is that what you had in mind?"

To his surprise, Sam Yeager made the affirmative gesture. "As a matter of fact, yes," he replied. "We have feared the

Race now for ninety years—ninety of ours, twice as many of yours. Mutual fear is not the worst thing in the world. It may keep both sides from doing anything irrevocably stupid."

Atvar's mouth fell open in a laugh. "I see you look on the bright side of things. My guess would be that nothing is sure to keep both sides from doing anything irrevocably stupid."

"My guess would be that you are right," the Big Ugly replied. "I am still allowed to hope, though."

"There I cannot disagree," Atvar said. "If we did not hope, one side or the other would have destroyed Tosev 3 by now."

"Truth," Yeager said. "Now you of the Race have to remember that all the time, as we have had to do since the year we call 1942. And you have to remember it can apply to your planets, not just to the one we live on."

That, no doubt, was part of what he meant by respect. To Atvar, it seemed perilously close to arrogance. That the Race had the same feeling never entered his mind. His mental horizon had expanded a great deal since he first came to Tosev 3, but he remained a part of his culture. For the Race to pressure other species seemed natural to him. For others to do the same to his kind did not.

He had the sense to see a change of subject might be a good idea. "Why did you not go sightseeing with the other Tosevites?" he asked.

"Please do not misunderstand me," the Big Ugly replied. "I will be pleased to see as much of your planet as I can. If the Doctor were in charge now, I would be out with the others. But I have more responsibility than I thought I would. I need to talk with you—with your government—about how we can all get along now that things have changed and you really need to recognize our fundamental equality."

Atvar laughed again. "You assume what you wish to prove, something I have seen a great many Tosevites do. We have sent fleets to Tosev 3. You have sent one ship here, and a slow one at that. This, to me, does not argue in favor of fundamental equality. The balance has changed. There is a new weight on your side of the scale. But the two sides do not match."

"Maybe not." The corners of Sam Yeager's mouth turned up. That could be a gesture of amiability or of something else masquerading as amiability. "When we do fly a fleet here, are you sure you will want to meet us? You will know I mean no disrespect when I tell you our technology changes much faster than yours." That said what sort of gesture the upturned mouth corners were, all right.

"You have been stealing from us since we first came to Tosev 3, you mean," Atvar said.

"Truth," Sam Yeager said again, surprising Atvar, but he also made the negative hand gesture. "But what we know for ourselves and what we have discovered has also grown, and we have already started doing things with what we have learned from you that you never thought of."

He told another truth there. The fleetlord wished he hadn't. Reports that came in at light speed kept talking about Tosevite advances in electronics, in biochemistry, and in many other areas. It was indeed worrisome. *Why could you not have gone sightseeing?* the fleetlord thought resentfully.

Karen Yeager found herself enjoying a winter day near the South Pole of Home. It felt like an April day in Los Angeles: a little chilly for the T-shirt and shorts she had on, but not bad. The guide, a female named Trir, seemed more interested in the Tosevites she had charge of than in the scenery around her. Her eye turrets kept going every which way, staring at the Big Uglies.

In a distracted voice, Trir said, "Conditions here today are relatively mild. On rare occasions, water has been known to freeze and fall to the ground in strange crystals that are known as *snow*. . . . What is that appalling noise?"

"They are laughing," Kassquit told her. "That is the noise they make to show amusement."

"Why?" the female of the Race asked. "Do they not believe me?"

"We believe you. We do not laugh to offend you," Karen said. "We laugh because our planet is cooler than Home. Snow is common on many parts of it. We are more familiar with it than members of the Race." She said that even though she'd been a little girl the last time it snowed all over Los Angeles (though of course she didn't know what had happened while she was in cold sleep).

"I see," Trir said . . . coldly. The female acted as if she were in the company of a group of tigers that walked on their hind legs and wore business suits. Maybe the Big Uglies wouldn't shoot her or devour her, but she wasn't convinced of it.

"They speak the truth," Kassquit said.

"I see," Trir said again, no more warmth in her tone. As far as she was concerned, Kassquit must have been about as barbarous as a wild Big Ugly, even if she wore body paint instead of clothes. It was definitely chilly to be walking around in nothing but body paint and a pair of sandals. Karen Yeager had a hard time feeling much sympathy for the Race's pet human.

Trying to be a diplomat, Frank Coffey said, "Shall we go on?"

"I thank you. Yes. That is an excellent idea," Trir said. "Please follow me." She walked along a well-defined trail. Every couple of hundred yards, signs at the height of Lizard eye turrets urged members of the Race to stay on the trail and not go wandering away into the wilderness. Karen had to smile when she saw them. They reminded her of those in some of the busier national parks back in the United States.

"What happens to the local plants and animals when it snows?" Jonathan Yeager asked.

"Some plants go dormant. Some animals hibernate," the guide answered. "Most survive as best they can or simply perish under those harsh conditions."

In broad outline, the South Polar region of Home reminded Karen of the country around Palm Springs and Indio, or perhaps more of the Great Basin desert of Nevada and Utah. Plants were scattered randomly across the landscape, with bare ground between most of them and with occasional clumps growing wherever the soil was especially rich or where there was more water than usual. The plants looked like desert vegetation, too: their leaves were small and shiny, and they didn't get very big. A lot of them were armed with spikes and barbs to make life difficult for herbivores.

Something skittered from one clump of plants to another. Karen didn't get the best look at it, but it reminded her of a small-l lizard. Of course, since all the land creatures on Home seemed to be scaly, they would remind her of lizards—unless they reminded her of dinosaurs instead.

She and the rest of the humans walked along in Trir's wake, admiring the scenery. It was beautiful, in a bleak way. A few of the plants showed Home's equivalent of flowers, which had black disks at their heart that attracted pollinators. Karen went up to one and sniffed at it. It didn't smell like anything in particular.

"Why do you do that?" Trir asked.

"I wanted to find out if it had an odor," she answered.

"Why would it?" The guide didn't sound as if she believed the explanation.

"Because many plants on Tosev 3 use odors to attract flying animals that spread their sex cells," Karen replied, realizing she had no idea how to say *pollinators* in the language of the Race.

"How very peculiar," Trir said, and added an emphatic cough to show she thought it was very peculiar indeed.

Something rose from a bush and flapped away: one of the bat-winged little pterodactyloids that did duty for birds here. It was the same greenish gray as the leaves from which it had emerged. Protective coloration was alive and well on Home, then. When the flying beast landed in another bush, it became for all practical purposes invisible.

Bigger fliers glided overhead. Karen's shadow stretched long off to one side. Tau Ceti—more and more, Karen was just thinking of it as *the sun*—shone not very high in the north. She wondered what happened during the long, dark winter nights when the sun didn't rise at all.

When she asked, though, Trir stared at her with as little comprehension as if she'd used English. "What do you mean?" the Lizard asked. "There is a time when the sun does not rise above the horizon, yes, but there is always light here."

That left Karen as confused as Trir had been. "But—how?" she asked.

Frank Coffey explained it for both of them. Speaking in the Race's language, he said, "Tosev 3 has the ecliptic inclined to the equator at twenty-six parts per hundred." The Lizards didn't use degrees; they reckoned a right angle as having a hundred divisions, not ninety. "Here on Home, the inclination is only about ten parts per hundred. On our world, the far north and the far south can be altogether dark for a long time.

There must always be at least twilight here during the day, because the sun does not get so far below the horizon."

"That, at least, is a truth," Trir said. "You . . . Tosevites must come from a very peculiar world indeed."

Karen hid her amusement. The guide had almost said *Big Uglies,* but had remembered her manners just in time. The sky wouldn't have fallen if she'd slipped, but she didn't know that. Just as well she didn't, probably. The more polite the Race and humanity were to each other, the better things were likely to go. And that was all to the good, since each side could reach the other now.

She did say, "To us, Home seems the peculiar world."

"Oh, no. Certainly not." Trir used the negative gesture and an emphatic cough. "Home is a normal world. Home is the world against which all others are measured. Rabotev 2 and Halless 1 come fairly close, but Tosev 3 must be much more alien."

"Only because you come from Home is this world normal to you," Karen said. "To us, Tosev 3 is the standard."

"Home is the standard for everyone in the Empire," Trir insisted.

"Except for Kassquit here, we are not citizens of the Empire," Karen said. "We come from the United States, an independent not-empire."

Trir must have been briefed about that, but it plainly meant nothing to her. She could not imagine intelligent beings who did not acknowledge the Emperor as their sovereign. And she would not admit that the choice of Home as a standard for how worlds should be was as arbitrary as that of Earth. Even Kassquit weighed into the argument on Karen's side. She couldn't convince Trir, either. And the guide did seem to find her just as alien as she found the Americans.

In English, Jonathan said, "If this is the Race's attitude, we're going to have a devil of a time making them see reason."

"The higher-ups, the males and females we'll be dealing with, have better sense," Tom de la Rosa said, also in English.

"I hope so," Jonathan said. "But down deep, they're still going to feel the same way. They're the center of the universe, and everything revolves around them. If they think that's how it ought to be, we're going to have a hard time persuading them they're wrong."

"Atvar will help there," Karen said. "After all the time he spent on Earth, he knows what's what."

"What are these preposterous grunts and groans?" Trir demanded.

"Our own language," Karen answered. "We know yours, and on our planet many males and females of the Race have learned ours."

"How extremely peculiar." The Lizard used another emphatic cough. "I assumed all intelligent beings would naturally speak our language. That is so throughout the Empire."

"But we do not belong to the Empire," Karen said. "I already told you that. When the Empire tried to conquer our not-empire, we fought it to a standstill and forced it to withdraw from the territory we rule."

"As time goes on, you will be made into contented subjects of the Empire, as so many Tosevites already have been," Trir replied.

She sounded perfectly confident. That was the attitude the Race had taken back on Earth, too. Were the Lizards right? They thought they had time on their side. They were very patient, far more patient than humans. They routinely thought and planned in terms of thousands of years.

Hadn't that hurt them more than it helped, though? They'd first examined Earth in the twelfth century. If they'd sent the conquest fleet then, humanity wouldn't have been able to do a thing about it. People really would be contented citizens of the Empire now. But the Lizards had waited. They'd got all their ducks in a row. They'd made sure nothing could go wrong.

Meanwhile, Earth had had the Industrial Revolution. By the time the Race arrived, people weren't pushovers any more. And why? Because the Lizards had planned too well, too thoroughly.

He who hesitates is lost. If that wasn't a proverb the Race should have taken to heart while dealing with humanity, Karen couldn't think of one that was.

Kassquit said, "In my opinion, Senior Tour Guide, the issue you raise is as yet undetermined."

"Well, what do you know?" Trir retorted. "You are just another one of these Big Ugly things yourself." She could lose her temper after all.

Karen had never expected to sympathize with Kassquit, but she did here. Trir might as well have called Kassquit a nigger. In essence, she had. Kassquit said, "Senior Tour Guide, I am a citizen of the Empire. If that does not happen to please you, you are welcome to stick your head even farther up your cloaca than it is already." She did not bother with an emphatic cough. The words carried plenty of emphasis by themselves.

Had Trir been a human, she would have turned red. As things were, her tailstump quivered with fury. "How dare you speak to me that way?" she snarled.

"I dare because I am right." Now Kassquit did use an emphatic cough.

"Truth!" Karen said. She used another one. "Judge males and females for what they are, not for what they look like."

"I thank you," Kassquit said.

"You are welcome," Karen answered. They both sounded surprised at finding themselves on the same side.

Atvar had just finished applying fresh body paint when the telephone hissed for attention. He laughed as he went to answer it. Jokes as old as the unification of Home insisted that it always hissed right when you were in the middle of the job. He felt as if he had beaten the odds.

"This is Atvar. I greet you," he said.

"I greet you, Exalted Fleetlord. I am Protocol Master Herrep," said the male on the other end of the line. "You recently petitioned for an imperial audience?"

"Yes?" Atvar made the affirmative gesture.

"Your petition has been granted. You are ordered to appear at the imperial court tomorrow at noon so that you may be properly prepared for the ceremony." Herrep broke the connection. He did not ask if Atvar had any questions or problems. He assumed there would be none.

And he was right. When the Emperor commanded, his subjects—even subjects with rank as high as Atvar's—obeyed.

Preffilo, the imperial capital, lay halfway around the planet. That did not matter. An imperial summons took precedence

over everything else. Atvar called the wild Big Uglies and
canceled the session he had scheduled for the next day. Then
he arranged a shuttlecraft flight to Preffilo. When he announced he was traveling to an audience with the Emperor,
the usual fee was waived . . . after the shuttlecraft firm checked
with the imperial court. Every so often, someone tried to steal
a free flight to Preffilo.

Court officials awaited Atvar at the shuttlecraft port. "Have
you enjoyed the privilege of an imperial audience before, Exalted Fleetlord?" one of them asked.

"I should hope I have," Atvar answered proudly. "It was
with his Majesty's predecessor, more than two hundred years
ago now, not long before I took the conquest fleet to Tosev 3."

"I see." The courtier's tone was absolutely neutral. Not the
faintest quiver of tailstump or motion of eye turrets showed
what he was thinking. And yet, somehow, he managed to convey reproach. Atvar should have returned to Home as Atvar
the Conqueror, who had added a new world to the empire. Instead, he might have been called Atvar the Ambiguous, who
had added just over half a world to the Empire, and who had
left the other half full of independent, dangerous wild Big
Uglies.

Atvar remained convinced he'd done the best he could
under the circumstances. Conditions on Tosev 3 were nothing
like the ones the conquest fleet had been led to expect. Anyone with half a brain should have been able to see that. His recall and the scorn heaped on him since he'd come back only
proved a lot of males and females had less than half a brain.
So he believed, anyhow—and if this courtier didn't, too bad.

"Come with us," the courtier said. "We will refresh you on
the rituals as we go."

"I thank you," Atvar replied. Every youngster learned the
rituals of an imperial audience in school, on the off chance
they might prove useful. Unlike the vast majority of males
and females, Atvar actually had used what he'd learned. But,
even discounting a round trip in cold sleep, that had been a
long time ago. He welcomed a chance to review. Embarrass-
ing yourself before the Emperor was as near unforgivable as
made no difference.

Most of the buildings in Preffilo were the usual utilitarian boxes. Some had a little more in the way of ornament than others. None was especially out of the ordinary. The imperial palace was different. Ordinary buildings came and went. The palace went on forever. It had stood in the same spot for more than a hundred thousand years. It wasn't quite the oldest building on Home, but it was the oldest continuously inhabited one.

It looked like a fortress. In the early days, before Home was unified, it had been a fortress. It had bastions and outwalls and guard towers, all in severe gray stone with only tiny, narrow windows. Here on peaceful Home, most of the travelers who came to see the palace thought of it only as ancient, not as military. No one on Home thought of matters military on first seeing any building. Atvar had had to worry about military architecture, both that of the Race and Tosevite, on Tosev 3. He could appreciate what the builders here had done.

And he could appreciate the gardens in which the palace was set. Almost as many males and females came to see them as came to see the palace. With multicolored sand, carefully placed rocks of different sizes, colors, and textures, and an artistic mixture of plants, they were famous on three planets. To most Big Uglies, Atvar thought, they would have been nothing special. The Tosevites had an embarrassment of water on their native world. They appreciated great swaths of greenery much more than the Race did. This spare elegance would not have appealed to them.

But there were exceptions to everything. While fleetlord, he had learned that photographs of the gardens around the imperial palace were wildly popular in the Tosevite empire—and it really was an empire—of Nippon. The Nipponese Big Uglies practiced a somewhat similar gardening art of their own . . . although Atvar doubted whether the gardeners or courtiers here would have appreciated the comparison.

As soon as he entered the palace, he assumed the posture of respect. He held it till one of the courtiers gave him leave to straighten. Then he went on to the cleansing chamber, where a female known as the imperial laver removed the body paint he'd applied only the day before. He felt as bereft as an unwrapped wild Big Ugly, but only for a moment. Another court figure, the imperial limner, painted on the special pattern worn only by petitioners coming before the Emperor.

"I am not worthy," Atvar said, as ritual required.

"That is a truth: you are not," the imperial limner agreed. An emphatic cough showed how unworthy Atvar was. She continued, "You are granted an audience not because of your worth but by grace of the Emperor. Rejoice that you have been privileged to receive that grace."

"I do." Atvar used an emphatic cough of his own.

"Advance, then, and enter the throne room," the imperial limner said.

"I thank you. Like his Majesty, you are more gracious, more generous, than I deserve." Atvar assumed the posture of respect again. The imperial limner did not return the courtesy. She represented the sovereign, and so outranked any official not connected with the court.

The throne room held banners seen nowhere else on Home. After a hundred thousand years, it held reproductions of the original banners that had once hung between the tall, thin windows. Awe made Atvar suck a deep breath into his lung. He knew what those banners stood for. They were the emblems of the empires *the* Empire had defeated in unifying the planet and the Race. Everywhere else on Home, they were forgotten. Here, where conquest had begun, the Emperor and those who served him remembered. There were also newer insignia from Rabotev 2 and Halless 1, and some, newer still, from Tosev 3. But other banners Atvar knew well from the Big Uglies' world were conspicuously absent.

All the throne room was designed to make a male or female advancing to an audience feel completely insignificant. Colonnades led the eye up to the tall, distant, shadowy ceiling. The path up to the throne lay in shadow, too, while the throne itself was gorgeous with gold and brilliantly illuminated. The spotlights glowed also from the gilding that ornamented the Emperor's chest and belly. The 37th Emperor Risson did not need ornate patterns of body paint to display his rank. He simply glowed.

In ancient days, Atvar had heard, the Emperor had been thought to represent the sun on Home. He didn't know whether it was true or simply an explanation of why the Emperor wore solid gold body paint. It sounded as if it ought to be true, which was good enough.

Two large males in gray paint as simple as the Emperor's suddenly stepped into the aisle, blocking Atvar's progress. He gestured with his left hand. "I too serve his Majesty," he declared. That sent them away; they slunk back into the shadows from which they had sprung. They represented what had once been a more rigorous test of loyalty.

At last, Atvar dropped into the posture of respect before the throne. He cast his eye turrets down to the ground. The stone floor here was highly polished. How many males and females had petitioned how many Emperors in this very spot? The numbers were large. That was as far as Atvar was willing to go.

"Arise, Fleetlord Atvar," the 37th Emperor Risson said, from somewhere up above Atvar.

"I thank your Majesty for his kindness and generosity in summoning me into his presence when I am unworthy of the honor." Atvar stuck to the words of the ritual. How many times had how many Emperors heard them?

"Arise, I say again," Risson returned. Atvar obeyed. The Emperor went on, "Now—enough of that nonsense for a little while. What are we going to do about these miserable Big Uglies, anyway?"

Atvar stared. The previous Emperor had *not* said anything like that when the fleetlord saw him before going into cold sleep. "Your Majesty?" Atvar said, unsure whether to believe his hearing diaphragms.

"What are we going to do about the Big Uglies?" Risson repeated. "They are here, on Home. We have never had a problem like this before. If we do not make the right choices, the Empire will have itself a lot of trouble."

"I have been saying that for a long time," Atvar said dazedly. "I did not think anyone was listening."

"I have been," the Emperor said. "Some of the males and females who serve me are . . . used to doing things as they have been done since the Empire was unified. For the situation we now have, I do not think this is adequate."

"But if you speak, your Majesty—" Atvar began.

"I will have a reign of a hundred years or so—a little more, if I am lucky," Risson said. "The bureaucracy has been here for more than a hundred thousand. It will be here at least as much longer, and knows it. Emperors give orders. We even have them obeyed. It often matters much less than you would think. A great many things go on the same old way when you cannot keep both eye turrets on them—and you cannot, not all the time. Or was your experience as fleetlord on Tosev 3 different?"

"No, your Majesty," Atvar said. "But I am only a subject, while you are the Emperor. My spirit is nothing special. Yours will help determine if your subjects have a happy afterlife. Do not the males and females who serve you remember this?"

"Some of them may," the Emperor said. "But a lot of them have worked with me and with my predecessor, and some even with his predecessor. Much more than ordinary males and females, they take their sovereigns for granted."

Atvar had heard more startling things in this brief audience than in all the time since awakening again on Home. (He'd heard plenty of startling things on Tosev 3, but everything startling seemed to hatch there.) "I would not think anyone could take your Majesty for granted," he said.

"Well, that is a fine compliment, and I thank you for it, but it does not have much to do with what is truth," Risson said. "And I tell you, Fleetlord, I want you to do everything you can to make peace with the Big Uglies. If you do not, we will have a disaster the likes of which we have never imagined. Or do you believe I am wrong?"

"I wish I did, your Majesty," Atvar replied. "With all my liver, I wish I did."

Kassquit had an odd feeling when she came back to Sitneff after the excursion to the park near the South Pole. Whenever she was alone with members of the Race, she always stressed that she was a citizen of the Empire, and no different from any other citizen of the Empire. She made members of the Race believe it, too, not least because she believed it herself.

But when she found herself in the company of other Tosevites, she also found herself taking their side in arguments with males and females of the Race. Part of that, there, had hatched from Trir's outrageous rudeness. Kassquit understood as much. The rest, though? She looked like a wild Big Ugly. Her biology was that of a wild Big Ugly. In evolutionary terms, the Race's body paint was only skin deep. Beneath it, she remained a Tosevite herself.

"This concerns me, superior sir," she told Ttomalss in his chamber in the hotel where the American Big Uglies also dwelt. "I wonder if my advice to the Race is adequate. I wonder if it is accurate. I have the odd feeling of being torn in two."

"Your words do not surprise me," her mentor said. Kassquit was relieved to hear it. He understood her better than any other member of the Race. Sometimes, though, that was not saying much. He went on, "Since your cultural and biological backgrounds are so different, is it much of a surprise that they often conflict? I would think not. What is your view?"

"I believe you speak the truth here," Kassquit said, relieved to have the discussion persist and not founder on some rock of incomprehension. "Perhaps this accounts for some of my intense curiosity whenever I find myself around wild Big Uglies."

"Perhaps it does," Ttomalss agreed. "Well, no harm indulging your curiosity. You are not likely to betray the Race by doing so. Nor are you likely to go back into cold sleep and return to Tosev 3. Or do you think I am mistaken?"

"No, superior sir, I do not. And I thank you for your patience and understanding," Kassquit said. "I hope you will forgive me for saying that I still find this world strange in many ways. Living on the starship orbiting Tosev 3 prepared me for some of it, but only for some. The males and females here are different from those I knew back there."

"Those were picked males—and, later, females," Ttomalss said. "The ones you meet here are not. They are apt to be less intelligent and less sophisticated than the males and females chosen to travel to the Tosevite solar system. Would you judge all Big Uglies on the basis of the ones the not-empire of the United States chose to send to Home?"

"I suppose not," Kassquit admitted. "Still, that is a far smaller sample than the one the Race sent in the conquest and colonization fleets."

"Indeed it is," Ttomalss replied. "The reason being that we

can send two large fleets to Tosev 3, while the wild Big Uglies have just managed to send a single starship to Home."

"Yes, superior sir," Kassquit said dutifully. But she could not resist adding, "Of course, when the Race first came to Tosev 3, the wild Big Uglies could not fly beyond their own atmosphere, or very far up into it. In what short period has the Race shown comparable growth?"

For some reason, that seemed to upset Ttomalss, who broke off the conversation. Kassquit wondered why—so much for his patience and understanding. Only the next day did she figure out what had gone wrong. He had compared Tosevites to the Race in a way that slighted her biological relatives. And what had she done in response? She had compared her species and the Race—to the advantage of the wild Big Uglies.

Things were as she'd warned him. Altogether without intending to, she'd proved as much. She was more like the Race than wild Big Uglies—and she was more like wild Big Uglies than the Race.

Males and females of the Race stared at her whenever she ventured out in public. Some of them asked her if she was a wild Big Ugly. That was a reasonable question. She always denied it politely. The males and females who kept talking with her after that were often curious how a Tosevite could be a citizen of the Empire. That was reasonable, too.

But then there were the males and females who had no idea what she was. Video had been coming back from Tosev 3 for 160 of Home's years, but a good many members of the Race did not seem to know what a Big Ugly looked like. She got asked if she was a Hallessi, and even if she was a Rabotev. One of the ones who did that was wearing false hair to pretend to be a Big Ugly himself. Kassquit hadn't imagined such ignorance was possible.

And males and females who did recognize her for a Tosevite kept sidling up to her and asking her if she could sell them any ginger. They got angry when she said no, too. "But you are from there!" they would say. "You must have some of the herb. You must!" Some of them were trembling in the early stages of ginger withdrawal.

At first, she tried to reason with them. "Why would I have

any ginger?" she would ask. "It does nothing for my metabolism. For me, it is a spice, not a drug. And I have never tasted it; it was forbidden on the starship where I lived."

Reasoning with members of the Race who craved ginger quickly proved impractical. It wasn't Kassquit's fault. She was willing, even eager, to go on reasoning. The males and females who were desperate for the herb weren't.

"I will do anything. Anything!" a female said. Her emphatic cough was the most unnecessary one Kassquit had ever heard. "Just let me have some of the herb!" She would not believe Kassquit had none.

After a meeting with the wild Big Uglies, Kassquit asked them, "Do the males and females of Home cause you difficulties?"

They looked from one to another without answering right away. At last, the dark-skinned male, the one named Frank Coffey, said, "It is only to be expected that they are curious about us. Except for you, they have never seen a real live Big Ugly before."

"You do not seem upset at the Race's name for your folk," Kassquit said.

Coffey shook his head, then remembered to use the negative hand gesture. "I am not," he said. "We have our own name for the Race, you know, which is no more flattering to them than 'Big Uglies' is to us. And besides, I have been called worse things than a Big Ugly in my time."

"Have you?" Kassquit said. This time, Coffey remembered right away to use the Race's affirmative gesture. She asked him, "Do you mean as an individual? Why would anyone single you out as an individual? You do not seem much different from any other wild Tosevite I have met."

"In some ways, I am typical. In other ways, I am not." The Big Ugly tapped his bare left forearm with the first two fingers of his right hand. "I was not so much singled out as an individual. I was singled out because of this."

"Because of what? Your arm?" Kassquit was confused, and did not try to hide it.

Frank Coffey laughed in the loud, uproarious Tosevite style. So did the other American Big Uglies. Coffey was so uproarious, he almost fell off the foam-rubber chair on which

he was sitting. Shaped chunks of foam made a tolerable substitute for the sort of furniture Big Uglies used. The Race's
stools and chairs were not only too small but also made for
fundaments of fundamentally different shape.

"No, not on account of my arm," Coffey said when at last
he stopped gasping and wheezing. "Because of the color of
the skin on it."

He was a darker brown than the other wild Big Uglies on
Home, who had a good deal more pale tan and pink in their
complexions. Kassquit was darker than they were, too, though
not to the same degree as Frank Coffey. She said, "Ah. I have
heard about that, yes. But I must say it puzzles me. Why
would anyone do such an irrational thing?"

"How much time do you have?" Coffey asked. "I could tell
you stories that would make your hair as curly as mine." The
rest of the wild Big Uglies took their leave, one by one.
Maybe they had heard his stories before, or maybe they didn't
need to.

Kassquit's hair was straight. She had never thought about it
much one way or the other. The dark brown Big Ugly's hair,
by contrast, grew in tight ringlets on his head. She had noticed that before, but, again, hadn't attached any importance
to it. Now she wondered if she should. "Why would a story
make my hair curl?" she asked. Then a possible answer occurred to her: "Did you translate one of your idioms literally
into this language?"

Coffey made the affirmative gesture. "I did, and I apologize. Stories that would appall you, I should have said."

"But why?" Kassquit asked. Then she held up a hand in a
gesture both the Race and the Big Uglies used. "Wait. During
the fighting, the Race tried to recruit dark-skinned Big Uglies
in your not-empire. I know that."

"Truth," Coffey said. Kassquit was not expert at reading
tone among Big Uglies, but she thought he sounded grim. His
next words pleased her, for they showed she hadn't been
wrong: "They were able to do that because Tosevites of that
race—that subspecies, you might say—had been so badly
treated by the dominant lighter group."

"But the experiment failed, did it not?" Kassquit said.

"Most of the dark Tosevites preferred to stay loyal to their own not-empire."

"Oh, yes. They decided being Tosevite counted most of all, or the large majority of them did, and they deserted the Race when combat began," Frank Coffey said. "But that they joined the Race at all says a lot about how desperate they were. And, although we in the United States do not like to remember it, some of them did stay on the Race's side, and they fought against my not-empire harder than the soldiers from your species did."

Was he praising or condemning them? Kassquit couldn't tell. She asked, "Why did they do that?"

Coffey's expression was—quizzical? That would have been Kassquit's guess, again from limited experience. He said, "You have never heard the word 'nigger,' have you?"

"Nigger?" Kassquit pronounced the unfamiliar word as well as she could. She made the negative gesture. "No, I never have. It must be from your language. What does it mean?"

"It means a dark-skinned Tosevite," Coffey answered. "It is an insult, a strong insult. Next to it, something like 'Big Ugly' seems a compliment by comparison."

"Why is there a special insulting term for a dark-skinned Tosevite?" Kassquit asked.

"There are special insulting terms for many different kinds of Tosevites," Frank Coffey said. "There are terms for those with different beliefs about the spirit. And there are terms based on what language we speak, and those based on how we look. The one for dark-skinned Tosevites . . . One way to subject a group is to convince yourself—and maybe that group, too—that they are not fully intelligent creatures, that they do not deserve to share what you have. That is what 'nigger' does."

"I see." Kassquit wondered if she did. She pointed to him. "Yet you are here, in spite of those insults."

"So I am," the wild Tosevite said. "We have made some progress—not enough, but some. And I am very glad to be here, too."

"I am also glad you are here," Kassquit said politely.

☆ 5 ☆

Though Sam Yeager had not gone to the South Pole, there were times when he wanted to see more of Home than the Race felt like showing him. Because the Lizards had insisted on him as ambassador when the Doctor didn't wake up, they had a hard time refusing him outright. They did do their best to make matters difficult.

Guards accompanied him wherever he went. "There are many males and females here who lost young friends on Tosev 3," one of the guards told him. "That they should seek revenge is not impossible."

He wished he could afford to laugh at the guard. But the female had a point. Friendship ties were stronger among the Race than in mankind, family ties far weaker. Save in the imperial family, kinship was not closely noted. In a species with a mating season, that was perhaps unsurprising.

Going into a department store was not the same when you had a guard with an assault rifle on either side of you. Of course, Sam would have stood out any which way: he was the alien who was almost tall enough to bump the ceiling. But that might have made members of the Race curious had he been alone. As things were, he frightened most of them.

Their department stores frightened him—or perhaps awed would have been the better word. Everything a Lizard could want to buy was on display under one roof. The store near the hotel where the Americans were quartered was bigger than any he'd ever seen in the USA: this even though Lizards were smaller than people and even though there was no clothing section, since the Race—except for the trend setters and weirdos who imitated Big Uglies—didn't bother with clothes. If the Lizards wanted a ball for a game of long toss, a fishing net (what they caught weren't quite fish, but the creatures did swim in water), a new mirror for an old car, something to read, something to listen to, something to eat, something to feed their befflem or tsiongyu, a television, a stove, a pot to put on the stove, a toy for a half-grown hatchling, an ointment to cure the purple itch, a sympathy card for someone else who had the purple itch, a plant with yellow almost-flowers, potting soil to transplant it, body paint, or anything else under Tau Ceti, they could get what they needed at the department store. The proud boast outside—WITH OUR MART, YOU COULD BUILD A WALL AROUND THE WORLD—seemed perfectly true.

The clerks wore special yellow body paint, and were trained to be relentlessly cheerful and courteous. "I greet you, superior sir," they would say over and over, or else, "superior female." Then they would add, "How may I serve you?"

Even in the face of a wild Big Ugly flanked by guards with weapons rarely seen on Home, their training did not quite desert them. More than one did ask, "Are you a male or a female, superior Tosevite?" And a couple of them thought Sam was a Hallessi, not a human. That left him both amused and bemused.

"I am a male, and the ambassador from the not-empire of the United States," he would answer.

That often created more confusion than it cleared up. The clerks did not recognize the archaic word. "What is an ambassador?" they would ask, and, "What is a not-empire?"

Explaining an ambassador's job wasn't too hard, once Sam got across the idea of a nation that didn't belong to the Empire. Explaining what a not-empire was proved harder. "You make your choices by counting snouts?" a clerk asked him. "What if the side with the most is wrong?"

"Then we try to fix it later," Sam answered. "What do you do if the Emperor makes a mistake?"

He horrified not only the clerk but also his guards with that. "How could the Emperor make a mistake?" the clerk demanded, twisting his eye turrets down to the ground as he mentioned his sovereign. "He is the *Emperor*!" He looked down again.

"We think he made a mistake when he tried conquering Tosev 3," Sam said. "This caused many, many deaths, both among the Race and among us Tosevites. And the Empire has gained very little because of it."

"It must have been for the best, or the spirits of Emperors past would not have allowed it," the clerk insisted.

Again, the guards showed they agreed. Sam only shrugged and said, "Well, I am a stranger here. Maybe you are right." The Lizards seemed pleased. They thought he had admitted the clerk *was* right. He knew he'd done no such thing. But, more than a hundred years before, while he was growing up on a Nebraska farm, his father had always loudly insisted there was no point to arguing about religion, because nobody could prove a damned thing. The Race had believed what it believed for a *lot* longer than mankind had clung to any of its faiths—which again proved exactly nothing.

When he and the guards left the department store, one of them asked, "Where would you like to go now, superior Tosevite? Back to your hotel?" He sounded quite humanly hopeful.

Sam made the negative hand gesture. He stood out in the middle of the vast parking lot surrounding the department store. Lizards driving in to shop would almost have accidents because they were turning their eye turrets to gape at him instead of watching where they were going. The weather was—surprise!—hot and dry, about like an August day in Los Angeles. He didn't mind the heat, or not too much. It felt good on his old bones and made him feel more limber than he really was.

"Well, superior Tosevite, if you do not want to go back to the hotel, where *would* you like to go?" the guard asked with exaggerated patience. Plainly, the Lizard thought Sam would have no good answer.

But he did: "If you would be so kind, would you take me to a place that sells old books and periodicals?"

His guards put their heads together. Then one of them pulled out a little gadget that reminded Sam of a Dick Tracy two-way wrist radio, but that they insisted on calling a telephone. It did more than any telephone Yeager had ever imagined; they could even use it to consult the Race's Home-spanning electronic network.

Here, the Lizard simply used it as a phone, then put it away.

"Very well, superior Tosevite. It shall be done," she said. "Come with us."

His official vehicle had been—somewhat—adapted to his presence. It had almost enough leg room for him, and its seat didn't make his posterior too uncomfortable. Still, he wasn't sorry whenever he got out of it. The guards had taken him to an older part of Sitneff. How old did that make the buildings here? As old as the Declaration of Independence? The discovery of America? The Norman conquest? There were towns in Europe with buildings that old. But had these been around for the time of Christ? The erection of Stonehenge? Of the Pyramids? Lord, had they been around since the domestication of the dog? Since the last Ice Age? If the guards had said so, Sam would have been in no position to contradict them. He saw old, old sidewalks and weathered brick fronts on the buildings. How long would the brickwork have taken to get to look like that? He had not the faintest idea.

The sign above the door said SSTRAVO'S USED BOOKS OF ALL PERIODS. That certainly sounded promising. Sam had to duck to get through the doorway, but he was just about used to that. An electronic hiss did duty for the bell that would have chimed at a shop in the United States.

An old Lizard fiddled around behind the counter. On Earth, Sam hadn't seen really old Lizards. The males of the conquest fleet and males and females of the colonization fleet had almost all been young or in their prime. Even their highest officers hadn't been elderly, though Atvar and some others had long since left youth behind. But this male creaked. His back was bent. He moved stiffly. His scales were dull, while his hide hung loose on his bones.

"I greet you," he said to Sam Yeager, as if Yeager were an ordinary customer. "What can I show you today?"

"You are Sstravo?" Sam asked.

"I am," the old male replied. "And you are a Big Ugly. You must be able to read our language, or you would not be here. So what can I show you? Would you like to see a copy of the report our probe sent back from your planet? I have one."

That report went back almost nine hundred years now. Was it a recent reprint, or did the Race's paper outlast most of its Earthly equivalents? Despite some curiosity, Sam made the negative gesture. "No, thank you. I have seen most of that report in electronic form on Tosev 3. Can you show me some older books that are unlikely to have made the journey from your world to mine? They can be history or fiction. I am looking for things to help me understand the Race better."

"We often do not understand ourselves. How a Big Ugly can hope to do so is beyond me," Sstravo said. "But you are brave—though perhaps foolish—to make the effort. Let me see what I can find for you." He doddered over to a shelf full of books with spines and titles so faded Sam could not make them out and pulled one volume off it. "Here. You might try this."

"What is it called?" Sam asked.

"Gone with the Wind," Sstravo answered.

Sam burst out laughing. Sstravo stared at him. That loud, raucous sound had surely never been heard in this shop before. "I apologize," Sam said. "But that is also the title of a famous piece of fiction in my world."

"Ours dates from seventy-three thousand years ago," Sstravo said. "How old is yours?"

Even dividing by two to turn the number into terrestrial years, that was a hell of an old book. "Ours is less than two hundred of your years old," Sam admitted.

"Modern art, is it? I have never been partial to modern art. But ours may interest you," Sstravo said.

"So it may," Sam said. "But since I only know your language as it is used now, will I be able to understand this?"

"You will find some strange words, a few odd turns of phrase," the bookseller said. "Most of it, though, you will follow without much trouble. Our language does not change quickly. Nothing about us changes quickly. But our speech has mostly stayed the same since sound and video recording carved the preferred forms in stone."

"All right, then," Sam said. "What is the story about?"

"Friends who separate over time," Sstravo answered. One of the guards made the affirmative gesture, so maybe she'd read the book. Sam kept thinking of Clark Gable. Sstravo went on, "What else would one find to write about? What else is there to write about?"

"We Tosevites feel that way about the attraction between

male and female," Sam said. Sstravo and the guards laughed. Sam might have known—he had known—they would think that was funny. He held up the copy of *Gone with the Wind* that owed nothing to Margaret Mitchell. Cro-Magnons hadn't finished replacing Neanderthals when this was written. "I will take this. How do I make arrangements to pay you?"

"I will do it," one guard said. "I shall be reimbursed."

"I thank you," Sam said. The guard gave Sstravo a credit card. The bookseller rang up the purchase on a register that might have been as old as the novel. It worked, though. *"Gone with the Wind,"* Sam murmured. He started laughing all over again.

Jonathan Yeager hadn't seen his father for seventeen years. For all practical purposes, his father might as well have been dead. Now he was back, and he hadn't changed a bit in all that time. Jonathan, meanwhile, had gone from a young man into middle age. Cold sleep had a way of complicating relationships just this side of adultery.

At least his father also recognized the difficulty. "You've changed while I wasn't looking," he said to Jonathan one evening as they sat in the elder Yeager's inadequately air-conditioned room.

"That's what you get for going to sleep while I stayed awake," Jonathan answered. He sipped at a drink. The Lizards had given them pure ethyl alcohol. Cut with water, it did duty for vodka. The Race didn't use ice cubes, though, and seemed horrified at the idea.

His old man had a drink on the low round metal table beside him, too. After a nip from it, he nodded. "Well, I was encouraged to do that. They didn't come right out and say so, but I got the notion it was good for my life expectancy." He shook his head in wonder. "Since I'm heading toward a hundred and twenty-five now, I guess it must have been—assuming I ever woke up again, of course."

"Yeah. Assuming," Jonathan said. He'd got used to not having his father around, to standing on the front line in the war against Father Time. Now he had some cover again. If his father was still around, he couldn't be too far over the hill himself, could he? Of course, his father had stood still for a while, even as he'd kept going over that hill himself.

"They wanted to get rid of me, and they did," his dad said. "They might have made sure I had an 'accident' instead, if they could have sneaked it past the Race. If I hadn't taken cold sleep, they probably would have tried that. But after Gordon tried to blow my head off and didn't quite make it, the warning they got from the Lizards must have made them leery of doing it if they didn't have to."

"So here you are, and you're in charge of things," Jonathan said. "That ought to make them start tearing their hair out when they hear about it ten-plus years from now."

"I thought so, too, when I woke up and the Doctor didn't," his father replied. "But now I doubt it. I doubt it like hell, as a matter of fact. They'll be into the 2040s by the time word of that gets back to Earth. By then, it will have been more than sixty years since I went into cold sleep and more than seventy-five since I made a real nuisance of myself. Hardly anybody will remember who I am. If I do a decent job of dealing with the Lizards, that's all that'll matter. Time heals all wounds."

Jonathan thought it over, then slowly nodded. "Well, maybe you're right. I sure hope so. But I still remember what happened in the 1960s, even if nobody back there will. What they did to you wasn't right."

"It was a long time ago—for everybody except me," his father said. "Even for me, it wasn't yesterday." He finished his drink, then got up and fixed himself another. "See? You've got a lush for an old man."

"You're no lush," Jonathan said.

"Well . . . not like that," Sam Yeager admitted. "When I was playing ball . . . Sweet Jesus Christ, some of those guys could put the sauce away. Some of 'em drank so much, it screwed them out of a chance to make the big leagues. And some of 'em knew they weren't ever going to make the big leagues because they just weren't good enough, and they drank even harder so they wouldn't have to think about that."

"You weren't going to," Jonathan said incautiously.

"And I drank some," his father answered. "I might have made it to the top if I hadn't torn up my ankle. That cost me most of a season and most of my speed. Hell, I might have made it if the Lizards hadn't come. I could still swing the bat some, and I was 4-F as could be—they wouldn't draft me with full upper and lower plates. But even if it was the bush leagues, I liked what I was doing. The only other thing I knew how to do then was farm, and playing ball beat the crap out of that."

Jonathan took another pull at his glass. It didn't taste like much, but it was plenty strong. He said, "You like what you're doing now."

"You bet I do." His father dropped an emphatic cough into English. "There hasn't been a really big war with the Lizards since the first round ended the year after you were born. The Germans were damn fools to take 'em on alone in the 1960s, but then, the Nazis *were* damn fools. If there's another fight, it won't just take out Earth. Home will get it, too."

"And the other worlds in the Empire," Jonathan said. "We wouldn't leave them out."

His father nodded. "No, I don't suppose we would. They could hit back if we did. That's a lot of people and Lizards and Rabotevs and Hallessi dead. And for what? For what, goddammit?" Every once in a while, he still cussed like the ballplayer he had been. "For nothing but pride and fear, far as I can see. If I can do something to stop that, you'd better believe I will."

"What do you think the odds are?" Jonathan asked.

Instead of answering straight out, his father said, "If anything happens to me here, the Lizards are liable to ask for you to take over as our ambassador. Are you ready for that, just in case?"

"I'm not qualified, if that's what you mean," Jonathan answered. "I'm not telling you any big secrets; you know it as well as I do. The only reason they might think of me is that I'm your kid."

"Not the only reason, I'd say." His father drank another slug of ersatz vodka. "I've been studying ever since they revived me, trying to catch up on all the stuff that happened after I went into cold sleep. From everything I've been able to find out, you were doing a hell of a job as Lizard contact man. They wouldn't have asked you to come on the *Admiral Peary* if you and Karen weren't good."

"Oh, we are." The hooch had left Jonathan with very little modesty, false or otherwise. "We're damn good. And all those years of dealing with Mickey and Donald gave us a feel for the Race I don't think anybody could get any other way. But neither one of us is as good as you are."

That wasn't modesty. That was simple truth, and Jonathan knew it even if he didn't like it. He and Karen and most human experts on the Race learned more and more over the years about how Lizards thought and behaved. No doubt his old man had done that, too. But his father, somehow, wasn't just an expert on the Race, though he was that. Sam Yeager had the uncanny ability to think like a Lizard, to become a Lizard in all ways except looks and accent. People noticed it. So did members of the Race. So had Kassquit, who was at the same time both and neither.

He had the ability. Jonathan didn't. Neither did Karen. They were both outstanding at what they did. That only illustrated the difference between being outstanding and being a genius.

With a wry chuckle, the genius—at thinking like a Lizard, anyhow—who was Jonathan's father said, "That's what I get for reading too much science fiction. Nothing like it to kill time on a train ride or a bus between one bush-league town and the next." He'd said that many times before. He claimed the stuff had loosened up his mind and helped him think like a Lizard.

But Jonathan shook his head. "I used to believe that was what did it for you, too. But I read the stuff. I started younger than you, 'cause we had it in the house and I knew ever since I was little what I wanted to do. I liked it, too. It was fun. And I got to study the Race in college, where you had to learn everything from scratch. You're still better at it than I am— better than anybody else, too."

"When I was a kid, I wanted to be Babe Ruth," his father said. "The only times I ever got into a big-league ballpark, I had to pay my own way. You're playing in the majors, son, and you're a star. That's not bad."

"Yeah. I know." Jonathan had his own fair share of the gray, middle-aged knowledge that told him he'd fallen somewhat short of the place he'd aimed at when he was younger. That was somewhat mitigated because he hadn't fallen as far short as a lot of people did. But that his father held the place he'd aimed for and couldn't quite reach . . . "I do wonder how Babe Ruth's kid would have turned out if he'd tried to be a ballplayer. Even if he were a good one, would it have been enough?"

"I think Ruth had girls," his father said.

Jonathan sent him an angry look. *How could he misunderstand what I was saying like that?* he wondered. And then, catching the gleam behind his old man's bifocals, Jonathan realized he hadn't misunderstood at all. He'd just chosen to be difficult. "Damn you, Dad," he said.

His father laughed. "I've got to keep you on your toes somehow, don't I? And if Babe Ruth's son turned out to be Joe DiMaggio, he wouldn't have one goddamn thing to be ashamed of. Do you hear me?"

"I suppose so," Jonathan said. In a way, being very good at what he'd always wanted to do was not only enough but an embarrassment of riches. He'd been good enough—and so had Karen—to get chosen to come to Home, as his father'd said. But that wasn't all of what he'd wanted. He'd wanted to be the *best*.

And there was his father, sitting in this cramped little Lizard-sized room with him, slightly pie-eyed from all that almost-vodka he'd poured down, and he *was* the best. No doubt about it, they'd broken the mold once they made Sam Yeager.

How many human ballplayers had sons who couldn't measure up to what they'd done? A good many. Most of them you never even heard about, because their kids couldn't make the majors at all. How many had had sons who were better than they were? Few. Damn few.

His father said, "When it comes to this stuff, I can't help being what I am, any more than you can help being what you are. We both put in a lot of hard work. I know what all you did while I was awake to see it. I don't know everything you did while I was in cold sleep, but you couldn't have been asleep at the switch. You're here, for heaven's sake."

"Yeah," Jonathan said in what he hoped wasn't too hollow a voice. "I'm here." He *was* an expert on the Race. He *had* busted his hump in the seventeen years after Dad went into cold sleep. And if expertise didn't quite make up for genius, he couldn't help it. His father was right about that.

"I'm going to ask you one thing before I throw you out and flop," Sam Yeager said, finishing his drink and standing up on legs that didn't seem to want to hold him. "If you want to blame fate or God or the luck of the draw for the way things are, that's fine. What I want to ask you is, don't blame me. Please? Okay?"

He really sounded anxious. Maybe that was the booze talking through him. Or maybe he understood just what Jonathan was thinking. After all, he'd had to deal with failure a lot larger than Jonathan's.

What would he have done if the Lizards hadn't come? For all his brave talk, odds were he wouldn't have made the big leagues. Then what? Played bush-league ball as long as he could, probably. And after that? If he was lucky, he might have hooked on as a coach somewhere, or a minor-league manager. More likely, he would have had to look for ordinary work wherever he happened to be when he couldn't get around on a fastball any more.

And the world never would have found out the one great talent he had in him. He would have gone through life—well, not quite ordinary, because not everybody could play ball even at his level, but unfulfilled in a certain ultimate sense. Jonathan couldn't say that about himself, and he knew it. He nodded. He smiled, too, and it didn't take too much extra effort. "Okay, Dad," he said. "Sure."

Although Ttomalss had gone into cold sleep after all the Big Uglies who'd come to Home, he'd been awake longer than they had. His starship had traveled from Tosev 3 to Home faster than their less advanced craft. He called up an image of their ramshackle ship on his computer monitor. It looked as if it would fall apart if anyone breathed on it hard. That wasn't so, of course. It *had* got here. It might even get back to Tosev's solar system.

The psychologist made the image go away. Looking at it only wasted his time. What really mattered wasn't the ship that had brought the Tosevites here. What mattered was that they were here—and everything that had happened back on Tosev 3 since they left.

He still didn't know *everything,* of course—didn't and wouldn't. Radio took all those years to travel between Tosev's system and this one. But, in the communications both Fleet-lord Reffet, who led the colonization fleet, and Shiplord Kirel, who headed what was left of the conquest fleet after Atvar's recall, sent back to Home, Ttomalss found a rising note of alarm.

It had been obvious even to Ttomalss, back during his time on Tosev 3, that the Big Uglies were catching up with the Race in both technology and knowledge. He'd assumed the Tosevites' progress would plateau as time went on and they finally did pull close to even with the Race. He'd assumed, in other words, that the Race knew everything, or almost everything, there was to know.

That was turning out not to be true. Reports from both Reffet and Kirel talked about Tosevite scientific advances that had the psychologist wondering whether he fully understood the news coming from Tosev 3. He also began to wonder whether Reffet and Kirel and the males and females working under them fully understood what was happening on Tosev 3.

When he said as much to Atvar, the former fleetlord of the conquest fleet responded with the scorn Ttomalss had expected from him: "Reffet never has understood anything. He never will understand anything, and he never can understand anything. He has not got the brains of a retarded azwaca turd."

"And Kirel?" Ttomalss asked.

"Kirel is capable enough. But Kirel is stodgy," Atvar said. "Kirel has brains enough. What Kirel lacks is imagination. I have seen kamamadia nuts with more." He rolled out one striking phrase after another that morning.

"What would you do, were you still in command on Tosev 3?" Ttomalss asked.

Atvar swung both eye turrets toward him. They were sitting in one of the small conference rooms in the hotel where the Big Uglies were staying. How many other conference rooms all across Home were just like this one, with its sound-absorbing ceiling tiles, its greenish brown walls—walls not far from the color of skin for the Race, a soothing color—its writing board and screen and connection to the planetwide computer network, its stout tables and not quite comfortable chairs? Only the fact that some of the chairs now accommodated Tosevite posteriors—not quite comfortably, from what the Big Uglies said—hinted at anything out of the ordinary.

After a pause, Atvar said, "Why do you not come for a walk with me? It is a nice enough day."

"A walk?" Ttomalss responded as if he'd never heard the words before. Atvar made the affirmative gesture. With a shrug, the researcher said, "Well, why not?"

Out they went. It *was* a nice enough day. Atvar let out what sounded like a sigh of relief. "We were certain to be recorded in there," he said. "Now that I am no longer in charge on Tosev 3, I do not wish to be quoted on what to do about it by anyone who could substantiate the record."

"I see," Ttomalss said. "Well, since I am not in a position to do that, what is your opinion on what to do in aid of Tosev 3?"

"That Reffet and Kirel are cowards." Atvar's voice went harsh and hard. "The Big Uglies are gaining an advantage on us. You know this is true. So do I. So does everyone else with eyes in his eye turrets. But the males allegedly leading on Tosev 3 have not the courage to draw the proper conclusion."

"Which is?"

"You were there. You already know my view. We cannot afford to let the Big Uglies get ahead of us. They are already here with one ship. That is bad enough, but tolerable. All this ship can do is hurt us. If they send fleets to all our solar systems, though, they can destroy us. They can, and they might. We attacked them without warning. If they have the chance, why should they not return the favor? And so, as I proposed many years ago, our best course is to destroy them first."

"That would also mean destroying our own colony," Ttomalss said.

"Better a part than the whole." Atvar used an emphatic cough. "Far better."

"I gather Reffet and Kirel do not agree?"

"They certainly do not." Atvar spoke with fine contempt. "They fail to see the difference between the purple itch, for which a soothing salve is all the treatment needed, and a malignancy that requires the knife."

"You are outspoken," Ttomalss observed.

"By the spirits of Emperors past, Senior Researcher, I feel here what Straha must have felt back on Tosev 3 before he tried to oust me," Atvar exclaimed.

Ttomalss hissed in astonishment. Shiplord Straha had been so disgusted over the way the conquest fleet was being run that, after his attempt to supplant Atvar failed, he'd defected to the American Big Uglies. He'd later returned to the Race with news from Sam Yeager that the Americans had been the ones to attack the colonization fleet. Nothing less than news like that could have restored him to the fleetlord's good graces, or even to a semblance of them.

Atvar made the affirmative gesture. "By the spirits of Emperors past, it is a truth. During the fighting, Straha saw how genuinely dangerous the Big Uglies were, and wanted to use radical measures against them. I, in my infinite wisdom, decided this was inappropriate—and so we did not completely defeat them. Now I am the one who sees the danger, and no one here on Home or on Tosev 3 appears willing to turn an eye turret in its direction."

"Exalted Fleetlord, you are not the only one who sees it," Ttomalss said. "Looking at the reports coming from Tosev 3, what strikes me is their ever more *frightened* tone."

"Another truth," Atvar said. "All the more reason for us to eliminate the menace, would you not agree? I have had an audience with the Emperor. Even he realizes we have to find some way to deal with the Big Uglies."

"Some years ago, I think, annihilating the Big Uglies might well have been the appropriate thing to do," Ttomalss replied. Atvar hissed angrily. He liked hearing disagreement no better than he ever had. Ttomalss said, "Listen to me, if you please."

"Go on." Atvar did not sound like a male who was going to listen patiently and give a reasoned judgment on what he heard. He sounded much more as if he intended to tear Ttomalss limb from limb.

All the same, the psychologist continued, "Unless I am altogether mistaken in my reading of the reports from Tosev 3, I think one reason Reffet and Kirel hesitate to apply your strategy is that they fear it will not work, and it will provoke the independent Tosevites."

"What do you mean, it will not work?" Atvar demanded. "If we smash the not-empires, they will stay smashed. The Empire will no longer have to worry about them—and a good thing, too."

"It might well be a good thing, if we could be sure of doing it," Ttomalss said. "By the latest reports from Tosev 3, though, the Big Uglies are now ahead of us technologically in many areas, ahead of us to the point where Reffet and Kirel are close to despair. We are not innovators, not in the same way the Tosevites are. And we have only a small scientific community on Tosev 3 in any case. It is a colonial world. The center of the Empire is still Home. At the moment, unless I am badly mistaken, the Big Uglies could beat back any attack we might try. Whether we could do the same if they attacked us is a different question, and likely one with a different answer."

"Has it come to that so soon?" Atvar said. "I would have believed we had more time."

"I am not certain, but I think it has," Ttomalss said. "I am also not certain the Big Uglies fully realize their superiority. If they were to defeat an attack from the Race . . ."

"They would become sure of something they now only suspect? Is that what you are saying?"

Ttomalss paused till a female wearing blue false hair between her eye turrets got too far away to hear. Then, unhappily, he used the affirmative gesture and said, "Exalted Fleetlord, I am afraid it is. If not, then I am misreading the reports beamed here from Tosev 3."

"I have been reading those same reports," Atvar said. "I did not have that impression. And yet . . ." He paused, then strode out ahead of Ttomalss, his tailstump twitching in agitation. The psychologist hurried to catch up with him. Atvar swung one eye turret back toward Ttomalss. With obvious reluctance, the fleetlord slowed. When Ttomalss came up beside him once more, he asked, "Have you also been reading translations of the reports the American Big Uglies have sent this way for the benefit of their starship and its crew?"

"I have seen some of those translations," Ttomalss said cautiously. "I do not know how reliable they are."

"Well, that is always a concern," the fleetlord admitted. "We have sent back an enormous amount of data on Tosev 3, including video and audio. But none of the so-called experts here has ever seen a real live Big Ugly before now except possibly Kassquit, the irony being that she speaks only the language of the Race."

"Kassquit is . . . what she is. I often marvel that she has as much stability as she does," Ttomalss said. "Hoping for more would no doubt be excessive. But I am sorry. You were saying?"

"I was saying that, having read the translations, I was struck by how confident the American Big Uglies seem," Atvar said. "They appear to respect the Race's power on Tosev 3—as who not utterly addled would not?—but they do not appear to be in the least afraid of it." His tailstump trembled some more. "This may support your view."

"Are any officials who have never been to Tosev 3 aware of these concerns?" Ttomalss asked. "The ones pertaining to conditions on the planet, I mean, not those involving the American Big Uglies here."

Atvar's mouth fell open in a laugh. He waggled his lower jaw back and forth, which meant the laugh was sardonic. "Officials here who have never been to Tosev 3 are not aware of anything, Senior Researcher," he said. "Anything, do you hear me? Why do you suppose they have you and me and even Kassquit negotiating with the wild Big Uglies? They are not competent."

"At least they know that much," Ttomalss said. As reassurances went, that one fell remarkably flat.

Colonel Glen Johnson floated in the *Admiral Peary*'s control room, watching Home go round below him. That was an illusion, of course; the starship revolved around the planet, not the reverse. But his habits and his way of thinking were shaped by a language that had reached maturity hundreds of years before anyone who spoke it knew about or even imagined spaceflight.

He shared the control room with Mickey Flynn. "Exciting,

isn't it?" Flynn remarked. He yawned to show just how exciting it was.

"Now that you mention it, no." Johnson peered out through
the coated glass. There might have been nothing between him
and the surface of Home. The Lizards' world had less in the
way of cloud cover than Earth, too, so he could see much
more of the surface. Grasslands, mountains, forests, seas, and
lots and lots of what looked like desert to a merely human eye
rolled past. On the night side of the planet, the Race's cities
shone like patches of phosphorescence. He said, "I used to
love the view from up high when I was in a plane or a ship in
Earth orbit. Hell, I still do. But . . ." He yawned, too.

"I never thought I would know how Moses felt," Flynn
said.

"Moses?" Johnson contemplated his fellow pilot instead of
the ever-changing landscape down below. "I hate to tell you
this, but you don't look one goddamn bit Jewish."

"No, eh? I'm shocked and aggrieved to hear it. But I wasn't
thinking of looks." Flynn pointed down to Tau Ceti 2. "We've
brought our people to the Promised Land, but we can't go into
it ourselves."

"Oh." Johnson thought that over, then slowly nodded. "Yeah.
I've had that same thought myself, as a matter of fact, even
though it's been a hell of a long time since I went to Sunday
school." It was a pretty fair comparison, no matter who made
it. He wondered how long he'd last under full gravity. Not
long—he was sure of that. And he wouldn't have much fun
till the end finally came, either.

Mickey Flynn said, "I wonder if God reaches this far, or if
the spirits of Emperors past have a monopoly here."

"The Lizards are sure their spirits reach to Earth, so God
better be paying attention here just to even things out," Johnson said.

When he was a kid, even when he was a young man, he'd
really believed in the things the preacher talked about in Sunday sermons. He wondered where that belief had gone. He
didn't quite know. All he knew was, he didn't have it any
more. Part of him missed it. The rest? The rest didn't much
care. He supposed that, had he cared more, he wouldn't have
lost his belief in the first place.

His gaze went from the ever-unrolling surface of Home to the radar screen. As always, the Lizards had a lot of traffic in orbit around their homeworld. The radar also tracked several suborbital shuttlecraft flights. Those looked a lot like missile launches, so he noticed them whenever they went off. As long as the alarm that said something was aimed at the *Admiral Peary* didn't go off, though, he didn't get too excited.

Actually, by comparison with the orbital traffic around Earth, Home was pretty tidy. The Lizards were neat and well organized. They didn't let satellites that had worn out and gone dead stay in orbit. They cleaned up spent rocket stages, too. And they didn't have any missile-launching satellites cunningly disguised as spent rocket stages, either. Home wasn't nearly so well defended as Earth. The Lizards hadn't seen the need. Why should they have seen it? They were unified and peaceful. No other species had ever paid them a call in its own starships. Till now . . .

"In the circus of life, do you know what we are?" Flynn said out of the blue.

"The clowns?" Johnson suggested.

"You would look charming in a big red rubber nose," the other pilot said, examining him as if to decide just how charming he would look. Flynn seemed dissatisfied—perhaps not charming enough. After that once-over, he went on with his own train of thought: "No, we are the freaks of the midway. 'Step right up, ladies and gentlemen, and see the amazing, astonishing, and altogether unique floating men! They glide! They slide! They sometimes collide! And after one touch—one slight touch—of gravity, they will have died! One thin dime, one tenth part of a dollar, to see these marvels of science perform for *you*!' " He pointed straight at Johnson.

"If I had a dime, I'd give it to you," Johnson said. "I remember the carnival barkers back before the war. Sweet Jesus Christ, that's more than ninety years ago now. But you sound just like 'em."

Mickey Flynn looked pained. " 'Talkers.' The word is 'talkers,' " he said with what seemed exaggerated patience. "Only the marks call them 'barkers.' "

"How do you know that?" Johnson asked. After so long living in each other's pockets on the *Lewis and Clark,* he thought

he'd heard all the other pilot's stories. Maybe he was wrong.
He hoped he was. Good stories were worth their weight in
gold.

"Me?" Flynn said. "Simple enough. Until I was three years
old, I was a pickled punk, living in a bottle of formaldehyde
on a sideshow shelf. It gave me a unique perspective—and
very bad breath."

He spoke with the same straight-faced seriousness he
would have used to report the course of a Lizard shuttlecraft.
He had no other tone of voice. It left Glen Johnson very little
to take hold of. "Anyone ever tell you you were out of your
tree?" he asked at last.

"Oh yes. But they're all mad save me and thee—and I have
my doubts about thee," Flynn said.

"I've had my doubts about you—thee—a lot longer than
the other way round, I'll bet," Johnson said.

"Not likely," the other pilot replied. "When you came aboard
the *Lewis and Clark,* I doubted you would live long enough to
doubt me or anything else ever again. I thought Healey would
throw you right out the air lock—and keep your spacesuit."

Since Johnson had wondered about the same thing, he
couldn't very well argue with Mickey Flynn. He did say, "Nobody believes I had electrical problems at just the wrong
time."

"Healey believed you—or he wasn't quite sure you were
lying, anyhow," Flynn said. "If you hadn't done such a good
job of faking your troubles, he *would* have spaced you, and
you can take that to the bank." He eyed Johnson once more. It
made his expression look odd, since they floated more or less
at right angles to each other. "Don't you think you can 'fess
up now? It was more than ten light-years and almost seventy
years ago."

Johnson might have confessed to Mickey Flynn. Flynn was
right; what he'd done in Earth orbit hardly mattered here in
orbit around Home. But Brigadier General Walter Stone
chose that moment to come into the control room. Johnson
was damned if he would admit anything to the dour senior
pilot. He had the feeling that Stone wouldn't have minded
spacing him, either. And so he said, "I told you—I had wiring

troubles at the worst possible time, that's all. There is such a thing as coincidence, you know."

Stone had no trouble figuring out what the other two pilots were talking about. With a snort, he said, "There is such a thing as bullshit, too, and you've got it all over your shoes."

"Thank you very much—sir." If Johnson was going to keep up the charade of innocent curiosity, he had to act offended now. "If you will excuse me . . ." He reached for a handhold, found it, and pulled himself from one to another and out of the control room.

Internally, the ship was laid out like a smaller version of the *Lewis and Clark*. Corridors had plenty of handholds by which people could pull themselves along. Intersecting corridors had convex mirrors that covered all approaches. Johnson used them, too. He'd seen some nasty collisions—Mickey Flynn hadn't been kidding about that—and he didn't want to be a part of one. You could get going at quite a clip. If you didn't happen to notice that somebody else was barreling along, too . . .

His cabin was a little larger than the cramped cubicle that had gone by the name in the *Lewis and Clark*. His bunk was nothing more than a foam mattress with straps to keep him from drifting away. In weightlessness, what more did anyone need? A few people had nightmares of falling endlessly, but most did just fine. Johnson was glad he was, for once, part of the majority.

He didn't feel like sleeping just now, though. He put a *skelkwank* disk into a player and started listening to music. *Skelkwank* light—a coherent beam of uniform frequency— was something humanity hadn't imagined before the Lizards came. English had borrowed the word from the language of the Race. All sorts of humans had borrowed—stolen—the technology.

Johnson remembered records. He wondered if, back on Earth, even one phonograph survived. Maybe a few stubborn antiquarians would still have them, and museums. Ordinary people? He didn't think so.

So much of the *Admiral Peary* used pilfered technology. Humanity had had radar before the Lizards came. People were beginning to work on atomic energy. But even there, the

Race's technology was evolved, perfected. Stealing had let humans evade any number of mistakes they would have made on their own.

Where would we be if the Race hadn't come? Johnson knew where he would be in this year of our Lord 2031: he would be dead. But where would people be? Would the Nazis still be around, or would the USA and the Russians and England have smashed them? He was pretty sure the Germans would have gone down the drain. They were, after all, taking on the rest of the world without much help.

But even beaten, they were a formidable people. In the real world, they'd pulled themselves together after the Race's invasion and again after the fight they'd stupidly picked with the Lizards over Poland in the 1960s. That had been a disastrous defeat, and had cost them much of their European empire. But they'd been recovering even when Johnson went into cold sleep, and reports from Earth showed they were working hard to reestablish themselves as a power to be reckoned with.

The Lizards worked hard to keep the *Reich* from violating the terms of the armistice they'd forced upon it. They had kept Germany from returning to space for a long time. But the *Reich* had quietly rearmed to the point where pulling its teeth now would only touch off another war. The Lizards didn't want that. The last one had hurt them even though they won it. The Germans, by acting as if they weren't afraid to take the chance of another scrap—and maybe, given Nazi fanaticism, they weren't—had won themselves quite a bit of freedom of action.

Bastards, Johnson thought. *But tough bastards.* For the time being, though, the Germans would trouble the Race only back on Earth. Things were different for the Americans. They were here. Just a few minutes before, Johnson had watched Home through the glass of the control room.

And more American ships would be coming. The pilot was as sure of that as he was of his own name. The USA wasn't a country that did things by halves. What would the Lizards do when almost as many American ships—and Russian ships, and maybe Japanese ships, too—as those of the Race flew back and forth between the Sun and Tau Ceti? For that matter, what would humanity do when that came true?

* * *

Ttomalss blamed his talk with Fleetlord Atvar for the worried interest with which he approached evidence of the Big Uglies' growing scientific progress in the reports reaching Home from Tosev 3. And the more he looked, the more evidence he found. That didn't surprise him, but didn't leave him happy, either.

Some of the most recent reports alarmed him in a new way. When he'd stayed on Tosev 3, the worry had been that the Big Uglies were catching up with the Race in this, that, or the other field. That wasn't what the scientists in the colonization fleet were saying now. Instead, they were writing things like, *The Big Uglies are doing this, that, or the other thing, and we don't know how.* More and more often, the Race was falling behind.

Everything his own people did was refined and perfected and studied from every possible angle before it went into large-scale use. Their technology hardly ever malfunctioned. It did what it was supposed to do, and did it well. If something didn't do what it was supposed to do, and do it all the time, they didn't use it. They went into the unknown one finger-claw's width at a time.

The Big Uglies, by contrast, charged into the unknown with great headlong leaps. If something worked at all, they'd try it. If it was liable to fail and kill large numbers of the individuals who used it, they seemed to take that as part of the price of doing business. They scoffed at danger, even obviously preventable danger. When the Race came to Tosev 3, the Big Uglies had been making motor vehicles for a fair number of years. They'd made them, but they hadn't bothered including safety belts. How many lives had that cost them? How many injuries? Whatever the number, the Tosevites hadn't included them.

Their cold sleep followed the same pattern. It worked . . . most of the time. If the Tosevite called the Doctor died on the way to Home, well, that was unfortunate, but the Big Uglies hadn't wanted to wait till the process got better. If they had waited, they wouldn't have launched their starship in the first place.

Whenever Ttomalss found evidence of Tosevite advances

beyond anything the Race could match, he passed it on to males and females in the Imperial Office of Scientific Management. And those males and females, as far as he could tell, promptly forgot all about it. Whenever he asked for follow-up, they acted as if they had no idea what he was talking about. They didn't quite laugh at him to his face. He would have bet they laughed at him behind his back.

He had spent a lot of years on Tosev 3. Maybe he'd picked up some small streak of perverse independence from the Big Uglies he'd studied for so long. Whatever the reason, he decided to forget about the males and females in the Imperial Office of Scientific Management. He used the computer network to find the name and number of a physicist who taught at the local university.

Pesskrag didn't answer the phone. Ttomalss left a message on her machine and waited to see if she would call him back. If she didn't, he vowed to call another working scientist and, if necessary, another and another till he found somebody who would listen to him.

To his relief, the physicist did return his call the next day. When he saw her on the monitor, her youth astonished him. "I greet you, Senior Researcher," she said. At least she wore no wig. "Do you really mean to tell me these Big Ugly things have made discoveries we have not? Excuse me, but I find that very hard to believe."

"If you are interested, I would be pleased to send you the data to evaluate for yourself," Ttomalss answered. "Please believe me when I tell you that you will not wring my liver if you persuade me I am worrying over nothing."

"Send the data, by all means," Pesskrag said. "I was amazed that these creatures could fly a starship, even a slow one. But that, after all, is something they learned from us. I will be even more surprised if they do prove to have learned anything we do not know."

"I will send the data I presently have. More comes in all the time. Decide for yourself," Ttomalss said. "One way or the other, I look forward to your evaluation."

He transmitted the recent reports from Tosev 3. Technically, he probably wasn't supposed to do that. The Imperial Office of Scientific Management had irked him enough that he didn't care so much whether he was supposed to. He wanted answers, not proper bureaucratic procedures. *Yes, the Big Uglies have corrupted me,* he thought.

This time, Pesskrag did not call back for several days. Ttomalss wondered if he ought to try to get hold of the physicist again. That, he convinced himself, would show Big Ugly–style impatience. He made himself wait. He told himself he'd waited for years in cold sleep. What could a few days matter now? But when he'd lain in cold sleep, he hadn't known he was waiting. Now he did. It made a difference.

He had just come back to his room from a negotiating session with the wild Tosevites when the telephone hissed for attention. "Senior Researcher Ttomalss. I greet you," he said.

"And I greet you. This is Physics Professor Pesskrag."

Excitement tingled under Ttomalss' scales. One way or the other, he would find out. "I am glad to hear from you," he said, and barely suppressed an emphatic cough. "Your thoughts are . . . ?"

"My thoughts are confused. My thoughts are very nearly addled, as a matter of fact," Pesskrag said. "I had expected you to send me a pile of sand, to be honest with you."

"I am not a physicist myself. I have no sure way of evaluating it," Ttomalss said. "That is why I sent it to you. All I can say is, males and females with some expertise were concerned about it on Tosev 3. Did they have reason to be?"

"Yes." Pesskrag used an emphatic cough. "The Big Uglies are making experiments that never would have occurred to us. Some of these are large and elaborate, and will not be easy to duplicate here. Do you have more data than you provided me, by any chance?"

"I am sorry, but I do not," Ttomalss said.

"Too bad," the physicist told him. "Most of what you have given me is descriptive only, and not mathematical: it appears to be taken from the public press, not from professional journals. Even so, I would dearly love to see the results from some of these trials."

"Is that a truth?" the psychologist asked.

"That *is* a truth." Pesskrag used another emphatic cough.

"In that case, maybe you should see if you can duplicate these experiments here," Ttomalss said. "Maybe you should pass this information on to other physicists you know. If you do not have the facilities to duplicate what the Big Uglies are doing, maybe a colleague will."

"Do I have your permission to do that?"

"Mine? You certainly do." Ttomalss did not tell the physicist his might not be the only permission required. He did say, "If they decide to attempt this research, I would appreciate it if they got word of their results back to me."

"Yes, I can see how you might. Ah . . ." Pesskrag hesitated. "You do realize these experiments will not be attempted tomorrow, or even within the next quarter of a year? Colleagues will have to obtain materials and equipment, to say nothing of funding and permissions. These wings will spread slowly."

"I see." Ttomalss did, too—all too well. "Please bear in mind, though, and please have your fellow physicists also bear in mind, that these are liable to be the most important experiments they ever try. Please also bear in mind that the Big Uglies tried them years ago. The news is just now reaching us, because of light speed and because of whatever delay there was between the experiments themselves and when the Race learned of them. What you will be doing has been done on Tosev 3. Do we want to fall behind the Big Uglies? Do we dare fall behind them?"

"Until I looked at this, I would have said falling behind those preposterous creatures was impossible," Pesskrag said. "Now I must admit this may have been an error on my part. Who would have believed that?" Amused and amazed, the physicist broke the connection.

Ttomalss was neither amused nor amazed. He knew the Big Uglies too well. He was alarmed. The natives of Tosev 3 had been bad enough when they knew less than the Race. They'd used everything they did know, and they'd had an overabundant supply of trickery, not least because, being disunited, they'd spent the last centuries of their history cheating one another whenever they saw the chance. They'd pulled one even a while ago. Their current presence on Home proved that. If they ever got ahead . . .

If they ever get ahead, how will we catch up? Ttomalss wondered. The Big Uglies had started far behind, but they ran faster. They'd caught up. Could the Race hope to pick up its pace if the Tosevites ever got ahead? That was part of what Ttomalss was trying to find out.

What he did find out failed to encourage him. A few days after he sent the data to Pesskrag, he got an angry telephone call from a male called Kssott. Kssott worked in the Imperial Office of Scientific Management. "You have been distributing information that should have stayed confidential," he said in accusing tones.

"Why should it stay confidential?" Ttomalss demanded. "Do you think that if you bury it in the sand it will never hatch? I can tell you that you are wrong. Among the Big Uglies, it has hatched already."

"*That* is the information we most need to grasp with our fingerclaws and hold tight," Kssott said.

"Why? It is a truth whether you admit it or not," Ttomalss said angrily. "And if you do admit it, maybe you—we—can do something about it. If not, the Tosevites will keep on going forward, while we stay in the same place. Is that what you want?"

"We do not want to introduce unexamined changes into our own society," Kssott said. "That could be dangerous."

"Truth," Ttomalss agreed sarcastically. "Much more dangerous than letting the Big Uglies discover things we have not. I have heard that the Big Uglies worry the Emperor himself. Why do they not worry you?"

Kssott said, "You are misinformed."

"I most assuredly am not," Ttomalss said, appending an emphatic cough. "I have that directly from a male who has it straight from the Emperor's own mouth."

All he got from Kssott was a shrug. "We have been what we are for a very long time. The Race is not ready for rapid change, nor capable of it. Would you disrupt our society for no good purpose?"

"No. I would disrupt it for the best of good purposes: survival," Ttomalss said. "Would you keep it as it is so that the Big Uglies can disrupt it for us?"

"You find this a concern," Kssott said. "The Imperial Office of Scientific Management does not. Our views will prevail. You may rest assured of that, Senior Researcher. Our views *will* prevail." He sounded very certain, very imperial, very

much a high-ranking male of the Race. Ttomalss wanted to
kill him, but even that wouldn't have done much good. There
were too many more just like him.

As chief negotiator for the Americans, Sam Yeager sometimes had to put his foot down to be included on the junkets
the other humans got to take. "I did not come here to sit in a
conference room all day and talk," he told one of the Lizards'
protocol officers. "I could do that back on Tosev 3, thank you
very much. I want to see some of this world."

"But did you not come here to negotiate?" the protocol officer asked. "I did not believe the purpose of your crossing interstellar space was tourism."

The female had a point . . . of sorts. But Sam was convinced
he did, too. "If Fleetlord Atvar and your other negotiators
want to talk with me, I will gladly talk with them," he said.
"But let them come along on the journey, too."

To the protocol officer, that must have seemed like heresy.
But stubbornness won the day for Sam. And, once he'd won,
once he was whisked off to the port city of Rizzaffi, he rapidly wished he'd let the protocol officer have her way. The
prospect of visiting a seaside city on Home had seemed irre-
sistible . . . till he got there.

To the Lizards, whose world was more land than water,
ports were afterthoughts, not the vital centers they so often
were on Earth. Rizzaffi, which lay on the shore of the Sirron
Sea, proved no exception.

It also proved to have the nastiest weather Sam had ever
known—and he'd played ball in Arkansas and Mississippi.
Home was a hot place. The Lizards found Arabia comfortable. But most of this world was dry, which made the climate
bearable for a mere human being.

Rizzaffi was a lot of things. Dry wasn't any of them. Nige-
ria might have had weather like this, or the Amazon jungle, or
one of the nastier suburbs of hell. You couldn't fry an egg on
the sidewalk, but you could sure poach one. Most of the
buildings in the port were of highly polished stone. Things
that looked like ferns sprouted from their sides anyway.
Mossy, licheny growths spread across them and even grew on
glass.

The Lizards routinely used air conditioning in Rizzaffi, not to cut the heat but to wring some of the water out of indoor air. That did them only so much good. Every other advertisement in the town seemed to extol a cream or a spray to get rid of skin fungi.

"You know what this place is?" Frank Coffey said after their first day of looking around.

"Tell me," Sam said. "I'm all ears."

"This is where athlete's foot germs go to heaven after they die."

"If you think I'll argue with you, you're nuts," Sam said. It had never quite rained during the first day's tour. But it had never quite not rained, either. It was always mist or drizzle or fog, the sky an ugly gray overhead.

Rizzaffi reminded him of a classic science-fiction story about the mad jungles of Venus, Stanley Weinbaum's "Paradise Planet." Venus wasn't like that, of course, but Weinbaum hadn't known it wasn't. He'd died a few years before the Lizards came to Earth. He'd barely made it to thirty before cancer killed him. News of his death had hit Sam hard; they'd been close to the same age.

He thought about mentioning "Paradise Planet" to Coffey. After a moment, he thought again. The younger man hadn't been born when the story came out. To Coffey, Venus had always been a world with too much atmosphere, a world with the greenhouse effect run wild, a world without a chance for life. He wouldn't be able to see it as Weinbaum had imagined it when jungles there were not only possible but plausible. And that, to Sam, was a shame.

As he discovered the next day, even the plants in Rizzaffi's parks were like none humanity had ever seen. The trees were low and shrubby, as they were most places on Home. They had leaves, or things that might as well have been leaves, growing directly from their branches rather than from separate twigs or stalks. But those leaves were of different color and shape from the local ones with which Sam was familiar. Stuff that looked something like grass and something like moss grew on the ground below the treeish things. An animal that resembled nothing so much as a softshell turtle with a red

Joseph Stalin mustache jumped into a stream before Sam got as good a look at it as he wanted.

"What was that thing?" he asked their guide.

"It is called a fibyen," the Lizard answered. "It feeds in the mud and gravel at the bottom of ponds and creeks. Those tendrils above its mouth help tell it what its prey is."

Frank Coffey said, "It looked like something I'd see Sunday morning if I drank too much Old Overcoat Saturday night."

He spoke in English. The guide asked him to translate. He did, as well as he could. The translation failed to produce enlightenment. After a good deal of back-and-forth, the guide said, "Alcohol does not affect us in this particular way, no matter how much of it we drink."

"Lucky you," Coffey said.

Before that could cause more confusion still, Sam said, "I have a question."

"Go ahead," the Lizard replied with some relief.

"You have sent many of your creatures from a dry climate from Home to Tosev 3, to make parts of our planet more like yours," Yeager said. The guide made the affirmative gesture. Sam went on, "Why have you not also sent creatures like the fibyen and the plants here in Rizzaffi? Tosev 3 has many areas where they might do very well."

"Why? I will tell you why: because you Tosevites are welcome to areas like this." The guide's emphatic cough said how welcome humans were to such places. "Some of us must live here in this miserable place, but we do not like it. I do not believe anyone who was not addled from hatching could like it. And that reminds me. . . ." The Lizard's eye turrets swiveled in all directions, though how far he could see through Rizzaffi's swirling mist was a good question.

"Yes?" Sam asked when the guide didn't say anything for some little while.

"Have you Big Uglies got any ginger?" the Lizard demanded. "That wonderful herb helps me forget what a miserable, damp, slimy hole this is. I would give you anything you like for a few tastes, and I am sure I am far from the only one who would."

"Well, well," Frank Coffey said. "Isn't that interesting?"

This time, he didn't translate from English to the Race's language.

"That's one word," Sam said, also in English. This wasn't the first time humans had got such a request. He wondered how to answer the guide. Really, though, only one way was possible: "I am very sorry, but we are diplomats, not ginger smugglers. We have no ginger. We would not give it out if we did, because it is against your laws." What else could he say, when he wasn't sure if this Lizard was an addict or a provocateur?

The guide let out a disappointed hiss. "That is most unfortunate. It will make many males and females very unhappy."

"A pity," Sam said, meaning anything but. "Perhaps we should go back to the hotel now."

"Yes," the Lizard said. "Perhaps we should."

With the air conditioning going full blast, the hotel was merely unpleasant. After hot wet weather, hot dry weather seemed a godsend. The sweat that had clung greasily to Sam's skin evaporated. Then salt crusts formed instead, and he started to itch. For a human, showering in a stall made for Lizards was an exercise in frustration. Apart from the force of the stream, it involved bending low and banging one's head against the ceiling over and over. Yeager wouldn't have liked it when he was young. Now that he was far from young and far from limber, it became an ordeal. But he endured it here for the sake of getting clean.

He ate in the hotel refectory. He didn't think it deserved to be called a restaurant. As usual, the food was salty by Earthly standards. That probably wasn't good for his blood pressure, but he didn't know what he could do about it. He fretted about it less today than he would have most of the time. He'd sweated out enough salt to need replenishing.

And he could get pure alcohol and dilute it to palatability with water. Nobody here knew anything about ice cubes. The Race cared nothing for cold drinks. But warm vodka was better than no vodka at all.

His son had a sly look in his eye when he asked, "Well, Dad, aren't you glad you came along?"

"If Home needed an enema, they'd plug it in right here," Sam replied, which made Jonathan choke on his drink. The older Yeager went on, "Even so, I *am* glad I came. When will I ever get the chance to see anything like this again? How many people have ever seen a fibyen?"

"*I* didn't even get to see it," Jonathan said. "But you know what else? I'm not going to lose any sleep about missing it."

"I lose enough sleep to sleeping mats," Sam said. "Kassquit may not have any trouble with them, but she's been sleeping on them all her life. Me?" He shook his head and wiggled and stretched. Something in his back crunched when he did. That felt good, but he knew it wouldn't last.

Outside, lightning flashed. Now real rain started coming down—coming down in sheets, in fact. Sam knew the Lizards did a good job of soundproofing their hotels. The thunderclap that followed hard on the heels of the lightning still rattled his false teeth.

Karen Yeager said, "This is a part of Home none of the Lizards who came to Earth ever talked much about."

"I can see why, too," Jonathan said. "How many people brag about coming from Mobile, Alabama? And this place makes Mobile look like paradise."

Sam, who'd been through Mobile playing ball, needed to think about that. Mobile was pretty bad. But his son had it right. And if that wasn't a scary thought, it would do till a really spooky one came along.

"Makes you see why the Race doesn't care much about ships, too," Jonathan added. "I wouldn't want to live here, either."

"I had the same thought," Sam said. "But their ports can't all be like this. Sure, Mobile is a port, but so is Los Angeles."

"Good point," Jonathan allowed. He suddenly grinned. "They've sent us to the South Pole, and now to this place. Maybe they're trying to tell us they really don't want us gallivanting all over the landscape."

"Maybe they are. Too bad, in that case," Sam said. "Even Rizzaffi is interesting, in a horrible kind of way."

"Sure it is," his son said. "Besides, the more the Race shows us they don't want us to do something, the likelier we are to want to do it. Sort of reminds me of how I felt about you and Mom when I was sixteen."

"It would," Sam said darkly, and they both laughed. They

could laugh now. Back then, Sam had often wanted to clout his one and only son over the head with a baseball bat. It had probably been mutual, too. *Sure it was,* Sam though. *But, by God, he was the one who really had it coming. Not me. Of course not me.*

☆ 6 ☆

Kassquit liked Rizzaffi no better than did the wild Big Uglies. She probably liked it less, and found it more appalling. The Tosevites who'd come to Home on the *Admiral Peary* were at least used to weather, to variations on a theme. They'd lived on the surface of a planet. She hadn't. The air conditioning aboard a starship had no business changing. If it did, something was badly wrong somewhere.

Even ordinary weather on Home disconcerted her. The change in temperature from day to night seemed wrong. It felt unnatural to her, even though she knew it was anything but. But in Sitneff the change from what she was used to hadn't been extreme. In Rizzaffi, it was.

She felt as if she were breathing soup. Whenever she left the hotel, cooling moisture clung to her skin instead of evaporating as it did in drier climates. She envied the Race, which did not sweat but panted. Ordinary males and females kept their hides dry—except for contact with the clammy outside air. She couldn't. And if her sweat didn't evaporate, she wasn't cooled, or not to any great degree. She not only breathed soup; she might as well have been cooking in it.

The wild Big Uglies kept going out in the horrible weather again and again. Kassquit soon gave up. They really were wild to get a look at everything they could, and came back to the hotel talking about the strange animals and stranger plants they had seen. Their guide seemed downright smug about what an unusual place Rizzaffi was. Kassquit recognized the difference between unusual and enjoyable. The Americans didn't seem to.

When Sam Yeager talked about the fibyen, Kassquit read about the animal and saw a picture of it at the terminal in her room. Having done that, she knew more about it than he did. He'd seen one in the flesh, and she hadn't, but so what? To her, something on a monitor was as real as something seen in person. How could it be otherwise when she'd learned almost everything she knew about the universe outside her starship from the computer network?

Almost everything. She kept looking at the way Jonathan and Karen Yeager formed a pair bond. She eyed Linda and Tom de la Rosa, too, but not so much and not in the same way. When she looked at Sam Yeager's hatchling and his mate, she kept thinking, *This could have been mine.*

That it could have been hers was unlikely. She knew as much. But Jonathan Yeager had been her first sexual partner—her only sexual partner. Ttomalss had offered to bring other wild Big Ugly males up from the surface of Tosev 3, but she had always declined. She could not keep them on the starship permanently, and parting with them after forming an emotional bond hurt too much to contemplate. She'd done it once, with Jonathan, and it had been knives in her spirit. Do it again? Do it again and again? Her hand shaped the negative gesture. Better not to form the bond in the first place. So she thought, anyway.

She also noticed Karen Yeager watching her. She understood jealousy. Of course she understood it. It gnawed at her whenever she saw Jonathan and Karen happy and comfortable together.

You have him. I do not. Why are you jealous? Kassquit wondered. Because she hadn't been raised as a Big Ugly, she needed a long time to see what a wild Tosevite would have understood right away. *You have him, but I had him once, for a little while. Do you wonder if he wants me back?*

She took a certain sour pleasure in noting those suspicious glances from the wild female Tosevite. She also realized— again, much more slowly than she might have—why Karen Yeager had wanted her to put on wrappings: to reduce her attractiveness. Males and females of the Race could demonstrate such foolishness during mating season, but happily did without it the rest of the year. But Big Uglies, as Kassquit knew too well, were always in season. It complicated their lives. She wondered how they'd ever managed to create any kind of civilization when they had that kind of handicap.

A good many members of the Race remained convinced that the Big Uglies hadn't created any kind of civilization. They were certain the Tosevites had stolen everything they knew from the Race. That would have been more convincing if the Big Uglies hadn't fought the conquest fleet to a standstill when it first came to Tosev 3. Kassquit had occasionally pointed this out to males and females who mocked the Big Uglies—mocked her, in effect, for what was she if not a Big Ugly by hatching?

They always seemed surprised when she did that. They hadn't thought it through. They *knew* they were superior. They didn't have to think it through.

No one in Rizzaffi had ever seen a Big Ugly before, except in video. Wild or citizen of the Empire didn't matter. At the hotel, the staff treated her about the same as the American Tosevites. She wasn't convinced the staff could tell the difference. She didn't say anything about that. She feared she would find out she was right.

She sat glumly in the refectory, eating a supper that wasn't anything special. The starship where she'd lived for so long had had better food than this. She didn't stop to remember that that food had mostly Tosevite origins, though after the colonization fleet arrived some of the meat and grain came from species native to Home.

As often happened, she was eating by herself. The American Big Uglies did not invite her to join them. To make matters worse, they chattered among themselves in their own language, so she couldn't even eavesdrop. She told herself she didn't want to. She knew she was lying.

And then a surprising thing happened. One of the wild Tosevites got up and came over to her table. She had no trouble recognizing him, thanks to his brown skin. "I greet you, Researcher," he said politely.

"And I greet you, Major Coffey," Kassquit answered.

"May I sit down?" the Tosevite asked.

"Yes. Please do," Kassquit said. Then she asked a question of her own: "Why do you want to?"

"To be sociable," he replied. "That is the word, is it not?—sociable."

"That is the word, yes." Kassquit made the affirmative gesture.

Coffey sat down. The table, like most in the refectory, had been adapted—not very well—to Tosevite hindquarters and posture. The wild Big Ugly said, "What do you think of Rizzaffi?"

"Not much," Kassquit answered at once. That startled a laugh out of Coffey. She asked, "What is your opinion of this place?"

"About the same as yours," he said. "When I was a hatchling, I lived in the southeastern United States. Summers there are very warm and very humid. But this city beats any I ever saw." He added an emphatic cough to show Rizzaffi was much worse than any other place he knew.

He used the Race's language in the same interesting way as Sam Yeager. He spoke fluently, but every once in a while an odd or offbeat phrase would come through. Kassquit suspected those were idioms the wild Big Uglies translated literally from their own language. Had they done it often, it would have been annoying. As things were, piquant seemed the better word.

Kassquit said as much. Major Coffey's face showed amusement. Kassquit wished her own features made such responses. But Ttomalss hadn't—couldn't have—responded to her when she tried to learn to smile as a hatchling, and the ability never developed. Coffey said, "So you find us worth a laugh, then?"

"That is not what I meant," Kassquit said. "Some of your ways of putting things would make fine additions to the language."

"I thank you," the wild Big Ugly said. "Your language has certainly hatched many new words in English."

"Yes, I can see how that might be—words for things you did not have before you met the Race," Kassquit said.

"Many of those, certainly," Coffey agreed. "But also others. We sometimes say *credit,* for instance, when we mean *money.*" The first word he stressed was in the Race's language, the second in his own. He went on, "And we will often use an interrogative cough by itself when we want to say,

'What do you mean?' or an emphatic cough to mean something like, 'I should say so!' "

"But that is a barbarism!" Kassquit exclaimed. "The Race has never used the coughs by themselves."

"I know. But we are not talking about the Race's language right now. We are talking about English. What would be a barbarism in your language is just new slang in ours. English is a language that has always borrowed and adapted a lot from other tongues it has met."

"How very strange," Kassquit said. "The Race's language is not like that."

"No, eh?" Frank Coffey laughed a noisy Tosevite laugh. "What about *ginger*?"

"That is something the Race did not have before it came to Tosev 3," Kassquit said, a little defensively. Even more defensively, she added, "To me, it would only be a spice. Biologically, I am as much a Tosevite as you are."

"Yes, of course." Coffey laughed again, on a different note. "Back on Tosev 3, though, I would not have expected to sit down to supper with a female without wrappings; I will say that."

"Well, you are not on Tosev 3," Kassquit replied with some irritation. "I follow the Empire's customs, not yours. Karen Yeager already bothered me about this. I say your view is foolishness. You are the guests here; the Empire is your host. If anything, you should adapt to our customs, not the other way round."

"I was not complaining," the wild Big Ugly said. "I was merely observing."

Kassquit started to accept that in the polite spirit in which it seemed to have been offered. Then she stopped with her reply unspoken. She sent Frank Coffey a sharp look. How had he meant what he'd just said? Was he making an observation, or was he observing . . . her?

And if he was observing her, what did he have in mind? What did she think about whatever he might have in mind? Those were both interesting questions. Since Kassquit wasn't sure *what* she thought about whatever he might have in mind, she decided she didn't need to know the answers right away.

Without even noticing she'd done it, she made the affirmative gesture. She didn't need to know this instant, sure enough. Frank Coffey would spend a lot of time—probably the rest of his life—on Home.

And if he was interested, and if *she* was interested, they both might pass the time more pleasantly than if not. Or, on the other hand, they might quarrel. No way to know ahead of time. That helped make Tosevite social relationships even more complicated than they would have been otherwise.

Was the experiment worth attempting, then? She knew she was getting ahead of herself, reading too much into what might have been a chance remark. But she also knew Tosevite males probably *would* show interest if an opportunity presented itself. And she knew she probably would, too. Compared to Tosevite males, Tosevite females might be less aggressive. Compared to the Race . . . She was a Tosevite, no doubt about it.

Atvar watched with a certain wry amusement as the shuttlecraft returned from Rizzaffi. Nothing could have persuaded him to go there. He knew better. You could come down with a skin fungus just by sticking your snout outdoors. The place made much of Tosev 3 seem pleasant by comparison.

He wondered if suggesting they visit Rizzaffi had been an insult of sorts, one too subtle for them to understand. That was risky. Sam Yeager had a feeling for such things. Atvar shrugged. He'd find out.

One after another, the Big Uglies came off the shuttlecraft. Even from the terminal, Atvar had no trouble recognizing Kassquit, because she did not wear wrappings the way the wild Tosevites did. She was a strange creature, as much like a female of the Race as a Big Ugly could be. The more Atvar got to know her, the more he wondered if she came close enough. If all the Big Uglies on Tosev 3 were like her, would they make satisfactory citizens of the Empire?

He sighed. He really couldn't say. She remained essentially Tosevite, essentially different, in a way the Rabotevs and Hallessi didn't. With them, cultural similarity overwhelmed biological differences. They were variations on a theme also expressed in the Race. Big Uglies weren't. No matter what cultural trappings were painted on them, they remained different underneath.

Here they came, the wild ones and Kassquit, on a cart that had its seats adapted to their shape. The cart stopped just outside the terminal. A gate opened. The Tosevites hurried inside.

Atvar walked forward. After all these years dealing with Big Uglies, he still had trouble telling one from another. Here, he had trained himself to look for Sam Yeager's white head fur. If the Tosevite ever put on a hat, Atvar wasn't sure he could pick him out from the others. As things were, though, he managed.

"I greet you, Ambassador," he said.

"And I greet you, Fleetlord," Yeager replied. "I still find it very strange to be called by that title. Do you understand?"

"Perhaps," Atvar said. "Life does not always give us what we expect, though. Consider my surprise when the conquest fleet came to Tosev 3 and I discovered we would not have a walkover on our hands."

Sam Yeager let out several yips of barking Tosevite laughter. "There you have me, Fleetlord, and I admit it. You must have found that a lot stranger than I find this."

"To tell you the truth, I was never so horrified in all my life," Atvar said, and Sam Yeager laughed again. The former head of the conquest fleet asked, "And what did you think of Rizzaffi?"

"Interesting place to visit," Yeager said dryly—not the fitting word, not when speaking of the port city. "I would not care to live there."

"Only someone addled in the eggshell would," Atvar said. "I marvel that you chose to visit the place at all." There. Now he'd said it. He could try to find out if someone really had insulted the Big Uglies by suggesting they go there.

But Sam Yeager shrugged and said, "It is an unusual part of your planet."

"Well, *that* is a truth, by the spirits of Emperors past!" Atvar used an emphatic cough.

"Fair enough," the Tosevite ambassador said. "I, for one, would like to see unusual places. We will see enough of the ordinary while we are here. And if the unusual is not always pleasant—we can leave. And I am glad we have left. But I am also glad we went."

"If you go to Rizzaffi with that attitude, you will do all right," Atvar said. "If you go to Rizzaffi with any other attitude—any other attitude at all, mind you—you will want to run away as fast as you can."

"Not so bad as that," Yeager said. "It does have some interesting animals in the neighborhood. That fibyen is a queer-looking beast, is it not?"

"Well, yes," Atvar admitted. "But I would not go to Rizzaffi for interesting animals alone. If I wanted to see interesting animals, I would go to the zoo. That way, I would not grow mildew all over my scales."

He got another loud Tosevite laugh from Sam Yeager. "When I put on corrective lenses outside to see something up close, they steamed over," Yeager said.

"I am not surprised," Atvar replied. "When you go back to your hotel, we will talk of things more interesting than Rizzaffi. The Emperor himself has taken an interest in your being here, you know." He cast down his eye turrets.

"We are honored, of course," Yeager said. Polite or ironic? Atvar couldn't tell. The Big Ugly went on, "He probably wants to figure out the smoothest way to get rid of us, just like the rest of you."

"No such thing!" Atvar had to work hard not to show how appalled he was. Was the Race so transparent to Tosevites? If it was, it was also in a lot of trouble. Or was that just Sam Yeager proving once again that he could think along with the Race as if he had scales and eye turrets and a tailstump? Atvar dared hope so. Other Big Uglies often didn't listen to Yeager, no matter how right he usually proved.

Now he asked, "Is there any chance I might have an audience with the Emperor myself?"

"Would you like to?" Atvar said in surprise, and Sam Yeager made the affirmative gesture, for all the world as if he were a male of the Race. The fleetlord replied, "I cannot arrange that. You must submit a request to the court. The courtiers and the Emperor himself will make the final decision."

"I see." Yeager eyed Atvar in a way that made him uncomfortable despite the Big Ugly's alien, nearly unreadable features. "I suspect a recommendation from someone of fleet-lord's rank would not hurt in getting my request accepted," Yeager said shrewdly. "Or am I wrong?"

"No, you are not wrong. Influence matters, regardless of the world," Atvar said. "I will make that recommendation on your behalf. If it is accepted, you will have to learn some fairly elaborate ceremonial."

"I can do that, I think," Sam Yeager said. "And I thank you for your kindness. I expect you will want something for it one of these days, which is only right. I will do what I can to arrange that. Influence runs both ways, after all. We have a saying: 'You scratch my back and I will scratch yours.' "

"I understand your meaning," Atvar said. "This saves me the trouble of raising such a delicate topic."

"I am glad," Yeager said, and that *was* irony. "I also hope the Emperor will be kind enough to forgive any breaches of protocol I might accidentally commit. I am only an ignorant alien who knows no better."

Had any other alien ever known so much about the Race? Atvar had his doubts. He said, "Yes, there is precedent for such forgiveness from the days when the first Rabotevs and Hallessi came to reverence sovereigns long ago."

"Well, I am very glad to hear it," the Big Ugly said. "What is the usual penalty for botching the rituals in front of the Emperor?"

He would not cast down his eyes when he named the sovereign. That proved him foreign—a word the Race hadn't had to think about for a long time before invading Tosev 3. It also irritated Atvar no end. With a certain sour amusement, then, he answered, "Traditionally, it is being thrown to the beasts."

There, he took Sam Yeager by surprise. "Is it?" he said. "Forgive me for saying so, but that strikes me as a trifle drastic." He paused. "What are the beasts these wicked males and females are thrown to?"

"You are too clever," Atvar said. "In the ancientest days, long before Home was unified, they were sdanli—large, fierce predators. Ever since, though, they have been courtiers in sdanli-skin masks who tell the incompetent wretches what fools and idiots they are and how they did not deserve their audiences."

"Really?" Sam Yeager asked. Atvar made the affirmative gesture. The wild Big Ugly laughed. "I like that. It is very . . . symbolic."

"Just so," Atvar said. "The pain, perhaps, is less than that of actually being devoured. But the humiliation remains. Males and females have been known to slay themselves in shame after such a session with the courtiers. For most of them, of course, one audience with the Emperor"—he cast down *his* eye turrets—"is all they will ever have, and is, or would be, the high point of their lives. When it suddenly becomes the low point instead, they can think only of escape."

An audience with the Emperor would in a sense be wasted on a wild Big Ugly. He wouldn't appreciate the honor granted him. Without a hundred thousand years of tradition behind it, what would it mean to him? A meeting with a sovereign not his own, a meeting with a sovereign he reckoned no more than equal to his own. Back on Tosev 3, Atvar had had to pretend he believed the Big Uglies' not-emperors to be of the same rank as *the* Emperor. Here on Home, he didn't have to go through that farce. But for Sam Yeager, it was no farce. It was a truth.

The Big Ugly said, "Well, you would not have to worry about that with me."

"No, I suppose not," Atvar said; Yeager had just gone a long way toward confirming his own thoughts of a moment before. Even so, the fleetlord went on, "I will, as I said, support your request if you like. How the courtiers and the Emperor respond to it, though, is not within the grip of my fingerclaws."

"I would be very grateful for your support, Fleetlord, very grateful indeed." Yeager used an emphatic cough. "Back on Tosev 3, the Race's ambassador would meet with my not-emperor. Only seems fair to turn things around here."

He truly did believe a wild Big Ugly chosen for a limited term by an absurd process of snoutcounting matched in importance the ruler of three and a half inhabited planets spread over four solar systems.

Ah, but if the Emperor had only ruled four planets . . . ! Since he didn't, Atvar had to put up with Yeager's provincial arrogance. "Again, Ambassador, I will do what I can on your behalf."

Maybe the Emperor would reject the idea. But maybe he wouldn't. He was certainly interested in the Big Uglies and concerned about them. Atvar suspected the audience, if granted, would not be publicized. Too many males and females would envy the Big Ugly.

Yeager said, "You know we American Big Uglies"—he used the Race's slang for his species without self-consciousness— "have a literature imagining technological achievements of which we are not yet capable?"

"I have heard that, yes," Atvar replied. "Why do you mention it now?"

"Because there are times when my being here on Home feels as if it came from one of those stories," the Tosevite said. "If I were to meet the Emperor of another intelligent species, how could it seem like anything but what we call science fiction?" He laughed. "I probably should not tell you that. I am sure the Doctor never would have said anything so undiplomatic."

"You are honest. You are candid," Atvar said. *And, no matter how well you can think like one of us, you are not, and I fear, never will be.*

After some little while on Home, Karen Yeager was getting used to being stared at whenever she went out on the streets of Sitneff. The Lizards didn't come right up and harass her and Jonathan and the de la Rosas, but eye turrets always swiveled toward the humans. Some males and females would exclaim and point. Karen didn't like it, but she supposed it was inevitable.

Sometimes she stared right back—mostly at the males and females who wore wigs and T-shirts and sometimes even shorts: shorts ventilated for their tailstumps. Did they have any idea how ridiculous they looked? Probably about as ridiculous as humans with shaved heads and body paint, but she didn't dwell on that.

And then one day, like the most curious Lizard, she was pointing and exclaiming at the little green man—that was what he looked like—coming out of a shop. "Look!" she exclaimed in English. "A Halless!" She felt as if she'd spotted a rare and exotic species of bird.

The Halless was about as tall as a Lizard, which meant he came up to her chest. He was the green of romaine lettuce, though his hide was scaly, not leafy. He stood more nearly erect than Lizards did. His feet were wide and flat, his hands—only three fingers and a thumb on each—spidery and delicate.

Like the Rabotev shuttlecraft pilot they'd met, he had a shorter snout than did males and females of the Race. Unlike the Rabotevs and the Lizards, he had ears: long, pointed ones, set high up on his round head. His eyes were on stalks longer than those of the Rabotevs, and could look in different directions at the same time.

None of the Lizards paid any special attention to him. They were used to Hallessi. He stared at the humans with as much curiosity as the members of the Race showed. In a high, thin, squeaky voice, he said, "I greet you, Tosevites."

"And we greet you, Halless," Karen answered, wondering what she sounded like to him. "May I ask your name?"

"Wakonafula," he answered, which didn't sound like a handle a Lizard would carry. "And you are . . . ?"

Karen gave her name. So did her husband and Tom and Linda de la Rosa. They seemed willing to let her do the talking, so she did: "We have never met anyone from your world before. Can you tell us what it is like?"

Wakonafula made the negative gesture. "I am sorry, but I cannot, not from personal experience. I was hatched here on Home, as were several generations of my ancestors. I have seen videos of Halless 1, but I suppose you will have done that, too. And I have also seen videos of Tosev 3. How can you possibly exist on such a miserably cold, wet world?"

"It does not seem that way to us," Tom de la Rosa said. "We are evolved to find it normal. To us, Home is a miserably hot, dry world."

"That strikes me as very strange," Wakonafula said. "When it is so pleasant here . . . But, as you say, you are adapted to conditions on Tosev 3, however nasty they may be."

"Why did your ancestors leave their planet and come to Home?" Karen asked.

"A fair number of students come here from Halless 1—and also from Rabotev 2, for that matter—for courses not available on other worlds," the Halless answered. "Home still has the best universities in the Empire, even after all these millennia. And some students, having completed their work, choose to stay here instead of going back into cold sleep and back to the worlds where they hatched. We are citizens of the Empire, too, after all."

Back when India belonged to Britain and not to the Race, some of its bright youngsters had traveled halfway around the world to study at Oxford and Cambridge. Not all of them went back to their homeland once their studies were done, either. Some stayed in London and formed an Indian community there. Funny to think that the same sort of thing could happen so many light-years from Earth.

"May I ask you a question?" Linda de la Rosa asked.

Now Wakonafula used the affirmative gesture. "Speak," he urged.

"I thank you," Linda said. "Does it not trouble you that Home has the best universities? If your folk ruled Halless 1 instead of the colonists from Home, would it not have the very best of everything?"

Trir, the humans' Lizard guide, spluttered indignantly. She sounded like an angry tea kettle. Karen had trouble blaming her. If Linda wasn't preaching sedition, she was coming mighty close.

But Wakonafula said, "You have asked several questions, not one. Let me answer like this: if it were not for the Race, we would still be barbarians. We would die of diseases we easily cure today, thanks to the Race. We would go to war with one another; our planet had several rival empires when the conquest fleet came. Thanks to the Race, we live at peace. If Halless 1 is not equal to Home in every way—and it is not, as far as I can tell from here—it is far closer than it was before the conquest. In the fullness of time, it will catch up."

He sounded calmly confident. In the fullness of time . . . How many humans had ever had the patience to wait for the fullness of time? The Race did. Back on Earth, the Lizards had always insisted that Hallessi and Rabotevs thought more like them than like humans. Judging by Wakonafula, they had a point. Humans commonly preferred kicking over the apple cart now to waiting for the fullness of time.

On the other hand, how reliable was Wakonafula? Was he a chance-met Hallessi, as he seemed to be? Or was he a plant, primed to tell the Big Uglies what the Race wanted them to hear? How could anyone be sure? That was a good question. Karen knew she had no certain answer for it.

"If you will excuse me, I must be on my way," the Halless said now, and left. Yes, he might well have had—probably did have—business of his own to take care of. But that casual departure roused Karen's suspicions.

And then Trir said, "You see that all species within the Empire are happy to be a part of it."

Once roused, Karen's suspicions soared. This was pretty clumsy propaganda—but then, the Lizards never had been as smooth about such things as people were. More than a little annoyed, she said, "I am very sorry, but I do not see anything of the sort."

"How could you not?" the guide asked in what sounded like genuine surprise. "The Halless said—"

"I heard what he said," Karen broke in. "But his saying it does not have to make it a truth. He could easily have received instructions from superiors about what he was to tell us."

"That is a shocking suggestion," Trir exclaimed.

Karen's husband made the negative gesture. "I do not think so," Jonathan Yeager said. "Such things happen all the time on Tosev 3. No reason they should not happen here as well."

"Why should we resort to such trickery?" Trir asked.

"To make us believe things in the Empire are better than they really are," Karen said. "Do you not agree that would be to your advantage?"

Trir let out an indignant hiss. "I will not even dignify such a claim with a response. Its foolishness must be as obvious to you as it is to me."

Was there any point to arguing more? Reluctantly, Karen decided there wasn't. The Lizard was not going to admit anything. Maybe Trir really didn't see there was anything to admit. Karen wouldn't have been surprised, only saddened, to find that was so. Plenty of humans couldn't see their superiors' ulterior motives, either.

And the guide also seemed perturbed, saying, "Perhaps we should go back to the hotel. That way, no more unfortunate incidents can take place."

"This was not unfortunate. This was interesting," Tom de la Rosa said. "We learned something about the Hallessi and something about the Empire." *And if we didn't learn exactly what you wanted us to, well, too bad,* Karen thought. But Trir was unlikely to see things like that.

A genuinely unfortunate incident did happen not long before they got to the hotel. A Lizard skittered up to them and said, "You things are what they call Big Uglies, right? You are not Hallessi or Rabotevs? No—you cannot be. I know what they look like, and you do not look like that. You must be Big Uglies."

"Go away. Do not bother these individuals," Trir said sharply.

"It is not a bother," Karen Yeager said. "Yes, we are from Tosev 3. Why do you ask?"

"Ginger!" The stranger added an emphatic cough. "You must have some of the herb. I will buy it from you. I will give you whatever you want for it. Tell me what that is, and I will pay it. I am not a poor male." Another emphatic cough.

Such things had happened before, but never with such naked, obvious, desperate longing. "I am sorry," Karen said, "but we have no ginger."

"You must!" the Lizard exclaimed. "You must! I will go mad—utterly mad, I tell you—if I do not get what I need."

"Police!" the guide shouted. Hissing out a string of curses, the Lizard who wanted drugs scurried away. Trir said, "Please ignore that male's disgraceful conduct. It is abnormal, depraved, and altogether disgusting. You should never have been exposed to it."

"We know about the Race and ginger," Karen said. "The problem on Tosev 3 is far larger and far worse than it is here."

"Impossible!" Trir declared, proving Lizards could be parochial, too.

"Not only not impossible, but a truth," Karen said, and tacked on an emphatic cough. "Remember—on our home planet ginger is cheap and easily available. A large number of colonists there use it. In fact, it is beginning to change the entire society of the Race there."

"A drug? What a ridiculous notion. You must be lying to me on purpose," Trir said angrily.

"She is not." Now Jonathan Yeager used an emphatic cough. "Remember, ginger brings females into their season. If females are continuously in season, males also come into season continuously. On Tosev 3, the Race's sexuality has grown much more like ours."

The guide's tailstump quivered in agitation. "That is the most disgusting thing I have ever heard in my life."

"Which does not mean that it is anything but a truth," Karen said. "A little investigation on your computer network will prove as much."

"I do not believe it," Trir said in a voice like a slamming door. Karen did not believe the Lizard would do any investigating. Among the Race as among humans, clinging to what one was already sure of was easier and more satisfying than finding out for oneself. Trir pointed. "And here is the hotel." *Here is where I can get rid of you and your dangerous ideas.*

"There's no place like home," Karen said in English. Her husband and the de la Rosas laughed. Trir was bewildered. Since Karen was annoyed at her, she didn't bother translating, and left the Lizard that way.

The scooters aboard the *Admiral Peary* easily outdid the ones the *Lewis and Clark* had carried. The little rockets had the advantage of thirty years' development in electronics, motors, and materials. They were lighter, stronger, faster, and better than the ones Glen Johnson had used in the asteroid belt. They carried more fuel, too, so he could travel farther.

In principle, though, they remained the same. They had identical rocket motors at front and back, and smaller maneuvering jets all around. Get one pointed the way you wanted it to go, accelerate, get near where you were going, use the nose rocket to decelerate the same amount, and there you were. Easy as pie . . . in theory.

Of course, lots of things that were easy in theory turned out to be something else again in reality. This was one of those. Even with radar, gauging distances and vectors and burn times wasn't easy. But Johnson had started as a Marine pilot flying piston-engined fighters against the Race. He'd been shot down twice, and still carried a burn scar on his right arm as a souvenir of those insane days. If he hadn't been recovering from his wounds when the fighting stopped, he would have gone up again—and likely got shot down again, this time permanently. Life for human pilots during the invasion had been nasty, brutish, and almost always short.

And Johnson had done as much patrol flying in Earth orbit as any man around before . . . joining the crew of the *Lewis and Clark*. And he'd taken a scooter from the *Lewis and Clark* to one rock in the asteroid belt or another, and from rock to rock as well. If any human being was qualified to fly one while orbiting Home, he was the man.

He discovered spacesuit design had changed while he was in cold sleep, too. The changes weren't major, but the helmet was less crowded, instruments were easier to read, and there were fewer sharp edges and angles on which he could bang his head. All of this was the sort of thing the Lizards would have done automatically before they ever let anybody into a spacesuit. People didn't work that way. If things weren't perfect, people went ahead regardless. That was why the *Admiral Peary* had got to the Tau Ceti system—and why the Doctor hadn't.

"Testing—one, two, three," Johnson said into his radio mike. "Do you read?"

"Read you five by five, scooter," a voice replied in his ear. "Do you read me?"

"Also five by five," Johnson said. "Ready to be launched."

"Roger." The outer door to the air lock opened. Johnson used the maneuvering jets to ease the scooter out of the lock and away from the ship. Only after he was safely clear of the *Admiral Peary* did he fire up the rocket at the stern. It gave him a little weight, or acceleration's simulation of weight. He guided the scooter toward the closest Lizard spaceship.

"Calling the *Horned Akiss,*" he said into his radio mike. An akiss was a legendary creature among the Race—close enough to a dragon for government work. *Horned Akiss* made a pretty good name for a military spacecraft, which that one was. "Repeat—calling the *Horned Akiss*. This is the *Admiral*

Peary's number-one scooter. Requesting permission to approach, as previously arranged."

"Permission granted." A Lizard's voice sounded in his ear. "Approach air lock number three. Repeat—number three." To guide him, red and yellow lights came on around the designated air lock. The Lizard continued, "Remember, you and your scooter will be searched before you are permitted into the ship."

"I understand," Johnson said. The males and females aboard the Lizards' ship weren't worried about weapons. If he tried a treacherous attack on the *Horned Akiss,* the rest of the Race's ships would go after the *Admiral Peary.* What they were worried about was ginger smuggling.

The radar and computer would have told Johnson when to make his deceleration burn and for how long—if he'd paid any attention to them. He did it by eye and feel instead, and got what was for all practical purposes the same result: the scooter lay motionless relative to the air lock. When the outer door opened, he eased the scooter inside with the maneuvering jets, the same way as he'd brought it out of the *Admiral Peary's* air lock.

Behind him, the outer door closed. The Lizard on the radio said, "You may now remove your spacesuit for search." Before Johnson did, he checked to make sure the pressure in the air lock was adequate. The Lizard hadn't been lying to him. Even so, he was cautious as he broke the seal on his face plate, and ready to slam it shut again if things weren't as they seemed.

They were. The air the Race breathed had a smaller percentage of oxygen than the Earthly atmosphere, but the overall pressure was a little higher, so things evened out. He could smell the Lizards: a faint, slightly musky odor, not unpleasant. The *Horned Akiss'* crew probably didn't even know it was there. When he got back to the *Admiral Peary,* he'd smell people the same way for a little while, till his nose got used to them again.

The inner airlock door opened. Two Lizards glided in, moving at least as smoothly weightless as humans did. "We greet you," one of them said. "Now—out of that suit." He added an emphatic cough.

"I obey," Johnson said. Under the suit, he wore a T-shirt and shorts. He could have gone naked, for all the Race cared. The Lizards in charge of security had long wands they used to sniff out ginger. One went over the spacesuit, the other Johnson and the scooter. Only after no alarm lights came on did Johnson ask, "Are you satisfied now?"

"Moderately so," answered the one who'd examined him. "We will still X-ray the scooter, to make sure you have not secreted away some of the herb in the tubing. But, for now, you may enter the *Horned Akiss*. If you prove to be smuggling, you will not be allowed to leave."

"I thank you so much!" Johnson exclaimed, and used an emphatic cough. "And I greet you, too."

Both Lizards' mouths fell open in silent, toothy laughs. Johnson was laughing, too. He'd visited the Race's spacecraft before. Their searches were always as thorough as this one. They didn't know whether the *Admiral Peary* had ginger aboard. They didn't believe in taking chances, though.

Together, they said, "We greet you. We like you. If you are carrying the herb, we will like you too well to let you leave, as we have said. Otherwise, welcome."

Except for that, Mrs. Lincoln, how did you like the play? Johnson thought wryly. "I thank you so very much!" he repeated, tacking on another emphatic cough. For good measure, he also bent into the posture of respect.

That made the Lizards laugh again. "You are more sarcastic than you have any business being," one of them said.

"Oh, no." Johnson used the Race's negative gesture. "You are mistaken. This is normal for Big Uglies."

They laughed one more time. "No wonder your species is so much trouble," said the one who'd spoken before.

"No wonder at all," Johnson agreed. "Now, come on—take me to your leader." He did some laughing of his own. "I always wanted to say that."

Neither of the Lizards got the joke. But they understood irony as well as he did. Both of them assumed the posture of respect. They chorused, "It shall be done, superior Big Ugly!"

As a matter of fact, by their body paint and his own eagles, Johnson did outrank them. It was pretty damn funny any which way. And they *did* take him to their leader.

The corridors in the *Horned Akiss* were narrower and lower than those aboard the *Admiral Peary*. Not surprising, not when Lizards were smaller than people. The handholds were of a slightly different shape and set at distances Johnson found oddly inconvenient. But he managed with minimal difficulty. The laws of the universe operated in the same way for the Lizards as they did for mankind. The differences between spacecraft were in the details. The broad brush strokes remained the same.

Medium Spaceship Commander Henrep's office even reminded Johnson of Lieutenant General Charles Healey's. It had the same sense of carefully constrained order. Henrep looked even more like a snapping turtle than Healey did, too, but he couldn't help it—he was hatched that way. Fixing Johnson with both eyes, he asked, "What is the real purpose of this visit?"

"Friendship," Johnson answered. "Nothing but friendship."

"An overrated concept," Henrep declared—yes, he did have a good deal in common with Healey.

Johnson used the negative gesture again. "I think you are mistaken, superior sir. The Race is going to have to learn to get along with wild Tosevites, and wild Tosevites are going to have to learn to get along with the Race. If we do not, we will destroy each other, and neither side would benefit from that."

Henrep remained unimpressed. "The Race can certainly destroy your species. Just as certainly, you cannot destroy us. You can, no doubt, ruin Tosev 3. You can, perhaps, damage Home. You cannot harm Halless 1 or Rabotev 2. The Empire would be wounded, yes. But even at the worst it would go on."

"That is the situation as we here know it now, yes," Johnson replied. "But how do you know my not-empire has not sent starships to Rabotev and Halless to attack their inhabited planets in case of trouble elsewhere between your kind and mine? Are you sure that is not so?"

By the way Henrep glowered, the only thing he was sure of was that he couldn't stand the human floating in front of him. His tailstump quivering with anger, he said, "That would be vicious and brutal beyond belief."

"So it would. So would destroying us," Johnson said. "We

can do each other a lot of damage. That is why it would be better to live as friends."

"It would have been better to destroy you before you had any chance of threatening us," Henrep said angrily. He not only acted like Lieutenant General Healey, he thought like him, too.

"Maybe it would—though I would not agree with that," Johnson said. "But it is much too late to worry about that now. And so, superior sir . . . friendship."

A phone on Henrep's desk hissed before he could tell Johnson just where to put his friendship. The Lizard listened, spoke a quick agreement, and hung up. One of his eyes swung back to Johnson. "You have no ginger." He sounded almost as accusing as if the human had tried to smuggle twenty tons of the herb.

"I could have told you that. I *did* tell you that."

"So you did. But you are a Big Ugly. That makes you a liar until proved otherwise." Henrep's second eye turret moved toward Johnson. "How long do you think your slow, homely excuse for a ship could survive if we really went after it?"

"Long enough to smash up your planet, superior sir." Johnson turned what should have been a title of respect into one of contempt. "And if you do not believe me, you are welcome to find out for yourself."

Henrep sputtered like a leaky pot with a tight lid over a hot fire. Johnson swallowed a sigh. *So much for friendship,* he thought.

Jonathan Yeager held up a hand. The guide waggled an eye turret in his direction to tell him he might speak. He asked, "How old did you say that building back there was?"

"Why did you not pay closer attention when I spoke before?" Trir snapped.

"Well, excuse my ignorance," Jonathan said.

In English, Karen said, "What's her problem? She's supposed to be telling us what's what. That's her job. If we want to find out more, she should be happy."

"Beats me," Jonathan said, also in English.

That didn't seem to suit Trir, either. The guide said, "Why

do you not speak a language a civilized person can understand?"

"Maybe I will," Jonathan answered, returning to the Race's tongue, "when I see you acting like a civilized person."

Trir sputtered and hissed indignantly. "That's telling her," Tom de la Rosa said in English. His wife nodded.

Karen said, "I think we all need to behave ourselves better." She used the language of the Race, and looked right at Trir.

The guide made a gesture Jonathan had not seen before, one obviously full of annoyance. "You Big Uglies have to be the most foolish species ever to imagine itself intelligent," she said. "Do you not even understand what is going on around you?"

All the humans exchanged confused looks. "It could be that we do not," Jonathan said. "Perhaps you would be generous enough to explain the situation—whatever the situation is—to us?"

That produced an exasperated snort from Trir. "That such things should be necessary . . ." she muttered, and then, reluctantly, used the affirmative gesture. "Oh, very well. There does seem to be no help for it. Can you not sense that, along with other females in this region, I am approaching the mating season? This is its effect on my behavior. Before long, the males' scent receptors will start noting our pheromones, and then life will be . . . hectic for a little while."

"Oh," Jonathan said. The Lizards went through mating seasons on Earth, too, but there were so many ginger-tasters there that the rhythm of their life wasn't so well defined as it was here on Home. He went on, "Apologies. I did not know it. Your pheromones mean nothing to us, you know."

"Tosevites," Trir said, more to herself, he judged, than to him. She gathered herself. "Well, that *is* the situation. If you cannot adjust to it, do not blame me."

She still sounded far more irritable than Lizards usually did. Jonathan said, "We will try to adjust. Perhaps you should do the same, if that is possible for you."

"Of course it is possible." Trir sounded furious. "How dare you presume it is anything but possible?"

"Well, if it is, suppose you tell me once more how old that building back there is," Jonathan said.

"If you had been listening—" But the Lizard caught herself. "Oh, very well, since you insist. It was built in the reign of the 29th Emperor Rekrap, more than seven thousand years ago—fairly recently, then."

"Fairly recently," Jonathan echoed. "Oh, yes, superior female. Truth." Seven thousand of the Race's years were about thirty-five hundred of Earth's. So that building wasn't older than the Pyramids. It was about the same age as Stonehenge. Old as the hills as far as mankind was concerned. Nothing special, not to the Race.

Tom de la Rosa asked, "What are the oldest buildings in this city?"

"Here in Sitneff?" Trir said. "Most of the construction here dates from modern times. This is a region with some seismic activity—not a lot, but some. Few of the structures here go back much beyond twenty-five thousand years."

All the humans started to laugh. Frank Coffey said, "Even dividing by two, that's not what I call modern." He spoke in English, but tacked on an emphatic cough just the same.

And he wasn't wrong. What had people been doing 12,500 years ago? Hunting and gathering—that was it. They were just starting to filter down into the Americas. The latest high-tech weapons system was the bow and arrow. They might have domesticated the dog. On the other hand, they might not have, too. No one on Earth knew how to plant a crop or read or write or get any kind of metal out of a rock.

And the Race? The Race, by then, had already conquered the Rabotevs. Lizards were living on Epsilon Eridani 2 as well as Tau Ceti 2. Life here on Home had changed only in details, in refinements, since then.

They're still doing the same things they did back then, and doing them the same old way, pretty much, Jonathan thought. *Us? We got from nowhere to here, and we got here under our own power.*

Trir looked at things differently. "It is because rebuilding is sometimes necessary in this part of the world that Sitneff enjoys so few traditions. It is part of the present but, unfortunately, not really part of the past." As the humans laughed again, the guide's eye turrets swung from one of them to the next. "Do I see that you are dubious about what I have said?"

Laughing still, Jonathan said, "Well, superior female, it all depends on what you mean by the past. Back on Tosev 3, our whole recorded history is only about ten thousands of your years old."

That made Trir's mouth drop open in a laugh of her own. "How very curious," she said. "Perhaps that accounts for some of your semibarbarous behavior."

"Maybe it does," Jonathan said. He thought Trir's rudeness was at least semibarbarous, but he was willing to let it pass. This wasn't his planet, after all.

Linda de la Rosa saw things differently. "What sort of behavior do you call it when you insult the guests you are supposed to be guiding? We did not need nearly as long as you did to learn to travel among the stars, and we deserve all proper respect for that." She finished with an emphatic cough.

Trir's nictitating membranes flicked back and forth across her eyes: a gesture of complete astonishment. "How dare you speak to me that way?" she demanded.

"I speak to you as one equal to another, as one equal telling another she has shown bad manners," Linda de la Rosa answered. "If you do not care for that, behave better. You will not have the problem any more in that case, I promise you."

"How can you be so insolent?" Trir's tailstump quivered furiously.

"Maybe I am a semibarbarian, as you say. Maybe I just recognize one when I hear one," Linda told her.

That didn't make Trir any happier. In tones colder than the weather even at Home's South Pole, she said, "I think it would be an excellent idea to return to your lodgings now. I also think it would be an excellent idea to furnish you with a new guide, one more tolerant of your . . . vagaries."

They walked back to the hotel in tense silence. Trir said nothing about any of the buildings they passed. The Race might have signed its Declaration of Independence in one and its Constitution in the next. If it had, the humans heard not a word about it. The buildings remained no more than piles of stone and concrete. Whatever had happened in them in days gone by, whatever might be happening in them now, would remain forever mysterious—at least if the humans had to find out from Trir.

And things did not improve once Jonathan and the rest of the Americans got back to the hotel. A sort of tension was in the air. Trir was far from the only snappy, peevish Lizard Jonathan saw. The scaly crests between the eyes of males, crests that normally lay flat, began to come up in display.

"Nobody's going to want to pay any attention to us for the next few weeks," Jonathan said to Karen after they went up to their room.

She nodded. "Sure does look that way, doesn't it? They aren't going to pay attention to anything but screwing themselves silly."

"Which is what they always say we do," Jonathan added. With any luck at all, the Lizards snooping and translating would be embarrassed—if the jamming let their bugs pick up anything. "Either they don't know us as well as they think they do, or they don't know themselves as well as they think they do."

"Maybe," Karen answered. "Or maybe they just took their data from you when you were in your twenties."

"Ha!" Jonathan said. "Don't I wish!" He paused, then added, "What I really wish is that I could do half now of what I did then. Of course, there's not a guy my age who wouldn't say that."

"Men," Karen said, not altogether unkindly. "You just have to make up in technique what you lose in, ah, enthusiasm."

"Is that what it is?" Jonathan said. She nodded. In an experimental way, he stepped toward her. The experiment proved successful enough that, after a little while, they lay down on the sleeping mat together. Some time after that, he asked, "Well, did I?"

"Did you what?" Karen's voice was lazy.

"Make up in technique what I've lost in enthusiasm?"

She poked him in the ribs. "Well, what do you think? Besides, you seemed enthusiastic enough to me."

"Good."

Later, after they were both dressed again, Karen remarked, "The funny thing is, we talk about sex even more than we do it. The Lizards?" She shook her head. "They talk about it even less than they do it. It's like they try to forget about mating season when it isn't happening."

"Hell, they *do* forget about it when it isn't happening,"

Jonathan said. "If something had happened to the colonization fleet so it never got to Earth, the males from the conquest
fleet wouldn't have cared if they never mated again, poor bastards. Without the pheromones, it just doesn't matter to
them."

"That isn't quite what I meant. They don't write novels
about what goes on during mating season, or plays, or songs,
or much of anything. They don't care, not the way we do."

Jonathan thought that over. Slowly, he said, "When they're
not in the mating season, they don't care about sex at all." He
held up a hasty hand. "Yes, I know you just said that. I wasn't
done. When they *are* in the season, they don't care about anything else. They're too busy doing it to want to write about it
or sing about it."

"Maybe," Karen said.

Jonathan suddenly laughed. She sent him a quizzical look.
He said, "Back on Earth, if they keep using ginger the way
they were, they really will get to where they're a little horny
all the time, the way we are. I wonder if they will start writing
about it then back there, and what the Lizards here on Home
will think of them if they do."

"Probably that they're a bunch of perverts," Karen said.
"They already think that about us."

"Yeah, I know, you old pervert, you," Jonathan said. "But
we have fun."

Atvar tried to keep his mind on the discussion. Sam Yeager
had presented some serious proposals on ways in which the
Race and the wild Big Uglies could hope to keep the peace,
both back on Tosev 3 and in the solar systems that made up
the Empire. He'd also pointed out the obvious once more:
now that the Big Uglies had interstellar travel of their own,
trade with the Empire would take on a new footing. The Race
would have to start taking steps to accommodate Tosevite
starships.

Those were important points. Certain males and females
here on Home had realized as much years earlier. Nothing
had been done about that realization, though. No one seemed
to know when or if anything would be taken care of. Nothing
moved quickly here. Nothing had had to, not for millennia.

But anyone who delayed while dealing with the Big Uglies would be sorry, and in short order. Atvar knew that. He made the point whenever he could, and as forcefully as he could. Hardly anybody seemed to want to listen to him.

And he had trouble listening to Sam Yeager right now. The scales on his crest kept twitching up. They were not under his conscious control. He had pheromones in the scent receptors on his tongue. Next to that, ordinary business, even important ordinary business, seemed pallid stuff.

At last, when he realized he hadn't heard the last three points the wild Big Ugly had brought up, he raised a hand. "I am sorry, Ambassador," he said. "I am very sorry indeed. But even for an old male like me, mating season is here. I cannot keep my mind on business while I smell females. We can take this up again when the madness subsides, if that is all right with you."

Sam Yeager laughed in the loud, barking Tosevite way. "And we can take it up again when the madness subsides even if that is not all right with me," he said. "The Race may not have mating on its mind most of the year, but you sure make up for lost time when you do."

Ruefully, Atvar made the affirmative gesture. "That is a truth, Ambassador. It is not a truth we are particularly proud of, but it is a truth."

"You do not offend me. You are what you are," the Big Ugly said. "I will remind you that you needed much longer to say the same thing about us."

"That is also a truth," Atvar admitted. "And it is a truth that your habits still strike us as unhealthy and repulsive. But your biology has made you what you are, as ours has done with us. We can accept that. What is particularly unhealthy and repulsive to us is the way ginger has made us begin to imitate your sexual patterns. Our biology has not adapted us to be continuously interested in mating."

"Well, you can borrow some of our forms from us," Sam Yeager replied. "Back on Tosev 3, you already seem to have discovered the idea of marriage—and the idea of prostitution." The two key words were in English; the language of the Race had no short, exact term for either.

Atvar had heard both English words often enough before

going into cold sleep to know what they meant. He despised the words and the concepts behind them. The Race had brought civilization to the Rabotevs and the Hallessi—and to the Tosevites. What could be more humiliating than borrowing ways to live from barbarians? Nothing he could think of.

But right now he could hardly think at all—and he did not much want to, either. "If you will excuse me . . ." he said, and rose from his chair and hurried out of the conference chamber.

Somewhere not far away, a female was ready to mate. That was all he needed to know. He turned his head now this way, now that, seeking the source of that wonderful, alluring odor. It was stronger that way. . . . He hurried down a corridor. His hands spread, stretching out his fingerclaws as far as they would go. Males often brawled during mating season. Some of the brawls were fatal. Penalties for such affrays were always light, and often suspended. Everyone understood that such things happened under the influence of pheromones. It was too bad, but what could you do?

There! There she was! And there was another male—a miserable creature, by his body paint a hotel nutritionist, second class—headed for her. Atvar hissed furiously. Of their own accord, the scales that made up his crest lifted themselves from the top of his head. That was partly display for the female's sake, partly a threat gesture aimed at the hotel nutritionist.

"Go away!" the nutritionist said, hissing angrily.

Instead of answering with words, Atvar leaped at him, ready to claw and bite and do whatever he had to do to make his rival retreat. The hotel nutritionist was much younger, but not very spirited. He snapped halfheartedly as Atvar came forward, but then turned and fled without making a real fight of it.

Atvar let out a triumphant snort. He turned back to the female. "Now," he said urgently.

And now it was. She bent before him. Her tailstump twisted to one side, out of the way. He poised himself above and behind her. Their cloacas joined. Pleasure shot through him.

Still driven by the pheromones in the air, Atvar would have

coupled again. But the female skittered away. "Enough!" she said. "You have done what you needed to do."

"I have not yet done everything I want to do," Atvar said. The female ignored him. He hadn't expected anything different. He might have hoped, but he hadn't expected. And his own mating drive was less urgent than it had been in his younger days. He trotted off. If that hotel nutritionist, second class, made a sufficiently aggressive display to this female, he might yet get a chance to mate with her. *But my sperm are still in the lead,* Atvar thought smugly.

He went out into the street. It was chaos there, as he'd thought it would be. Males and females coupled on the sidewalk and even in the middle of traffic. Sometimes, males overwhelmed by pheromones would leap out of their vehicles and join females. Or females in cars and trucks would see a mating display and be so stimulated that they would stop their machines, get out, and assume the mating position in the middle of the road.

Accidents always skyrocketed at this time of year, along with the brawls. It was no wonder that the Race didn't care to think about the mating season when it finally ended. Males and females simply were not themselves, and they knew it. Who would want to remember a time like this, let alone celebrate the mating urge the way the Big Uglies did? Incomprehensible.

Atvar coupled with another female out in front of the hotel. Then, sated for the moment, he watched the show all around him. It was interesting for the time being, but he knew he was pheromone-addled. When the pheromones wore off, so would the appeal of the spectacle.

Overhead, a pair of squazeffi flew by. They were conjoined. A lot of creatures mated at this time of year. That way, the eggs the females laid would hatch in the springtime, when the chance for hatchlings' survival was highest. Like other flying creatures on Home, they had long necks, beaky mouths full of teeth, and bare, membranous wings with claws on the forward margin. Their hides were a safe, sensible green-brown, not much different from the color of his own skin.

Tosev 3 had nothing like squazeffi. Similar animals had once existed there, but were millions of years extinct. Instead, the dominant fliers there were gaudy creatures with feathers. Atvar had never got used to birds, not in all the time he'd spent on the Big Uglies' homeworld. They looked more like something a gifted but strange video-game designer might imagine than anything real or natural.

He wondered what the Tosevites thought of squazeffi and other proper flying things. If he still remembered after mating season—by no means certain, not with the pheromones addling him—he would have to ask them. In the meantime . . .

In the meantime, he ambled back into the hotel. A Big Ugly—the dark brown one named Coffey—walked past him. Like Rabotevs and Hallessi, the Tosevite was oblivious to the pheromones filling the air around him. He said, "I greet you, Exalted Fleetlord," as if Atvar weren't thinking more of females than of anything else.

The fleetlord managed to reply, "And I greet you." Frank Coffey smelled like a Tosevite—a strange odor to a male of the Race, but not one to which he would pay much attention during mating season.

Then Atvar spotted Trir. The guide saw him at the same time. His crest flared erect. He straightened into a display a male used only at this time of year. Trir might not have intended to mate with him. But the visual cues from his display had the same effect on her as females' pheromones had on him. She bent into the mating posture. He hurried around behind her and completed the act. After his hiss of pleasure, she hurried away.

Frank Coffey had paused to watch the brief coupling. "May I ask you a question, Exalted Fleetlord?" he said.

"Ask." Still feeling some of the delight he'd known during the mating act, Atvar was inclined to be magnanimous.

"How does the Race get *anything* done during mating season?" the wild Big Ugly inquired.

"That is a good question," Atvar answered. "Females too old to lay eggs help keep things going, and there are a few males who, poor fellows, do not respond to pheromones. Rabotevs and Hallessi are useful in this role, too, now that we can bring them back here. They have mating seasons of their own, of course, but we do not need to take those into account here as much as we do on their home planets."

"I suppose not," Coffey said, and then, thoughtfully, "I wonder how many intelligent species have mating seasons and how many mate all through the year."

"Until we got to know about you Tosevites, we thought all such species were like the Race," Atvar said. "The first two we came to know certainly were, so we thought it was a rule. Now, though, the tally stands at three species with seasons and one without. I would have to say this sample is too small to be statistically significant."

"I would say you are bound to be right." The Tosevite looked up toward the ceiling—no, up beyond the ceiling, as his next words proved: "I wonder how many intelligent species the galaxy holds."

"Who can guess?" Atvar said. "We have probed several stars like Home with no planets at all, and one other with a world that supports life but is even colder and less pleasant for us than Tosev 3: not worth colonizing, in our judgment. One of these days, we will find another inhabited world and conquer it."

"Suppose someone else finds the Empire?" Coffey asked.

Atvar shrugged. "That has not happened in all the history of the Race, and by now our radio signals have spread across most of the galaxy. No one from beyond has come looking for us yet." He swung his eye turrets toward the wild Big Ugly. "I think we would do better to worry about the species with which we are already acquainted." Coffey did not presume to disagree with him.

☆ **7** ☆

Most of the time, the Race mocked Tosevite sexuality. For a small stretch of each year, though, males and females here far outdid the wildest of wild Big Uglies in sheer carnality. Kassquit had seen two mating seasons before this one. They astonished and appalled her. The creatures she'd thought she knew turned into altogether different beings for a little while.

She had seen mating behavior in the starship orbiting Tosev 3 after the colonization fleet brought females to her homeworld. Some of those females had come into season on their own. Others, ginger-tasters, had had chemical help. That was disruptive enough, as their pheromones sent males all over the ship into heat. But this . . . this was a world gone mad.

And it was a madness of which she had no part. The Race scorned Tosevite sexuality, yes. Kassquit knew that only too well. She'd been on the receiving end of such comments more times than she could count back in the starship orbiting Tosev 3. She hadn't heard so many since waking up on Home. It wasn't that males and females here were more polite. If anything, the reverse was true. But a lot of them were simply ignorant of how Big Uglies worked.

For the time being, Kassquit could have done the mocking. Males and females coupled on the streets. They coupled in the middle of the streets. Males brawling over females clawed and bit one another till they bled. Yes, Kassquit could have done the mocking—had she found anyone to listen to her.

The Race paid no attention. Right now, males and females were too busy joining to worry about anything else. Later, once the females' pheromones wore off, everyone would try to pretend the mating season had never happened. Kassquit had already seen that. And, once the females' pheromones

194

had worn off, males and females would go back to disparaging the Tosevites for their lascivious and disgusting habits. She'd seen that, too.

Now, though, she could talk with the American Big Uglies. They hadn't come down to the surface of Home when she watched the two previous mating seasons. The server in the hotel refectory was a female. She skittered about as if she'd tasted too much ginger, but Kassquit did not think that was the problem. Unless she was wrong, the female had to hurry to get her work done before some male interrupted her.

To Frank Coffey, Kassquit said, "This is a difficult time."

"Truth." The wild Big Ugly laughed. "We Tosevites do not do things like this. The Race must think about nothing but mating. What a perverse and depraved sexuality its males and females must have."

For a moment, Kassquit thought he was serious in spite of that laugh. He sounded exactly like a pompous male grumbling about the Big Uglies. Then she realized he had to be joking, no matter how serious he sounded. That made the jest all the more delicious. She laughed, too, at first the way the Race did and then noisily, like any other Tosevite. She did that only when she thought something was very funny.

Frank Coffey raised an eyebrow. "Do you disagree with me? How can you possibly disagree with me? I wonder how we Big Uglies can hope to deal with creatures so constantly obsessed with mating."

That only made Kassquit laugh harder. "Do you have any idea how much you sound like some kind of self-important fool of a male pontificating about Tosevites?"

"Why, no," Coffey said.

Again, Kassquit needed a couple of heartbeats to be sure he was kidding. Again, the brief doubt made the joke funnier. She got out of her seat and bent into the full posture of respect. "I thank you," she said.

"For what?" Now the brown Big Ugly seemed genuinely confused, rather than playing at confusion as he had a little while before.

"For what?" Kassquit echoed. "I will tell you for what. For puncturing the pretensions of the Race, that is for what."

"You are grateful for that?" Coffey asked. Was his surprise

here genuine or affected? Kassquit couldn't tell. The wild Big Ugly went on, "Since you are a citizen of the Empire, I would have thought that you would be angry at me for poking fun at the Race."

Kassquit made the negative gesture. "No," she said, and added an emphatic cough. "The Race can be foolish. The Race can be very foolish. Sometimes they realize it, sometimes they do not. But being a citizen of the Empire is more, much more, than being a member of the Race."

"That is not how it has seemed to us Tosevites," Coffey said.

"Well, no," Kassquit admitted. "But that is because of the special circumstances surrounding the occupation of Tosev 3."

"Special circumstances?" Now Frank Coffey did the echoing. "I should say so!"

"I have never denied them," Kassquit said. "I could not very well, could I? But you will have seen, I think, that the Empire treats all its citizens alike, regardless of their species. And we all have the spirits of Emperors past looking after our spirits when we pass from this world to the next."

She looked down for a moment when she mentioned the spirits of Emperors past. Coffey didn't. None of the wild Big Uglies did. He said, "I will admit you are better at treating all your citizens alike than we are, though we do improve. But you will understand we have different opinions about what happens after death."

The Tosevite opinions Kassquit had studied left her convinced they were nothing but superstition. How could a being like a male Big Ugly with preposterous powers have created the entire universe? The idea was ridiculous. And even if such a being had done such a thing, why had he not seen fit to tell the Big Uglies about the Race and the Empire before the conquest fleet arrived? No, the notion fell apart the moment it was examined closely.

But mocking Tosevite superstitions only hatched hatred and enmity. Kassquit said, "In this case, I think we will have to agree to disagree."

"Fair enough," Coffey replied. "That is an idiom in English. I did not know the Race's language also used it."

For her part, Kassquit was surprised the Big Uglies could come up with such a civilized concept. She did not say that, either, for fear of causing offense. She did say, "You wild Tosevites have proved less savage than many here on Home expected."

That set Frank Coffey laughing. "By our standards, we are civilized, you know. We may not be part of the Empire, but we are convinced we deserve to stand alongside it."

"Yes, I know you are," Kassquit replied, which kept her from having to state her own opinion about American convictions.

Evidently, though, she did not need to, for the wild Big Ugly said, "You do not think we are right."

"No, I do not. Home has been unified for a hundred thousand years. The Race has been traveling between the stars for twenty-eight thousand years. When the Race came to Tosev 3, you Tosevites were fighting an enormous war among yourselves. You are still not a unified species. All this being true, how do you presume to claim equality with the Empire?"

"Because we have won it," the wild Big Ugly answered, and used an emphatic cough. "I do not care how old the Race is. In America, the question to ask is, what have you done yourself? No one cares what your ancient ancestor did. Here is what we did in the United States: when the Race attacked us without warning, we fought the invaders to a standstill. We won our independence, and we deserve it. You said as much yourself to Trir down by the South Pole. I admired you for your honesty, for I know we are not altogether your folk."

"Admired . . . me?" Kassquit wasn't used to hearing such praise. Home had plants that always turned toward the sun. She turned toward compliments in much the same way. "I thank you. I thank you very much."

"You are welcome," Frank Coffey said. "And I will tell you one other reason why we deserve to stand alongside the Empire." He waited. Kassquit made the affirmative gesture, urging him to go on. He did: "Because you and I are sitting here in the refectory of a medium-good hotel in Sitneff, on Home, and I, at least, did not come here on a starship the Race built. Is that not reason enough?"

I am proud of the Empire, Kassquit thought, *but the wild*

Big Uglies have their pride, too, even if it is for smaller achievements. "Perhaps it is—for you, at any rate," she said. She would not admit the Tosevites' deeds matched those of the Race. That would have gone too far.

"All right. I suspect we are also agreeing to disagree here." Coffey shrugged. "That too is part of diplomacy."

"I suppose it is." Kassquit hesitated, then said, "There are times when I wish I did not have to deal with my own species as if it were made up of aliens. But, to me, it is. I do not know what to do about that."

"You have a real problem there," Frank Coffey said gravely. "I have had some trouble with some part of my own species, because I am dark in a not-empire dominated by pale Tosevites. That was more true when I was young than it is now." He laughed at himself. "Than it was when I went into cold sleep, I should say. I would expect it to be better still now, but I have no data. And I was never as cut off from my own kind as you are."

"No. You have a common language with other American Tosevites, a common set of beliefs, a common history. All I share with Tosevites are my looks and my biochemistry. There are times when I wish we could meet halfway: I could become more like a wild Big Ugly and you wild Tosevites could become more like citizens of the Empire."

"We have changed a good deal since the Race came to Tosev 3," Coffey said. "Maybe we will change more. But maybe the whole Empire—not just you—will need to change some to accommodate us." The sheer arrogance of that made Kassquit start to flare up. Coffey held up a hand to forestall her. "You know that the Race has done this on Tosev 3. I admit ginger has driven some of the change, but it is no less real on account of that."

Males and females of the Race did act differently there from the way they did here on Home. Kassquit had seen that. It wasn't just ginger, either. On Tosev 3, the Race moved faster than it did here. It had to, to try to keep up with the surging Big Uglies.

"You may have spoken a truth," Kassquit said slowly. "That is most interesting."

"If you do not mind my saying so, you are most interest-

ing," Coffey said. "You balance between the Race and us Tosevites. I know you are loyal to the Empire. But have you ever
wondered what living as an ordinary Big Ugly would be
like?"

"I should say I have!" Kassquit added an emphatic cough.
"I thank you for thinking to ask. I thank you very much.
Sometimes, perhaps, biology can more readily lead to empa-
thy than culture can."

"Perhaps that is so," Frank Coffey said.

Mating season distracted Ttomalss no less than Atvar. If
anything, it distracted the psychologist more. He was younger
than the fleetlord, and so more able and more inclined to dis-
tribute his genes as widely as he could. He knew he should
have paid more attention to the wild Big Uglies and to
Kassquit, but everything went to the befflem during mating
season. The Race understood that. So did the Hallessi and
Rabotevs, who had mating seasons of their own. If the Tosevites couldn't figure it out, well, too bad for them.

At supper one day, Linda de la Rosa asked Ttomalss, "Our
guide will regain her usual disposition after mating season is
over?"

"Yes, yes," he answered distractedly; pheromones in the air
still left him half addled.

"Well, that is good," the wild Tosevite said, "because Trir
turned into a first-class *bitch* once it started." She added an
emphatic cough. The key word was not in the language of the
Race, but from its tone Ttomalss had no trouble realizing that
it was imperfectly complimentary.

He shrugged. "Hormonal changes can produce mood swings
among us. Do you Tosevites know nothing similar?"

Tom de la Rosa looked up from his zisuili chop in herbs.
"Oh, no, Senior Researcher, we are altogether unfamiliar
with such things." He laughed a raucous Tosevite laugh. His
mate poked him in the ribs with her elbow. That only made
him laugh harder.

The byplay puzzled Ttomalss. He studied a videotape of it
several times. Only when his wits sharpened with the end of
the mating season did he figure it out. Kassquit's mood could
swing considerably during her fertility cycle, and swing in a

fairly regular way. The alterations were less extreme than the ones the Race went through during mating season, but they were there. (The Race's physicians never had figured out why Tosevite females bled about once every twenty-eight days. Had that not been universal, they would have thought it pathological.)

Linda de la Rosa asked, "How much longer will your mating season last? How much longer until we can get down to serious business again?"

"Or even serious sightseeing?" Tom de la Rosa added. "As things are now, Trir is useless, and I do not suppose any other guide, male or female, would be much better."

"About another ten days," Ttomalss answered. "Already, things are less frenzied than they were when the season began."

"If you say so," Tom de la Rosa replied. Was that agreement or sarcasm? Ttomalss couldn't tell. Being unable to tell annoyed him.

He went upstairs to his room. The air there was fairly free of pheromones. He could think, after a fashion. He knew from experience he would have to redo half the work he did at this season of the year. But if he didn't do anything, he would have even more to catch up on once the mating madness ebbed.

When he checked his computer for messages and new data, he let out an interested hiss. A report from Senior Researcher Felless had just come in from Tosev 3. Felless had imagined herself an expert on Big Uglies before ever setting foot on their home planet. Once there, she'd promptly got addicted to ginger. She'd mated with Ttomalss, and once, in a scandalous scene, with the Race's ambassador to the Deutsche and several officials who were visiting him.

Little by little, she had acquired real expertise on the Big Uglies. Ttomalss noted that she hadn't been recalled to Home, though. Males and females trusted his judgment more than hers. He wondered how much she resented being stuck on a world whose only redeeming feature for her was a drug.

Of course, Felless was a contrarian by nature. Not liking a place might help set up a perverse attraction for it in her. And she was truly addicted to ginger. Here on Home, the herb was scarce and, because it was scarce, expensive. Not on Tosev 3.

On the Big Uglies' homeworld, Ttomalss sometimes thought it easier to taste ginger than not to. Felless would have agreed with him; he was sure of that.

Ginger-taster or not, though, Felless had become a keen observer of the Tosevite scene. Here was her image, with a little static hashing it from the journey across the light-years. She was saying, "I wish we would have brought more scientists with the colonization fleet, but who would have thought we would have needed them? Those we do have here are nearly unanimous in saying the wild Big Uglies have surpassed us in electronics, and are on their way to doing so in physics and the mathematics relating to physics."

The camera cut away to a picture of a Tosevite journal, presumably one dealing with some science. Felless' voice continued in the background: "I am also informed that the problem may be even more severe than was realized until quite recently. Our scientists have not kept close watch on the Big Uglies' scientific and mathematical publications, not least because the Tosevites use mathematical notation different from ours. Our experts say the Big Uglies' symbology is for the most part neither better nor worse than ours, simply different. But, because few of our experts have become familiar with their notation, some of their advances were not noted until years after they occurred."

"Give me some examples, please," Ttomalss said, as if Felless could reply at once. Even had he been speaking into a microphone hooked up to a transmitter to Tosev 3, he would have had to wait all the years for his signal to cross between this solar system and Tosev's, and then just as long for her answer to come back. He knew that. Maybe the stresses of the mating season were leaving him less rational than usual. Or maybe he had realized that these journal articles amplified what had been in the public press and caught the physicist Pesskrag's interest even then. Now maybe she would have the chance to learn more about what the Big Uglies really were up to when it came to physics.

As if listening to him even though she'd spoken years before, Felless did start giving examples. They impressed Ttomalss less than she'd plainly expected they would. Had she claimed the Big Uglies were building weapons systems the Race could not hope to match, he would have been alarmed. So would the governing bureaucrats here on Home, and so would Reffet and Kirel back on Tosev 3.

Advances in theoretical physics, though? Ttomalss was a psychologist, not a physicist; he wasn't sure what Felless was talking about half the time. For that matter, she was a psychologist, too. He wondered how well she understood the material that had agitated her.

Again, she addressed the very point that had concerned him: "Several theoreticians will be submitting their own reports on these topics before long. They are still working to discover all the implications of the new data. They are unanimous, however, that these implications are startling."

"If the Big Uglies want to muck around on experiments that will never have any practical use, they are welcome and more than welcome to do just that," Ttomalss said. "It distracts them from the sort of engineering that could actually prove dangerous to us."

When he checked to see if anyone else on Home had evaluated Felless' latest report, he was amused but not astonished to discover that one male and two females had already submitted reports whose essence was what he'd just said. One of the females made a cautious addition to her report: "Not being familiar with the physical sciences or with Tosevite notation, I am not ideally suited to judge whether Felless' concerns are justified."

Ttomalss called that female and asked, "Do we have anyone here on Home who *is* familiar with the Tosevites' notation?"

She shrugged. "Senior Researcher, I have not the faintest idea. Why would anyone wish to learn such things, though, when our own notation has served us well for as long as Home has been unified and probably longer?"

"A point," the psychologist admitted. "Still, at the moment it could be relevant simply in terms of threat evaluation."

"That is a truth—of sorts," the female said. "If, however, there is no threat to evaluate, then the issue becomes irrelevant." She hung up. Maybe the question did not interest her. Maybe, like Ttomalss, she was still at the tag end of the mating season, and not inclined to take anything too seriously if she didn't have to.

At the moment, about the only ones not half addled by the urge to reproduce were the Big Uglies. Even in his present state, Ttomalss felt the irony there. One evening at supper, he approached Sam Yeager and said, "I greet you, superior Tosevite. May I ask you a few questions?"

"And I greet you, Senior Researcher," the ambassador from the United States replied. "Go ahead and ask. I do not guarantee that I will answer. That depends on the questions. We can both find out."

"Truth," Ttomalss said. "What do you know of theoretical physics and Tosevite mathematical notation?"

Sam Yeager laughed. "Of theoretical physics, I know nothing. I do not even suspect anything." He used an emphatic cough to show how very ignorant he was. "Of mathematical notation, I know our numbers and the signs for adding, subtracting, multiplying, and dividing." He held up a finger in a gesture the Big Uglies used when they wanted to add something. "Oh, wait. I know the sign for a square root, too, though I have not had to extract one since I got out of school, which is a very long time ago now."

"Somehow I do not think this is what concerns our scientists on Tosev 3," Ttomalss said.

"Well, what does concern them?" the Big Ugly asked.

"Possible Tosevite advances in theoretical physics," Ttomalss answered. "I do not know all the details myself."

"I do not know any of them," Sam Yeager said with what sounded like a certain amount of pride. "I never thought theoretical physics could be important until we had to figure out how to make atomic bombs to use against the Race. Back during the fighting, I was involved in that project, because I was one of the few Tosevites who had learned enough of the Race's language to interrogate prisoners."

"Even if you do not know the details, then, you are aware that these theoretical advances can be important," Ttomalss said.

The Tosevite ambassador made the affirmative gesture. "Yes, I know that. I said I knew that. But I also said I have no idea what American physicists are working on back on Tosev 3, and that too is a truth."

"Very well," Ttomalss said, though it was anything but.

Sam Yeager must have sensed that. Laughing again in his noisy way, he said, "Senior Researcher, I would have been ignorant about these things before I went into cold sleep. Now the scientists have worked for all these years without me. It only makes me more ignorant still."

He sounded as if he was telling the truth about that. Ttomalss wasn't sure how far to trust him, though. One thing worried the psychologist: the American Big Uglies were not broadcasting news of what their physicists had learned toward Home and their starship in orbit around it. Why not, if they were making such advances? Ttomalss saw one possible reason: they knew the Race would be deciphering their signals, and did not want it learning too much.

That worried him. That worried him a lot.

Mickey Flynn watched Glen Johnson climbing into his spacesuit. "Teacher's pet," Flynn said solemnly—the most sobersided jeer Johnson had ever heard. "Look at the teacher's pet."

Johnson paused long enough to flip the other pilot the bird. "The Lizards know quality when they see it."

Flynn pondered that, then shook his head. "There must be some rational explanation instead," he said, and then, "Why do they want to see you again so soon, anyhow? Haven't they got sick of you by now? I would have, and they're supposed to be an intelligent species."

Instead of rising to that, Johnson just kept on donning the suit. As he settled the helmet on its locking ring, he said, "The one advantage of this getup is that I don't have to pay attention to you when I've got it on." With the helmet in place, he couldn't hear Flynn any more. That much was true. But Flynn went right on talking, or at least mouthing, anyhow. He looked very urgent while he was doing it, too. Were this the first time Johnson had seen him pull a stunt like that, he would have been convinced something urgent was going on and he needed to know about it. As things were, he went on into the air lock and began checking out the scooter.

He didn't expect to find anything wrong with the little local rocket ship, but he made all the checks anyhow. Any pilot who didn't was a damn fool, in his biased opinion. It was, after all, his one and only neck.

Everything checked out green. Yes, he would have been surprised if it hadn't, but life was full of surprises. Avoiding the nasty ones when you could was always a good idea.

The outer airlock door swung open. He used the scooter's maneuvering jets to ease it out of the lock, then fired up the stern motor to take it in the direction of the nearest Lizard spacecraft, the *Pterodactyl's Wing* (that wasn't an exact translation, but it came close enough). He had no idea why the Lizards wanted to talk with him, but he was always ready to get away from the *Admiral Peary* for a little while.

As he crossed the double handful of kilometers between his spaceship and theirs, he got one of those surprises life was full of: a Lizard scooter came out to meet him. "Hello, scooter of the Race. I greet you," Johnson called on the Lizards' chief comm frequency. "What is going on?"

"I greet you, Tosevite scooter," the Lizard pilot answered. "You are ordered to stop for inspection before approaching the *Pterodactyl's Wing*."

"It shall be done," Johnson said. On the radio, nobody could see him shrug. "I do not understand the need for it, but it shall be done." He applied the same blast to the forward engine as he'd used in the rear to make his approach run to the Lizards' ship. With his motion towards it killed, he hung in space between it and the *Admiral Peary*.

He watched the Lizards' scooter approach on the radar screen and by eye. It was bigger than the one he flew. He had room for only a couple of passengers. The other scooter could carry eight or ten members of the Race. At the moment, though, it had just two aboard. Whoever was piloting it had a style very different from his. Instead of a long blast precisely canceled, the Lizard flew fussily, a little poke here, a little nudge there, his maneuvering jets constantly flaring like fireflies. Any human pilot would have been embarrassed to cozy up like that, but the Lizard got the job done. After what seemed like forever, the two scooters floated motionless relative to each other and only a few meters apart.

"I am going to cross to your scooter for the inspection," one of the spacesuited Lizards said. The male—or possibly female—waved to show which one it was.

"Come ahead." Johnson waved back.

The Lizard had a reaction pistol to go from yon to hither. The gas jet pushed it across to Johnson's scooter, where it braked. "I greet you, Tosevite pilot," resounded in Johnson's headphones. "I am Nosred."

"And I greet you." Johnson gave his own name, adding, "This is unusual. Why have you changed your procedures?"

"Why? I will tell you why." Nosred leaned toward Johnson. When their helmets touched, the Lizard spoke without benefit of radio: "Turn off your transmitter." Direct sound conduction brought the words to Johnson's ears.

He flipped the switch and took another precaution. If Nosred wanted a private chat, the human was willing to find out why, and the precaution wouldn't be noticeable from the outside. Their helmets still touching, Johnson said, "Go ahead."

"I thank you. What I want to discuss with you is the possibility of your bringing ginger out of your starship the next time you come forth," Nosred said.

I might have known, Johnson thought. The Race figured Big Uglies were obsessed with sex. The way it looked to people, Lizards were obsessed with ginger—which sometimes led them to be obsessed with sex, but that was a different story.

Not without a certain pang, Johnson made the negative gesture. "I do not have any. The ship does not have any."

Nosred made the negative gesture, too. "I do not believe you, Tosevite pilot. Ginger is too valuable a commodity and too valuable a weapon for you Big Uglies to have left it all in your own solar system. You must have brought some with you. Logic requires it."

"This is your own opinion. This is not a truth," Johnson said. He knew more than he was telling. One of the things he knew was that he couldn't tell whether this Lizard was setting a trap for him. Till he knew that, he had no intention of trusting Nosred—or any other male or female of the Race.

"You do not think I am reliable," Nosred said in accusing tones. "That is the truth here, that and nothing else."

He was right. Being right wouldn't get him any ginger. Johnson said, "It would be best if I proceeded on to the *Pterodactyl's Wing* now. Your own folk will begin to wonder why we linger here without any communication they can monitor."

With an angry hiss, Nosred pulled back. His radio came to life: "Our preliminary inspection here reveals no ginger, Tosevite pilot. You have permission to proceed on to our ship."

"I thank you. It shall be done." Johnson had to remember to turn his own radio back on. He used his steering jets to reorient the scooter's nose toward the *Pterodactyl's Wing,* then made his acceleration and deceleration burns by eyeball and feel. He was good at what he did. That deceleration burn left him motionless with respect to the Lizard spaceship and only a few meters from the air lock.

Nosred and his silent friend arrived several minutes later, after another series of small, finicky burns. The Lizards took them back aboard first, though, which meant Johnson had nothing to do but twiddle his thumbs till the airlock master condescended to let him into the *Pterodactyl's Wing.*

"I thank you so very much," Johnson said, and tacked on an emphatic cough so very emphatic, he sprayed the inside of his faceplate with spit. Somehow, though, he doubted whether the Lizard appreciated or even noticed the sarcasm.

His scooter and his person got the same sort of painstaking search they had the last time he went aboard one of the Race's spacecraft. A small machine floated out of his spacesuit. He snagged it. "What is that?" the airlock master demanded suspiciously.

"A recorder," Johnson answered. "Go ahead and examine it. You will find no hidden ginger." The Lizard ran it through a sniffer and an X-ray machine. Only after he was satisfied did he return it to Johnson. The pilot bent into the posture of respect. "Again, you have my most deep and profound gratitude." He used another nearly tubercular emphatic cough.

"You are welcome," the Lizard said complacently. Johnson wondered if anything short of a kick in the snout would penetrate that unconscious arrogance. The airlock master went on, "Medium Spaceship Commander Ventris wishes to speak with you now."

"Does he?" Johnson said. "Well, then, it shall be done, of course." Once more, the Lizard in charge of the air lock took that for obedience, not irony.

Ventris let out a warning hiss when Johnson floated into his office. The Lizard's tailstump twitched angrily, in anger or a good bureaucratic simulation thereof. "What is this I hear from Scooter Copilot Nosred about your trying to sell him ginger while he inspected you out beyond my ship?"

"What is it?" Johnson echoed. "Sounds like nonsense to me."

"I think not," Ventris said. "I think you Big Uglies are involved in more of your nefarious schemes."

"I think it is nonsense," Johnson repeated. "What is more, superior sir, I think you are a fool for believing it. And what is still more, I can prove what I say. I would like to see Nosred do the same."

When Ventris' tailstump twitched now, it was in genuine fury. "Big talk comes easy to Big Uglies," he said.

Johnson pulled the little recorder from the front pocket of his shorts. Ventris stared at it as if he'd never seen anything like it before. He probably hadn't. It was an American design, not one taken directly from the Race. "Here. Your own hearing diaphragms will tell you what you need to know." He punched the PLAY button. The recorder gave back a somewhat muffled version of the conversation Johnson and Nosred had had while their helmet radios were off. When the recording ended, Johnson shut off the machine and put it back in his pocket. "You see?"

"I see that Scooter Copilot Nosred will soon regret that he was ever hatched," Ventris said heavily.

"Good," Johnson said. "But do you also see that you owe me an apology? Do you see you owe my entire species an apology?"

"You are either joking or addled," Ventris said with a scornful hiss.

"Shall I take a recording of your remarks about Big Uglies and nefarious schemes to our ambassador, superior sir?"

Johnson had no such recording, but Ventris didn't need to know that.

By the way Ventris looked, he might have stepped in a large pile of azwaca droppings. "I am sorry . . . that you Big Uglies are here. I am sorry . . . that I have to have anything to do with you. I apologize . . . that Nosred has been corrupted by a vile Tosevite herb. If your ambassador is unhappy about these sentiments, too bad. Let him start a war."

Sam Yeager wouldn't start a war on account of a male who couldn't stand Big Uglies. Johnson knew it. And Ventris was only saying what a lot of Lizards felt. Johnson knew that, too. He said, "Well, superior sir, I just think there is something you ought to know."

"And that is?" Ventris asked icily.

"We love you, too."

"Good," Ventris said. He got the irony there with no trouble at all. "Here is a basis for understanding." Johnson had tried talking about friendship with Henrep, the commandant of the *Horned Akiss*. It hadn't worked. Maybe mutual loathing would.

Sam Yeager misspelled a word. He muttered something disgusted, wadded up the paper, and flung it in the direction of the wastebasket. It didn't go in. He got up, walked over, grabbed it, and dropped it in. Then he went back to the table, got a fresh sheet, and started over. A petition for an audience with the Emperor had to be written by hand, and it had to be perfect. If you didn't care enough to do it right, you didn't deserve to see the sovereign. That was how the Lizards saw it, and he was in no position to persuade them they were wrong.

Writing such a petition was easy for them. They learned how in school. Even though their writing system was perfectly phonetic, it wasn't the one Yeager had grown up with—and some of the language required for the petition was so old-fashioned, it wasn't used on anything *but* petitions to the Emperor. So Sam had already made errors on four sheets of paper.

After some more muttering, he started writing again. At least half the petition involved proclaiming his own unworthiness, over and over again. He laughed as he went through that part. Males and females of the Race probably felt their own unworthiness as they wrote. This was a much bigger deal for them than it was for him. He wondered what would happen to him after he died. When you got to be seventy, you couldn't very well help wondering. In the not too indefinite future, you'd find out. But unlike the Lizards, he didn't believe spirits of Emperors past were likely to be involved.

Then he laughed again, this time on a more sour note. The Lizards had run up temples to spirits of Emperors past in their own territory on Earth and wherever independent countries would let them. Thanks to the First Amendment, the United States hadn't tried to stop them, and human reverence for the spirits of Emperors past was stronger in the USA—and especially in California, and most especially in Los Angeles—than anywhere else in the world. That so many years of so many crude jokes had been so solidly confirmed never failed to irk an adopted Angeleno like him.

He went back to the petition. Only a few lines to go now. He felt like a pitcher working on a no-hitter. Nobody would mention it, for fear of putting in the jinx. Here it came, the last line. No mistakes yet. Three more words, two more words, one more word—done! Sam felt like cheering. He waited for his infielders to come up and slap him on the back.

They didn't, of course. Nobody else knew he'd finished the petition. Jonathan and Karen knew he was working on it. So did Atvar. But here it was, done, all in the form the Race required. He didn't see how the most finicky protocol master could turn him down.

Trouble was, the Lizardly equivalent of dotting every *i* and crossing every *t* might not be enough. The protocol masters might turn him down because he wasn't scaly enough to satisfy them. Or they might turn him down for the hell of it—after all, they turned down most Lizards who petitioned for an audience with the Emperor.

He still hoped they wouldn't. When was the last time a foreign ambassador had come before an Emperor? Before Home was unified, surely. That was a *long* time ago now, back when Neanderthals still squatted in caves in Europe. Since then, Rabotevs and Hallessi had come to Home to pay their respects to the rulers of the folk who'd conquered them, but that was different. That didn't count. They'd already been conquered. A subject's greetings weren't worth as much as an equal's.

So Sam thought, anyway. The Lizards were liable to have different ideas. Equality didn't mean to them what it did back in the United States. Back home, it was an excuse to let everybody run like hell, aiming at the top. Here on Home? Here on Home, equality meant everybody staying in place and being content to stay in place. The USA had been a growing concern for 250 Earth years. Home had been unified for two hundred times that long.

Two hundred U.S. histories, all laid end to end . . . Say what you pleased about the Lizards, but this society *worked*. No human culture had been around long enough to make that claim—which didn't stop any number of human cultures from proclaiming their magnificent wonderfulness at the top of their lungs.

But in the space of one U.S. history, people had gone from sailing ships to starships. How long had the Race needed to make the same jump? A hell of a lot longer; of that Sam was sure.

He telephoned Atvar. Would the fleetlord answer, or was he out enjoying the last little stretch of the mating season? His image appeared on the monitor. "I greet you, Fleetlord," Sam said.

"And I greet you, Ambassador," Atvar answered. "What is the occasion for this call?"

"May I come to your room?" Yeager asked. "I have prepared my petition for an imperial audience, and I would like a member of the Race to check it for mistakes before I submit it."

"I will gladly do this," Atvar said, "though I doubt it will be necessary. You use our language very well. Even when you do not speak just as we do, you often speak as we would if we were a little more interesting."

"I thank you." Sam hoped that was a compliment. "I thank you, but I would still like you to look the petition over. I speak your language pretty well, yes, but it is not the one I learned from hatchlinghood. And I have to try to write it much less often than I speak it, and the language of this petition is different from what the Race usually uses. All these things being so . . ."

"Well, come ahead," Atvar said. "I still think you are worrying about having your clutch of eggs stolen by a beast that is not there, but you are right that it is better to be too careful than not careful enough."

"See you very soon, then." Sam broke the connection. His guards waited in the hall outside the door. "I am only going to visit Fleetlord Atvar, two floors down," he told them.

"We have our orders, superior Tosevite," one of the guards replied. That sentence implied even more blind obedience among the Lizards than it would have in the most spit-and-polish military outfit back on Earth. Arguing would have been pointless. Sam didn't try. He just walked down the hall. The guards accompanied him.

The floor was hard. With their scaly feet, the Lizards had never seen as much need for carpets as people did. The walls were painted a muddy greenish brown that never would have passed muster on Earth. The ceiling was too low; Sam had to duck whenever he walked by a lighting fixture. But it was unmistakably a hotel. The rows of identical doors with numbers on them, the indifferent paintings on the walls (some of them all the more indifferent to his eyes because the Race saw two colors in what was the near infrared to him)—what else could it be?

He went down the stairway. The steps weren't quite the right size and spacing for his legs, and the handrail was too low, but he got down without a stumble. One of the guards skittered ahead of him. The other followed.

More guards stood outside Atvar's door. They bent into the posture of respect. "We greet you, superior Tosevite," they said.

"And I greet you," Sam answered. "The fleetlord is expecting me."

As if to prove him right, Atvar opened the door just then. The U.S. ambassador and the Lizard exchanged polite greetings. Atvar said, "Please come in." Yeager did. His guards, for a wonder, didn't follow. Even they could see no assassins were likely to lurk in Atvar's room.

Atvar had a human-style chair in the room. He waved Sam

to it. "I thank you," Sam said. He handed the petition to the fleetlord. "Is everything as it ought to be? If it is not, I will copy it over again." *Or maybe I'll just jump out a window, depending,* he thought.

"Let me have a look at this. As you know, it must be perfect," Atvar said. Sam made the affirmative gesture. He knew that all too well. Atvar went on, "Your handwriting is not bad. It is not particularly fluid, but it is clear. I have seen plenty of males and females with worse. They are in a hurry, and they scribble. You obviously took pains over this."

"I should hope I did!" Sam used an emphatic cough. "When I did not take enough pains, I made mistakes and had to start over."

"The process is not supposed to be easy," Atvar said. "It is designed to weed out those who seek an audience for only frivolous reasons. Let me see here. . . . I do believe, Ambassador, that everything is as it should be. I cannot see how the protocol masters could reject this petition on any stylistic grounds."

At first, that so delighted Sam, he thought Atvar had said the petition was sure to be approved. After a moment, though, he realized Atvar hadn't said any such thing. "What other reasons are there for rejecting it?" he asked. He'd come up with a few of his own—what would the fleetlord find?

"If the Emperor does not care to see you, there is no more to be said," Atvar answered. "I do not believe this to be the case, but it may be. If certain courtiers do not wish you to see the Emperor, that is also a difficulty. But in that case, there may be ways around it."

"Such as?" Sam asked. Lizard politics at this intimate level was a closed book to humans. How *did* members of the Race get what they wanted in the face of opposition?

"If we are able to learn who has set out to addle your egg, perhaps we can appeal to a higher-ranking opponent," Atvar answered. "Such ploys are not guaranteed to succeed, but they are not hopeless."

"This is very much the same sort of thing I would do in a Tosevite factional squabble," Sam said. "In some ways, our two species are not so very different."

"In some ways, possibly not," the fleetlord said. "In oth-

ers . . . In others, the difference is as large as the distance between our sun and the star Tosev."

"It could be." Something occurred to Sam. "I have a question," he said. Atvar made the affirmative gesture. Sam asked,
"Since I do not wear body paint, how will the imperial laver
and the imperial limner deal with me?"

Atvar started to answer, then stopped short. "How do you
know about the imperial laver and the imperial limner? Have
you been researching imperial audiences on the computer
network?"

Sam made the negative gesture. "No. As a matter of fact,
I have been reading *Gone with the Wind*. Have you ever
read it?"

Atvar's mouth dropped open in a startled laugh. "That old
kwaffa berry? By the spirits of Emperors past, I had to go
through it in a college literature course. I have hardly thought
about it from that day to this, either. How did you ever get
your fingerclaws on it?"

"I found it in a secondhand bookstore," Yeager answered. "I
do not suppose imperial ceremonial would have changed
much from that time to this." There was one area where humanity and the Race differed widely.

"No, probably not," Atvar agreed. He took endless millennia of unchanging ceremonial for granted. *"Gone with the
Wind?"* He laughed again. "And how do you like it?"

"Quite a bit, actually," Sam answered. "What did you think
of it?" They spent the next hour happily picking the novel to
pieces.

The Race's cooks were willing to scramble eggs for the
Americans, though they didn't eat eggs themselves. Karen
Yeager worked hard not to remind herself that the creatures
these eggs came from would have scared the hell out of a
chicken. The flavor was about three-quarters of what it should
have been. Put enough salt on them and they weren't bad.
Speaking of salt, she also had a couple of slices of aasson on
her plate. Aasson was smoked and salt-cured zisuili meat. It
came closer to bacon than the eggs did to hen's eggs, but it
was salty as the devil.

Nothing on Home took the place of coffee. Instant came

down from the *Admiral Peary*. The Lizards thought the stuff was nasty, but they—mostly—stayed polite about it. Karen and Jonathan wouldn't have been polite if they couldn't have it. They both drank it without cream: Jonathan plain, Karen with sugar. The Race used sugar, though less than people did. Tom and Linda de la Rosa liked their coffee light. That they couldn't have. Except for the Americans' lab rats, they were the only mammals on the planet. To the Lizards, the very idea of milk was revolting.

"Nasty," Tom said, not for the first time. "But I'd be even nastier without my caffeine fix. Might as well be ginger for me." He sipped from his mug, made a horrible face, and then sipped again.

Trir came into the hotel refectory. "I greet you, Tosevites," she said cheerfully. "Today we are going to go for a bus ride out into the country. Does that not sound pleasant?" She couldn't smile and simper the way human tour guides did; her face wasn't made for it. But she did the best with what she had.

In English, Jonathan murmured, "Has she forgotten how snotty she acted when mating season was just getting started?"

"She probably has," Karen answered. "I don't think she had any control over that."

Her husband made the sort of face Tom de la Rosa had. "I didn't have much control over the urge to kick her in the teeth," he muttered.

"What is that you are saying?" Trir asked. She didn't sound angry or contemptuous, the way she had before when she heard English. She just seemed curious.

The humans in the refectory all looked at one another. Karen knew what everybody else had to be thinking: how do we tell her what a monster she was, and do we tell her anything at all? The best diplomacy might have been just to keep quiet. Try as she would, though, Karen couldn't stomach that. She said, "We could not help but notice how much friendlier you are now than you were when your mating season began."

"Oh, that." Trir fluttered her fingers in what couldn't have been anything but embarrassment. "Take no notice of it. Mating season is a time when ordinary rules and ordinary behavior go running out the door." A human would have said they flew out the window. It came down to the same thing. The guide went on, "If I did or said anything to offend, please accept my apologies." She bent into the posture of respect.

If she'd done or said anything to offend? For a little while there, she hadn't done or said anything that didn't offend. But she didn't seem to remember how nasty she'd been, and she did seem sorry for it.

"Let it go, then," Karen said. Jonathan and Linda de la Rosa made the affirmative gesture. What else could you do, short of kicking the guide in the teeth as Jonathan had wanted?

"I thank you," Trir said. "Now, as I was telling you, we are going to go out into the country this morning, out to a zisuili ranch. Zisuili are domestic animals valuable for their meat and hides, and they—"

"We know something about zisuili," Linda de la Rosa broke in. "The colonization fleet brought them to Tosev 3."

"Ah, yes, of course—it would have," Trir agreed brightly. "They are some of our most important meat animals." She pointed to Karen's aasson. "As you see."

"They have also caused some of the most important environmental damage on our planet," said Tom de la Rosa, who'd made a career out of the environmental effects Home's imported plants and animals were having on Earth. "They eat everything, and they eat it right down to the ground."

"They are efficient feeders," Trir agreed, which meant the same thing but sounded a lot better.

"I want to go see the zisuili," Jonathan said in English. "I've seen Lizards with wigs, by God. Now I want to see them riding around on whatever they use for horses. I want to see them with ten-gallon hats on their heads and with six-shooters in their holsters. I want to hear them hissing, 'Yippee!' and playing zisuiliboy music around their campfires."

That produced a pretty good stunned silence. After half a minute or so, Karen broke it: "I want to see you committed to an asylum for the terminally silly." Jonathan didn't come out with quite so many absurd remarks as his father did, but the ones he turned loose were doozies.

"What is a zisuiliboy?" Trir asked. She must have recognized the word—or, here, part of a word—from her language in the midst of the English.

"Believe me, you do not want to know," Karen told her. Trir plainly believed nothing of the sort. Karen sighed and went on, "It is nothing but a joke—and a foolish joke at that." She sent Jonathan a severe look. He seemed notably deficient in anything resembling a sense of shame.

About forty-five minutes later, all the Americans rode with Trir toward the zisuili ranch. Kassquit came along, too. She hadn't seen much more of Home than the Americans had, and she was bound to be at least as curious.

The bus had windows that were easy to see out of but hard to see into. That kept members of the Race from gawking, and possibly from causing accidents. The ride out to the ranch took a little more than an hour. The border between city and country was not abrupt. Buildings gradually got farther and father apart. The countryside looked not too different from the way it did in the rural areas outside of Los Angeles. It was scrubland and chaparral, with bushes giving way here and there to patches of what Home used for trees.

And then Karen almost fell off her seat. She pointed out the window. Sure as hell, there was a Lizard mounted on something that looked like a cross between a zebra and a duck-billed dinosaur. The creature was striped in a pattern of gold and dark brown that probably helped it fade into the background at any distance. To her vast relief, the Lizard on its back sported neither cowboy hat nor Colt revolver, nor even a wig. Even so, when she glanced over to Jonathan she saw him looking almost unbearably smug.

"What is the name of that riding beast?" she asked Trir. If she sounded slightly strangled, well, who could blame her?

"That is an eppori," the guide answered. "Epporyu still have their uses, even after all these years of mechanical civilization. They require no fuel, and they can go places where wheeled vehicles would have difficulties. And some males and females enjoy riding them, though the attraction has always been beyond me."

"We have animals like that back on Tosev 3," Sam Yeager said. "When I was a hatchling, I lived on a farm. Back then, many more animals were in use than powered vehicles. I learned to ride—I had to."

"Would you care to ride an eppori?" Trir asked.

"Maybe briefly," he answered. "I was never one who enjoyed riding animals much. Vehicles are much more comfortable."

"This is also my attitude," Trir said. Her eye turrets swiveled over the other humans. "Perhaps some of your colleagues—or even you, Kassquit—would be interested in trying this."

Kassquit promptly made the negative gesture. "I thank you, but no. I am happy enough with mechanical civilization. I do not have any of these atavistic impulses you mentioned."

"I will try, unless my odor frightens the epporyu," Tom de la Rosa said. "I have ridden back on Tosev 3, for most of the reasons you mentioned. Riding animals find their own fuel, and they can travel almost anywhere—certainly anywhere the larger animals from Home that I study are likely to go."

One by one, the rest of the Americans agreed to make the effort. Karen was anything but enthusiastic. She hadn't been on a horse for at least twenty years before going into cold sleep. Jonathan also looked dubious. *The things we'll do to keep from letting our friends down,* Karen thought.

The zisuili were not a problem. They looked like ankylosaurs with turreted eyes. All the Americans had seen them in person before, and knew they paid no particular attention to people. What the epporyu would do when they met humans might be a different story. People weren't just going to look at them. They were going to try to get on their backs—if the animals would put up with it.

Sam tried to be the first human on an eppori. Everybody had been willing to let him set foot on Home first. And everyone was just as unanimous in telling him he couldn't ride first now. "You're the one we can't afford to lose," Frank Coffey said in English, and added an emphatic cough. "Let 'em run away with one of us or trample him, but not you." The other Americans nodded.

"I'm outvoted," Karen's father-in-law said.

"You bet you are, Dad," Jonathan told him.

Tom de la Rosa tried to claim first ride by saying he was the best horseman among them. The others—including Linda—pointedly observed that being able to ride a horse might not have thing one to do with riding an eppori. They settled who *would* ride first by a method that fascinated Trir—stone, paper, scissors. And when Karen's stone smashed Frank Coffey's scissors, she won the prize.

Once she had it, she wasn't sure she wanted it. "If it weren't for the honor of the thing, I'd rather walk," she said. But she walked toward the eppori that a zisuiliboy named Gatemp was holding for her.

When she started to go to the creature's left side, Gatemp made the negative gesture. "We mount from the right," he said.

"You would," Karen muttered. The eppori swiveled an eye turret her way as she came up beside it. It made a snuffling noise that might have meant anything. She set a hand on its scaly hide. It felt like living, breathing crocodile leather. She asked Gatemp, "Is it all right to get up?"

"I think so," he answered. "Why not find out?"

"Yes, why not?" Karen said grimly. She would have been awkward mounting from the left side. She was worse than awkward from the right. Gatemp's mouth fell open in a laugh. She would have bet it would. A Lizard stirrup had only a bar on the bottom. Members of the Race could grip it with their toes. Karen couldn't, but her foot did fit on it.

Fortunately, the eppori seemed good-natured. It snuffled again, but didn't buck or jump or do anything else too very horrifying. It plodded forward for a couple of strides, then turned one eye turret back toward her as if asking, *Well, what do you want me to do now?*

The saddle was uncomfortable as could be. She ignored that; she wouldn't be on long. "How do I control it?" she asked Gatemp.

"With the reins, and with your legs, and with your voice." He might have been talking about a horse, sure enough. After he gave her the basic instructions, he said, "Now you try. Make the eppori walk and go to the left."

"It shall be done," she said, and hoped it would. She squeezed the scaly body with her knees and twitched the reins as he'd told her. The eppori walked. Karen felt like cheering. She tugged the reins to the left. The animal turned in that direction. She hadn't come more than ten light-years to go riding, but by God she could!

* * *

On the bus on the way back to Sitneff, Jonathan Yeager turned to his wife and said, "You smell like an eppori."

"So do you," Karen answered. "We all do."

"Well, no," Jonathan said. "Tom smells more like zisuili. But then, he was the one who stepped in it."

"You guys are never going to let me live that down, are you?" Tom de la Rosa's voice rose in mock anger.

"You'll be famous on four planets, once the word gets around," Jonathan's father said. They'd been speaking English. He translated for Kassquit and Trir.

"Being around animals larger than I am makes me nervous," Kassquit said. "Who knows what they will do next? They are animals, after all." By the way she spoke, that should have been obvious to anybody.

Jonathan, who'd grown up in the city, had a certain amount of sympathy for her point of view. But Kassquit had never even seen an animal in person, not till she got to Home. No wonder she was hinky about them now. Jonathan didn't say any of that, though. The less he said that involved agreeing with Kassquit, the less trouble he'd have with Karen.

Frank Coffey said, "Animals—most animals, I should say; I do not mean large carnivores or anything of the sort—are not so bad once you get to know them and to know what they are likely to do. Until that happens, though, it is only natural to be wary near them."

"Truth," Sam Yeager said. "As I told you, I grew up on a farm, so I ought to know. We had the meanest mule in the county. A mule is a work animal and can be a riding animal, and is often stubborn. I was very careful around him until I figured out what he would put up with and what made him angry. After that, we got along well enough."

"I never heard that story before," Jonathan said.

"No? Well, maybe it is because you are stubborn as a mule yourself, and would not listen even if I told it."

Karen snickered. Jonathan gave her a dirty look, which only made her snicker again. But when he turned around and glanced at his father, Sam Yeager tipped him a wink. What was that supposed to mean? It wasn't anything either Kassquit or Trir would notice. Was his old man making up the story about the mule so Kassquit would feel better? That would have been Jonathan's guess, but he couldn't prove it.

They came to the outskirts of Sitneff just in time for the evening rush hour. It was crowded on the highway, but things didn't coagulate the way they did in Los Angeles. The roads were adequate for the number of cars that used them. Jonathan sighed. There were times when seeing how smoothly the Lizards managed things made him feel very much the barbarian.

When the bus stopped in front of the hotel, some small flying things were making small, rather sweet-sounding chirps from the shrubbery in front of the building. Jonathan listened with interest. He hadn't heard many animals with even remotely musical calls on Home. Birdsong was unknown here. Till this moment, he hadn't realized how much he missed it.

The chirping went on. "What are those creatures making that noise?" he asked Trir.

"Those are called evening sevod," the guide answered. "They are related to squazeffi and other such fliers. They always call about the time the sun goes down."

"Evening sevod." Jonathan repeated the name so he'd remember it. "I thank you. They sound very pleasant."

"Well, so they do," Trir said. "Several of our musical composers have used their calls as thematic models."

"Really?" he said. "Musicians on Tosev 3 sometimes do the same thing with the sounds of our animals."

"That is interesting," Trir said. "Forgive me, but I had not thought you Tosevites would know anything of music."

Jonathan laughed at himself. *I'm not the only one who thinks we're a bunch of barbarians.* "We do," he said. "If you want details, I am sure Senior Researcher Ttomalss can give them to you. I have no idea whether any of our music would please you. We have many different styles."

"You are more diverse than we are. I have noticed that in my research on Tosev 3," Trir said.

"Home has been unified for a long time. That means the Race has been homogenized for a long time," Jonathan said. "Back on Tosev 3, our different cultures are still *very* different from one another."

"I know from my research on your species that this is a truth. It strikes me as very strange even so," Trir said.

"No stranger than tens of thousands of years of sameness seem to a Tosevite," Jonathan replied. The evening sevod kept piping in the bushes. Finally, one of them flew out. He'd never imagined a robin-sized pterodactyl. If not for the light streaming out of the hotel lobby, he wouldn't have got more than the faintest fleeting glimpse. The little creature made one more musical squeak and then disappeared.

Trir said, "But unity is natural. Unity is inevitable. Seeing what a species is like before the inevitable occurs is unusual."

Was she right? Jonathan started to make the negative gesture, but checked himself. Even before the Lizards came, cultures based on ideas and technology from Western Europe had become the strongest ones on Earth. To stay independent, other countries had had to adopt Western European techniques. If they didn't, they would go under, as Africa and India had done. China had struggled with Western ideas as it now struggled against the Race. Japan had succeeded in holding its own after Commodore Perry made it open up to the wider world, but it had done so by adopting Western methods—and it might have failed, too.

"Technology, I think, is more important than culture," Jonathan's father said—the two Yeagers had been thinking along with each other.

"But would you not agree that in large measure technology dictates culture?" Trir asked.

"In large measure, but not completely," Sam Yeager replied. "Different cultures and different species can use the same technology in different ways. We Big Uglies, by now, have access to almost the same technology as the Race does, but I do not think we are quite the same."

His grin meant nothing to Trir, but she did catch his ironic tone. "That is a truth," she said, "but you and we are biologically distinct. This is not the case with various cultures belonging to the same species."

She had a point. She could be annoying, but she wasn't stupid. Jonathan said, "You have to understand that it has only been a little more than a thousand of your years since we first went all the way around Tosev 3. It has only been half that time since one culture on our world got ahead of the others technologically to any great degree. And, of course, it has been less than two hundred of your years since the Race came. Maybe we will grow more alike as time goes by. But not enough time has passed yet for that to happen."

"Only a thousand years since you circumnavigated your world . . ." Trir let out a soft hiss full of wonder. "I had read this, mind you. In the abstract, I knew it. But to be reminded of it in that way . . ." She hissed again.

Kassquit said, "Is there any possibility that we could circumnavigate the refectory? I am very hungry."

"I am not so sure about circumnavigating it," Frank Coffey said. "We could probably sit down in it."

"That might do," Kassquit said.

Trir's eye turrets went from one of them to the other. It was a shame, Jonathan thought, that Lizards didn't play tennis. The crowds on Home could have followed the action without moving their heads back and forth. While he woolgathered, the guide said, at least half to herself, "Tosevites are very peculiar."

Since he'd just been thinking about tennis, of all the useless things, he could hardly quarrel with her. His father didn't even try. "Truth—we *are* peculiar," Sam Yeager said. "And the Race is peculiar. And when we get to know Rabotevs and Hallessi better, I am sure we will find they are peculiar, too."

Trir probably hadn't been thinking about the idiosyncracies of the different intelligent species. She'd been thinking Big Uglies were bizarre. But all she said now was, "Supper does seem a good idea."

The refectory featured krellepem from the Ssurpyk Sea. Finding out what krellepem were took some work. Jonathan finally gathered they were something like crabs or lobsters. He ordered them. So did the rest of the humans, Kassquit included.

Trir wanted nothing to do with them. "When we evolved, we left the seas and came up on land," she said. "I am not interested in eating anything that did not bother to evolve."

Jonathan had heard all sorts of excuses for not eating all sorts of things—quite a few of them from his sons when they were little—but never one that Darwin would have approved of. He admired Trir's creativity.

When the krellepem came, they looked more like trilobites than anything else Jonathan had ever seen. They'd evolved even less than he'd expected. The servers brought special tools for eating them—tools that put him in mind of a hammer and chisel. Each segment of shell had its own chunk of meat inside.

"This is a savage way of feeding oneself," Kassquit said as the pile of broken bits of krellep shell in front of her grew taller.

"Possibly," Frank Coffey said. "But the results are worth it."

"Truth," Jonathan agreed. The krellepem tasted something like oysters, something like scallops. He discovered they had meat inside their skinny little legs, too, and sucked it out one leg at a time. The others started imitating him.

"How do you do that?" Trir asked, watching them. Jonathan demonstrated. Trir said, "We would have to use tools to get at that meat. Our mouthparts are not flexible enough to do what you are doing."

She was right, though Jonathan hadn't thought about it till that moment. Lizards didn't have lips, not the way humans did. The edges of their mouths were hard. They couldn't suck meat out of a tubular leg, they couldn't kiss. . . . *They can't make fart jokes,* Jonathan thought, and realized he was even more tired than he'd suspected.

"What is funny?" Karen asked when he snorted. He told her.

"What is a *fart joke*?" Trir asked; the relevant phrase had been in English.

"Something that proves my mate is seriously deranged," Karen told her.

"I thank you. I thank you very much." Jonathan used an emphatic cough.

"You Tosevites can be most confusing," Trir said.

All the Americans chorused, "We thank you. We thank you very much." They all used emphatic coughs. Trir was . . . most confused.

☆ 8 ☆

Glen Johnson looked down on Home from his orbital path in the *Admiral Peary*. He shared the control room with Mickey Flynn and Dr. Melanie Blanchard. Flynn eyed him and said, "I don't believe the Lizards are going to want to let you aboard any more of their spacecraft. I told you bathing before you went would have been a good idea."

"Funny. Ha, ha. I laugh," Johnson said. "Hear me laugh?"

He glanced over toward the doctor. She smiled, but she wasn't laughing. That left him relieved. She said, "They really are anxious about ginger, though, aren't they?"

"Anxious about it and eager for it, both at the same time," Johnson answered. "That one scaly bastard who went helmet-to-helmet with me . . ."

"Good thing you had the recorder going," she said.

"If somebody wants to talk off the record, that's usually the time when it's a good idea to make sure he's on," Johnson said. "As soon as he told me to turn off my radio, I figured he had to have ginger on his miserable little mind. And as soon as I knew that, I knew he was liable to try to diddle me if I didn't have any to give him."

"Did the captain of the Lizard ship ever apologize for seizing you?" Dr. Blanchard asked.

"Ventris? Oh, hell, yes—pardon my French—finally, in a way, once I browbeat him into it. Then he made it sound like it was our fault his scooter pilot got trapped by the wicked herb. To hear him talk, it was like ginger came after that Lizard with a gun. *He* didn't have anything to do with it, of course."

"Why, heaven forfend," Mickey Flynn said. "The very idea is ridiculous. That anything could possibly be a Lizard's fault . . . ?" He shook his head. "Next thing you know, there'll be Big Uglies traveling between the stars."

"Don't hold your breath for that," Johnson said.

Melanie Blanchard looked from one of them to the other. "I can see how both of you'd be welcome guests on the surface of Home."

"Certainly," Flynn said. "The Lizards wouldn't kill me. They'd let their planet do it for them." He mimed being squashed flat.

"When are you going down to the surface?" Johnson asked the doctor.

"I don't know yet," she answered. "I'll have to take it easy down there for a while—I do know that. I spent too long weightless aboard the *Lewis and Clark*."

"Is it safe for you to go?" he said.

"I think so," Dr. Blanchard answered. "If I have any doubts when the time comes, I'll get a second opinion."

"What if the other docs lie to you because they want to be the ones who go down there?" Johnson asked.

She looked startled, then shook her head. "No, they wouldn't do that," she said. "They need to know they can count on me, too."

"Wouldn't be so good if the doctor who was treating you might want you dead instead of better," Flynn observed.

"Wanted—dead more than alive," Johnson intoned solemnly.

She glared at each of them in turn. Had she been a Lizard with eye turrets that moved independently, she would have glared at both of them at the same time. "Thanks a lot, guys," she said, mostly in jest. "Thanks a hell of a lot. Now I'll be looking back over my shoulder whenever I see anybody else wearing a white coat."

"Well, spread the word around," Flynn said. "That way, the others will be looking over their shoulders at you, too."

"Helpful," Melanie Blanchard said. "Very goddamn helpful." To show how helpful it was, she glided out of the control room.

"There—now look what you did," Flynn said to Johnson. "You scared her away."

"Me?" Johnson shook his head. "I thought it was you."

Her voice floated up the hatchway by which she'd departed: "It was both of you, as a matter of fact."

The two pilots looked at each other. They pointed at each other. Johnson started to laugh. Mickey Flynn, refusing to yield to such vulgar displays of emotion, looked even more impassive than before. That only made Johnson laugh harder than ever. He said, "No wonder we confuse the damned Lizards. We confuse each other, too."

"You don't confuse me a bit," Flynn declared.

"That's because you were confused to begin with," Johnson answered. "And if you don't believe me, ask Stone. He'll tell you."

Flynn shook his head. "He thinks he's not confused, which only makes him the most confused of all."

Johnson raised an eyebrow. "I have to think that one over."

"I hope nothing breaks," Flynn said helpfully. "But if it will assist in your cogitations, let me remind you that he still more than half wants to see how long you'll last if you go out the air lock without a suit."

Since he was right yet again, Johnson did the only thing a sensible man could do: he changed the subject. "Well," he said, "one of these days, the Lizards are going to get in an uproar about ginger that has something behind it."

"How can they do that?" the other pilot replied. "Everybody knows there is no ginger aboard the *Admiral Peary.*"

"Yeah, and then you wake up," Johnson said scornfully. "Missiles with bombs in their noses are weapons. We brought plenty of those. Ginger is a weapon, too. You think we don't have any?"

Flynn shrugged. "I know about missiles. I know where they fit on the plans for the ship. I know how to arm them. I know how to launch them. I know how to tell the ship to do all that automatically in about nothing flat, so we can get the missiles away even if we're under attack. Nobody has briefed me about ginger, which is the sum total of what I know about it. I will also point out that it's the sum total of what you know about it, too."

He was right again, of course. That didn't mean Johnson wasn't also right, not this time. "We can addle half the scaly so-and-sos down on that planet," he insisted. "There's got to be a way to get the herb from hither to yon."

"You are assuming what you want to prove," Mickey Flynn said. "If you'd gone to the same sort of school I did, the nuns would have rapped your knuckles with a steel yardstick for a breach of logic like that."

"If I'd gone to the kind of school you did, I'd have to drop my pants if I wanted to count to twenty-one," Johnson retorted.

Flynn eyed him with mild astonishment. "You mean you don't? Truly, you are a fount—or at least a drip—of knowledge."

"Thank you so much." Johnson suddenly snapped his fingers. "I've got it!"

"I hope you can take something for it," Flynn said with well-simulated concern.

Johnson ignored him. "I know where I'd put the ginger if I were designing the *Admiral Peary*." He held up a hand. "If you make that particular suggestion, I'm going to be very annoyed at you."

With dignity, the other pilot said, *"Moi? Je ne comprende pas."*

"Of course you don't," Johnson said. "Listen, how many people in cold sleep is this ship carrying?"

"Seventeen," Flynn answered. "Or was it forty-six thousand? I forget."

"Heh," Johnson said. "Funny. But the point is, you don't know for sure. I don't, either. And neither do the Lizards. What looks like space for people in cold sleep could be space for the herb just as easily."

"You have a low, nasty, suspicious mind," Flynn told him.

"Why, thank you," Johnson said.

"I don't know. Why not thank me?"

Johnson scowled. "I'd throw something at you, but I might miss you and hit something valuable instead."

Flynn assumed a look of injured innocence. By his face, his innocence had suffered enough injuries to end up on the critical list. Then he said, "You know, if you keep speculating about all these things we haven't got, you won't make our esteemed and benevolent commandant very happy with you."

"Who's going to tell him?" Johnson asked. "You?"

"Certainly not," Mickey Flynn replied. "But the walls have ears, the ceilings have eyes, and the floors probably have kidneys or livers or something else you wouldn't want to eat unless your stomach were rubbing up against your backbone."

Walls with ears were a cliché. Ceilings with eyes at least made sense. As for the rest . . . "Your mother dropped you on your head when you were little."

"Only when I needed it," Flynn said. "Of course, there were times when she needed to be retrained. Or was that restrained? Amazing how one's entire childhood can revolve around a typographical error."

"That's not all that's amazing," Johnson said darkly, but Flynn took it for a compliment, which spoiled his fun.

Over the next few days, he wondered if the commandant would summon him to his office to give him a roasting. Then, when that didn't happen, he wondered why it didn't. Because the *Admiral Peary* carried no ginger, and the idea that it might was ridiculous? Or because the ship was full of ginger, and the less said about the herb, the better? The one thing that didn't occur to Johnson was that Healey hadn't heard his speculation. The floors did indeed have kidneys, or maybe livers.

Dr. Blanchard worked with grim intensity in the exercise chamber, doing her best to build up her strength for the trip down to the surface of Home. Johnson spent stretches on the exercise bicycle, too, but he didn't get excited about them the way she did. He was in pretty good shape for a man who'd spent the last twenty years of his life weightless. He could exercise till everything turned blue and not be fit enough to face gravity.

He said, "I wish they'd send one of the other docs down, not you."

"Why?" she demanded, working the bicycle harder than ever so that her sweaty hair plastered itself against the side of her face. "I'll be damned if I want to go through all this crap for nothing."

"Well, I can see that," he said, pedaling along beside her at his own slower pace—one of the great advantages of a stationary bike. "But you're a hell of a lot better looking than they are."

"Not right now, I'm not," she said, which wasn't true, at least not to someone of the male persuasion. She added, "Besides, I must smell like an old goat," which was.

Johnson denied it anyway, saying, "I'm the old goat."

"What you are is a guy with too much time on his hands," she said. "Exercise more. That'll help some."

"Thanks a lot," he muttered. "Some problems, you know, you're not really looking for a cure."

"Well, you'd better be," Dr. Blanchard said, and that was effectively that.

"I greet you, Ambassador," Atvar told Sam Yeager when he met the Big Ugly in the hotel conference room. "And I am pleased to tell you congratulations are in order."

"And I greet you. I also thank you. What kind of congratulations, Fleetlord?" the American Tosevite inquired.

"Your petition for an audience with the Emperor has been granted," Atvar answered. "This news comes through me and not directly to you because I have been appointed your sponsor, so to speak."

"That is excellent news. Excellent!" Sam Yeager not only used an emphatic cough, he also got out of his chair and bent into the posture of respect. "I am in your debt for the help you gave me. Ah . . . what does being a sponsor entail?"

He was pleased. Atvar knew that. But the wild Big Ugly was not overjoyed, as a proper citizen of the Empire would have been. He was just pleased—much too mild a reaction. His question, though, was reasonable enough. Atvar said, "A sponsor does about what you would expect. He trains his hatchling—that is the technical term—in responses and rituals required in the audience. If the hatchling disgraces himself, the sponsor is also disgraced. Not all those who win audiences have a sponsor. Getting one is most common among those least likely to have their petitions accepted and so least likely to be familiar with the rituals."

"Among the poor and the ignorant, eh?" Sam Yeager laughed in the noisy fashion of his kind. "Which am I?"

"You are ignorant, of course, Ambassador. Will you deny

it?" Atvar said. "I suppose I was chosen as your sponsor not only because I know you but because I am familiar with Tosevites in general and because I have had a recent audience with his Majesty. I will do my best to help you avoid the pitfalls."

"Again, I thank you," Sam Yeager said. "I do hope the Race will remember that I really am ignorant, that I am only a poor, stupid wild Big Ugly who knows no better. If I make a mistake, I will not be doing it on purpose."

"I believe that is understood, yes," Atvar said. "If the Emperor and his court did not understand it, your petition would have been rejected."

"Good." The Tosevite paused. "And something else occurs to me. The Emperor ought to grant Kassquit an audience."

That took Atvar by surprise. Both his eye turrets swung sharply toward Yeager. "Interesting," he said. "Why do you propose this?"

"For the good of the Empire—and for Kassquit's own good," Sam Yeager answered. "She is a citizen of the Empire, after all, and she is proud of being a citizen of the Empire. The Empire might do well to show that it is proud to have her as a citizen."

"What an . . . interesting idea indeed," Atvar said. "You realize we may do this and use it in propaganda aimed at the Tosevites under our control on Tosev 3? It would show them they can truly become part of the Empire themselves."

"Oh, yes. I realize that," the wild Big Ugly replied. "I will take my chances nonetheless. For one thing, it will be more than twenty of your years before those pictures arrive at Tosev 3." He stopped.

Atvar eyed Yeager with amused scorn. The Tosevite thought of the interval signals took to go from Home to Tosev 3 as a long time. If it wasn't happening right now, it wasn't real for a Big Ugly. But then Atvar looked at Sam Yeager in a different way. Say what you would about him, he was not a fool. And . . . "You said, 'For one thing,' Ambassador, but you did not go on with any more after the first. What were your other points?"

"Ah, you noticed, did you?" Sam Yeager shrugged. "Well, I suppose I can tell you. My one other point would have been simply that Kassquit's audience with the Emperor might do you less good than you would expect if you were to broadcast it widely in the areas of Tosev 3 that you rule."

"Oh? And why do you say that?" Atvar wondered if Yeager was going to try to spout some persuasive nonsense to keep the Race from doing what was really in its best interest to do. But the wild Big Ugly answered, "Because you will be photographing a Tosevite female without her wrappings. This will perhaps arouse some of your audience. It will scandalize a great deal more. I suspect, though, that it will have the desired effect on very few."

Atvar's hiss of dismay was altogether heartfelt. "I had forgotten about that," he admitted. "You are a very clever Tosevite."

Sam Yeager shook his head. Atvar understood the gesture. The American Big Ugly said, "Not at all, Fleetlord. But I do know my own kind. I had better, would you not agree?"

"Well, perhaps," Atvar said, which made Sam Yeager come out with another of his noisy laughs. But then the fleetlord brightened. "I may be able to persuade her to wear wrappings for the purpose of the audience."

"Good luck," Sam Yeager said.

At first, Atvar thought he meant that sincerely. Then he suspected irony. Judging such things when they came from one of another species, another culture, was never easy. And then Atvar thought about how stubbornly Kassquit had refused to wear wrappings when the wild Big Uglies asked it of her. She was proud to be a citizen of the Empire, and would not want to conform to the usages common among wild Tosevites. She did not seem to notice that her stubbornness was one of the most Tosevite things about her.

"Maybe I can persuade her," Atvar said at last. "An audience with the Emperor would be something she highly desired."

"That is a truth," Sam Yeager said. "But she would desire it as a citizen of the Empire. Would she desire it as nothing but a propaganda tool?"

"I think finding out may be worth my while," Atvar said. "If you will excuse me . . ."

He rang up Kassquit on the conference-room phone. "Yes,

Exalted Fleetlord, I would be pleased to see you," she said. Her intonation when speaking the Race's language differed only slightly from Sam Yeager's. He had a language of his own. She didn't. But her Tosevite mouthparts were the most important factor in determining how she sounded.

Atvar said his farewells to Yeager and went up to her room. It had, he saw, been modified in the same ways as had the wild Big Uglies'. That made sense; biology outweighed culture when it came to comfort. "I greet you," Atvar said. "I hope all is well?"

"As well as it can be when one is neither azwaca nor fibyen," Kassquit replied. "How may I help you today?"

"How would you like to present yourself before the Emperor?" Atvar asked.

Kassquit's small, narrow, immobile eyes widened. That was a sign of astonishment in Tosevites. Citizen of the Empire or not, Kassquit shared reflexes with the rest of her species. *Only natural,* Atvar thought. Kassquit said, "There is nothing I would like better, Exalted Fleetlord, but why would the Emperor wish to see one such as me?"

"What do you mean?" Atvar asked, though he knew perfectly well. Pretending he did not, he went on, "Are you not a citizen of the Empire like any other?"

"You know what I am," Kassquit said bleakly. "I am a Big Ugly. I am a citizen of the Empire not like any other."

She had reason to sound bleak. She was perfectly right. As she'd said, she was a citizen of the Empire unlike any other. She was not and could not be a wild Big Ugly. The Race had made sure of that. Atvar sounded resolutely cheerful: "That is all the more reason for his Majesty to wish to grant your petition—to show that every citizen of the Empire is like every other citizen once out of the shell."

The cliché held good for members of the Race, for Rabotevs, and for Hallessi. It did not hold good for Tosevites, as Atvar remembered just too late. Kassquit rubbed his snout in the mistake, saying, "I remind you, Exalted Fleetlord, that I did not hatch from an egg."

"Well, soon there will be millions of citizens who did not hatch from eggs," Atvar said resolutely. "You are the first—

truth. But you will not be the last. Far from it." He used an emphatic cough.

"Possibly not." Kassquit spoke with the air of one making a great concession. Then she hesitated. "Would my audience be used for propaganda purposes with the wild Big Uglies on Tosev 3?"

She might have been—she was—betwixt and between, but that did not make her a fool. Atvar reminded himself of that once more. Had she been less bright, she would have had much more trouble coping with her situation than she did in fact. Cautiously, the fleetlord answered, "It might. That would depend in part on whether you are willing to put on wrappings for the occasion. An unwrapped female might cause more, ah, controversy than approval among the wild Tosevites."

Kassquit made the negative gesture. "Why should I accommodate myself to the prejudices of barbarians?" she demanded. "I *am* a citizen of the Empire. Let the wild Big Uglies see what that means." She did not use an emphatic cough. Her words were quite emphatic enough.

Atvar answered her question, though no doubt she'd posed it rhetorically: "Why should you accommodate yourself to barbarians? Because in so doing you would serve the Empire's interests."

But Kassquit used the negative gesture again. "The Empire should not accommodate itself to the wild Big Uglies, either. It should find ways to get them to accommodate themselves to it."

"Having them see another Tosevite treated as an equal here on Home would go some way toward that end," Atvar said.

"Then let them see me treated as an equal, and not artificially wrapped," Kassquit said firmly. "If the Emperor is willing to accept my petition under those circumstances, I will submit it. If not"—she shrugged—"not."

"Submit it in any case," Atvar urged. "His Majesty and the court may well accept it come what may, simply because of the services you have already rendered the Empire." He was careful not to say, *the Race.*

"Well, then, it shall be done, Exalted Fleetlord, and I thank you for the suggestion," Kassquit said.

"Sam Yeager urged me to propose this to you," Atvar said, knowing she would hear as much from one of the wild Big Uglies if not from him. "His opinion is that your petition will probably be accepted whether or not you wear wrappings."

"He is a clever male. I hope he is right here," Kassquit said.

"In my opinion, he probably is," Atvar said. "The Emperor should have a special interest in meeting a Tosevite subject, especially as he will also be meeting with the ambassador from these independent Big Uglies."

"I would hope he might accept my petition even if I were not—" But Kassquit broke off and made the negative gesture. "That is pointless. I am a special case. I have been made into a special case, and I can do nothing about it. No matter what I hope for, there is no point to hoping for normality."

"If I could tell you you were wrong, I would. But you are right, and telling you otherwise would be not only pointless but untrue," Atvar said. "Since you are special, however, you should exploit that for all it is worth."

"That, no doubt, is a truth," Kassquit replied. "It is a truth I have been reluctant to use, however. I do want to be valued for myself, not as . . . as a curiosity, you might say."

"There will be many more Tosevite citizens of the Empire in years to come," Atvar said. "There may even be some on Tosev 3 now. But I do not think there will ever be another one as completely acculturated as you are."

"I would disagree with you," Kassquit said. "Some hundreds or thousands of years from now, after Tosev 3 is firmly incorporated into the Empire, all the Big Uglies there will be as I am."

"I have my doubts about that," Atvar said. "Thanks to ginger and to the strong native civilizations, I suspect Tosev 3 will always be something of a special case, a world apart, in the Empire. Tosevite cultures will not be subsumed to the same degree as those of the Rabotevs and Hallessi have been."

"And, of course, I knew nothing of any Tosevite culture when I was a hatchling," Kassquit said. "I thought of myself as a misshapen female of the Race. I kept wishing I would grow scales and eye turrets. When it did not happen, I wondered what I had done to be so bad."

Atvar had authorized Ttomalss' experiment with Kassquit. He'd followed it with interest. Not only had it been interesting, it had also been necessary. He'd always been convinced of that. Up till now, he'd never felt guilty about it. He wondered why not.

"Write your petition," he said. "I fear we have done you an injustice in the past, one we cannot possibly make up to you. But what we can do, we will. By the Emperor, by the spirits of Emperors past, I promise you that."

"Yes, of course," Ttomalss said in some surprise, staring at Kassquit's image in the monitor. "I would be pleased to review your petition for an audience with the Emperor. But why, if you do not mind my asking, is this the first that I have heard of your submitting such a petition?"

"Fleetlord Atvar suggested that I do so." Kassquit's features showed no expression, but excitement sang in her voice. "He said he had the idea from Sam Yeager. The wild Big Ugly reasoned that, if the Emperor would consent to see him, he might also consent to seeing a Tosevite citizen of the Empire—*the* Tosevite citizen of the Empire now living on Home."

Ttomalss didn't need to think that over for very long before deciding Sam Yeager was bound to be right. The propaganda value of such an audience was obvious—once someone pointed it out. Ttomalss' tailstump quivered in agitation. "I should have thought of this for myself."

"Truth—you should have." Kassquit could be particularly liverless when she chose. She went on, "But, as long as someone has thought of it, who does not matter very much. May I bring you the petition now?"

"Please do," Ttomalss said, trying his best to hide the vaguely punctured feeling he had. "I am sure you will have written it out without a flaw. After all, the language we are speaking, the language we both write, is as much yours as mine."

"So it is, superior sir," Kassquit said. "For better and for worse, so it is. I will be there very shortly."

She was, as usual, as good as her word. When the door button hissed, Ttomalss let her in. "I greet you," he said.

"And I greet you," she replied, bending into the posture of

respect. Then she handed him the papers. "Please tell me if everything is in order."

"Certainly." Ttomalss' eye turrets flicked back and forth, back and forth, as he read through the petition. When he looked at it, he saw nothing that showed a Big Ugly rather than a female of the Race had written it. He occasionally raised one eye turret to look at Kassquit. She was, of course, what she had always been. Physically, she was a Tosevite. Culturally, she belonged to the Empire. "As far as I can see, this is perfect. I congratulate you."

"I thank you," Kassquit said.

"I am given to understand Sam Yeager had some trouble completing his petition," Ttomalss said.

"I have spoken to him about this while I was preparing mine," Kassquit replied. "He tells me he has some trouble with formal written composition in a language not his own. He is certainly fluent enough while speaking, and in informal postings on electronic bulletin boards."

"Yes, that is a truth," Ttomalss agreed. Back on Tosev 3, Sam Yeager had electronically masqueraded as a member of the Race for some time before Kassquit realized what he was. The Big Uglies, generally speaking, were better at languages than the Race. They had to be, with so many different tongues on their planet. The last time the Race had had to deal with languages other than its own was during the conquest of Halless 1, and that was ten thousand years ago now. Except for a handful of scholars, no one knew anything about the Hallessi languages any more. That of the Race had supplanted them within a few centuries after the conquest.

However much Ttomalss hoped that would happen on Tosev 3, he had his doubts about whether it would. English, in particular, was flourishing like a weed. Members of the Race had had to learn it not to administer a conquered people but to treat with equals. Conservatives balked at doing so, and more and more often were getting left behind.

Kassquit said, "Since you confirm that this petition is in proper format and correct, superior sir, I am going to give it to Fleetlord Atvar, in the hope that his name will help win approval for it."

That jabbed a dagger of jealousy under Ttomalss' scales.

Kassquit was his protégée, not Atvar's. A moment's thought made him see the sense of Kassquit's plan. Atvar had recently earned an imperial audience himself. He was serving as Sam Yeager's sponsor, preparing the wild Big Ugly for his encounter with the 37th Emperor Risson. That all had to mean the imperial courtiers—and perhaps even the Emperor himself—thought well of the former fleetlord of the conquest fleet.

Ttomalss had petitioned for an imperial audience not long after coming back to Home. The court had not accepted his petition. That hadn't left him particularly downlivered; he knew how many petitions were submitted, how few accepted. Still, he had not imagined that the Big Ugly he'd raised from a hatchling might win an audience ahead of him.

She was a grown individual now. Tosevite literature was full of references to generational struggles, to young asserting their authority—no, their right to wield authority—against those who had raised them. Such conflicts were much less common among the Race, where hatchlings were physically able to care for themselves at an early age, and where those who mated to produce them were unlikely to be the ones who reared them.

Such different social structures were bound to make acculturation more difficult. That had been obvious since early in the invasion. What ginger did to the Race and its mating patterns, though, came as a rude surprise. And the Race's adoption of Tosevite institutions on Tosev 3 reversed tens of thousands of years of precedent. Such adoptions made thoughtful observers—or perhaps just worried observers— wonder which was in fact the dominant species on Tosev 3. That had nothing to do with the Big Uglies' rapidly advancing technology, either. It was an altogether separate concern.

Just what we need, Ttomalss thought sourly. He returned the petition to Kassquit. She left his room. He went back to trying to figure out just where the Tosevites stood in terms of technology. Were the Race's experts right to be as alarmed as they were? Or were they even underestimating the danger because of their unfamiliarity with so much of what was being printed in Tosevite scientific journals?

And what was *not* being printed in those scientific journals? What were the Big Uglies trying to keep secret? Penetrating their computer networks was far harder now than it had been even when Ttomalss went into cold sleep. When the conquest fleet arrived, the Big Uglies had had no computer networks. They'd had no computers, not in the sense that the Race did.

We should have knocked them flat, Ttomalss thought, not for the first time. *We almost did. We should have finished the job. I think we could have.*

He laughed, not that it was really funny. Shiplord Straha had urged an all-out push against the Big Uglies. Most males in the conquest fleet had reckoned him a maniacal adventurer. He hadn't succeeded in toppling Atvar and imposing his program. In hindsight, it didn't look so bad.

Could things have turned out worse had Straha got his way? Ttomalss made the affirmative gesture. If Tosev 3 taught any lesson, it taught that things could always turn out worse. *I Told You So* would have been a good title for an autobiographical account written by the planet itself.

Ttomalss laughed again, this time at the conceit. But it wasn't really funny, either. No one who'd left Home for Tosev 3 in the conquest fleet had dreamt the Big Uglies would be able to put up a hundredth of the fight they had. No one who'd been on Tosev 3 at the time of the invasion would have dreamt the Big Uglies would have interstellar travel within a male's lifetime . . . but here they were.

Where will they be in one lifetime more? Ttomalss wondered uneasily.

That led to another question. *Will they be anywhere at all?* Atvar had always considered the possibility of a war of extermination against the Tosevites, to make sure they could not threaten the Empire even if they took the technological lead. He would have left his plans behind for Reffet and Kirel. He would have left those plans behind, yes, but would the current commanders have the nerve to use them? Both males struck Ttomalss as less resolute than Atvar.

Every day they waited, though, made a successful cleansing less certain. *Even if we try to annihilate the Big Uglies, could we do it?* Ttomalss shrugged. He was no soldier, and he had incomplete data. Thanks to the limitations light speed

caused, everyone here on Home had incomplete data about
Tosev 3. The trouble there was, not everyone seemed to realize it. Males and females here were used to change that
stretched over centuries, and didn't stretch very far even in
such lengths of time. Tosev 3 wasn't like that, no matter how
much trouble members of the Race who'd never been there
had remembering as much.

And, more and more, Ttomalss was growing convinced that
even the males and females of the Race who actually lived on
Tosev 3 were operating on incomplete data in their evaluation
of what the Big Uglies were up to. Part of that was the Race's
trouble with languages not its own, part the different mathematical notation the Tosevites used, and part, he suspected,
was a case of willful blindness. If you didn't believe down
deep in your liver that another species could come to know
more than you did, how hard would you look for evidence that
that was in fact coming to pass? Not very, he feared.

He checked his computer and telephone records to see
whether Pesskrag had ever called him back. As he'd thought:
no. He made a note to himself to call the physicist soon.

Having made the note, he looked at it and deleted it. Delay
was the very thing he'd worried about, and there he was,
telling himself to delay. Instead of waiting, he telephoned
Pesskrag that very moment.

It did him no good. He got the female's out-of-office announcement. He recorded a message of his own, finishing, "I
hope to hear from you soon. The more time goes by, the more
I am convinced this issue is urgent."

Pesskrag did call back the next day, and found Ttomalss in
his room. She said, "I apologize for not getting back to you
sooner, Senior Researcher. I will blame part of the delay on
the mating season, which always disrupts everything."

"Truth." Ttomalss admitted what he could hardly deny.
"But it is over now. What have you and your colleagues done
with the data I provided you?"

"We are still evaluating them, trying to decide if they can
possibly be credible. We are making progress on the notation," the physicist answered. "The mathematics does appear
to be internally consistent, but that does not make it easy to
follow or easy to believe."

"Can you test it experimentally?" Ttomalss asked. "You were hoping to do that when we spoke last."

"And we still hope to," Pesskrag said. "But funds, permissions, and equipment have all proved harder to get than we expected."

"I see," Ttomalss said. And he did. He saw that the Race *would* go at its own pace. Nothing would hurry it. Normally, that was good. If it really needed to hurry . . . Maybe the lessons it most needed to take from the Big Uglies had nothing to do with technology.

Kassquit came down to the refectory walking on air. Several of the American Tosevites were there eating breakfast. Kassquit wished her features could match the mobility theirs had. Since they couldn't, she had to show her happiness in other ways.

She went up to Sam Yeager and bent into the posture of respect before him. "I thank you, Ambassador," she said, and added an emphatic cough.

"For what?" Sam Yeager asked. Before she could answer, though, he pointed to her. "They accepted your petition for an audience with the Emperor?"

"They did!" Kassquit made the affirmative gesture. "I thank you so much for suggesting it! This is probably the proudest day of my life."

"I am pleased for you, and I congratulate you," the white-haired Big Ugly said. "If he would see me, I thought it was likely he would see you, too. After all, you are one of his, and I am not."

"To meet the Emperor!" Kassquit exclaimed. "To show I really am a citizen of the Empire!"

She wondered if the wild Tosevites truly understood how important and exciting this was for her. Whether they did or not, they congratulated her warmly. Frank Coffey said, "This must mean a great deal to you, even if it would not mean so much to one of us."

"Truth. That is a truth," Kassquit said. The dark brown Big Ugly did see what was in her liver: intellectually, at least, if not emotionally. "What could be a greater mark of acceptance than an imperial audience?"

"Ah—acceptance." Now Coffey made the affirmative gesture. "Acceptance is something I can appreciate." To show how much he could appreciate it, he too added an emphatic cough. "For me, Researcher, what showed I had truly been accepted by my society was getting chosen to join the crew of the *Admiral Peary*."

Tom de la Rosa laughed a loud Tosevite laugh. "Oh, yes, Frank, this *does* show acceptance." He made his emphatic cough ironic at the same time. "Everyone back in the United States loved you so much, you got sent all these light-years just so you could be part of the society there."

Even Kassquit saw the joke in that. The American Tosevites all thought it was very funny. Frank Coffey laughed as loud as any of the others. He said, "That sounds ridiculous. I know it sounds ridiculous. But the odd thing is, no matter how ridiculous it sounds, it is a truth, and an important truth. Had I been less of an equal, I would still be back on Tosev 3."

"And you would probably be having more fun back there than you are here, too," de la Rosa replied.

"Maybe I would. Of course, I would be old back there, and I am . . . not so old here," Coffey said. "This has its compensations."

"If not for cold sleep, I would surely be dead," Sam Yeager said. "Given the choice, I prefer this."

Kassquit said, "And you will also go before the Emperor."

"Well, so I will. But I have to tell you, I know it means less to me than it does to you," the American ambassador said. "For one thing, I have already met several of our not-emperors—*presidents,* we call them."

"I have heard the word, yes," Kassquit said coolly. Did he really imagine a Big Ugly chosen by snoutcounting was the equal to *the* Emperor? By all the signs, he did, however absurd she found the notion.

He said, "There is something else, too, something that shows how different from the Empire we truly are. Here, the goal is to meet the Emperor. In the United States, the goal is to *become* the president. Do you see what I mean?"

Now Kassquit had to try to understand emotionally something that was plain enough intellectually. American Big Uglies could aspire to become the ruler of their not-empire.

She knew those not-emperors ruled for only a limited period, and had other checks on their power. Even so . . .

She tried to imagine a male or female of the Race setting out to become the Emperor. The picture refused to form in her mind. Oh, such things had happened in the days of ancientest history, though they weren't much mentioned in the lessons hatchlings learned at school. And once, even after Home was unified, a deranged male had tried to murder an Emperor (that was mentioned even less often).

But that a member of the Race, a Rabotev, a Halless, or even a Tosevite could aspire to supplant the Emperor and rule the Empire now . . . Automatically, her hand shaped the negative gesture. She said, "I do not believe your not-emperors have control over the afterlife as well as this life."

"Well, no, neither do I, though some of them would probably be happy enough to claim authority like that," Sam Yeager said. The other American Big Uglies laughed again, which was the only thing that told Kassquit he didn't mean it. He went on, "And what you need to grasp, Researcher, is that I do not believe your Emperors have control over the afterlife, either."

The Race's language did not have a word precisely equivalent to *blasphemy*. It had never needed a word like that, because the idea of denying that the spirits of Emperors past controlled the existence yet to come had not hatched on Home. But, even without a word for it, Kassquit understood the idea as soon as she heard it.

She said, "Many billions of individuals of several different species have accepted what you reject."

That didn't faze Sam Yeager. He said, "A great many individuals have believed a great many things that eventually turned out not to be so." He held up a hand before Kassquit could speak. "I do not say this *is* true for the spirits of Emperors past. I say it *may* be true. As far as I know, no one has found a way to bring certain truth back from the next world."

"So many who have believed make a strong argument for truth all by themselves," she said.

"No." He shook his head before remembering and using the Race's negative gesture. "As I said before, many can believe something that is not a truth. On Tosev 3, for centuries, most males and females—almost all, in fact—believed the planet was flat, and that the star Tosev revolved around it instead of the other way round. Belief does not make truth. Evidence makes truth. And belief does not make evidence."

Had he been talking about anything but belief in the afterlife, Kassquit would have agreed with him without hesitation. As things were . . . As things were, she held that belief in a mental compartment separate from the rest of her life and the rest of her attitudes. Almost every citizen of the Empire did the same. Belief in the spirits of Emperors past and in what they could do in the world to come was deeply ingrained in the Race, the Rabotevs, the Hallessi . . . and Kassquit.

Angrily, she said, "How can you tell me the beliefs of many do not matter when your not-empire counts snouts to run its affairs?"

To her annoyance, that did not irritate the wild Big Uglies. It amused them. Jonathan Yeager said, "She has got you there, sire of mine."

"Oh, no. She is sly, but she is not sly enough to trick a gamy old zisuili like me," Sam Yeager answered. He turned back to Kassquit. "Snoutcounting is not about evidence. It is about beliefs. There is no sure evidence for the future, and providing for the future is what a government does. There are only beliefs about what is likely to happen next and what ought to happen next. When it comes to beliefs, snoutcounting is fine. But beliefs are not truths, no matter how much you might wish they were."

"He is right," Karen Yeager said. She, of course, could be counted on to side against Kassquit. She continued, "On Tosev 3, we have many different beliefs about what happens after we die. They cannot all be true, but how can we tell for certain which ones are false?"

Kassquit's opinion was that they were all false, and that citizens of the Empire held the only true belief. She knew she had no evidence for that, though, not evidence of the sort that would help her in this argument. She did the best she could: "From what I have heard, a growing number of Tosevites are accepting the Empire's beliefs. This is true not only in the regions where the Race rules but also in your own not-empire. Or is that not so?"

The wild Big Uglies started laughing again. Kassquit was confused and furious at the same time. Before she could say anything more, Tom de la Rosa said, "Some American Big Uglies want to believe in the spirits of Emperors past because they are not happy with the beliefs they had before. Some want to believe in them because they like to imitate the Race any way they can. And some want to imitate them because they are fools. Or do you have no fools in the Empire?"

"We have fools." Kassquit wished she could deny it, but the language of the Race wouldn't let her. It had the word, and the word pointed infallibly to the thing. Besides, anyone who saw a male or female of the Race topped with red or green false hair almost infallibly spotted a fool. With such dignity as she could muster, she added, "But we do not believe the word applies to those who reverence the spirits of Emperors past."

"I do not believe it does, either, if they have been brought up in their beliefs since hatchlinghood," de la Rosa said. "But those who change their beliefs later in life, those who change them as a Big Ugly changes his wrappings—individuals like that are often fools."

He sounded reasonable. Kassquit cherished reason. She clung to it. Clinging to it had helped her stay as close to sane as she had. There were times when she wondered how close that was. With her cultural and biological heritages so different, was it any wonder her stability often balanced on the point of a fingerclaw? The wonder, perhaps, was that she had any stability to balance.

Here, Tom de la Rosa's reason threatened that stability. The thought that her spirit would be sustained by the spirits of Emperors past in the world to come had also helped sustain her when things did not go well in this world. Even the slightest hint that that might not happen left her feeling threatened.

Frank Coffey said, "Pale Tosevites used to believe dark Tosevites were inferior just because they were dark. Some pale Tosevites still believe that."

"I used to believe it," Sam Yeager said. "It was something I was taught from hatchlinghood. But there is no evidence to support it, and I hope I know better now."

"I hope you do, too." Coffey sounded jocular, but he did not laugh. He nodded to Kassquit. "By your looks, I would say you are Chinese." Sam Yeager said something in English. Coffey nodded again, then went on, "He tells me you are. Pale Tosevites have shown these misplaced beliefs against Chinese, too."

"And Chinese against pale Tosevites," Tom de la Rosa added. "It is not all the fault of my kind of Big Ugly. A lot of it is, but not all."

"Believe what you will," Kassquit said. "What I believe is, I am proud to have been granted an audience with the Emperor. And, come what may, I will go right on being proud." And she did.

Lizards always stared at Jonathan Yeager and the other Americans when they left their hotel for any reason. Jonathan didn't suppose he could blame them. People had done plenty of staring at Lizards when they first met them. *He* hadn't. Because of what his father and mother did, he'd grown up around Lizards, and took them as much for granted as he did humans.

Being neither a mad dog nor an Englishman, he tried not to go out in Home's noonday sun. Oh, it wouldn't have killed him, any more than a hot summer day in Los Angeles would have. It wasn't much over a hundred, and, as Angelenos were endlessly fond of saying, it was a dry heat. But, while that made it more or less bearable, it didn't make it pleasant.

Early morning *was* pleasant. Sitneff cooled down into the seventies at night—another consequence of low humidity. Jonathan enjoyed going to the park not far from the hotel, finding a bench in the shade of the shrubby treeish things, and watching Home go by.

Lizards on the way to work drove past in cars and buses that didn't look too different from the ones he would have seen in the United States. These were smaller, because Lizards were smaller. They had smoother lines, and the differences between one model and another seemed smaller than in the USA. Maybe he was missing subtleties. Or maybe, because the Race valued efficiency more than people did, their vehicles just deviated less from ideal designs than human machines did.

Males and females skittered by on the sidewalk, too, some

of them no doubt on the way to work, others moving faster for the sake of exercise. Some of the runners would stop short when they noticed him. Others would keep one eye turret trained on him till they got out of sight. They would use the other eye to watch where they were going. There they had an advantage over mankind. It wasn't necessarily an enormous advantage, as Jonathan saw when a Lizard watching him banged into another coming the other way. Watching didn't just mean seeing. It also meant paying attention. Anyone of any species could fail that test.

Other males and females trotted through the park. Some were regulars, and had seen him and the other humans there before. A few would call out, "I greet you, Tosevite!" as they went by. Jonathan always waved and answered when they did. *Friendly relations, one Lizard at a time,* he thought.

Every so often, a Lizard would stop what he was doing and want to talk. The ones with wigs and T-shirts were more likely to do that than the ones who didn't try to imitate people. That made sense—they'd already proved their interest in mankind. Jonathan was glad whenever it happened. It let him—he hoped it let him—get an unfiltered view of what life on Home was like. Maybe Lizards who paused and came up to talk were government plants, but Jonathan didn't think so. In the USSR or the *Reich,* he would have been suspicious of what strangers told him. He didn't think the Race was so sophisticated about propaganda.

One very ordinary, unwigged, unclothed Lizard didn't seem sophisticated at all. After looking Jonathan over from head to foot (his moving eye turrets made the process obvious), the male said, "So you are one of those things they call Big Uglies, are you?"

Jonathan hid a smile, not that the Lizard would have known what one meant. He made the affirmative gesture. "Yes, I am a Big Ugly," he agreed gravely.

"Do you by any chance know a male called Telerep?" the Lizard asked. "He went to Tosev 3 with the conquest fleet. He was a landcruiser gunner, and a friend of mine."

"I am sorry, but no." Sorry or not, Jonathan couldn't help smiling now. "For one thing, I was hatched near the end of the fighting. For another, Tosev 3 is a planet the size of Home, even if it does have more water. Do you know where your friend served? It might have been halfway around the world from me."

"No, I do not know that," the male said. "Tosev 3 does not seem so big. I often wonder what happened to Telerep, and if he came through all right. He was a good fellow. We had some fine times together. I know a few males and females who have heard from friends who joined the conquest fleet, but not many. For most, well, it is a long way between here and your world."

"That is a truth," Jonathan said. "When I see our sun in the night sky as just another star, I realize how far it is."

"Tosev, yes. Hard for me to think of it as anything but a star, you understand," the Lizard said, and Jonathan made the affirmative gesture again. The Lizard went on, "We call the constellation Tosev is in the Sailing Ship. What is your name for it?"

"To us, it is the Herder," Jonathan answered; that was as close a translation of Boötes as he could manage in the Lizards' language. "Of course, when we see that constellation, we do not see our own sun in it."

The Lizard drew back half a pace in surprise. Then his mouth fell open. "That is funny. I had not thought of it so, but you would not, would you? What do you call the constellation in which you see our sun?"

"That is the Whale," Jonathan told him. He had to explain the key word, which came out in English: "A whale is a large creature that swims in our seas. Your sun is dimmer than ours. I mean no offense when I tell you it seems faint when we see it on Tosev 3."

"I understand," the Lizard replied. "Even if you are a wild Big Ugly, I must say you sound quite civilized."

"I thank you," Jonathan replied, not without irony. "So do you."

That line drew different responses from different Lizards. This one laughed once more. "And I thank you, superior Tosevite." His mouth dropped down yet again. "Are you a superior Tosevite or an inferior Tosevite? You have only those wrappings—no body paint to let me see what your rank is."

He straightened a little to show his own paint to Jonathan. "As you can tell, I am an optician, second grade."

Actually, Jonathan couldn't have told that without a chart. The Race's system of using body paint to mark social distinctions went back to before Home was unified. It had been getting more complex since the days when men weren't even painting mammoths on cave walls. Every seniority level in every occupation had its own distinctive pattern and colors. Lizards—and Rabotevs and Hallessi—read body paint as easily as they read the characters of their written language. Some humans were nearly that good. Jonathan wasn't bad, but optician wasn't one he recognized offhand.

He said, "If I had body paint, it would say I was an ambassador's assistant."

"Ambassador!" Another laugh came from the Lizard. "There is a very old-fashioned word, superior Tosevite. There have been no ambassadors since the days of ancientest history."

"Again, I mean no offense, but I must tell you you are mistaken," Jonathan said. "On Tosev 3, there have been ambassadors to and from the Race for nearly ninety years—ninety of ours, twice as many of yours. Where independent empires and not-empires meet as equals, they need ambassadors."

"Independent empires and not-empires," the male echoed. "What an . . . interesting phrase. I suppose I can imagine an independent empire; after all, you Big Uglies did not know about *the* Empire till we came. But what might a not-empire be? How else would you govern yourselves?"

"Well, there are several ways," Jonathan said. "The not-empire we are from, the United States, is what we call a *democracy.*" He said that word in English, then returned to the Race's language: "That means giving all adult males and females a voice in how they are governed." As best he could, he explained voting and representative government.

"Snoutcounting!" the optician exclaimed when Jonathan was done, and tapped his own snout with a fingerclaw. If Jonathan had had a nickel for every time he'd heard that derisive comment from a Lizard, he could have damn near bought the *Admiral Peary.* This male went on, "But what happens when the males and females being snoutcounted make a mistake?"

"We try to fix it," Jonathan answered. "We can choose a new set of representatives if we are not happy with the ones in power. What happens when *your* government makes a mistake? You are stuck with it—is that not a truth?"

"Our government makes very few mistakes," the Lizard said. On Earth, that would have been a boast with no truth behind it, a boast the USSR or the *Reich* would have made. Here on Home, it might well have been true.

But very few mistakes were different from no mistakes at all. Jonathan said, "I can think of one mistake your government made."

"Speak. What could that be?" the male asked, plainly doubting it was anything of much weight.

"Trying to conquer Tosev 3," Jonathan answered.

The Lizard said, "Well, that may be a truth, superior Big Ugly. Yes, it may be. Actually, I would say trying was not the difficulty. I would say the difficulty was failing."

"A nice point." Jonathan smiled again. "Are you sure you are not an attorney?"

One of the optician's eye turrets rolled downward, as if he were examining his own body paint. "No, I seem to be what I am. So you Tosevites make jokes about attorneys, too, do you? We say they are the only males and females who can go into a revolving door behind someone else and come out ahead."

He and Jonathan spent the next ten minutes trading lawyer jokes. Jonathan had to explain what a shark was before the one about professional courtesy made sense to the Lizard. Once the male got it, his mouth opened enormously wide—the Race's equivalent of a belly laugh.

He said, "If you Big Uglies tell stories like those, you really will convince me you are civilized."

"I thank you, though I was not worrying about it very much," Jonathan answered. "Back on Tosev 3, we have stayed independent of the Race. We have come to Home in our own starship. If things like that do not make us civilized, can a few silly jokes do the job?"

"You never can tell," the Lizard answered. "That is a truth, superior Big Ugly: you never can tell. Those other things may prove you are strong. Jokes, though, jokes show you can enjoy yourselves. And if being able to enjoy yourself is not a part of civilization, what is?"

Jonathan thought that over. Then he got off the bench and bent into the posture of respect before the startled Lizard. He got sand on his knees, but he didn't care. "That is also a truth, and a very important one," he said. "I thank you for reminding me of it."

"Happy to be a help," the Lizard said. As Jonathan straightened, the male added, "And now, if you will excuse me, I must be on my way." He skittered off down the path.

Had he been an ordinary Lizard in the street, or had the government sent him by? After thinking that over, Jonathan slowly nodded to himself. A plant, he judged, would have been more likely to call him a Tosevite all the time, simply for politeness' sake. This male either hadn't known or more probably hadn't cared that *Big Ugly* might be insulting. That argued that he was genuine. Jonathan hoped so. He'd liked him. He went back to the hotel room to write up the encounter while it was still fresh in his memory.

In the room they shared, Karen Yeager read her husband's notes. "Get into a revolving door in back of you and come out in front of you?" she said. "*We* tell that one."

"I know," Jonathan answered. "We can't swap dirty jokes with the Lizards. We—"

"*Too* bad," Karen broke in. "I can just see a bunch of guys and a bunch of males standing around in a bar, smoking cigarettes, and trading smut. Men!"

"Tell me gals don't talk dirty when guys aren't around to listen to it," Jonathan said. Karen gave him a sour look, because she couldn't. He laughed. "Told you so. Anyway, we can't swap dirty jokes with the Race, because they don't work the way we do, not for that. But jokes about the way society goes along—those are different."

"I see." Karen went a little farther in the notes. "So he liked the one about professional courtesy, did he?"

"I thought he'd bust a gut," Jonathan answered. "I bet he'll be telling it all over Sitneff today, changing the shark to one of their dangerous animals. They don't have a lawyer joke just like that one, the way they do with some of the others."

"They don't have as many dangerous animals as we do, ei-ther," Karen answered. "Maybe that's why."

"Maybe they don't have as many dangerous lawyers." With pretty good timing, her husband shook his head. "Nah, not likely."

Karen made a horrible face. "If you want to tell dumb jokes with the Lizards, that's fine. Kindly spare me."

"It shall be done, superior female," Jonathan said, dropping into the language of the Race. He didn't bother returning to English as he went on, "When my father goes to see the Em-peror, I wonder what we will be doing."

"Probably seeing the rest of the capital with Trir or some other guide." Karen stuck to English. Perhaps incautiously, she added, "We may not have Kassquit with us for a while, ei-ther. She'll be studying for her audience, too."

Jonathan nodded. "That's true. I had nothing to do with it, either. Dad suggested it to Atvar and Atvar suggested it to Kassquit, and it went from there."

"I know. Did I say anything else?" Karen knew her voice had an edge to it.

"No, you didn't *say* anything." Jonathan had heard it, too. "But would you say anything if she were going to walk off a cliff?"

I'd say good-bye. But that wasn't what Jonathan wanted to hear, and would only start trouble. She might have wanted to start trouble if he'd sniffed after Kassquit like a male Lizard smelling a female's pheromones. But he really hadn't, even if Kassquit went right on showing everything she had—and even if, thanks to cold sleep, she literally was better preserved than she had any business being.

All that went through Karen's head in something less than a second. Jonathan probably didn't even notice the hesitation before she said, "Kassquit isn't my worry here. She's playing on the Race's team."

She wondered if her husband would push it any further. He just said, "Okay." There were reasons they'd stayed married for thirty years. Not the smallest of them was that they both knew when they shouldn't push it too far.

"I wonder what's happening back on Earth right now,"

Karen said. "I wonder what the boys are doing. They're older than we are. That seems very strange."

"Tell me about it!" Jonathan said, and she knew he wasn't thinking about Kassquit any more. "Their kids may have kids by now. I don't think I'm ready to be a great-grandfather yet."

"If we ever do make it back to Earth, you may be able to tack another *great* onto that," Karen said. Her husband nodded. She got up from the foam-rubber seat and looked out the window. When she first came down from the *Admiral Peary*, she'd marveled at the cityscape every time she saw it. Why not, when her eyes told her she was on a brand new world? Now, though, she took the view for granted, as she'd take the view from the front window of her house back in Torrance for granted. It was just what she saw from the place where she lived. Familiarity could be a terrible thing.

When she said that to Jonathan, he looked relieved. "Oh, good," he said. "I was afraid I was the only one who felt that way."

"I doubt it. I doubt it like anything," Karen said. "We can ask Frank and the de la Rosas at lunch, if you want to. I bet they'll all say the same thing."

"Probably," Jonathan said. "Dad, too, I bet. He's seen more different things out of windows than all of us put together." He blinked. "If we make it back to Earth, he's liable to be a great-great-great-grandfather. You don't see that every day."

"We're going to be a bunch of Rip van Winkles when we get back to Earth," Karen said. "If we'd fallen asleep when your father was born and woke up when the colonization fleet got there, we'd think we'd gone nuts."

Jonathan excitedly snapped his fingers. "There *were* people like that, remember? A few who'd gone into comas in the twenties and thirties, and then they figured out how to revive them all those years later. They didn't think *they'd* gone nuts—they thought everybody around them had. Invaders from another planet? Not likely! Then they saw Lizards, and they had to change their minds."

"They made a movie out of that, didn't they?" Karen said. "With what's-his-name in it . . . Now that's going to bother me."

"I know the guy you mean," her husband said. "I can see

his face, plain as if he were standing in front of me. But I can't think of his name, either."

"Gee, thanks a lot," Karen said.

"Somebody down here will remember it," Jonathan said. "Or else somebody on the *Admiral Peary* will."

"And if they don't, we can radio back to Earth and find out—if we don't mind waiting a little more than twenty years."

Jonathan grinned. "You're cute when you're sarcastic."

"Cute, am I?" She made a face at him. He laughed at her. She made another face. They both laughed this time. Their marriage had its strains and creaks, but they got along pretty well.

Karen forgot to ask about the actor at lunch, which only annoyed her more. She remembered to try at dinner. "I saw that movie on TV," Linda de la Rosa said. "It was pretty good."

"Who was the guy?" Karen asked.

"Beats me," Linda said.

Sam Yeager said, "I remember that one, too. My old friends, Ristin and Ullhass, played a couple of the Lizards. They did all kinds of funny things to make a living once they decided they liked staying with us and didn't want to go back to the Race."

Karen knew Ristin and Ullhass, too. She hadn't recalled that they were in that movie. She said, "But who the devil played the lead? You know, the doctor who was bringing those people out of their comas after all those years?"

"Darned if I know." Her father-in-law shrugged.

Tom de la Rosa and Frank Coffey couldn't come up with it, either. Tom did say, "The guy had that TV show for a while. . . ." He frowned, trying to dredge up the name of the show. When he couldn't, he looked disgusted. "That's going to itch me till I come up with it."

"It's been itching me all day," Karen said. "I was hoping one of you would be able to scratch it." She threw her hands in the air in frustration.

They'd been speaking English. They were talking about things that had to do with the USA, not with the Race—with the exception of Sam Yeager's two Lizard friends. They went on in English even after Kassquit came into the refectory.

Karen didn't know about the others, but she thought of Kassquit as more Lizard than human . . . most ways.

As usual, Kassquit sat apart from the Americans. But when
they kept trying and failing to remember that actor's name,
she got up and walked over to them. "Excuse me for asking,"
she said, "but what is this commotion about?"

"Something monumentally unimportant," Sam Yeager answered. "We would not get so excited about it if it really mattered."

"Is it a riddle?" she said.

"No, just a frustration," he told her. "There was an actor in
a motion picture back on Tosev 3 whose name none of us can
recall. We know the film. It would have come out some time
not long before I went into cold sleep, because I saw it. This
is like having food stuck between the teeth—it keeps on being
annoying."

"Did this film involve the Race?" Kassquit asked.

"Only a little." Sam Yeager explained the plot in three sentences. "Why?"

Kassquit didn't answer. She went back to her supper and
ate quickly. *Queer thing,* Karen thought. *She really isn't very
human. I just wish she'd wear clothes.* She gave a mental shrug
and started eating again herself. She hardly noticed when
Kassquit left the refectory, though she did notice Jonathan
noticing.

She was a little surprised when Kassquit not only came
back a few minutes later but also came over to the Americans
again. "James Dean," Kassquit said, pronouncing the name
with exaggerated care.

Everybody exclaimed. She was right. As soon as Karen
heard it, she knew that. Frank Coffey bent into the posture of
respect. "How did you find out?" he asked.

"It was in the computer network," Kassquit answered. "The
Race has a good deal of information on Tosevite art and en-
tertainment that concern it. How wild Tosevites view the
Race is obviously a matter of interest to males and females on
Tosev 3, and also to officials here on Home. I hoped it might
be so when I checked."

"Good for you," Linda said. "We thank you."

"Truth," Sam Yeager said. "James Dean. Yes, that is the

name. When he first started out, I could not stand him as an actor. I thought he was all good looks and not much else. I have to say I was wrong. He kept getting better and better."

Karen thought her father-in-law's age was showing. She'd always admired Dean's looks—along with most of the other women in the English-speaking world—but she'd always thought he had talent, too. It was raw talent at first. She wouldn't deny that. Maybe that was why he didn't appeal so much to the older generation, the generation that had Cary Grant and Clark Gable as its ideals. But it was real, and the rawness of it only made it seem more real. And Sam Yeager was right about one thing: he'd got even better with age.

"Too bad you did not get to see some of the films he made after you went into cold sleep," she said. "*Rescuing Private Renfall* is particularly good."

"The computer network mentions that film," Kassquit said. "It was set during the Race's invasion, was it not?" She waited for agreement, then went on, "It has been transmitted to Home for study. You could probably arrange to see it, if you cared to."

"Films from our home?" Sam Yeager said. "That *is* good news!" He used an emphatic cough. Karen and the other Americans all made the gesture of agreement.

9

When Sam Yeager let Atvar into his room, the fleetlord swung an eye turret toward the monitor. "What *are* you watching there?" Atvar asked.

"A film from the United States," Yeager answered. "Until a few days ago, I did not know any of them had been transmitted to Home. One of the actors here gives a truly memorable performance."

Atvar watched for a couple of minutes. *Rescuing Private Renfall* had its original English sound track; the Race had reinvented subtitles to let Lizards who didn't speak English know what was going on. After a bit, Atvar said, "Much of this is inaccurate. You were a soldier yourself, Ambassador. You will see the inaccuracies just as I do."

Sam could hardly deny it. He'd noticed several. He said, "Drama compresses and changes. Do all of your films show reality just as it happened?"

"Well, no," the fleetlord admitted. "But why do your filmmakers show the Race as either vicious or idiotic? We were doing what we thought was right when we came to Tosev 3, and we were doing it as best we could. If we had been inept and vicious as this film shows us to be, not a male of the Race would have been left alive on your planet."

He was right about that, too. But Sam said, "I have seen some of the productions your colonists made after they came to our world. They are as unkind to Tosevites as we are to the Race. Will you tell me I am wrong?"

He watched Atvar squirm. Plainly, the fleetlord wanted to. As plainly, he knew he couldn't. With a sigh, Atvar said, "Well, perhaps neither you Tosevites nor the Race are as kind as possible to those who were, after all, opponents."

"That is a truth," Sam said, and turned off the video. "And now, Fleetlord, I am at your service."

Atvar made the negative gesture. "On the contrary, Ambassador. I am at your service. It is a great honor to go before the Emperor. It is almost as great an honor to help prepare another for an audience. This says, more plainly than anything else can, that my conduct when I was in his Majesty's presence was acceptable, and that he would be willing to have someone else imitate me."

"Try to imitate you, you mean," Sam said. "I am only an ignorant Big Ugly. I will do my best not to embarrass myself, but I do not know if I can be perfect. I fear I have my doubts."

"Whether or not you have confidence in yourself, I have confidence in you," Atvar said. "You will do well. You think like one of us. When the time comes, you will think like one of us in the Emperor's presence."

"I hope so," Sam said. Atvar reminded him of one of his managers sending him in to pinch-hit with the game on the line, saying, *I know you can rip this guy.* And sometimes Sam would, and sometimes he wouldn't. He always had hope. He always had a chance. He didn't always succeed. If he failed here, the consequences would be larger than those of striking out with the tying run on third base in the ninth.

"And we do have these videos to take you through the procedure," Atvar said. "They are not, of course, videos of actual audiences, but they should serve well enough for the sake of rehearsal. Real imperial audiences are very rarely televised. It is possible that Kassquit's will be, and I am certain yours will, however, as it marks an extraordinary occasion."

Sam grinned crookedly, not that the fleetlord was likely to note the nuances of his expression. "Thanks a lot. Make sure you put no pressure on me. Am I going to have a billion males and females with both eye turrets on everything I do?"

"Maybe more," Atvar said. "This would attract considerable interest among the Race. And, of course, this event would also be broadcast to Rabotev 2 and Halless 1—and, I suppose, to Tosev 3 as well. But speed of light means viewers on other worlds will not see your performance for some years."

"Oh, good," Sam said. "That means I would not be known

as an idiot on four worlds all at the same time. It would take a while for the news to spread."

Atvar might not have recognized a crooked grin for what it was, but he knew sarcasm when he heard it. He laughed. "The simplest way not to have this problem would be to do well in the audience."

"Easy for you to say," Sam muttered darkly. But then, bones creaking, he bent into the posture of respect. "I am at your service, superior teacher. Let us watch these videos. You can explain the fine points to an ignorant foreigner like me."

"Foreigner," Atvar repeated in musing tones. "You may have noticed some archaic words in *Gone with the Wind*. Well, *foreigner* is much more old-fashioned than any of those. If not for the conquests of the Rabotevs and Hallessi, it would have entirely disappeared from the language."

"This is not necessarily bad," Sam said. "We Big Uglies have always needed the word. Foreigners are the individuals you fight with—when you are not fighting with friends and relations instead."

"Our conquest would have been easier if you had not fought among yourselves," Atvar said. "You already had armies mobilized and factories producing military hardware as fast as you could."

"Truth. Friends of mine were thinking about going to work in them when the Race came," Sam said. "But now—the videos."

"It shall be done," Atvar said, obedient and ironic at the same time.

He spoke to the computer, and done it was. Sam watched the ceremony—or rather, the simulation of the ceremony— over and over. He could pause whenever he wanted, go back and look at something again whenever he needed to, and skip whatever he already had down. After a while, he said, "I notice the male playing the role of the Emperor wears an actor's body paint, not the gold paint the real Emperor uses."

"Truth. In dramas and films, we allow that only on a case-by-case basis," Atvar replied. "Here, it was judged inessential. Everyone knows whom the male is impersonating, whether the actual gold is seen or not." He turned an eye turret toward Sam. "I suppose you will mock us for this sort of discrimination."

"Not me." Yeager used the negative gesture. "Instead of special body paint, our emperors would often wear special wrappings that no one else was allowed to use. That was one way you told emperors from ordinary males and females." Ermine, the purple . . . If you wanted to paint your belly gold instead, why not? He couldn't help adding, "In the United States, though, our not-emperor is just an ordinary citizen with a special job."

"Snoutcounting," Atvar said disdainfully. "Why you think this is a suitable way to rule a state of any size is beyond me. Why should a mass of males and females added together be wiser than the decision a ruler makes after consulting with experts in the field under consideration? Answer me that, if you please."

"First, experts can be wrong, too. Look what the Race thought about Tosev 3," Sam Yeager said. If that wasn't a baleful stare Atvar sent him, he'd never seen one. He went on, "And second, Fleetlord, who says rulers who do not need to answer to those who chose them always consult with experts before they make their choices? Sometimes—often—they just do as they please. This is a truth for us Big Uglies. Is it any less a truth for the Race?"

"Perhaps a little," Atvar answered, and Sam thought he might have a point. Except during mating season, Lizards were a little calmer, a little more rational, than people. As Sam had seen, both back on Earth and here on Home, they made up for it then. The fleetlord continued, "We are sometimes guilty of arbitrary behavior. If you will tell me the snoutcounting United States is not also sometimes guilty of it, I must say you will surprise me. You have seen the contrary for yourself."

"Well, so I have," Sam said gruffly. He'd almost paid with his neck for President Warren's arbitrary decision to attack the colonization fleet. "We think our system does better than others in reducing such behavior, though."

"You have been snoutcounting for how long in your not-empire?" Atvar asked.

Sam had to stop and think. To him, the Bicentennial had

happened quite recently—but that ignored his cold sleep. It was 2031, not 1977. "A little more than five hundred of your years," he answered.

Atvar's hiss was a small masterpiece of sarcasm. "When you have five thousand—or, better, twenty-five thousand—years of experience with it, then you may claim some small credit for your system. Meanwhile . . . Meanwhile, shall we go back to preparing you for your audience with his Majesty?"

"Maybe that would be a good idea." Sam had no idea whether democracy could lead humans to a state stable for millennia like the Empire. He had no idea whether any system could lead humans to a state stable for millennia. Humans were more restlessly changeable than Lizards.

Or, at least, humans with cultures springing from Western Europe had been more restlessly changeable than Lizards for the past few hundred years. That wasn't always so elsewhere on Earth. It hadn't been so in Western Europe before, say, the fifteenth century, either. If the Lizards had chosen to come not long after they sent their probe, they would have won everything their livers desired. That thought had given a lot of human statesmen and soldiers nightmares over the years.

Atvar started the video again. He made it pause in the middle of the ceremony. In thoughtful tones, he said, "I still do not know what we are going to do about the imperial laver and limner."

"I am not going to go before the Emperor naked," Yeager said. "That is not our custom. And I am not going to wear the body paint of a supplicant. I am not a supplicant. I am the representative of an independent not-empire, a not-empire with all the same rights and privileges as the Empire has. My *president*"—he used the English word, which Atvar understood—"is formally the equal of the Emperor."

"You make too much of yourself here," Atvar said stiffly. "He is not as powerful as the Emperor."

"I did not say he was. Back on Tosev 3, we had many not-empires and empires before the Race came. Some were large and strong, others small and not so strong. But they were independent. A strong one did not have the right to tell a weak one what to do. That principle was part of why we were fighting a war among ourselves when you came. The president is not as powerful as the Emperor. But he is independent of him, and sovereign in his own land."

Atvar's tailstump wiggled in agitation. "I am not the one to answer this. The protocol masters at the imperial court will have to decide."

"Do please remind them that the United States is an independent not-empire," Yeager said. "Males and females who have never been to Tosev 3 are liable to have a hard time understanding that on their own."

"Believe me, Ambassador—I am painfully aware of this," Atvar replied. "I will tell them to consult their records from ancientest history, from the days before Home was unified, when there were still other sovereignties here besides the Empire. I do not know what survives from those times, but they will."

"I thank you." Sam didn't want to push Atvar too far. Not many Lizards here on Home had experience back on Earth. No point to antagonizing the highest-ranking one who did. "This is important for both my not-empire and the Race." He knew more than a little relief when the fleetlord made the affirmative gesture.

Kassquit told the video on her monitor to pause. She asked Atvar, "You say these are the same images Sam Yeager is using to prepare for his audience with the Emperor?"

"Yes, that is correct," the fleetlord told her. "If you practice diligently, you should do well enough."

"Oh, I will!" Kassquit promised. "I can think of no greater honor than to have the imperial laver remove my ordinary body paint and the imperial limner put on the new."

To her surprise, Atvar laughed. Hastily, he said, "I mean no offense, Researcher. But your reaction there is the opposite of the wild Big Ugly's. He refuses to have anything to do with the laver and the limner."

"What?" For a moment, Kassquit could hardly believe her ears. She'd never liked them; the Race's hearing diaphragms were much neater. Whenever they told her something she had trouble believing, she mistrusted them. "Did I hear you correctly, Exalted Fleetlord?"

"You did. You must remember—Sam Yeager is at pains to

make sure everyone remembers—the American Tosevites are not imperial subjects, and are proud of not being imperial subjects. The pride may be misplaced, but it is no less real on account of that."

"Eventually, they will outgrow their presumption," Kassquit said.

"Perhaps. Such is the hope, at any rate." Atvar's voice was dry. "Meanwhile, let me see you go through this section of the ceremony once more."

"It shall be done, Exalted Fleetlord." Kassquit bent herself into several positions related to but not identical with the posture of respect. She looked to the left. She looked to the right. She looked behind her. None of that was as easy for her as it would have been for a member of the Race, for she had to turn her whole head to do it since she did not have eye turrets. As with her ears, there were still times when she resented having physical equipment different from that of the Race. She did not let her resentment show, though, or even dwell on it, for she had to concentrate on the responses she was supposed to make to courtiers who were not in fact in the hotel room with her.

When she finished, she looked to Atvar. When the fleetlord did not say anything for some little while, fear bubbled up in her. Had she made such a dreadful mess of it? She hadn't thought so, but how much did she really know? Every so often, she got forcefully reminded that, even if she was a citizen of the Empire, she was not a member of the Race.

At last, his voice neutral, Atvar said, "You did this without previous study of these videos?"

"Yes, Exalted Fleetlord," Kassquit replied unhappily. "I used sources that described the ceremony, but I have not seen it up until now. Did I . . . did I do it very badly?"

To her astonishment, Atvar made the negative gesture. "No. Except that you have no tailstump to move to right and left to accompany your head, you did it perfectly. The protocol masters have assured me that this is no impediment: you cannot move what you do not have. I congratulate you, and all the more so because you learned this on your own."

"Really?" Kassquit said in amazement. The fleetlord made

the affirmative gesture again. Kassquit whispered, "I thank you."

"For what?" Atvar said. "Yours is the hard work, yours the achievement. You receive the praise you have earned. Now— do you know the next part of the ceremony as well as you know this one?"

"I . . . I believe I do, Exalted Fleetlord."

Atvar swung his eye turrets away, then aimed them both right at her: a sign he was paying close attention. "Let me see."

"It shall be done." Kassquit went through the next portion. She hadn't seen the videos for it, and wasn't quite perfect; Atvar found a couple of small things to correct. She said, "I will improve them before the audience." That didn't seem enough, so she added, "I will improve them before you see me again."

"Do not be upset," Atvar told her. "You are doing quite well, believe me. Now—on to the portion that follows." On to that portion they went. Kassquit imagined her way through the whole ceremony. At last, Atvar said, "You have done everything very well up to this point. Now you have come before the Emperor's throne. You offer him your greetings." Kassquit bent into the special posture of respect reserved for the Emperor alone. It was awkward for a Tosevite—her back was too straight—but she managed it. Atvar didn't criticize her, so she must have done it right, or right enough. Then he said, "Now the Emperor speaks to you. How do you respond?"

"The Emperor . . . speaks to me?" Kassquit quavered. "Is that likely to happen?"

"It can happen," Atvar answered. "When I left Home to take the conquest fleet to Tosev 3, my audience with his Majesty was purely formal. When I saw the present Emperor not long ago, there was some informal talk. It is up to his Majesty, of course. The present Emperor, I think, is more inclined to talk than his predecessor was."

"He would not care to talk to the likes of me," Kassquit said. "I am an individual of no importance."

"There I would disagree with you," Atvar said. "You are not an individual of high rank. But you are important. Never doubt it. You are the first—so far, the only—Tosevite to be reared entirely within the culture of the Empire. You are the shape of the future. We hope you are the shape of the future, at any rate."

"How could I not be?" she asked.

"If things go wrong on Tosev 3, it would be all too easy for you not to be," Atvar answered. "There may be no Tosevites following any cultural models, in that case."

"What do you think the odds are?" Kassquit asked.

Atvar shrugged, a gesture the Race and Big Uglies shared. "Who can guess? It all depends on how dangerous the wild Tosevites become." He did his best to brush aside the question: "That is not something on which it is profitable to speculate. Back to business. Should the Emperor speak to you, how would you respond?"

"Exalted Fleetlord, I might be too much in awe to respond at all," Kassquit answered honestly.

"Well, silence is probably acceptable, but if his Majesty does choose to speak to you, I think he would hope for some kind of response." Atvar might have been trained as a soldier, but he had learned a good deal about diplomacy, too.

Kassquit recognized as much. "If he speaks to me informally, I suppose I will try to answer the same way," she said. "Since the setting would be informal, I do not suppose I can know in advance just what I would say."

"All right." The fleetlord made the affirmative gesture. "That will do. We do not expect miracles. We hope for effort. You need not worry on that score, Researcher. You have made your effort very plain."

"I thank you. This is important to me." Kassquit used an emphatic cough to show how important it was.

"Good." Atvar used another one. "Your loyalty does you credit. It also does credit to Ttomalss, who inculcated it in you."

"Yes, I suppose it does," Kassquit said. "Please forgive me. My feelings toward Ttomalss are . . . complex."

"How so?" Had the fleetlord made the question perfunctory, Kassquit would have given it the same sort of answer. But Atvar sounded as if he was truly curious, and so she thought for a little while before speaking.

At last, she said, "I think it is yet another conflict between my biology and my upbringing. When wild Big Uglies are small, they fixate on those who sired and hatched them. This is necessary for them, because they are helpless when newly hatched. But the Race does not form that kind of bond."

"I should hope not," Atvar said. "Our hatchlings can take care of themselves from the moment they leave the egg. Why not? If they could not, they would have soon become prey in the days before we were civilized."

"Yes, I understand that," Kassquit said. "It is only natural that Ttomalss should have had trouble forming such a bond with me. I give him credit: he did try. But it was not natural, as it would have been for wild Big Uglies. And I noticed his incomplete success—things being as they are, I could hardly help noticing. I could hardly help resenting what he could not give me, either."

"All this was some while ago, though," Atvar said. "Surely your resentment has faded over the passing years?"

"To some degree—but only to some degree," Kassquit replied. "You will know, I am sure, that there have been times when Ttomalss has treated me as much as an experimental animal as a friend or someone else with whom he should have forged a bond of trust. This failure has naturally kept resentment alive in me. Am I an autonomous individual, or only an object of curiosity?"

"You are both," Atvar said, which struck Kassquit as basically honest—at least, it was the same conclusion she'd reached herself. The fleetlord went on, "Because of your biology and your upbringing, you will always be an object of interest to the Race. By now, I suspect you have also resigned yourself to this."

"To some degree—but only to some degree," Kassquit repeated, adding an emphatic cough to that. "For example, the Race held me in cold sleep for years instead of reviving me and letting me become acquainted with Home. This decision was made for me; I had no chance to participate in it myself."

"There is some truth in that, but only some," Atvar said. "One of the reasons the decision was made for you, as you say, is that we admire your professional competence and value your ability in dealing with the wild Big Uglies. We wanted to do our best to make sure you would be in good health when they arrived."

Kassquit made the negative gesture. "You do not understand, Exalted Fleetlord. You did that for your benefit, for the Race's benefit, for the Empire's benefit, and not for mine. There is a difference, like it or not."

The fleetlord sighed. "I can see that you might think so. But are you not a citizen of the Empire? You have certainly said so often enough."

"Yes, I am a citizen of the Empire. I am proud to be a citizen of the Empire." Kassquit used another emphatic cough. "But does the Empire not have a certain obligation to treat its citizens justly? If it does not, why is being a citizen any sort of privilege?"

"You *are* an individual." By Atvar's tone, he did not mean it as a compliment. "You also—forgive me—sound very much like a Tosevite. Your species is more individualistic than ours."

"Maybe the Empire needs more Tosevite citizens," Kassquit said. "Perhaps things here have been too tranquil for too long."

Atvar laughed at her. "Things have not been tranquil since we found out what wild Big Uglies were capable of. They will not be tranquil again for a long time to come. But you may be right. I think his Majesty believes you are. That is part of the reason you are receiving this audience."

"Whatever the reason, it is a great honor," Kassquit said. "Shall we rehearse the ceremony again, Exalted Fleetlord? I want everything to be perfect." She used yet another emphatic cough.

Ttomalss liked talking with Major Frank Coffey. His reason for liking that particular American had nothing to do with the Big Ugly's personality, though Coffey was pleasant enough. It wasn't even rational, and Ttomalss knew it wasn't. Knowing as much didn't make it go away.

He liked Coffey's color.

He knew exactly why, too. The officer's dark brown hide reminded him of the green-brown of his own scaly skin. It made the wild Big Ugly seem less alien, more familiar, than the pinkish beige of the other American Tosevites. He wasn't, of course. Ttomalss understood that full well. Understanding didn't make the feeling go away.

Coffey got up from the chair made for a Big Ugly's hindquarters in one of the hotel's conference rooms. He stretched and sighed. "It was kind of you to make this furniture for us," he said, "but you would never get rich selling chairs back on Tosev 3."

"I am sure that is a truth," Ttomalss said. "Some of the things Tosevites make for the Race are also imperfect. No species can ever be completely familiar with another. The Rabotevs and Hallessi still surprise us every now and again."

"Interesting. And I believe you. Even different cultures on Tosev 3 run up against this same difficulty," Coffey said. "I am glad you said it, too. It brings me to one of the fundamental troubles in the relationship between my not-empire and the Empire, one that needs to be solved."

"Speak. Give forth," Ttomalss urged. "Is that not why you have come: to solve the difficulties between the United States and the Empire?" Had he been a Big Ugly himself, the corners of his mouth would have curled up in the Tosevites' facial gesture of benevolent amiability. He *liked* Frank Coffey.

He also made the mistake of assuming that, because he liked Coffey, the wild Big Ugly would not say anything he did not like. Coffey proceeded to disabuse him of that assumption. "The difficulty is that the Race *does not* recognize Tosevite not-empires as equals," he declared, and added an emphatic cough. "This *must* change if relations between us are to find their proper footing." He used another one.

"But that is not so," Ttomalss protested. "We have equal relationships with the United States, with the SSSR, with the Nipponese Empire, with Britain—even with the *Reich*, though we defeated it. How can you complain of this?"

"Very easily," Frank Coffey answered. "You say that we are your equals, but down deep in your livers you do not believe it. Can you tell me I am mistaken? You thought from the beginning that we were nothing but sword-swinging savages. Down deep, you still believe it, and you still act as if you believe it. Will you make me believe I am wrong?"

Ttomalss thought that over. He did not have to think for very long. The wild Big Ugly had a point. The Race was proud of its ancient, long-stable civilization. What could wild Big Uglies be but uncouth barbarians who were good at fighting and treachery but very little else?

Slowly, the psychologist said, "This is perceptive of you. How did you come to realize it?"

Frank Coffey laughed a loud Tosevite laugh. "It is plain enough to any Tosevite with eyes to see. And it is especially obvious to a Tosevite of my color." He brushed a hand along the skin of his forearm, a gesture he made with the air of one who had used it before.

"What do you mean?" Ttomalss asked.

"You will know that pale Tosevites have discriminated against those of my color," Coffey said, and waited. Ttomalss made the affirmative gesture. The American went on, "This discrimination is now illegal in my not-empire. We are all supposed to be equal, legally and socially. Supposed to be, I say. There are still a fair number of pale Big Uglies who *would* discriminate against dark ones if only they could get away with it. These days, showing that too openly is not acceptable in the United States. But one of us usually has no trouble telling when pale Tosevites have such feelings, even when they try to hide them. And so you should not be surprised when I recognize the symptoms of the disease in the Race as well."

"I see," Ttomalss said slowly. "How did you persuade the pale Big Uglies to stop discriminating in law against you darker ones?"

" 'Discriminating in law,' " Frank Coffey echoed. "That is a nice phrase, a very nice phrase. We had two advantages. First, the *Reich* discriminated against groups it did not like, discriminated very blatantly—and we were at war with the *Reich,* so whatever it did looked bad to us, and became something we were embarrassed to imitate. And then the Race tried to conquer all Tosevites. To resist, the United States had to draw support from all its own inhabitants. Discriminating in law became something we could not afford to do, and so we stopped."

"Back in ancientest history, I believe the Race was also divided into subspecies," Ttomalss said. "But long years of mixing have made us highly uniform. I suspect the same may happen with you."

Coffey shrugged. "So it may. But it will not happen soon, even by the way the Race reckons time. During your mating seasons, your males and females are not too fussy about mating partners. That helps you mix. With us, it is different."

"I suppose it would be," Ttomalss said. "So social discrimination also lingers in mating, even though discrimination in law does not?"

"Yes, it does," the American Big Ugly replied. "Now I praise you for your perceptiveness. Not many from another culture, from another biology, would have seen the implications of that."

"I thank you," Ttomalss said. "I have been studying your species and its paradoxes for some years now. I am glad to be reminded every now and then that I have gained at least a little insight. Perhaps my close involvement with Kassquit has also helped."

Coffey nodded. He started to catch himself and add the Race's gesture of agreement, but Ttomalss waved for him not to bother. The Tosevite said, "I can see how it might have. Kassquit is a remarkable individual. You did a good job of raising her. By our standards she is strange—no doubt of that—but I would have expected any Tosevite brought up by the Race to be not just strange but hopelessly insane. We are different in so many vital ways."

"Again, I thank you. And I will not lie to you: raising Kassquit was the hardest thing I have ever done." Ttomalss thought about what he'd just said. He had spent some time in the captivity of the Chinese female, Liu Han. She'd terrorized him, addicted him to ginger, and made him think every day in her clutches would be his last. Had raising Kassquit been harder than *that*? As a matter of fact, it had. "Is imperfect gratitude always the lot of those who bring up Tosevites?"

Major Coffey laughed again, this time loud and long. "Maybe not always, Senior Researcher, but often, very often. You need not be surprised about that."

"How do those who raise hatchlings tolerate this?" Ttomalss asked.

"What choice have they—have we—got?" the wild Big

Ugly said. "It is one of the things that come with being a To-sevite."

"Do you speak from experience? Have you hatchlings of your own?"

"Yes and no, respectively," Coffey replied. "I have no hatchlings myself. I am a soldier, and I always believed a soldier would not make a good permanent mate. But you must recall, Senior Researcher—I was a hatchling myself. I locked horns with my own father plenty of times."

" 'Locked horns,' " Ttomalss repeated. "This must be a translated idiom from your language. Does it mean, to quarrel?"

"That is exactly what it means."

"Interesting. When you Tosevites use our tongue, you enliven it with your expressions," Ttomalss said. "Some of them, I suspect, will stay in the language. Others will probably disappear."

"Your language has done the same thing to English," Major Coffey said. "We use interrogative and emphatic coughs. We say, 'Truth,' when we mean agreement. We use other phrases and ways of speaking of yours, too. Languages have a way of rubbing off on one another."

"You would know more about that than I do," Ttomalss told him. "Our language borrowed place names and names for animals and plants from the tongues of Rabotev 2 and Halless 1. Past that, those tongues did not have much of an effect on it. And, of course, the Rabotevs and Hallessi speak our language now, and speak it the same way as we do."

"You expect the same thing to happen on Tosev 3, don't you?" Coffey said.

Ttomalss made the affirmative gesture. "Yes, over the course of years. It may—it probably will—take longer there than with the Rabotevs and Hallessi. Your leading cultures are more advanced than theirs were." He held up a hand. "You were going to say something about your equality. Let me finish, if you please."

"It shall be done, Exalted Researcher," the wild Big Ugly said with a fine show of sarcasm. "By all means, go on."

"I thank you so very much," Ttomalss said, matching dry for dry. "What I wanted to tell you was that the process has already begun in those parts of Tosev 3 the Race rules. That is more than half the planet. Your not-empire may still be independent, but you cannot claim it is dominant."

"I do not claim that. I never have. The United States never has," Coffey replied. "But the Race seems unwilling to admit that independence means formal equality. The Emperor may have more power than the President of the United States. As sovereigns, though, they both have equal rank."

That notion revolted Ttomalss. It would have revolted almost any member of the Race. To say the Emperor was no more than equal to a wild Big Ugly chosen for a limited term by snoutcounting . . . was absurd. Even if it was true under the rules of diplomacy (rules the Race had had to resurrect from ancientest history, and also to borrow from the Tosevites), it was still absurd.

That he should think so went a long way toward proving Frank Coffey's point. If Ttomalss hadn't spent so many years working with the Big Uglies, he wouldn't even have realized that. Realizing it made him like it no better.

"You are very insistent on this sovereign equality," he said.

"And so we ought to be," Coffey answered. "We spilled too much of our blood fighting to keep it. You take yours lightly because it has never been challenged till now."

Ttomalss started to make a sharp reply: Coffey was presumptuous if he imagined the American Tosevites truly challenged the Race. At the last moment, though, the psychologist held his peace. Not for the first time, dealing with the Tosevites made him feel as if he were trying to reach into a mirror and deal with all the reversed images he found there. That the American Big Uglies could be as proud of their silly snoutcounted temporary leader as the Race was of the Emperor and all the tradition behind his office was preposterous on the face of it . . . to the Race.

But it was not preposterous to the Americans. Ttomalss had needed a long time to realize that. The Big Uglies might be as wrong about their snoutcounting as they were about the silly superstitions they used in place of due reverence for the spirits of Emperors past. They might be wrong, yes, but they were very much—*very* much—in earnest. The Race needed to remember that.

It made dealing with the American Tosevites more complicated and more difficult. But, when dealing with Tosevites, what wasn't difficult?

Karen Yeager looked at her husband. She said, "Do you know what I'd do?"

"No, but you're going to tell me, so how much difference does that make?" Jonathan replied with the resigned patience of a man who'd been a husband for a long time.

She sniffed. Resigned patience wasn't what she wanted right now. She wanted sympathy. She also wanted ice cubes. "I'd kill for a cold lemonade, that's what I'd do," she declared.

"Now that you mention it, so would I," Jonathan said. "But you haven't got any, and I haven't got any, either. So we're safe from each other, anyway. Besides, we're more than ten light-years from the nearest lemon."

"A cold Coke, then. A cold glass of ippa-fruit juice. A cold anything. *Ice* water, for heaven's sake." Karen walked over to the window of their hotel room and stared out. The alien landscape had grown familiar, even boring. "Who would have thought the Race didn't know about ice?"

"They know. They just don't care. There's a difference," Jonathan said. "And besides, we already knew they didn't care. We've spent enough time in their cities back on Earth."

He was right. Karen sniffed again anyhow. She didn't want right. She *really* wanted ice cubes. She said, "They don't care what we like. That's what the problem is. They know we like cold things, and they haven't given us a way to get any. You call that diplomacy?"

"Some of them know we like ice, yeah. They know it here." Her husband tapped his head. "But they don't know it here." He set a hand on his stomach. "They don't really believe it. Besides, I can guaran-damn-tee you there's not a single ice-cube tray on this whole planet."

"And this is a real for-true civilization?" Karen exclaimed. Jonathan laughed, but she went on, "Dammit, there's bound to be something they could use to make ice cubes. Gelatin molds, maybe—I don't know. But we ought to be asking for them, whatever they are, and for a freezer to put them in."

"Talk to the concierge," Jonathan suggested. "If that doesn't work, talk to Atvar. If he can't do anything about it, you're stuck."

The concierge was a snooty Lizard named Nibgris. He understood about freezers; the Race used them to keep food fresh, just as humans did. But the idea that someone might want small bits of frozen water flummoxed him. "What would you use them for, superior Tosevite?" he asked, using the honorific with the same oily false politeness hotel people laid on back on Earth.

"To make the liquids I drink colder and more enjoyable," Karen answered.

Nibgris' eye turrets aimed every which way but right at her. That meant he thought she was crazy but was too polite to say so out loud. "How can a cold drink possibly be more enjoyable than one at the proper temperature?" he asked.

"To Tosevites, cold drinks *are* proper," she said.

"What do you expect me to use to hold the bits of water?" he inquired.

"I do not know," Karen said. "This is not my world. It is yours. I was hoping you might help me. Is that not why you are employed here?"

"Perhaps, superior female, you might use a few tens of measuring cups." Nibgris' mouth fell open in a laugh. He didn't expect to be taken seriously.

Karen didn't care what he expected. Briskly, she made the affirmative gesture. "They would do excellently. I thank you. Please bring a small freezer and the measuring cups up to my room at once."

The concierge's tailstump quivered in agitation. "We have not got that many cups in the entire establishment!"

"Do you suppose you could send someone out to buy them?" Karen asked. "I am sure your government would reimburse you. Even if it did not, though, I doubt the expense would bankrupt the hotel."

Nibgris jerked as if a mosquito had bitten him. A sarcastic Big Ugly seemed to be the last thing he knew how to face. "It is not the expense," he said plaintively. "It is the ridiculousness of the request."

"Is any request that leads to making a guest more comfortable ridiculous?" Karen asked.

"Well . . . no." Nibgris spoke with obvious reluctance. People who worked in hotels always claimed their first goal was making their guests comfortable. More often than not, it was really making things more convenient for themselves. That didn't seem much different here on Home.

"I would do it myself, but I do not have any of your money," Karen said. "It would be a great help to me and to my mate and to all the other Tosevites. We would be most grateful." She added an emphatic cough.

By the way Nibgris' tongue flicked in and out, he cared nothing for humans' gratitude. But the resigned sigh that followed was amazingly manlike. "It shall be done, superior Tosevite."

"I thank you," Karen said sweetly. She could afford to be sweet now. She'd got what she wanted—or thought she had.

Nibgris took his own sweet time about having the Lizards who served him bring up the freezer. When Karen called the next day to complain, the concierge said, "My apologies, superior Tosevite, but there has been a certain disagreement with the kitchens. The cooks claim that anything connected with food or drink in any way is their province, and they should be the ones to bring the freezer and the measuring cups to you."

"I do not care who does it. I only care that *someone* does it." Karen used another emphatic cough. "Transfer my call to the head of the kitchens, if you would be so kind. I will see if I can get some action out of that male—or is it a female?"

"A female—her name is Senyahh." Nibgris transferred the call with every sign of relief.

Senyahh seemed startled to see a Big Ugly staring out of the monitor at her. "Yes? You wish?" she asked in tones just this side of actively hostile.

"I wish the freezer Nibgris promised me yesterday, and the measuring cups in which to freeze water." Karen was feeling just this side—or perhaps just the other side—of hostile herself. Snarling at one more Lizard functionary was the last thing she wanted to do, but by then she would have crawled through flames and broken glass to get her hands on ice cubes.

"Why do you think I am responsible for fulfilling Nibgris'

rash promises?" Senyahh demanded. "I see no necessity for such a bizarre request."

"That is because you are not a Tosevite," Karen said.

"By the spirits of Emperors past, I am glad I am not, too." Senyahh tacked on a scornful emphatic cough.

Karen's temper snapped. "By the spirits of Emperors past, Senyahh, I am glad of the same thing. You would be as much a disgrace to my species as you are to your own." The head of the kitchens hissed furiously. Ignoring her, Karen went on, "I expect the freezer and the cups inside of a tenth of a day. If they are not here, I shall complain to Fleetlord Atvar, who has the hearing diaphragm of the present Emperor. Once Atvar is through with you, you may find out more about the spirits of Emperors past than you ever wanted to know. A tenth of a day, do you hear me?" She broke the connection before Senyahh could answer.

As she angrily stared at the blank monitor, she wondered if she'd gone too far. Would fear of punishment persuade the head of the kitchens to do as she wanted? Or would Senyahh decide Atvar was unlikely to side with a Big Ugly and against a fellow Lizard? Karen would know in a couple of hours.

"Being mulish?" Jonathan asked—a word he must have got from his father.

"I'll say!" The trouble Karen had had poured out of her. She finished, "Do you think I antagonized the miserable Lizard?"

"Probably—but so what?" Jonathan sounded unconcerned. "If you act like a superior, the Lizards will think you are. It works the same way with us, only a little less, I think. And if you don't have a freezer inside a tenth of a day, you really ought to give Atvar a piece of your mind. He'll back you."

"Do you think so?" Karen asked anxiously.

"You bet I do." Jonathan used an emphatic cough even though they were speaking English. "If he tells you no, you can sic Dad on him, and you'd better believe he doesn't want that."

Karen judged Jonathan was right. Atvar had enough important things to quarrel and quibble about with Sam Yeager that something as monumentally trivial as ice cubes would only prove an irritation. If she were Senyahh, she wouldn't have cared to risk the fleetlord's wrath.

Time scurried on. Just before—*just* before—the deadline, the Race's equivalent of a doorbell hissed for attention. Two Lizards with a square metal box on a wheeled cart stood outside. A cardboard carton full of plastic cups lay on top of the metal box. "You are the Tosevite who wanted a freezer?" one of the Lizards asked. He sounded as if he couldn't have cared less one way or the other.

"I am," Karen said.

"Well, here it is," he said, and turned to his partner. "Come on, Fegrep. Give it a shove. As soon as we plug it in, we can go do something else."

"Right," Fegrep said. "Pretty crazy, a freezer in a room. And why does the Big Ugly want all those stupid cups?" He'd just heard Karen speak his language, but seemed to think she couldn't understand it. Or maybe he just didn't care.

Under other circumstances, Karen might have got angry. As things were, she was too glad to see the freezer to worry about anything else. The workmales wheeled it into the room, eased it down off the cart, and plugged it in. Then they left. Karen opened the freezer. It was cold in there, sure enough. She started filling the measuring cups full of water and sticking them inside the freezer. "Ice cubes!" she told Jonathan. "All we have to do is wait."

"They're round," he observed. "How can they be ice cubes?"

She corrected herself: "Ice cylinders. Thank you, Mr. Webster's Dictionary of the English Language." Her husband might have got angry, too. Instead, he took a bow. As he must have known it would, that annoyed her even more.

After she started making ice cubes (she refused to think of them as cylinders) she kept opening the freezer every so often to see how they were doing. "You're letting the cold air out," Jonathan said helpfully.

"I know I am," she answered. "I don't care. I've been waiting all this time. I can wait a little longer."

Some small stretch of time after she would have had ice cubes if she'd been patient, she had them anyhow. Coaxing them out of the measuring cups wasn't so easy, but she managed. She put five of them in a glass of room-temperature—

which is to say, lukewarm—water, then waited for them to do
their stuff. After five minutes, she rested the glass against her
cheek for a moment.

"Ahh!" she said. Then she drank. "Ahhhh!" she said. She'd
never thought of ice water as nectar of the gods, but it would
do. It would definitely do.

"Let me have some," Jonathan said.

"Get your own glass," Karen told him. "I earned this one."
He bent into the posture of respect and gave her an emphatic
cough. Her snort turned into a laugh. Jonathan fixed himself
a glass of ice water. He made the same sort of ecstatic noises
as she had. She laughed again. She'd known he would.

Atvar gave only half a hearing diaphragm to Senyahh's
complaints. When the female finally paused to draw more air
into her lung, he cut her off: "Hear me, Kitchen Chief. Any
reasonable requests from these Tosevites are to be honored.
Any—do you hear me?"

Senyahh glared at him out of the monitor. "I do not call a
request for a freezer and a swarm of measuring cups reasonable, Exalted Fleetlord."

Members of the Race were more patient than Big Uglies.
At times like this, Atvar wondered why. "Let me make myself
very plain. Any request is reasonable that does not involve
major expense—a yeartenth's hotel revenues, let us say—or
danger to a member of the Race. Anything within those limits, your only proper response is, 'It shall be done, superior
Tosevite.' And then you do it."

"That is outrageous!" Senyahh exclaimed.

"I am sorry you feel that way," Atvar replied. "But then,
your record at this hotel has been good up until now. I am sure
that will help you gain a new position once you are released
from this one. For you *will* be released from this one if your
insubordination continues for even another instant. Do I
make myself plain enough for you to understand, Kitchen
Chief?"

"You do. You are not nearly so offensive as the Big Ugly I
dealt with, though," Senyahh said.

"Is that a resignation?" Atvar asked.

With obvious reluctance, the kitchen chief made the negative gesture. "No, Exalted Fleetlord. It shall be done." She broke the connection.

Atvar hoped he had put the fear for a happy afterlife into her. He wouldn't have bet anything he worried about losing, though. If she'd tried so hard to obstruct one Tosevite request, she was liable to do the same or worse with another. Some males and females enjoyed being difficult. *She might as well be a Big Ugly,* Atvar thought. His mouth fell open in a laugh. A moment later, he wondered why and snapped it shut. That wasn't funny.

But the real trouble with the Big Uglies wasn't that they reveled in making nuisances of themselves. The real trouble was that they were too good at it. He'd thought that too many times back on Tosev 3. That he had reason to think it here on Home only proved he'd been right to worry on the other world, and that the males and females who'd recalled him hadn't known what they were doing.

It proved that to Atvar, anyhow. Several of the officials who'd ordered him back from Tosev 3 still held their posts. By all appearances, they were still satisfied they'd done the right thing. That they now had to deal with Big Uglies here on Home should have given them a hint that the problem on Tosev 3 hadn't been Atvar. It should have, but had it? Not likely, not as far as the former fleetlord could see.

The trouble—well, *a* trouble, anyhow—with the Big Uglies was that they were too good at whatever they set their minds to. The way Kassquit and Sam Yeager were approaching their imperial audiences was a case in point. He hadn't said so to either one of them, but few members of the Race could have matched how much they'd learned, or how quickly.

He hissed softly. That thought reminded him of something he had to do. He called the protocol master in the capital. The male's image appeared on the screen. "This is Herrep. I greet you, Exalted Fleetlord."

"And I greet you, Protocol Master," Atvar replied politely. "I wonder whether your staff has yet finished researching the question I put to you not long ago. The time for the wild Big Ugly's audience with his Majesty fast approaches."

"I am aware of that, yes," Herrep said. He was an old male, older even than Atvar, and had held office a long time. His scales had the dusty tone age gave them, and sagged slightly on his bones. Because of their looser hides, old males and females looked a little more like Tosevites than younger members of the Race did. Herrep went on, "I hope *you* understand this is a matter from the very ancientest days, and not one to be researched in the same way as one from more recent times."

"Why not?" the fleetlord asked. "Research is research, is it not? So it would seem to me, at any rate."

But the protocol master made the negative gesture. "Not necessarily. For most research, anyone with a computer connected to the network and a certain curiosity can do as well as anyone else. But much of the material we are looking through is so old, it never went into the computer network at all. We have to locate it physically, to make sure we do not destroy it by examining it, and sometimes also to interpret it: the language is so very old, it has changed a good deal between that time and this."

Atvar let out another low hiss, this one of wonder. "I did not realize your material was as old as that. You have my apology. You might as well be dealing with the same sort of situation as the Big Uglies do when they go through their archives."

"I do not know what sort of research the Big Uglies do, or what sort of archives they have," Herrep said. "But I do know I have an answer for you, or the beginnings of an answer."

"Do you?" Atvar said eagerly. "Tell me, please!"

"However little I care to admit it, your wild Big Ugly of an aspirant appears to be correct," the protocol master replied. "The imperial laver and imperial limner are *not* involved in the ceremony when the representative from an independent empire greets the Emperor. In ancientest days, before Home was unified, the Emperor sometimes sent out ambassadors of his own to other emperors. Their lavers and limners—for they too had such officials—were not involved, either."

"I thank you," Atvar said. "So independence is what matters? I do not suppose that Sam Yeager's coming from a not-empire would affect the situation?"

"A not-empire?" Herrep said. "Please forgive me, Exalted Fleetlord, but I am unfamiliar with the term." As best he could, Atvar explained the American Tosevite penchant for snoutcounting. The protocol master's eye turrets moved in a way that said the idea revolted him. It revolted Atvar, too, but the Big Uglies seemed to thrive on it. Herrep asked, "On Tosev 3, such a temporary, snoutcounted sovereign is considered the equal of any other?"

"That is a truth. You need have no doubt of it whatever." Atvar used an emphatic cough. "Not-empires are more common than empires there. The United States is one of the oldest ones; it has used this system for more than five hundred of our years."

Herrep hissed scornfully. "And this is supposed to be a long time?"

"By our standards, no. By the standards Big Uglies use, Protocol Master, it *is* a fairly long time," Atvar answered.

"You realize I would have to stretch a point, and stretch it a long way, to consider the representative of such a sovereign equal to an ambassador from a true empire," Herrep said. "There is no precedent for such a thing."

"There may not be any precedent on Home, but there is a great deal of it on Tosev 3," Atvar said.

The protocol master made the negative gesture. "On Tosev 3, there is precedent for fleetlords treating with such individuals. There is none for *the Emperor* to do so."

"If you refuse—and especially if you refuse at this stage— you offer the American Big Uglies a deadly insult. This is the sort of insult that could prove deadly in the most literal sense of the word," Atvar said. "As for stretching a point—there is all the Tosevite precedent for empires dealing with not-empires. If we recognize the United States as independent— and what choice do we have, when it *is*?—we have to recognize that precedent, too. And remember, the American Big Uglies are *here*. They are also as formidable as that implies."

"I do not want to do what is expedient," Herrep said. "I want to do what is right."

Alarm coursed through Atvar. He wished he'd never uttered the word *not-empire* in the protocol master's hearing. By the nature of his job, Herrep cared more for punctilio than for the real world. The real world hadn't impinged on the imperial court for more than a hundred thousand years. But it was here again. One way or another, Herrep was going to have to see that.

Carefully, the fleetlord said, "If helping to ensure peace not just between two independent entities"—that took care of empires and not-empires—"is not right, what is? And if you consult with his Majesty himself, I think you will find he has a lively interest in meeting the ambassador from the United States."

On the monitor, Herrep stirred uncomfortably. "I am aware of that. I had, for a moment, forgotten that you were as well." Atvar almost laughed, but at the last moment kept his amusement from showing. That struck him as a particularly revealing comment. The protocol master went on, "Very well, Exalted Fleetlord. I have no good reason to accept Tosevite precedents, but you remind me I have no good reason to reject them, either. We shall go forward as if this wild Big Ugly represented a proper empire."

"I thank you," Atvar said. "By the spirits of Emperors past, I think you are doing that which is best for the Empire."

"I hope so," Herrep said dubiously. "But I wonder about the sort of precedent *I* am setting. Will other wild Big Uglies from different not-empires come to Home seeking audience with his Majesty? Should they have it if they do?"

"It is possible that they may," replied Atvar, who thought it was probable that they would. A starship from the SSSR was supposed to be on the way, in fact—but then, the SSSR's rulers had killed off their emperor, something the fleetlord did *not* intend to tell Herrep. "If they succeed in coming here, they will have earned it, will they not? One group of independent Big Uglies, the Nipponese, have an emperor whose line of descent, they claim, runs back over five thousand of our years."

"Still a parvenu next to *the* Emperor," Herrep said. Atvar made the affirmative gesture. The protocol master sighed. "Still, I could wish they had got here first. We shall just have to endure these others."

"They are all nuisances, whether they come from empires or not-empires," Atvar said. With a sigh of his own that came from years of experience, much of which he would rather not have had, he went on, "It may almost be just as well that many of them have kept their independence. They are too different from us. We had little trouble àssimilating the Rabotevs and Hallessi, and we thought building the Empire would always be easy. Even if we do eventually succeed with the Big Uglies, they have taught us otherwise."

"You would know better than I," Herrep said. "Aside from the obvious fact that snoutcounting is ridiculous, everything I have seen of these Big Uglies—the ones who have come to Home—suggests they are at least moderately civilized."

Atvar made the affirmative gesture. "Oh, yes. I would agree with you. The American Tosevites sent the best they had. I was not worried about their lack of civilization, especially not here on Home. I was worried about how fast they progress in science and technology, and about how different from us they are sexually and socially. I do wonder if those two difficulties are related."

"What could we do if they are?"

"As of now, nothing has occurred to me—or, so far as I know, to anyone else."

"Then why waste time wondering?"

"You are a sensible male, Protocol Master. Of course this is what you would say," Atvar replied. "The trouble is, the Big Uglies make me wonder about the good sense of good sense, if that makes any sense to you." By Herrep's negative gesture, it didn't. Atvar wasn't surprised. Nothing about Tosev 3 really made sense to the Race. Trouble? Oh, yes. Tosev 3 made plenty of trouble.

Dr. Melanie Blanchard and Mickey Flynn were floating in the *Admiral Peary*'s control room when Glen Johnson pulled himself up there. Johnson felt a small twinge of jealousy listening to them talk as he came up the access tube. He knew that was idiotic, which didn't prevent the twinge. Yes, Dr. Blanchard was a nice-looking woman—one of the nicer-looking women for more than ten light-years in any direction— but it wasn't as if she were his. And she would be going down to the surface of Home before long, a journey on which neither he nor Flynn could hope to follow.

"It's too bad," she was saying when Johnson emerged. "That is really too bad."

"What is?" Johnson asked.

"News from Earth," Mickey Flynn said.

Johnson waited. Flynn said no more. Johnson hadn't really expected that he would. With such patience as the junior pilot could muster, he asked, "*What* news from Earth?"

"An Arab bomb in Jerusalem killed Dr. Chaim Russie," Melanie Blanchard said. "He was the grandson of Dr. Moishe Russie, the man for whom the Lizards' medical college for people is named."

"Did you know this Chaim Russie?" Johnson asked.

"I met him once. He was still a boy then," she answered. "I knew Reuven Russie, his father, a little better. He'd married a widow. She had a boy, and they'd had Chaim and another son of their own, who I think was also a doctor, and they were happy." She shook her head. "Reuven Russie would have been up in his eighties when this happened, so he might not have lived to see it. For his sake, I hope he didn't."

Johnson nodded. The news was fresh here, but all those years old back on Earth. Dr. Blanchard had taken that into account. A lot of people didn't. Johnson said, "Was the bomb meant for Lizards or for Jews?"

"Who knows?" she answered. "I don't think the bombers were likely to be fussy. They weren't before I went into cold sleep, anyhow."

"No, I suppose not." Johnson looked at Flynn. "There were advantages to being out in the asteroid belt for so long. News from Earth had to be big to mean much to us. When the Lizards fought the Nazis, that mattered—especially because they blew up the Germans' spaceship."

"The *Hermann Göring*," Flynn said.

"Yeah." Glen Johnson felt a certain dull surprise that the name didn't rouse more hatred in him than it did. Back in the vanished age before the Lizards came, Hitler had been public enemy number one, and the fat *Luftwaffe* chief his right-hand man. Then all of a sudden the Nazis and the USA were on the same side, both battling desperately to keep from being enslaved by the Race. Göring went from zero to hero in one swell foop. If the Germans started shooting missiles at the Lizards, more power to 'em. And if they'd been building the missiles to shoot them at England or the Russians, well, that was then and this was now. Nothing like a new enemy to turn an old one into a bosom buddy.

That was then and this was now. *Now* was unimaginably distant for anybody old enough to remember the days before the Lizards came: the most ancient of the ancient back on Earth, and a handful of people here who'd cheated time through cold sleep. He looked out through the antireflection-coated glass. That was Home unwinding beneath him, in its gold and greens and blues: seas surrounded by lands, not continents as islands in the world ocean. The *Admiral Peary* was coming up toward Sitneff, where Sam Yeager and the rest of the American delegation were staying.

"Looks like a pretty good dust storm heading their way," Johnson said. The gold-brown clouds obscured a broad swath of ground.

"That kind of weather is probably why the Lizards have nictitating membranes," Dr. Blanchard said.

"Gesundheit," Mickey Flynn responded gravely. "I've heard the term before, but I never knew quite what it meant."

Why, you sandbagging so-and-so, Johnson thought. If that wasn't bait to get the nice-looking doctor to show off and be pleasant, he'd never heard of such a thing. He only wished he'd thought of it himself.

Melanie Blanchard was only too happy to explain: "It's their third eyelid. A lot of animals back on Earth have them, too. It doesn't go up and down. It goes across the eye like a windshield wiper and sweeps away the dust and grit."

"Oh," Flynn said. He paused, no doubt for effect. "I always thought it had something to do with cigarettes."

"With cigarettes?" Dr. Blanchard looked puzzled.

Johnson did, too, but only for a moment. Then he groaned. His groan made the doctor think in a different way. She groaned, too, even louder. Flynn smiled beatifically. He would have seemed the picture of innocence if he hadn't been so obviously guilty.

"That's one more thing these evil people did when they shanghaied me," Johnson told Dr. Blanchard. "I used to spend more of my time on Earth than I did in space, and I used to smoke. So when they tied me up and carried me away on the *Lewis and Clark,* I had to quit cold turkey."

"Take a good look at him," Flynn told the doctor. "Can you imagine anyone who'd want to tie him up and carry him away? Anyone in his right mind, I mean?"

She ignored that and replied to Johnson: "In a way, you know, they did you a favor. Smoking tobacco is one of the dumbest things you can do if you want to live to a ripe old age. Lung cancer, heart disease, stroke, emphysema . . . All sorts of pleasant things can speed you out the door."

"I liked it," Johnson said. "Nothing like a cigarette after dinner, or after . . ." He sighed. It had been a very, very long time since he'd had a cigarette after sex. He tried to remember just how long, and with whom. Close to seventy years now, even if he'd managed to dodge a lot of them.

Now Mickey Flynn surveyed him with an eye that, if it wasn't jaundiced, definitely had some kind of liver trouble. He knew why perfectly well. He'd managed to hint about sex in front of Dr. Blanchard. If he hinted about it, he might make her interested in it, perhaps even with him.

Or he might not. Doctors were unflappable about such matters. And Melanie Blanchard didn't like—really didn't like—cigarettes. "Damn things stink," she said.

"Been so long now since I've had one, I'd probably say you were right," Johnson admitted. "But I sure used to like them."

"Lots of people did," she answered. "Lots of people back on Earth are paying for it, too. Back when disease was likely to kill you before you got old, I don't suppose there was anything much wrong with tobacco. Something else would get you before it did. But now that we know something about medicine, now that most people can expect to live out their full span, smoking has to be one of the stupidest things anybody can do."

Johnson busied himself with looking out the window. He hadn't had a cigarette in something close to fifteen years of body time. If a kindly Lizard offered him a smoke, though, he suspected he would take one. A male of the Race who hadn't been able to enjoy a taste of ginger in a long time probably felt the same way about his chosen herb.

Johnson never got tired of the view. One of the reasons he'd become a flier was so he could look down and see the world from far above. Now he was looking down at another world from even farther above. As such things went, Home was an Earthlike planet. A lot of the same geological and biological forces were at work both places. But, while the results they'd produced were similar enough for beings evolved on one planet to live fairly comfortably on the other, they were a long way from identical. The differences were what fascinated him.

He got so involved staring at an enormous dry riverbed, he almost missed the intercom: "Colonel Johnson! Colonel Glen Johnson! Report at once to Scooter Bay One! Colonel Johnson! Colonel Glen Johnson! Report at once to—"

" 'Bye," he said, and launched himself down the tube he'd ascended a little while before. As long as nobody was screaming at him to report to Lieutenant General Healey's office, he'd cheerfully go wherever he was told. He'd go to see Healey, too; he was military down to his toes. But he wouldn't be cheerful about it.

"Good—you got here fast," a technician said when he came gliding up.

"What's going on?" Johnson asked.

"We got a Mayday call from the Lizards, if you can believe it," the tech answered. "Their stuff is good, but it looks like it isn't quite perfect. One of their scooters had its main engines go out not far from us. We're closer than any of their ships, and they ask if we can bring the scooter crew back here till they make pickup."

"I'll go get 'em," Johnson said, and started climbing into the spacesuit that hung by the inner airlock door. He paused halfway through. Laughing, he went on, "They'll fluoroscope every inch of those poor Lizards before they let 'em into their ships. Gotta make sure they aren't smuggling ginger, you know."

"Well, sure," the technician said. "They'll probably send that Rabotev for the pickup, too. He doesn't care anything about the stuff—though he might care about the money he can bring in for smuggling it."

"There's a thought." Johnson finished getting into the spacesuit. He ran diagnostic checks on the scooter as fast as he could without scanting them. He didn't want to get in trouble out there and need rescuing himself. When the outer airlock door opened he guided the scooter out with the steering jets. The tech gave him a bearing on the crippled Lizard scooter. His own radar identified the target. He fired a longish blast with his rear motor. The *Admiral Peary* shrank behind him.

He used the Lizards' signaling frequency: "I greet you, members of the Race. Are you well? Do you need anything more than transportation? This is a scooter from the Tosevite starship, come to pick you up." Partly by eye and partly by radar, he decided when to make the burn that would bring him to a halt near the Lizard craft in difficulties.

"We thank you, Tosevite. Except for engine failure, we are well." The Lizard who'd answered was silent for a moment, probably pausing for a rueful laugh. "These things are not supposed to happen. They are especially not supposed to happen when you Big Uglies can make fun of us for bad engineering."

"Yours is better than ours, and everyone knows it." Johnson peered ahead. Yes, that was a scooter of the sort the Race built. "Nobody's engineering is perfect, though. We already know that, too."

"You are generous to show so much forbearance," the Lizard replied. "Were our roles reversed, we would mock you."

"If you like, you may think of me as laughing on the inside," Johnson said. "Meanwhile, why not leave your scooter and come over to mine once I kill my relative velocity? I will take you back to my ship. Your friends can pick you up at their convenience."

"It shall be done, superior sir," the Lizard said. By the way the two members of the Race handled themselves as they pushed off from their disabled craft, they were experienced in free fall. Johnson put one of them in front of him and one behind, so as not to disturb his scooter's center of mass too much.

As he burned for the *Admiral Peary,* he made the same sort of remark he had with the technician: "They will fumigate you before they let you back on any of your own ships." His passengers were silent. They would have been silent if they were laughing, too. He looked at each of them in turn. Laughing, they weren't.

10

Jonathan Yeager was glad his father had talked the Race into letting him and the rest of the American delegation come along to Preffilo for the imperial audience, and not only because a dust storm filled the air in Sitneff with a brown, gritty haze. The humans had been to a lot of places on Home, but not to the imperial capital. Except for the trip to the park near the South Pole, Jonathan had been less impressed than he'd expected. If you'd seen one Lizard city, you'd damn near seen them all. They varied among themselves much less than American towns did.

Figuring out why wasn't hard. Cities in the USA were only a few centuries old, and showed wildly different influences of geography and culture. Cities here on Home differed one from another in geography. In culture? Not at all. They'd all been part of the same culture since long before modern man took over from the Neanderthals. They'd all been improved and reworked time and again, and they all felt pretty much the same.

Preffilo wasn't like that, anyhow. Jonathan had expected a bustling imperial capital, something on the order of London in Victoria's day or Moscow when he went into cold sleep. But Preffilo wasn't like that, either. Home had its bureaucrats, its males and females who ran things, and they came to the imperial capital to hear their sovereign's wishes. They didn't make a swarming mess out of the city, though. And the reason they didn't was simple: the Emperor didn't want them to.

In a way, Preffilo was like Kyoto in the days when the Emperor of Japan was a figurehead and the shogun ran things. It preserved the way things had been a long time before (here, a long, long, *long* time before), back when what was now only symbolic had been real.

Stretching Earthly comparisons, though, went only so far. The Emperor here was no figurehead. He'd never been a figurehead, not—so far as Jonathan knew—throughout the whole long history of the Race. Most Emperors tempered their authority with common sense. It was a strong custom that they should. The Race respected custom more than any humans, even the Japanese, did. But there were occasional exceptions scattered through the Lizards' history, some glorious, others— rather more—horrible. If an Emperor wanted to stir things up, he could.

Along with feeling like the beating heart of a power greater than any Earth had ever known, Preffilo also felt *old.* Even to the Lizards, for whom everything within the scope of written human history seemed no more antique than month before last, their capital felt old. Some Englishman had earned immortality of a sort by calling vanished Petra *a rose-red city half as old as time.* (It was immortality only of a sort, for nobody bothered to remember the rest of the poem these days, or even the Englishman's name.)

There were similar poems about Preffilo in the language of the Race. The differences were twofold. For one thing, Preffilo wasn't just half as old as time. It had been a going concern for thousands of years before Home was unified. In those days, mammoths and cave bears must have seemed about as likely to inherit the Earth as skulking human beings. And, for another, Preffilo wasn't a vanished city. It was still a going concern, and looked forward to the next hundred thousand years with only minimal changes.

Geography, again, played a role in that. The Race's capital happened not to lie in earthquake country. Only how well a building was built said how long it would stay up. The Lizards commonly built very well. Along with the palace, a fair number of structures in Preffilo were supposed to be older than the unification of Home, going back to what the Race called ancientest history. Jonathan was hardly in any position to disagree with what the guide told him.

The humans' guide here was a male named Jussop. Jonathan liked him better than Trir. He didn't seem to take questions as personal affronts, the way she sometimes did. Of course, not many folk came to see Sitneff; the tour guide business there was underdeveloped. Things weren't like that in the capital. Lizards, Rabotevs, and Hallessi all visited here. Humans? They might be out of the ordinary, but Jussop would accommodate them.

Once they were settled in their hotel, he took them to the mausoleum where urns holding the ashes of eons' worth of past Emperors were on display. Jonathan wasn't sorry to escape the hotel. The Race had tried to keep its guests comfortable, but it hadn't done the best job in the world. The rooms back in Sitneff were a lot more inviting. Considering how much they left to be desired, that wasn't good news.

Even the little bus that took them from the hotel to the mausoleum had seats that fit human backsides worse than those on the bus in Sitneff. Jonathan grumbled, but in English. His father might have been diplomacy personified. Ignoring the miserable seats, Sam Yeager asked Jussop, "How did you arrange for us to have a private viewing of the mausoleum? I hope we do not inconvenience too many males and females who want to commune with the spirits of Emperors past."

"Well, you must understand I did not personally make these arrangements, Ambassador," the guide replied. Sam Yeager's title seemed natural in his mouth, though except in historical fiction it had fallen out of the Race's language not long after the unification of Home. Jussop went on, "His Majesty's government does wish to extend you every courtesy. You must also understand it is not, perhaps, strictly a private viewing."

"What does that mean?" Karen asked sharply, before Jonathan could. "It was supposed to be."

Jussop made a vaguely conciliatory gesture. "You will not be swarmed with these others who seek to commune with spirits of Emperors past. The other superior Tosevite is right about that, never fear." He left it there, in spite of other questions from the rest of the Americans.

The bus rounded a corner and silently stopped. The questions stopped at the same time. "That's amazing," Jonathan whispered. The rest of the humans stared as avidly as he did. If you had set the Parthenon in the middle of an enormous Japanese garden, you might have created a similar effect. The mausoleum didn't really look like the Parthenon, but it had that same exquisite simplicity: nothing in excess, and everything that was there perfect without being ostentatious. The landscaping, with open ground, stones of interesting color and shape, and a few plants strategically placed and intriguingly trimmed, came a good deal closer to its Earthly counterpart.

"Lovely," Sam Yeager said to Jussop. "I have seen pictures, but pictures do not do it justice. For some things, only being there will do."

"That is a truth, Ambassador," the guide replied. "It is an important truth, too, and not enough folk realize it. We walk from here. As we go along the path, the view will change repeatedly. Some even say it improves. But the walk to the mausoleum is part of the experience. You are all capable of it? . . . Good."

It was somewhere between a quarter mile and half a mile. The path—made very plain on the ground by the pressure of who could say how many generations of feet—wound and curved toward the entrance. Every so often, Jussop would silently raise a hand and wave to signal that they had come to a famous view. The perspective did change. Did it improve? Jonathan wasn't sure. How did you go about measuring one magnificence against another?

And then, when they'd drawn close to the mausoleum, the Race proved it could make mistakes to match any mere humanity ever managed. A hiss from behind made Jonathan look back over his shoulder to see what was going on. A horde of reporters and cameramales and -females hurried after them on the path like a swarm of locusts. Some of the Lizards with cameras wore wigs, which seemed not just ridiculous but—here—a desecration. "Is this building not marvelous?" one of the reporters shouted.

"Is it not inspiring?" another demanded.

"Does it not make you seek to reverence the spirits of Emperors past?" a third yelled. The closer they came, the more excited and vehement they got.

A fourth reporter said, "Tell me in your own words what you think of this mausoleum." Then, without giving any of the Americans a chance to use their own words, the Lizard went on, "Do you not feel this is the most holy, most sacred site on four worlds? Do you not agree that nowhere else is the same combination of serenity, power, and awe-inspiring beauty? Would you not say it is unmatched in splendor, unmatched in grandeur, unmatched in importance?"

"Get them out of here," Tom de la Rosa told Jussop, "before I pick up one of these sacred rocks and bash in their heads—assuming they have any brains there, which does not seem likely."

Before the guide could do anything, the reporters and camera crews had caught up with the humans. The reporter who wanted to put words in everyone's mouth thrust his—or possibly her—microphone in Jonathan's face. "I will not comment about the mausoleum, since I have not yet been inside," Jonathan said, "but I think *you* are unmatched in rudeness, except possibly by your colleagues."

"I am the ambassador," his father said, and the archaic word seemed to have some effect even on the jaded reporters. Sam Yeager went on, "My hatchling speaks truth. We did not come to this place for publicity. We came to see what is here to see, and to pay our respects to your beliefs even if we do not share them. Will you kindly have the courtesy and decency to let us do that—undisturbed?"

"But the public needs to know!" a Lizard shouted.

"This is not a public matter. It is private, strictly private," Jonathan's father said. "And if you do not go away, the protest I make when I have my audience with the Emperor will be most public indeed."

Jussop had been quietly speaking into a handheld telephone. The Race's police were most efficient. No more than two or three minutes went by before they hurried up to escort the reporters away. "Come on, come on," one of them said. "The Big Uglies do not want you around. This is not a traffic accident, where you can ask bloodthirsty questions of some poor male who has just lost his best friend."

Spluttering protests, the reporters and camera crews reluctantly withdrew. Most reluctantly—some of them kept shouting inane questions even as the police pushed them away from the Americans. "I apologize for that, superior Tosevites," Jussop said. "I apologize with all my liver. I did not think it would be so bad."

Maybe he was telling the truth, maybe he wasn't. Short of making a worse scene, the Americans couldn't do much about it now. Major Frank Coffey said, "Let us just go on, then, and hope the moment is not ruined."

It turned out not to be. The only reason it turned out not to be was that the mausoleum was wonderful enough inside to take the bad taste of the reporters out of Jonathan's mouth—and, by what he could see, from everyone else's, too. Tau Ceti's buttery light poured through windows and glowed from granite and marble. Urns of Hellenic simplicity and elegance but not of a shape any human potter would have chosen held the last remains of a couple of thousand Emperors. The sequence was spotty before Home was unified; it seemed to be complete after that.

Nobody said anything for a long time. People wandered where they would, looking, admiring. Even footfalls rang monstrously loud here. Because the Americans were representatives of an independent country, they had special permission to take pictures inside the mausoleum. Permission or not, no one touched a camera. It would have profaned the place. Karen quietly squeezed Jonathan's hand. He nodded. Not even the memorial to Washington, D.C., in Little Rock had affected him like this. Whatever the many differences between mankind and the Race, the Lizards understood majesty.

Sam Yeager paused outside the imperial palace to admire the grounds. They were landscaped with the same spare elegance that informed the gardens surrounding the imperial mausoleum. He turned to Atvar, who as his sponsor walked one neat pace behind him and to his right, and who had stopped at the same time as he had. "I hope you will not be angry if I tell you that these grounds remind me of something the Nipponese might do," Sam said.

The fleetlord made the negative gesture. "I am not angry, for the same thing has occurred to me. I think you would do better, though, not to make this comparison to the courtiers within."

That made Sam chuckle. "No doubt you speak truth. I suppose they would say the Race had the idea first, and that too would be a truth."

"Indeed it would. These grounds have been more or less as they are for a very long time, even by the standards of the Race—much longer than all of Tosevite history put together," Atvar said. "And now, shall we proceed?"

"One moment, if you please," Sam said after glancing at his watch. "I left the hotel early so I could gawk a bit before the ceremony starts. We have time. I will not disgrace the United States by being late." When he was playing minor-league ball—in a vanished century, in a vanished time that had not known the Lizards—he'd never once missed the train or the bus to the next town. Half of getting anywhere in life was simply showing up on time.

Atvar also wore a watch. Like every other Lizard timepiece Sam Yeager had ever seen, his was digital. Their style had started a fad among humans for the same kind of watches, and even for clocks. Yeager was old-fashioned. He went right on wearing a watch with hands (even if this one had been made for Home's day, which was about an hour and a quarter longer than Earth's, and for keeping time by tenths).

But that was a small thing. The palace in front of him was anything but. Unlike most of the Race's buildings, it had been designed when those within had to worry about their safety, and it looked the part. Sam wouldn't have wanted to attack it with anything short of an armored division. Where the grounds looked Japanese, the palace seemed more Russian than anything else. He supposed the onion domes topping some of the gray stone towers put that thought in his mind. But the palace wasn't really Russian, any more than the mausoleum was really a match for the Parthenon. Those were just comparisons his human mind groped for. The Race's architecture had its own logic, and not all of it followed anything he was used to.

He looked at his watch again, then gathered himself. "I am ready," he said. "It is time. Let us go on."

On they went. The entry door was made of some flame-colored, tiger-striped wood truly unearthly in its beauty. It had been polished till it shone. The ironwork of the hinges and latch looked massive enough to stop a charging elephant. Sam laughed at himself. This door might have been built to stop a great many things, but elephants weren't one of them.

The great portal silently swung open. Herrep, the protocol master, stood just inside. Sam took a deep breath. He'd faced up to presidents. He'd faced up to hard-throwing kids who'd stick one in your ear just because they had no idea where the lousy ball would go once they let loose of it. And he could damn well face up to this snooty Lizard.

He took one more deep breath, then crossed the threshold. As soon as he did, he assumed the posture of respect. He had to work to keep from laughing again. *I'm an old man. I must look like a real idiot crouched down here with my butt in the air.* No air conditioning, either, not even what passed for it among the Lizards. Sweat rolled off him.

"You may rise," Herrep said.

"I thank you." Sam's back creaked as he got to his feet. "In the name of the people of the United States, in the name of the President of the United States, I thank you. I come in peace. In the name of peace, I convey my folk's greeting to the Emperor, and wish him good health and many years."

"In his name, I thank you, and I accept the greeting in the spirit in which you offer it," the protocol master said. "Now, if you would be so kind as to follow me . . ."

"It shall be done," Sam said. Remote-control cameras on the ceiling and the wall swung with him as he moved: no baying swarm of cameramales and -females here, as there had been at the mausoleum. Sam was old enough to remember the ballyhoo days of the 1920s. They had nothing on what the Lizards had done there.

Herrep led him past an elderly female who sat with a basin of water and a scrubbing brush: the imperial laver. Then the protocol master walked past another female, just as ancient, this one with a fancy set of body paints: the imperial limner. Sam sketched the posture of respect to each of them in turn without fully assuming it. They both returned the gesture. He recognized them as important parts of the imperial court; they recognized him as someone who did not require their services. It was a quiet compromise, and one that did not show how much argument lay behind it. Proper compromises seldom did.

After leaving the imperial limner behind a bend in the corridor, Herrep paused for a moment. "We are not on camera here," he said. "I just wanted to tell you, researching this ceremonial was endlessly fascinating. I believe the Emperors of ancientest days would recognize what we do here. It might not be exactly what they were used to seeing, but they would recognize it."

"I am glad to hear you say so," Yeager replied politely. "It is also not too different from the ceremonies we use on Tosev 3."

Herrep waved that aside, as if of no account. That was, no doubt, how he felt about it. To him, Big Uglies were barbarians, and how could what barbarians did among themselves matter to a civilized male? The answer to that was simple: it began to matter when the barbarians grew too strong for a civilized male to ignore. And that was what had happened here.

"Shall we proceed, then?" the protocol master said.

"We can hardly stop now. Males and females would talk," Sam answered. Herrep's eye turrets swung sharply toward him. Sam Yeager only waited. He wasn't surprised to discover that the protocol master had no idea what to make of levity, even of the mildest sort. Herrep pointed forward. Sam made the affirmative gesture. As soon as he turned the next corner, he knew he would be back on camera.

Knowing this was all part of a fancy charade did not, could not, keep awe from prickling through him. The audience chamber was designed to make anyone of any species coming before the Emperor feel small and unworthy. The eons-dead males and females who'd done the designing had known their business, too. Up near the shadow-filled ceiling, a small flying thing chittered shrilly. Long colonnades of shining stone drew the eye up and drew it on toward the throne at the far end of the hall.

A courtier appeared before Sam. He carried on a staff an American flag. Data transmissions from Earth meant the Race knew what the Stars and Stripes looked like. As Sam and the flagbearer walked down the aisle toward the throne, a recording of "The Star-Spangled Banner" blared out. No doubt Lizard commentators would be quietly explaining to their audience what the strange music meant.

Atvar had said that the banners displayed in the audience hall belonged to empires extinguished by *the* Empire here on Home, on Rabotev 2, on Halless 1—and on Earth. Yeager recognized the Mexican flag, and the Australian, and the Brazilian, and the Chinese. He could not stop to look for and look at others.

Spotlights gleamed from the gilded throne—or was it solid gold? They also gleamed from the Emperor's gilded chest and belly. Sam thought that was funny. No doubt the Lizards found human royal regalia just as ridiculous.

Two large Lizards—they came up past the middle of his chest—in plain gray body paint stepped out to block his path. They were imperial guards: an ancient survival in an empire where no one had tried to assassinate a sovereign in tens of thousands of years. Like the Swiss Guards who protected the Pope, they looked as if they still knew how to fight, even if they didn't have to.

"I come in peace," Sam assured them. They drew back.

Yeager advanced to the end of the aisle, just in front of the throne. The spotlights on the 37th Emperor Risson made his all-gold body paint glow. That might have awed any Lizard who came before him. It didn't do much for Sam one way or the other. He assumed the special posture of respect reserved for the Emperor, there on the stone smoothed by uncounted tens of thousands of males and females of the Race, the Rabotevs, and the Hallessi who'd done the same thing on the same spot.

From the throne, the Emperor said, "Arise, Ambassador Sam Yeager."

"I thank you, your Majesty," Sam replied, and again rose creakily to his feet. "I bring peaceful greetings from my not-emperor and from the males and females of the United States. Our hope is for trade, for mutual prosperity, and for mutual respect."

"May this be so," Risson said. "It has been a very long time since an independent ambassador came before an Emperor of the Race."

"Everything changes, your Majesty," Sam said. "Some things change quickly, some very slowly. But everything changes."

Most members of the Race would have argued with him. Change here happened at a pace to make a snail into a bullet. It was seldom visible within the course of a single lifetime. For the Lizard in the street, that meant it might as well not have happened at all. But appearances deceived.

"Truth," Risson said simply. Yeager was relieved the Emperor knew what he was talking about. Risson went on, "One thing I hope will never change, though, is the friendship and peace between your not-empire and the Empire."

"Your Majesty, that is also my fondest hope." Sam got to try out an emphatic cough for all the Lizards across the planet who might be watching.

"Excellent," the Emperor replied. "So long as there is good will on both sides, much can be accomplished. I hope to converse with you again on other occasions, Sam Yeager of the United States." Risson had been rehearsing, too; he pronounced the name of Sam's country as well as any Lizard could.

And he spoke the words of dismissal as smoothly and politely as anyone could have. Yeager assumed the special posture of respect once more. This time, he could rise without waiting for permission. The flagbearer preceded him up the aisle, away from the imperial throne. The audience was over.

Risson had more personality than he'd expected. The gold paint and all the ceremonial hemming in the Emperor made him seem more a thing than an individual. Plainly, making any such assumption about Risson would be rash. Despite the role he played, he was very much himself.

"I thank you for your help," Sam quietly told the Lizard who'd carried the Stars and Stripes.

"Ambassador, it was my privilege," the Lizard replied, which might have meant that he was proud to have played a role, no matter how small, in history—or might have meant someone had told him to carry the flag and he'd done it.

He peeled off where he had joined the American. Yeager continued into the bend in the corridor where, Herrep had assured him, he was not being filmed. The protocol master waited for him there. "I congratulate you, Ambassador," Her-rep said. "Your performance was most satisfactory."

"I thank you," Sam answered. Not splendid or magnificent or brilliant or anything like that. Most satisfactory. He nodded to himself. Under the circumstances, and from such an exacting critic, it would definitely do.

Kassquit watched Sam Yeager's audience from a hotel room in Preffilo. She had not come to the imperial capital with the delegation of wild Big Uglies, but separately. She did not want her audience with the 37th Emperor Risson to be seen as merely an afterthought to that of the American ambassador. It probably would be—she was, after all, a Big Ugly herself, even if not a wild one—but she wanted to distance it as much as she could.

She studied the ambassador's performance with a critical eye. Since he represented an independent not-empire, the ceremony was somewhat different for him. He did more than well enough, remembering his responses and acting with dignity. He also seemed unaware that billions of eyes would be upon him, here on Home and then on the other worlds fully ruled by the Empire and on Tosev 3. He surely wasn't, but seeming that way was all that mattered.

She hoped she would be able to bring off such an unaffected performance herself. She remembered hearing that Sam Yeager, when he was younger, had been an athlete of some sort. Perhaps that gave him an edge in seeming natural, for he would already have appeared before large audiences.

Let me not disgrace myself, Kassquit thought. *Spirits of Emperors past, show all the worlds that I truly am a citizen of the Empire.* She was not used to the idea of prayer, but it seemed more natural here in Preffilo than it ever had before. After all, the remains of the past Emperors were here. Surely their spirits would linger here as well.

She visited the mausoleum a few days after the American Tosevites had done so. The guide, a male named Jussop, said, "We had a little trouble with the wild Big Uglies. Some reporters got their livers all in an uproar when it came to asking questions. That will not happen with you."

"I am glad to hear it," Kassquit answered. She recognized

the need for publicity every now and again, but faced the prospect without enthusiasm. Having had no privacy whatever as a hatchling and young adult, she jealously clung to what she'd been able to accumulate since.

With a disapproving hiss, Jussop went on, "Another thing is, those wild Big Uglies thought the mausoleum was handsome and everything like that—they said all the right things— but you could tell it did not *mean* anything to them, the way it is supposed to."

"They have different beliefs," Kassquit said. "They know no better. In a way, I am sorry for them."

"Well, you sound like a proper person, a person with the right kind of attitude," Jussop said. "Come along, then, and I will show you what there is to see."

"I thank you." Kassquit sketched the posture of respect without fully assuming it.

She went into the full posture once she got inside the mausoleum. It might not have meant much to the wild Big Uglies, but it certainly did to her. It was, in fact, the most spiritual moment of her life. Surrounded by the ashes of Emperors past, she also felt surrounded by their spirits. And they seemed to accept her; she seemed to belong there. She might have the body of a Tosevite, but she was part and parcel of the Empire.

Slowly, reverently, she walked from one urn to the next, glancing briefly at the memorial plaque by each. So many sovereigns, so many names . . . Some she knew from history. Some she'd never heard of. No doubt no one but scholars or collectors of trivia would have heard of them. Well, that was fine, too. They were all part of the ancient, magnificent edifice that was the Empire. All of their spirits would cherish her when she passed from this world.

The Americans will never know this certainty, she thought sadly. *Yes, I am sorry for them.*

At last, when her liver was full of peace, she turned to Jussop. "I thank you. I am ready to leave now. This has been the most awe-filled day of my life. I do not see how anything could surpass it."

"You are going to have an audience with the Emperor, are you not?" the guide asked. Kassquit made the affirmative gesture. Jussop said, "In that case, you would do well not to speak too soon."

Kassquit thought about it, then made the affirmative gesture again. "Truth. I stand corrected."

Which counted for more, she wondered as she lay down on the sleeping mat of her hotel room: the spirits of Emperors past or the actual physical presence of the reigning Emperor? She had trouble deciding, but she knew she would be one of the lucky few who *could* decide, for she would soon meet the 37th Emperor Risson in the flesh.

A few reporters did wait outside the imperial palace when she and Atvar were driven up to it. She wondered if it was built like a fortress to hold them at bay. She wouldn't have been surprised. "How does it feel to be the second Tosevite granted an audience with his Majesty?" one of them called as she and her sponsor got out of their car.

"I would rather think of myself as the first Tosevite citizen of the Empire granted an audience with his Majesty," Kassquit answered.

"How did you become a citizen of the Empire?" another reporter asked, while the camera crews came closer and closer.

"I was only a hatchling at the time. You would do better to ask Senior Researcher Ttomalss, who arranged it," Kassquit said. "And now, if you will excuse me, I must proceed. I cannot be late for the audience."

They could not have cared less whether she was late. All they wanted was a story from her. Her being late and being disgraced would make as good a story as her audience. It might make a better one, since another Big Ugly had just come before the Emperor. Sam Yeager was a wild Big Ugly, of course, not a citizen, but would the male or female in the street care? One Tosevite looked just like another, as far as the Race could tell.

She ignored the further shouted questions from the reporters, and walked into the entryway by which she'd been told to go in. An involuntary sigh of relief escaped her when the closing door shut off their queries.

"You did well there," said a male waiting inside.

After reading his body paint, Kassquit bent into the posture of respect. "I thank you, Protocol Master."

"You are welcome. You earned the praise," Herrep replied. "Reporters will eat your life if you give them half a chance—even a quarter of a chance. So . . . are you ready to proceed with your audience?"

"I hope so, superior sir," Kassquit said. "I shall do my best not to embarrass you or myself or Fleetlord Atvar, who lent me so much help."

"I thank you," Atvar said. "But I believe you would have done well without me, too."

Herrep made the affirmative gesture. "I have confidence in you," he said. "I have heard excellent reports of your preparation, and the American ambassador's audience left nothing to be desired. Your species may differ from ours in many ways, but you seem competent. Not knowing your kind, I was hesitant before. Now, though, I see my qualms were as empty as a hatched egg."

He did not seem like a male who said such things lightly. "I thank you, Protocol Master," Kassquit said again.

Herrep's only reply was, "Let the ceremony begin."

Unlike Sam Yeager, Kassquit not only had to come before the imperial laver and limner but counted doing so a privilege. She gave them the ritual thanks. The soap the laver used to remove her everyday body paint was harsh on her soft skin. So was the brush with which the old female rubbed off the last traces. Kassquit would have endured far worse than that to come before her sovereign.

The imperial limner was even older than the laver. She poked with a fingerclaw one of the glands intended to produce nutritive fluid for a Tosevite hatchling. "How am I supposed to get the pattern right when you have these bumps here?" she complained.

That wasn't ritual. It was just ordinary grumbling. Kassquit wondered if she dared answer it. After brief hesitation, she decided she did. "Please do the best you can. I cannot help my shape, any more than you can help yours."

"I do not have this trouble with Rabotevs or Hallessi." The limner heaved a sigh. "Oh, well. Might as well get used to it. I suppose more and more of you Big Ugly things will come see his Majesty." She might have been old, but she was an artist with the brush. Despite Kassquit's shortcomings in shape, the pattern for an imperial supplicant rapidly covered her torso.

"I thank you, gracious female," Kassquit said when the limner finished. That *was* ritual. Getting back to it felt good. She went on, "I am not worthy."

"That is a truth: you are not," the limner agreed, and added an emphatic cough. "You are granted an audience not because of your worth but by grace of the Emperor. Rejoice that you have been privileged to receive that grace."

"I do." Kassquit used her own emphatic cough.

"Advance, then, and enter the throne room."

"I thank you. Like his Majesty, you are more gracious, more generous, than I deserve." Kassquit bent into the posture of respect. The limner did not.

When Kassquit and Herrep paused in a jog in the corridor before she went out into the audience chamber proper, the protocol master said, "Fear not. Your talk with the limner will be edited before it is broadcast. She has done so many of these ceremonies, they have lost their grandeur for her."

"Really? I had not noticed," Kassquit said. Herrep started slightly, then saw the joke and gave her a polite laugh. Kassquit asked, "May I proceed, superior sir?" Herrep made the affirmative gesture, and she stepped out into that vast, shadowed, echoing hall.

For a moment, awe almost paralyzed her. This was where the Empire became *the* Empire upon the unification of Home. This was where the Rabotevs and Hallessi acknowledged the Emperor's sovereignty and made the Empire more than worldwide. And now, in a smaller way, she too was becoming part of imperial history. Of itself, her back straightened. Pride filled her as she walked toward the throne.

She almost gasped when the Emperor's gray-painted guards suddenly appeared out of the shadows and blocked her path. Kassquit gestured with her left hand, declaring, "I too serve the Emperor." The guards silently withdrew. She advanced.

In the spotlight, the Emperor and his throne blazed with gold. Kassquit averted her eyes from the radiance as she assumed the special posture of respect before her sovereign. From above her, the 37th Emperor Risson said, "Arise, Researcher Kassquit."

Her name in the Emperor's mouth! She held the posture, saying, "I thank your Majesty for his kindness and generosity in summoning me into his presence when I am unworthy of the honor." Ritual steadied her, as she'd hoped it would.

"Arise, I say again," the Emperor replied, and Kassquit did. The Emperor's eye turrets swung up and down as he examined her. He said, "I am greatly pleased to welcome my first Tosevite citizen to Home. I have heard that you are very able, which gladdens my liver."

"I thank you, your Majesty," Kassquit said dazedly. No one had told her Risson would say anything like *that*! When he made the gesture of dismissal, she might have invented antigravity, for she did not think her feet touched the floor even once as she withdrew.

Along with the rest of the Americans, Sam Yeager watched Kassquit's audience on television. "She goes through all the rituals of submission you talked them out of," Tom de la Rosa said to him.

"For her, they're all right," Sam answered. "The Emperor's her sovereign. But he's not mine, and I wasn't going to pretend he is."

"Looks like she's got all the moves down pat," Frank Coffey remarked.

Sam nodded. "I'm not surprised. Jonathan and I met her years before we went into cold sleep. She's not quite human, poor thing, but she's plenty smart." He dropped into the Lizards' language for a one-word question for his son: "Truth?"

"Truth," Jonathan agreed. He didn't add an emphatic cough, as Sam Yeager had thought he might. But then, Karen was sitting right there next to him, and wouldn't have appreciated any such display of enthusiasm. As far as Karen was concerned, Kassquit was entirely too human. But Sam had been talking about the way she thought, not the way she was made.

Linda de la Rosa said, "The Emperor paid her a nice compliment there."

"That's the point of the audience," Sam said. "He wants to show everybody—the Lizards here on Home, and eventually

Rabotevs and Hallessi and humans, too—that they're really just one big, happy family. The Race isn't as good at propaganda as we are, but they've got the right idea for that."

"What did you think of Risson, Dad?" Jonathan asked.

"We all right?" Sam asked Major Coffey. Only after Coffey's nod showed electronics were foiling the Race's bugs did he go on, "He impressed me more than I figured he would. Most of what he said was stuff he had to say, but the way he said it made me sit up and take notice. He's got brains, I think. He's not just sitting up there because he's descended from the last Lizard who had the job."

"The succession is about the only place where family ties really matter to the Race, isn't it?" Karen said.

"Looks that way to me," Sam agreed. "The Emperor has his own—harem, I guess you'd call it—of females, and one of the eggs one of those females lays hatches out the next Emperor. And how they go about deciding which egg it is, they know and God knows, but I don't."

He laughed. Back before he went into cold sleep, he'd never worried about how the Lizards dealt with the imperial succession. It hadn't seemed like anything that could matter to him. Which only went to show, you never could tell. He laughed again. It wasn't as if he hadn't already known that. His whole career since the day he met his first Lizard—a slightly wounded prisoner somewhere south of Chicago—had been a case of *you never can tell.*

The door hissed for attention. Sam didn't know about the rest of the Americans, but he missed a good, old-fashioned doorbell. His knees ached as he got to his feet. He wondered if the Lizards were going to complain about the bug suppressor. If they did, he intended to send them away with a flea in their hearing diaphragm. Bugging ambassadors' residences was impolite, even if it happened all the time.

But the Lizard who stood in the hallway wore the body paint of an assistant protocol master. Sam recognized it because it was similar to Herrep's but a little less ornate. "Yes?" he said, as neutrally as he could. "What can I do for you?"

"You are the ambassador? Sam Yeager?" Lizards had as much trouble telling people apart as most people did with members of the Race. If Sam hadn't been the only human on the planet with white hair, the assistant protocol master wouldn't have had a chance.

I ought to dye it, he thought irreverently. But heaven only knew what the Race used for dyes. He made the affirmative gesture. "Yes, I am the ambassador."

"Good. You will come with me immediately."

"What? Why?" Yeager was primed to tell the assistant protocol master that he still had a thing or two—dozen—to learn about diplomacy. You didn't order an ambassador around like a grocery boy.

But he never got the chance, for the female said, "Because you are summoned to a conference by the Emperor."

"Oh," Sam said. A sovereign *could* order an ambassador around like a grocery boy. He gave the only reply he could under the circumstances: "It shall be done."

"What are they up to, Dad?" Jonathan asked in English.

"Beats me. This one isn't in the rules, or not in the part they showed me, anyhow," Sam answered in the same language. "If I'm not back in two days, call the cops." He was joking— and then again, he wasn't. His own government had kidnapped him. It wasn't completely inconceivable that the Race might do the same. If the Race did, though, he was damned if he knew what the humans here could do about it—this side of starting a war, anyhow.

The assistant protocol master hissed. For a bad moment, Sam feared she understood English. Some Lizards here did— even that Rabotev shuttlecraft pilot had. But the female said only, "Please be prompt."

She led Yeager out of the hotel and into a car with darkened windows. No one looking in could see the car held a human. No reporters waited at the curb. None waited outside the imperial palace, either. Sam was impressed again. Whatever this was, it wasn't a publicity stunt.

"This will be a private audience?" he asked the assistant protocol master.

"Semiprivate," the Lizard replied. "And it will be a conference, not an audience. Ceremony will be at a minimum."

"All right. I am sure it is a great honor to be called like this." Sam didn't say whether it was an honor he wanted. That was part of diplomacy, too.

"You are the first ambassador so summoned in more than a hundred thousand years," the assistant protocol master said. The Race hadn't had any independent ambassadors come before it in all that time. Yeager thought about pointing that out, but forbore. Diplomacy again.

He almost laughed when he found the conference room nearly identical to those in the hotel back in Sitneff. All across the USA, such rooms looked about the same. Evidently, that also held true on Home. The walls were a green-brown not far from the color of a Lizard's hide. The table in the middle was too low to be quite comfortable for humans.

There were a couple of chairs more or less made for people in the conference room. Yeager sat down in one of them. A few minutes later, Kassquit came in and took the other. "I greet you, Ambassador," she said politely.

"And I greet you," Sam replied. How many conferences back on Earth had featured a naked woman? Not many—he was sure of that. Jumping out of a cake afterwards, maybe, but not at the conference itself.

When the door opened again, the Emperor came in. His gilding marked him off from his subjects. Kassquit sprang out of her chair and assumed the special posture of respect. Sam followed suit more slowly. He did everything more slowly these days.

"Rise, both of you," the 37th Emperor Risson said. "The reason I called you here was to see whether we could progress toward settling the differences between the Race and the American Tosevites."

He didn't think small. In a sovereign, that was, or could be, an admirable quality. Sam returned to the chair that wasn't quite right for his shape. "I hope we can, your Majesty," he said. "That would be wonderful."

The 37th Emperor Risson turned one eye turret toward him, the other toward Kassquit. "Which of us is outnumbered, Ambassador?" he asked.

"Both of us," Yeager replied. "Two Big Uglies, one male of the Race. Two citizens of the Empire, one American."

"No Emperor has ever been outnumbered by Tosevites before," Risson said. Even though Sam had used the Race's slang for humans, the Emperor was too polite to imitate him.

Risson went on, "And yet, Tosevites have occupied the Race's thoughts, and the thoughts of the Emperors, for a good many years now."

"Well, your Majesty, we have been paying a fair amount of attention to the Race ourselves lately," Sam said in a dry voice.

He wondered whether Risson would catch the dryness. When the Emperor's mouth dropped open in a laugh, Sam knew he had. Matching dry for dry, Risson said, "Yes, I can see how that might possibly be so." The Lizard leaned forward. "And now, can you tell me what you American Tosevites require from the Race, since it has drawn your notice?"

"Yes, I can tell you that," Sam Yeager answered. "I can tell you in one word, as a matter of fact. We want equality."

"Do you not believe you should wait until you have earned it?" the 37th Emperor Risson returned. "Eighteen hundred years ago, when we first discovered your kind, you were savages." He spoke a word of command. A hologram of a knight sprang into being in the air.

Sam had seen that image a thousand times. He was, by now, good and sick of the blond Crusader. "I have never denied that the Race was civilized long before we were," he said. "But that male is long dead, and I sit here on your home planet talking with you, your Majesty. I came here in my not-empire's ship, too."

"If we fought, you would lose," Risson said.

"If we fought, we would hurt you badly," Sam said. "We have been able to hurt you badly for some time now, and grow more able every year. But I thought we were here to talk about peace."

"So we are," the Emperor said. "Equality? Do you truly know what you ask?"

"Yes, your Majesty. I think I do," Sam answered. A Japanese might have understood the demand—might have made the demand—more fiercely. The Empire looked at the USA the way the USA and Europe had looked on Japan when she muscled her way into the great powers. The Japanese weren't white men. They were wogs, nothing else but. After they got strong enough, though, it stopped mattering.

Yeager shook his head in slow wonder. The day after Pearl

Harbor, he'd tried to join the Army and fight the Japs. (Because of his false teeth, the Army turned him down then, though they'd been glad enough to take him when the Lizards came a little more than five months later.) Now here he was, sympathizing with Japan. Life could be very strange.

Kassquit said, "Your Majesty, I understand the Race's pride, the Empire's pride. Do you fully understand the Tosevites' pride?"

"The *Tosevites'* pride?" By the way the 37th Emperor Risson said it, that had never once crossed his mind. Sam wasn't surprised. The Race did look down their snouts at Big Uglies, just as Americans and Europeans had looked down their noses at the Japanese. But Risson went on, "Researcher, it is possible that I do not. I thank you for pointing it out to me."

"I am pleased to serve your Majesty," Kassquit murmured. Sam smiled. Her face didn't show anything, but if that wasn't pride of her own, he'd never heard it.

"Equality. Pride," Risson said, perhaps half to himself, and then, "I am glad I had this talk. It has given me a great deal to think about." That was dismissal: polite dismissal, but dismissal even so. As the Lizards whisked Sam back to his hotel, he found he too had a lot to think about.

Ttomalss was one of the few members of the Race who understood what being a parent involved. That was what all his patient years of raising Kassquit from a hatchling had got him. And now he was going through the part of parenthood that seemed strangest. The hatchling he'd raised had taken wing on her own. Not only had Kassquit enjoyed an audience with the Emperor, but she'd also conferred with him in private.

Because the conference was and stayed private, the male in the street never found out about it. To most members of the Race, Kassquit remained just another Big Ugly. But a female at the imperial court let Ttomalss know. "Are you not proud of what you accomplished?" she asked.

"Yes, I am. Very much so," Ttomalss answered, and broke the connection in a hurry.

It wasn't that he was lying. On the contrary. He *was* proud of Kassquit. All the same, he also felt himself surpassed, and that was an odd and uncomfortable feeling. It wasn't so much that Kassquit had had the audience with the 37th Emperor Risson. Ttomalss saw the propaganda value there. But that Risson had summoned her back to confer . . . Yes, that got under the psychologist's scales.

Ttomalss had never won an imperial audience himself. He didn't particularly expect one. He was prominent, but not that prominent. He thought he might have been worthy of consultation, though. If the Emperor thought otherwise, what could he do about it? Not a thing. Not a single, solitary thing.

Yes, Kassquit had spread her wings, all right. They had proved wider and stronger than Ttomalss ever expected— maybe wider and stronger than his own. He knew Big Uglies often had this experience. He wondered how they stood it without being torn to pieces. It couldn't be easy.

Of course, they had biological and cultural advantages he didn't. They knew such things were liable to happen. Some of them even hoped their hatchlings would surpass them. Under other circumstances, Ttomalss might have admired such altruism. He had more trouble practicing it himself.

To keep from thinking about Kassquit and her triumphs, he telephoned Pesskrag. Getting hold of the physics professor wasn't easy. Returning calls might have been a custom from another world, as far as she was concerned. Ttomalss hoped she was busy in the laboratory, not off to the South Pole with friends. Her messages would follow her either way, of course, but she might be more inclined to answer them if she was working and not out having a good time.

When she didn't call back for two days, Ttomalss began to get not only annoyed but worried. He wondered if something had happened to her. He called her department chairfemale, only to learn that that worthy had just gone into the hospital with a prolapsed oviduct. *Excesses of the mating season,* he thought sourly. No one else in the department seemed to know anything about where Pesskrag was or what she was doing. He wondered if he ought to get hold of the police.

Pesskrag finally did call him the next day. When Ttomalss saw her image in the monitor, he still wondered if he ought to get hold of the police. Her nictitating membranes were swollen and puffy with exhaustion. She looked as if she'd just escaped a kidnapping attempt. She said, "I apologize for being so very hard to reach, Senior Researcher," and then she yawned right in Ttomalss' face.

Seeing that teeth-filled gape of jaw made Ttomalss want to yawn, too. That desire to imitate a yawn was almost a reflex in the Race. Idly, Ttomalss wondered if the Big Uglies had anything similar. That would have to wait, though. It would probably have to wait for years. This, on the other hand . . . "What have you been doing?" Ttomalss asked.

"Experimenting," Pesskrag said, and yawned again. This time, Ttomalss did yawn back. The physicist shut her mouth with an audible snap. She pointed at him. "And it is your fault, too—yours and the Big Uglies'."

"All right. I accept my share of the blame," Ttomalss said. "Do you have any results from your experiments yet?"

"Only very preliminary ones," she answered, and gave forth with another yawn. She seemed on the point of falling asleep where she sat. Gathering herself, she went on, "Full computer analysis will take some time. It always does. Pre-liminary results do suggest that the Big Uglies probably are correct."

"How interesting," Ttomalss said, and Pesskrag made the affirmative gesture. The psychologist went on, "You are the expert in this matter. If the Big Uglies *are* correct, what are the implications?"

"Again, much of this will have to wait for full analysis," Pesskrag replied. Ttomalss impatiently lifted a hand. The psy-chologist opened her mouth again—this time for a laugh, not a yawn. She might have been drunk with weariness as she continued, "But we are going to see some changes made."

"What sort of changes?" Ttomalss asked.

"How should I know?" she said. "Would you judge a hatch-ling's whole career when it is still wet from the juices of its egg?"

Ttomalss did his best to sink his fingerclaws into patience. "Let me ask you a different way," he said. "Is this a matter that will only matter in learned journals and computer discus-sion groups, or will it have practical meaning?"

"Sooner or later, a lot of what is discussed in learned jour-nals and computer groups has practical meaning," Pesskrag said stiffly. But then she relented: "All right. I know what you mean. I would say this will have practical meaning. Just how soon, I am less certain. We will need to confirm what we think we have found, and that too will take some time. Then, assuming we do confirm it, we will have to see what sort of engineering the physics leads to."

"How long do you suppose that will take?" Ttomalss asked.

"Years, certainly. I would not be surprised if it took centuries," the physicist answered. "We will have to be very careful here, after all. Everything will have to be worked out in great detail. We will have to make sure these changes do not disrupt our society, or do so to the smallest possible degree. Deciding what the safest course is will of course be the responsibility of planners, not scientists."

"Of course," Ttomalss echoed. "Tell me one thing more, if you would be so kind: how soon could something like this pass from physics to engineering if those in charge cared nothing for change or disruption?"

"What an addled notion!" Pesskrag said. Ttomalss did not argue. He only waited. She went on, "I cannot imagine the circumstances under which such a thing would be permitted. I certainly hope the males and females in charge of such things are more responsible than you seem to believe."

"If such matters were gripped by the fingerclaws of our males and females alone, I would agree with you," Ttomalss said. "Do please remember the source of your inspiration here, though. Let me ask my question in a different way: what do you suppose the Big Uglies have been doing with the data you are just now discovering?"

"The Big Uglies?" Pesskrag spoke as if she were hearing of Tosevites for the first time. After some thought, she shrugged. "I am sorry, Senior Researcher, but I have not the faintest idea. How matter and energy behave is my province. How these strange aliens act is yours."

"I will tell you how to estimate their behavior," Ttomalss said.

"Please do." The physicist sounded polite but skeptical.

"Make the most radical estimate of possibilities you have the power to invent in your own mind," Ttomalss said. He waited again. When Pesskrag made the affirmative gesture, he went on, "Once you have made that estimate, multiply its capacity for disaster by about ten. Having done that, you will find yourself somewhere close to the low end of Tosevite possibilities."

Pesskrag laughed. Ttomalss didn't. He didn't say anything at all. After a little while, Pesskrag noticed he wasn't saying anything. She exclaimed, "But surely you must be joking!"

"I wish I were," the psychologist said. "If anything, I am not giving the Big Uglies enough credit—or maybe blame is more likely to be the word I want."

"I do not understand," Pesskrag said.

"Let me show you, then. You may possibly have seen this image before." Ttomalss called up onto the screen the picture of the Tosevite warrior the Race's probe had snapped. He said, "Please believe me when I tell you this was the state of the art on Tosev 3 eighteen hundred years ago—eighteen hundred of our years, half that many by the local count."

"Oh. I see," Pesskrag said slowly. "And now . . ." Her voice trailed away.

"Yes. And now," Ttomalss said. "And now several of their not-empires have kept their independence in spite of everything the Race could do. And now they are making important discoveries in theoretical physics before we are. Do you still believe I am joking, or even exaggerating?"

"Possibly not," Pesskrag said in troubled tones. "We would not have made *this* discovery for a long time, if ever. I am convinced of that. So are my colleagues. Even imagining the experiment requires a startling radicalism."

"And the Race is not radical," Ttomalss said. Pesskrag hesitated, then used the affirmative gesture once more. So did the psychologist. He went on, "I need to tell you, I need to make you understand in your belly, that by our standards the Big Uglies are radical to the point of lunacy. If you do not understand that, you cannot hope to understand anything about them. Let me give you an example. During the fighting after the conquest fleet landed, they destroyed a city we held with an atomic weapon—a weapon they had not had when the fighting started. Do you know how they did it?"

"By remote control, I would assume," Pesskrag replied.

Ttomalss made the negative gesture. "No. That is how we

would do it. That is how they would do it now, I am sure. At the time, their remote-control systems were primitive and unreliable. They sailed a boat that travels underwater—one of their military inventions—carrying the bomb into this harbor. When the boat arrived, a brave male on it triggered the bomb, killing himself and the rest of the crew in the process."

"Madness!" the physicist said.

"Yes and no," Ttomalss answered. "Remember, it did us much more harm than it did the Big Uglies. And so they did not count the cost. They have a way of proceeding without counting the cost. That is why I asked where this discovery might go, and how long it might take to get there."

The way Pesskrag's eye turrets twitched told how troubled she was. "I am sorry, Senior Researcher, but I still cannot say for certain. We are going to have to modify a good deal of theory to account for the results of this experiment. We will also have to design other experiments based on this one to take into account what we have just learned. I do not know what sort of theoretical underpinnings the Big Uglies already have. If this was an experiment of confirmation for them, not an experiment of discovery . . . If that turns out to be so, they may have a bigger lead than I believe."

"And in that case?" Ttomalss always assumed the Tosevites knew more and were more advanced than the available evidence showed. He was rarely wrong about that. He did sometimes err on the conservative side even so. Since he was trying to be radical, that worried him. But no member of the Race could be as Radical as a Big Ugly. Realizing that worried him, too.

"I need to do more work before I can properly answer you," Pesskrag said. Her words proved Ttomalss' point for him. That worried him more still. A Tosevite physicist wouldn't have hesitated before answering. And that worried him most of all.

Lieutenant General Healey gave Glen Johnson a baleful stare as the two of them floated into the *Admiral Peary*'s small, cramped refectory. "Too bad sending you down to the surface of Home would kill you," the starship commandant rasped. "Otherwise, I'd do it in a red-hot minute."

"Since when has that kind of worry ever stopped you?" After a long, long pause, Johnson added, "Sir?" He didn't have to waste much time being polite to Healey. As far as he knew, the *Admiral Peary* had no brig. He didn't need to worry about blowing a promotion, either. What difference did it make, when he never expected to see Earth again? He could say whatever he pleased—and if Healey felt like baiting him, he'd bait the commandant right back.

Healey's bulldog countenance was made for glowering. But the scowl lost a lot of its force when its owner lost the power to intimidate. "You are insubordinate," the commandant rasped.

"Yes, sir, I sure am," Johnson agreed cheerfully. "You'd be doing me a favor if you sent me down to Home with the doctor, you know that? I'd be keeping company with a nice-looking woman till gravity squashed me flat. You'd be stuck up here with yourself—or should I say stuck on yourself?"

That struck a nerve. Healey turned the glowing crimson of red-hot iron. A comparable amount of heat seemed to radiate from him, too. He got himself a plastic pouch of food and spent the rest of supper ignoring Johnson.

The meal was a sort of a stew: bits of meat and vegetables and rice, all bound together with a gravy that was Oriental at least to the extent of having soy sauce as a major ingredient. A spoon with a retracting lid made a good tool for eating it.

Johnson did wonder what the meat was. It could have been chicken, or possibly pork. On the other hand, it could just as well have been lab rat. How much in the way of supplies had the starship brought from Earth? The dietitians no doubt knew to the last half ounce. Johnson didn't inquire of any of them. Some questions were better left unanswered.

When he reported to the control room the next morning, Brigadier General Walter Stone greeted him with a reproachful look. "You shouldn't ride the commandant so hard," the senior pilot said.

"He started it." Johnson knew he sounded like a three-year-old. He didn't much care. "Did you tell him he should stay off my back?"

"He has reasons for being leery of you," Stone said. "We both know what they are, don't we?"

"Too bad," Johnson said. "We both know his reasons never amounted to a hill of beans, too, don't we?"

"No, we don't know that," Walter Stone said. "What we know is, nobody ever proved those reasons have anything to do with reality."

"There's a reason for that, too: they don't." Johnson had stuck with his story since the 1960s.

"Tell it to the Marines," said Stone, an Army man.

Since Johnson had been a Marine now for something approaching ninety years, he chose to take umbrage at that—or at least to act as if he did. He got on fine with Mickey Flynn; he and Stone had been wary around each other ever since he involuntarily joined the crew of the *Lewis and Clark.* They would probably stay that way as long as they both lived.

Stone wasn't obnoxious about his opinions, the way Lieutenant General Healey was. That didn't mean he didn't have them. To him, Johnson would always be below the salt, even if they'd come more than ten light-years from home.

Prig, Johnson thought, and then another word that sounded much like it. The first was fair enough. The second wasn't, and he knew as much. Stone was extremely good at what he did. Johnson knew himself to be unmatched at piloting a scooter. No human being was better than Walter Stone at making a big spaceship behave. Johnson had seen that with both the *Lewis and Clark* and the *Admiral Peary.* If the other man had a personality that seemed to be made of stamped tin . . . then he did, that was all.

"Hello!" Dr. Melanie Blanchard floated up into the control room, and Johnson forgot all about Stone's personality, if any. The doctor went on, "I'm making my good-byes. The shuttle-craft will take me down to Home tomorrow."

"We'll miss you," Johnson said, most sincerely. Stone nodded. The two of them had no quarrel about that.

Dr. Blanchard said, "No need to. The doctors aboard will be able to take care of you just fine in case anything goes wrong. They'll do better than I could, in fact. My specialty is cold-sleep medicine, and they tend to people who are actually warm and breathing to begin with."

Johnson and Stone looked at each other. Johnson could see he and the senior pilot shared the same thought. He spoke before Stone could: "We weren't exactly thinking of your doctoring."

"Oh." Melanie Blanchard laughed. "You boys say the sweetest things." She was careful to keep her tone light. She'd been careful for as long as Johnson had known her. He was sure he and Stone weren't the only men aboard the *Admiral Peary* who thought of her not just as a physician. He was pretty sure nobody'd had the chance to do anything but think. The ship was big enough to fly from Earth to Home, but not big enough to keep gossip from flying if there were anything to gossip about. If anything could travel faster than light, gossip could.

No gossip had ever clung to Dr. Blanchard. Johnson wished some would have; it would have left him more hopeful. He smiled at her now. "You think we talk sweet, you should give us a chance to show you what we can do."

"Take no notice of him," Walter Stone told the doctor. "I agree with everything he says, but take no notice of him anyway." Johnson looked at Stone in surprise. Flynn wouldn't have disdained that line. Johnson hadn't thought Stone had it in him.

Melanie Blanchard laughed. "Flattery will get you—not as much as you wish it would," she said, the laugh taking any sting from the words. "Being noticed is nice. Having people make nuisances of themselves isn't." She held up a hand. "You two haven't. I could name names. I could—but I won't."

"Why not?" Johnson asked. "If you do, we'll have something interesting to talk about."

"You'll be talking about me behind my back whether I name names or not," she said. "I know how things work. If you were going down there, they'd talk about you, too. Oh, not the same way—you aren't women, after all—but they would. Will you tell me I'm wrong?"

"Sure," Johnson said. "If we were going down to Home, they'd talk about *him*." He jerked a thumb at Walter Stone.

"Me? Include me out," Stone said.

"Thank you, Mr. Goldwyn," Johnson said. Stone grimaced. He looked as if he hadn't wanted to give Johnson even that much reaction. Johnson turned back to Melanie Blanchard.

"Five gets you ten your shuttlecraft pilot won't be a Lizard. Rabotevs and Hallessi don't care about ginger."

"They don't care about taking ginger," she said. "I bet they'd like the money they'd make for smuggling it—you've said that yourself. Of course, we haven't got any ginger to give them, so it doesn't matter."

"Of course," Johnson and Stone agreed together.

Johnson didn't know for sure whether the *Admiral Peary* carried ginger, whatever might his suspicions. He could think of three people who might: Sam Yeager, Lieutenant General Healey, and Walter Stone. He didn't ask the senior pilot. He was sure of one thing—the Lizards thought the humans' starship was full of the stuff from top to bottom.

Come to think of it, Dr. Blanchard might know the truth about the herb, too. Had she just come out and told it, or was she operating on the principle that the Race might have managed to bug the *Admiral Peary* and needed to be told what they already wanted to hear?

She said, "I'm going to go below and make sure I've got everything I'll need down on the surface of Home. In the meantime . . ." She glided over to Johnson and gave him a hug and a kiss. Then she did the same thing with Walter Stone. And then, waving impartially to both of them, she was gone.

"Damn," Johnson said: a reverent curse if ever there was one. The memory of her body pressed against his would stay with him a long time. At his age, sex wasn't such an urgent business as it had been when he was younger. That didn't mean he'd forgotten what it was all about.

Walter Stone looked amazingly lifelike as he stared toward the hatchway down which Dr. Blanchard had gone. He shook himself like a man coming out of cold water. "Now that you mention it, yes," he said.

"Lot of woman there," Johnson observed. "I'd run into somebody like that, I probably would have stayed married and stayed on Earth."

He waited for Stone to point out that he'd be dead now in that case. The other man didn't. He only nodded.

With a sigh, Johnson added, "Of course, you notice she isn't married herself. Maybe she's not as nice as she seems."

"Or maybe she thinks men are a bunch of bums," Stone

said. "You've got an ex-wife. Maybe she's got an ex-husband or three."

That hadn't occurred to Johnson. Before he could say anything, a Lizard's voice spoke from the radio: "Attention, the Tosevite starship. Attention, the Tosevite starship. We have launched a shuttlecraft to pick up your physician. This is the object you will discern on your radar."

Sure enough, there it was: a blip rising from Home toward the *Admiral Peary.* "We thank you for the alert, Ground Control," Stone said in the language of the Race.

A little later, the shuttlecraft pilot's face appeared in the monitor. As Johnson had guessed, he was (or perhaps she was) a dark-skinned, short-faced Rabotev with eyes on stalks, not in turrets. "I greet you, Tosevites," the pilot said. "Please give me docking instructions."

"Our docking apparatus is the same as the Empire uses," Stone said. He had, no doubt, almost said *the same as the Race uses,* but that wouldn't do with a Rabotev. "Lights will guide you to the docking collar. Call again if you have any trouble."

"I thank you," the shuttlecraft pilot replied. "It shall be done."

The Rabotev was certainly capable. He—she?—docked with the *Admiral Peary* with a smooth efficiency anyone who'd flown in space had to respect. With the duty in the control room, Johnson couldn't give Dr. Blanchard another personal good-bye. He sighed again. Memory wasn't a good enough substitute for the real thing.

☆ **11** ☆

Karen Yeager was starting to get to know the Sitneff shuttle-craft port. It wasn't as familiar to her as Los Angeles International Air- and Spaceport, but she had some idea which turns to take to get to the waiting area. The shuttlecraft port also had one great advantage over LAX: she was a VIP here, not one more cow in a herd. She and Jonathan got whisked through security checkpoints instead of waiting in lines that often doubled back on themselves eight or ten times.

"I could get used to this," she said as they took their seats in the waiting area. If the seats weren't perfectly comfortable—well, they wouldn't be here very long.

Her husband nodded. "Could be worse." In English, he added, "Only drawback is everybody staring at us."

"Well, yes, there is that," Karen said. She too felt as if every eye turret in the waiting area were turned her way. That wasn't quite true, but it wasn't far wrong, either. Lizards attracted much less attention at airports back on Earth. Of course, there were millions of Lizards on Earth, and only a handful of humans here on Home.

She shifted in her seat. No, it wasn't comfortable at all. Back on Earth, some airports had special seating areas for the Race. Karen didn't plan on holding her breath till the Lizards returned the favor here.

A shuttlecraft landed. Its braking rockets roared. The Race was better at soundproofing than mere humans were, but she still felt that noise in her bones. Three Lizards got out of the shuttlecraft. Their friends or business colleagues or whatever they were greeted them when they came into the terminal.

After glancing at his watch, one of the Americans' guards said, "Your fellow Tosevite should be grounding next."

"I thank you." Karen and Jonathan said the same thing at the same time. As couples who've been married for a long time will, they smiled at each other.

The guard was right. The groundcrew at the port moved the last shuttlecraft off the flame-scarred tarmac. A few minutes later, another one landed a hundred yards off to the left. This time, the pilot who emerged was a Rabotev. The Lizards in the waiting area paid no particular attention to him (or her); they were used to Rabotevs. But they exclaimed and pointed when Dr. Melanie Blanchard came down the landing ladder after him.

"She's moving as if she's got the weight of the world on her shoulders, isn't she?" Jonathan said.

"She probably feels that way, too," Karen said. "She's been out of gravity for quite a while now."

Dr. Blanchard trudged across the concrete toward the waiting area. Lifting each foot and then putting it down took an obvious effort. A Lizard scurried into the shuttlecraft and came out with a pair of suitcases of Earthly manufacture. He hurried after the human. Carrying her luggage wasn't very hard for him. By the way things looked, it might have killed her.

Turning to the guards, Karen said, "Can you please keep the reporters away from her? She is too tired to answer questions right away."

"It shall be done, superior sir." The Lizards still had as much trouble telling humans' sexes apart as people did with them. Karen couldn't get too annoyed, though, because the guards did do what she'd asked. The reporters shouted their questions anyhow, but they had to do it from a distance.

Dr. Blanchard waved to them. That took effort, too. "I am glad to be here," she called in the language of the Race. She didn't look or sound glad. She looked as if she wanted to fall over. And when she got to Karen and Jonathan, she sank into one of the seats by them regardless of how uncomfortable it was. "Whew!" she said. Sweat gleamed on her face. "Can I rest for a little while before we go on?"

"Sure," Jonathan said. "How are you?"

"Hammered," she answered frankly. "I remember I used to take gravity for granted. What I don't remember is how. I feel like I've got two great big football players strapped to my back."

"You'll get used to it again," Karen said.

Melanie Blanchard nodded. Even that looked anything but easy for her. "I suppose I will," she said. "In the meantime, though, I'm a shambling wreck—only I can't shamble for beans, either."

One of the Lizard guards came up to her and bent into the posture of respect. "I greet you, superior female. Shall we now return to the hotel where your species stays?"

"I thank you, but please let me rest first," she replied. "I have been weightless for a very long time, and I need a little while to get used to being back in gravity again."

The guard made the affirmative gesture. "As you say, so shall it be." He went back to holding off the reporters.

"I wish it were, 'As you say, so shall it be,'" Dr. Blanchard said in English. "Then I'd tell myself everything was fine, and it would be—'physician, heal thyself.' I'd love to. Only problem is, I can't."

"When we do go back to the hotel, you can stretch out on a sleeping mat," Karen said. "Then come over to our room, if you've got the energy. We've got ice cubes. As near as I can tell, they're the only ones on the planet." She spoke with what she hoped was pardonable pride.

"And we've got the Race's equivalent of vodka," Jonathan added. "What they use for flavored liquor is amazingly nasty—of course, they think the same thing about scotch and bourbon. But this is just ethyl alcohol cut with water. You can drink it warm, but Karen's right—it's better cold."

"Vodka over ice sounds wonderful. Getting up off the sleeping mat and going to your room . . ." Dr. Blanchard laughed ruefully and shook her head. "Maybe if I say pretty please, you'll bring me a drink instead?"

"That might be arranged," Karen said.

"We'll be friends forever if it can," Melanie Blanchard said. "Is the car back to the hotel very far from here?"

"About as far as it was from the shuttlecraft to where you are," Jonathan answered.

The doctor heaved herself to her feet. She wobbled for a moment. Jonathan held out his arm. She took it, but then steadied and stood on her own. To the guard, she called, "I am ready to go to the car now, as long as I do not have to move too fast."

"Set whatever pace you please, superior female," the Lizard replied. "Our orders are to accommodate ourselves to your needs."

"I thank you. That is very kind." Dr. Blanchard dropped back into English to tell Karen and Jonathan, "Why don't you lead the way? You know where you're going, and I haven't got the faintest idea."

"I don't think we'll lead. I think we'll go one on each side of you, in case you need propping up," Jonathan said. That turned out to be a good idea. Dr. Blanchard walked as if she were a St. Bernard plowing through thick snow. Home's gravity field seemed harder for her than drifts after a blizzard were for a dog. The Lizard carrying her suitcases followed, while the guards spread out on all sides.

When they reached the car, she sank down into a seat with a groan of pleasure. "This one even fits my butt," she said happily. "All the time in the world on an exercise bike up there isn't the same as ten minutes in gravity, believe you me it isn't."

She seemed a little better by the time they got back to the hotel. That relieved Karen; she'd feared the doctor would be in no shape to take care of herself, let alone anybody else. But Melanie Blanchard walked more easily than she had before, and even paused briefly to talk with reporters waiting outside. She might need a while to do a thorough job of adjusting, but it seemed likely she would.

When the humans went into the lobby, Karen's father-in-law met them with an expression she found hard to fathom. Was it grim, or was he swallowing a belly laugh? He sounded grim when he said, "We have a . . . situation here."

"What's up, Dad?" Jonathan asked.

"A cleaning crew went into your room while you were out meeting Dr. Blanchard," Sam Yeager answered. "They were fooling with the rats' cages. We've had an escape."

"Oh, dear," Melanie Blanchard said. "I was hoping to do some work with them."

"That's not the problem," Karen said, which was, if anything, an understatement.

Sam Yeager nodded. "No, it's not. The Race told us they'd raise holy hell if anything of ours got loose on Home. We promised on a stack of Bibles we wouldn't let the critters loose—and we didn't."

"They don't care what they've done to Earth's ecology," Karen said. "They claim that's not their worry. But if we return the favor, it's a different story. How many got away?"

"Eight or ten, I think," her father-in-law answered. "You'll know better than I do when you see your room, because you have a better notion of how the cages were laid out. But as of now, I'm open to suggestions."

"Why should we worry?" Karen said. "It's the Lizards' own fault. If they want to catch the rats, tell 'em to buy a cat."

Everybody laughed. Dr. Blanchard said, "Excuse me," and sat down on the edge of a table. That was probably more comfortable than perching in what the Race used for chairs. The table was flat, not curved the wrong way for a human fundament.

"They are setting traps," Sam Yeager said. "I have no idea how much good that will do. Can they find something rats really want to eat? Can the rats find something to eat and drink on their own?" He spread his hands. "I don't know about that, either. Stay tuned for the next exciting episode, and we'll find out."

"They'll have vermin of their own." Dr. Blanchard looked and sounded happier sitting down. "They'll have creatures that hunt vermin, too. The next interesting question may be whether those creatures feel like hunting rats."

"Befflem, tsiongyu, and their wild cousins, I'd expect," Jonathan said. "Yes, that could be mighty interesting. Befflem have turned into godawful nuisances back on Earth. There'd be a sort of poetic justice if rats did the same thing here."

"I doubt the Race would appreciate it," his father said dryly. "But they can't blame us for the escape. They did it themselves. I wouldn't want to be one of those cleaners right now, not for all the tea in China I wouldn't."

"If I wake up and find *myself* nose to nose with a rat, I'll probably scream," Karen said.

"If I wake up and find *myself* nose to nose with a rat, I'll probably scream, too," Sam Yeager said. "That'll scare the rat out of a year's growth, but I don't suppose it'll do much else."

"If anything Earthly can establish itself on Home, I'd bet on rats," Dr. Blanchard said thoughtfully. "They've evolved to live anywhere and eat anything. And they've evolved to live in cities alongside people. They might feel right at home here on Home."

"That occurred to me, too," Sam Yeager said. "I don't know if it's fully occurred to the Race yet. You have to have lived on Earth for a while before you understand just what pests rats can be, and there aren't that many Lizards here who have."

"If they don't get it now, they will pretty soon," Karen said.

"They may, anyhow," Jonathan said. "Maybe rats *can't* make it here. Maybe they won't find anything to eat. Maybe the exterminators will get 'em. Maybe something local will think they're delicious."

"Maybe," Dr. Blanchard said. "But nobody's ever gone broke betting on rats."

Senyahh held a strange creature by the tail. The creature was deceased. The bandage on the kitchen chief's other hand said it hadn't perished without putting up a fight. "What *is* this horrible thing, Exalted Fleetlord?" Senyahh demanded.

Atvar eyed it with a grim sense of recognition. The tail was long and naked and scaly, which made the animal seem a little less alien. The creature's body, though, was soft-skinned and furry. Its head had the flaps of skin Tosevite creatures used to concentrate sound waves for their hearing diaphragms. The head was, at the moment, somewhat the worse for wear.

"What did you hit it with?" Atvar inquired.

"A frying pan," Senyahh answered. "It bit me anyhow. And I almost missed it. It is as fast as a beffel, but I never saw anything like it before. What is it?"

"I believe it is called a *rat*." Atvar pronounced the unfamiliar word as well as he could. "It is one of the escaped Tosevite animals. Congratulations on killing it."

"Oh, one of those horrible creatures," Senyahh said. "I

thought they would be bigger and uglier and go around on their hind legs."

"This is quite ugly enough, in my opinion," Atvar said. "And I meant those congratulations. We believe the house-keeping staff let eight or ten *rats* escape. This is the first one of which we have seen the slightest trace."

Senyahh swung the dead beast by the tail. "It will cause no more trouble," she declared, a hunter's pride in her voice.

"This one will not, no," Atvar agreed. "But what of the others? What if they breed? What if they flourish? On Tosev 3, they are major pests. Do they have any diseases or predators here? I have my doubts."

The head of the kitchens had her own concerns. She asked, "Are they good to eat?"

"I believe so, but the Big Uglies do not commonly consume them." Atvar pointed to the female. "You are welcome to experiment on your own, but do not, *do not*, serve the results of your experiment to the American Tosevites—not even to Karen Yeager, with whom you quarreled." He used an emphatic cough. "The cleaning crew that freed the *rats* has been sacked. If you give the Americans *rat* to eat, you will envy their fate. Do you understand me? Do I make myself plain?"

"Yes, Exalted Fleetlord. It shall be done. Or rather, it shall not be done, no matter how tempting it may be. You have my word on it," Senyahh declared.

"All right. Take the miserable creature away, then," Atvar said. "I am more familiar with these animals than I ever wanted to be."

After the kitchen chief left his room, Atvar said several pungent things. He did not blame the female who had killed the rat. She was only doing her job. The cleaning crew . . . Had it been up to him, they would have got worse than the sack. Their foolishness had endangered all of Home. Yes, Atvar knew more about rats than he wanted to. He knew much more about rats than any male or female who'd never been to Tosev 3.

He hadn't wanted the animals to come down to the surface of Home in the first place. He'd wondered if the Big Uglies had brought them here to wage their own brand of ecological warfare. He'd warned. He'd fussed. And he'd been undone not by the American Tosevites but by the hotel's housekeeping staff. They'd decided they felt like playing with the animals. Now everyone would have to pay for it.

Then Atvar made the negative gesture. The Big Uglies wouldn't have to pay a thing. They might have got what they wanted. He couldn't prove that, no matter how it seemed to him. But it hadn't been their fault. That was only too obvious.

He tried to look on the bright side of things, an exercise with which he'd had frequent practice on Tosev 3. Species from Home were making the Big Uglies' planet more livable, more comfortable, for the Race. The Tosevites couldn't make that sort of arrangement here on Home. All they could do was make nuisances of themselves. That, unfortunately, was an exercise with which *they'd* had frequent practice on Tosev 3.

As if to prove the point, Sam Yeager chose that moment to telephone him. "I greet you, Ambassador," Atvar said resignedly. "What can I do for you this morning?"

"I would like to request permission to bring down another ten *rats* from the *Admiral Peary* to replace the ones that were allowed to escape," the ambassador replied.

"Oh, you would?" Atvar said.

"Yes, please," Sam Yeager said. "They are very useful to us because they let us test foods easily and conveniently. We were sorry to lose the ones the housekeepers released."

He made sure that got under Atvar's scales. Atvar couldn't do anything about it, either, because he'd earned the right. The fleetlord tried to stall: "I cannot decide this on my own. I will have to consult with local authorities."

"Back on Tosev 3, Fleetlord, we call that *passing the buck*." Sam Yeager used three words of English. "It means seeking to evade responsibility. That is not like you. I hope to hear an answer very soon. Good day." He broke the connection.

Atvar hissed angrily. Some of the anger was aimed at the Big Ugly, the rest at himself. The ambassador was right: he did seek to evade responsibility for letting more *rats* come down to the surface of Home. Unlike the males and females who had never left this planet, he had a pretty good notion of how damaging the Tosevite creatures could be. Letting more of them come here, even caged, was not in the Race's best interest.

But if it was in the Big Uglies' best interest . . . Atvar hissed again. Sam Yeager had come right out and said it was. The only way the Race could reject the ambassador's request would be to insult the American Tosevites and possibly to jeopardize their health. Atvar did not care to be responsible for that. He did not think any other male or female would care for it, either.

He wondered if he ought to make some calls anyhow, on the off chance he was wrong. His hand shaped the negative gesture. That struck him as pointless—and also as *passing the buck,* as Sam Yeager had put it.

Instead of telephoning members of his own species, he called the Big Ugly back. "Why, hello, Fleetlord. I greet you," Sam Yeager said, as politely as if they hadn't been sparring not long before.

"And I greet you," Atvar replied, trying—with indifferent success, he feared—to match that politeness.

"What can I do for you now?" the American Tosevite asked, still smoothly. "Does this have to do with what we were talking about a little while ago, or is it about something else?"

"The same topic." Atvar respected the Big Ugly for coming to the point, and respected him even more for doing so in an inoffensive way. "You have permission to bring ten more of these *rats* here. They are to remain caged at all times, as their predecessors were to have done."

"I thank you, Fleetlord, and I do understand the restrictions," Sam Yeager said. "We agreed to them from the beginning. We have not violated them, either. It was your own folk who freed the *rats* still—I suppose—in this hotel."

Atvar didn't like that *I suppose.* He also wasn't happy that Sam Yeager was completely correct. With luck, the housekeepers who'd got more curious than they should have would have trouble finding work anywhere for the rest of their lives. Atvar would have loved to fine or imprison them, but they hadn't done anything criminal—so the local prosecuting attorney assured him. Whether they'd done anything damaging was a different question, worse luck.

"Will any special Tosevite bait attract these creatures?" the fleetlord asked. "If so, we will use it in our traps."

"Our traditional bait is *cheese,*" Sam Yeager answered.

Then he had to explain to Atvar what cheese was. The explanation left the fleetlord as much revolted as enlightened. The idea of milk was disgusting enough to the Race. The idea of deliberately letting it rot before eating it was worse. Trying to suppress nausea, Atvar inquired, "Do you have any of this stuff closer than the Tosevite solar system?"

"We have none here on the surface of Home—I know that," the American ambassador said. "There may be some aboard the *Admiral Peary*. If you like, I will ask the ship to send some down with the *rats* if there is."

"I thank you," Atvar said. "I thank you very much, in fact. That would be generous of you, and greatly appreciated."

Sam Yeager sounded wryly amused: "Unlike a certain species I could name, we do not deliberately seek to disrupt the ecology of another world."

"You have made your political point, Ambassador." Atvar, on the other hand, sounded sour. "We have sought to make Tosev 3 more Homelike and friendly to ourselves. You have done the same on certain parts of the planet."

"Never so drastically as your folk are doing," the Tosevite ambassador said. "And we know better now. You brag about the Race's long spell of civilization, but it does not seem to have made you sensitive to ecological concerns."

The Race was chiefly interested in shaping ecologies to its own needs. It had done so on Rabotev 2 and Halless 1, and was still busy doing it on Tosev 3. Sam Yeager's attitude made Atvar less proud of that than he might have been.

He did not intend to let the wild Big Ugly see what he was thinking. Bitter experience on Tosev 3 had taught him that revealing anything to the Big Uglies was a mistake. They never took such revelations as simple confidences, but always as signs of weakness. And they exploited such signs for all they were worth. Would Sam Yeager do the same? Atvar did not doubt it for an instant.

"We see nothing wrong in manipulating the environment for our own benefit," the fleetlord said. "That is one of the hallmarks of an intelligent species, would you not agree?"

"Manipulation is one thing, destruction something else altogether," the American ambassador insisted.

"Very often, the difference lies in the point of view," Atvar said. "Or will you tell me I am mistaken?" He waited. Sam Yeager used the negative gesture. Atvar respected his honesty. He went on, "This being so, you accuse us of being strong enough to make ourselves comfortable on a new world. To this I must plead guilty."

"Who gave you the right to do that?" Sam Yeager asked.

"We gave it to ourselves, by being strong enough to do it," Atvar replied.

Yeager studied him. "You say these words, Fleetlord, and you seem pleased with them. And I suppose you have reason to be pleased with them—now. But I tell you this: when I hear them, they are to me nothing to be pleased with. They are a judgment on your kind, a judgment on the whole Race. And judgments like that have a way of being fulfilled."

Atvar stared at him in astonishment. He sounded more like one of the mullahs who'd made life so unpleasant for the Race on Tosev 3's main continental mass than the highly civilized being the fleetlord knew him to be. "Do you threaten me, Ambassador?" Atvar demanded.

"No, Fleetlord," the wild Big Ugly replied. "I do not threaten you if I say the sun will rise tomorrow, either. I simply observe."

"If that is the sort of observation you are going to make, you would do better to keep it to yourself," Atvar said coldly.

"As you wish, Fleetlord," Sam Yeager said. "But have you not seen that the truth will come and find you regardless of whether anyone points it out to you ahead of time?"

Yes, he did sound like a mullah. "What I have not seen, in this particular instance, is that you are speaking truth," Atvar said. Sam Yeager only shrugged. He spread his hands, as if to say, *You will find out.* Atvar deliberately turned his eye turrets away from those hands. To his annoyance, the American ambassador only laughed—a loud, grating Tosevite laugh.

At supper in the refectory that evening, Jonathan Yeager listened to his father's account of the conversation with Atvar. Sam Yeager was speaking English: "I tell you, I felt like Daniel in the Old Testament. I was doing everything but shouting and waving my arms and yelling, 'Thou art weighed in the balances, and art found wanting.'"

"How did he take it?" Dr. Melanie Blanchard asked.

"He got mad," Sam answered. "I would have got mad, too, if somebody talked to me like that. But I still don't think I'm wrong. If you're that arrogant, it usually comes back and bites you."

"As far as I'm concerned, you handled it just right," Tom de la Rosa said. "What they've done to ecosystems back on Earth is a shame and a disgrace. They'd better not think we're happy about it."

"But now the shoe is on the other foot," Jonathan said. "Now they're worried about rats here, not zisuili and azwaca and befflem and all their plants back on Earth. The shoe pinches more when it's on their foot."

"Oh. The rats." Dad snapped his fingers. "Almost forgot. We do have permission to bring down replacements."

"You insulted Atvar, and you still got away with that?" Frank Coffey said. "Not bad, Ambassador. Not bad at all." He clapped his hands together.

"I didn't insult him till after he'd agreed." Sam Yeager grinned. "Aren't I sly?"

Everybody laughed. Jonathan said, "He didn't change his mind afterwards?"

"Nope," his father answered. "Or if he did, he didn't tell me. If they shoot down the shuttlecraft with the rats in it, then we'll know he was *really* angry." That drew more laughs. Tom de la Rosa hoisted his glass of more-or-less vodka in salute. All the Americans drank.

A couple of tables away, Kassquit sat by herself. Sometimes she joined the other humans when they ate, sometimes she didn't. That seemed to fit her betwixt-and-between nature: stuck between what she'd been born as and what she'd been raised as. Having watched Mickey and Donald grow from their eggs into . . . fair copies of human beings, Jonathan thought he understood that better than most.

He scratched his head, which reminded him he needed to shave it again soon. Was he wrong, or had Kassquit been more standoffish than usual lately? After a moment's thought, he nodded to himself. Unless he was wrong, she hadn't eaten with the Americans since Dr. Blanchard came down from the *Admiral Peary.*

He switched to the language of the Race, calling, "Say, Researcher, will you not come over and eat with us?"

Karen gave him a hard look. He pretended not to notice. This had nothing to do with the fact that he and Kassquit had been lovers up on her starship in the early 1960s. He and Karen hadn't been married yet, or even engaged. They had been going together, though, and his . . . research had almost spelled the end of that. This was just social. Jonathan really meant that. Because of what she was, Kassquit was to a certain degree isolated from everyone around her, humans and Lizards alike. Getting her to mingle wasn't just diplomacy; it also felt like psychotherapy.

As usual, Kassquit's face showed nothing. She might have been joyful, furious, gloomy—you couldn't tell by looking. She said, "I did not think you would want me there, not when you were so busy using your own language."

"We will speak yours if you do join us." That wasn't Jonathan—it was Melanie Blanchard. "We have no problem speaking the Race's language, even if we are a little more comfortable with our own. The familiar is often welcome, especially when one is far from home."

"Well, I suppose that could be a truth, if one had known anything resembling a home in one's past," Kassquit said. "I have concluded that a cubicle in a starship makes an inadequate substitute."

"No doubt you are right," Sam Yeager said, trying to smooth things over. "But if you join us, you may make a closer approach to something homelike than you would with the Race. Or, of course, you may not. But how will you know unless you try the experiment?"

"I do not think I can have a true home either with the Race or with you wild Tosevites," Kassquit said unhappily. "If there were more Tosevite citizens of the Empire—not Tosevites raised as I was, necessarily, but those who live in the Empire's culture despite their species—I might find more in common with them than I do with you or the Race."

"There are probably a fair number of such persons on Tosev 3 now," Jonathan's father said. "This, of course, does you no good at all here."

"Truth," Kassquit said. "And if I were to go back into cold

sleep and seek them out on Tosev 3, who knows how things would change there by the time I arrived? Variability, I think, is the key to Tosevites generally."

That was undoubtedly how humans seemed from the Race's point of view—the one Kassquit naturally adopted as her own. But a lot of Lizards refused to see that changes in the way humans did things could affect them. Kassquit didn't make that mistake, anyhow.

Frank Coffey said, "Do come sit with us, Kassquit."

"You ask me this?" she said. "Are you certain you desire my company?"

Major Coffey made the affirmative gesture. "Of course I am," he said, and added an emphatic cough.

Kassquit's face still showed nothing. But she brought her plate to the table where the Americans were sitting. "Do you mind if I ask what you were talking about before?" she inquired.

"Mostly about the *rats* that were released here, and about bringing more of them down from the *Admiral Peary* so we can go on testing food," Jonathan answered.

"Is that still necessary?" Kassquit asked. "Have the animals found many problems for you? I had no such aids when I woke up on Home, but I have eaten the food here and I am still well."

"We would rather not take chances we do not have to take," Dr. Melanie Blanchard said. "We would also rather avoid unpleasant surprises if we can. The Race can eat almost anything we Tosevites can eat on our world, but who would have expected the trouble ginger causes them?"

That seemed only common sense to Jonathan. He thought Kassquit would make the affirmative gesture; she was nothing if not logical. Instead, she let out an audible sniff. "How likely is this?"

Dr. Blanchard shrugged. The motion seemed easier and less of an effort than it would have right after she came down to the surface of Home. Little by little, she was getting reacquainted with gravity. She said, "Who knows? What is certain is that we would like to prevent it if possible. Do you object? Few members of the Race would, not on those grounds. The Race is more cautious than we Tosevites are."

"I do not object on the grounds of prudence," Kassquit said. "I do wonder if one of the reasons you wanted to bring *rats* here was in the hope that they might escape and establish themselves. That would let you pay the Race back for ecological changes caused by creatures from Home on Tosev 3."

"Not fair," Jonathan said. "If *we* had released the *rats,* you could accuse us of that. But members of the Race did it. We kept the animals caged. We were going to keep them caged, too. We know just what sort of pests they can be."

Kassquit considered that. At last, reluctantly, she did use the affirmative gesture. "From you, Jonathan Yeager, I will believe this."

"Why would you not also believe it from Dr. Blanchard?" Jonathan asked. "She knows much more about these things than I do."

"Yes—why?" Melanie Blanchard echoed. "I mean you no harm, Researcher. In fact, I would like to examine you, if you do not mind. I probably know less about medicine as a whole than a physician from the Race, but I know a lot more about being a Tosevite. I might find something a physician from the Race would miss."

Had Jonathan been in Kassquit's shoes, he could have been grateful for that offer. If she got sick, what could the Lizards do about it? Not much, not that he could see. A human doctor, though, had to know how people ticked.

But Kassquit looked at Dr. Blanchard as if she'd just suggested vivisection. "I thank you, but no," she said. "The Race's techniques have always been adequate up until now."

"No doubt," Dr. Blanchard said. "But then, you have never been very ill, have you? You are still young, and you were never exposed to most Tosevite diseases. You are now beginning to reach the age where your body will show the wear it has accumulated. More regular examinations are a good idea."

"I thank you, but no," Kassquit repeated. "I will continue in my present way of doing things until it shows itself to be unsatisfactory."

"This is not a good idea," Jonathan told her. "Technicians maintain computers and other machines. You should also maintain yourself."

"And so I do. And so I shall—with the Race," Kassquit said. "If this proves inadequate, as I told you, I shall consider other options."

Her determination was unmistakable. Jonathan scratched his head again. It didn't add up—not to him, anyway. But Karen whispered in his ear in English: "She doesn't like the doctor."

Jonathan blinked. That hadn't occurred to him. Once his wife pointed it out, though, it seemed so obvious that he wondered why it hadn't. He also wondered why Kassquit didn't like the doctor. They'd hardly had anything to do with each other.

Frank Coffey asked, "Would a member of the Race want a Tosevite doctor?"

"Certainly not." Kassquit didn't use an emphatic cough, but her tone of voice left no doubt about how she felt.

"All right, then." Coffey was unperturbed. "Why would you want to use a physician of a different species when you have another choice?"

Kassquit looked at him. "You too would recommend that I trust myself to Dr. Blanchard?" She had a little trouble pronouncing the name, but less than a Lizard would have. When Coffey made the affirmative gesture, Kassquit sprang to her feet. "You are all against me!" she exclaimed, and stormed out of the refectory. The only reason she didn't slam the glass door behind her was that its mechanism wouldn't let her.

"What was that all about?" Linda de la Rosa asked in English.

"Is it me she doesn't want to deal with, or is it because I'm a human being and not a Lizard?" Melanie Blanchard asked in the same language.

I think it may be you, went through Jonathan's mind. He glanced at his wife, and would have bet she was thinking the same thing. Neither he nor Karen said anything, though. They might have been wrong. Even if they turned out to be right, who could guess why Kassquit felt the way she did? She was a riddle—sometimes, Jonathan suspected, even to herself.

His father said the same thing a different way: "Kassquit takes some getting used to. It's not her fault she is the way she is, God knows. I do think she's got a good heart."

Jonathan nodded. Karen let out a distinct sniff. Among the Americans, though, she found herself outvoted. *Snoutcounting,* Jonathan thought. He was amused, but knew neither his wife nor Kassquit would have been.

Kassquit wanted nothing more than to avoid the wild Big Uglies. She wished she could have nothing to do with them. They did not understand her, they mocked her. . . . So it seemed from her point of view, at any rate.

No matter what she wanted, though, she had to deal with the Tosevites. She'd been brought to Home to deal with them. No matter how revolting they acted, she couldn't just walk away from her work with them. More than once, she thought, *If I were a female of the Race, I could.* Being what she was, she had fewer choices. She could not abandon the wild big Uglies. Half the time—more than half the time—members of the Race couldn't tell her apart from them anyway.

She tried to avoid them at mealtimes. That didn't always work, because they didn't all eat at the same times every day. She stayed as far from them in the refectory as she could. That probably would have sufficed with the Race, whose members were sophisticated enough to recognize a good sulk. The Big Uglies, though, were as nosy as so many befflem, and just about as enthusiastic.

Because the American Tosevites usually ate breakfast early, Kassquit had started eating late. She didn't like that, because she got hungry. She did it even so. But when Frank Coffey came in for a snack, he found her there. She hoped he would take care of what he wanted and leave her alone.

He didn't. He came over to the table where she was sitting and said, "May I join you?"

"If you insist," Kassquit said coldly.

A male of the Race would have taken the hint. She would have thought the Big Ugly might also; she hadn't been subtle. But Coffey just said, "I thank you," and sat down. Then he asked, "Why are you angry at Dr. Blanchard? What has she done to you? How could she have done anything to you? She just got here."

"I am not angry at Dr. Blanchard!" Kassquit said—angrily. The wild Big Ugly sitting across the table from her did not respond. He just let the words hang in the air. They seemed so manifestly false, Kassquit felt she had to modify them: "She has not done anything to me—not directly."

"Ah?" Yes, Frank Coffey was like a beffel that had taken a scent. "What has she done indirectly, then?"

"You ought to know." Kassquit did not bother to hide the bitterness she felt.

"I do not have any idea what you are talking about," the American Big Ugly said.

"A likely story," Kassquit said. "You do not need to lie to me, you know. That is nothing but a waste of time on your part."

"Lie about what?" Coffey asked. "You have completely confused me. I am sorry, but that is a truth. I wish I believed in the spirits of Emperors past. I would swear by them to convince you. What oath would you like me to use?"

"For a truthful person, oaths do not matter. For one who is not truthful, they do not help," Kassquit snapped.

The Big Ugly made the affirmative gesture. "That is well said. You have known me since I came down to the surface of Home. I have been here most of a year now. What is your opinion of me? Have you believed me to be a truthful person, or one of the other sort?"

"Up until now, I believed you to be truthful," Kassquit said. "Your behavior here, though, makes me doubt it very much."

"What behavior here? What have I done?" Frank Coffey asked. "As I say, I confess that you have baffled me."

Kassquit took a deep breath. "Your pretending not to know why I dislike Dr. Blanchard and what grievance I hold against her."

"I do not know that. I do not understand it." He used an emphatic cough. "That is a truth, Kassquit. For the sake of your own health, I think you would be wise to let her examine you. If you do not like her, I can see how you might be reluctant, but I do not know why you do not like her. She seems friendly enough, and she is a capable physician."

"Friendly enough. *Friendly* enough!" Kassquit all but spat the words. "Yes, I can see why you would say so. I certainly can."

"And what is that supposed to mean?" Did the American Tosevite make his interrogative cough sound sarcastic, or was that just a trick of Kassquit's overheated imagination? She recognized the possibility, but she didn't think so.

"As if you do not know," she said furiously. "You all got along fine down here without the services of a physician. None of you has needed a physician." Coffey started to say something—probably that you never could tell when someone *would* need a physician. She overrode him: "The real reason she came down to Home is obvious enough."

"Not to me," he said. "You had better tell me what this 'real reason' is."

"Why, to provide you with a mating partner from among your fellow wild Big Uglies, of course," Kassquit said.

Frank Coffey stared at her. Again, he started to say something. Kassquit didn't stop him this time. He stopped himself—by starting to laugh. And once he started, he could not stop. Raucous Tosevite mirth poured out of him. Kassquit thought it would never end. Finally, after what seemed like forever, the torrent slowed.

"I see nothing funny about it," Kassquit said in icy tones.

That only started the wild Tosevite laughing again. This time, the fit did not last quite so long. But when it ended, tears left bright streaks down Coffey's cheeks. "Oh, dear," he said, wheezing and gasping for breath. "I think I hurt myself. But I could not help it. I am very sorry, Kassquit, but you packed an impressive amount of misunderstanding into one sentence there."

"I do not believe I misunderstood anything," Kassquit said. "You had better explain to me why you think I did."

"It shall be done, superior female." Coffey began ticking off points on his fingers. "Dr. Blanchard did *not* come down here to become my mating partner. The two of us have *not* mated. We have never discussed mating, not even once. We have not made advances at each other. I have no idea whether she would be interested in mating with me. If I had to guess, I would doubt it. I know for a fact that I am not particularly interested in mating with her."

"So you say," Kassquit jeered.

Coffey nodded. Then he used the Race's affirmative gesture. "Yes. So I say. And it is a truth, too. I see you *are* a citizen of the Empire. You certainly do not understand how things work among wild Big Uglies. And I ought to ask you a question of my own: why do you care about what Dr. Blanchard and I may or may not do?"

"Because I was hoping to mate with you myself," Kassquit answered. Had she been raised as a wild Big Ugly, she might not have been so blunt. But then, had she been raised as a wild Big Ugly, she would have been different in so many ways, the question wouldn't have arisen in that form.

"Oh," Frank Coffey said, and then, "Oh," again in an altogether different tone of voice.

When he didn't say anything else for some little while, Kassquit asked, "Well? What do you think of that?"

He wasn't laughing any more. Kassquit didn't think she could have borne it if he were. Despite her prodding, he didn't answer right away. When he did, he spoke slowly and thoughtfully: "I think you know I would be lying if I said the idea of mating with you had never crossed my mind."

"I had *thought* that, yes," Kassquit agreed. "That was why I was so upset when Dr. Blanchard came down from your starship. She is one of your kind in a way that I cannot be. I thought—I feared—she would make a better partner for you."

The brown Big Ugly did laugh then, but, Kassquit judged, much more at himself than at her. He said, "I have trouble believing anyone named Melanie could make a good partner for me—but to understand that you would need to know the American *Gone with the Wind,* not the Race's book of the same name."

Kassquit *didn't* understand; the American *Gone with the Wind* meant nothing to her. She did finally start to believe that he wasn't eager to mate with Dr. Blanchard. And if he wasn't . . . "This idea had crossed your mind, then, you say? And what did you think of it when it did?"

"Obviously, part of me liked it very much—but that part has never been what anyone would call fussy," he replied. No matter how far removed from the affairs of wild Big Uglies she was, she had no trouble figuring out what he meant. He went on, "The rest of me was not nearly so sure—is not nearly so sure—that would be a good idea. You are isolated from our ways of doing things. I was very much afraid I would be taking advantage of you."

"Why?" Kassquit asked in genuine puzzlement. "Would we not both take pleasure from this? How is that more advantageous to you than to me?"

"Things are more complicated than that—or they often are, anyway, back on Tosev 3," Coffey said. "We do not have a mating season the way the Race does, and emotional attachments between partners are usual with us. In fact, mating among us does not just spring from previously existing emotional attachments. The act of mating, the pleasure of mating, giving pleasure to another in mating, helps *cause* emotional attachments. Do you have any idea what I am talking about?"

"Oh, yes," Kassquit said softly. She remembered all too well how bereft she had felt when Jonathan Yeager left the Race's starship and returned to the surface of Tosev 3, and how devastated she was when she learned he was making a permanent mating arrangement with Karen Yeager. That had seemed like betrayal—nothing less. If Frank Coffey were to abandon her for a wild Tosevite female, too . . . She shoved that thought aside and made the affirmative gesture. "I understand exactly what you mean."

Her tone must have carried conviction, for Coffey did not argue with her any more. He just said, "Knowing all this, you would still wish to go forward?"

"I would," she answered. "I may end up unhappy. I understand that. But I feel empty now. Next to empty, even unhappy does not seem so bad."

"That . . . makes more sense than I wish it did," the wild Big Ugly said. He nodded—again, Kassquit thought, more to himself than to her—and laughed quietly. "In that case, superior female, there is an English expression that seems to fit here: my place or yours?"

Kassquit needed a moment to figure out what that meant, but only a moment. "Why not mine?" she said.

They rode up the elevator together. Kassquit hung the PRIVACY, PLEASE sign in front of her room. Then Frank Coffey said, "Wait. I had better make sure you do not become gravid. Let me get a sheath. I will be back right away."

He took a little longer than Kassquit had expected, but not long enough for her to complain when he returned. It had been a long time since she lay down with a male Tosevite, but she remembered what to do. And he knew how to stimulate her. He turned out to know better than Jonathan Yeager had. At first, that surprised her. Then she realized Jonathan Yeager must have been almost as inexperienced as she was. And then she stopped caring about such things.

Afterwards, Frank Coffey was careful to keep his weight on his elbows and knees and not on her. "The Race's language does not have words for this," he said. " 'I thank you' is not nearly strong enough." He kissed her. "I hope that says something."

"Oh, yes." Kassquit felt near tears. She hadn't realized how much she'd missed this. "*Oh,* yes." She used an emphatic cough. It didn't seem adequate, either. She kissed him this time. A member of the Race wouldn't have understood. He seemed to.

Ttomalss knew he had too many things going on all at the same time. He kept waiting to hear whether Pesskrag and her fellow physicists were making progress in their experiments. He monitored what the wild Big Uglies were up to, and reported back on that to Atvar. The retired fleetlord also seemed to be running in too many directions at once.

"*Rats!*" he said to Ttomalss out of a clear sky. "We have got to find those creatures and get rid of them, Senior Researcher, or this entire world will suffer on account of them."

"Truth," Ttomalss agreed. "Maybe you should clear everyone out of this hotel and fumigate it, the way you would for pests of our own."

"I have discussed this matter with Sam Yeager," Atvar said unhappily. "He is not enthusiastic about moving. He is not obstructive—he will relocate if we insist. But he is not enthusiastic. Diplomacy is, or can be, a nuisance. I hesitate to displace him if I can accomplish my goals by other means."

"How many more rats have you recovered?" Ttomalss asked.

Even more unhappily, Atvar answered, "One after that which Senyahh killed. And it was not captured here in the hotel but in the park across the way. That is another reason I hesitate to displace the wild Big Uglies: it may already be too late."

It may already be too late. Ttomalss didn't respond to that. It was the Race's usual lament when dealing with the Tosevites. Here, it was liable to be true in more ways than Atvar had meant it.

After leaving the fleetlord's suite, Ttomalss left a message for Pesskrag. The physicist took her time about calling him back. Maybe she was busy experimenting. Maybe she'd finished experimenting but had nothing new to tell him. Maybe she was just sick and tired of him. Till she did eventually answer, he couldn't say.

What with everything else that was going on, Ttomalss hardly had the chance to turn an eye turret toward Kassquit every now and then. Her room in the hotel was not electronically monitored, as were those of the wild Big Uglies (not that those microphones had yielded much; the American Tosevites appeared to have antimonitoring electronics of their own). Not only was she assumed to be on the Emperor's side, but she had also strongly objected to being monitored back on the starship orbiting Tosev 3.

Without that continuous monitoring, Ttomalss had to rely on what he observed when he and Kassquit were together. He would have done better observing one of his own species. He knew that. However acculturated Kassquit was, her basic responses remained Tosevite, and alien.

One morning at breakfast, he said, "You will correct me if I am wrong, but do you not seem more cheerful than usual?"

Kassquit paused to take a bite of aasson. After she swallowed, she answered, "You might say so. Yes, superior sir, you might say so."

"Good. I am glad to hear it." Ttomalss was also glad he had seen it. "Do you happen to know why you are more cheerful?" If she did, he would do his best to make sure conditions did not change for her.

"Yes, superior sir, I do know," Kassquit said, and said no more.

Trying not to show the exasperation he felt, Ttomalss asked, "Do you mind telling me why you are more cheerful than usual? Is it by any chance the aftereffect of your audience with the Emperor?" He felt proud of himself for being so insightful.

And he felt correspondingly deflated and annoyed when Kassquit used the negative gesture. "No, superior sir, I do not mind telling you," she replied. Ttomalss brightened, hoping that was why she'd used it. But she went on, "Though I am and always will be proud the Emperor received me, I must confess that that is not the main reason why I am more cheerful these days."

Once more, she didn't elaborate. This time, Ttomalss did let out an irked hiss. "I ask again: why are you, then?"

"Do you truly want to know?" Kassquit inquired—perhaps ironically, though that did not occur to the psychologist till later. At the time, he just made the affirmative gesture. Kassquit said, "Very well, then, superior sir—I will tell you. I am more cheerful than usual because I have begun mating again. I find it much more satisfactory and much more enjoyable than self-stimulation. Do you have any other questions?"

Ttomalss didn't. He finished breakfast in a hurry and left the refectory as fast as he could. That didn't take him far enough away. He left the hotel, too, and strode at random down the streets of Sitneff. He hoped immersing himself in his own kind would take the bad taste of Tosevites off his tongue.

Even Kassquit! Or was it, especially Kassquit? She had everything the Race and the Empire could give her. She had a reasonable rank and more than adequate wealth. She even had the privilege of an imperial audience, which Ttomalss himself did not enjoy. And what did she value? What made her happy—made her so happy, Ttomalss couldn't help but notice? Tosevite mating behavior—and that even after she was warned against it!

It hardly seemed fair.

She is a Big Ugly after all, Ttomalss thought sadly. *In spite of everything we have done for her, she is still nothing but a Big Ugly.* That was a liverbreaking notion. Air whooshed out of his lung in a long, sad sigh. She was as much a citizen of the Empire as any Tosevite could possibly be, more than any other Tosevite was likely to be for thousands of years, if ever. But her biology still drove her in ways no member of the Race could fully understand.

Or was that true? Back on Tosev 3, there was a small but growing number of males and females who used ginger to simulate the Big Uglies' year-round sexuality. Some of them had even adopted the Tosevite custom of permanent exclusive mating bonds. To most of the Race, they were perverts, even more depraved than the Big Uglies themselves. But might they not one day serve as a bridge between the Empire on the one hand and the wild and stubbornly independent Tosevites on the other? And might Kassquit not be part of that same bridge?

Ttomalss could dare hope. But Tosev 3 had dashed the Race's hopes again and again ever since the conquest fleet arrived. In a Tosevite legend, hope was the last thing to emerge from a box of troubles. The legend didn't say what happened next. Ttomalss' guess was that the troubles leaped on new-hatched hope and devoured it.

An automobile warning hissed at him. He sprang in the air in surprise and skittered back to the curb. He'd walked off against traffic, something he never would have done if he hadn't been so gloomy and distracted. *If that car had smashed me, it would have been your fault, Kassquit.*

The audience with the Emperor made her proud. But mating with a wild Big Ugly (and with which?—she hadn't said) made her happy. Ttomalss wondered if he ought to see which American Tosevite seemed unusually happy these days. But would a wild Big Ugly show it the way Kassquit did? The Americans were used to mating in a way she wasn't.

She would rather be pleased in this way by her own kind than honored by the Empire. A stray beffel beeped at Ttomalss. He was usually kind to animals, but he made as if to kick this one. The beffel had been a stray for a while. It recognized that gesture, and scrambled away on its short, strong legs before the blow could connect. He wouldn't have actually kicked, but the beffel couldn't know that.

My superiors will have to hear of this, but how am I sup-

posed to put it in a report? Ttomalss wondered. *How can I phrase it so that it does not reflect badly on Kassquit—or on me?* Atvar would understand. He'd seen how things were on Tosev 3, and he had some notion of normal Tosevite sexual behavior. But most of the so-called experts here on Home had no direct experience with Big Uglies. They would be offended or disgusted—or maybe they would be offended *and* disgusted. Ttomalss didn't want Kassquit punished for what was, to her, normal behavior. That wouldn't be fair.

He stopped, so abruptly that a female in a blue wig that looked nothing like any real Big Ugly's hair almost ran into him. She said something rude. He ignored her, which made her say something even ruder. He still paid her no attention. He stood there on the sidewalk in front of a meat market. *If Kassquit's behavior is normal for her, why are you getting so upset about it?*

Because she took me by surprise. No, the answer there wasn't very hard to find, was it? The Race did not approve of surprises or respond well to them—another reason Tosev 3 had caused it so many headaches. Males and females liked to know how everything worked, how all the pieces fit together, and exactly what their part was in the bigger scheme of things.

To the Race, Big Uglies sometimes seemed to act almost at random. Part of that was because Tosevites worried less about the future than did members of the Race. If they saw present opportunity, they grabbed with both hands. And their sexual and family ties made them do things inexplicable to the Race.

"Sexual ties." Ttomalss muttered the words out loud. A male going by kept one eye turret on him till he passed out of sight. Again, the psychologist hardly noticed, though in other circumstances he would have been mortified to draw so much attention. He still didn't know with which American male Kassquit had mated.

Only four candidates. Two of them had permanent mating contracts with females. Ttomalss had learned, though, that Big Uglies respected such contracts only imperfectly. And Jonathan Yeager had been Kassquit's first partner, all those years before. Would they have returned to each other?

Or would Tom de la Rosa have forsaken his partner? As

an ecological expert, de la Rosa was formidable. In sexual terms . . . Ttomalss had no idea what he was like in sexual terms.

He knew just as little about Major Frank Coffey in that context. Dark brown Big Uglies had a formidable sexual reputation among paler ones, but that reputation appeared to be undeserved. Under the skin, Tosevite subspecies were remarkably similar.

Then there was Sam Yeager himself. He had been mated, but his longtime partner was dead. Would he be looking for sexual opportunities now? How could a member of the Race hope to know?

You could ask him, Ttomalss thought. Then he made the negative gesture. The American ambassador would not get angry at the question. Ttomalss was reasonably sure of that. But Yeager would laugh at him. He was pretty sure of that, too. He was no more fond of making a fool of himself than anyone else of any species.

Just when he had decided he couldn't make a reasonable guess about the candidates, he realized he hadn't really considered all of them. Big Uglies occasionally became intimate with members of their own sex. Because of pheromones and crest displays, such behavior was much rarer among the Race. Could Kassquit have experimented with a female?

Kassquit *could* have done almost anything. What she *had* done, she knew and Ttomalss didn't. He also had to admit to himself that he couldn't figure it out from the evidence he had. Maybe a Big Ugly could have. He wouldn't have been surprised. But, despite all his years studying the Tosevites, he was no Big Ugly himself.

He was glad of that, too. Imagine putting a sexual liaison ahead of an audience with the Emperor! If that didn't prove how different the Tosevites were, what would?

He did his best to look on the bright side of things. Sooner or later, the truth would come out. His store of data would grow. The bright side turned darker. No matter how much data he had, would he ever really understand?

The Americans had been living in one another's pockets ever since they got to Home. They had few secrets from one another. Keeping secrets wasn't easy, and they hardly ever bothered. Even so, not everything got talked about right out in the open. Karen Yeager was probably the last one to realize Major Coffey and Kassquit had started sleeping together.

When she did, she was horrified. "Isn't that treason or something?" she demanded of her husband.

"I doubt it," he answered. "I can't see Frank giving secrets away to the Lizards no matter what. Can you? It would take a lot more than a what-do-you-call-it—a honey trap, that's what they say—to get him to do anything like that."

Karen considered. Reluctantly, she decided Jonathan was right. She made herself an almost-vodka, chilling it with ice she'd fought so hard to win. "Well, maybe so," she said. "But it's still disgusting. She's hardly even human."

Jonathan didn't say anything. That was no doubt smart on his part. Karen remembered, just too late, that he hadn't found anything disgusting about sleeping with Kassquit. If men could, they would, or most of them would.

"She really isn't," Karen said, as if Jonathan had contradicted her.

"I know she's not," he answered uncomfortably. "But she does try. It makes her more . . . more pathetic than if she didn't. Part of her wants to be—I think a lot of her wants to be. But she doesn't know how. How could she, seeing the way she was raised? She's crazy, yeah, but she could be a lot crazier. And you know what the saddest thing is?"

"Tell me." Ominous echoes filled Karen's voice.

Her husband usually heeded those echoes. Not today. He spoke as if he hadn't heard them: "The saddest thing is, she knows how much she's missing. And she knows she's never going to get it—not from us, and not from the Lizards, either. How do you go on after you've figured something like that out?"

"She seems to have found some way to amuse herself," Karen said.

"That's not fair, hon," Jonathan said. "If you hadn't done anything for twenty years—and I don't think Kassquit has, not since me—wouldn't you grab the chance if it came along?"

Karen thought about twenty years of celibacy. Going without was easier for most women than for most men, but even so.... "Maybe," she said grudgingly.

No matter how grudgingly she said it, Jonathan had to know how big an admission that was. "Give her a break, will you?" he said. "She needs all the breaks she can get, and she hasn't caught very many of them."

"Maybe," Karen said again, even more grudgingly than before. "But what about Frank? What's he thinking? *Is* he thinking?"

"There are four women on this planet," Jonathan said. "As far as I know, he's never come on to you or Linda. If he has, nobody's said anything about it."

"He hasn't with me, anyway," Karen said.

"All right, then. Let's figure he hasn't with Linda, either," Jonathan said. "Melanie Blanchard just got here. That leaves . . ." He didn't finish the sentence, but he didn't have to.

Every word he said made good logical sense. But this wasn't a matter for logic—or it didn't feel like one to Karen, anyhow. When she said, "It's Kassquit!" she summed up everything that wasn't logical about it.

Jonathan only shrugged. "I can't do anything about it. I haven't done anything about it, either, and you know darn well I haven't. If you don't like it, take it up with Frank. And good luck to you."

He wasn't often so blunt. Karen wished he hadn't been this time, either. She said, "I couldn't do that!"

"Okay, fine," her husband said. "In that case, wouldn't you say it's none of your beeswax? And if it isn't, what are you worrying about?"

"Talk about not being fair!" Karen exclaimed. "How long have you known without telling me?"

"A while," he said, which told her less than she wanted to know. He went on, "If you watch them, you can kind of tell. It's the way they look at each other when they think nobody else is paying any attention."

Karen had always paid as little attention to Kassquit as she could while staying polite, or maybe even a little less than that. And she evidently hadn't paid as much to Frank Coffey as she should have. "I still have trouble believing it," she said.

"Oh, it's true," Jonathan said. "If it weren't, why would Frank have started taking rubbers from the medical supplies?"

For that, Karen had no answer. She did wonder how her husband knew Coffey was doing that. Had he actually seen him? Or did he know how many he and Tom de la Rosa were likely to use, and figure the excess must have gone to Frank? Karen decided she wasn't curious enough about that to ask.

She said, "I still don't think it can be good for what we're trying to do here. It's . . . sleeping with the enemy, that's what it is."

"Sorry, hon, but I don't think you're right," Jonathan told her. "Anything that keeps us from going nuts here is pretty good, far as I'm concerned. Kassquit's no more Mata Hari than she is Martha Washington. If anybody gives anything away in pillow talk, she's likely to be the one."

He was altogether too likely to be right about that. Because he was, Karen didn't try to contradict him. She just said, "The whole idea is repulsive, that's all."

Jonathan said nothing at all. No, sleeping with Kassquit hadn't repelled him. That wasn't anything Karen didn't already know; after all, he'd done it before they were married. Since he hadn't tried doing it since, she didn't suppose she ought to mention it. But biting her tongue wasn't easy.

In the face of that silence from her husband, she said, "I'm going down to the refectory. It's just about time for lunch."

"Go ahead," Jonathan answered. "I'm not hungry yet. I'll come down in a while. I've got some paperwork I need to catch up on."

Maybe he did and maybe he didn't. Karen wouldn't have bet one way or the other. Plainly, though, he didn't want to go on talking about Kassquit and Frank Coffey. Karen didn't see what she could do about it short of ramming the topic down his throat. That wouldn't accomplish anything but starting a fight. Life was too short . . . wasn't it? With a twinge of regret, she decided it was.

"I'll see you later, then," she said. "I *am* hungry." That wasn't a lie. She left the room and walked down the hall to the elevators.

When one arrived, it announced itself with a hiss, not a

bell. She wondered if she would ever hear a bell again when a door opened. Sometimes small things made all the difference between feeling at home and being forcibly reminded you were on an alien world. She got into the elevator. It was smoother than any Earthly model she'd ever known.

She braced herself for more alienness in the refectory. The food there, or most of it, wasn't bad, but it wasn't what she was used to, either. She supposed a Japanese traveling through South Dakota had the same problem. If so, she sympathized.

Some of the booths had been adapted to accommodate humans. The adaptations were clumsy but functional. A Lizard came up to her with a menu. "Here are today's offerings, superior Tosevite," the server said.

"I thank you." Karen read through it. "Ah, you have the azwaca cutlets again. Bring me those, please."

"It shall be done, superior Tosevite. And to drink?"

"The ippa-fruit juice. Chilled, if you have it." Ippa-fruit juice had a citrusy tartness to it.

"We do." The server made the affirmative gesture. "We would not for ourselves, but we have seen how fond of cold things you Tosevites are. Please wait. I will take your order to the cooks. It will not be long."

"Good," Karen said. For the moment, she had the refectory to herself. That suited her. She wasn't in the mood to face anyone else just then anyhow. She wished the refectory were cooler. She wished all of Home were cooler.

Of course, what she wished had nothing to do with how things really worked. She knew that, even if she didn't like it very much. The Race had cooled the refectory even this far only to accommodate her kind. The Lizards liked things hot. The heat of a medium summer's day in Los Angeles wasn't heat to them at all. It was chill.

The server brought the ippa-fruit juice. It wasn't as cold as lemonade would have been back on Earth, but it was chilled. The tangy sweetness pleased her. Had the Race brought ippa fruit to Earth? If so, a trade might easily spring up. Plenty of people would like it. *I'll have to ask Tom,* she thought. If anyone here would know, he was the man.

When she finished the juice, the server refilled her glass from a pitcher. In a lot of ways, restaurants on Earth and Home were similar. "Your meal will come very shortly," he assured her two or three times, sounding much like a human waiter anxious to preserve his tip. The Americans didn't need to worry about tipping, though, not while they ate in the hotel refectory. Karen didn't even know if Lizards were in the habit of tipping. If they were, the government took care of it here.

The server had just brought her the cutlets—and some roasted tubers on the side—when Kassquit walked into the refectory. Karen nodded, not in a friendly way (that was beyond her), but at least politely. She wanted to see how Kassquit would behave and what, if anything, she had to say for herself.

Kassquit nodded back with that same wary politeness. "I greet you," the half-alien woman said.

"And I greet you," Karen answered. "I hope you are well and happy?"

"I am well, yes. I thank you for asking." Kassquit considered the rest of the question. "Happy? Who can say for certain? There certainly were times in the past when I was more unhappy."

What was that supposed to mean? "Ah?" Karen said: the most noncommittal noise she could make, but one that invited Kassquit to keep talking if she wanted to.

She must have, for she went on, "I suppose even ordinary wild Tosevites are often unhappy when they are young, for they do not yet know how they will fit into their society." She paused. Karen made the affirmative gesture; that was true enough. Kassquit continued, "It was, I think, worse for me, for I knew I did not fit in at all, not in biology, not in appearance, not in speaking—not in anything, really—and I was often reminded of this. No, I was not happy."

Karen felt ashamed of disliking Kassquit. No other human being in the history of the world had gone through what Kassquit had. *And a good thing, too,* Karen thought. "And now?" she asked.

"Now I have a place of my own. I have some acceptance— even the Emperor does not find me altogether unworthy. And

I am not completely cut off from my biological heritage, as I was for so long."

Again, what did she mean? That she and Frank Coffey were fooling around, as Jonathan had said? Karen couldn't think of anything else that seemed likely. She surprised herself when she nodded again and said, "Good."

☆ **12** ☆

Atvar heard from Ttomalss that Kassquit and the wild Big Ugly had become physically intimate. "We instructed her not to do this. What is it likely to mean, Senior Researcher?" he inquired. "Will she abandon us for the Americans?"

"I do not believe so, Exalted Fleetlord," Ttomalss replied. "This is just another complication, not—I hope—a catastrophe."

"Just another complication." Atvar let out a weary, hissing sigh. "I have heard those words or words much like them too often for my peace of mind." He laughed. "I remember when I once had peace of mind."

"Before you went to Tosev 3?" Ttomalss asked.

"Certainly," Atvar said. "Not afterwards, by the spirits of Emperors past!" He cast down his eye turrets. "Never afterwards."

"I believe that, Exalted Fleetlord," the psychologist said. "And, all things considered, you were fairly lucky. The Big Uglies never captured you."

"That is a truth." Atvar had forgotten about Ttomalss' ordeal. He returned to the business before him: "Ironic that Kassquit should form this attachment so soon after her audience with the Emperor."

"Indeed," Ttomalss said morosely. "I asked her about this myself, in fact. She said the audience was a source of pride, but the liaison was a source of satisfaction. Tosevite sexuality is different from ours, and there is nothing much to be done about it."

That was another truth. The Race had wasted a lot of time and energy on Tosev 3 trying to get the Big Uglies to change their customs before deciding it *was* wasting its time and energy. The Tosevites were not going to change what they did, any more than the Race would.

The fleetlord wished that thought hadn't occurred to him. Ginger had made a significant part of the Race change its sexual patterns. Atvar let out a sudden, thoughtful hiss. "Do you know, Senior Researcher, I believe we may have missed a chance on Tosev 3."

"In what way?" Ttomalss asked.

"I wonder if, through drugs, we might make the Big Uglies' sexual patterns more like ours and those of the other species in the Empire," Atvar said. "As far as I know, this was never investigated."

"I believe you are right, Exalted Fleetlord," Ttomalss said. "The work might prove worthwhile. If you send a message now, researchers there can begin experimenting before too many more years have passed."

"I may propose that," Atvar said. "If they find such a drug, well and good. If they fail to find it, we are no worse off."

"Just so." Ttomalss made the affirmative gesture. "And now, if you will excuse me . . . I did want to let you know about Kassquit's situation."

"For which I thank you." Atvar laughed again, sourly. "Though why I should thank you for exercising my liver is beyond me. This is one of those times when politeness and truth part company, I fear."

"I understand." Ttomalss left the fleetlord's room.

The psychologist could go. The problem he had posed would stay. He had to be annoyed that Kassquit would choose her biological heritage over her cultural one. As far as Atvar could tell, though, that was the extent of Ttomalss' annoyance. He didn't have to worry about the effect Kassquit's possible shift of allegiance would have on negotiations with the wild Big Uglies.

Atvar thought about commanding her to stop mating with Frank Coffey. Only the suspicion—the near certainty—that she would ignore such a command held him back. She was no less headstrong than any wild Tosevite. Stubbornness, especially about sexual matters, was in their blood. He also thought about removing her from his party and sending her halfway round the world.

He could do that. He had the authority. But it would mean depriving the Race of Kassquit's insights into the way Tosevites functioned. At the moment, she was demonstrating how they functioned. Atvar wondered if that had even occurred to her. He doubted it. Tosevites let their sexual desires dictate their behavior to a degree the Race found ridiculous and unimaginable—except during mating season, at which time males and females had their minds on other things.

"No," he said, more to himself than to anyone else. He would keep Kassquit here in Sitneff. That might mean he would have to weigh carefully anything she said about the American Tosevites. Fair enough. Weighing data was something he was good at. He realized he would also have to weigh what he got from Ttomalss, who would not be anything close to objective about his former ward.

Sending a message to Tosev 3 was another matter. Atvar no longer had authority to do it on his own. He hadn't since his recall. But altering the Big Uglies' sexuality might be important. He was even willing to go through channels to make sure the idea reached the distant colony.

He was willing, yes, but he wasn't enthusiastic. Years of handling affairs on Tosev 3 himself as the Emperor's autonomous viceroy had left him impatient with the idea of gaining others' permission before acting. He was convinced he knew enough to do what needed doing on his own. Anyone who thought otherwise had to be misguided.

Of course, the entire cumbersome bureaucracy here on Home had eventually decided otherwise. Atvar remained convinced those bureaucrats were fools. When he talked to them here, he did his best not to show it. Ttomalss was right—this was an important idea. It was even more important than getting even with the bunglers who'd recalled him. So he told himself, anyhow.

His Majesty's chief scientific adviser was a female named Yendiss. She heard Atvar out and then asked, "What assurance do you have that researchers can actually discover or synthesize a drug of this sort?"

"Assurance? Why, none," Atvar answered. "But I have one contrary assurance to offer you, superior female."

"Oh?" Yendiss said. "And that is?"

"If researchers do not look for a drug of this sort, they are guaranteed not to find it," Atvar said.

In the monitor, Yendiss' eye turrets swung sharply toward him. "Are you being sarcastic, Fleetlord?" she demanded.

"Not at all." Atvar made the negative gesture. "I thought I was stating a simple and obvious truth. If such a drug is there to be found, we ought to find it. Making the Big Uglies more like us would reduce some acute sociological strains on Tosev 3. It would make assimilating the Tosevites much easier. Is that not an important consideration?"

The scientific adviser did not answer directly. Instead, she asked, "Do you have any idea how expensive this research might be?"

"No, superior female," Atvar answered resignedly. "But whatever it costs, I am convinced making it will be cheaper than not making it."

"Send me a memorandum," Yendiss said. "Make it as detailed as possible, listing costs and benefits." By the way she said that, she plainly thought costs the more important consideration. "Once I have something in writing, I can submit it to specialists for their analysis and input."

"It shall be done." Atvar broke the connection. He let out a loud, frustrated hiss. The Race had done business like this for a hundred thousand years. That was fine—when the business had nothing to do with the Big Uglies. How many years would go by before the specialists made up their minds? Yendiss wouldn't care. She would say getting the right answer was the most important thing.

Sometimes, though, the right answer seemed obvious. Getting it quickly began to matter. Anyone who'd dealt with Tosev 3 knew that. How many centuries had the Race spent preparing the conquest fleet after its probe showed that the Big Uglies were ripe for the taking? Enough so that, by the time the conquest fleet arrived, the Tosevites weren't ripe any more.

Would this be more of the same? "Not if I have anything to do with it," Atvar declared, and made another call.

Before long, the imperial protocol master looked out of a monitor at him. "I greet you, Fleetlord," Herrep said. "I doubt this is strictly a social call, so what do you want of me?"

"I would like to speak with the Emperor for a little while," Atvar replied. "This has to do with affairs on Tosev 3."

"Are you trying to leap over some functionary who obstructs you?" Herrep asked.

"In a word, yes."

"His Majesty rarely lets himself be used that way," the protocol master warned.

"If he refuses, I am no worse off, though the Race may be," Atvar said. "He does see the Big Uglies as a real problem for the Race, though, which not many here seem to do. Please forward my request to him, if you would be so kind. Let him decide. I believe it is important."

"Very well, Fleetlord," Herrep said. "Please note that I guarantee nothing. The decision is in the grip of his Majesty's fingerclaws."

"I understand, and I thank you," Atvar answered. "Whatever he chooses, I shall accept." *Of course I shall. What choice have I got?*

The protocol master broke the connection. Too late, Atvar realized Herrep hadn't said when he would forward the request to the Emperor or how long it might be till Risson called back—if he did. A delay of a few days wouldn't matter. A delay of a few months or even a few years wouldn't be anything out of the ordinary for the Race. That kind of delay might be unfortunate, but who without firsthand experience of the Big Uglies would realize exactly how unfortunate it might be?

Atvar's telephone hissed frequently. Whenever it did, he hoped it would be the Emperor returning his call. Whenever it wasn't, he felt an unreasonable stab of disappointment. And then, four days after he'd spoken with Herrep, it was. The female on the line spoke without preamble: "Assume the posture of respect so you may hear his Majesty's words."

"It shall be done," Atvar replied, and he did it. The female disappeared from the monitor. The 37th Emperor Risson's image replaced her. Atvar said, "I greet you, your Majesty. I am honored to have the privilege of conversation with you."

"Rise, Fleetlord. Tell me what is on your mind," Risson replied. He sometimes stood on hardly more ceremony than the Big Uglies did. "Herrep seems to think you have come up with something interesting."

"I hope so, your Majesty." Atvar explained.

Risson heard him out, then asked, "What are the chances for success?"

"I would not care to guess about them, because I have no idea," Atvar replied. "But they must be much greater than zero: our biochemists are skilled, and on Tosev 3 they will have studied the Big Uglies' metabolism for many years. If we do not make the effort, what hope do we have of success? That I can guess: none."

"Truth," Risson said. "Very well. You have persuaded me. I shall issue the necessary orders to pass this idea on to our colony on Tosev 3. Let us see what the colonists do with it. If the Big Uglies were more like us, they would certainly be easier to assimilate. We should do all we can to try to bring that about."

"I think you are right, your Majesty, and I thank you very much," Atvar said. "You will also have seen for yourself by now how little inclined toward compromise the wild Big Uglies are. This may eventually give us a new weapon against them, one we can use when we would hesitate to bring out our bombs."

"Let us hope so, anyhow," the Emperor said. "Is there anything more?" When Atvar made the negative gesture, Risson broke the connection. *He* does *take the Big Uglies seriously,* Atvar thought. *If only more males and females did.*

Dr. Melanie Blanchard poked and prodded Sam Yeager. She looked in his ears and down his throat. She listened to his chest and lungs. She took his blood pressure. She put on a rubber glove and told him to bend over. "Are you sure we need a doctor here?" he asked.

She laughed. "I've never known anybody who enjoys this," she said. "I do know it's necessary, especially for a man your age. Or do you really want to mess around with the possibility of prostate cancer?"

With a sigh, Sam assumed the position. The examination was just as much fun as he remembered. He said, "Suppose I've got it. What can you do about it here?"

"X rays, certainly," Dr. Blanchard answered. "Chemotherapy, possibly, if we can get the Race to synthesize the agents we'd need. Or maybe surgery, with Lizard physicians assisting me. I'm sure some of them would be fascinated." She took off the glove and threw it away. "Doesn't look like we need to worry about that, though."

"Well, good." Sam straightened up and did his best to restore his dignity. "How do I check out?"

"You're pretty good," she said. "I'd like it if your blood pressure were a little lower than 140/90, but that's not bad for a man your age. Not ideal, but not bad. You used to be an athlete, didn't you?"

"A ballplayer," he answered. "Never made the big leagues, but I put in close to twenty years in the minors. You could do that before the Lizards came. I've tried to stay in halfway decent shape since."

"You've done all right," Dr. Blanchard told him. "I wouldn't recommend that you go out and run a marathon, but you seem to be okay for all ordinary use."

"I'll take that," Sam said. "Thanks very much for the checkup—or for most of it, anyhow."

"You're welcome." She started to laugh. Sam raised an eyebrow. She explained, "I started to tell you, 'My pleasure,' but that isn't right. I don't enjoy doing that, no matter how necessary it is."

"Well, good," he said again, and got another laugh from her. She packed up her supplies and walked out of his room. Sam laughed, too, though he was damned if he was sure it was funny. The closest, most intimate physical contact he'd had with a woman since his wife died—and he'd been on the wrong end of a rubber glove. If that wasn't mortifying, he didn't know what would be.

He didn't usually worry about such things. He didn't usually get reminded about them quite so openly, though. He was still a man. His parts did still work. He laughed once more. They would work, anyhow, if he could find himself some company.

Major Coffey had managed. Sam shrugged. No accounting for taste. Kassquit had always fascinated him, but he'd never thought she was especially attractive. He shrugged again.

Jonathan would have told him he was wrong—and Karen would have hit Jonathan for telling him that.

Someone knocked on the door. That meant an American stood in the hall. A Lizard would have pressed the button for the door hisser. Sam looked around. Had Dr. Blanchard forgotten something? he wondered hopefully. He didn't see anything that looked medical. Too bad.

He opened the door. There stood Tom de la Rosa. Sam aimed an accusing forefinger at him. "*You're* not a beautiful woman," he said.

De la Rosa rubbed his mustache. "With this on my upper lip, I'm not likely to be one, either."

"Well, come on in anyhow," Sam said. "I'll try not to hold it against you."

"I'm so relieved." Tom walked past Yeager and over to the window. "You've got a nicer view than we do. See what you get for being ambassador?"

Sam had come to take the view for granted. Now he looked at it with fresher eyes. It was pretty impressive, in a stark, Southwestern way. "Reminds me a little of Tucson, or maybe Albuquerque."

"Somewhere in there," Tom de la Rosa agreed. "If we don't get what we need here, you know, Tucson and Albuquerque are going to look a lot more like this. They look a lot more like this now than they did when we went into cold sleep."

"I do know that," Sam said. "Arizona and New Mexico are just about perfect country for plants and animals from Home."

"And if they crowd ours out, I don't know how we're going to get rid of them," Tom said. "The Lizards don't show a whole lot of give on this one."

"You've got that wrong," Sam said. De la Rosa sent him a questioning look. He spelled out what he meant: "The Lizards don't show any give at all on this one. As far as they're concerned, they're just making themselves at home—or at Home—on Earth."

De la Rosa winced at the audible capital letter. When he recovered, he said, "But it's not right, dammit. They've got no business imposing their ecology on us."

"Starlings and English sparrows in the United States. And Kentucky bluegrass. And Russian thistle, which is what a lot of tumbleweeds are," Sam said mournfully. "Rats in Hawaii. Mongooses—or is it mongeese?—too. Rabbits and cats and cane toads in Australia. I could go on. It's not as if we haven't done it to ourselves."

"But we didn't know any better. Most of the time we didn't, anyhow," Tom de la Rosa said. "The Race knows perfectly well what it's doing. It knows more about ecology than we'll learn in the next hundred years. The Lizards just don't give a damn, and they ought to."

"They say they haven't introduced anything into territory we rule. They say what they do on territory they rule is their business—and if their critters happen to come over the border, they don't mind if we get rid of them."

"Mighty generous of them. They'd tell King Canute he was welcome to hold back the tide, too," Tom said bitterly. "The only thing they wouldn't tell him was how to go about it."

"Well, Tom, here's the question I've got for you," Sam said. "If the Lizards don't want to change their minds—and it doesn't look like they do—is this worth going to war to stop?"

"That's not the point. The point is getting them to stop," de la Rosa said.

Sam shook his head. "No. They don't want to. They don't intend to. They've made that as plain as they possibly can. As far as they're concerned, they're moving into a new neighborhood, and they've brought their dogs and cats and cows and sheep and some of their flowers along with them. They're just making themselves at home."

"Bullshit. They understand ecological issues fine. They don't have any trouble at all," Tom said. "Look at the fit they pitched about the rats. Have they caught any besides the first two? It'd serve the Race right if the damn things did get loose."

"As far as I know, those are the only ones they've got their hands on," Sam said. "But you still haven't answered my question. Is this something we fight about? Or is it already too late for that? You can't put things back in Pandora's box once they're loose, can you?"

"Probably not." De la Rosa looked as disgusted as he sounded. "But the arid country on Earth—everywhere from

Australia to the Sahara to our own Southwest—is never going to be the same. The least we can do is get an agreement out of them not to introduce any more of their species to Earth. That's locking the barn door after the horse is long gone, though."

"I've been over this with Atvar before. He's always said no. I don't think he's going to change his mind." Sam Yeager sighed. He saw Tom's point. He'd seen with his own eyes what creatures from Home were doing in and to the Southwest—and things had only got worse since he went into cold sleep. He sighed again. "Atvar will tell me the Race is as sovereign in the parts of Earth it rules as we are in the USA. He'll say we have no right to interfere in what the Lizards do there. He'll say we complain about being interfered with, but now we're meddling for all we're worth. It's not a bad argument. How am I supposed to answer him?"

"Throw the rats in his face," Tom suggested. "That will get him to understand why we're worried."

"He already understands. He just doesn't care. There's a difference," Sam said. "No matter what happens from our point of view, the Lizards get major benefits by importing their animals and plants. If we try to tell them they can't, we're liable to have to fight to back it up. *Is this worth a war?*"

Tom de la Rosa looked as if he hated him. "You don't make things easy, do you?"

"Atvar's told me the same thing. From him, I take it as a compliment. I'll try to do the same from you," Sam said. "But you still haven't answered my question. The Lizards are changing the planet. I agree with you—that's what they're doing. Do we wreck it to keep them from changing it?"

"That's not a fair way to put things," Tom protested.

"No? That's what it boils down to from here," Sam said. "We can have a damaged ecology, or we can have a planet that glows in the dark. Or else you'll tell me it's not worth a war. But nothing short of war is going to make the Lizards change their policy about this."

Instead of answering, de la Rosa stormed out of the room. Yeager wasn't particularly surprised or particularly disappointed. Tom was a hothead. You needed to be a hothead to get involved in ecological matters. Every so often, though, even hotheads bumped up against the facts of life. Sometimes the cost of stopping a change was higher than the cost of the change itself.

He looked out the window again. He imagined saguaros putting down deep roots here. He imagined owls nesting in the saguaros, and roadrunners scurrying here and there in the shade of the cactuses snapping up whatever little lizardy things they could catch. He imagined sidewinders looping along. He imagined how the Lizards would feel about all of that—especially the ones who had the misfortune to bump into sidewinders. Would they go to war to keep it from happening? They might.

But it was already happening back on Earth. Too late to stop it now. And, whatever else happened, he couldn't imagine an American colonization fleet crossing the light-years and coming down on Home. The Race had the population to spare for that sort of thing. The USA didn't.

He wondered how much he'd accomplished by coming here. That he'd got here alive was pretty impressive, too. He'd had the audience with the Emperor and the private meeting afterwards. But what had he gained that he couldn't have got from Reffet and Kirel back on Earth? Anything?

If he had, he was hard pressed to see it. He understood Tom de la Rosa's frustration. He had plenty of frustration of his own. The Lizards here on Home were less inclined to compromise than the ones back on Earth had been. They thought they were right, and any miserable Big Ugly had to be wrong.

One thing the flight of the *Admiral Peary* had proved: humans could fly between the stars. The Race couldn't ignore that. The Lizards would have to be wondering what else might be on the way. Maybe the colonists back on Earth could radio ahead and let Home know other starships were coming, but maybe not, too. If humans wanted to send secret expeditions, they might be able to.

Sam grimaced. The *Reich* might do that. And any German expedition would come with guns not just handy but loaded. The Nazis owed the Lizards for a defeat. After all this time, would they try to pay them back?

How am I supposed to know? Sam asked himself. All he knew about what the *Reich* was like these days, he got from the radio bulletins beamed Homeward by America and by the Lizards themselves. It didn't seem to have changed all that much—and there was one more thing to worry about.

Whenever Jonathan Yeager saw Kassquit, he wanted to ask her if she was happy. She certainly gave all the signs of it, or as many as she could with a face that didn't show what she was thinking. Frank Coffey seemed pretty happy these days, too. Jonathan had no great urge to ask him if he was. That was none of his business, not unless Coffey felt like making it his business.

Jonathan wondered what the difference was. That he'd been intimate with Kassquit all those years ago? He thought there was more to it than that. He hoped so, anyhow. He had the strong feeling that Major Frank Coffey could take care of himself. He wasn't nearly so sure about Kassquit. She couldn't be a Lizard, however much she wanted to, but she didn't exactly know how to be a human being, either. She was liable to get hurt, or to hurt herself.

And what can you do about it if she does? Jonathan asked himself. The answer to that was only too obvious. He couldn't do a damn thing, and he knew it. He also knew Karen would grab the nearest blunt instrument and brain him if he tried.

He sighed. He couldn't blame Karen for being antsy about Kassquit. To his wife, Kassquit was The Other Woman, in scarlet letters ten feet high. Kassquit wasn't at her best around Karen, either.

It came as something of a relief when Trir said, "Would any of you Tosevites care for a sightseeing tour today?" at breakfast one morning.

"What sort of sights do you have in mind showing us?" Linda de la Rosa asked.

"Perhaps you would like to go to the Crimson Desert?" the guide said. "It has a wild grandeur unlike any other on Home."

"I want to go," Tom de la Rosa said. "I would like to see what you term a desert on this world, when so much of it would be a desert on Tosev 3."

All the Americans volunteered—even Jonathan's father, who said, "None of the negotiations going on right now will addle if we pause. Pausing may even help some of them."

Jonathan knew his dad wasn't happy with the way things were going. He hadn't expected him to come out and say so, though.

Then Kassquit asked, "May I also come? I too would like to see more of Home."

"Yes, Researcher. You are welcome," Trir said. "We will leave from in front of the hotel in half a daytenth. All of you should bring whatever you require for an overnight stay."

"The Crimson Desert," Karen said musingly. "I wonder what it will be like."

"Hot," Jonathan said. His wife gave him a sardonic nod. Had they been going to the desert on Earth, he would have warned her to take along a cream that prevented sunburn. As a redhead, she needed to worry about it more than most people did. But Tau Ceti wasn't the sun. It put out a lot less ultraviolet radiation. Even in the warmest weather, sunburn wasn't so much of a worry here.

They boarded the bus that had taken them out to the ranch. The driver left the hotel's lot and pulled out into traffic. They were off. The bus' dark windows kept Lizard drivers and passengers in other vehicles from gaping at Big Uglies. It didn't keep the Americans from looking out. Whenever Jonathan saw a Lizard in a wig—or, every once in a while, a Lizard in a T-shirt—he had everything he could do not to howl with laughter. Then he'd run a hand over his own shaven skull and think about sauces and geese and ganders.

In the halfhearted Lizard way, the bus was air-conditioned. That meant it was hot inside, but not quite stifling. Jonathan's father started to laugh. "What's funny, Dad?" Jonathan asked.

"Another bus ride," his father answered. "I used to think I'd taken the last one when I quit playing ball, but I was wrong."

"I bet you never expected to take one on another world," Jonathan said.

"Well, that's a fact," Sam Yeager agreed. "All the same, though, a bus ride is a bus ride. Some things don't change. And I keep looking for greasy spoons by the side of the road. I don't suppose the Race knows anything about chop-suey joints or hot-dog stands."

"Probably a good thing they don't," Jonathan said.

"Yeah, I suppose," his father said. "But it hardly seems like a road trip without 'em. I've been spoiled. I have this idea of how things are supposed to work, and I'm disappointed when they turn out different."

"You probably expect flat tires, too," Jonathan said.

His father nodded. "You bet I do. I've seen enough of them. Heck, I've helped change enough of them. I wonder what the Lizards use for a jack."

"Let's hope we don't find out," Jonathan said. To his relief, his father didn't argue with him.

They had no trouble getting to the Crimson Desert. The bus rolled south and east out of Sitneff, into open country. By any Earthly standards, that would have been desert. By the standards of Home, it wasn't. It was nothing but scrub. Treeish things were few and far between, but smaller plants kept the ground from being too barren. Every once in a while, Jonathan spotted some kind of animal scurrying along, though the bus usually went by too fast to let him tell what the creature was.

Mountains rose ahead. The bus climbed them. The road grew steep and narrow; Jonathan got the feeling not a whole lot of vehicles came this way. He hadn't thought Home would have roads to nowhere, but the one they were on sure gave that feeling. Up and up it went. The bus' engine labored a little. The driver turned off the air conditioning, but it kept getting cooler inside the bus anyhow. It might have dropped all the way down into the seventies. It was the coolest Jonathan had been anywhere on Home this side of the South Pole.

A few minutes later, they came to what was obviously the crest of the grade. Trir said, "This is the third-highest pass on all of Home." Without checking an atlas, Jonathan had no idea whether she was right, but nothing about the place made him want to disbelieve her.

The bus seemed relieved to find a downhill slope. The driver knew her business. She never let it get going too fast, but she was never too obvious about riding the brakes, either. The change in the weather on the other side of the mountains was immediate and profound. Before long, three or four Americans and Kassquit all called for the driver to turn the air conditioning on again. With a sigh, she did. It suddenly seemed to be fighting a much more savage climate.

"There!" Trir pointed ahead, out through the windshield. "Now you can see why this place got its name."

Jonathan craned his neck for a better look. Sure enough, the cliffsides and the ground were of a reddish color, brighter than rust. He wouldn't have called most of it crimson, but he wouldn't have revoked anyone else's poetic license, either. And color names didn't translate perfectly between the Race's language and English to begin with.

Down went the bus, into the middle of the desert. By the noises the air conditioning made, it was working harder and harder. By the way sweat ran down Jonathan's face, it wasn't working hard enough. "How hot is it outside?" he asked.

"Probably about fifty-five hundredths," Trir answered.

The Race divided the distance between water's freezing and boiling points into hundredths—the exact equivalent of Celsius degrees. The USA still routinely used Fahrenheit. Jonathan was struggling to do the conversion in his head when Frank Coffey spoke in horrified English: "Jesus! That's just the other side of 130!"

It could get that hot on Earth . . . just barely. But Trir spoke as if this was nothing out of the ordinary. What was that line about mad dogs and Englishmen? Noel Coward had never heard of Lizards when he wrote it.

Ten minutes later, the bus stopped. Air like a blast furnace rolled inside. *It's a dry heat,* Jonathan thought in something not far from despair. That worked fine when the temperature was in the nineties. Over a hundred, it wore thin. At the moment, all it meant was that Jonathan would bake instead of boil.

Trir seemed perfectly happy. "Is it not a bracing climate?" she said. "Come out, all of you, and look around." She skittered out of the bus and down onto the ground.

Major Coffey wasn't the only human being who said, "Jesus!" But they'd come all this way. There wasn't—Jonathan supposed there wasn't—much point just staying in the bus. He got to his feet and went out into the Crimson Desert.

Jesus! didn't begin to do it justice. Jonathan found he had to keep blinking almost as fast as he could. If he didn't, his eyeballs started drying out. In between blinks, he looked around. The place did have a stark beauty to it. Wind and dust had carved the crimson cliffs into a cornucopia of crazy shapes. Not all the shades of red were the same. There were bands and twists of rust and scarlet and crimson and carmine and magenta. Here and there, he spotted flecks of white all the brighter for being so isolated. Tau Ceti beat down on him out of a greenish blue sky.

"Does anything actually live here?" Tom de la Rosa asked. "*Can* anything actually live here?" He didn't sound as if he believed it. Jonathan had trouble believing it, too.

But Trir made the affirmative gesture. "Why, certainly. You can see the saltbushes there, and the peffelem plants."

Jonathan couldn't have told a saltbush from a peffelem plant if his life depended on it. Both varieties looked like nothing but dry sticks to him. "Where do they get their water?" he asked. The inside of his mouth was drying out, too.

"They have very deep root structures," the guide replied.

All the way to China didn't seem to apply, not here on Home. Or maybe it did. By the way the air and the ground felt, plants might have needed ten light-years' worth of roots to draw any water to these parts.

But then, to his amazement, something moved under those sticklike caricatures of plants. "What was that?" he said, his voice rising in surprise.

"Some kind of crawling thing," Trir answered indifferently. "There are several varieties in these parts. Most of them live nowhere else on Home."

"They come already cooked, too, I bet," Jonathan's father said in English.

When he translated that into the Race's language, Trir laughed. "It is hot, certainly, but not so hot as all that."

"I agree," Kassquit said.

She'd been raised to take for granted the temperatures Lizards normally lived with. This probably felt the same for her as it did for Trir. The Americans, though, were used to Earthly weather. Dr. Blanchard said, "Be careful of heat-stroke. I'm glad I made sure we brought plenty of water."

"Can we go back inside the bus, please?" Linda de la Rosa said. "I'm feeling medium rare, or maybe a little more done than that."

"But I wanted to talk about the famous fossils not far from

here," Trir said. "These are some of the fossils that the famous savant Iffud used to help establish the theory of evolution." She paused. "You Tosevites are familiar with the theory of evolution, are you not?"

"Why, no," Major Coffey said, straight-faced. "Suppose you tell us what it is. It sounds as if it might be interesting."

"Cut it out, Frank," Jonathan said in English, and poked him with an elbow. Then he went back to the language of the Race: "He is joking, Senior Tour Guide. We have known of the theory of evolution for more than three hundred of your years."

"*We* have known of it for more than 110,000 years," Trir said starchily.

So there, Jonathan thought. But the trip to the Crimson Desert had turned out to be interesting in ways he hadn't expected. And he told himself he would never complain about the weather in Sitneff again, no matter what.

Mickey Flynn gazed out of the *Admiral Peary*'s control room at Home below. "I feel . . . superfluous," he remarked. "Not a great deal for a pilot to do here. Now that I contemplate matters, there's nothing for a pilot to do here, as a matter of fact."

"You buzz around on a scooter, same as I do," Glen Johnson said.

"Oh, huzzah." Joy and rapture were not what filled Flynn's voice. "I'm sure Mickey Mantle played catch with his little boy, too, after he retired. Do you suppose he got the same thrill as he did when he played for Kansas City?"

"Not fair," Johnson said, but then he liked flying a scooter. The difference between him on the one hand and Flynn and Stone on the other was that he was a pilot who could fly a starship, while they were starship pilots. To them, scooters were like rowboats after the *Queen Mary.* Johnson went on, "With a little luck, you'll have the chance to fly her back to Earth, too."

"Well, yes, there is that," Flynn agreed. "How very antiquated do you suppose we'll be, there at the tail end of the twenty-first century? Like Civil War veterans when the Lizards came—that's the comparison that springs to mind."

"There were a few," Johnson said. "Not many, but a few."

"So there were." Flynn nodded ponderously. "But at least they lived through the time in between. They saw the changes happen with their own eyes. When we get back, we'll have been on ice most of the time. Everything we run into will be a surprise."

"You're in a cheerful mood today, aren't you?" Johnson said, and the other pilot nodded again. Some of those worries had occurred to Johnson, too. He didn't see how he could have avoided them. Alone in his bunk in the wee small hours, all these light-years from Earth, what did he have to do but worry? After a bit, he added, "Something else makes me wonder."

"Speak. Give forth," Flynn urged.

"Okay. Here it is: how come there aren't any other American starships here? Or starships from anywhere else, come to that?"

"We started first. You may possibly have noticed this," Flynn said. "Then again, since you were in cold sleep for so long, you may have given up noticing things for Lent."

"Oh, yeah. We started first. I knew that—knew it once I woke up, anyway," Johnson said. "But so what? The *Admiral Peary*'s not as fast as a Lizard starship. You'd figure the state of the art back on Earth would get better. They'd build faster ships, and we'd have company. Only we don't."

"Who knows what's on the way?" Flynn said.

"Well, I don't," Johnson admitted. "But radio's twice as fast as a Lizard ship—I suppose that means it's twice as fast as anything we're likely to make, too. There's the *Molotov*, but have you heard about starships besides her on the way?"

"No one has whispered anything into my pink and shell-like ear," Flynn replied. Johnson snorted. Ignoring the noise, Flynn continued, "This is not to say our beloved commandant and the Race don't know more than I do."

Flynn's comment about their beloved commandant was worse than insubordinate. It was downright mutinous. Johnson clucked in mild reproach. Flynn cared very little. He said, "The Lizards might tell us what's going on. You think Healey ever would?"

"Oh, ye of little faith," Johnson said, which was and wasn't an answer at the same time.

"That's me," Flynn agreed. "That's me right down to the ground. And I ask you, where's our next starship after the *Molotov*? Where's the new American ship, or the Japanese one? Hell, the Nazis are liable to be back in space again."

"Maybe they're waiting for news from us to get back to Earth," he said. "Maybe they didn't know if the cold sleep worked as well as they thought. Maybe the HERE BE DRAGONS notices printed on all the road maps made them think twice. But now they'll have to think that if we can do it, anybody can do it."

"Maybe," Johnson said. "That makes more sense than anything I thought of."

"Why am I not surprised?" Flynn asked.

"Ha. Funny." Johnson gave him a dirty look. It bounced off his armor of irony. Muttering, Johnson continued, "If you're right, though, things have changed back on Earth. The Germans solve problems by throwing bodies at them till they go away—or they used to, anyhow."

"Takes a lot of bodies to stretch from Earth to Tau Ceti," Flynn observed. "And everyone who found out about a failure would laugh at the failed party. The Nazis always did have a hard time seeing a joke when it was on them."

"Mm. Maybe," Johnson said again. Once more, the other pilot had an answer for him. Whether it was *the* answer . . . Well, how could he say when he was in orbit around Home and *the* answer, whatever it was, lay back on Earth?

He looked down at the Lizards' world. The landscape down there was almost as familiar as Earth's by now. With less cloud cover than was usual on Earth, he could see better, too. They were coming up on Sitneff. The dust storm that had plagued the city where the Americans were staying had subsided. "I wonder how Melanie's doing down there," he said.

"Pretty well, by all the reports," Flynn said. "Why? Did you think she couldn't live without you?"

"Actually, I thought she'd be so glad to get away from you that she'd start dancing too soon and hurt herself," Johnson answered.

"Have I been reviled? Have I been insulted? Have I been

slandered? Have I been traduced? Have I been given the glove? Have I been slammed? Have I been cut? Have I—?" Flynn went on pouring out synonyms till anyone would have thought him the second coming of the illustrious Dr. Roget.

"Enough, already!" Johnson exclaimed by the time it was much more than enough.

Mercifully, the other pilot fell silent. Johnson enjoyed the quiet for about five minutes. Then the intercom summoned him to Lieutenant General Healey's office. He enjoyed that not at all. He would rather have gone to the dentist.

By all the signs, Healey was less than enamored of having him there. The commandant growled, "Congratulations. You've managed to make the Lizards love you."

"Sir?" Johnson said woodenly. If he wasn't baiting Healey, Healey would be baiting him. He didn't want to give the other man a handle if he could help it.

But Healey only nodded, which made his J. Edgar Hoover jowls wobble. "That's right. Your rescue mission with the scooter impressed the hell out of them. And so we've arranged a cultural exchange mission with the Race."

"Sir?" Johnson said again, this time in surprise.

"We're going to trade them one of our scooters for one of theirs," Healey said. "There's not a damn thing on one of our scooters that can help them militarily, and they must feel the same way about theirs. So we'll swap, and look them over, and see if we learn anything."

"Oh." Johnson knew he still sounded startled. Had anyone but Healey told him that, he wouldn't have been. But he'd always figured Healey would sooner swap missiles with the Lizards than information.

"I'm so glad this meets with your approval." The commandant's sarcasm would have stung more if Johnson hadn't already been on the receiving end of it so often. Healey said, "The scooter is waiting at Lock Two. The sooner you fly it to the *Horned Akiss,* the sooner we'll get a Lizard scooter to play with."

"All right," Johnson said. "Now that I know where I'm going, I expect I can get there. It does make things easier, you know."

Healey waved that away. He waved away almost everything

Johnson said, whether or not the motion showed. "Go on," he said.

Johnson went. He enjoyed flying the scooter. Had Lieutenant General Healey known how much he enjoyed it, the commandant probably would have chosen someone else for the job. Healey never had wanted him to have any fun.

Well, too bad for the redoubtable lieutenant general. Johnson got into his spacesuit, then ran checks on the scooter. Everything came up green. He hadn't *thought* Healey would want him to have an unfortunate accident, but you never could tell.

The outer airlock door opened. Johnson used the scooter's little steering jets to ease it out into space. As soon as he did, he started to laugh. He knew exactly how the little spacecraft was supposed to respond when he goosed it. It was definitely slower than it should have been, which meant it was heavier than it should have been.

"You sandbagging son of a bitch!" he exclaimed, having first made sure his radio was off. Before sending the Lizards a scooter, Healey had made sure it didn't perform as well as it might have. He wanted the Race to keep right on underestimating what humans could do. That struck Johnson as singularly pointless way the hell out here. If he said anything about it, though, the commandant would probably order him back and clap him in irons.

Instead, he called the *Horned Akiss* on one of the Race's signaling frequencies. He found out the Lizards there *were* expecting him. That came as a relief. It would have been just like Healey to send him out and hope the Race would shoot him down. Evidently not—not this time, anyway.

Once Johnson got clear of the *Admiral Peary,* he aimed the scooter at the *Horned Akiss* and fired up the rear engine. Sure enough, the little rocketship was lugging an anvil; its acceleration wasn't a patch on what it should have been. Inside his suit, he shrugged. Sooner or later, he'd get there.

And, in due course, he did. He wasn't invited aboard the Lizards' ship. Instead, one of their scooters waited for him. "I greet you, Tosevite," the Lizard aboard it called. "Shall we exchange craft?"

"That seems to be the point of the exercise." Johnson

brought his scooter up alongside the bigger one and killed relative velocity. By then, he'd stopped worrying about the extra weight he was carrying; it was like flying with a couple of passengers, and he'd done that often enough.

He read the Race's language, so the controls on the other scooter made sense to him. He had to explain his to the Lizard, who might never have heard of English or of Arabic numerals. Fortunately, the male—or was it a female?—didn't get flustered, saying, "It all seems straightforward enough."

"It is," Johnson agreed. "Just take it slow and easy, and you will do fine."

"Good advice. I had not thought a Tosevite would be so sensible," the Lizard replied. "The same also goes for you. Slow and easy, as you say."

"Oh, yes." Johnson made the affirmative gesture.

He *was* cautious flying the Lizards' scooter back to the *Admiral Peary*. He had to get used to it. It performed about the way he'd expected, though. He hoped the Lizard pilot wouldn't be too disappointed with the logy machine the Big Uglies had sent to the Race.

And then, when Johnson was almost back to the American starship, he said something about the commandant that would have made all his earlier remarks fit for a love letter. He couldn't prove a thing, but he had a feeling. He shook his fist in the direction of Lieutenant General Healey's office. Healey couldn't see him, of course, any more than the commandant could hear him. *Too damn bad,* he thought.

Sam Yeager was sick and tired of the conference rooms in the hotel in Sitneff. One morning, he asked Atvar, "Fleetlord, would it offend you if we moved our discussions across the way to the park for a while?"

"Would it offend me? No," the Lizard replied. "I do not think we would be so efficient there, though. And will you not grow uncomfortable as the day warms up?"

"That's why I said 'for a while,'" Yeager told him. "But I do not think it will be too bad. Sitneff is not that much warmer than Los Angeles, the city where I settled not long after the fight with the conquest fleet ended."

"Well, then, Ambassador, let it be as you wish," Atvar said.

"Maybe changing where we talk will also change the direction in which our talks are going."

"I must say that also occurred to me," Sam agreed. "I am afraid their direction could use some changing."

The way he looked at things, the problem was that his talks with Atvar had no direction. He would propose things. The fleetlord would either reject them, talk around them, or say they needed more study before anything could be settled. To the Race, more study often meant a delay of decades if not centuries.

Sam had been reluctant to point that out, not wanting to derail things altogether. But he had concluded that things were already about as derailed as they could be. He wondered whether Atvar felt the same way, or whether the Lizard was satisfied to stall. Sam hoped not. One way or the other, it was time to find out.

Cars and trucks and buses halted when Yeager appeared at the crosswalk. Drivers and passengers all turned their eye turrets his way. "I enjoy being with you in public," Atvar remarked as they crossed. "It is not easy for me to be anonymous, not with the body paint I put on. Next to you, though, I am invisible. Most refreshing."

"Glad to be of service," Sam said dryly. Atvar laughed.

When they got to the park, Sam led them to some tables and benches screened from the morning sun by the treelike shrubs behind them. "Are you sure you are comfortable, Ambassador?" Atvar asked.

"I thank you for your concern, but I am fine," Sam said. He nodded politely to a Rabotev walking along the path. The dark-skinned alien hopped in the air in surprise. Sam Yeager turned back to Atvar. "I am fine as far as comfort goes, anyhow. I am less happy with the direction of our talks, to use your term."

"I am sorry to hear that. It makes my liver heavy," Atvar said.

"If it does, Fleetlord, a little more real cooperation might work wonders," Sam said bluntly. "From my point of view, the Race seems to be doing its best to make these discussions go nowhere while appearing to make progress."

"What an extraordinary notion," Atvar exclaimed. "How

can you possibly say that when you have conferred with the Emperor himself?" He cast his eye turrets down toward the pale, sandy soil beneath his feet.

"I can say it because it appears to me to be a truth. I am honored the Emperor said he wanted to help settle the differences between the Race and the United States. I am honored, yes, but I am not very impressed. He offered no proposals, only his good will. Good will is valuable; I do not reject it. But good will by itself does not solve problems."

"You must not expect haste from us," Atvar said. "Remember, we are not used to dealing with independent not-empires." He laughed again. "We are not used to dealing with not-empires at all."

"I understand that. I have tried to take it into account," Sam said. "I am sorry, but it does not seem to be a good enough explanation. If you do not deal with us through diplomacy, we will end up fighting. Am I wrong?"

"Probably not," Atvar answered. "If we do fight, the Race will win. Am I wrong?"

"You would have been right when I went into cold sleep, Fleetlord. I know that," Sam said. "Now? Now I am not so sure any of your planets would get away untouched. You have been able to reach Tosev 3 for a long time. Now we can also reach you. You would do well to remember that."

"Is this diplomacy, or only a threat?" Atvar asked.

"It is diplomacy. It is also a threat," Yeager answered. "I do not try to deny it. You did not worry about threatening us when you came to Tosev 3. You went ahead and did it, and not just with words. You invaded my not-empire. You occupied parts of it for years. You dropped nuclear weapons on Washington and Seattle and Pearl Harbor. These are truths, even if perhaps you would rather not remember them now. If we fight again, your worlds will learn what sort of truths they are."

He waited. There was a chance that Atvar would stand up and spit in his eye. If that happened, he didn't know what he'd do. Resign the ambassadorship, maybe, and go back up to the *Admiral Peary* and back into cold sleep. Someone else would have a better chance of getting a worthwhile agreement out of the Lizards.

Atvar's tailstump lashed in agitation. Whatever he'd expected to hear, what Sam had just told him wasn't it. At last, he answered, "Ambassador, you fought in that war. How can you speak of visiting its like on Home and the other worlds of the Empire?"

"You still do not see my point, Fleetlord, or not all of it," Sam said. "The prospect bothers you more *because now it might happen to you, too.*" He added an emphatic cough. "It did not bother you at all when it could only happen to Big Uglies. And that is what I am trying to tell you: you were wrong not to be bothered under those circumstances. We have a saying: 'what goes around comes around.' Do you understand that? I had to translate it literally."

"I think I do," Atvar said. "It is another way of saying that what we did to you, you can now do to us."

"That is part of it, but only part of it," Yeager said. "You did it to us, and you thought you were right to do it to us. Why should we not think we are also right to do it to you?"

He watched the fleetlord's tailstump quiver again. He could make a pretty good guess about what Atvar was thinking: *because we are the Race, and you are nothing but a pack of wild Big Uglies.* But that was the sort of thinking that had sent the conquest fleet out. It might have made some sense against an opponent who couldn't hit back. The Lizards didn't face that kind of opponent any more. If they didn't keep it in mind, everybody would be sorry.

When Atvar still didn't say anything, Sam spoke again, quietly: "This too is what equality means."

To his surprise, Atvar's mouth fell open in a laugh, though the Lizard was anything but amused. "You know, of course, that Shiplord Straha almost cast me down from my position. His reason for doing so was that I had not prosecuted the war against the Tosevites hard enough to suit him. He felt that, if we did not do everything we could, regardless of consequences, to overcome Tosevite resistance, we would regret it one day. Enough of the assembled shiplords thought him wrong to let me keep the job. I reckoned him a maniac. Again, you know of this."

"Oh, yes. I know of this." Sam made the affirmative gesture. After Straha defected to the USA one jump ahead of Atvar's vengeance, the exile and Yeager had become good friends. Sam didn't remind Atvar of that; it would have been rude. Instead, he said, "But now I have to say I am not sure I see your point."

"It is very simple—not complicated in the least," Atvar answered. "My point is, Straha was right. Here we are, all these years later, and Straha was right. Irony has a bitter taste."

This time, Sam had to think hard before deciding what to say next. He had heard Straha say the same thing. For all he knew, the shiplord was saying it right now back on Earth. "Does Straha still live?" he asked. "I was in cold sleep a long time, and have not heard."

"I do not know if he *still* lives, but the signal that he has died has yet to reach Home," Atvar replied. Sam used the affirmative gesture again. When news took years to travel from one sun to the next, *still* could be a nebulous notion. The fleetlord went on, "Are you not grateful for my mistaken moderation?"

"Are you sure it was mistaken?" Yeager said. "There is no guarantee you would have won a great and final victory with Straha in command. By what I recall, you were fighting pretty hard as things were."

"We will never know, will we?" Atvar said. "Could the result have been much worse for my species than what in fact occurred?"

"I think it could have," Sam Yeager said. "If you had not won, you would have had all the surviving Tosevite not-empires and empires mad for revenge against you. The fighting on Tosev 3 might never have stopped."

Atvar shrugged. "And so? Even with constant fighting on Tosev 3, we probably would not have had to worry about Tosevites visiting Home."

"Fleetlord, we really have a problem here, and you need to recognize it," Yeager said. "If the Race cannot get used to the idea that we Big Uglies are doing things only you have been doing for thousands of years, then the two sides *will* collide. They cannot help but collide. And that will not be to anyone's advantage."

"Better to no one's advantage than to yours alone," Atvar said.

"I do not believe an agreement on even terms that everyone

adheres to would be to anyone's disadvantage," Sam said. "If I am wrong, no doubt you will correct me. I think the Emperor would also want an equitable agreement. That was my impression from my meetings with him. Again, you will correct me if I am wrong."

"You are not wrong. Where we differ, Ambassador, is in determining what goes into an equitable agreement."

"An equitable agreement is one where both sides have the same duties and the same obligations," Sam said.

"Why should that be so, when one side is stronger than the other?" Atvar came back. "Our superior strength should be reflected in any treaty we make."

Sam used the negative gesture. What he felt like doing was tearing his hair, but he refrained. "First, all independent empires and not-empires have the same rights and duties," he said. "This is true on Tosev 3, and it used to be true on Home as well. Ask the protocol master if you do not believe me. And second, as I have pointed out before, how much stronger you are is no longer obvious, the way it was when I went into cold sleep. Whether you are stronger at all is no longer obvious, in fact."

He waited. He had to wait quite a while. At last, Atvar said, "This may not prompt a treaty, you know. This may prompt an effort to exterminate you while we still can."

"The Race has been talking about that for a long time." Sam did his best not to show how alarmed he was. "I do not believe exterminating us would be easy or cheap. I do believe you might end up exterminating yourselves in the process."

"Possibly. But if we could be rid of you without destroying ourselves altogether, the price might well be worth paying."

"Is this your opinion, the government's opinion, or the Emperor's opinion?" Sam asked. The answer to that might tell him where these talks were going—if they were going anywhere. He waited.

"It is my opinion," Atvar said. "Perhaps I am mistaken. Perhaps peace will prove a benefit to all concerned, and not merely a breathing space in which you Tosevites gather yourselves for a blow against the Race. Perhaps this is a truth. But the evidence from Tosev 3 makes me doubt it."

"Why am I here, then?" Sam asked. This time, Atvar did not answer him at all.

Atvar had begun to hope he never again saw the park across the way from the hotel in Sitneff. After his talk there with Sam Yeager, he pictured bombs bursting on Tosev 3, and on Home, and on the Empire's other two worlds. How strong *were* the Americans? No way to know, not for certain. All he could know was how strong they had been when the latest signals left Tosev 3.

The Race had comfortably run the Empire at light speed for thousands of years. Delays of signals from one planet to the next had mattered little. But Tosev 3 was farther from Home than either Rabotev 2 or Halless 1, which made delays longer, and the Tosevites changed far faster than any species in the Empire, which made those delays more critical.

Maybe there was a good answer to the problem, but Atvar failed to see it.

He was worried enough to telephone the Emperor again. He didn't get through to Risson. He hadn't expected to, not at once—things simply didn't work that way. He did hope the message he left would persuade Risson to call him back. His Majesty's courtiers knew the Emperor took a keen interest in Tosevite affairs.

Half a day later, Atvar did get a call from Preffilo. That female was on the line again. Atvar assumed the special posture of respect as the Emperor's image appeared on the monitor. As Risson had before, he said, "Rise, Fleetlord, and tell me what is on your mind."

"It shall be done," Atvar said once more, and summarized what he and Sam Yeager had had to say to each other. He finished, "What are we going to do, your Majesty? It strikes me that our choices are to grant the Big Uglies privileges they have not earned and do not deserve, or else to face a devastating war. Neither seems satisfactory."

"Will the American Tosevites fight if we refuse to make these concessions?" the Emperor asked. "Are they as strong as their ambassador claims?" He didn't sound the least bit self-conscious at using the old, old word to describe Sam Yeager's status.

"As for your first question, your Majesty, they might,"
Atvar answered. "Pride pushes them more strongly than it
does us." That he might find it harder to recognize the Race's
pride than the Big Uglies' had never occurred to him. He
went on, "As for the second question, how can we be certain
where the Tosevites are these days?" He reminded the Emperor of the problem with communicating with Tosev 3.

Risson made the affirmative gesture. "Yes, I know the difficulty. It has always been next to impossible to administer
Tosev 3 from Home. As you say, the lag is much more important there than with our other two worlds."

Back when the Race first discovered the Big Uglies were
much more advanced than anyone on Home had thought, the
conquest fleet had dutifully radioed the news from Tosev 3 to
Home. All those years later—more than twenty of Tosev 3's
turns around its star—detailed orders had started coming
back from Home and the bureaucrats here. The only problem
with them was, they were ridiculously unsuited to the situation as it had developed. Atvar had had the sense to ignore
them. The males and females here had taken a lot longer to
have the sense to stop sending them.

"What do you recommend now?" Risson persisted. "Do
you believe making the concessions the American Tosevites
demand is necessary to ensure peace? Do you believe it *will*
ensure peace, or will it only encourage the Big Uglies to demand more from us later?"

"With the Big Uglies, that second possibility is never far
from the surface," Atvar said. "They have only those dull
nails in place of fingerclaws, but they grab fiercely even so."

"That has also been my impression," the Emperor said. "If
we reject their demands, would they truly fight on that account?"

"I am not certain. I wish I were. In the short run, I am inclined to doubt it. But they would surely arm themselves
more powerfully. They would build more starships. We might
decide on a preventive war against them. There is no certainty
that war would succeed now. The longer we wait, the less our
likelihood of victory. That, I would say, *is* certain."

Risson hissed unhappily. "You are telling me our best
choice would be to order all-out war against them now?"

Our best choice would have been to order all-out war against them as soon as the first round of fighting stopped, Atvar thought grimly. But he couldn't have done that. It might have left Tosev 3 uninhabitable, and the colonization fleet was on the way. After muttering Straha's name under his breath, he said, "When it comes to dealing with the wild Big Uglies, your Majesty, there are no good choices. We have to thread our way through the bad and try to avoid the worst."

"I see," the Emperor said. "I always saw, but the coming of this starship has poked my snout in it more strongly than ever." He paused. "Sam Yeager struck me as being a reasonable individual."

"Oh, he is," Atvar agreed. "But he has his duty, which is to represent his not-empire, and he does that quite well. When you consider that he also views the world from an alien perspective, dealing with him becomes all the more difficult."

"An alien perspective," Risson echoed. "We are not used to that. Sam Yeager speaks our language well. He adapted to the ceremonial of the audience as well as a citizen of the Empire could have done."

"Truth. I was proud to be his sponsor. I do not say he is unintelligent—on the contrary," Atvar said. "But he is *different*. His differences are to some degree disguised when he speaks our language. The assumptions behind his thoughts are not assumptions we would make. We believe otherwise at our peril."

"What are we going to do? Can we annihilate the independent Big Uglies even if we want to?" Risson asked.

"I do not know," Atvar answered. "I simply do not know. Conditions on Tosev 3 are different from the way they were when the latest signals reached us. How they are different, who can guess? But they *are* different. Whatever the difference is, I doubt that it redounds to our advantage."

"This is a disaster," the Emperor said. "A disaster, nothing less. We would have done better not to land on Tosev 3 at all, to leave the Big Uglies to their own devices. Maybe they would have destroyed themselves by now. They would not have had any external rivals then, so they might have gone on with their local wars."

"It could be, your Majesty," Atvar said. "Unfortunately, this is not a choice we can make now. We have to deal with the situation as it is, not as it was when the conquest fleet arrived."

"I understand that," the 37th Emperor Risson said. "But am I not allowed to wish it were otherwise?"

"Why not, your Majesty? We all have wishes about what might have been when it comes to the Big Uglies. How could it be otherwise? The way things really are is less than satisfactory."

"Truth," the Emperor said. "Now tell me this, if you would be so kind—suppose we grant every concession the American Big Uglies seek from us. If we give them everything they say they want, will that be enough to make them keep whatever agreement they may make with us?"

"They are, in their own way, honorable. They would *intend* to stick to the terms of a treaty, your Majesty," Atvar said. "The trouble with them is that, unlike us, they are *changeable*. In twenty years, or fifty years, or at most a hundred years, they will not be what they are now. They will look at the treaty, and they will say, 'This is not relevant, because we are not the same as we were. We are smarter. We are stronger. You need to change this, that, and the other thing to reflect these new conditions.' And you may be sure the new terms they demand will be to their advantage, not ours."

"We do change. But we change slowly and sensibly," Risson said. "By all the signs, they change for the sport of changing."

"Oh, they do, your Majesty. They admit it," Atvar replied. "Change has become ingrained in their culture in a way it never did with us. Their motorcars look different from year to year—not because the new ones run better, though they often do, but merely so it can be seen that they *are* new. They change the style of their cloth wrappings in the same way, and for the same reason. It is as if we changed the style of our body paint every few years."

"We could not do that! It would hatch chaos!" Risson exclaimed.

"I understand that. It is one of the reasons I find our young males and females with their false hair and even their wrappings so disturbing. But the Big Uglies embrace change, where we mostly endure it," Atvar said. "Anyone who does not see that does not see the first thing about them. It drives us mad. That we are so different often drives the Big Uglies mad, I think. But their variability has proved a great source of strength for them."

The Emperor let out another unhappy hiss. "Again, you are telling me war now may be our best hope."

"It . . . may be," Atvar said unwillingly. "But it also may not. If war comes, it will cost us more than we have paid in the whole history of the Empire. I do not believe Sam Yeager was lying or bluffing when he said the American Big Uglies would attack all our worlds in case of war. I do not believe we will be able to block all their attacks, either. They will hurt us. They will hurt us badly. Whether the other independent Tosevites will join them against us, I cannot say. If they do, that would make a bad situation worse. How much worse, I am not prepared to guess."

"And what will happen to Tosev 3 if war breaks out between us and the independent Big Uglies?" Risson asked.

"Well, your Majesty, I am not there. In his wisdom, the previous Emperor, your illustrious predecessor, chose to recall me." Atvar could not keep acid from his voice. He went on, "My opinion, however, for what it may be worth, is that the Big Uglies should never get another chance to start a war if they are addled enough to fight now. And if that means leaving Tosev 3 uninhabitable for us and for them, so be it. Up until this time, they were local menaces, restricted to their own solar system. That, unfortunately, is no longer the case."

"It is too late now to send you back to Tosev 3," the Emperor said. Atvar bent into the special posture of respect. Risson had just done what no one else had done before him: he'd admitted the Race had made a mistake in recalling the fleetlord. He gestured for Atvar to rise, then went on, "Do all you can to promote a peaceful resolution of our difficulties. If that fails . . . If that fails, we will do what becomes necessary, and we will do our best."

"It shall be done, your Majesty," Atvar said.

"I hope it shall," Risson replied. "As I say, we shall attempt it, at any rate."

He is not confident we can beat the Big Uglies if it comes to war, Atvar realized. The fleetlord would have been more shocked had he been more confident himself. What had the Tosevites learned in the years since the latest signals from Tosev 3 reached Home? What would they learn in the years while the order to attack was speeding from Home to Tosev 3? Whatever it was, how would they apply it to weapons? Would the Race be able to keep up, to counter them?

"If the spirits of Emperors past are with us, we will not have to do that," Atvar said.

"Let us hope they are. Let us hope we do not have to," Risson said. "But let us also be as ready as we can, so we will see trouble as it hatches and before it grows . . . too much." Atvar wished the Emperor hadn't added the last two words, but made the affirmative gesture anyway.

☆ **13** ☆

Ttomalss had stopped stalking around Sitneff looking for bef-flem to boot. Kassquit would do whatever she did. If it brought her emotional and physical satisfaction, well and good. If it brought her emotional travail . . . she was an adult, and would have to cope with it as best she could.

So the psychologist told himself, anyhow. If a small, mean part of him rather hoped his former ward ran into emotional travail, he had the grace to be ashamed of that part. He did his best not to let it affect his thinking or his actions.

It wasn't as if he had nothing else on his mind. One morning—*early* one morning—Pesskrag telephoned him and said, "I hope you know you are responsible for commencing the unraveling of work thought to be truth for tens of millennia."

"Am I?" Ttomalss said around a yawn. "And how should I feel about this—besides sleepy, I mean?"

"You are—you and that other psychologist back on Tosev 3, that Felless," Pesskrag said. "If you two had not brought the Big Uglies' research to our attention, we might have remained ignorant of these developments . . . forever."

"Now that you know of them, what can you do with them?" Ttomalss' eye turrets were beginning to decide they would work together after all. Once he got some breakfast, he probably would be capable of rational thought. He wouldn't have bet on that when the telephone first hissed for his attention.

"That is why my colleagues and I have been experimenting so diligently: to begin to find out what we can do," the physicist answered. She went on, "We are not altogether sure we believe what we are finding."

"I have asked you before—just what is so startling about

these Tosevite discoveries?" Ttomalss said. "Are you in a better position to tell me than you were the last time we spoke?"

"We may see more change in the next two to five hundred years than we have seen at any time in our history since Home was unified," Pesskrag said.

"What *sort* of change?" Ttomalss demanded. "*How* will things be different?" He hoped for concrete answers.

Pesskrag remained resolutely abstract. "Senior Researcher, at present I have no idea. But, as we evaluate each experiment, it will suggest others, and we will probably have a much better notion of exactly where we are going in a few more years."

"There are times when I believe you are doing your best to addle me with frustration," Ttomalss said. Pesskrag laughed and made the negative gesture. Ttomalss made the affirmative one. "Yes, I do believe that. Will you not give me at least some idea of how much you have learned since we last spoke?"

Laughing still, the physicist replied, "It shall be done, superior sir. Last time we spoke, I believe I said our knowledge was like a new hatchling, still wet with the juices from its egg. We have indeed advanced from that point. Now, in my opinion, our knowledge is like a new hatchling on which the sun has dried the juices from its egg."

"I thank you so very much." Ttomalss' pungent sarcasm set Pesskrag laughing all over again. Ttomalss stubbornly persisted: "How far is the gap from fascinating experiment to workable new technology?"

"I am very sorry, Senior Researcher, but I have no way to judge that," Pesskrag replied. "It will be a while. Technology that induces such major changes will have to be investigated with unusual care. That will slow its implementation. We will need a good many lifetimes before we can fully evaluate it."

She'd said that before, too. "Suppose we were reckless. Suppose we were reckless to the point of being addled." Ttomalss tried to force on her a mental exercise he'd used before. "Suppose we knew whatever it is you now think we know. Suppose we cared nothing for consequences, only for getting the maximum use from this new knowledge. How soon after your discoveries *could* we have workable new technology?"

He had to give Pesskrag credit. She did try to imagine that, though it was alien to all her thinking patterns. "We would have to be completely addled to work in that way," she said. "You do understand as much?"

Ttomalss used the affirmative gesture. "Oh, yes. That is part of the assumption I am asking you to make."

"Very well." Pesskrag's eye turrets both turned up toward the ceiling. Ttomalss had seen that gesture in many males and females who were thinking hard. He used it himself, in fact. After a little while, the physicist's eyes swung toward him again. "You understand my estimate is highly provisional?"

Now Ttomalss had all he could do not to laugh. However wild Pesskrag was trying to be, she remained a typical, conservative female of the Race. He could not hold it against her. "Yes, I understand that," he said gently. "I am only looking for an estimate, not a statement of fact."

"Very well," she said. "Always bearing that in mind, if I were as wild as a wild Big Ugly—for that is what you have in mind, is it not?—I might find something useful within, oh, a hundred fifty years. This assumes no disasters in the engineering and no major setbacks."

"I see. I thank you." Ttomalss was willing to bet the Tosevites would be faster than that. The question was, how much faster than that would they be? Pesskrag was pretending to a wildness she did not have. The Big Uglies did not have a great many things, but they had never lacked for wildness. She'd given Ttomalss an upper limit. He had to figure out the lower limit for himself.

She said, "I thought I would shock you. I see I do not."

"No, you do not," Ttomalss agreed. "Your expertise is in physics. Mine is in matters pertaining to the wild Big Uglies. I admit the field lacks the quantitative rigor yours enjoys. Even so, what I do know of the Tosevites persuades me that your answer is believable."

"That is truly frightening," Pesskrag said. "I have trouble taking my own estimate seriously, and yet it fazes you not at all."

"Oh, it fazes me, but not quite in the way you mean,"

Ttomalss said. How long had the Big Uglies been working on this line of experiments before Felless noticed they were doing it? How much of their research had never got into the published literature for fear of drawing the Race's notice—or, come to that, for fear of drawing rival Tosevites' notice? Those were all relevant questions. He had answers to none of them. He found another question for Pesskrag: "If the Big Uglies do succeed within the timeframe you outline, could we quickly match them?"

"Maybe." Her voice was troubled. "If so, though, we would have to abandon the caution and restraint we have come to take for granted. That would produce even more change than I have outlined."

"I know," Ttomalss said.

Pesskrag said, "If we are forced to change as rapidly as the Big Uglies, will we become as unstable as they are?"

"I doubt it. I doubt we could. But we would have to become more changeable than we are, I think. To some degree, this has already happened with the colonists on Tosev 3," Ttomalss answered.

"As far as I am concerned, that is not a recommendation," Pesskrag said. "I have read of the colonists' strange perversions inspired by Tosevite drugs. I have even read that some of them prefer living among the wild Big Uglies to staying with their own kind. Can such things be true?"

"They can. They are," Ttomalss said. "As is often true when examining social phenomena, though, causation is more complex than it is in the purely physical world."

"I do not care," Pesskrag said stoutly. "Why would any sensible male or female want to live among alien barbarians? Anyone who does such a thing cannot possibly be worthwhile, in my opinion."

"Why? Some males and females who were good friends beforehand became addicted to ginger together. They formed mating bonds like those common among the Big Uglies," Ttomalss said. Pesskrag let out a disgusted hiss. Ttomalss shrugged. "Like them or not, these things have happened on Tosev 3. For a long time, we reckoned such mated pairs perverts, as you say, and were glad to see them go—"

"As well we should have been!" Pesskrag broke in.

"Perhaps. We certainly thought so when these pairs first came to our attention," Ttomalss said. "But ginger is widespread on Tosev 3, and a surprising number of close friends of opposite sexes have become more or less permanent mating partners: so many that we saw we were losing valuable males and females to the Big Uglies by driving all such pairs into exile. These days, there is a sort of tacit tolerance for them on Tosev 3, as long as they do not behave too blatantly in public."

"Disgusting!" Pesskrag added an emphatic cough. "Bad enough that the Big Uglies have revolting habits. But they are as they have evolved to be, and so I suppose they cannot help it. If our own males and females on that planet are no longer fit to associate with decent members of the Race, though, we have a real problem."

"Tosev 3 has presented us with nothing but problems ever since the conquest fleet got there," Ttomalss said. "And yes, I think our society on that world will be different from the way it is elsewhere in the Empire—unless ginger becomes so widespread here and on our other worlds that we begin to match patterns first seen there."

"I hope with all my liver that this does not happen," Pesskrag said.

"So do I. I am a conservative myself, as any sensible male past his middle years should be," Ttomalss said. "But you were the one who said we would see change in the relatively near future. Is it a surprise that some of this change would be social as well as technological?"

"I understand technological change. I understand how to manage it," Pesskrag said. "I am not sure anyone knows how to manage social change. Why should anyone? The Race has little experience with it, and has not had any to speak of since Home was unified."

"Do you know who has experience managing social change?" Ttomalss asked.

Pesskrag made the negative gesture, but then said, "The colonists on Tosev 3?"

"That is astute, but it is not quite what I meant. Close, but not quite," the psychologist said. "As a matter of fact, I had in mind the Tosevites themselves. Their whole history over the past thousand of our years has involved managing major social changes. They have gone from slave-owning agrarians to possessors of a technical civilization that rivals our own, and they have not destroyed themselves in the process."

"Too bad," the physicist said.

"You may be right. If we had stayed away for another few hundred years, they might have solved our problem for us," Ttomalss said. "Then again, if we had stayed away for another few hundred years, they might have come to Home anyway. In that case, all the problems we have with them now would seem trivial by comparison."

"All the problems we have now, yes," Pesskrag said. "The problems on the horizon are not small. Believe me, superior sir—they are not."

"Please give me a written report, in language as nontechnical as you can make it," Ttomalss said.

"As things are, I would rather not put any of this in writing until my colleagues and I are ready to publish," the physicist said.

"Do you believe others will steal your work? I am sure we can discourage that," Ttomalss said.

"Until we know more, I am afraid to let this information out at all," Pesskrag said, and Ttomalss could not make her change her mind.

"Excuse me." The Lizard who spoke to Jonathan Yeager in the lobby of the hotel in Sitneff was not one he had seen before. The male was evidently unfamiliar with his kind, too, continuing, "You would be one of the creatures called Big Uglies, would you not?"

"Yes, that is a truth." Jonathan's amusement faded as he got a look at the Lizard's rather sloppily applied body paint. "And you would be a police officer, would you not?"

"Yes, that is also a truth." The Lizard had a quiet, almost hangdog air. He seemed embarrassed to make the affirmative gesture. "I am Inspector Second Grade Garanpo. I have a few questions to ask you, if you would be so kind."

"Questions about what?" Jonathan asked.

"Well, about the ginger trade, superior sir, if you really

want to know," Garanpo answered. "Ginger comes from your world, does it not?"

"Yes, of course it does," Jonathan said. "But I do not know why you need to ask me about it. I have been here ever since the American diplomatic party came down to the surface of Home. We had no ginger with us then, and we have none now."

"Which of the Tosevites would you be? Meaning no offense, but you all look alike to me," the inspector said. Jonathan gave his name. Garanpo sketched the posture of respect without fully assuming it. "I thank you. I want to know because when there is ginger, one naturally thinks of you Tosevites."

"Why?" Jonathan asked. "Unless I am mistaken, there has been ginger on Home for many years. It must have been brought here by males and females of the Race, because this is the first Tosevite starship to come here. Perhaps you should be looking closer to home, so to speak, than you are."

"Perhaps we should. Perhaps we are. You are a very clever fellow, to make a joke in our language." Garanpo's mouth dropped open in what was obviously a polite laugh. "But perhaps we should also come to the source, you might say."

"Why?" Jonathan asked again. "Whatever your latest problem with ginger is, why do you think it has anything to do with me?"

"With you personally, superior sir? I never said a thing about that," Garanpo said. "I never said it, and I do not mean it. But I think it does have something to do with you Big Uglies, and that is a truth."

"For the third time, Inspector, what is your evidence?"

"Oh, my evidence? I thank you for reminding me." The police officer made as if to assume the posture of respect again, then checked himself. "Well, my evidence is that the price of ginger on the streets lately has fallen right on its snout, if you understand what I am saying."

"I understand what you mean, yes, Inspector," Jonathan answered. "I do not understand why you think this has anything to do with us Big Uglies, though. One of your starships is much more likely to have done the smuggling."

"But we did not have any new ships come in from Tosev 3 just before the price of the herb tumbled," Garanpo said.

Damn, Jonathan thought. But he said, "You have not had any new Tosevite ships come in, either. Why blame the *Admiral Peary*? Our ship has been peacefully orbiting Home for some time now."

"There was recently contact between your ship and one of ours. This was shortly before the price change in ginger," Garanpo said. "No one has found ginger on the *Horned Akiss*—which is the name of our ship—and no one can prove it got from the *Horned Akiss* to the surface of Home, but that is the way things look. No one can prove it *yet,* I should say. Yes, I should say that. But we are working on it, which is also a truth."

Damn, Jonathan thought again. This time, he said, "I think you had better tell my sire, the ambassador, what you have just told me. I think you had better tell him the abridged version of it, too."

"Do you know, superior Tosevite, my supervisor often says the very same thing to me," the Lizard replied. " 'Abridge it, Garanpo,' he says, and so I do my best, but somehow I find myself pining for the details. Have you ever had that feeling, where you are pining to tell all you know because some little part of it may turn out to be *the* important part? And of course you never know which part ahead of time, so. . . ."

He went on for some time. The feeling Jonathan had was guilt at inflicting him on his father. However unpleasant that might be, though, he feared it was necessary. Garanpo had some circumstantial evidence, anyhow.

"Your sire, you tell me?" Garanpo said as he and Jonathan rode up the elevator together. "Now that is interesting, very interesting. I cannot think of many members of the Race who could name their own sires. I am sure I cannot. Are you sure you can?"

He doesn't know he's just insulted me and my mother, Jonathan reminded himself. He made the affirmative gesture and said, "Yes, Inspector, I am sure. Our mating customs differ from yours."

"Well, they must," Garanpo said. "I do not know much about you Big Uglies, I admit." If he was like any human cop

Jonathan had ever met, he was sandbagging like a mad bastard. He went on, "Do you really choose your leaders by snoutcounting? It does not strike me as a very efficient system."

"We really do. It seems to work for us," Jonathan answered. The elevator stopped. The door slid open. Jonathan got out. Without being told, Garanpo turned left, the direction in which Sam Yeager's room lay. Jonathan nodded to himself. Yes, the Lizard knew a good deal more than he was letting on.

After a couple of strides, Garanpo seemed to realize Jonathan wasn't following. One of his eye turrets swung back toward the American. "I do need you to show me the way, you know," he said testily.

"Yes, of course, Inspector," Jonathan said. If Garanpo didn't know his father's room number—and probably his hat size, too—he would have been amazed.

"Hello, son," Sam Yeager said in English after he let Jonathan and Garanpo in. He switched to the language of the Race to ask, "Who is your friend?" Jonathan introduced the policemale. His father said, "I greet you, Inspector. I am pleased to meet you. And what can I do for you today?"

Garanpo did a better job of summing up the ginger situation than Jonathan had thought he could. He finished, "And so, your, uh, Ambassadorship—that is a funny word, is it not?—now you know why I think some of the Big Uglies up in space may have been involved in all this."

"I can see why you think so, yes," Sam Yeager replied. "I can also see that you have nothing resembling proof. Members of the Race out in space might have held ginger to release it at a time when the price was to their liking, too, you know."

"Oh, yes. That is a truth, your Ambassadorship," Garanpo said. "They might have. But they might not have, too. The timing makes me think they did not. And if they did not, what do you propose to do about it?"

"I am not going to answer a hypothetical question. If you have proof Tosevites are involved in this business, by all means come and see me again," Jonathan's father said. "I do want to point out, though, that possession and sale of ginger are not illegal for us. Among Tosevites, it is only a spice, not a drug."

"Is conspiracy illegal?" Garanpo asked, and then waved away his own question. "Never mind. Forget I said that. I will do just what you say, your Ambassadorship, and I thank you for your time. A pleasure to meet you as well, Jonathan Yeager." He sketched the posture of respect to both Americans—a little more deeply to Jonathan's father—and left the room.

"What do you think, Dad?" Jonathan asked.

"I don't know." Sam Yeager checked the antibugging gadgetry on the table between them, then nodded to himself. "Okay. Inspector Garanpo didn't manage to plant anything new in here. That's a relief. I guess we can talk pretty freely. What do I think? I think somebody upstairs screwed up. I think whoever it is better not screw up again, or we'll have trouble diplomatic immunity won't even start to get us out of. What do *you* think?"

"I've got the feeling you're right," Jonathan said in a troubled voice. "I'd be surprised if the *Admiral Peary* didn't have ginger along."

"I'd be *amazed* if the *Admiral Peary* didn't have ginger along," his father agreed. "It's not just a weapon—it's a can opener, too. It can help us find out all kinds of things we wouldn't know about otherwise."

"It can get us into all kinds of trouble we wouldn't know about otherwise, too," Jonathan said.

"Oh, you bet it can." His father added an emphatic cough even though they were speaking English. "It can, and I'd say it just has."

"What are we going to do about it?" Jonathan asked.

Sam Yeager made a sour face. "Only one thing I can think of to do: I've got to have a little heart-to-heart with Lieutenant General Healey. All things considered, I'd rather have a drunk tree surgeon yank my appendix without anesthetic."

Jonathan winced. He couldn't help himself. "You don't *like* Lieutenant General Healey, do you?"

"What gave you that impression?" his father said. They grinned at each other. Sam Yeager went on, "Why, I think the commander is a Swell Old Boy." The capital letters thudded into place. He dropped his voice. When he muttered, "Brass hat," Jonathan wasn't sure he was supposed to hear. But evidently he was, for his father continued, "Healey's the sort of guy who would have cheered his head off when we blew up Lizard colonists in cold sleep. He's the sort of guy who—" He broke off.

By his expression, though, Jonathan had a good notion of what was in his mind. His father probably figured Healey was the sort of guy who would have locked him up and lost the key after he let the Lizards know what the USA had done. There were a lot of people like that. Quite a few of them, understandably, held high military rank.

With a sigh, Sam Yeager said, "Well, it's just got to be done. I don't think the Race can unscramble our communications. Our gear was state of the art in 1994, and better than anything they had on Earth. I wonder what we've got now. Probably walks the message up to the ship and whispers in Healey's ear."

"I'd like to be a fly on the wall when you do talk to him," Jonathan said.

"Nope. No flies. This has got to be between him and me," his father said. "Officially, I don't know anything. Officially, I don't even suspect anything. I'm just calling to check. That's how it's got to be . . . officially. The rest is . . . officially . . . off the record."

There were times, Jonathan knew, when arguing with his father was useless. He could tell this was one of those times. Since his hint hadn't worked, he just said, "Okay, Dad. You know what you're doing." He hoped his father would let him know how things had gone somewhere later on.

Sam Yeager sent him a look of mingled surprise and gratitude. *He thought I was going to squawk,* Jonathan realized. And Jonathan might well have squawked if he were the age he had been when his father went into cold sleep. But he'd done some growing and changing of his own in the seventeen years till they put him on ice.

He set a hand on his father's shoulder. "It really is okay. I'll just stay tuned for the next exciting episode, that's all. We'll find out who done it then, right?"

"Well, sure," his father answered. "Right before the last commercial break. That's how it always works, isn't it?" They both smiled. Jonathan wished life really were so simple. Who didn't? Who wouldn't?

He went back down to the lobby. He more than half expected to find Inspector Garanpo poking around there, looking for signs of ginger. But the Lizard had left. Garanpo had a disorganized air that was also disarming. Jonathan had the feeling a keen brain lurked behind that unimpressive façade.

With a sigh, he went into the refectory. He couldn't do anything about whatever Garanpo found out. He hoped his father could. Whether anyone up on the *Admiral Peary* would pay attention to the American ambassador was an interesting question. Sam Yeager was a civilian these days, while the starship was a military vessel. Would Lieutenant General Healey remember he was supposed to take orders from civilians? If he didn't, what could Dad do about it?

Frank Coffey was sitting in the refectory talking with Kassquit. Jonathan would have liked to hash out some of his worries with the major, but he couldn't now. What he would have to say wasn't for Kassquit's ears. Jonathan hoped Coffey did remember not to tell his new lady friend too much. Then he laughed at himself. He'd assured Karen that that couldn't possibly happen, and now *he* was worrying about it.

Kassquit and Frank Coffey laughed. They had not a care in the world—not a care in more than one world. Jonathan envied them more than he'd thought he could. *He* had worries, sure enough. So did Coffey, as a matter of fact. The only difference was, he didn't know it yet.

How stupid *had* they been, up on the *Admiral Peary*?

When Sam Yeager had a long conversation with Lieutenant General Healey, nobody aboard the *Admiral Peary* except the commandant officially knew what they talked about. That didn't keep rumors from flying, of course. If anything, it made them fly faster than ever. As soon as Glen Johnson heard a rumor involving Healey and ginger, he just nodded to himself.

Sure as hell, the scooter hadn't performed the way it should have when he took it over to the *Horned Akiss*. Sure as hell, it had seemed as if the little rocketship was heavier than usual. It *had* been heavier than usual. Somebody must have figured out a way to pack it full of ginger while fooling the Race's sensors—or maybe the Lizards using those sensors had been well paid not to notice anything out of the ordinary. Such arrangements were common enough on Earth; no doubt they could be cooked up here, too.

Johnson felt like kicking himself because he hadn't figured out what was going on before he delivered the scooter. He didn't like thinking of himself as a chump or a jerk. What choice did he have, though? Not much.

He wasn't the only one on the starship to work out what had probably happened, either. When he came up to the control room to take a shift less than a day after Yeager and Healey talked, Mickey Flynn greeted him with, "And how is everyone's favorite drug smuggler this morning?"

"I haven't the faintest idea," Johnson answered. "You can't mean me."

"I can't? Why not?"

"Because that would violate regulations, and I'd get a spanking if I violated them."

"This has, of course, been your abiding concern since time out of mind."

"Why, certainly," Johnson said. "Would I be here if it weren't?"

"The mind reels at the possibilities," Flynn replied. "Even if you were smuggling drugs to the Race, though, why would you worry about it?"

That was a good question. In truth, Johnson didn't much care how the Lizards amused themselves in their spare time. He wouldn't have minded sending them ginger . . . if it had been his idea. His voice roughened as he answered, "I'll be damned if I want that shithead in charge of us making me do his dirty work for him."

"I'm shocked—shocked, I tell you. Anyone who didn't know better would think you'd conceived a dislike for the man."

What Johnson said to that had something to do with conceiving, but not much. His opinion of Lieutenant General Healey was certainly less than immaculate.

It seemed like fate, then—and not a very benign sort of fate, either—that the commandant of the *Admiral Peary* summoned Johnson to his office as the pilot came off his shift. Mickey Flynn said, "There, you see? He was listening all along."

"I don't care. He already knows what I think of him," Johnson answered, which was true enough. But, however little he wanted to, he did have to find out why Lieutenant General Healey wanted to see him.

Healey greeted him with the usual unfriendly glare. But he said nothing about what Johnson had said in the control room. Instead, fixing him with a glare, the commandant barked, "Are you ready to fly the Lizards' scooter back to the *Horned Akiss*? We've learned everything we're likely to from it."

"That depends, sir," Johnson answered.

Healey's bulldog glower only got angrier. "Depends on what?" he demanded, hard suspicion in his voice.

"On whether you've loaded it up with ginger, the way you did with ours. If you have, you can find yourself another sucker, on account of the Lizards are going to land on whoever tries to pull the same stunt twice like a ton of bricks."

"You're the best scooter pilot we've got. It's almost the only thing you're good for. I can order you to fly that scooter," the commandant said.

"Yes, sir, you sure can," Johnson agreed cheerfully. "And you can fling me in the brig for disobeying orders, too, because I won't take it out of the air lock till you tell me the truth about it."

"I always knew you and that Lizard-loving Yeager were two of a kind," the commandant snarled.

That answered Johnson's question without directly answering it. "Why don't you send Stone, sir?" he asked in turn. "He's always happy to do anything you say."

"He is the senior pilot," Healey said stiffly.

"You mean you can't afford to lose him but you can afford to lose me?" Johnson said. "Well, sir, I've got news for you: *I* can't afford to lose me. So when you send that scooter over, find yourself another boy to ride herd on it."

The commandant glowered at him. Healey had come to expect insubordination from him over the years. Outright insurrection was something else again. "Consider yourself under arrest, Colonel," Healey said. "Report to the brig at once."

"Happy to, sir," Johnson answered. "Only one question: where the hell is it? I haven't gone looking for it till now. I didn't even think we had one."

"We do, and you have so," Healey said. "It's on B deck, room 227. Enjoy yourself."

"Sir, I won't be talking to you, so I expect it'll be a pleasure."

Johnson also had the pleasure of leaving before the commandant could reply. He headed straight for the brig. It proved to be a compartment like any other on the starship. The only difference was, it had a door that wouldn't open from the inside once he closed it after himself. That could be no fun at all in case of emergency, but Johnson refused to dwell on unpleasant possibilities. He strapped himself onto the standard-issue bunk and took a nap.

Nobody bothered him. He began to wonder if Healey'd told anyone he was jugged. Then he wondered if anybody would come by and feed him. He had visions of someone finding a starved, shriveled corpse in the brig the next time Healey decided to throw someone in there, which could be years from now.

He told himself he was being silly. Stone and Flynn would notice he wasn't showing up for his shift. They'd ask where he was . . . wouldn't they? Healey would have to tell them . . . wouldn't he? It all seemed logical enough. But when logic and Lieutenant General Healey collided, all bets were off.

Three hours later, the door to the cell opened. It was Major Parker, Healey's adjutant. Johnson looked at him and said, "I want a lawyer."

"Funny, Colonel. Funny like a crutch," Parker answered.

"What, you think I'm kidding?" Johnson said. "My ass, pardon my French."

"And where are you going to find a lawyer here?" the other officer asked in what he evidently intended for reasonable tones. He looked dyspeptic. Anyone who had to listen to Healey all the time had a good reason for looking dyspeptic, as far as Johnson was concerned.

He said, "Okay, fine. Screw the lawyer. Let me talk to Ambassador Yeager. That ought to do the job. By God, that ought to do it up brown."

Parker looked as if he'd asked for the moon. "The commandant sent me here to let you out as long as you give me your word of honor you'll keep your mouth shut."

"Sorry." Johnson shook his head. "No deal. He's the one who got into this mess, and got me into it with him. He ought to be making me promises, not asking for them. I'd just as soon stay here. How long before the whole ship starts wondering why? How long before the Lizards start wondering why, too?"

"Colonel, you are deliberately being difficult," the adjutant said, his voice starchy with disapproval.

"You noticed!" Johnson exclaimed. Parker turned red. Johnson nodded. "You bet your left nut I'm being difficult, Major. Healey still thinks this is my problem, and he's dead wrong. It's his, and he'd better figure that out pretty damn quick."

"I'll be back." Parker made it sound like a threat. "The commandant won't be very happy with you."

"Well, I'm not very happy with him, either," Johnson said, but he didn't think the other officer heard him.

Another two hours went by. They were not the most exciting time Glen Johnson had ever spent. He wondered if Healey knew how potent a weapon boredom could be. Leave him in here long enough and he'd start counting the rows of thread in his socks for want of anything more interesting to do. Maybe he should have agreed when Parker offered him the deal.

No, goddammit, he thought. Healey had played him for a patsy. He wouldn't be the commandant's good little boy now.

The door opened again. There floated Parker, his face as screwed up as if he'd bitten into a persimmon before it was ripe. He jerked a thumb toward the corridor behind him. "Go on," he said. "Get out."

Johnson didn't move. "What's the hitch?" he asked.

"No hitch," Parker said. "Your arrest is rescinded. Officially, it never happened. You're restored to regular duty, effective immediately. What more do you want, egg in your beer?"

"An apology might be nice," Johnson said. If he was going to be difficult, why not be as difficult as he could?

Healey's adjutant laughed in his face. "You'll wait till hell freezes over, and then twenty minutes longer. Do you want to?" He made as if to close the door once more.

"No, never mind," Johnson said. He hadn't actually demanded one, only suggested it. He didn't have to back down, or not very far. He pushed off from the far wall of the brig and glided out into the corridor. "Ah! Freedom!"

"Funny," Parker said. "Har-de-har-har. You bust me up."

"You think I was kidding?" Johnson said. "Well, you probably would."

"What's that supposed to mean?" the other man said. "I'm just as much an American as you are. I know what freedom's worth."

"You sure don't act like it," Johnson said. "And your boss wouldn't know what it was if it piddled on his shoes."

The two-word answer Healey's adjutant gave was to the point, if less than sweet. Johnson laughed and blew him a kiss. That only seemed to make Parker angrier. Johnson wasn't about to lose any sleep on account of it. He pushed off again and returned to the land of the free and, he hoped, the home of the brave.

He brachiated to the refectory. Walter Stone was there, eating a sandwich and drinking water out of a bulb. The senior pilot waved to Johnson, who glided over to him and grabbed a handhold. "I hear you've been naughty again," Stone said.

"Not me." Johnson shook his head. "It's our beloved skipper. He told me to smuggle more ginger to the Lizards, and I'm afraid I turned him down. Fool me once, shame on you. Fool me twice, shame on me."

"You haven't got the right attitude," Stone said.

"Sorry, but I'm afraid I do," Johnson said. "Healey wants me to give the Lizards ginger? Okay, fine. He doesn't care if they catch me and toss me in one of their clinks for the next thirty years? That's not fine, not by me, not when the Race knows what we're up to. And the Lizards do know. You can't tell me any different."

Stone looked as if he would have liked nothing better. He

didn't, though. And if he couldn't, Johnson thought, nobody could.

Kassquit was happy. She needed a while to recognize the feeling. She hadn't known it for a while—a long while. She'd known satisfaction of a sort, most commonly at a job well done. Sometimes that masqueraded as happiness. Now that she'd run into the genuine article again, she recognized the masquerade for what it was.

She knew sexual satisfaction was part of her happiness. So she'd told Ttomalss—and she'd taken a different kind of satisfaction at discomfiting him. But the longer the feeling lasted, the more she noticed other things that went into it.

Chief among them was being valued for her own sake. That was something she'd seldom known among the Race. By the nature of things, it wasn't something she could easily know in the Empire. To Ttomalss and to the other males and females who dealt with her, she was about as much experimental animal as she was person. She couldn't be a proper female of the Race, and she couldn't be a normal Big Ugly, either.

But Frank Coffey made her feel as if she were. He talked with her. Members of the Race had talked to her. Looking back, she thought even Jonathan Yeager had talked to her. Now she discovered the difference.

But to Frank Coffey, what she said mattered at least as much as what he said. And that held true whether they were talking about something as serious as the relations between the Empire and the United States or as foolish as why her hair was straight while his curled tightly.

"There are black Tosevites in the United States whose hair is straight," he said one day.

"Are there?" she said, and he made the affirmative gesture. "And are there also Tosevites of my type with hair like yours?"

This time, he used the negative gesture. "No, or I have never heard of any. The black Tosevites I mentioned artificially straighten theirs."

"Why would they want to do such a foolish thing?" Kassquit asked.

"To look more like the white Tosevites who dominate in the

United States." Coffey sounded a little—or maybe more than a little—grim.

"Oh." Kassquit felt a sudden and altogether unexpected stab of sympathy for wild Big Uglies she'd never seen. "By the spirits of Emperors past, I understand that. I used to shave all the hair on my body to try to look more like a female of the Race. I used to be sorry I had these flaps of skin—*ears*—instead of hearing diaphragms, too. I even thought of having them surgically removed."

"I am glad you did not," he said, and leaned over to nibble on one of them. Kassquit liked that more than she'd thought she would. After a moment, Frank Coffey went on, "You know more than I do about being a minority. That is something surprising for a black American Tosevite to have to admit. But I was never a minority of one."

"Never till now," Kassquit pointed out.

"Well, no," he said. "For once, though, I feel more isolated simply because I am a Tosevite than because I am a black Tosevite. That, I admit, is an unusual feeling."

"You are not black," Kassquit said "You are an interesting shade of brown—a good deal darker than I am, certainly, but a long way from black." His skin tone showed up to fine advantage against the smooth white plastic of the furniture in the refectory.

"Sometimes my shade of brown has proved more interesting than I wished it would," he said, laughing. This time, Kassquit heard no bitterness in his voice. He added, "You and I are part of the default setting for Tosevites, after all."

"The default setting?" Kassquit wondered if she'd heard correctly, and also if Coffey had used the Race's language correctly.

He made the affirmative gesture. He meant what he'd said, whether it was correct or not. Then he explained: "Most Tosevites have dark brown eyes and black hair. Skin color can vary from a dark pinkish-beige like Tom de la Rosa through Tosevites like you to those a little darker than I am, but the hair and eyes stay the same. The default setting, you see? Only in the northwestern part of the main continental mass did Tosevites with very pale skins, light eyes, and yellow or reddish hair evolve. They have colonized widely—they were the ones who developed technological civilization on our planet—but they hatched in a limited area."

"The default setting." Kassquit said it again, thoughtfully this time. "This makes me one of the majority?"

"As far as Tosevites are concerned, it certainly does." Coffey made the affirmative gesture. "You were hatched in China, I believe, and there are more Chinese than any other kind of Tosevite."

"I have heard this before," Kassquit said. "When I was all alone among the Race, it did not seem to matter much. Now that I am not alone any longer, it means more."

Now that I am not alone any longer. Those words meant more than she'd ever dreamt they could. Maybe that was the secret of her new happiness. No, not maybe—without a doubt. Except for the brief, bright segment of her life when Jonathan Yeager came aboard her starship, she hadn't kept company with other Big Uglies throughout her life. She didn't realize how much she missed that company till she had it again. Being among her own biological kind simply felt right.

Maybe that was because wild Big Uglies understood her in ways the Race couldn't. For all she knew, it was just because Tosevites smelled subconsciously right to her. Pheromones didn't play as obvious a role with Tosevites as they did with the Race, but that didn't mean they weren't there.

Whatever the reason, she liked it.

Quietly, Frank Coffey said, "When I set what I have gone through in my lifetime against what you have suffered, I am embarrassed that I have ever complained. Next to you, I am nothing but a beginner."

"Most of it has not been . . . so bad," Kassquit said. "When you are in a situation that never changes, you do your best to get used to it, whatever it is. Only when you have something to compare it against do you begin to see it might not have been everything you wished it would be."

"Truth—not a small truth, either," Coffey said. "That is probably why so many dark brown Tosevites accepted second-class status in the United States for so long." He smiled. "You see? I said 'dark brown.' But they did not see anything else was possible, and so they complained less than they might have. When pale Tosevites' attitudes about us began to change, we took as much advantage of it as quickly as we could."

"And, as you have said yourself, you proved you deserve to be included in your Tosevite society by isolating yourself here on Home," Kassquit said.

He shrugged. "Some things are worth the price. From what I have heard in the signals sent out from Tosev 3, relations between dark and pale Tosevites in the United States are smoother now than they were when I went into cold sleep."

"Do you think you are responsible for that?" Kassquit asked.

"Maybe a little—a very little," Coffey answered. "I would like to think that I have made a difference in my not-empire, even if the difference is only a small one." He pointed to her. "You, now, you have made a difference in the Empire."

"Oh, yes, a great difference." Kassquit wished she weren't being ironic, but she was. "The Race has had to figure out what to do with one Big Ugly who does not know what to do with herself."

"Considering how you were raised, you have done very well." The American Tosevite added an emphatic cough.

"I thank you," Kassquit said. "I tell myself this. I have told myself this a great many times. I wish I could persuade myself it is a truth."

"Well, it is, if my opinion is worth anything," Coffey said. "You are highly educated and highly capable."

"I am highly abnormal, in a great many ways." Kassquit tacked on an emphatic cough of her own. "I know this. You will not offend me by agreeing with it. Truth is truth, with me as with anyone else."

"Have you ever wondered what you would have been like if Ttomalss had not got you from your mother?" Coffey asked.

"Only ten thousand times!" she exclaimed. "I could have been an average Big Ugly!" Part of her, a large part, irresistibly yearned for that. Just to be someone like everyone else around her . . . What would that be like? It seemed wonderful, at least to one who had never known the feeling.

"You could have been an average female Chinese Big Ugly not long after the conquest fleet came," Frank Coffey said. "This is a less delightful prospect than you may believe. You would have had only about a fifty percent chance of living past the age of five—Tosevite years, of course. You probably would not have learned to read, let alone anything more. You would have worked hard all your life, and likely would have been mated to a male who did as he pleased but would not give you the same privilege. Sex differences in social roles are much larger among us than they are in the Race."

He spoke truths—Kassquit knew as much. Even so, she said, "I would have been myself, the self I was meant to be. Here, now, the way I am, what am I? Nothing! I cannot even speak a Tosevite language."

"No matter what language you speak, you make yourself understood," Coffey said. "Not only that, but you have something worth saying. What else matters?"

"I thank you again," Kassquit said. "Whenever we speak, you make me feel good. This is a pleasure worth setting alongside the pleasure you give me when we lie together."

The wild Big Ugly mimed the beginnings of the posture of respect, just the way a member of the Race might have done. "I thank *you*," he said. "It is mutual, you know, as such things should be. It is not just that you do not dislike me or look down on me because I have dark skin. I do not think the other Americans here do that. But it has never occurred to you that disliking or looking down on me because of my skin is even a possibility. That is not and cannot be true of them, not with society in the United States being as it was when we all went into cold sleep."

"Do you suppose it can be true of society in your not-empire as it is now?" Kassquit asked.

"I do not think so," Coffey answered. "More change still will have come, I suppose, by the time I get back to Tosev 3. Maybe then . . . and maybe not, too."

Kassquit didn't want to think about his leaving. She remembered how unhappy she'd been after Jonathan Yeager went back down to the surface of Tosev 3. She was happier now than she had been with him. Would she be unhappier without Frank Coffey in proportion to the degree she was happier with him? Probably. That seemed logical, even if logic didn't always play a large role in emotional dealings.

I am happy now. By the spirits of Emperors past, I will

enjoy being happy now. I will savor it. And if I am unhappy later, I suppose I will end up savoring that, too.

As if reading her thoughts, Coffey said, "I am not going anywhere for a while."

"Good," Kassquit said, and used one more emphatic cough.

By now, a fair number of shopkeepers in Sitneff were used to having Big Uglies drop in on them. Karen Yeager ignored her husband's teasing about having no clothes to shop for here. She knew Jonathan wouldn't have minded watching her or any other reasonably good-looking woman who wore body paint and nothing else.

Because she couldn't shop for clothes (like any good teasing, Jonathan's held a grain of truth), she had to improvise. Bookstores fascinated her, as they fascinated her father-in-law. Very often, one of her guards would pull out a transaction card and buy something for her. Sooner or later, his superiors would pay him back. Since none of the guards grumbled about how much money Karen cost, she guessed the repayment arrangements were more efficient than they would have been in the USA.

The Race's printed lines ran from top to bottom of the page and from right to left across it. Lizards opened books at what would have been the back by American standards and worked their way forward. Other than that, their volumes were surprisingly similar to the ones humans used. They stored a lot of data electronically, but they hadn't abandoned words on paper.

"Why should we?" a bookstore clerk responded when she remarked on that. "Books are convenient. They are cheap. They require no electronic support. Why make things more complicated than necessary?"

Back on Earth, the answer would have been, *Because we can.* Sometimes the Race was wise enough not to do what it had the technical ability to do. Not so many humans had that kind of wisdom.

One of her guards said, "If a beffel chews up a book, that is an annoyance. If a beffel chews up an electronic reader, that is a larger annoyance and a larger expense."

"Befflem *are* nuisances," another guard said. "I often wonder why we put up with them. They run wild and get into everything."

He swung his eye turrets toward Karen, then looked away again a moment later. She knew what that meant. Lizards often compared humans to befflem. She didn't think of it as an insult, though the Race often meant it that way. She liked the small, feisty creatures the Lizards kept as pets. She would have liked them even better if they hadn't gone feral and made nuisances of themselves over such a broad part of Earth.

"Are you finished here, superior Tosevite?" the first guard asked her.

She made the affirmative gesture. "I am," she said. "Since we have been speaking of befflem, would you be kind enough to take me to a pet store?"

"It shall be done, superior Tosevite." Did the guard sound amused or resigned? Karen couldn't quite tell. She would have bet on the latter, though.

She didn't care. She enjoyed the Race's pet shops at least as much as bookstores. The bookstores did smell better. Pet shops on Earth were often full of earthy odors. Pet shops on Home were full of unearthly odors, sharper and more ammoniacal than their equivalents back in the USA. Karen didn't mind all that much. The odors weren't dreadful, and after a few minutes she always got used to them.

Befflem in cages scurried around and squabbled with one another and beeped at anyone who went by and stuck out their tongues to help odors reach their scent receptors. They also beeped at the larger, more dignified tsiongyu, the Race's other favorite pets. The tsiongyu usually ignored the befflem. Every once in a while, though, they lost their air of lordly disdain and tried to hurl themselves through the wire mesh of their cages at the low-slung, scaly beasts that annoyed them. When they did, the befflem only got more annoying. A beffel's chief purpose in life often seemed to be getting someone or something angry at it.

Karen fascinated the befflem. Just as the odors in the pet store were alien to her, her smell was nothing they'd ever met before. They crowded to the front of their cages. Their tongues flicked in and out, in and out, tasting the strange odors of

Earth. Their beeps took on a plaintive note. The befflem might almost have been asking, *What are you? What are you doing here?*

The tsiongyu, by contrast, pretended Karen wasn't there. They were long-legged, elegant, and snooty. *Too smart for their own good* was how she thought of them. They ignored the members of the Race in the pet shop, too. They could be affectionate, once they got to know somebody. With strangers, though, it was as if they were society matrons who hadn't been introduced.

There were also cages with evening sevod and other flying creatures in them. They stared at Karen out of turreted eyes. It wasn't evening, so the sevod weren't singing. The other flying animals squawked and hissed and buzzed. Karen wouldn't have wanted anything that made noises like that in her house. By the prices on the cages, the Lizards didn't mind the racket at all.

Farther back in the store were aquariums filled with Home's equivalent of fish. They looked much less different from fish on Earth than land creatures here did from land creatures on Karen's home planet. Water imposed more design constraints on evolution than air did. But the turreted, swiveling eyes went back a long, long way in the history of life on Home, for the fishy things used them, too.

One silver variety swam along just below the surface of the water. It had unusually long eye turrets. They stuck up into the air, as if they were twin periscopes on a submarine. A guard said, "When the shooter sees a ffissach or some other prey on a leaf over its stream, it spits water at it, knocks it down, and eats it."

"Truth?" Karen said. The male made the affirmative gesture. Karen came closer and looked at the little watery creatures with new interest—till one of them, literally, spat in her eye. She jumped back in a hurry, dabbing at her face with the sleeve of her T-shirt.

The guards all laughed. They thought that was the funniest thing they'd ever seen. Once Karen had dried off, she did, too. "You see, superior Tosevite?" said the guard who'd told her about shooters.

"I do see," Karen said. "But why did the shooter spit water

at me? I was not sitting on a leaf." The guards thought that was pretty funny, too.

As they left the pet shop, the manager called, "Would you not like a beffel of your own, superior Tosevite? Life with a beffel is never dull." Karen believed that. She didn't rise to the sales pitch, though.

Out on the sidewalk, a Lizard came up to her and said, "Excuse me, but are you not one of the creatures called Big Uglies?"

"Yes, that is what I am," Karen agreed. Most of the time, members of the Race used the name without even thinking it might be insulting. She wondered how often whites had said *nigger* the same way around Frank Coffey.

Then, suddenly, she had other things to worry about. The Lizard opened his mouth wide and bit her in the arm.

She screamed. She pounded the Lizard on the snout. She kicked him. She grabbed his arm when he tried to claw her, too. After a heartbeat of stunned surprise, the guards jumped on the Lizard and pulled him off her.

"Big Uglies killed both my best friends on Tosev 3!" he shouted. "I want revenge! I have to have revenge!"

"You are as addled as an unhatched egg abandoned in the sun," a guard said.

Karen paid next to no attention. Lizards' teeth were sharp and pointed. She bled from at least a dozen punctures and tears. On Earth, improvising a bandage would have been easy, for cloth was everywhere. Not so here. She pulled her T-shirt off over her head and wrapped it around her arm. Seeing her in a bra and shorts wouldn't scandalize the Lizards. They thought she was peculiar any which way.

Two guards dragged off the Lizard who'd bitten her. The third one bent into the posture of respect, saying, "I apologize, superior Tosevite. From the depths of my liver, I apologize. That male must be deranged."

Karen's arm hurt too much for her to care about the Lizard's psychiatric condition. Through clenched teeth, she said, "Take me back to the hotel. I want to have our physician look at these wounds and clean them."

"It shall be done, superior Tosevite," the guard said, and done it was.

Back at the hotel, both Lizards and humans exclaimed when they saw her with a bloody shirt wrapped around her arm. They exclaimed again when she told them how she'd got hurt. "Please get out of the way," she said several times. "I need to see Dr. Blanchard."

"Well, this is a lovely mess," the physician said when she got a good look at Karen's injuries. She cleaned them, which hurt. Then she disinfected them, which hurt worse. "A couple of those are going to need stitches, I'm afraid."

"Will they get infected?" Karen asked.

"Good question," Dr. Blanchard said. She didn't answer right away, reaching for the novocaine instead. That hurt going in, but numbed things afterwards. Before she started suturing, though, she went on, "We haven't seen much in the way of germs here on Home that bother us. But I'll tell you, I wish you hadn't picked this particular way to try the experiment."

"So do I," Karen said feelingly. "The Lizard must have been storing up resentment since the days of the conquest fleet—well, since the days when word from the conquest fleet got back from Home. And the first Big Ugly he saw, he just went *chomp!* Good thing he didn't have a gun."

"Probably a very good thing," Melanie Blanchard agreed. "Um, you may not want to watch this."

"You're right. I may not." Looking was making Karen woozy. "Do you think a tetanus shot would help?"

"I doubt it. They won't have tetanus here. They'll have something else instead," the doctor answered, which made an unfortunate amount of sense. "I will give you a bunch of our antibiotics, though. I hope they'll do some good, but I can't promise you anything."

"Why not give me some of the ones the Lizards use, too?" Karen asked.

"I would, except I think they're more likely to poison you than help you," Dr. Blanchard answered. "I don't know of any that have been tested on us. I don't think anyone ever saw the need before."

"Oh, joy," Karen said. "If I start breaking out in green and purple blotches—"

"If you do, all bets are off," Melanie Blanchard said. "But I don't want to try anything like that before I have to, because it *is* dangerous for you. I think I'd better consult with some of the Race's doctors, to find out which drugs I ought to use just in case."

"I didn't come here intending to be a guinea pig," Karen said.

"People hardly ever do intend to become guinea pigs," Dr. Blanchard observed. "Sometimes it happens anyway."

"What do you think the chances are?" Karen asked.

Dr. Blanchard sent her a severe look. "Guinea pigs don't get to ask questions like that. They find out." *Oh, joy,* Karen thought again.

When Jonathan Yeager went into cold sleep, he never thought he would have to worry about whether his wife came down with a wound infection. He'd imagined a nuclear confrontation between the *Admiral Peary* and the forces of the Race, but never an angry Lizard with a long-festering grudge and a nasty set of teeth. He wished he hadn't thought of the grudge in those terms—not that he could do anything about it now.

"How are you?" he asked Karen every morning for a week.

"Sore. Nauseated, too," she would answer—she was taking a lot of antibiotics.

At the end of the week, Jonathan's heart began coming down from his throat. His wife seemed to be healing well. Dr. Blanchard took out the stitches. She gave a cautious thumbs-up, saying, "With luck, no more excitement."

"I'd vote for that," Karen said. "Excitement isn't why I came here. And good old dull looks nice right now."

"You've got apologies from everybody but the Emperor himself," Jonathan said.

His wife shrugged. "I'd rather not have got bitten in the first place, if it's all the same to you."

"Well, yes, I can see that," Jonathan said. "I'm glad you seem to be healing all right."

"*You're* glad!" Karen exclaimed. "What about me? I was joking with the doctor about breaking out in green and purple blotches—and I was hoping I *was* joking, if you know what I mean."

"Our germs don't seem to bother the Lizards, so it's only fair the ones on Home should leave us alone," Jonathan said.

"That's what Melanie told me. That's nice and logical," his wife replied. "When it's your arm, though, logic kind of goes out the window."

"The crazy Lizard could have raised an even bigger scandal," Jonathan said.

"How? By biting your father?" Karen said. "That would have done it, all right. He's the ambassador, after all, not just an ambassador's flunky like yours truly."

"Well, I'm just an ambassador's flunky, too," Jonathan said, a little uneasily. Comparisons with his father made him nervous. He was good enough to get here. His father was good enough to head up the American embassy. Not a lot of difference, but enough. He shook his head. That wasn't what he wanted to think about right now. He went on, "I had something else in mind. What if the crazy Lizard had bitten Kassquit?"

"Kassquit?" Karen thought about it, then started to giggle. "Yes, that would have been a hoot, wouldn't it? Poor Lizard is angry at the Big Uglies because his friends got killed during the fighting, and then he would have hauled off and bitten the only Big Ugly who wishes she were a Lizard and has the citizenship to prove it? That would have been better than man bites dog."

The Lizard's story was pathetic, if you looked at it from his point of view. Here he'd nursed his grief and his grudge all these years—it would have been close to eighty of the Earthly variety since he got the bad news—and what had he got for it? One snap—at a human who hadn't been more than a baby when the fighting stopped. Oh, yes: he'd got one more thing. He'd got all the trouble the Race could give him. They'd lock him up and eat the key, which was what they did instead of throwing it away.

Jonathan didn't worry about going into Sitneff even after his wife's unfortunate incident. His guards asked him about it once. He said, "Any male of the Race who bites me will probably come down with acute indigestion. And, in my opinion, he will deserve it, too."

That startled the guards into laughing. One of them said, "Superior Tosevite, do you taste as bad as that?"

"Actually, I do not know," Jonathan answered. "I have never tried to make a meal of myself." The guards laughed again. They didn't try to restrict his movements, and keeping them from doing that was what he'd had in mind.

Like Karen, he prowled bookstores. He read the Race's language even better than he spoke it. Words on a page just sat there. They could be pinned down and analyzed. In the spoken language, they were there and gone.

Since word of the conquest fleet's arrival on Tosev 3 got back to Home, the Lizards had spent a good deal of time and ingenuity writing about humans, their customs, and the planet on which they dwelt. Much of that writing was so bad, it was almost funny. Jonathan didn't care. He bought lots of those books. No matter how bad they were, they said a lot about what the Lizard in the street thought of Big Uglies.

The short answer seemed to be, *not much.* According to the Race's writers, humans were addicted to killing one another, often for the most flimsy of reasons. Photographs from the *Reich* and the Soviet Union illustrated the point. They were also sexually depraved. Photographs illustrated that point, too, photographs that wouldn't have been printable back on Earth. Here, the pictures were likelier to rouse laughter than lust. And humans were the ones who grew ginger.

Ginger had spawned a literature of its own. Most of that literature seemed intended to convince the Lizards of Home that it was dreadful stuff, a drug no self-respecting member of the Race should ever try. Some of it put Jonathan in mind of *Reefer Madness* and other propaganda films from before the days he was born—his father would talk about them every now and again. But there were exceptions.

One Life, One Mate was by the defiant female half of a permanently mated Lizard pair: permanently mated thanks to ginger and what it did to female pheromones. The pair was, for all practical purposes, married, except the idea hadn't occurred to the Lizards till they got to Tosev 3. The female described all the advantages of the state and how it was superior to the ordinary friendships males and females formed. She was talking about love—but, again, that was something the Lizards hadn't known about till they bumped into humanity.

She went on almost endlessly about how the mixture of friendship and sexual pleasure produced a happiness unlike any she'd known at Home (the ginger might have had something to do with that, too, but she didn't mention it). Rhetorically, she asked why such an obvious good should be reserved for Big Uglies alone. She complained about the Race's intolerance toward couples that had chosen to create such permanent bonds with ginger. The biographical summary at the back of the book (it would have been the front in one in English) said she and her mate were living in Phoenix, Arizona. Jonathan knew not all permanently mated pairs were expelled from the Race's territory these days. The author and her partner, though, had done as so many others had before them, and found happiness as immigrants in the USA.

Jonathan's guards had a low opinion of *One Life, One Mate*. "Bad enough to be a pervert," one of them said. "Worse to brag about it."

"Meaning no offense, superior Tosevite," another added. "This kind of mating behavior is natural for you. We of the Race thought it was peculiar at first, but now we see that is an inescapable part of what you are. But our way is as natural for us as yours is for you. Would any Tosevites want to imitate our practices?"

Hordes of lust-crazed women not caring who joined with them, panting and eager for the first man who came along? Dryly, Jonathan said, "Some of our males might not mind so very much."

"Well, it would be unnatural for them," the second guard insisted. "And your way is unnatural for us. Next thing you know, this addled female will want each pair to take care of its own eggs and hatchlings, too." His mouth fell open and his jaw waggled back and forth in derisive laughter.

"That is how we do things," Jonathan said.

"Yes, but your hatchlings are weak and helpless when they are newly out of the egg," the guard said, proving he'd done some—but not quite all—of his homework about Big Uglies. "Ours need much less care."

"Truth," the first guard said.

Was it the truth? The Race took it as gospel, but Jonathan wasn't so sure. His folks—and then he and Karen—had raised Mickey and Donald as much as if they were human beings as possible. The little Lizards had learned to talk and to act in a fairly civilized way much faster than hatchlings seemed to do among the Race. Maybe giving them lots of attention had its advantages.

And maybe you don't know what the devil you're talking about, Jonathan thought. Mickey and Donald were no more normal Lizards than Kassquit was a normal human. With her example before them, the Americans had gone ahead anyway. Jonathan had been proud of that when the project first began. He wasn't so proud of it any more. His family had done its best, but it couldn't possibly have produced anything but a couple of warped Lizards.

He had more sympathy for Ttomalss than he'd ever dreamt he would. That was something he intended never to tell Kassquit.

"I have a question for you, superior Tosevite," the second guard said. "Ginger is common and cheap on your world. Suppose all the males and females of the Race there fall into these perverted ways. How will we deal with them? How can we hope to deal with them, when they have such disgusting habits?"

The question was real and important. It had occurred to humans and to other members of the Race. The answer? As far as Jonathan knew, nobody had one yet. He tried his best: "I do not believe all members of the Race on Tosev 3 will change their habits. More of them use ginger there than here, yes, but not everyone there does—far from it. And those who keep to their old habits on Tosev 3 have learned to be more patient and respectful toward those who have changed their ways. Perhaps members of the Race here should learn to do the same. Sometimes different is only different, not better or worse."

All three of his guards made the negative gesture. The one who had not spoken till now asked, "How do you Tosevites treat the perverts among you? I am sure you have some. Every species we know has some."

"Yes, we do," Jonathan agreed. "How do we treat them?

Better than we used to, I will say that. We are more tolerant than we were. Perhaps you will find that the same thing happens to you as time goes by."

"Perhaps we will, but I doubt it," that third guard said. "What is right is right and what is wrong is wrong. How can we possibly put up with what anyone sensible can tell is wrong with a single swing of the eye turret?" His companions made the affirmative gesture.

"Your difficulty is, the Race's society has not changed much for a very long time," Jonathan said. "When anything different does come to your notice, you want to reject it without even thinking about it."

"And why should we not? By the spirits of Emperors past, we know what is right and proper," the guard declared. Again, his comrades plainly agreed with him. Jonathan could have gone on arguing, but he didn't see the point. He wasn't going to change their minds. They were sure they already had the answers—had them and liked them. He'd never thought of the Lizards as Victorian, but he did now.

☆ 14 ☆

The Race didn't arrest Walter Stone after he returned their scooter to them. Glen Johnson assumed that meant whatever ginger had been aboard was removed before they got it back. Stone said, "What would you do if I told you they didn't even search the scooter?"

"What would I do?" Johnson echoed. "Well, the first thing I'd do is, I'd call you a liar."

Stone looked at him. "*Are* you calling me a liar?" His voice held a distinct whiff of fists behind the barn, if not of dueling pistols at dawn.

Johnson didn't care. "That depends," he answered. "*Are* you telling me the Lizards didn't search the scooter? If you are, you're damn straight I'm calling you a liar. They aren't stupid. They know where ginger comes from, and they know damn well the Easter Bunny doesn't bring it."

"You're the one who brought it the last time," Stone observed.

"Yeah, and you can thank our beloved commandant for that, too," Johnson said. "I've already thanked him in person, I have, I have. He played me for a sucker once, and he wanted to do it again. Do you think the Lizards would have given me thirty years, or would they have just chucked me out the air lock?"

"They didn't find any ginger on the scooter," Stone said, tacitly admitting they had looked after all.

"They didn't find it when you took it over," Johnson said. "Suppose there hadn't been that delay before you flew it. Suppose I'd taken it when Healey told me to. What would they have found then?"

"I expect the same nothing they found when I got to their

ship." Stone sounded unperturbed, but then he usually did. He'd been a test pilot before he started flying in space. It wasn't that nothing fazed him, only that he wouldn't admit it if something did.

Being a Marine, Johnson had a dose of the same symptoms himself. That inhuman calm was a little more than he could take right now, though. "My ass," he said. "And it would have been my ass if I'd taken the scooter over to the *Horned Akiss*. You've got a lot of damn nerve pretending anything different, too."

"If you already know all the answers, why do you bother asking the questions?" Stone pushed off and glided out of the control room.

Resisting the impulse to propel the senior pilot with a good, swift kick, Johnson stayed where he was. Home spun through the sky above, or possibly below, him. He went around the world every hour and a half, more or less. What would things have been like for the Lizards in the days when they were exploring Home? Seas here didn't all connect; there was no world-girdling ocean, the way there was on Earth. The first Lizard to circumnavigate his globe had done it on foot. How long had it taken him? What dangers had he faced?

The Race could probably answer all those questions as fast as he could ask them. It didn't matter that woolly mammoths and cave bears had seemed at least as likely as people to inherit the Earth when the first Lizard went all the way around Home. The data would still be there. Johnson was as sure of that as he was of his own name. The Race had more packrat genes in it than humanity did.

But Johnson didn't call the *Horned Akiss* or one of the Race's other orbiting spacecraft to try to find out. He didn't want chapter and verse. He wanted his own imagination. What would that Lizard have thought when he got halfway around? The animals and plants would have been strange. So would the Lizards he was meeting. They would have spoken different languages and had odd customs.

None of that was left here any more, not even a trace. Home was a much more homogenized place than Earth. Lizards everywhere spoke the same language. Even local accents had just about disappeared. From everything Johnson could tell, all Lizard cities except maybe the capital—which was also a shrine, and so a special case—looked pretty much alike. You could drop a female from one into another on the far side of Home and she'd have no trouble getting along.

Is that where we're going? Johnson wondered. Even nowadays, someone from Los Angeles wouldn't have much trouble coping in, say, Dallas or Atlanta. But Boston and San Francisco and New York City and New Orleans were still very much their own places, and Paris and Jerusalem and Shanghai were whole separate worlds.

Thinking of separate worlds made Johnson shake his head. You could take that imaginary female of the Race and drop her into a town on Rabotev 2 or Halless 1, and she still wouldn't miss a beat. Oh, she'd know she wasn't on Home any more; there'd be Rabotevs or Hallessi on the streets. But she'd still fit in. They'd all speak the same language. They'd all reverence the spirits of Emperors past. She wouldn't feel herself a stranger, the way a woman from Los Angeles would in Bombay.

And the Lizards didn't seem to think they'd lost anything. To them, the advantages of uniformity outweighed the drawbacks. He shrugged. Maybe they were right. They'd certainly made their society work. People had been banging one another over the head long before the Race arrived, with no signs of a letup any time soon. If the Race had stayed away, they might have blown themselves to hell and gone by now.

If the Lizards had come to Earth now, in the twenty-first century, humans probably would have beaten the snot out of them. If they'd come any earlier than they did, they would have wiped the floor with people. Only in a narrow range of a few years would any sort of compromise solution have been possible. And yet that was what had happened. It was pretty strange, when you got right down to it.

Fiction has to be plausible. Reality just has to happen. Glen Johnson couldn't remember who'd said that, but it held a lot of truth.

Most of Home was spread out before him. As usual, there was less cloud cover here than on Earth. Deserts and mountains and meadows and seas were all plainly visible, as if displayed on a map. Johnson wondered what effect Home's geography had had on the Race's cartography. Back on Earth, people had developed map projections to help them navigate across uncharted seas. Hardly any seas here were wide enough to be uncharted.

He shrugged. That was one more thing the Lizards could probably tell him about in great detail. But he didn't want to know in great detail. Sometimes, like a cigar, idle curiosity was only idle curiosity.

Counting cold sleep, he hadn't smoked a cigar in close to seventy years. Every now and then, the longing for tobacco still came back. He knew the stuff was poisonous. Everybody knew that these days. People still smoked even so.

He laughed, not that it was funny. "Might as well be ginger," he muttered, "except you can't have such a good time with it."

All things considered, the Indians had a lot to answer for. The Europeans had come to the New World and given them measles and smallpox, and it didn't look as if America had sent syphilis back across the Atlantic in return. But tobacco was the Indians' revenge. It had probably killed more people than European diseases in the Americas.

The insidious thing about tobacco was that it killed slowly. Back in the days before doctors knew what they were doing, you were likely to die of something else before it got you. That meant people got the idea it was harmless, and the smoking habit—the smoking addiction—spread like a weed.

But with diseases like typhoid and smallpox and TB knocked back on their heels, more and more people lived long enough for lung cancer and emphysema and smoking-caused heart attacks to do them in. And kicking the tobacco habit was no easier than it had ever been. Once the stuff got its hooks in you, hooked you were. Some people said quitting heroin was easier than quitting tobacco.

Johnson hadn't had any choice. He was healthier than he would have been if he'd kept on lighting up. He knew that. He missed cigars and cigarettes even so. He'd never smoked a pipe. He managed to miss those, too.

Then something else occurred to him. Humanity and the Race were both liable to be lucky. While European diseases had devastated the natives of the Americas, Lizards and people hadn't made each other sick. They'd shot one another, blown one another up, and blasted one another with nuclear weapons. But germ warfare didn't seem to work out. *Thank God for small favors,* he thought.

Mickey Flynn came up the access tube and into the control room. "A penny for your thoughts," he said. "I know I'm overspending, but such is life."

"Thank you so much. I'm always glad to be around people who respect my abilities," Johnson said.

"As soon as I find them, you may rest assured I'll respect them," Flynn replied. "Now—are you going to earn your stipend, or not?"

"I hate to risk bankrupting you, but I'll try," Johnson said. With Flynn, you had to fight dryer with dryer. Johnson expanded on his musings about tobacco and disease. When he finished, he asked, "How did I do?"

The other pilot gravely considered. "Well, I have to admit that's probably worth a penny," he said at last. "Who would have believed it?" He reached into the pocket of his shorts and actually produced a little bronze coin—the first real money Johnson had seen aboard the *Admiral Peary.* "Here. Don't spend it all in the same place." Flynn flipped the penny to Johnson.

"I do hope this won't break you," Johnson said, sticking it in his own pocket. "Why on earth did you bring it along, anyhow? How did they let you get away with it?"

"I stuck it under my tongue when I went into cold sleep, so I could pay Charon the ferryman's fee in case I had to cross the Styx instead of this other trip we were making," Flynn answered, deadpan.

"Yeah, sure. Now tell me another one," Johnson said.

"All right. I won it off the commandant in a poker game." Flynn sounded as serious with that as he had with the other.

"My left one," Johnson said sweetly. "Healey'd give you an IOU, and it wouldn't be worth the paper it was written on."

"Don't you trust our esteemed leader?" Flynn asked.

Johnson trusted Lieutenant General Healey, all right. That it was trust of a negative sort had nothing to do with anything—so he told himself, anyhow. He said, "When I have the chance, I'll buy you a drink with this."

As far as he knew, there was no unofficial alcohol aboard the *Admiral Peary*. He wouldn't have turned down a drink, any more than he would have turned down a cigar. Flynn said, "While you're at it, you can buy me a new car, too."

"Sure. Why not?" Johnson said grandly. What could be more useless to a man who had to stay weightless the rest of his days?

"A likely story. What's your promise worth?" Flynn said.

"It's worth its weight in gold," Johnson answered.

"And now I'm supposed to think you a wit." Flynn looked down his rather tuberous nose at Johnson. "I'll think you half a wit, if you like. You filched that from *The Devil's Dictionary*. Deny it if you can."

"I didn't know it was against the rules," Johnson said.

"There's an old whine in a new bottle," Flynn said loftily.

"Ouch." Johnson winced. He was a straightforward man. Puns didn't come naturally to him. When he went up against Mickey Flynn, that sometimes left him feeling like a one-legged man in an ass-kicking contest. All of a sudden, he laughed. The Lizards probably felt that way about the whole human race.

When Pesskrag called Ttomalss, the female physicist was more agitated than he had ever seen her. "Do you know what this means?" she demanded. "Do you have the faintest idea?"

"No. I am not a physicist," Ttomalss said. "Perhaps you will calm yourself and tell me. I hope so, at any rate."

"Very well. It shall be done. It shall be attempted, anyhow." In the monitor, Pesskrag visibly tried to pull herself together. She took a deep breath and then said, "This has taken the egg of the physics we have known since before Home was unified, dropped it on a rock, and seen something altogether new and strange hatch out of it. Each experiment is more startling than the last. Sometimes my colleagues and I have trouble believing what the data show us. But then we repeat the experiments, and the results remain the same. Astonishing!" She used an emphatic cough.

"Fascinating." Ttomalss wondered if he was lying. "Can you tell someone who is not a physicist what this means to him?"

"Before we understood—or thought we understood—the nature of matter and energy, we threw rocks and shot arrows at one another. Afterwards, we learned to fly between the stars. The changes coming here will be no less profound."

"You suggested such things before," Ttomalss said slowly. "I take it that what you suggested then now seems more likely?"

"Morning twilight suggests the sun. Then the sun comes over the horizon, and you see how trivial the earlier suggestion was." Pesskrag might have been a physicist by profession, but she spoke poetically.

However poetically she spoke, she forgot something. Ttomalss said, "The Big Uglies dropped this egg some time ago. What sort of sunrise are they presently experiencing?"

"I do not know that. I cannot know that, being so many light-years removed from Tosev 3," Pesskrag replied. "I must assume they are some years ahead of us. They made these discoveries first. From what you say, they are also quicker than we to translate theory into engineering."

"Yes, that is a truth," Ttomalss agreed. "If anything, that is an understatement. I asked you this before. Now I ask it again: can you prepare a memorandum telling me in nontechnical terms what sort of engineering changes you expect to hatch from these theoretical changes?"

This time, Pesskrag made the affirmative gesture. "I think I had better now. We are further along than we were, so what I say will be much less speculative than it would have the last time you asked me. I should send it to you by the day after tomorrow."

"That will do. I thank you. Farewell." Ttomalss broke the connection.

He knew memoranda often hatched more slowly than their authors thought they would. This one, though, came when Pesskrag promised it. Ttomalss read it on the monitor before printing a hard copy. Once he had read it, his first impulse was to conclude that Pesskrag had lost her mind. But she had evidence on her side, and he had only his feelings. He was, as he'd said, no physicist himself.

He was also alarmed. If she did know what she was talking about . . . If the Big Uglies knew the same sorts of things, and more besides . . . Ttomalss printed out the memorandum and took it to Atvar's chamber. He was glad to find the retired fleetlord there. "This is something you should see, Exalted Fleetlord," he said, and held out the paper.

"What is it, Senior Researcher?" Atvar seemed distracted, uninterested. "You will forgive me, I hope, but I have other things on my mind."

"None of them is more important than this," Ttomalss insisted.

"No?" Atvar swung one eye turret toward him. "I am concerned with the survival, or lack of same, of both the Race and the Big Uglies. Do you still hold to your claim?"

"I do, Exalted Fleetlord," Ttomalss replied.

Slowly, Atvar's other eye turret followed the first. "You really mean that," he observed, astonishment in his voice. Ttomalss made the affirmative gesture. Atvar held out his hand in a way that suggested he was about as ready to claw as to grab. "Very well. Let me see this, so I can dispose of it and go on to other things."

"Here, Exalted Fleetlord." Ttomalss handed him the printout. Atvar began to read with one eye turret, as if to say the memorandum deserved no more. Ttomalss waited. Before long, the fleetlord was going over the document with both eyes, a sign it had engaged his interest. Ttomalss made the affirmative gesture again, this time to himself. He'd expected nothing less.

At last, Atvar looked up from the printout. "You really believe this will happen, Senior Researcher?"

"Pesskrag has never struck me as one who exaggerates for the sake of winning attention," Ttomalss replied. "She believes this will happen. So do her colleagues. If it does, it will be important."

"If it does, it will turn the world—several worlds—upside down," Atvar said. Ttomalss could hardly disagree with that. The fleetlord went on, "Did I note that this is information derived from experiments modeled after those the Big Uglies have already carried out?"

"You did, yes." Ttomalss waited to see how Atvar would respond to that.

The fleetlord let out a furious hiss. "We are going to have our work cut out for us, then, are we not?"

"It would appear so." Ttomalss wondered how large an understatement that was.

Atvar said, "Do your pet physicists have an idea how long this will need to go from experiment to production?"

"This report does not state it," Ttomalss answered. "The last time I asked Pesskrag the same question, she gave me an estimate—hardly more than a guess, she said—of at least a hundred fifty years."

"That was her estimate for us?" Atvar asked. When Ttomalss showed that it was, Atvar asked a grimly sardonic question: "How long will it take the Big Uglies?"

"Again, Exalted Fleetlord, I have no idea. I am only a messenger here. Pesskrag would not offer an estimate for that."

"Of course she would not." Yes, irony had its claws in the fleetlord, all right. "What do she and her colleagues know of Tosevites? About what I know of physics. They could hardly know less than that, could they?"

"Well, they could know as little as *I* know about physics," Ttomalss said.

He startled a laugh out of Atvar. "Either way, they do not know much. And that is the problem, would you not agree? Even those of us with some understanding of the Big Uglies too often underrate them. The less the physicists' knowledge, the greater their tendency to do so."

"The less the physicists' knowledge of Big Uglies, the greater their tendency to think the Tosevites are just like us," Ttomalss replied.

"We both said the same thing, in slightly different ways," Atvar said. Ttomalss wished he could disagree with that, but knew he could not. The fleetlord continued, "We are going to have some interesting times, are we not? Not pleasant, necessarily, but interesting."

"I would think so, yes," Ttomalss said. "Forgive me, but you seemed out of sorts when I brought you this report."

"Did I? I suppose I did," Atvar said. "Talks with the Big Uglies are not going as well as I wish they were. Sam Yeager simply does not have a realistic view of the situation."

"Are you sure, Exalted Fleetlord?" Ttomalss asked. "From

all I have seen, the American ambassador is about as reasonable a Tosevite as was ever hatched."

"This has also been my view," Atvar replied. "He has also been as friendly to the Race as any Tosevite could be expected to be. That makes his present intransigence all the more disappointing. I fear he must have instructions that constrain him, for he is not at all yielding, even on small points."

"How much have you yielded to him?"

"What I am allowed to," Atvar said. "He pushes the notion of formal equality to ridiculous extremes, though. If one believes his assumptions, there is no difference between the Empire and the United States in sovereignty and in obligations, none whatever."

"What is the likely result if these talks fail?" Ttomalss asked.

"War. What else?" Atvar sounded particularly bleak.

"Then they had better not fail. Or do you disagree?"

"Oh, no." The fleetlord used the negative gesture. "I think you are absolutely right. The Emperor agrees with you, too. But if the wild Big Uglies present impossible demands, what are we supposed to do? Yield to them? I am very sorry, Senior Researcher, but I think not."

"One more question, Exalted Fleetlord, and then I will leave," Ttomalss said. "Do the Tosevites think our requirements are as ridiculous as we think theirs? If they do, perhaps both sides should be more flexible and seek some sort of compromise solution."

"Easier to propose a compromise than to propose compromise terms both sides would find acceptable," Atvar said coldly. "Farewell."

That was an unmistakable dismissal. "Farewell," Ttomalss said, and left the fleetlord's chamber. He had done what he could. The Race as a whole had done what it could. The wild Big Uglies, no doubt, would loudly insist that they had done what they could. And what was the likely result of all that? The same disaster that would have appeared if everyone had gone into these talks with the worst will imaginable. *So much for good intentions,* the psychologist thought. There was some sort of Tosevite saying about what good intentions were worth. He couldn't recall the details, but remembered thinking that the phrase, when he'd heard it translated, held more truth than he wished it did.

The elevator ride down to the lobby felt like a fall, perhaps a fall straight into despair. Hoping to make himself feel better with some food, Ttomalss went into the refectory. The result was not what he'd hoped for. Oh, the food would be pleasant enough; the hotel had a good kitchen. But Kassquit and Frank Coffey were in there ahead of him, sitting in a couple of chairs designed for Big Uglies.

It wasn't that Ttomalss begrudged his former ward's happiness. So he told himself, at any rate. Still, seeing her so obviously pleased with the company of her fellow Tosevite got under his scales. If behavior sprang from biology more than from culture, perhaps conflict with the wild Big Uglies *was* inevitable—a conclusion he would rather not have reached just then.

He did his best to reach a different conclusion. Maybe their happiness together showed that citizens of the Empire and wild Tosevites could get on well despite their cultural differences. That sounded reassuring, but he couldn't make himself believe it. It would have been a truth had all citizens of the Empire been Tosevites. Had Kassquit been a member of the Race, Frank Coffey would not have been interested in her in the way he was. *Tosevite sexuality makes cultural differences less important,* he judged. But that was an argument for biological primacy, not against it, and one he wished he had not thought of.

The server brought his zisuili ribs. They were tender and meaty, the sauce that covered them tart on his tongue. He savored them less than he wished he would have. His mind was on other things. Atvar had always been on the optimistic side when it came to dealing with the Big Uglies. If even he feared a clash was inevitable, maybe it was.

Sam Yeager knew the commandant of the *Admiral Peary* was the sort of man who would have disposed of him like a crumpled paper towel for letting the Lizards know who was responsible for the attack on the colonization fleet. That was one reason Yeager hated talking with Lieutenant General Healey.

And the commandant despised him right back. He knew it. As far as Healey was concerned, he was a traitor and a Lizard-lover, somebody who cared about the Race more than he did about humanity or his own country. Their mutual lack of affection had made their conversation about ginger not long before particularly unpleasant.

Healey could have worked much more easily with the Doctor. Nobody had ever questioned the Doctor's patriotism. And the Doctor would have figured Healey was a useful tool, and treated him with the respect required to keep him . . . useful. (Nobody, Yeager was convinced, could have kept Healey happy. The capacity for happiness simply was not in the man.)

But the USA was stuck with one Sam Yeager as ambassador. It meant Lieutenant General Healey had to take him seriously, for his position if not for himself. And it also meant that, now and again, like it or not, Sam had to deal with Healey.

"Are you sure this conversation is secure?" Healey growled. Yeager might have guessed those would be the first words out of his mouth.

"As sure as my instruments will let me be," he answered. Of course the Race would try to monitor conversations between the ground and the *Admiral Peary*. The scrambling equipment was human-made, the best around in 1994. That put it a little ahead of anything the Lizards owned. But they had a whole solar system's worth of electronics here to try to tease signal out of noise. Maybe they could. Sam felt he had to add, "Life doesn't come with a guarantee, you know."

"Yes, I am aware of that." By Healey's sour rasp, he was wishing he were having this conversation with the Doctor. He muttered something Sam couldn't make out, which was probably just as well. Then he gathered himself. "Tell me what's on your mind, Ambassador." In his own crabbed way, he was making an effort. If he dealt with Sam Yeager the ambassador, he wouldn't have to think so much about Sam Yeager the man—the man he couldn't stand.

"I think you would do well to stay alert for anything unexpected." Sam picked his words with as much care as he could.

"We always do," Healey said, as if Sam couldn't be trusted

to know that for himself. But then his tone sharpened: "Are you telling me there may be some special reason we need to be alert?" He was narrow. He was sour. He was also professionally competent, however little Yeager cared to acknowledge that.

And Yeager had to answer, "Yes, I'm afraid there may be."

"Suppose you tell me more," the commandant rapped out.

"There are . . . sovereignty issues," Sam said unhappily. "Free-trade issues. The Race has most-favored-nation status in commerce with the United States. It doesn't want to see that there are reciprocity issues. If tariffs keep us from carrying on any sort of trade with the planets in the Empire—"

"Then we have a problem," Healey broke in, and Sam couldn't disagree with him. Healey went on, "All right, Ambassador. I suppose I have to thank you for the heads-up. I promise you, we won't be caught napping. Anything else?"

"I don't think so," Sam said. "Out." He broke the connection. It was his turn to do some muttering. One reason the *Admiral Peary* had come to Home heavily armed was to remind the Race war with the United States didn't just mean war within the Sun's solar system. War could come home to the other worlds the Empire ruled.

Healey was probably the right man to be up there, too. If he had to fight for his ship, he would do it till the Lizards overwhelmed him. Inevitably, they would, but they'd know they'd been in a scrap, too.

They'd never had anybody insist on full equality with them before. They didn't know how to respond. No, that wasn't true. They couldn't see that they needed to agree. That came closer to the truth.

Shaking his head, Sam left his room. He went down to the lobby, where he found Tom de la Rosa and Frank Coffey good-naturedly arguing about, of all things, a blown call in the 1985 World Series. De la Rosa rounded on him as he came up. "What do you think, Sam? Was the guy safe or out?"

"Beats me," Sam said. "I'd been on ice for years."

"So had that stupid umpire," Coffey said. "The only difference is, they ran him out there anyway."

Yeager looked around. There weren't any Lizards close

by—just a couple of guards at the door. But the Race was bound to have bugged the area. He would have, in the Lizards' place. Any edge you could get was better than none. He said, "Come on back up to my room, gentlemen, if you'd be so kind." The Lizards had bugs there, too. The difference was, those bugs didn't work—Sam didn't think they did, anyhow.

"What's up?" Tom asked. Yeager only shrugged, pointed at a wall, and tapped his own ear. The Lizards could have all the bugs they wanted down here, but they wouldn't get everything that was going on.

De la Rosa and Coffey certainly knew what Sam was saying. They kept on hashing out the blown call—or maybe the good call, if you believed Tom—all the way up the elevator. By the time they got off, Sam found himself wishing he'd seen the play. He wondered if people back on Earth were still arguing about it, too.

But everyone's manner changed when the three of them got back to the hotel room. "What's up?" de la Rosa asked again, this time in a much less casual tone of voice.

Before answering, Sam checked the bug sniffer. Only after he saw everything was green did he ask what was on his mind: "Which is better, a treaty that doesn't give us everything we ought to have or a fight to make sure we get it?"

"Whether 'tis nobler in the mind to suffer
The slings and arrows of outrageous fortune,
Or to take arms against a sea of troubles,
And by opposing end them?" Frank Coffey quoted.

De la Rosa grinned at him. "You're a lot of things, Major, but I'll be damned if I can see you as a melancholy Dane."

"You're right—I'm too cheerful," Coffey said. De la Rosa and Yeager both made faces at him.

"It's a serious question, though." Sam got back to business. "It looks more and more as if the Lizards aren't going to give us full equality all over the Empire. So what do we do about that? Do we settle for something less, or do we go to war and blow everything to hell and gone?"

"Can't very well phone home for instructions, can you?" de la Rosa said.

"Not unless I want to go back into cold sleep till the answer comes in twenty-odd years from now," Yeager answered. "And there's not much point to sending out an ambassador if you're going to do it all by radio, is there?"

"You're the man on the spot," Coffey agreed. "In the end, it all comes down to you."

Sam knew that. He wished Frank Coffey hadn't put it so baldly. He wished the Doctor had revived. He wished for all sorts of things he wouldn't get. The weight lay on *his* shoulders. *He* was responsible for billions of lives scattered among four different species. Nobody since the Emperor who'd sent the conquest fleet to Earth had borne that kind of burden—and the Lizard hadn't known he bore it.

"If we accept an inferior treaty now, maybe we can get it fixed when we're stronger," Tom said. "We're getting stronger all the time, too."

"Other side of that coin is, maybe the Lizards will think they have a precedent for holding us down," Coffey said. "What are your orders, Ambassador?"

He was a military man. To him, orders were Holy Writ. Sam had lived in that world for a long time. He understood it, but he didn't feel bound by it, not any more. He said, "The first thing my orders are is out of date. Tom said it: I can't phone home. I'm the man on the spot. If my orders tell me to insist on complete equality no matter what and I see that means war, I'm going to think long and hard before I follow them."

"Are you saying you *won't* follow them?" Coffey asked. That was a dangerous question. If he saw somebody wantonly disobeying orders . . . well, who could guess what he might do?

"No, I'm not saying I won't follow them," Yeager answered carefully. "But war on this scale is something nobody's ever imagined, not even the people who were around when the conquest fleet landed." He was one of those people. There were a few more up on the *Admiral Peary*. Back on Earth? Only the oldest of the old, and even they would have been children back then.

A good many Lizards who'd been active then were still

around. That wasn't just on account of cold sleep, either. They lasted longer than people did. But did they understand what they might be setting in motion? Sam didn't think so.

"What will make up your mind, one way or the other?" Frank Coffey didn't want to let it alone. He was capable. He was dutiful. He made Sam want to kick him in the teeth.

Still picking his words with care, Sam said, "If they say, 'You have to do it our way, or we'll go to war with you right now,' I don't see that I have any choice. We let them know we'll fight. You can't let them get away with that kind of threat. If they think they can, they'll own us."

"No doubt about that," Coffey said. Tom de la Rosa nodded.

"Okay," Sam said. "But if they say something like, 'We want to stay peaceful, but this is the only kind of treaty we can accept,' that may be a different story. Then it might be a better idea to say, 'Well, we're not real happy with this, but we'll make the deal for now,' and figure our grandchildren can finish picking the Lizards' pockets."

"I like that, or most of me does," Tom said. "It won't stop the ecological damage, but a lot of that's already done."

Coffey stayed dubious. "I don't want them thinking they can push us around at all. They're like anybody else who's got power and wants more: give 'em an inch and they'll take a mile. And who knows who'll be doing the pushing around fifty years from now, or a hundred and fifty?"

"It hasn't come to ultimatums yet," Yeager said. "I'm still hoping it doesn't."

"But you wouldn't have warned the *Admiral Peary* if you weren't worried," Major Coffey said. "I know you, Ambassador. You wouldn't give Lieutenant General Healey the time of day if you weren't worried." He was too obviously right to make that worth denying. When Sam didn't say anything, Coffey asked his question again: "What are your orders?"

They weren't Sam's. They were intended for the Doctor. He would have had no qualms about carrying them out. Yeager was sure of that. "Basically, to ensure our freedom and independence," he answered. "That's what this is all about. Past the basics, I've got a lot of discretion. I have to. The home office is a hell of a long way from here."

"You're right about that," Tom said.

"Sure are," Frank Coffey said. "But you don't get anywhere against oppression by bowing down and saying, 'Thank you,' to the fellow with the bullwhip. No offense, Ambassador, but that just doesn't work." Sam would have been happier had he thought the black man was wrong.

When the phone hissed for attention, Atvar had just come out of the shower. That was a smaller problem for a member of the Race than it would have been for a wild Big Ugly; he didn't need to worry about decking himself with wrappings before he went to answer. But it was an annoyance even so.

Shaking a last couple of drops of water off the end of his snout, he sat down in front of the monitor and let the camera pick up his image. "This is Atvar. I greet you," he said.

"And I greet you, Fleetlord."

The face on the screen made Atvar hiss in surprise. "Your Majesty!" he exclaimed, and began to fold into the special posture of respect reserved for the Emperor.

"Never mind that," the 37th Emperor Risson said, holding up a hand. "We have serious matters to discuss."

Atvar made the affirmative gesture. "As always, your Majesty, I am at your service."

"Good," Risson said. "How seriously do you take this new report from Senior Researcher Ttomalss and the physicists he has recruited?"

"Seriously enough to pass it on in the hope that your eye turrets would move across it," Atvar answered. "I cannot fully comment on the quality of the research. There I have to rely on the scholars involved. But, by their reputations, they are first-rate males and females."

"Yes." Risson used the affirmative gesture, too. "This being so, what they say is probably right. What do we do about that?"

"I think perhaps you should ask the physicists and not me," Atvar said. "My own view is, we push ahead with this research as hard as we can. The Big Uglies already have a considerable start on us."

"That is also a truth." Risson used the same gesture again.

"How likely is it, in your opinion, that we will be able to catch up?"

There was an interesting question—so interesting, Atvar almost wished the Emperor hadn't asked it. The Race had had a head start on the Tosevites in technology. It didn't any more. The Big Uglies moved faster than the Race did. If they had found something new and the Race had to make up lost ground . . .

The Emperor deserved the truth. Indeed, he required the truth. With a sigh, Atvar answered, "While it may not be impossible, I do not believe it will be easy, either. We are more sensible than they are, but without a doubt they are more nimble."

"I was hoping you would tell me something else," Risson said with a sigh of his own. "Your view closely matches those of my other advisers. This being so, our view of negotiations with the American Big Uglies necessarily changes, too, would you not agree?"

"I would," Atvar said. "I have begun to take a less compromising line with Sam Yeager. We are likely to be stronger now than in the future. Any bargains we make should reflect our current strength."

"Good. Very good. Again, I agree," Risson said. "I also wonder how much the Big Uglies here know about the research back on their own planet. Our monitoring has not picked up much in the way of information on it coming from the wild Tosevites on their home planet. Speculation is that Tosevite leaders know we are listening to their transmissions and do not wish to give us any data they do not have to."

"That strikes me as reasonable," Atvar said. "I wish it did not, but it does. The Tosevites are more accustomed to secrecy than we are. They have internal rivalries the likes of which we have not known since before Home was unified."

"So I am given to understand." The 37th Emperor Risson sighed again. "You know I want peace with the Big Uglies. Who could not, when war would prove so destructive?" He waited. As far as Atvar was concerned, agreement there was automatic. The Emperor went on, "But if war should become necessary, better war when we are stronger than when we are weaker."

"Just so, your Majesty—thus the harder line," Atvar replied. "I do not relish it. Who could? But better on our terms than on the Tosevites' terms. So far, Sam Yeager has been intransigent when it comes to the Americans' demands. If we cannot get what we require by other means, shall we proceed to whatever forceful steps prove necessary?"

"War is only a last resort," Risson said. "Always, war is only a last resort. But if it becomes necessary . . ."

"They will have some warning," Atvar warned. "When the signals from their own ship fall silent, they will know something has gone wrong."

"Why should those signals fall silent?" the Emperor asked. "We can continue with negotiations here as always. If the Big Uglies in our solar system fail to detect the outgoing signals, then we have many years before any come back here from Tosev 3 to alert them. Is that not a truth?"

Before answering, Atvar had to stop and think that over. Once he had, he bent not into the special posture of respect that applied to the Emperor alone but into the more general posture one gave not only to superiors but also to anyone who said something extraordinarily clever. "I do believe that would serve, your Majesty . . . provided the Big Uglies do not learn about the scheme ahead of time."

"How likely are they to do so?" Risson asked.

"I am not certain. No one is quite certain," Atvar replied. "I would suggest, though, that you do not mention this any more when calling me here. Tosevite electronics are good enough to keep us from monitoring their conversations in their rooms and most of their conversations with their starship. How well they can monitor ours is unknown, but we should exercise caution."

"What they have here can defeat our electronics?" Risson said. Atvar made the affirmative gesture. The Emperor went on with his own thought: "What they have on Tosev 3 will be more advanced than what they have here?"

"That is also bound to be a truth, your Majesty," Atvar agreed. "Our technology is stable. Theirs advances by leaps and bounds. This is, no doubt, one of the reasons why they have the arrogance to believe themselves our equals."

"Indeed," Risson said. "And it is one of the reasons we

should strike first, if we must strike. If they get too far ahead of us, we have no hope of fighting them successfully. Again, you know I would rather have peace."

"I do, your Majesty." Atvar's emphatic cough showed how well he knew it.

"And yet my first duty is to preserve the Empire and the Race," Risson continued. "If the only way I can do that is through a preventive war, then I must consider one, no matter how distasteful I find it. If we ever reach a position where the wild Big Uglies can dictate the terms of engagement to us, we are lost."

"Another truth," Atvar said. "When I administered our lands on Tosev 3, I often contemplated preventive war against the Tosevites. I always held off on launching it, both in the hope that we would be able to live peacefully alongside them and out of fear for the damage such a war would have caused even then. Perhaps I was wrong to hold back."

"Perhaps you were, Fleetlord," Risson said. "But it is too late to dwell on that now. We have to make the best of the present situation, and to make sure the future is not worse than the present."

"Just so, your Majesty," Atvar said.

"If these physicists prove to know what they are talking about, we have less time to make up our minds than I wish we did," the Emperor said. "I will do everything in my power to drive our research efforts forward. I am not a scientist, though. All I can offer is moral suasion."

Atvar made the negative gesture. "No, your Majesty, there is one thing more, and something much more important."

"Oh? And that is?"

"Funding."

Risson laughed, though Atvar hadn't been joking. "Yes, Fleetlord, that is bound to be a truth, and an important one, as you say. Believe me, the appropriate ministries will hear that this is a project of the highest priority. It will go forward."

"I am glad to hear it, your Majesty," Atvar said. Risson said a few polite good-byes, then broke the connection. Atvar stared thoughtfully at the monitor. The Emperor was worrying about the new developments, which was good. Atvar still wondered how much difference it would make. The Big

Uglies had a lead, and they moved faster than the Race. How likely was it that the Race could catch up? Not very, Atvar feared. Which meant . . .

"Which means trouble," the fleetlord muttered. Like the 37th Emperor Risson, he vastly preferred peace. Unlike his sovereign, he'd seen war and its aftermath at first hand, not just as signals sent across the light-years. More war now would be dreadful—but more war later might be worse.

One of his eye turrets swung toward the ceiling. Somewhere up there, out past all the stories above him, the Tosevite starship spun through space. When the conquest fleet first came to Tosev 3, the Big Uglies hadn't been able to fly out of their stratosphere. Two generations before that, they'd had no powered flight at all. And now they were here.

Their nuclear weapons were here, too. If it was possible to keep the wild Big Uglies on that ship from finding out the Race had gone to war against the United States, that might save Home some nasty punishment. Or, on the other hand, it might not. Something might go wrong, in which case the starship would strike the Race's home planet. The Big Uglies might launch other starships, too. For that matter, they might already have launched them. There was one of Atvar's nightmares.

Signals flew faster than ships between the stars. That had been true ever since the Race first sent a probe to the Rabotevs' system, and remained true today. Atvar hoped he would have heard if more Tosevite ships were on the way. He hoped, but he wasn't sure. The Race could keep the American starship here from knowing an attack order had gone out. Back in the Tosevite system, the Big Uglies might be able to keep the Race from learning they'd launched ships. Because they'd been cheating one another for as long as they'd been more or less civilized, they were more practiced at all forms of trickery than the Race was.

And what was going on in *their* physics laboratories? How long before abstract experiments turned into routine engineering? Could the Big Uglies turn these experiments into engineering at all? Could anyone?

We'll find out, Atvar thought. He laughed. Before leaving for Tosev 3, he'd been used to knowing how things worked, what everything's place was—and everyone's, too. It wasn't like that any more. It never would be again, not till the last Big Uglies had been firmly incorporated into the Empire— and maybe not even then.

Atvar made the negative gesture. One other possibility could also bring back order. It might return when the last Big Uglies died. It might—if the Tosevites didn't take the Race (to say nothing of the Rabotevs and Hallessi) down with them.

They would do their best. The fleetlord was sure of that. How good their best might be . . . As Atvar did so often in his dealings with the Big Uglies, he trembled between hope and fear. More often than not, the Race's hopes about Tosev 3 had proved unjustified. The Race's fears . . .

He wished that hadn't occurred to him.

Karen Yeager wondered why Major Coffey had called all the Americans on the surface of Home to his room. He'd never done that before. He was the expert here on matters military. If he had something to say, he usually said it to Karen's father-in-law. What was so important that everyone needed to hear it?

At least Kassquit wasn't here. Karen had half wondered if she would be. In that case, Frank Coffey wouldn't have been talking about military affairs, but about his own. Could he have been foolish enough to ask Kassquit to marry him? People far from home did strange things, and no one had ever been farther from home than the people who'd flown on the *Admiral Peary*. Even so—

"People, we have a problem." Coffey's words cut across Karen's thoughts. The major paused to check the antibugging gadgets, then nodded to himself. He went on, "The Lizards have come up with something sneaky." He went on to explain how the Race could order war to start back on Earth without leaving the humans on and orbiting Home any the wiser.

Though the room was warm—what rooms on Home weren't warm, except the ones that were downright hot?—ice walked up Karen's back. "They can't do that!" she exclaimed. She felt foolish the moment the words were out of her mouth.

The Lizards damn well *could* do that, which was exactly the problem.

"What do we do about it?" Linda de la Rosa asked.

Sure enough, that was the real question. "Whatever we do is risky," Sam Yeager said. "If we sit tight, the Lizards may get away with their scheme. If we don't, we let them know we're tapping their phone lines. They may not like that at all."

"What can they do? Throw us off the planet?" Karen asked. "Even if they do, how are we worse off?"

"We have to make sure they don't order their colonists to sucker-punch the United States without our knowing it," Frank Coffey said.

"It would be nice if they didn't order the colonists to sucker-punch the United States even if we do know about it," Tom de la Rosa said. Karen had a devil of a time disagreeing with that.

Melanie Blanchard said, "I don't see how we can stop them from sending the order secretly. All they have to do is transmit from a ship that's gone outside this solar system. They'd have the angle on any detectors we could put out."

That held the unpleasant ring of truth. Jonathan said, "All things considered, we're probably lucky they didn't think of this sooner. They haven't had to worry about these kinds of problems for a long, long time. They're a little slow on the up-take."

"So what do we do?" Sam Yeager asked. "We let them know we know what they've got in mind?"

"That would show them our electronics are better than theirs," Coffey said. "It might make them think twice about taking us on. Who knows how far we've come since the *Admiral Peary* left, and how far we will have come by the time their signal gets to Earth?"

"We might make them more eager to jump us, though, to make sure they don't fall further behind," Tom said. "From what you told us, the Emperor and Atvar were talking about that."

"And what are these experiments they were talking about?" Karen asked. "It sounds like they're trying to catch up with some sort of discovery that got made on Earth a while ago. Do we know anything about that?"

Nobody answered, not right away. At last, Major Coffey said, "People back on Earth may not have transmitted anything about it to us, just to make sure the Lizards didn't intercept . . . whatever it is."

That made a fair amount of sense. It also argued that the discovery, whatever it was, was important. Jonathan said, "The Lizards must have spotted it on their own, then. Has the *Admiral Peary* picked up anything that would give us a clue?"

"There's a lot of electronic traffic coming from Earth to Home—an awful lot," Coffey said. "We're the Race's number-one interest right now. There's more than our starship can keep up with. This bit might have slipped through without even being noticed—or it might have been encrypted. We haven't broken all the Lizards' algorithms, not by a long shot."

"What kind of search can we run?" Sam Yeager held up a hand. "Never mind. I don't need to know right now. But whatever they can do on the ship, they ought to start doing it. The more we know, the better off we'll be."

"Maybe we can shame the Lizards into behaving," Linda said. Then she laughed. "I know—don't hold my breath."

"I'll try. It's one more weapon. What's that line? Conscience is the still, small voice that tells you someone may be watching," Sam said. "The other thing the ship has to do is send a warning back to the States that there might be a surprise attack. After Pearl Harbor and the strike against the colonization fleet, Earth has seen too much of that kind of thing."

Major Coffey stirred, but didn't say anything. More than a few people in the military still felt the strike against the colonization fleet had been legitimate because the United States carried it out. Frank Coffey had never shown any signs of being one of those officers—never till now. He probably still deserved the benefit of the doubt.

"Are we agreed, then?" Sam Yeager asked. "I will protest to Atvar and the Emperor and anyone else who'll listen. I'll let them know we're sending back a warning, so they won't catch us napping."

"They'll deny everything," Jonathan predicted.

"We would," Tom de la Rosa said. "They may not even

bother—they haven't had as much practice at being hyp-ocrites as we have. Any which way, though, the more compli-cated we make their lives, the better."

"Amen," Karen said. Several other people nodded.

"All right, then. We'll try it like that." Sam Yeager shook his head. "I wish I were talking about getting my car to start, not rolling the dice for everybody on the planet—for everybody on four planets."

"You're the one the Lizards wanted when the Doctor didn't wake up," Karen said. "If they won't listen to you, they won't listen to anybody."

Her father-in-law nodded, not altogether cheerfully. "That's what I'm afraid of—that they won't listen to anybody. Well, we'll find out." On that note, the meeting broke up.

"Happy day," Jonathan said as the Americans filed out of Frank Coffey's room.

"Uh-huh." Karen felt numb, drained. "I wonder just how much trouble there's going to be." She looked around, as if expecting the hotel corridors to go up in a radioactive cloud any minute now. That had always been possible, though they'd all done their best not to think about it. Now it felt appallingly probable.

"If anybody can get us out of it, Dad's the one," Jonathan said. "You were right about that." He plainly meant it. At a moment like this, he didn't waste time on jealousy of his father, the way he often did. Even when jealous, though, he didn't try to tear down his father's abilities; he only wished his own measured up to them.

"We'll see." Karen did her best to look on the bright side of things, if there was one. "It sounds like a lot's been going on back on Earth that we don't know much about. I do won-der what those experiments the Lizards were talking about mean."

Jonathan waved her to silence. She bit down on the inside of her lower lip, hard enough to hurt. She'd let her mouth run away with her. The Race was bound to be bugging the corri-dors. The Americans didn't even try trolling for eavesdrop-ping devices there; the job was too big.

"They'll know we know soon enough," she said.

"Oh, yeah." Jonathan didn't argue with that. "And we'll never get a nickel's worth of useful intelligence by tapping the phones again." He shrugged. "What can you do? Sometimes that stuff is useless if you don't cash it in."

Lunch in the refectory was . . . interesting. Kassquit knew the Americans had gathered, and wanted to know why. Nobody wanted to tell her. Her face never showed anything much. Even so, Karen had no trouble telling she was getting angry. "Why will you not let me know what you talked about?" she demanded of all of them—and of Frank Coffey in particular.

Like so many lovers through the eons, she assumed her beloved would tell her everything because they were lovers. Karen had wondered about that herself. But Coffey said what he had to say: "I am sorry, but this was private business for us. When we decide to talk about it with the Race, we will."

"But I am not a member of the Race. You of all males ought to know that," Kassquit said pointedly.

"You are a citizen of the Empire," Coffey said. "That is what I meant. We Americans often think of the Empire as belonging only to the Race. I realize that is wrong, but it is our first approximation."

"I am also a member of the Empire's team of negotiators," Kassquit pointed out. "If anyone on Home is entitled to know, I am."

Sam Yeager made the negative gesture. "This is a matter for the fleetlord, and perhaps for the Emperor himself."

Karen wondered if that said too much. It was enough to make Kassquit's eyes widen in surprise: one expression she did have. "What could be so important? Our talks are not going perfectly, but they have not suffered any great crisis."

That only proved she was out of the loop for some of the things going on around her. Karen eyed her with an almost malicious satisfaction. *You're not as smart as you think you are. We know things you don't.* She stopped herself just before she tacked on a couple of mental *Nyah-nyahs.*

"You will hear soon enough," Sam said.

"Why will you not tell me now?" Kassquit asked.

"Because high officials in the Empire need to know first, as I said before," Sam Yeager answered, more patiently than

Karen would have. "They will tell you what you need to know. If they do not tell you enough, ask me. I will speak freely then. Until I have followed protocol, though . . ." He made the negative gesture.

Karen thought Kassquit would get angry at that, but she didn't. She *was* reasonable, sometimes even when being reasonable was unreasonable. Not letting her emotions run wild probably helped her in dealing with the Race. Lizards operated differently from people; Kassquit would have been banging her head against a stone wall if she'd tried getting them to respond on her terms. But her chilly rationality was one of the things that made her seem not quite human.

Now she said, "Very well, Ambassador. I understand the point, even if I do not like it. I shall be most interested to learn what your concerns are."

"I thank you for your patience," Karen's father-in-law said, letting her down easy.

In English, Tom de la Rosa said, "She's not going to wait for Atvar and Ttomalss. She's going to try to wheedle it out of you, Frank." He grinned to show Coffey he didn't mean that seriously.

"She can try," Coffey said, also in English. "I know what I can tell her, and I know what I can't."

Karen eyed Kassquit. Even if she didn't wear clothes, she probably wasn't cut out to be a spy. Karen sighed. Life was different from the movies. Here was a naked woman on the other side, and she *didn't* seem to be using her charms for purposes of espionage. What was the world—what were the worlds—coming to?

Kassquit stared at Ttomalss in something approaching horror. "The Big Uglies dared spy on the conversations of the Emperor himself?" She cast down her eyes at mentioning her sovereign.

Ttomalss also looked down at the floor for a moment as he made the affirmative gesture. "I am afraid that is a truth, yes. What is even more disturbing is that they were *able* to eavesdrop on the Emperor's conversation with Fleetlord Atvar. We have had no luck listening to their private conversations."

"That is not a matter of luck. It is a matter of technology," Kassquit pointed out.

"You are correct. I wish you were not," Ttomalss told her. "And the technology the wild Big Uglies brought here is bound to be years out of date on Tosev 3. Just how far out of date it may be is a matter of considerable concern to us."

"I understand that, yes," Kassquit agreed. "Can you tell me what the Emperor and the fleetlord were talking about, or are you going to be as obscure as the wild Tosevites?" She added the last bit as artlessly as she could. With luck, it would get Ttomalss to talk where he might otherwise have kept quiet.

And it did. He said, "In fact, their conversation does relate to advancing Tosevite technology. They were discussing whether that advancing technology made a preventive war necessary."

"Oh," Kassquit said, and then, "Oh, dear." She tried to gather herself. "The Race has talked about this for many years, but always abandoned the idea. Why is it back on the agenda now?"

Ttomalss hesitated. Then he shrugged. "The wild Big Uglies already know this, so there is no longer any reason why you should not. Do you remember my colleague back on Tosev 3, Senior Researcher Felless?"

"Yes," Kassquit said. "I must tell you I did not like her much."

"Felless is difficult for members of the Race to like, too—except when she has been tasting ginger, of course." Ttomalss qualified that with a fine, sarcastic, eye-turret-waggling leer. But he continued, "However difficult she may be, no one doubts her ability—when she is not tasting ginger. She noticed some unusual Tosevite technological development and sent word of it here."

"What sort of development?" Kassquit asked.

"We are not yet completely sure of that," Ttomalss answered. "But the physicists are convinced it will have important results at some point in the future."

"What sort of important results? How far in the future?"

"Again, we are not completely certain," Ttomalss said.

Kassquit eyed him. "Precisely what are you certain of, superior sir?"

Ttomalss shifted uneasily in his chair. "What do you mean? Do you intend that for sarcasm?"

"Oh, no, superior sir. How could I possibly be sarcastic because you are evading my questions? What do you suppose might provoke me into doing something of that sort?"

"This is not helpful." Ttomalss' voice was thick with disapproval.

"No, it is not," Kassquit agreed. "Your evasions are not helpful, either. The Tosevites evade my questions, too. I can understand that. They are not citizens of the Empire, and do not trouble their livers over its concerns. But I thought you and I were on the same side."

"Until the experiments progress further, I cannot offer you a report on them," Ttomalss said, which sounded like another evasion to Kassquit. Then he asked, "What questions are the Big Uglies evading?"

"The ones you would expect: the ones that have to do with dealings between the United States and the Empire. As I say, those evasions make sense. The ones you put forward strike me as absurd."

"You do not understand the full situation," Ttomalss said.

"That is a truth. I do not. And the reason I do not is that you will not tell me enough to let me understand it," Kassquit said angrily.

"When I am authorized to give you all the details, you may be assured that I will," Ttomalss said.

"Oh? And why may I be assured of that?" Kassquit snapped, even more angrily than before.

Ttomalss' tailstump quivered, so she'd succeeded in angering him, too. "If you do not care for my choices in this matter, I suggest that you take it up with Fleetlord Atvar, or with the Emperor himself."

"I thank you, superior sir. I thank you so very much." The way Kassquit bent into the posture of respect had no respect whatsoever in it. The way Ttomalss' tailstump quivered more than ever said he knew it, too. Kassquit went on, "It shall be done. Perhaps one of them has a certain minimal respect for the truth." She straightened, turned her back, and stalked out of his chamber.

She started to go to Atvar's room. Then she stopped in the

hallway and made the negative gesture. She would do that if all else failed. The 37th Emperor Risson had granted her an audience. Perhaps he would speak to her as well. And if he did, she intended to hurl that right into Ttomalss' snout.

Telephoning the Emperor, of course, was not so simple as putting a call in to the palace and expecting him to pick it up on the other end of the line. But it was easier for her than it might have been for a female of the Race. The sight of her Tosevite features in the monitor got her quickly transferred from a low-level functionary to a mid-level functionary to Herrep himself, for the males and females who served the Emperor remembered he had received two Big Uglies not long before.

The protocol master was made of sterner stuff. "What is the purpose of this call?" Herrep asked. His interrogative cough was the chilliest Kassquit had ever heard.

"To discuss with his Majesty relations between the Empire and the wild Big Uglies," Kassquit answered. "You will agree, superior sir, that this matter is of relevance—I should say, of unique relevance—to me."

Herrep could hardly deny that. She was a citizen of the Empire and a Big Ugly. No one else on Home could say both those things. She knew she wasn't wild. She wondered if Herrep would remember. To him, wouldn't one Big Ugly be the same as another?

"Wait," he said. "I will see if his Majesty wishes to speak to you." A pleasant, almost hypnotic moving pattern replaced his image on the monitor. Soft music began to play. Kassquit drummed her fingers on the desk in her room. They did not make sharp clicks, as those of a member of the Race would have done. Her fingerclaws were short and broad and blunt; she wore artificial ones to work the Race's switches and operate its keyboards.

She was beginning to wonder how patient she ought to be when the pattern vanished and the music fell silent. A male's face looked out at her. It wasn't Herrep's; it belonged to the 37th Emperor Risson. Kassquit scrambled to assume the special posture of respect. "I greet you, your Majesty. I thank you for taking the time to speak with me."

"You are welcome, Researcher," Risson replied. "We need not stand on much ceremony on the telephone. Am I correct in believing you have learned discussions with the wild Tose-vites have gone less well than we might have wished?"

"Yes, your Majesty," Kassquit said. "I have learned that. It dismays me. What dismays me even more is that I have been unable to learn why these talks have taken this unfortunate turn."

"There are two main reasons," the Emperor told her. "The first is Tosevite arrogance over issues of sovereignty and equality. Under other circumstances, this might be solved with patience and good will on both sides. I believe such patience does exist."

"What are these other circumstances, if I may ask?" Kass-quit said.

"The wild Big Uglies are pulling ahead of us technologi-cally," Risson said. "They rubbed our snouts in this recently, when they showed they could monitor our voice communica-tions and could keep us from monitoring theirs."

"A shocking breach of privacy," Kassquit said sympatheti-cally.

"Shocking because they were able to do it," Risson said. "After all, we have been trying to spy on them, too. But they succeeded and we failed. And their technology changes so much faster than ours. What do they currently have on Tosev 3? If we do not stop them now, will we be able to later?"

Kassquit knew those were all good questions. She also knew the Race had been debating them for years. "Why worry so much now?" she asked. "How has the situation changed for the worse?"

"In two ways," the Emperor said. "First, the wild Big Uglies can now reach us on our own planets. Any war against them would be Empirewide rather than confined to the system of Tosev 3. The longer we delay, the more harm they can do us, too." Kassquit used the affirmative gesture; that was an obvi-ous truth. Risson went on, "The second factor has grown more important as time passes. It is the growing fear that soon they will be able to hurt us and we will not be able to hurt them, as they can tap our telephones undetected till they admit it while we cannot monitor their conversations."

"Does this have to do with certain experiments that have been conducted on Tosev 3?"

Risson's eye turrets both swung sharply toward Kassquit. Yes, that had been the right question to ask. "You heard of this from . . . ?" he asked.

"I heard of their existence from Senior Researcher Ttomalss, your Majesty. I heard no more than that," Kassquit answered.

"Ah. Very well." Risson seemed to relax, which doubtless meant Ttomalss did have orders from on high not to say much about such things to Kassquit. The Emperor went on, "Yes, important experiments have taken place on Tosev 3. Just how important they are, our physicists are now trying to determine. We do not know how far or how fast the wild Tosevites have advanced from what we know they were doing some years ago. We do know we will have to try to catch up, and that will not be easy, since the Tosevites generally run faster than we do."

"What are the consequences if the Empire fails to catch up?" Kassquit asked.

"Bad. Very bad," Risson said.

That wasn't what Kassquit had expected to hear, but it told her how seriously the Emperor took the situation. She tried again: "In what way are these consequences bad, your Majesty?"

"In every way we can imagine, and probably also in ways we have yet to imagine," Risson replied. "It is because of these experiments that we view the current situation with such concern."

"Can you please tell me *why* you view them with such alarm?" Kassquit persisted. "The better I understand the situation, the more help I will be able to give the Empire."

"For the time being, I am afraid that this information is secret," Risson said. "We are still evaluating it ourselves. Also, the American Tosevites appear to be ignorant of what has taken place on their home planet. It would be to our advantage to have them remain ignorant. If they knew the full situation, their demands would become even more intolerable than they already are. And now, Researcher, if you will excuse me . . ." He broke the connection.

Kassquit stared at the monitor. Risson hadn't told her everything she wanted to know. But he had, perhaps, told her more than he thought he had. Whatever the wild Big Uglies back on Tosev 3 had discovered, it was even more important than she'd imagined.

☆ **15** ☆

Sam Yeager had faced plenty of frustrations on Home. He'd been ready for most of them—he knew what the Lizards were like and what they were likely to do as well as any mere human could. That (along with the Doctor's bad luck) was why he was the American ambassador today.

But one frustration he hadn't expected was having the Race know more about what was happening back on Earth than he did.

Things had worked out that way, though. Physicists back on the home planet seemed to be dancing a buck-and-wing about something. (Did anybody back on Earth dance a buck-and-wing about anything any more? Sometimes the phrases that popped into Sam's head made him feel like an antique even to himself.) The Race had a pretty good idea of what it was. None of the Americans on Home had even a clue.

His own ignorance made Sam call Lieutenant General Healey one more time. He relished that about as much as he would have a visit to the proctologist's. Sometimes, though, he had to bend over. And sometimes he had to talk to the *Admiral Peary*'s commandant. He consoled himself by remembering Healey liked him no better than he liked Healey.

"What's on your mind, Ambassador?" Healey growled when the connection went through. Then came the inevitable question: "And is this call secure?"

"As far as I can tell, it is," Yeager answered after checking the electronics in his room one more time.

"All right. Go ahead."

"Here's what I want to know: has the ship picked up any transmissions from the Lizards on Earth about human physicists' recent experiments, whatever they are? And have the

Lizards here on Home been blabbing about that kind of thing anywhere you can monitor them? I'd like to find out what's going on if I can."

"I don't remember anything like that." By the way Healey said it, it couldn't have happened if he didn't remember it.

More often than not, Sam would have accepted that just to give himself an excuse to get off the phone with a man he couldn't stand. That he didn't now was a measure of how urgent he thought this was. "Could you please check, General? Could you please check as carefully as possible? It's liable to be very important."

"How important is very important?" Healey asked scornfully.

"Peace or war important. I don't think it gets any more important than that. Do you?"

The commandant didn't answer, not for some little while. Yeager started to wonder if he really did think something else was more important. With Healey, you never could tell. At last, though, he said, "I'll see what I can find out."

"Thanks," Yeager said. Again, Healey didn't answer. A glance at the electronics told Sam the commandant had hung up on him. He laughed. The man was consistent. *Yeah, he's consistently a son of a bitch,* jeered the little voice inside Sam's head.

Talks with Atvar faltered. It was as if both the fleetlord and Sam were waiting for the other shoe to drop. Sam wasn't even sure what the other shoe was, but he had to wait—and he had to seem to know more than he did. At one point, Atvar said, "It would be better for all concerned if this turned out to be a dead end."

"Do you truly think so?" Yeager said, wondering what *this* was. "Our belief is that knowledge is never wasted."

"Yes, I understand that," the fleetlord answered. "You have this notion of what you call progress, of change as improvement. We think differently. When we think of change, we think of all the things that can go wrong, all the things that will need fixing. We are more realistic than you."

Sam made the negative gesture. "Meaning no disrespect, but I do not think so. The Race and Tosevites have different histories, that is all. You gained your technology slowly, one piece at a time, and that made you notice the disruptions it caused. We got ours over a couple of long lifetimes. It made things much better for us in spite of the disruptions."

"Did it?" Atvar asked. "Would the Jews the Deutsche exterminated agree with you? Without your newly advanced technology—railroads, poisons, and so on—the Deutsche could not have done as they did. This is not the only example. Will you deny it?"

"I wish I could," Sam answered. But that was not what Atvar had asked. Sam Yeager sighed. "No, I will not deny it. It is a truth. But you ignore, for example, the medical advances that allow most of us to live out our full spans without fear of the diseases that killed so many of us not long ago."

"I do not ignore them," Atvar said. Yeager thought he meant they also had a black side, as in the experiments Nazi doctors had undertaken while they were getting rid of Jews. But the fleetlord went down a different road: "Will your agriculture keep up with population growth? Will you regulate the number of hatchlings you are allowed to produce? Or will you simply start to starve because you do not think of difficulties until it is too late?"

Those were good questions. Sam had answers for none of them. All he could say was, "Tosevites have also predicted these disasters, but they have not happened yet. If progress continues, perhaps none of them will."

Atvar's mouth fell open. He knew Sam well enough to know he would not offend him by laughing at him. "There is such a thing as optimism, Ambassador, and there is such a thing as what we call drooling optimism."

"We would say wild-eyed optimism," Sam replied. "But you see optimism in general turning into that kind of optimism sooner than we do."

"No doubt you have come out with another truth," Atvar said. "As for me, I can speak only as a male of the Race. And one of the things I have to say is this: from the Race's perspective, your optimism leads to arrogance. You think you can ask for anything you want and everything will somehow turn out all right. I must tell you that *that* is not a truth, nor will it ever be." He added an emphatic cough.

"When you brought the conquest fleet to Tosev 3, you expected to find a bunch of sword-swinging barbarians," Sam said.

"Truth. We did," Atvar said. "I do not disagree. This is so."

"Forgive me, Fleetlord, but I have not finished," Sam said. "Instead of being sword-swinging barbarians, we were as you found us—"

"Barbarians with aircraft and landcruisers," Atvar broke in.

That stung. It also held some truth, more than Sam Yeager really cared to acknowledge. Refusing to acknowledge it, he went on as he had intended: "We were advanced enough to fight you to a standstill. You recognized some of us as equals, but you never truly meant it, not down in your livers, not even when we began to get ahead of you technologically. As long as we could not get out of our own solar system, you had some justification for this. But since we are talking here in Sitneff . . ."

"Everything you have said is a truth. It makes you more dangerous, not less. Why should we not try to rid ourselves of you while we still have the chance? If we do not, how long will it be before you try to get rid of us?"

There was the rub. The Race had always seen humans as nuisances. Now it saw them as dangerous nuisances. "We will fight to defend ourselves," Sam warned.

"That is not the issue," Atvar said. "Any species will fight to defend itself. You will fight to aggrandize yourselves. You will, but you will not do it at our expense."

"Was the conquest fleet fighting in self-defense?" Sam asked acidly.

"In the end, it certainly was," the fleetlord said, and Sam laughed in surprise. Atvar went on, "We had—and we paid for—a mistaken notion of where you Tosevites were in terms of technology. We knew as much before we landed on your planet. But if you had been what we thought you were, would you not agree you would have been better off if we had conquered you?"

Had the Lizards brought Earth from the twelfth century to the late twentieth in a couple of generations . . . "Materially, no one could possibly say we would not have been," Sam answered.

"There. You see?" Atvar said.

Sam held up a hand. "Excuse me, Fleetlord, but again I had not finished. The one thing you would have taken away from us forever is our freedom. Some of us would say that is too high a price to pay."

"Then some of you are fools," Atvar said with acid of his own. "You had freedom to murder one another, starve, and die of diseases you did not know how to cure. It is easy to speak of freedom when your belly is full and you are healthy. When you are starving and full of parasites, it is only a word, and one without much meaning."

That held some truth—more, again, than Yeager cared to admit. But just because it held some truth did not mean it was a truth. Sam said, "The Greeks invented democracy—snout-counting, if you like—more than fifteen hundred of our years before your probe came to Tosev 3: more than three thousand of yours. They were full of diseases. They were hungry a lot of the time. They fought among themselves. But they did it anyway. They believed—and a lot of us have always believed since—that no one has the right to tell anyone else what to do just because of who his sire was."

"Snoutcounting." As usual, Atvar filled the word with scorn. "My opinion remains unchanged: it is nothing to be proud of. And is this vaunted freedom of yours worth having when it is only the freedom to starve or to die or to impose your super-stition on others by force?"

"Who brought reverence for the spirits of Emperors past to Tosev 3?" Yeager inquired.

"That is not superstition. That is truth," Atvar said primly, sounding as certain as a missionary evangelizing an islander in the South Seas.

"Evidence would be nice," Sam said.

The fleetlord winced, but he answered, "We at least have the evidence of a long and prosperous history. Your supersti-tions have nothing whatever—nothing but fanaticism, I should say."

"We are a stubborn lot," Sam admitted.

"You are indeed." Atvar used an emphatic cough.

Sam said, "What you do not seem to understand is that we are also stubborn in the cause of freedom. Suppose you had sent the conquest fleet right after your probe and conquered us. You could have done it. No one would say anything else, not for a moment. Suppose you had, as I say. Do you not think that, once we learned about modern technology from you, we would have risen to regain our independence?"

He had often seen Atvar angry and sardonic. He had hardly ever seen him horrified. This was one of those times. The fleetlord recoiled like a well-bred woman who saw a mouse (which reminded Sam that the Lizards had yet to exterminate the escaped rats). Visibly gathering himself, Atvar said, "What a dreadful idea!" He used another emphatic cough. "You realize you may not have done your species a favor with this suggestion?"

He could only mean Sam had made humans seem more dangerous, which made a preventive war more likely. Sam wanted to scowl; that wasn't what he'd had in mind. He held his face steady. Atvar had probably had enough experience with humans to be able to read expressions. Picking his words with care, Sam said, "Whatever happens to us is also likely to happen to you. You know this is a truth, Fleetlord."

"I know that whatever happens now is likely to be better than what would happen in a hundred years, and much better than what would happen in two hundred." Atvar sighed. "I am sorry, Ambassador, but that is how things look out of my eye turrets."

"I am sorry, too." Sam used an emphatic cough of his own.

"Will it be war?" Jonathan Yeager asked his father.

Sam Yeager shrugged. "I don't know yet. But that's about as much as I can tell you." He shook his head. "No, that's not right. I can tell you one other thing: it doesn't look good right now."

"Everything seemed so fine when we got here," Jonathan said mournfully.

"I know," his father said. "But *that* we got here . . . It's just made the Lizards more nervous the longer they think about it. Now we can reach them. We can hit them where they live—literally. They're starting to figure that if they don't move to get rid of us now, they'll never have another chance. They worry we'll have the drop on them if they wait."

Jonathan looked out the window of his father's room. There

was Sitneff, the town he'd come to take for granted, with the greenish-blue sky and the dry hills out beyond the boxy buildings. It had been a comfortable place for Lizards to live since the Pleistocene, since before modern humans replaced Neanderthals. A female of the Race from those days wouldn't have much trouble fitting into the city as it was now. A Neanderthal woman dropped into Los Angeles might have rather more.

With a distinct effort of will, Jonathan pulled back to the business at hand, saying, "They may be right."

"Yeah, I know. It doesn't do us any good—just the opposite, in fact," his father said. "But if they do attack us, Earth isn't the only planet that'll suffer. You can bet your bottom dollar on that."

"Do you know for a fact that we've sent ships to Rabotev 2 and Halless 1?" As he usually did, Jonathan used the Race's names for the stars humans called Epsilon Eridani and Epsilon Indi. "Do you know that we've sent more ships here?"

"Know for a fact? No." Sam Yeager shook his head again. "The *Admiral Peary* hasn't got news of any other launchings except the *Molotov*. If the Lizards have, they aren't talking. But . . ." He sighed heavily, then repeated it: "But . . ." The one ominous word seemed a complete sentence. "If we did launch warships, we'd be damn fools to let the Lizards know we'd done it. If war does start, they're liable to get some horrendous surprises. And I have no idea—none at all—what the Russians and the Japanese and even the Germans might be able to do by now. There may be a fleet behind the *Molotov*. I just don't know."

"Madness," Jonathan said. "After you had your audience with the Emperor, I thought everything was going to fall into place. We'd have peace, and nobody would have to worry about things for a while." He chuckled unhappily. "Naive, wasn't I?"

"Well, if you were, you weren't the only one, because I felt the same way," his father said. "And I really don't know what queered the deal."

"That experiment back on Earth, whatever it was?"

"I guess so," his father said. "I'd like things a lot better if I knew what was going on there, though. The Lizards who do aren't talking." He paused to make sure the Race's listening devices were suppressed, then spoke in a low voice: "The Emperor wouldn't even tell Kassquit."

Jonathan whistled softly. "Kassquit is as loyal to the Empire as the day is long. Or do the Lizards think she'll spill everything she knows to Frank in pillow talk?" He threw his hands in the air to show how unlikely he thought that was.

"I don't know. I just don't know, dammit," Sam Yeager said. "That's possible—if the Lizards know us well enough to know what pillow talk is. But they do know we can bug their phone lines here, remember. That may be why Risson kept quiet. I can't say for sure. Nobody human on Home can say for sure. That worries me, too."

"Do they have any ideas on the *Admiral Peary*?" Jonathan asked.

"I asked Lieutenant General Healey." His father's mouth twisted, as if to say he considered that above and beyond the call of duty. "He hasn't found anything yet, but there's a hell of a lot of Lizard signal traffic between Earth and Home to sift through and sometimes try to decrypt, so who knows what he'll come up with once he does some real digging?"

"And in the meantime . . ."

"In the meantime, he's sending a war warning back to the USA," his father said grimly. "Whatever the Lizards do, they won't pull a Jap on us."

"Okay, Dad," Jonathan said. That was a phrase from Sam Yeager's generation. Jonathan understood it, though he wouldn't have used it himself. He wondered how many Americans living right now would have any idea what it meant. Not many, he suspected.

"Wish I had better news for you, son," his father said.

"So do I," Jonathan said. "If I can do anything, you sing out, you hear?"

"I will," his father promised. "That's what you're along for, after all. Right now, though, I have to tell you I don't know what it would be. That's not a knock on you. I don't know what more I can do myself. I wish to hell I did." Sam Yeager had always been a vigorous man who looked and acted younger than his years. But now the weight of worry made him seem suddenly old.

Jonathan walked over and set a hand on his father's shoulder. "Something will turn up."

"I hope so." His father sounded bleak. "I'll be damned if I know what it is, though. Of course, I would have said the same thing back in 1942, when the Lizards were knocking the crap out of us. Nobody had any idea what to do about them, either, not at first."

"That's what I hear," Jonathan agreed. "Of course, I wasn't around then. You were."

"If I hadn't been, you wouldn't be around now."

"Yeah," Jonathan said.

His father looked back across the years. "And if your mother hadn't been carrying you," he said, as much to himself as to Jonathan, "I probably wouldn't be *here* right now."

Jonathan raised a quizzical eyebrow. "What's that supposed to mean?"

Sam Yeager blinked. He seemed to realize what he'd just said. A long sigh escaped him. "You know your mother was married to another guy before she met me."

"Oh, sure," Jonathan said. "He got killed when the Lizards invaded, right?"

"Well, yeah." His father was staring into the past again. He looked . . . embarrassed? "It's—a little more complicated than we ever talked about, though."

"Whatever it is, I think you'd better spit it out, Dad," Jonathan said. "Do I have to come ten light-years to get all the old family scandals?"

"Well, it looks like you probably do." Sam Yeager not only looked embarrassed, he sounded embarrassed, too. "When your mother and I got married in beautiful, romantic Chugwater, Wyoming, we both thought her first husband was dead. That's the God's truth. We did."

"But he wasn't?" Jonathan said slowly. He didn't know how to take that. It was news to him.

His father nodded. "He sure wasn't. He was a physicist on our atomic-bomb project. Barbara—your mom—found out she was pregnant with you, and then she found out she wasn't a widow—bang! like that." Sam Yeager snapped his fingers.

"Jesus! You never told me any of this," Jonathan said.

"It's not exactly something we were proud of," his father

answered, which was probably the understatement of the year. "I always figured that, if she hadn't had a bun in the oven, she would have gone back to the other guy—Jens, his name was. I never asked her—you'd better believe I didn't!—but that's what I figure. She did, though, and so she ended up choosing me . . . and the rest is history."

"Christ!" Jonathan exclaimed. "Any *other* skeletons in the closet, as long as you're in a confessing mood?"

"I don't *think* so," his father answered. "I guess I should have told you this a long time ago."

"I guess you should have," Jonathan said feelingly. "What the hell happened to this other guy? Do you even know?"

"Yeah. I know." Sam Yeager's face went even more somber than it had been. "He kind of went off the deep end after that, and who can blame him? He shot a couple of people before they finally got him. And sometimes I wonder what I would have done. . . ." His voice trailed away.

"Oh, for God's sake, Dad!" Jonathan said. "You wouldn't have done anything that nutty. It's not your style, and you know it."

His father only shrugged. "How can you tell till something happens? You can't. Losing your mom screwed up the other guy's whole life. It sure wouldn't have done me any good. She was . . . something special." Now his voice broke.

For him, Barbara Yeager hadn't been dead long at all. He'd gone into cold sleep not long after she passed away. Jonathan had waited another seventeen years. He had scar tissue over the wound his father didn't. But the other things his old man had told him . . . "Why did you sit on all this stuff for so long? Didn't you think I had a right to know?"

Sam Yeager coughed a couple of times. "Well, part of it was that your mother never wanted to talk about it much. She always did her best to act as though it hadn't happened. I think she felt bad about the way things turned out for the other guy. I know I would have in her shoes. How could you help it? It wasn't even that she didn't love him, or hadn't loved him. That probably made it worse. Just—one of those things. She didn't have any perfect choices. She made the one she made, and then she had to live with it. We all had to live with it."

Except the other guy had turned out not to be able to.

Jonathan had always thought his mother's first husband was off the stage before she met his father. Nobody'd ever *said* so. It was just what he'd assumed, what his folks had wanted him to assume. He saw why they'd want him to—it was safe and conventional. The real story seemed anything but.

"Why tell me now?" he asked harshly.

"It's the truth. I figured you ought to know." His father's mouth tightened. "And I have no idea what the odds of our coming through all this are. We may not have a whole lot of time."

A deathbed confession? Not quite, but maybe not so far removed from one, either. Jonathan picked his words with care: "It must have been a crazy time, back when we were fighting the conquest fleet."

His father nodded. "You can say that again. We didn't know if we'd make it, or if we'd all get blown to hell and gone the next week or the next day or sometimes the next minute. A lot of us just . . . grabbed what we could, and didn't give a damn about tomorrow. Why, I remember—"

"Remember what?" Jonathan asked when his father broke off.

But Sam Yeager only said, "Never mind. That really isn't any of your business. I'm the only one left alive whose business it is, and I'll take it to the grave with me."

"Okay, Dad," Jonathan said, surprised by his father's vehemence. But that was just one surprise piled on top of a ton of others. He tried to imagine his father and mother falling in love, falling into bed, her thinking she was a widow. . . . He tried, and felt himself failing. The picture refused to form. They were his parents. They were so much older than he was.

His father wasn't so much older than he was as he had been before cold sleep. And once upon a time, long before cold sleep, his father had been younger still—and so had his mother. He still couldn't imagine it.

He couldn't imagine war with the Lizards, either. But that was liable to be every bit as real as his parents' sex life.

Kassquit asked Frank Coffey, "Do you know what sort of experiments you Tosevites are carrying out on your home planet?"

"No." The dark-skinned American Big Ugly made the negative gesture. "I know there are some, and I know the Race is worried about them. I was hoping you could tell me more."

She let her mouth fall open in a silent laugh. "I went up to the Emperor himself, and he would not tell me. And if I knew, I would hurt the Empire by telling you."

"If I knew, I might be hurting my not-empire by telling you," Coffey said. "And yet we both keep trying to find out. Either we are both spies, or we have become very good friends."

"Or both," Kassquit said.

The American Tosevite laughed, though she hadn't been joking. They lay on the sleeping mat in her room, both of them naked. They'd made love a while ago, but Frank Coffey hadn't shown any interest in putting his wrappings on again. When even an air-conditioned room on Home was warmer than Tosevites found comfortable, wrappings made no sense to Kassquit. She knew wild Big Uglies had strong prohibitions against shedding their wrappings in public. She knew, but she did not understand. However irrational they were, the prohibitions seemed too strong to overcome. She'd given up trying.

"Will it be war?" she asked. The question was being asked more and more often in the hotel in Sitneff, by more and more Tosevites and members of the Race.

"I cannot tell you that," Coffey answered. "I can tell you that the United States will not start a war against the Race. For us to start a war would make no sense. If the Race starts a war . . ." He shrugged. "We will fight back. We will fight back as hard as we can. You may rely on it."

"Oh, I do," Kassquit said. "The other part of the promise is what concerns me. The Deutsche tried a surprise attack against the Race."

"I remember. I was a boy then," Coffey said. That startled Kassquit for a moment. They seemed about the same age, but she'd come into adulthood when the Deutsche started the second major war between Big Uglies and the Race. Then she remembered she'd gone into cold sleep years before the American Tosevite had, and been kept in cold sleep till the *Admiral Peary* neared Home. Coffey went on, "They had radioactivity alerts every day. Depending on how bad the fall-out was, sometimes they would not let us go out and play."

"That sort of thing could happen here," Kassquit said.

"Truth," Coffey agreed. "Worse than that, much worse than that, could also happen here. And it could happen in my not-empire, too."

Kassquit cared very little about the United States. She remembered only belatedly that Frank Coffey cared very little about the Empire. That struck her as strange. It would have struck an average member of the Race as even stranger. For more than a hundred thousand years, the Race hadn't needed diplomatic relations with foreign empires. Those of the Rabotevs and Hallessi had fallen before earlier conquest fleets in the flick of a nictitating membrane.

Here as in everything else, the Big Uglies were different.

"If there is a war, Tosev 3 may not survive it," Kassquit said. "What would you do then?"

"Personally? I am not sure," Coffey answered. "I would not *know* the worst had happened for many years. That is something of a relief. But the question may be academic. The *Admiral Peary* and whatever other starships the United States is flying by then would do their best to make sure that whatever happened to Tosev 3 also happened to Home and the other worlds of the Empire."

Was he speaking as someone who was simply concerned, or as an American military officer who wanted to make sure the Race's military officers heard his words? He had to be sure Kassquit's room was monitored. Kassquit was sure of it herself. She hated it, but didn't know what she could do about it.

"How much damage could Tosevite starships do?" she asked, partly as a concerned citizen of the Empire and partly to make sure the Race's military officers heard his reply.

What he said, though, wasn't very informative: "How can I know for certain? I have been in cold sleep a long time. The state of the art back on Tosev 3 will have changed. I could not begin to guess the capabilities of the United States right now—or those of the other independent Tosevite empires and not-empires."

Or maybe that wasn't so uninformative after all. He'd managed to remind the Race it might not be fighting the United States alone. That was something military officers needed to think about, all right.

"If this war comes, it will be the worst anyone has ever known," Kassquit said.

"No one could possibly say that is not a truth," Coffey agreed gravely.

"Then why fight it?" Kassquit exclaimed.

"I speak for myself and for the United States when I say we do not want to fight it." Frank Coffey used an emphatic cough. "But I also have to say again that, if the Race attacks us, we will fight back, and fight back as hard as we can." He added another one.

"Where is the sense to it?" Kassquit asked.

"As for myself, I do not see that sense anywhere," the American Big Ugly said. "But I can tell you where I think the Race sees it."

"Where?"

"The Race fears that, no matter how bad the war would be if they fought it now, it would be even worse if they waited till later," Coffey answered. "This is a mistaken attitude. The United States is completely happy to be a good neighbor to the Empire—as long as the Empire stays a good neighbor to us."

That sounded both logical and reasonable. If Coffey meant it, if the United States meant it, the Empire and the Tosevites' snoutcounting not-empire *could* live side by side. If. One thing history had taught the Race, though, was that Big Uglies were least reliable when they sounded most reasonable and logical. They left it there. Where else could they take it?

After supper that evening in the refectory, Kassquit went over to Ttomalss and said, "Excuse me, superior sir, but may I speak with you for a little while?"

"Certainly," Ttomalss answered. "Will you come to my room?"

Kassquit made the negative gesture. "I thank you, but no. Do you not think it would be more pleasant to go outside and talk in the cool evening breezes?"

To her, those breezes were anything but cool. When she used the Race's language, though, she necessarily used the

Race's thought patterns, too. And, by the way Ttomalss' eye turrets swung sharply toward her face, he had no trouble figuring out what she really meant: if they talked outside the hotel, they would not—or at least might not—be talking into someone's hearing diaphragm.

The psychologist replied naturally enough: "We can do that if you like. Maybe the evening sevod are still calling. They are pleasant to hear—do you not think so?"

"Yes, very," Kassquit said.

They walked out of the hotel, Kassquit towering over the male who had raised her from a hatchling. Home's sun had set not long before. Twilight deepened, the western sky gradually fading toward the blue-black of night. The evening sevod were still twittering in the bushes around the building, though they sounded sleepier with each passing moment.

One by one, stars came out of the sky. The lights of Sitneff drowned out the dimmer ones, but the brighter ones still shaped the outlines of the constellations. Kassquit had often watched stars from the starship in orbit around Tosev 3. She'd had to get used to seeing them twinkle here; from space, of course, their light was hard and unwinking.

She stared and then pointed. "Is that not the star Tosev, superior sir?"

Ttomalss' eye turrets moved in the direction of her finger. He made the affirmative gesture. "Yes, I think so. Strange to see it as just another star, is it not?"

"Truth," Kassquit said, and then, "I ask you again: what sort of experiments are the wild Big Uglies working on there?"

"Ah," Ttomalss said. "I wondered why you wanted to speak behind the sand dune, as it were." He sounded more amused than annoyed. "If the Emperor did not tell you, why did you think I would?"

"You . . . know what his Majesty said to me?" Kassquit said slowly.

"I have a good notion of what he said, anyhow," Ttomalss replied. "You would have rubbed my snout in it had he told you. Will you not believe that if I had not been the one to bring this to the notice of those in authority here on Home, I would not be authorized to know of it, either?"

"What can possibly be as important as that?" Kassquit

asked. "Everyone makes it sound as if the sun will go nova to-morrow on account of it."

"Anything I say right now would only be speculation on my part," Ttomalss told her. "Until the physicists have spoken, I can tell you nothing. Until then, as a matter of fact, there really is nothing to tell."

Kassquit made the negative gesture. "I would not say that, superior sir. For instance, you could tell me what sort of ex-periments the physicists are working on."

Ttomalss used the negative gesture, too. "I could, but, as I say, I may not. The work is important and it is secret. If I were not directly involved in it, I repeat that I would be as ignorant as you. I wish I were."

The last four words made Kassquit eye him thoughtfully. She knew Ttomalss better than she knew anyone else alive. "Whatever the wild Big Uglies have found, you do not think we will be able to reproduce it."

"I never said that!" Ttomalss jerked as if she'd jabbed a pin under his scales. "I never said that, and I do not say it now. You have no right, none whatsoever, to make such assump-tions."

As was the way of such things, the more he protested, the more he convinced Kassquit she was right. She consoled him as best she could: "Whatever they do, superior sir, is bound to be limited to their own solar system for many years to come. The star Tosev is a long way away." She pointed up into the sky. Tosev seemed brighter now. That was an illusion, of course. Twilight had faded, and the sky around the star had grown darker. Kassquit had had to get used to that, too. In space, the sky was always black.

What she'd intended for consolation seemed to have the op-posite effect. Ttomalss twitched again. Then he spun and hur-ried back into the hotel, leaving her alone in the darkness outside. She couldn't remember the last time he'd been so rude. He was worried about something, all right—something to do with the Big Uglies and their experiments.

Whatever it was, Kassquit realized she probably wouldn't find out any time soon. If Ttomalss wouldn't give her the in-formation, no one would. She thought she was entitled to it.

If higher-ups in the Race disagreed with her, what could she do about it? Nothing she could see.

She followed Ttomalss back into the hotel. He wasn't waiting in the lobby for her. He'd gone upstairs—probably to report on her curiosity to some of those higher-ups. Kassquit shrugged. She couldn't do anything about that, either.

Ttomalss peered out of his hotel window into the night. That was not the ideal way to look at the stars. In a crowded town like Sitneff, there was no ideal way to look at them. Even for an urban setting, pressing your snout against some none-too-clean glass was less than optimal.

But Tosev was bright enough for him to spot in spite of everything. Just a sparkling point of light . . . Strange to think how something that small and lovely could cause so much trouble.

The psychologist made the negative gesture. It wasn't Tosev's fault. It was that of the annoying creatures infesting the star's third planet. If not for them, if not for that miserable world, Tosev would be . . . just another star, brighter than most but not bright enough to seem really special.

If. If not. But things were as they were. One way or another, the Race was going to have to deal with the Big Uglies. If that meant exterminating them, then it did. If the Race didn't exterminate the Big Uglies, weren't the Tosevites likely to do it to them first?

A star moving across the sky . . . But that wasn't a star, only a warning light on an airplane. It was deep in the red to Ttomalss' eyes. The Big Uglies might not have been able to see it at all. Their eyes could sense hues past deep blue, but did not reach as far into the red as the Race's did. Tosev was a hotter, brighter star than the sun. Tosevites were adapted to its light, as the Race was adapted to that of the sun. Hallessi, now, had names for colors at the red end of the spectrum that the Race could not see. Their star was cooler and redder than the sun, let alone Tosev.

With a sorrowful hiss, Ttomalss looked away from the window. The authorities on Tosev 3 had put him into cold sleep and sent him back to Home to work toward peace with the wild Big Uglies. He'd done everything he could toward that end, too. And what had it got him? Only the growing certainty that war was on the way.

He'd seen war on Tosev 3, and from orbit around the Big Uglies' home world. He tried to imagine *that* coming to the surface of Home. Peace had prevailed here since the planet was unified under the Empire: for more than a hundred thousand years. Males and females of the Race took it for granted. So did Rabotevs and Hallessi; they'd been freed from war since their worlds were brought into the Empire.

But if war was unimaginable to citizens of the Empire, it was anything but to the Big Uglies. They took it as much for granted as members of the Race took peace. And, because they did, responsible members of the Race also had to.

If war came now, it would ruin Tosev 3 and probably devastate the worlds of the Empire. What could be worse than that? The trouble was, Ttomalss feared he knew the answer. If war came later, it might only devastate Tosev 3 while ruining the worlds of the Empire.

How fast were the Big Uglies progressing? What did they know that Pesskrag and her colleagues were trying so hard to find out? Even more to the point, what did they know that Felless and other members of the Race on Tosev 3 didn't know they knew? Whatever it was, was it enough to tip the balance of power between the Empire and the independent Tosevites? If it wasn't now, would it be in a few years? In a few hundred years? What were the odds?

Would the independent Tosevites go to war with one another, and not with the Race? They'd been fighting one another when the conquest fleet arrived. Since then, the Race had seemed a bigger threat to them than they had to one another. But that wasn't necessarily a permanent condition. With the Big Uglies, no condition was necessarily permanent.

That went a long way toward making them as dangerous as they were.

So many questions. So few answers. Or maybe the answers were there on Tosev 3, but light's laggard speed simply hadn't brought them Home yet. Ttomalss let out another unhappy hiss. There were times when he wished Felless had never passed on the information she'd found.

The American Big Uglies had a saying: *if stupidity is hap-*

piness, it is foolish to be intelligent. That was how it went in the language of the Race, anyhow; Ttomalss suspected it lost something in the translation. Whatever truth it held depended on the status of the first clause—which suddenly seemed truer to the psychologist than it ever had before.

Ttomalss started to telephone Pesskrag, then stopped and made the negative gesture. He had almost been stupid, to say nothing of unintelligent, himself. The American Tosevites had shown they could monitor telephone calls inside the hotel. He didn't want them listening to anything he had to say to the physicist. He used an emphatic cough by itself, which showed how upset he was. No, he didn't want that at all.

He rode down to the lobby, and then went out into the night. His mouth fell open in a laugh. He did not have to worry about any of the Big Uglies sneaking after him. They would be as inconspicuous as an azwaca in a temple dedicated to the spirits of Emperors past. No, more so—an azwaca, at least, would belong to this world.

Ttomalss relished being one ordinary male among many ordinary males and females. This was where he belonged. These other members of the Race—even the occasional less than ordinary ones wearing false hair or wrappings—were his own kind. He might have spent many years studying the Big Uglies, but he knew them only intellectually. His liver belonged with his own.

He found a public telephone by a market whose sign boasted it was open all night. Passersby might hear snatches of his conversation. So what, though? Those snatches would mean nothing to them. If the Tosevites listened to everything he said . . . He made the negative gesture. They wouldn't. They couldn't, not now.

Before he could place the call, a skinny female sidled up to him. "Do you want to buy some ginger?" she asked.

He made the negative gesture. "No. Go away."

"You do not need to get huffy about it. Do you want to buy *me* some ginger? Then you can smell my pheromones and mate with me."

"No! Go away!" This time, Ttomalss used an emphatic cough.

" 'No! Go away!' " the female echoed mockingly. "You can

stuff that right on up your cloaca, too, pal." She skittered down the street.

He found himself quivering with anger. Ginger was a problem back on Tosev 3, certainly. That was where the stuff came from, so the scope of the problem there wasn't so surprising. To get his snout rubbed in it here on Home, though, when he'd just stepped away from the hotel for a little while . . . *Maybe we really ought to slag the Big Uglies' home planet. Then we would not have to worry about the herb any more.*

Or was that a truth? Wouldn't clever chemists start synthesizing the active ingredient? Getting rid of the trouble Tosevites caused might be even harder than getting rid of the Tosevites themselves. Somehow, that seemed altogether fitting to Ttomalss.

His fingerclaws poked in Pesskrag's number. He more than half expected to have to leave a message, but the physicist's image appeared on the screen. She said, "This is Pesskrag. I greet you."

"And I greet you. This is Ttomalss."

"Oh, hello, Senior Researcher. Good to hear from you. I was just thinking of you not long ago, as a matter of fact. What can I do for you?"

"Are you in a place where you can speak without being overheard?"

"Actually, I have had all my calls forwarded here to the laboratory. Some of my colleagues may hear what I say, but without their work I would not be able to tell you nearly so much as I can."

"All right. That will do." Ttomalss was impressed that she was working into the night. She recognized how important this research was, then. Good. The psychologist said, "I was wondering if you had gained any better idea of how long it might take to translate these new discoveries into real-world engineering."

"Well, I still cannot tell you I am certain about that," Pesskrag answered. "I presume you are asking based on the notion that speed counts for more than safety, and that the usual checks and reviews will be abandoned or ignored?"

"Yes, that is right," Ttomalss agreed.

"My opinion is that it will still be a matter of years, and

more of them rather than fewer. No one will walk confidently on this sand. There will be errors and misfortunes, and they will lead to delays. I do not see how they can help leading to delays."

That only proved she'd never watched Big Uglies in action. They charged right past errors and misfortunes. If those left dead or maimed individuals in their wake—well, so what? To the Tosevites, results counted for more than the process used to obtain them.

Asking the Race to imitate that sort of behavior was probably useless. No, it was bound to be useless. The Race simply did not and could not operate the way the Big Uglies did. Most of the time, Ttomalss thanked the spirits of Emperors past for that. Every once in a while, as now, it made him want to curse.

"Years, you say?" he persisted. "Not centuries?"

"I still say it should be centuries," Pesskrag replied. "It probably will not be, not with everyone pushing for speed at the expense of quality and safety, but it should be. There are too many variables we do not understand well. There are too many variables we do not understand at all."

"Very well. I thank you." Ttomalss broke the connection. He felt slightly reassured, but only slightly. Whatever the Race could do, the Tosevites were bound to be able to do faster. How much faster? *That* much faster? He despised the idea of preventive war, but. . . .

All of a sudden, he stopped worrying about preventive war. That ginger-peddling female was on her way back. She had two large, unfriendly-looking males with her, one of them particularly bizarre with a mane of yellow hair that had never sprouted from his skin. Ttomalss did not wait to find out if their personalities belied their appearance. He left, in a hurry.

"Hey, buddy, wait! We want to talk to you!" the male with the wig shouted after him.

Ttomalss didn't wait. He was sure the males—and that unpleasant female—wanted to do something to him. He was just as sure talking wasn't it. He swung one eye turret back toward them. To his enormous relief, the males weren't coming after him. The female wasn't relieved at that. She was furious. She clawed the male with the yellow false hair. He knocked her to the sidewalk. They started fighting.

My own people, Ttomalss thought sadly. *How are they any better than Big Uglies when they act like this?* But the answer to that was plain enough. They were *his.* Like them or not, he understood them. He understood them even if they wanted to hit him over the head and steal his valuables.

If the Big Uglies hit him over the head and stole his valuables, they weren't just robbers. They were alien robbers, which made them a hundred times worse.

And the Big Uglies wanted to hit the whole Race over the head and steal its valuables. Things had been peaceful and stable on Home for so long. It wouldn't last. It couldn't last, not any more. Maybe, once the Tosevites were gone for good, peace and stability would return . . . if anything was left of the Empire afterwards.

Existence or not—that is the question. So some Tosevite writer had put it. He'd been dead for hundreds of years, maybe even a thousand; Ttomalss didn't know as much as he would have liked about Tosevite chronology before the conquest fleet came. But that Big Ugly had got right to the liver of things. If existence for the Race and the Empire seemed more likely after a preventive war, then preventive war there should be. If not, not. Ttomalss feared he knew what the answer was.

Karen Yeager nodded politely to Trir. "I greet you," she told the tour guide.

"And I greet you," Trir said, also politely. The female had acted friendly enough lately; it wasn't close to mating season. Her eye turrets traveled up and down Karen's length. "I had thought there might be some future in escorting you Tosevites when you come to visit Home. Now I see that is unlikely to be so."

The hotel lobby was as warm as ever. Looking out through the big plate-glass windows, Karen could see the sun-blasted hills out beyond Sitneff. Despite all that, a chill ran through her. She hoped she was wrong as she asked, "What do you mean?"

"Why, that you Big Uglies probably will not be coming to

Home any more, and that I cannot expect to see shiploads of students and travelers. We are going to have to put you in your place, or so everyone says." Trir took the answer for granted.

More ice walked up Karen's back. "Who told you that, if I may ask? And what do you mean by putting us in our place?"

"We shall have to make certain you cannot threaten the Race and the Empire." By Trir's tone, that would be not only simple but bloodless. She had lived in peace all her life. Home had lived in peace since the Pleistocene. Males and females here had no idea what anything else was like.

Karen did. For better and for worse—more often than not, for worse—Earth's history was different from Home's. And the Race's soldiers had played no small part in that history since the conquest fleet arrived. "You are talking about a war, about millions—more likely, billions—dying," Karen said slowly. "I ask you again: who told you war was coming? Please tell me. It may be important." She used an emphatic cough.

"Everyone around here except maybe you Tosevites seems to think it will come," Trir replied. "And I do not think it will be as bad as you make it sound. After all, it will be happening a long way away."

You idiot! Karen didn't scream that at the Lizard, though she wanted to. She contented herself with making the negative gesture instead. "For one thing, war is no better when it happens to someone else than when it happens to you," she said, though she knew plenty of humans would have felt otherwise. "For another, I must tell you that you are mistaken."

"In what way?" Trir asked.

"This war, if there is a war, will ravage the Empire's worlds as well as Tosev 3. That is a truth." Karen added another emphatic cough.

"That would be barbaric!" Trir exclaimed, with an emphatic cough of her own.

"Why would it be more barbaric than the other?" Karen asked.

"Because this is the Empire, of course," Trir answered.

"I see." Karen hoped the Lizard could hear the acid dripping from her voice. "If you do it to someone else who is far away, it is fine, but it is barbaric if someone else presumes to do it to you right here."

"I did not say that. I did not mean that. You are confusing things," Trir said.

"I do not know what you meant. Only you can know that, down deep in the bottom of your liver," Karen replied. "But I know what you said. I know what I said. And I know one other thing—I know which of us is confused. Please believe me: I am not the one."

Trir's tailstump quivered with anger. "I think you have it coming, for telling lies if nothing else." She stalked away.

Karen felt like throwing something at her. That would have been undiplomatic, no matter how satisfying it might also have been. Karen thought hard about flipping Trir the bird. That would have been undiplomatic, too. She might have got away with it, simply because nobody here was likely to understand what the gesture meant.

And then, in spite of herself, she started to laugh. Could you flip somebody the bird here on Home? Wouldn't you have to flip her (or even him) the pterodactyl instead?

However much she wanted it to, the laughter wouldn't stick. That Trir seemed happy war would come was bad enough. That she seemed so sure was worse. And Karen muttered a curse under her breath. She hadn't got the guide to tell her who among the Lizard higher-ups was so certain war was on the way.

Did that matter? Weren't *all* the Lizards acting that way these days? She knew too well that they were. And if they acted that way, they were much more likely to bring it on.

An elevator opened, silently and smoothly. Everything the Race did was silent, smooth, efficient. Next to the Lizards, humans *were* a bunch of noisy, clumsy barbarians. But if they went down, they'd go down swinging, and the Empire would remember them for a long time—or else go down into blackness with them.

Kassquit came out of the elevator. She waved when she saw Karen in the lobby. She not only waved, she came over to her, saying, "I greet you."

"And I greet you," Karen answered cautiously. She and Kassquit still didn't usually get along. "What can I do for you today?" Would Kassquit be gloating at the prospect of war, too? She never got tired of bragging how she was a citizen of the Empire. As far as Karen was concerned, that was one of the things that made her less than human. She didn't *want* to be human, and wished she weren't.

But now Kassquit said, "If you know any way to keep the peace between your not-empire and the Empire, please speak of it to Sam Yeager and to Fleetlord Atvar. We must do whatever we can to prevent a war."

"I completely agree with you," Karen said—and if that wasn't a surprise, it was close enough for government work. *Government work is exactly the problem here,* she thought. She went on, "From my perspective, the problem is that the Race thinks war would be more to its advantage than peace." And how would Kassquit take *that*?

Kassquit used the affirmative gesture. "Truth. And a truth I do not know how to get around. My superiors are convinced they will have to fight later if they do not fight now, and they will be at a greater disadvantage the longer they delay. By the spirits of Emperors past, they must be addled!"

Karen wondered if they were. Humans progressed faster than Lizards. Both sides could see that. But . . . "If we can destroy each other, what difference does it make who has the fancier weapons? Both sides will be equally dead."

"That is also a truth." As usual, Kassquit's face showed nothing, but urgency throbbed in her voice. "Under such circumstances, war is madness."

"Yes," Karen said. "The United States has always held this view."

"After its experience when the colonization fleet came to Tosev 3 and in the unprovoked attack by the Deutsche, the Empire is not sure that is a truth," Kassquit said. "And, speaking of unprovoked attacks, consider the one your not-empire made against the colonization fleet not long after its ships went into orbit around your world. If you see a way to seize a victory cheaply and easily, will you not take it? This is the Race's fear."

"I do not know what to tell you, except that Sam Yeager is the one who made sure our unjust act would not go unpunished," Karen said. "I do not think we would make the same mistake twice. And I cannot help seeing that you have just made a strong case for war, at least from the Empire's point of view."

"I know I have. Making the case for war is easy—if one does not reckon in the dangers involved," Kassquit said. "My hope is that your not-empire has indeed changed from its previous aggressive stance. If I can persuade my superiors of that—and if you wild Tosevites work to convince them of the same thing—we may possibly avert this fight, even now."

"Would Sam Yeager be the American ambassador to the Race if we had not changed our ways?" Karen asked.

"Sam Yeager would not be your ambassador if the Doctor had survived," Kassquit pointed out. "The Doctor was a very able diplomat. No one would say otherwise. But no one would say he was a shining example of peace and trust, either."

She was right about that. If you were in a dicker with the Doctor, he would have had no qualms about picking your pocket. Not only that, he would have tried to persuade you afterwards that he'd done it for your own good. That talent had made him very valuable to the United States. Whether it had made him a paragon of ethics might be a different question.

"Do what you can with your own officials," Karen said. "I will speak to Sam Yeager. As you say, we have to try."

Kassquit used the affirmative gesture. They might not like each other, but that had nothing to do with anything right now. Karen rode up to her father-in-law's room and knocked on the door. When he opened it, he said, "You look like a steamroller just ran over your kitten."

She eyed him. "You don't look so happy yourself."

"To tell you the truth, I'm not," Sam Yeager said. "The small stuff is, Atvar is mad as hops because the Race found a rat—a half-grown rat—in a building a couple of miles from here. He keeps trying to make it out to be our fault, even though the cleaners let the darn things out."

"A half-grown rat? So they're breeding here, then," Karen said.

"Sure looks that way," Sam Yeager agreed. "And that's just the small stuff. The big stuff is . . . Well, you know about the big stuff."

"Yes, I know about the big stuff. That's why I wanted to talk to you." Karen summed up the conversations she'd just had with Trir and Kassquit. She went on, "What can we do? We have to be able to do *something* to convince the Lizards this war's not worth fighting. Something—but I don't know what."

Sam Yeager let out a long, weary sigh. "If they're bound and determined to go ahead and fight, I don't know what we can do about it but hit back as hard as we can. They look to have decided that this is going to be the best chance they've got." He shrugged. "They may even be right."

"Even if they are, it'll be a disaster!" Karen exclaimed.

Her father-in-law nodded. "I know that. I think they know it, too. If they don't, it's not because I haven't told 'em. But if they think it'll be a disaster now but maybe a catastrophe later . . ." He spread his hands.

"We don't want a war with them. We just *don't*," Karen said.

"Their attitude is, we may not want one now, but we're a bunch of changeable Big Uglies, and sooner or later we will," Sam Yeager said. "I don't know how to convince them they're wrong, either. And I'd better. If I can't . . ."

"Kassquit is trying the same thing on their side." Karen wasn't used to talking about Kassquit with unreserved approval—or with any approval at all—but she did now.

"Good for her. I hope it helps some, but I wouldn't bet the house on it," Sam Yeager said. "I hope something helps some. If it doesn't . . ." He paused again, and grimaced. "If it doesn't, we'll have a war on our hands."

"We can see it's madness. Kassquit can see it's madness. The Lizards are usually more reasonable than we are. Why not now?" Karen could hear the despair in her voice.

"It's what I told you before. They must think this is their best chance, or maybe their last chance. It doesn't look that way to me, but I'm not Atvar or the Emperor." Sam Yeager's scowl grew blacker. "I'm just a scared old man. If something big doesn't change in a hurry, four worlds are going to go up in smoke."

In the control room these days, Glen Johnson felt more as if he were in a missile-armed upper stage in Earth orbit, or even in the cockpit of a fighter heading for action against the

Lizards. Anything could happen, and probably would. He knew damn well that the Race could overwhelm the *Admiral Peary*. His job, and the job of everybody else on board, was to make sure they remembered they'd been in a fight.

The ship had a swarm of antimissiles that were supposed to be a hair better than the best the Race could fire. She also had close-in weapons systems—a fancy name for radar-controlled Gatling guns on steroids—to knock out anything the antimissiles missed. Put that together and it wouldn't keep the *Admiral Peary* alive. It wasn't supposed to. But it was supposed to keep her alive long enough to let her get her own licks in.

"What do you think?" Johnson asked Mickey Flynn. "Are we ready for Armageddon?"

Flynn gave that his usual grave consideration. "I can't say for sure," he replied at last. "But I do know that Armageddon sick and tired of worrying about it."

Johnson groaned, as he was no doubt intended to do. Mickey Flynn looked back blandly. Johnson was sick of worrying about it, too, which didn't mean he wasn't doing his share and then some. "What do we do if the balloon goes up?" he said.

This time, Flynn answered right away: "Well, it will be over in a hurry, anyhow." That was what the Lizards would have called a truth. By the way he said it, he thought Johnson was a damn fool for asking the question. After only a short pause, Johnson decided he'd been a damn fool, too.

In the background was the radio chatter among the Lizards' spaceships and orbiting stations and shuttlecraft. Johnson didn't know how much good monitoring that would do. Nobody was likely to give the attack order in clear language. It would be encrypted, so the Americans wouldn't realize what it was till things hit the fan.

Even so, the traffic was often fun to listen to. Lizards—and the occasional Rabotevs and Hallessi—bickered among themselves hardly less than humans did. Their insults revolved around rotten eggs and cloacas rather than genitals, but they used them with panache.

All at once, everything stopped. For about fifteen seconds, the radio waves might have been wiped clean. "What the hell?" Johnson said, in mingled surprise and alarm. He and Mickey Flynn had been talking about Armageddon. Had they just listened to the overture for it?

But then the Lizards returned to the air. Everybody was saying the same things: "What is that?" "Do you see that?" "Where did that come from?" "How did that get there?" "What could it be?"

Flynn pointed to the radar. It showed a blip that Johnson would have sworn hadn't been there before, about two million miles out from Home and closing rapidly. "What have we got here?" Johnson said, unconsciously echoing the Lizards all around the *Admiral Peary*. "Looks like it popped out of thin air."

"Thinner vacuum," Flynn said, and Johnson nodded—the other pilot was right.

The Lizards started sending messages toward the blip: "Strange ship, identify yourself." "Strange ship, please begin communication." And another one, surely transmitted by a worried member of the Race: "Strange ship, do you understand? Do you speak our language?"

Speed-of-light lag for a message to get to the strange ship—where the devil *had* it come from? out of nowhere?—and an answer to come back was about twenty-one and a half seconds. That, of course, assumed the answerer started talking the instant he—she? it?—heard the Lizards, which was bound to be optimistic.

"Do you think we ought to send something, too?" Johnson asked. Mickey Flynn was senior to him; it was Flynn's baby, not his. The other pilot shook his head. Johnson waved to show he accepted the decision. He found a different question: "Do you think it's a good thing we're at top alert?" Just as solemnly, Flynn nodded.

Close to a minute went by before the strange ship responded. When it did, the answer was in the Lizards' language: "We greet you, males and females of the Race." The individual at the microphone had a mushy accent. Even as Johnson realized it was a human accent, the speaker went on, "This is the starship *Commodore Perry*, from the United States of America. We greet you, citizens of the Empire. And we also greet, or hope we greet, our own citizens aboard the *Admiral Peary.*"

Johnson and Flynn both stabbed for the TRANSMIT button at the same time. Johnson's finger came down on it first. That was his only moment of triumph. Flynn, as senior, did the talking: "This is the *Admiral Peary,* Colonel Flynn speaking. Very good to have company. We've been out here by our- selves for a long time."

Again, there was a necessary wait for radio waves to travel from ship to ship. During it, Johnson wondered, *What's in a name?* The *Admiral Peary* recalled an explorer who'd pitted himself against nature and won. The *Commodore Perry* was named for the man who'd gone to Japan with warships and opened the country to the outside world no matter what the Japanese thought about it. The Lizards might not notice the difference, especially since *Peary* and *Perry* were pronounced alike even if spelled differently. But Johnson did. What did it mean?

This time, the person at the radio—a woman—replied in English: "Hello, Colonel Flynn. Good to hear from you. I'm Major Nichols—Nicole to my friends. We were hoping we'd find you folks here, but we weren't sure, because of course your signals from Home hadn't got back to Earth when we set out."

"I hope you've been picking up some of them as you fol- lowed our trail from Earth to Home," Flynn said. "And if you don't mind my asking, when *did* you set out?"

That was a good question. Here on the *Admiral Peary,* Johnson didn't feel like too much of an antique, even if he had been in cold sleep longer than most. But *these* whipper- snappers might not even have been born when Dr. Blanchard put him on ice. How much of an antique would he seem to them? *Do I really want to know?*

He had time to wonder about that again. Then Major Nichols' voice came back: "About five and a half weeks ago, Colonel."

Mickey Flynn drummed his fingers on his thigh in annoy- ance, one of the few times Johnson had ever seen him show it. "Five and a half weeks' subjective time, sure. But how long were you in cold sleep?" Flynn asked.

Johnson nodded: another good question. If the *Commodore Perry* was still slower than Lizard starships, that said one thing. If she matched their technology, that said something else—something important, too. And if she was faster, even a little bit . . .

The wait for radio waves to go back and forth felt maddening. After what seemed like a very long time, Major Nichols answered, "No, Colonel. No cold sleep—none. Total travel time, five and a half weeks. There've been some changes made."

Johnson and Flynn stared at each other. They both mouthed the same thing: *Jesus Christ!* The Lizards were bound to have somebody who understood English monitoring the transmission. The second that translator figured out what Major Nichols had just said, the Race was going to start having kittens, or possibly hatchling befflem. Johnson pointed to the microphone and raised an eyebrow. Flynn gave back a gracious nod, as if to say, *Be my guest.*

"This is Colonel Johnson, junior pilot on the *Admiral Peary,*" Johnson said, feeling much more senior than junior. "I hope you brought along some proof of that. It would be really useful. Things are . . . a little tense between us and the Race right now." He almost added an emphatic cough, but held back when he realized he didn't know how people of Major Nichols' generation would take that. After sending the message, he turned to Mickey Flynn. "Now we twiddle our thumbs while things go back and forth."

Flynn suited action to word. He said, "Why don't they have faster-than-light radio?" His thumbs went round and round, round and round.

"They do, in effect," Johnson said. "They've got the ships—if those are what they say they are. Einstein must be spinning in his grave."

"Colonel Johnson?" The voice of the woman from the *Commodore Perry* filled the control room again. "Yes, we have proof—all sorts of things that we know and the Race will hear about as its signals come in from Earth over the next few days and weeks. And we have a couple of witnesses from the Race aboard: a shuttlecraft pilot named Nesseref and Shiplord Straha."

"Oh, my," Johnson said. Even imperturbable Mickey Flynn looked a trifle wall-eyed. Straha had lived in exile in the USA for years. He'd been the third-highest officer in the conquest fleet, and then the highest-ranking defector after his effort to oust Atvar for not prosecuting the war against humanity vigorously enough failed. And he'd got back into the Lizards' good graces by delivering the data from Sam Yeager that showed the United States had launched the attack on the colonization fleet.

"I'd like to be a fly on the wall when Straha meets Atvar again," Flynn said.

"*Admiral Peary,* do you read me?" Major Nichols asked. "Are you there?"

"Where else would we be?" Flynn asked reasonably. "Ah, forgive me for asking, Major, but is the *Commodore Perry* armed?"

"That is affirmative," Nicole Nichols said. "We are armed." *She* used an emphatic cough, which answered that. "We did not know for certain that you had arrived when we departed, and we did not know what kind of reception we would get when we entered this solar system. Can you please summarize the present political situation?"

"I do believe I would describe it as a mess," Flynn said, a word that summed things up as well as any other for Glen Johnson. Flynn went on, "You'll need more details than that. I can put you through to Lieutenant General Healey, our commandant, and he can patch you through to Sam Yeager, our ambassador."

That produced a pause a good deal longer than required by speed-of-light. "Sam Yeager is your ambassador? Where is the Doctor?" Major Nichols asked. She used interrogative coughs, too.

"They couldn't revive him from cold sleep," Flynn said.

"I . . . see. How . . . unfortunate," Major Nichols said. "Well, yes, please arrange the transfer, Colonel, if you'd be so kind. Whoever the man on the spot has been, we'll have to deal through him."

Flynn fiddled with the communications controls. Lieutenant General Healey said, "It's about time I get to speak for myself, Colonel." Whatever he said after that, he said to

Major Nichols. Johnson and Flynn shared a look. If the commandant hadn't liked what the pilots were saying, he could have interrupted them whenever he pleased. But what really pleased him was complaining.

"Five and a half weeks from Earth to Home. Five and a half *weeks.* We can go back," Johnson said dizzily.

"Maybe we can go back," Flynn said. "If it's not weightless aboard the *Commodore Perry,* I wouldn't want to try it."

Johnson said something of a barnyard nature. That hadn't occurred to him. "I wonder how they did it," he said, and then, "I wonder whether I'd get it if they told me." Would his own great-grandfather have understood radio and airplanes? He doubted it.

Understood or not, though, the *Commodore Perry* was there. The Lizards were still trying to call it, a rising note of panic in their voices. One of them must have figured out what Major Nichols had said. And how would they like *that*?

☆ 16 ☆

Atvar awaited the shuttlecraft descending from orbit around Home with a sinking feeling in his liver. He made the negative gesture. No, that wasn't true. As a matter of fact, his liver felt as if it had already sunk all the way down to his toeclaws. Even in his wildest nightmares, he had never imagined a day like *this* might come.

And Straha had. Of all the males of the Race the Americans might have picked to rub Atvar's snout in his own failings, Straha was the prize example. Did they know that? Atvar laughed bitterly. Of course they did! They had to.

Faster than light! The Big Uglies could travel faster than light! The Race had decided that was impossible even before Home was unified, and hadn't worried much about it since. Some Tosevite physicist had come to the same conclusion, and the Big Uglies had believed him . . . while Atvar was on Tosev 3, anyhow. Unlike the Race, the Tosevites had kept worrying at the idea, though. The Race had got a scent of some of their earliest experiments, but. . . .

Yes. But, Atvar thought bitterly. The difference between what the Race had and what the Big Uglies had was the difference between a scent and the beast it came from. And the Big Uglies' beast was a starship.

Now what? the fleetlord wondered. Blasting the *Commodore Perry* would have been tempting—if another American starship might not be only days behind, might escape, and might bring word of war back to the United States long before the Race's colony on Tosev 3 could hope to hear about it. That was a recipe for disaster.

Preventive war seemed to have gone up in smoke. Too late, too late, too late. Again, how could you hope to attack some-

486

one who knew the bite was coming long before your teeth sank in—and who could bite you whenever he pleased? Home, at least, could defend itself. What about Rabotev 2 and Halless 1? If the Big Uglies wanted to, they could smash the Empire's other worlds before Home warned them they might be in danger.

Too late, too late, too late. The words tolled again, like a mournful gong inside Atvar's head.

After a moment, he realized not all that noise was internal. Some came through his hearing diaphragms. The terminal at the shuttlecraft port was efficiently soundproofed. All the same, the braking rockets' roar penetrated the insulating material and filled the building.

The windows facing the fire-scarred landing field were tinted. Even so, nictitating membranes flicked across Atvar's eyes to protect them from the glare. The shuttlecraft settled smoothly onto the concrete. Crashes were vanishingly rare; computer control made sure of that. Atvar wouldn't have minded seeing one of those rare, rare accidents now. No, he wouldn't have minded a bit. Watching Straha cook . . .

Didn't happen. The shuttlecraft's braking rockets cut off. Silence returned to the terminal. Atvar didn't quite let out a disappointed hiss. He hadn't really hoped the shuttlecraft would crash—or, if he had, he hadn't really expected it to.

Down came the landing ladder. The female who descended first wore the body paint of a shuttlecraft pilot. That would not be the pilot of this craft, but Nesseref, the traveler from Tosev 3. Behind her came a male of about Atvar's years. Straha had at least not had the effrontery to wear a shiplord's body paint, but rather the much plainer colors of an author. Last off the shuttlecraft was the Halless who'd brought it down from the *Commodore Perry*. Atvar forgot about the Halless right away; his attention was all on the newly arrived members of the Race.

Guards surrounded them and escorted them into the terminal. Straha said something to one of them. Her mouth fell open in a laugh. Straha had always been charming. That made Atvar like him no better.

Nesseref bent into the posture of respect as soon as she saw Atvar. "I greet you, Exalted Fleetlord," she said.

"And I greet you," he replied as she rose.

"Hello, Atvar," Straha said. "Well, now we know—it *could not* have turned out worse if I had been in charge." He added a sarcastic emphatic cough.

Atvar's fingerclaws started to shape the threat gesture one male used against another in the mating season. He forced them to relax. It wasn't easy. Neither was keeping his tone light as he answered, "Oh, I am not so sure of that. You might have lost the war against the Big Uglies instead of managing a draw. Then we could have had this to worry about even sooner."

Straha glared at him. "Do not project your incompetence onto me."

"I do not need to," Atvar said. "You have plenty of your own."

"Excuse me, superior sirs," Nesseref said, "but quarreling among yourselves will not help solve the problem the Race faces."

"Neither will *not* quarreling among ourselves," Straha replied, "and quarreling is much more fun."

"No, the shuttlecraft pilot speaks truth," Atvar said. "I thank you, Shuttlecraft Pilot. I need to know first of all how you are certain of the Big Uglies' claims about the speed of their starship."

"We were conscious throughout the flight," Nesseref said.

"Could you not have been drugged while asleep, put into cold sleep, and then revived the same way?" Atvar knew he was desperately searching for any escape from the Race's predicament.

Nesseref made the negative gesture. "I do not believe so, Exalted Fleetlord."

"Forget it, Atvar," Straha said. "For one thing, the Big Uglies already have word of things that will just be reaching Home now. Even as we speak, researchers here will be corroborating what they say. For another, when they go back to Tosev 3, they are willing to take more members of the Race along and then return them to Home. They are not willing to let them communicate with the colonists in any way, for fear you might do something foolish like order an attack, but if the males and females get there and come back here in something less than a large number of years, that should convince even the stubbornest—perhaps even you."

Atvar had not thought his liver could sink any lower. He discovered he was mistaken. Straha's sarcasm did not bother him. He and Straha had despised each other for many years. Each occasionally had to respect the other's competence, but that did not and would not make them friends. But the message about the American Tosevites' confidence that Straha delivered was daunting. They not only had this technique, they were sure it worked well.

"How do they do it?" Atvar asked. "*How* do they do it?"

"Neither one of us is a physicist," Straha said. Nesseref made the affirmative gesture. Straha went on, "They talk about doing things with space-time strings, about maneuvering or maybe manipulating them so that points normally distant come into contact with each other. What this means or, to tell you the truth, whether this means anything is not for me to say."

"Here I agree with the shiplord," Nesseref said. "They are very glib, as Big Uglies often are. But whether they told us these things to inform us or to mislead us, I am in no position to judge."

"I see." Atvar thought about telling them that the Race's physicists had begun work that might eventually let them catch up with the Big Uglies—assuming the Big Uglies hadn't moved on still further by then, which was not necessarily a good bet. He started to, yes, but his tongue did not flutter. Nesseref and Straha might blab to the Tosevites. They might be monitored by the Tosevites. Who could guess how far the Tosevites' electronics had come these days? Better to keep quiet.

"How is this world these days?" Straha asked. He then answered his own question, which was very much in character: "Not much different, or I miss my guess."

"In most ways, no. That is as it should be, in my opinion," Atvar said. "But you will see some things you would not have before you left: young males and females wearing false hair, for instance, and some of them even wearing wrappings."

"Really? Is that a truth?" Straha laughed. "So just as the Big Uglies on Tosev 3 have imitated us, we have also begun to imitate them? I had not thought we possessed even so much imagination as a species."

"The young are always unfathomable." Atvar did not mean it as a compliment.

"They think the same of us. Do you not remember when you could hardly wait for the old fools ahead of you to hop on the funeral pyre so *you* could hatch the egg of the world? It was all out there waiting for you, and you wanted to grab with all ten fingerclaws. Is that a truth, or is it not?"

"That is . . . some of a truth," Atvar answered. "I do not believe I was ever quite so vain as you show yourself to be, but I have long since suspected as much."

Straha irked him by laughing instead of getting angry. "You are still as stuffy as you always were, I see. Well, much good it has done you."

"*This* did not happen while I was in charge on Tosev 3. No one can blame me for *this*. The ministers here on Home decided Reffet would do better on Tosev 3 than I could," Atvar said. "That only shows how much they knew."

"Well, yes." Straha made the affirmative gesture. "Next to Reffet, you are a genius. This is not necessarily praise, you understand. Next to Reffet, a beffel smashed on the highway is also a genius." That startled a laugh out of Atvar, whose opinion of the fleetlord of the colonization fleet was not high, either. Straha went on, "You should have seen him when he learned of the *Commodore Perry*. He acted as if he wanted nothing more than to crawl back into his eggshell. That would be the best thing for him, if anyone wants to know what I think."

Nesseref said, "If anyone wants to know what *I* think, the best thing for the Race would be to stop all this vituperation and backbiting. We will have enough trouble catching up with the Big Uglies without that."

"No doubt you are a wise female," Straha said, but then he spoiled it by adding, "But you take a great deal of the enjoyment out of life."

"We have to catch up with the Big Uglies, and quickly." Atvar used an emphatic cough. "If we do not—"

"We are at their mercy," Straha broke in with a certain oppressive relish. "Do you suppose they might be interested in revenge for what the conquest fleet did to them?"

"Superior sir, you are not making this situation any better," Nesseref scolded.

"Truth. I cannot make it better, not now. No one can do that except possibly our physicists, and they have not done anything along these lines in the past hundred thousand years." Straha seemed to delight in pointing out unpleasant truths. "All I can do is bear witness to what the Big Uglies have done, the same way as you are. At that, I think I am more than good enough."

"I will bring you both to a hotel near the one where the American Big Uglies are staying," Atvar said.

"Why not to that hotel itself?" Straha asked. "It will be good to see Sam Yeager again. A male of sense and a male of integrity—the combination is too rare."

"I will not take you to that hotel itself because the American Tosevites can electronically monitor too much of what goes on inside," Atvar answered unhappily.

"Well, I cannot say that I am surprised," Straha said. "Even when their first starship set out, they were even or ahead of us in most electronics. That should have been a warning. They are further ahead of us now."

"I thank you for your encouragement." Atvar still had sarcasm as a weapon against Straha. But what weapons did he have now against the Big Uglies? None that he could see.

Ttomalss met Pesskrag at an eatery not far from the hotel where the wild Big Uglies dwelt. He hadn't been accosted going out to make the telephone call to invite her here, as he had the last time he'd tried speaking to her from a public phone. So far as he knew, the American Tosevites had no idea this place existed, which meant they couldn't monitor it.

"I greet you," Ttomalss said when Pesskrag sat down across from him in the booth.

"And I greet you," Pesskrag answered. "This is such an *exciting* time in which to have come out of the egg!" She used an emphatic cough. "And I owe you an apology, Senior Researcher. I did not believe what you told me about the Big

Uglies' relentless drive. I was mistaken. They must be all you claimed, and more."

A server came up and gave them both printouts of choices, adding, "We also have a special on zisuili ribs in a sauce of peffeg and other southern spices. You will enjoy it if you care for something that makes your tongue sit up and take notice."

"That will do very well," Ttomalss said. Pesskrag made the affirmative gesture. Ttomalss just wanted to get the server out from under his scales. Sometimes such individuals made too much of themselves. This male, mercifully, gathered up the printouts and went away.

Pesskrag kept on gushing about the Tosevites: "They went from experiment to theory to engineering in the flick of a nictitating membrane. We would never have been so impetuous—never, I tell you."

"We are going to have to be," Ttomalss said. "The military advantage this gives them is truly appalling. Until our signals reach Tosev 3, we are at their mercy. They have years to organize defenses against us and prepare their own surprise attack. Rabotev 2 and Halless 1 would never know what hit them. Even Home is vulnerable, though less so than it was before the *Admiral Peary* arrived."

"These are truths, Senior Researcher. I cannot deny it," Pesskrag said. "But this news holds other truths, too. These ships open much of this arm of the galaxy to colonization."

"At the moment, they open it to *Tosevite* colonization," Ttomalss said. "How long will we need to get such ships of our own?"

The physicist's eye turrets swung up toward the ceiling as she calculated. Her tongue flicked in and out. After a bit, she said, "Now that we know it can be done, I would estimate somewhere between fifty and a hundred years."

A pained hiss escaped Ttomalss. That wasn't far from what he'd thought himself. He'd hoped Pesskrag would tell him he was wrong. "Not sooner?" he said. "This is a very long time for the Big Uglies to have the capability while we do not."

"If we have to do the research and the engineering, that is my best guess," Pesskrag said. "I know the Big Uglies did it faster, but we are not Big Uglies."

"Truth—a truth that delights me most of the time. Here,

though, it could spell the end of us." Ttomalss paused. "Wait. You say *if* we do these things, it will take about this long. What else can we do?"

Before Pesskrag could answer, the server brought their meals. He had not been lying; the sauce that coated Ttomalss' zisuili ribs stung his tongue. He drank water to help quench the fire, then ate some more. The midday meal was not a gourmet's delight, but it was good enough of its kind. That sufficed; his mind wasn't fully on it anyhow.

After stripping the meat from a large rib with teeth and tongue, Pesskrag said, "We could save a lot of time by buying a ship from the Big Uglies, or at least acquiring some of the engineering know-how from them. Copying is faster than creating."

Ttomalss stared at her. That was also a truth, and a profound one. The Tosevites had caught up with the Race by imitating—stealing—technology from the conquest fleet. Of course, then the Big Uglies had proceeded to jump past their former mentors. Could the Race return the favor, or would the Empire live forever in the Tosevites' rapidly spreading shadow?

"There is one obvious problem," Ttomalss said. Pesskrag started eating another rib, but gestured for him to go on. He did: "It is not in the Big Uglies' interest to sell us this technology. The longer they have it and we do not, the greater their advantage."

"I cannot disagree with you," Pesskrag said. "But some individual Tosevites are bound to be corrupt. We can afford enormous rewards for information. And if we cannot openly buy these secrets, perhaps we can steal them."

"Perhaps we can," Ttomalss said. "You may well be right. We have to try."

"I still marvel that the Big Uglies made these experiments in the first place," Pesskrag said. "We had a hundred thousand years in which to try them, and we never did. We were convinced we knew everything worth knowing, and content with what we had."

"Big Uglies are never content. Never," Ttomalss said. "Discontent is their salient characteristic."

"This has proved to be to their advantage," Pesskrag observed.

"I do not deny it. I could not, could I?" Ttomalss replied. "Do you truly understand how they have done what they have done?"

"If I truly understood it, I would be able to duplicate it myself," the physicist said. "I cannot do that, Senior Researcher. At present, anyone who tells you he or she fully understands how the Big Uglies did this is either an optimist or a liar. I think my colleagues and I do begin to grasp the theory behind what they have done. Begin to, I stress." She used an emphatic cough. "I remain convinced that this is a useful first step."

"No doubt," Ttomalss said.

Pesskrag finished the second rib and began on a third. Ttomalss wished his appetite were as good. A Tosevite proverb floated through his mind: *the condemned male ate a hearty meal.* He wasn't condemned himself, but all the Race might be.

He started to say something, then had to lean back in a hurry as Pesskrag used the new rib like a lecturer's pointer and almost got sauce on his snout. "Oh, excuse me," the female said, "but I just thought of something else. Before long, I fear charlatans and maniacs will start crawling out from under every flat stone. They will all be shouting that they know how to travel faster than light. They will show us how if we transfer some large sum to their credit balance, or if we name them prime minister, or if the Emperor balances an egg on the end of his snout."

"An egg?" Ttomalss said, confused.

"These males and females will be addled. Just about all of them will either be addled or frauds," Pesskrag explained. "But we will have to investigate at least some of their claims, for fear of missing something profoundly important."

"I see." Ttomalss made the affirmative gesture. "I think I see, anyhow. There will also be some who travel on the opposite side of the road. Did you see Professor Kralk's memorandum, in which she states that the Big Uglies must be frauds, because faster-than-light travel is an obvious impossibility?"

"Oh, yes, I saw it. It would be pathetic if it were not so sad,"

Pesskrag said. "Kralk asserts this even though the signals from Tosev 3 are confirming in detail what the Big Uglies aboard the *Commodore Perry* said they would say." Pesskrag sighed. "It is too bad. Kralk was a sound female when she was younger. To be unwilling to change theory without justification is the mark of a scientist. To be unwilling to change theory even when there is abundant justification is the mark of someone whose thought processes have ossified."

They went their separate ways then, Pesskrag back to the laboratory to go on chasing the Big Uglies and Ttomalss back to the hotel to report to Atvar on what he had learned from the physicist. A young male wearing a wig of a greenish yellow like no Tosevite's real hair tried to sell him ginger. He snarled his rejection so fiercely, he frightened the petty criminal.

Can we change? he wondered. *Or have all our processes become ossified? We are going to find out. That is certain.*

He didn't talk to Atvar inside the hotel. Again, they feared the wild Big Uglies might be able to listen to what they said. They went over to the park where Sam Yeager liked to visit in the early morning or the late afternoon. They sat in the sunshine, not in the shade, also for fear the American ambassador might have planted little electronic hearing diaphragms wherever he went.

That was probably close to a delusion of persecution. Considering what had just happened to the Race, though, was any worry about the Big Uglies' abilities really delusional? Ttomalss feared it wasn't.

He told Atvar what Pesskrag had told him. The fleetlord hissed in dismay. "We cannot afford to wait so long. The Tosevites will not wait for us."

"The other alternative, as Pesskrag suggested, involves bribery and espionage," Ttomalss said. "It may well prove quicker, as she said. But it is far less certain."

"Nothing is certain any more," Atvar said sadly. "Nothing."

Ttomalss understood how he felt. The Empire was built on certainty and stability. It had been, for as long as it existed. Now all of that was likely to fly away like a swarm of startled evening sevod. "We should never have sent the conquest fleet to Tosev 3," the psychologist said.

"This same thought has occurred to me," Atvar answered.

"But who knows whether things would have turned out better or worse? If we had waited longer, the Big Uglies might have come upon us and caught us unawares. That would have been even worse than this. I will tell you what we should have done."

"What is that?" Ttomalss asked. "As far as I can see, all of our choices were bad."

"What we should have done, when our probe showed Tosev 3 to be inhabited, was send the conquest fleet at once. The Big Uglies really were primitives and savages then. We could have easily subdued them, and we would not have had to worry about any of this."

"Unless they rebelled after becoming part of the Empire and acquiring our technology," said Ttomalss, who no longer had any faith in the Race's ability to deal with the Tosevites.

Atvar only shrugged. "Yes, I have already heard this possibility mentioned. But I still believe doing that would have given us our best chance. Instead, we delayed—and the results of that are as we now see."

"So they are," Ttomalss replied. "Until we develop this technology for ourselves, we are at their mercy."

"Exactly." The fleetlord made the affirmative gesture. "I wonder if our best course might not be to fight the war anyway."

"But they would intercept our order. They would know about it years before our colony on Tosev 3 learned of it. Would that not be a disaster?"

Atvar sighed. "Probably. But what do we have now? A disaster of a different sort. We might have to sacrifice the colony."

"We would sacrifice the Rabotevs and the Hallessi, too. And who knows what the Big Uglies could do to Home itself?" Ttomalss said.

The fleetlord sighed again. "I suppose you are right. A war would have a certain finality to it, though. This way, we shall have to live with a difficult, dangerous, ambiguous future, with no guarantee that war, worse war, does not lie ahead."

"Anyone who has been to Tosev 3 knows that life is different, dangerous, and ambiguous more often than not," Ttomalss said, and Atvar made the affirmative gesture again.

* * *

Major Nicole Nichols was about the cutest little thing Sam Yeager had ever seen. She was just past thirty, which struck him as young for a major, but the *Commodore Perry* was bound to be full of hotshots. She was a light-skinned black woman with a bright smile, flashing eyes, and a shape he would have expected to see on a professional dancer, not a U.S. Air and Space Force officer.

She'd come down to Sitneff in the *Commodore Perry*'s own shuttlecraft. The Lizards were too rattled to refuse permission for that. They'd contented themselves with surrounding the shuttlecraft port with police and guards. If that shuttle was packed with ginger, smugglers would have a devil of a time getting to it unless some of the guards proved venal, which wasn't impossible.

Major Nichols was also all business. She heard Yeager's summary of what had gone on since the *Admiral Peary* reached Home, then nodded briskly. "We tried to get our ship built in time to get here before you, but it didn't quite happen," she said, and shrugged as if to say it couldn't be helped.

"That would have been awful!" Sam exclaimed. "We'd have revived and found out we were nothing but an afterthought."

"Yes, but *we* would have been in reasonably close touch with Earth, which you weren't," the major answered. That plainly counted for more with her. She eyed him as if he were a museum exhibit. To her, he probably was. And he wasn't even the right museum exhibit, for she went on, "Meaning no offense, but you *do* understand we'd expected to be dealing with the Doctor?"

"Oh, sure." He nodded. "And I'm not offended. I expected the same thing. But when he didn't wake up"—Sam shrugged—"the Lizards knew I was along, and they asked for me to represent the United States. I've done the best job I know how to do."

"No one has said anything different," Major Nichols assured him. For a moment, he took that as a compliment. Then he realized it meant the people from the *Commodore Perry* had been checking up on him. He supposed they would have checked on the Doctor, too, but probably not quite in the same way.

He said, "You're going to replace me, aren't you?"

"That was the plan," Major Nichols answered. "Someone who knows how things are now back on Earth has an advantage over you. I'm sure you've kept up with our broadcasts as best you could, but that still leaves you more than ten years behind the times." She spoke oddly. Her rhythm was different from what Sam was used to, and she used far more words and constructions from the Race's language as if they were English. By the way she used them, they *were* English to her.

"I know. As you say, it can't be helped." Sam smiled. "I'm looking forward to finding out what the United States *is* like these days."

Something changed in the major's face. "That . . . may be a little more complicated than you'd think, sir."

Yeager raised an eyebrow. "Oh?" Major Nichols nodded. Sam said, "Well, maybe you'd better tell me about it, then." If she were a man, he would have said, *Kiss me, 'cause I think you're gonna screw me.* Being of the female persuasion, though, she might not have taken that the right way.

"This is more complicated than we thought it would be," she repeated. "You have to understand, our instructions about you assumed you would be acting as the Doctor's assistant and adviser, not that you would be ambassador yourself."

"Okay. I understand that. It's simple enough," Sam said. "So what were these instructions that were based on that assumption?"

"That you were to stay here and continue to act as assistant and adviser to the Doctor's successor," Major Nichols answered.

"I . . . see," Sam said slowly. "And if I didn't want to do that? I wasn't born yesterday, you know, even if you don't count cold sleep. I was thinking I would enjoy retirement. I'm still thinking that, as a matter of fact."

The major looked unhappy. "Sir, there's no polite, friendly way to tell you this. You are to be . . . discouraged from coming back to Earth."

"Am I?" Sam said tonelessly. "Well, I don't have to be an

Einstein to figure out why, do I?" His voice went harsh and flat.

"You probably don't," she agreed. "You're . . . not remembered kindly in certain circles in the U.S. government."

"People who tell the truth often aren't," Sam said. "That's what I did, Major. That's what my crime was, back before you were born. I told the truth."

"They've rebuilt Indianapolis," Major Nichols said. She went on, "I have cousins there. I've been to Earl Warren Park. The memorial to the people who died is very touching." President Warren himself had died, by his own hand, when word of his role in the attack came out.

Sam made the affirmative gesture. He spoke in the language of the Race: "Where is the monument to those our not-empire wantonly destroyed? Do they not deserve some commemoration?"

She went right on speaking English: "It's because you say this kind of thing that some people thought you might be more comfortable staying here than coming back to the United States."

" 'Some people.' " Sam echoed that with an odd, sour relish. "I know what kind of people, too—the kind who think anybody who doesn't believe all the same things they do isn't a real American. Well, I happen to think I am, whether they like it or not."

Major Nichols didn't answer that right away. She studied Yeager instead. He had no idea what was going on behind her eyes. Whatever she thought, she kept to herself. He wouldn't have wanted to play poker against her; she would have taken the shirt off his back. At last, she said, "You're not what my briefings made me think you were going to be."

"No horns," he said. "No tail. No fangs, that's for sure— I've only got four of my own choppers. Lost the rest more than a hundred years ago, if you add cold sleep into it."

"They can do something about that now. They have what they call dental implants," she told him. "They go into your jawbone, and they're just about as good as real teeth."

"To tell you the truth, I hardly remember what real teeth are like," Sam said. "I've gone without 'em since I was a kid." Human teeth amazed and horrified the Lizards. They couldn't imagine why evolution made people go through life with only two sets. Like small-l lizards on earth, they replaced theirs continuously throughout their lives. And then Sam smiled sourly at the major from the *Commodore Perry.* "Besides, what difference does it make? You just said you're not going to let me go back to Earth anyway, didn't you?"

She flushed. Her skin wasn't dark enough to hide it. In a small voice, she said, "Me and my big mouth."

"You and your big mouth," he agreed. "Look, tell me something I want to know for a change, will you? How are my grandchildren? Do I have great-grandchildren yet? Great-great? And how are Mickey and Donald getting along?"

"One of your grandsons—Richard—is at Stanford University, heading the Interspecies Studies Department there," Major Nichols said. "The other—Bruce—runs a company that arranges cultural exchanges with the Lizards. They're both well, or they were when we left. You have five great-grandchildren—three boys and two girls—all told, and two great-great-granddaughters. Bruce is divorced. Richard had a brief failed marriage, then remarried and has stayed that way for almost thirty years."

"Lord!" Sam said softly. Jonathan's boys had been kids when he went into cold sleep. They'd been in college when Jonathan and Karen went on ice. It sounded as if they'd done pretty well for themselves since. By the way their bodies felt, they'd be older than their parents. If that wasn't bizarre, Sam didn't know what would be. "And what about Mickey and Donald?"

"Mickey is working with your grandson, Bruce," the major said. "He recently published his autobiography. He called it *Between Two Worlds.* He wrote it in English. It did well in the United States, and even better in translation with the Lizards. The translation is probably on its way here now at speed-of-light. There's talk of movie versions from Hollywood and from the Race."

"Wow!" Sam said. "That's not half bad—better than I expected, to tell you the truth, since he had two strikes against him the minute he hatched. What about Donald? You didn't say anything about him. Is he all right? If it's bad news, for God's sake spit it out. Don't try to sugarcoat it."

"Donald . . ." Nicole Nichols hesitated again. Again, Sam had trouble reading her face. Was that amusement sparking somewhere deep in her eyes? He thought so, but he couldn't be sure. She said, "The past five years, Donald has hosted something called *You'd Better Believe It.* It's the highest-rated game show in the USA and Canada. I wouldn't want to say whether it's the best—my tastes don't really run in that direction—but it has to be the most spectacular. And Donald, without a doubt, is the most spectacular thing in it."

Sam stared. Then he started to laugh. Then he started to howl. Donald had always been the more outgoing little Lizard. Now he wasn't a *little* Lizard any more. And he was evidently more outgoing than Sam had ever imagined.

"I'll be a son of a gun," he said; he still felt funny about swearing in front of a woman, even if she was a major, too. "Should I want to shake his hand or horsewhip him?"

"That's not for me to say," Major Nichols answered. "We ought to have a disk with some of the shows on it aboard the ship. They knew you and your son and daughter-in-law would want to see it."

"Well, good," Sam said. "That's something, anyhow. Once I see the shows, I wouldn't mind going back and telling him what I think of them. My grandsons and Mickey probably have a lot to teach me, too."

Major Nichols' face froze back into a perfect, unreadable mask. She'd acted amazingly lifelike there for a little while, when she was talking about Sam's family by blood and adoption. No more. She said, "As I told you, sir, that isn't in our present plans. I'm sorry."

I'll bet, Sam thought. "Once upon a time, I read a story called 'The Man without a Country,' " he said. "Darn good story. Seems as if I'm in that boat now, except the fellow in the story didn't want his country but it looks like my country doesn't want me."

"I'm sorry," Nicole Nichols said again: a polite, meaningless phrase. "In fact, the United States is grateful for everything you and the rest of the crew of the *Admiral Peary* have done here on Home."

"Just not grateful enough to want me back." Sam didn't bother trying to hide his bitterness.

"Circumstances are not just what we thought they'd be when we got our orders," she said. "Maybe the commandant will see that as justification for changing them. I must tell you, though, I doubt it. And I certainly don't have the authority to do so. If you will excuse me, sir . . ." She left his room before he could say whether he excused her or not. He stared around the place. Live here, or somewhere much like here, for the rest of his life? Live here while other humans zipped back and forth between the stars? Had any man ever had a crueler prison?

Karen Yeager slid the *skelkwank* disk into the player. Disk and player had been manufactured more than ten light-years apart by two different species, but the one fit perfectly into the other. Humans had borrowed the Lizards' standards along with their technology. A lot of what they made was interchangeable with what they'd taken from the Race.

"This ought to be fun," Jonathan said.

"This ought to be terrible," Sam Yeager said. "A gameshow host? My God, why didn't Donald just go out and start robbing banks?"

"I'll tell you what I want to see," Karen said. "I want to see what the clothes and the hairstyles look like. We've been out of touch for a long time."

"We'll be a bunch of frumps when we do get home," Melanie Blanchard said. Then she shrugged. "We would have been even worse frumps if we'd gone back in cold sleep."

All the Americans from the *Admiral Peary* crowded into Karen and Jonathan's room to watch the disk of *You'd Better Believe It.* The ice cubes Karen was so proud of were chilling a lot of Lizard-style vodka. Frank Coffey said, "At least we got here, by God. We were awake and doing our jobs when the *Commodore Perry* came in. There are bound to be ships behind us full of people in cold sleep. What they'll think when they wake up . . ." He shook his head.

"Little bit of a surprise," Sam Yeager said. He seemed subdued. He was drinking more than Karen would have expected, too. *Or am I just imagining things?* she wondered. She didn't want to ask if anything was wrong, not there in front of everybody. Her father-in-law had almost as strong a sense of privacy as a cat.

Instead, Karen said, "Shall I fire it up?"

"Yeah, do it." Tom de la Rosa raised his glass in salute. "Let's see what we came all these light-years to escape." Everybody laughed.

"Play," Karen said in the Race's language. That was one difference between local machines and those back on Earth: these didn't understand English. They didn't always understand a human accent, either. This time, though, the disk started spinning.

Music swelled. It sounded raucous and tinny to Karen, but what she listened to would have sounded the same to her grandparents. The computer graphics for the opening credits were at least as smooth and at least as fancy as anything the Lizards used. Sam Yeager looked impressed. That hadn't happened when he went into cold sleep in 1977. By the time Karen did, seventeen years later, people had pretty much caught up.

"And now," the announcer said in the slightly greasy tones of announcers everywhere and everywhen, "here are the lovely Rita and Donald and . . . *You'd Better Believe It*!"

The audience applauded frantically. The lovely Rita strutted out onto the stage. She *was* lovely: a statuesque brunette with a profile to die for. Karen, though, didn't think her husband or any of the other American males in the audience was paying attention to Rita's profile. The sparkling gown she wore trailed behind her on the floor . . . but was cut Minoan-style on top.

"Holy Jesus!" Tom said. "How'd you like to put makeup *there*?"

"I'd like it fine," Frank Coffey said. The guys bayed goatish laughter. Karen wanted to kick Jonathan. He hadn't said a word, but he was paying *close* attention to the screen.

When the camera went to the studio audience for a moment, Karen saw about half the younger women were topless. Some of them wore Lizard-style body paint, some didn't. That had been coming in Karen's time, but it hadn't got there yet. Plainly, it had now.

Back to Rita. She flashed a million-watt smile. "Now, folks," she said, "heeeeere's . . . Donald!"

He bounded out to center stage. The audience went nuts. All the Americans in the room in Sitneff started howling with glee. Donald was wearing a tuxedo—a painted-on tuxedo, perfect right down to the red-carnation boutonniere. Even his hands had been painted to make them seem a Caucasian's—though not a whole lot of Caucasians had fingerclaws.

"Hello, people!" he said. Energy came off him in waves. "Welcome to another session of—"

"*You'd Better Believe It!*" the audience shouted. They applauded themselves.

"That's right." Donald couldn't grin—his mouth wasn't made for it. But he gave the impression that he was grinning. He was a performer right down to the tip of his tailstump. "Now we're going to find out how much tonight's contestants don't know—and how much they'll pay for it." It was a throwaway line. The studio audience broke up anyway. Karen felt herself smiling, too. She couldn't help it. Donald pulled a smile out of her the way a magician pulled a rabbit out of a hat.

She looked around the room. She wasn't the only one smiling. Donald had even managed to distract the men from the lovely Rita. If that didn't prove he had what it took, nothing ever would.

Out came the first contestant, a short, dumpy, gray-haired woman from Great Falls, Montana. Donald contrived to grin at her, too. "Hello, Mrs. Donahue," he said. "What's your excuse for being here with us tonight? Exhibitionism? Or just greed?"

Mrs. Donahue blushed. "A little of both, maybe," she said.

"*You'd better believe it!*" the audience roared. She had to know that was coming, but she flinched anyway.

"Well, here we go," Donald said. "Why don't you climb into the hot seat, and we'll give you a whirl."

The hot seat had a seat belt. Karen rapidly discovered why: Donald had meant that whirl literally. The seat could spin on all three axes. It could also give electric shocks and do a wide variety of other unpleasant things. Mrs. Donahue had to answer questions while the chair and some really horrible sound effects discombobulated her. Not surprisingly, she didn't cover herself with glory.

"Too bad," Donald said when her ordeal was over. "No all-expense-paid trip to the Moon for you, I'm afraid. But you do have the new refrigerator and five hundred dollars in cash, so this didn't turn out too bad after all."

"You'd better believe it!" Mrs. Donahue said gamely, and the audience gave her a big hand.

Later on, a young man did win a trip to the Moon, and just about passed out from excitement. Back on Earth, going to the Moon evidently still wasn't something people did every day. Here from the Tau Ceti system, it didn't seem quite such a big deal. Karen glanced over at Sam Yeager. He'd been to the Moon. He'd had a photo on his wall to prove it. Karen never had. If you lived in Southern California, going to Home and not the Moon was like going to Madagascar without ever visiting Long Beach.

At the end of the show, Donald's eye turrets followed the lovely Rita's . . . visible assets as if he were a human male with some special girl-watching equipment. Then one of them swiveled back toward the camera for a moment. "I know the real reason—reasons—you watch, you crazy people out there. You can't fool me. We'll see you tomorrow—and you'll see us, too. So long." The screen went dark.

"Pause," Karen said in the Race's language. For a wonder, the player listened to her twice running. She went back to English: "Do we really want to watch another episode right away?"

"If it's got Rita in it, I'll watch it," Tom said. Linda planted a good, solid elbow in his ribs. He yelped, overacting—but he didn't overact half as much as Donald did.

"Well," Sam Yeager said, "it's nice to know he's making an honest living."

"You call that honest?" Jonathan asked.

"He's paying his own bills," the older man answered. "If that's the most popular game show in the country, he's probably making money hand over fist. Of course, if that's the most popular game show in the country, it's probably a judgment on us all, but that's a different story. But it's not illegal, no matter what else you can say about it."

"I think we've got the idea of what he does," Frank Coffey said. "I wouldn't mind leering at Rita some more—just don't tell Kassquit about it—but it can wait. Rita's a knockout, and Donald's pretty damn funny, but the *show*. . . ." He shuddered and knocked back his drink. Then he walked out of the room. Karen wondered if he realized he was whistling the theme song from *You'd Better Believe It*.

The de la Rosas and Dr. Blanchard also left. Sam Yeager got up, too, but only to fix himself another drink. "What's up, Dad?" Jonathan asked—he'd noticed something was out of kilter, too, then. "You're not just down in the dumps because Donald's making a buffoon of himself on national TV. You were low before we got the disk."

"Now that you mention it—yes," his father said. He stared down at the glass in his hand, as if expecting to find the answer there. Karen had never seen him do that before. It alarmed her. After a moment, still looking down into the glass, Sam went on, "They don't want to let me go home."

"What? Why not?" As soon as the words were out of Karen's mouth, she knew how silly they were. She knew damn well why not. She just hadn't imagined it would still matter, not after all these years.

Jonathan had no trouble figuring it out, either. "That's outrageous, Dad," he said. "You were *right*, by God."

"You'd better believe it," his father said, and laughed a sour laugh. "But what's that got to do with the price of beer?"

"What . . . exactly did Major Nichols tell you?" Karen asked.

"First off, they didn't expect to find me the ambassador. They figured I'd be minding the Doctor's p's and q's for him," Sam Yeager said. "They were going to have me go on minding p's and q's for whatever young hotshot they've brought to take over here. Told me there were still hard feelings back home over what I did. I wonder how big a villain I am in the history books." He swigged the almost-vodka.

"You shouldn't be," Karen said. "The people who ordered the attack on the colonization fleet were the villains."

Her father-in-law shrugged. "I think so, too. But if the powers that be don't . . ." He finished his drink. "I wonder if the *Commodore Perry* brought any real, live air conditioners for the new ambassador and his people. We should have thought of that ourselves, but we were too dumb." His mouth twisted. "Of course, even if they do have 'em, they probably wouldn't give me one."

"Oh, for the love of God, Dad!" Jonathan said.

"Yes, for the love of God." Sam Yeager sounded like something straight out of Edgar Allan Poe. Karen wondered if he did it on purpose.

She said, "Talk to their captain. Maybe he'll change his mind."

"Maybe." Her father-in-law sounded dubious in the extreme. He also sounded furious—just how much so, she didn't really understand till he went on, "I'd rather stay here than beg, though. Why should I have to beg for what I . . . darn well deserve anyway?" He held out his glass to her. "Fix me another one, would you? After all, I've got so much to celebrate."

Atvar climbed out of the shuttlecraft at the Preffilo port. Males and females in the body paint of the imperial court met him in the terminal and whisked him away to the palace. He hadn't been summoned to the capital for an audience with the Emperor, but for a working meeting with him. The ceremonial was much less involved. The honor might have been greater. A meeting with the Emperor meant he really wanted your opinion. An audience could mean anything at all. Champions at the biennial games got audiences with the Emperor.

Since it was only a meeting—if *only* was the right word—Atvar didn't have to worry about the imperial laver and limner. His own body paint would do. The courtiers whisked him into the palace through a side entrance. No reporters waited to shout asinine questions at him. Word had got out that a second Tosevite starship had come to Home. Word on what kind of starship it was hadn't, not yet. He wondered just how the males and females in charge of such things would get that across. He wondered if they could do it without touching off a panic. He would have panicked if he'd got news like that.

In fact, he had panicked when he got news like that. The Race was at the Big Uglies' mercy, if they had any. If that wasn't worth panicking about, what would be?

The 37th Emperor Risson sat in a conference room not much different from the ones in the hotel back in Sitneff, though the furniture was of higher quality. Atvar folded himself into the special posture of respect reserved for the Emperor alone. "Rise," Risson told him, the overhead lights gleaming from his imperial gold body paint. "Now that you have done that, Fleetlord, let us forget about ceremony for the rest of this session."

"Just as you say, your Majesty, so it shall be done," Atvar replied. That had been a truth for Emperors for a hundred thousand years. How much longer would it stay a truth? The answer wasn't in the Race's hands.

By the way Risson's eye turrets waggled, the same thought had occurred to him. Oddly, that relieved Atvar. He would not have wanted the Emperor blind to the consequences of what had happened here. Risson said, "Well, we have not seen an egg like this one since the days when Home was unified and we did not fight the last war among ourselves after all."

"I wish I could say you were wrong, your Majesty." Instead of saying that, Atvar made the affirmative gesture. "I only hope this one hatches as successfully. It will not be easy."

"No." Risson clicked his fingerclaws on the tabletop, as any thoughtful and not very happy member of the Race might have done. "By everything we can tell, the Big Uglies are not lying about what this new ship of theirs can do."

"I wanted to think they were. I did not really believe it," Atvar said.

"My reaction exactly," Risson said. "Neither Straha nor the shuttlecraft pilot—Nesseref—appears to have been drugged and deluded."

"In my opinion, Straha has long been deluded, but he thinks the same of me," Atvar said.

"I know something of the feuds that plagued the conquest fleet. I do not care to know more, from either side. They do not matter now," the Emperor said. "The only thing that matters is verifying the Big Uglies' claims. Straha and Nesseref tend to do that. So does the information we are receiving at speed-of-light from Tosev 3. The American Tosevites already know what we are hearing for the first time."

"Your Majesty, however much I tried to keep from doing

so, I thought I had to believe them as soon as that ship arrived," Atvar said. "For one thing, it seemed to come out of nowhere. For another, it is the culmination of something toward which the Big Uglies have been reaching for some time. Our physicists are behind theirs, but they are at least beginning to reach in the same direction."

"We are behind the Big Uglies. We change more slowly than they do. This does not bode well for us," Risson said.

"The same thought has occurred to me," Atvar said. "I would be lying if I said it filled my liver with delight."

"Immediate war might still be our best course," Risson said. "I do not want it. I do not think our chances are good. But if they only grow worse, perhaps we should send that message, no matter how many years it takes to arrive."

Atvar made the negative gesture. "No, your Majesty," he said, and used an emphatic cough. "This same thought occurred to me, but it would be a disaster. Consider: the Big Uglies must see this is one of our options. If they put one of their ships in line between our solar system and the star Tosev, they can intercept our signal, return to Tosev 3, and be ready to attack or defend against whatever we send from here, whichever suits them better, years before the colonists have any idea they are supposed to help us go to war."

Risson did consider, for some little while. At last, with obvious reluctance, he made the affirmative gesture. "Well, Fleetlord, that is a truth. It is not a palatable truth, but a truth it is."

"I can see one way around it," Atvar said. "If we were to have a passenger on their starship, that male or female could deliver a message to Fleetlord Reffet and Fleetlord Kirel. That way, the delay would be overcome."

"You are clever, Fleetlord. Unfortunately, the Big Uglies have thought of the same thing," Risson said. "They will let us have passengers, but they will not let them communicate with members of the Race on Tosev 3 in any way, citing exactly the danger you named."

With an unhappy hiss, Atvar said, "That cursed Straha told me the same thing. I had forgotten—my apologies, your Majesty. We have been too naive for too long; deceit does not come naturally to us any more."

"Instead of what we call diplomats, maybe we should have sent a shipload of azwaca-hide dealers to Tosev 3," the Emperor said. "They always have an eye turret on the main chance, and might have done better at getting what we need out of the Big Uglies."

"You should tell that one to your diplomatic aides, your Majesty. It holds much truth," Atvar said. Until the conquest fleet faltered on Tosev 3, Emperors had not needed diplomatic aides since Home was unified. The very word *ambassador* was obsolete in the Empire, preserved only in historical fiction. On Tosev 3, it had hatched out of the eggshell of dormancy once more.

"I would not wish to make them unhappy," Risson said. "They try their best. We have all tried our best. Sometimes . . . Sometimes things do not fall out as we wish they would. I have no idea what is to be done about this, except to go on doing the best we can."

"If we do not do that, we will fail," Atvar said. "Of course, even if we do, we may well fail anyhow."

"This thought has also crossed my mind," Risson said. "It is one of the reasons I have not slept well since this new starship came here. Having the other one in orbit above me, knowing some missile was bound to be aimed at this palace, was bad enough. But this one, this one we cannot imitate, let alone surpass—this is very bad. And do you know what else?"

"No, your Majesty. What else?" Atvar asked.

The 37th Emperor Risson let out an indignant hiss. "You will not be surprised to learn we have Tosevite encyclopedias here on Home," he said. "What better way to learn about the Big Uglies than through their own words? Some of our scholars who read English have investigated the American Tosevites after whom these two starships were named." He hissed again, even more irately than before.

"And?" Atvar asked, as the Emperor surely meant him to do.

"And the first ship, the *Admiral Peary,* is named for the Big Ugly who first reached the North Pole on Tosev 3," Risson said. "That was surely a Big Ugly who went into the unknown, and so his is a good name to give an early starship. But the *Commodore Perry* . . ." He hissed one more time.

"This Commodore Perry traveled by sea from the United States to the islands of Nippon, where he forced the Nipponese into concluding trade agreements with him because of the strength of his warships. Is this a deliberate insult to us? Do the Americans reckon us similar barbarians to exploit as they please?"

"Today, your Majesty, the Nipponese are no more—and no less—barbarous than any other wild Big Uglies," Atvar replied. "And—" He broke off.

Not soon enough. "Yes?" Risson prodded.

Atvar wished he'd kept quiet. Now he had to go on with his thought, such as it was: "I was going to say, your Majesty, that I understand the analogy the Big Uglies may have been drawing. Commodore Perry could travel by sea to the Nipponese. They could not travel by sea on their own to the land he came from. We are in a like situation in regard to that second starship."

Risson stiffened. Atvar wondered if he would be sent away, never to see his sovereign again. Then, to his vast relief, the Emperor laughed. "Well, Fleetlord, you have made your point, I must say. That analogy has more teeth than I wish it did. Until we can match the Tosevites' prowess, maybe we are in truth no better than semibarbarians."

"For many millennia, we have believed ourselves to stand at the pinnacle of biological and social evolution," Atvar said. "And why not? Our society was successful and stable. We easily overcame the other intelligent species we met and remolded their cultures and their worlds in the image of ours. Who could oppose us? Who could show us there were other ways of doing things?" He laughed, too, bitterly. "Well, now we know the answer to that."

"Yes. Now we know." Risson's voice was heavy with worry. "But thinking we were superior to all around us helped make us that way in fact . . . for a long time. Now that we see we are not at the pinnacle, as you said, will we begin to view ourselves as permanently inferior to the Big Uglies? That could also become a self-fulfilling prophecy, you know."

The fleetlord didn't answer right away. He'd had more experience worrying about Big Uglies than perhaps any other member of the Race. What worried him more than anything else was that they needed to be worried about. When the conquest fleet first landed, the Tosevites had used numbers and appalling heroism and even more appalling deceit to make up for their technological deficit. More appalling still was how fast that deficit had shrunk. And now . . . *Yes. And now,* Atvar thought.

"As you said, your Majesty, we have to do the best we can," he said at last. "They learned from us. For a while now, we will have to learn from them. And then, with a little luck, we can learn from each other. One thing this breakthrough will do: it will mean both the Tosevites and we can colonize much more widely than ever before. Both sides are vulnerable now because we are so concentrated. If we have colonies on hundreds of worlds rather than a handful, the situation changes."

It was Risson's turn to stop and think. "The Empire would not be the same. It would not, it could not, hope to hold together."

"Probably not, your Majesty," Atvar said. "But the Race would survive. In the end, is that not the most important thing?" Risson thought again, then used the affirmative gesture.

Now that Kassquit knew what Ttomalss had not wanted to tell her about, she also understood why her mentor and the Emperor had been so unwilling. Nothing would ever be the same again for the Empire. The Race, convinced faster-than-light travel was impossible, hadn't seriously looked for it. For the Big Uglies, *impossible* seemed nothing but a word to get around. And now they'd got around it. If the Race couldn't, it would find itself in deadly peril.

She'd wondered if she would have mixed feelings about what the American Tosevites had done. They were, after all, her own kin, far more than any members of the Race could have been. She might have shared some of the pride at their achievement. She had before, over smaller things.

But she didn't, not because of this. This terrified her. She could see the danger it represented to the Empire. As long as the Big Uglies had this technology and the Race didn't, the planets of the Empire lived on Tosevite sufferance.

"Do not worry, not on account of this," Frank Coffey told

her after she poured out her alarm to him in her room one afternoon. "Remember, this is the United States that has this technology. My not-empire will not do anything to touch off a war against the Race."

"No?" Kassquit said. "I am sure the millions your not-empire killed in the attack on the colonization fleet would be ever so relieved to hear that."

Coffey did have the grace to wince. He spread his hands, palms up. The paler skin there and on the soles of his feet, so different from the rest of his body, never failed to fascinate Kassquit. He said, "That was a long time ago. We would not do such a thing now."

"Oh? Are you certain? If your not-emperor gave the order, would your soldiers disobey it?" Kassquit asked. "Or would they do as they were told?"

"Our not-emperor would not give such an order," Coffey said, though he didn't tell her how he knew such a thing. "And if he—or she—did give it, not all soldiers would obey. Remember, Sam Yeager is our ambassador to the Race. He was a soldier who disobeyed."

"Yes, and was sent into exile because of it," Kassquit said. "He would not be ambassador if the Doctor had lived, and he will not stay ambassador now that the new ship is here. Nor will the newcomers allow him to go back to Tosev 3. So much for the respect he won for disobeying orders."

"You do not understand," Frank Coffey insisted.

Kassquit made the negative gesture. "On the contrary. I fear I understand much too well." She pointed toward the door. "I think you had better go. Otherwise, this conversation is all too likely to put an end to our friendship." It was more than a friendship, of course, but that was the strongest word the language of the Race had.

"We might do better to talk things out," Coffey said.

"No." Kassquit used the negative gesture again. "What is there to say? You are loyal to your not-empire, as you should be. I am loyal to the Empire. This is also as it should be, I believe. We will not change each other's minds. We will only quarrel, and what is the good of that?"

Coffey inclined his head. Kassquit understood that. It was what Big Uglies sometimes did instead of sketching the posture of respect. "No doubt you have found a truth. I will see you another time," he said. He put on the few wrappings American Tosevites insisted on wearing in public even in the warmth of Home, then left her room.

Only after he was gone did Kassquit let tears start sliding down her face. She had known he was unlikely to make a permanent mating partner. She had expected him to return to Tosev 3 when the *Admiral Peary* left. But the *Commodore Perry* changed everything. Now he might leave within days, or tens of days. When she found happiness, did she always have to see it jerked out from under her feet?

She remembered the attack by the *Reich* when Jonathan Yeager was up in the starship orbiting Tosev 3 with her. Actually, for a little while that had worked out well on a personal level. It meant they'd stayed together longer than they would have otherwise, because he couldn't go back down to the United States while the war lasted. But it had only made parting harder when the time finally came.

All at once, Kassquit wished she hadn't thought about the *Reich* and the Deutsche. The Race would be doing everything it could to learn to travel faster than light. But so, without a doubt, would the Deutsche. They were formidably capable engineers. And, as far as she could tell, their not-empire was governed by an equally formidable set of maniacs. What would they do if they succeeded before the Race did?

Maybe Frank Coffey had a point. Were the *Commodore Perry* a Deutsch starship, wouldn't it have announced its presence by launching missiles at Home? The United States could have been better. But it also could have been much worse.

Kassquit yawned. She didn't feel like thinking about it now. She felt like curling up and taking a nap. She lay down on the sleeping mat and did. When she woke up, she still felt more weary than she thought she should have. That had been happening more and more often lately. She wondered if something was wrong with her. Had she caught some Tosevite disease from Nicole Nichols or one of the other wild Big Uglies who'd come down from the *Commodore Perry*?

She went down to the refectory for a snack. That turned out to be a mistake. She'd always enjoyed spiced, chopped azwaca and niihau beans, but not today. They didn't smell right. They didn't taste quite right, either. And they sat in her stomach like a large, heavy boulder.

Then, quite suddenly, they didn't want to sit there at all any more. She bolted from the refectory with the plate of meat and beans still half full. She got to the cloacal station just in time. She bent over one of the holes in the floor and noisily gave back what she'd eaten.

She couldn't remember ever doing *that* before. It was one of the most disgusting experiences of her life. It brought a certain relief, but the taste! And the way it came out through the inside of her nose as well as her mouth!

She rinsed and spat, rinsed and spat. That didn't help as much as she wished it would have. "I *am* diseased. I *must* be diseased," she said, and used an emphatic cough. No one who was healthy could possibly do something so revolting.

She thought about going back to the refectory and finishing the chopped azwaca and beans. Then, with a shudder, she made the negative gesture. She didn't believe she would ever want that dish again. It tasted much better going down than it did coming up.

Instead, she went to her room and telephoned Dr. Melanie Blanchard. "I would like you to examine me, please," she said when the physician's face appeared in the monitor.

"I would be happy to," Dr. Blanchard said. "May I ask what has made you change your mind?" Her interrogative cough was a small masterpiece of curiosity. No member of the Race could have done that better.

"I am unwell," Kassquit said simply.

"All right," Dr. Blanchard said. "Come to my room, and I will see if I can figure out why you are."

"It shall be done." Kassquit broke the connection with no more farewell than that.

"I greet you," the American female said when Kassquit pressed the door hisser. "Before I start poking you and doing the other things physicians do, please tell me your symptoms." Kassquit did, in harrowing detail. Dr. Blanchard nodded. "All right—nausea and fatigue. Anything else?"

Now Kassquit hesitated. "I am not sure it is relevant."

"Tell me and let me be the judge," Melanie Blanchard

urged. "The more data I have, the better my diagnosis is likely to be."

"Yes, that does seem reasonable." Kassquit made the affirmative gesture, though still hesitantly. "My other notable symptom is that the blood which flows from my reproductive organs has not done so when it normally would have."

"Really?" the doctor said, in tones of strong surprise. Kassquit used the affirmative gesture again. Dr. Blanchard reached out and squeezed one of her breasts; Kassquit yelped. Dr. Blanchard asked, "Are they unusually tender?"

"Why, yes," Kassquit said. "How did you guess?"

"This set of symptoms is familiar to me. Sooner or later, it becomes familiar to most Tosevite females, regardless of whether they happen to be physicians. Unless I am very much mistaken, you are gravid."

Kassquit stared. "But that is impossible. Frank Coffey uses a sheath whenever we mate. He has not failed to do so even once."

"I am glad to hear that. It speaks well for him—and for you," Melanie Blanchard said. "But what you have described are the textbook early symptoms of gravidity. Sheaths are good protection against such accidents, but they are not perfect."

What Kassquit felt was irrational fury. The sheath's failure struck her as typical slipshod Tosevite engineering. Wild Big Uglies just did things. They didn't bother to do them right. Or maybe, considering that the prime purpose of mating was reproduction, Frank Coffey *had* done it right.

"There are other possibilities," the physician said. "All of them involve serious illness, and all of them are much less likely than simple gravidity. Some time not quite a local year and a half from now, I believe you will lay an egg." She laughed and used the negative gesture. "That is the first phrase that occurred to me in the Race's language. It is *not* what will happen. You will have a hatchling."

"A hatchling." Kassquit still struggled to take that in. "I know nothing about caring for hatchlings."

"I am sure the American Tosevites here on Home with you, whoever they turn out to be, will be glad to help you," Melanie Blanchard said. "Or, if you would rather, there is a medical procedure to terminate your gravidity. It is not very difficult, especially when done early."

"Do you recommend medically that I do this?" Kassquit asked.

"No," Dr. Blanchard said. "You are on the old side to be gravid, but you do not seem to be dangerously so. I will have to monitor you more closely than I would if you were younger, that is all. The procedure may become medically necessary, but I do not anticipate that it will. But other factors besides the merely medical are involved in whether you wish to rear a hatchling. This may be more true for you than for most Tosevite females. You have . . . less practice at being a Big Ugly."

"That is a truth," Kassquit said. "Still, if anything will teach me, this is likely to be the experience that would."

"You do not need to decide at once," Dr. Blanchard said. "During the first third of your gravidity, the procedure remains fairly simple. After that, as the hatchling grows inside you, it does become harder and more dangerous for you."

Kassquit set the palm of her hand on her belly. "I will think about it," she said, "but I believe I wish to go forward with this."

☆ 17 ☆

After Kassquit bolted from the refectory and came back looking wan two or three times, none of the Americans on Home had much doubt about what was ailing her. Frank Coffey sighed. He was careful to speak English: "I wonder how you say Broken Rubber in the Race's language."

"Congratulations—I think," Jonathan Yeager told him.

"Thanks—I think," Coffey said. "That isn't what I had in mind."

"Hey, you've given us something to talk about besides the *Commodore Perry*," Tom de la Rosa said. "And they said it couldn't be done."

Major Coffey sent him a slightly walleyed stare. "Thanks— I think," he said again, in the same tones he'd used with Jonathan. Everybody laughed.

Jonathan said, "Is she ready to be a mother?"

"Nobody's ever ready to be a mother till it happens to her." Karen Yeager spoke with great conviction. "Some people may think they are, but they're wrong. It's baptism by total immersion."

"Some people are *less* ready to be mothers than others, though," Dr. Melanie Blanchard said. "No offense, Frank, but I can't think of anybody who strikes me as less ready than Kassquit."

Karen nodded at that. Jonathan didn't, but he'd been thinking the same thing. Frank Coffey said, "We didn't intend for it to happen." He held up a hand. "Yeah, I know—nobody ever intends anything like that, but it happens all the time anyway." He sighed. "She's got nine months—well, most of nine months—to get used to the idea. And there will be more humans here to give her a hand." Another sigh. "She'll need one, heaven knows. I just hope—" He broke off.

Silence fell among the humans. Smiles faded from their faces. Jonathan knew what he'd started to say—*I just hope we don't go to war*—that or something like it. If they did go to war, what was one pregnant woman? No more than one pregnant woman had ever been in all the sad and sordid history of mankind.

"The Lizards wouldn't be that stupid, not now," Tom said. Nobody answered. Maybe he was right. On the other hand, maybe he wasn't. The Lizards had just got the biggest shock in their whole history. *They* probably didn't know how they were going to react to it. How could any mere humans guess along with them?

On the other hand, how could humans keep from trying?

People filed out of the refectory in glum silence. Jonathan looked out of the hotel's big plate-glass windows. He imagined the sun-bright flare of an exploding warhead right outside—and then darkness and oblivion.

"Penny for 'em," Karen said.

He shook his head. "You don't want to know." She didn't push him. Maybe she'd had thoughts like that herself.

"Ah . . . excuse me." That was in the language of the Race. An untidy-looking Lizard whose body paint could have used a touch-up went on, "Are you the Big Ugly I had the honor of meeting a while ago? Forgive me, but your name has gone clean out of my head. I really am a fool about such things."

"I greet you, Inspector Garanpo. Yes, I am Jonathan Yeager," Jonathan said. All at once, a visit from a Lizard detective hot on the trail of ginger seemed the least of his worries. "Inspector, let me present my mate, Karen Yeager. Karen, this is Inspector Garanpo. I told you about him the last time he visited us."

"Oh, yes, of course," Karen said. "I am pleased to meet you, Inspector." If she wasn't *very* pleased, the Lizard cop wouldn't know it.

Garanpo bent into the posture of respect. "It is an honor to make your acquaintance, superior female. Yes, indeed—an honor. Now I have met three of you Tosevites, and you seem pretty well civilized, you truly do. Not at all the sort of creatures I thought you might be when I found out there was a connection between your kind and the ginger trade."

"There is also a connection between members of the Race and the ginger trade," Jonathan pointed out. "Does that turn all males and females of the Race into monsters and criminals?"

"Well, no, I would not say that it does. I certainly would not say that." Garanpo made the negative gesture. Jonathan watched him with an odd sort of fascination. He'd never before seen a Lizard who reminded him of an unmade bed.

"Why are you here, Inspector?" Karen asked. "Has there been more ginger smuggling?"

"More? Oh, no, superior female, not that we have been able to find," Garanpo said. "What we do have, though, is more information on the ginger smuggling that previously took place. We have detected traces of ginger aboard the *Horned Akiss,* where the little rocket from your starship paid a call."

"Is that supposed to prove something, Inspector?" Jonathan said. "For all you know, there are ginger tasters in the crew."

"Here is what I know," Garanpo said. "I know that a shipment of ginger came down to Home not long after you Big Uglies and the Race traded little rocketships. And I know that you were going to trade them back again, but then there was a delay. After that delay, you did send back the one you got from us. There was no ginger inside it, or none to speak of, but we did detect traces of the herb inside some of the structural tubing. What have you got to say about *that,* superior Tosevite?" He flicked out his tongue, for all the world like one of his small Earthly namesakes.

What have I got to say? That we're lucky their scooter only had traces of ginger in it, and not enough to choke a horse. Those people upstairs came close as could be into walking into a buzz saw.

None of that seemed like anything the Lizard detective needed to hear. Jonathan put the best face on things he could: "I am sorry, Inspector, but this proves exactly nothing. Can you tell how old those traces of ginger are? How long has the *Horned Akiss* orbited Home? How many of your starships has it met? How long has ginger smuggling been going on?"

He could even have been right with his guesses, too. He

didn't think he was, but he could have been. A lawyer would have called it creating a reasonable doubt. He wasn't sure the Race's law had ever heard of the idea.

"Well, there has been ginger smuggling ever since starships started coming back from Tosev 3," Garanpo admitted. "But there has never been any so closely connected with the source of supply, you might say, until now."

"You do not know there is any such thing now," Jonathan said sharply. "You assume it, but you do not know it."

"We would, except that the officers on your ship refuse to let us do a thorough search and analysis of their little rocket-ship," Garanpo said. "That suggests a guilty conscience to me."

It suggested the same thing to Jonathan. Again, he wasn't about to say so. What he did say was, "Why should they? You yourself have told me that this little rocketship was in the Race's hands for some length of time. If you wanted to dis-credit us, you had the chance to do it."

Inspector Garanpo's eye turrets swiveled every which way before finally coming to rest on him again. "How are we sup-posed to show guilt when all you have to do is deny it?" the Lizard asked grouchily.

"How are we supposed to show innocence when all you have to do is claim we are guilty?" Jonathan asked in return.

Garanpo's eye turrets started swiveling again. He turned and skittered off, muttering to himself. "You did that very well," Karen said.

"Thanks," Jonathan said. "I wish I didn't have to. And you know what else I wish? I wish like hell I had a cold bottle of beer right now." The Race, unfortunately, had never heard of beer.

Karen said, "You can get their vodka at the bar. Or if you want it cold, we've got a bottle and ice cubes in the room."

Jonathan shook his head. "Thanks, hon, but it's not the same."

"Did that strange, shabby Lizard have any idea what he was talking about?"

"Of course not," Jonathan said, a little louder than he needed to. He cupped a hand behind his ear to remind Karen that they were in the lobby and the Lizards could monitor whatever they said. Her mouth shaped a silent *okay* to show she got the point. Jonathan went on, "On second thought, maybe vodka over ice isn't such a bad idea after all. You want to fix me one?"

"Sure," Karen answered. "I may even make one for myself while I'm at it."

They rode up to their room. As soon as Jonathan got inside, he checked the bug suppressors. When he was convinced they were working the way they were supposed to, he said, "You'd better believe we were smuggling ginger. If you want all the gory details, you can ask Dad."

"Good way to start a war," Karen observed.

She made him the drink. Once it was in his hand, he was damn glad to have it. Karen did fix one for herself, too. After a long pull at his, Jonathan coughed once or twice. It didn't taste like much—vodka never did—but it was strong enough to put hair on his chest. He said, "There have been wars like that—the Opium Wars in China, for instance. Opium was just about the only thing England had that the Chinese wanted. And when the Chinese government tried to cut off the trade, England went to war to make sure it went on."

"We wouldn't do anything like that," Karen said. Jonathan would have been happier if he hadn't heard the question mark in her voice. It wasn't quite an interrogative cough, but it came close.

"I hope we wouldn't," he said. "But it's a weapon, no two ways about it. The *Admiral Peary* wouldn't have carried it if it weren't. And if we're going to be able to start going back and forth between Earth and home every few weeks instead of taking years and years to do it . . . Well, the chances for smuggling go up like a rocket."

"And if we smuggle lots of ginger, and the Empire decides it doesn't like that . . ." Karen's voice trailed away. She got outside of a lot of her drink. As Jonathan had, she coughed a couple of times. "We could see the Opium Wars all over again, couldn't we?"

"It's crossed my mind," Jonathan said. "As long as we can go faster than light and the Lizards can't, they'd be like Chinese junks going up against the Royal Navy. Whether they understand that or not is liable to be a different question, though. And we have no idea what things are like back on Earth these days, not really."

"We can find out, though." Karen looked out the window, but her eyes were light-years from Home. "Grandchildren. Great-grandchildren. Our own sons—older than we are." She shook her head.

"Not many people will have to cope with that," Jonathan said. "The bottom just dropped out of the market for cold-sleep stock."

"It did, didn't it?" Karen said. "So many things we'll have to get used to."

"If Dad doesn't go back, I don't know that I want to," Jonathan said. "If all the people here decided to stay behind if the *Commodore Perry* wouldn't let him aboard, that would show the moderns how much we thought of him. I don't know what else we can do to change their minds."

"That . . . might work," Karen said slowly. She'd plainly been seeing Los Angeles in her mind, and didn't seem very happy about being recalled to Home—especially about being told she might do better staying here. Jonathan gulped the rest of his drink. She was Sam Yeager's daughter-in-law. The other Americans were just his friends. Would they sacrifice return tickets for his sake? *Will I have to find out?* Jonathan wondered.

The *Commodore Perry* excited Glen Johnson and the other pilots who'd come to the *Admiral Peary* from the *Lewis and Clark* much less than most other people. "What the hell difference does it make if we can go back to Earth in five weeks, or even in five minutes?" Johnson said. "We can't go home any which way."

"Wouldn't you like to see all the newest TV shows?" Mickey Flynn asked.

"Frankly, Scarlett, I don't give a damn, except maybe about the lovely Rita," Johnson answered, with feeling. What male couldn't like the lovely Rita?

"Wouldn't you like to see some new faces?" Flynn persisted. He pointed to Walter Stone. "The old faces are wearing thin, not that anyone asked my opinion."

Stone glowered. "I love you, too, Mickey."

"I'd like to see some young, pretty girls in person," Johnson said. "The only thing is, I don't think any young, pretty girls would be glad to see me."

"Speak for yourself, Johnson," Flynn said.

"That was his johnson speaking," Stone said. Johnson and Flynn both looked at him in surprise. He didn't usually come out with such things. He went on, "I want to know what they'll do with the *Admiral Peary*. We figured this crate would go obsolete, but we never thought it would turn into a dodo."

The comparison struck Johnson as only too apt. Next to the *Commodore Perry*, the *Admiral Peary* might as well have been flightless. She'd crossed more than ten light-years—and, except for her weapons and the ginger she carried, she was ready for the scrap heap. "They ought to put her in a museum," Johnson said.

"So our grandchildren can see how primitive we were?" Flynn inquired.

"That's what museums are for," Johnson said. "Our grandchildren are going to think we're primitive anyhow. My grandfather was born in 1869. I sure thought he was primitive, and I didn't need a museum to give me reasons why. Listening to the old geezer go on about how us moderns were going to hell in a handbasket and taking the whole world with us did the job just fine."

"And here he was, right all the time," Walter Stone said. "Way it looks now, we've got four worlds going to hell in a handbasket, not just one. Biggest goddamn handbasket anybody ever made."

"You really think the Lizards are going to jump us?" Johnson asked. He didn't get on well with Stone, but he had to respect the senior pilot's military competence.

"What worries me is that it might be in their best interest to try," Stone answered. "If they wait for us to build a big fleet of faster-than-light ships, their goose is cooked. Or we can cook it whenever we decide to throw it in the oven."

"How many FTL ships will we have by the time their attack order reaches Earth?" Mickey Flynn asked.

"Not as many as if they wait twenty years and then decide they're going to try to take us," Stone said. "They usually like to dither and look at things from every possible angle and take years to figure out the best thing they could do. Well, here the best thing they can do is not take years figuring it out. I wonder if they've got the brains to see that."

"It would be out of character," Johnson said.

"They've been worrying about us for a long time," Stone returned. "They were nerving themselves for something before the *Commodore Perry* got here. Would Yeager have had us send a war warning back to Earth if he weren't worried?"

"The question is, will the *Commodore Perry* make things better or worse?" Flynn said. "Will it make them think they can't possibly beat us, and so they'd better be good little males and females? Or will they think the way you think they'll think, Walter, and strike while the iron is hot?"

Stone didn't answer right away. Glen Johnson didn't blame him. How could you help pausing to unscramble that before you tried to deal with it? When Stone did speak, he confined himself to one word: "Right."

"Yes, but which?" Flynn asked.

"One of them, that's for damn sure," Stone said. "The other interesting question is, what sort of a wild card is the *Commodore Perry* when it comes to weapons? I know what *we've* got. Our stuff is a little better than what the Lizards use—not a lot, but a little, enough to give us a good fighting chance of making them very unhappy in case of a scrap."

"We had junk on the *Lewis and Clark,*" Johnson said.

Stone nodded. "Compared to this? You'd better believe it. Well, the *Commodore Perry* is more years ahead of us than the *Lewis and Clark* is behind us. So what is she carrying, and how much can she do to Home if she gets annoyed?"

Johnson whistled softly. "Think about the difference between World War I biplanes and what we flew when the Lizards got to Earth."

"There's another one," Stone agreed.

Flynn pointed down—up?—toward the surface of home. As it happened, the *Admiral Peary* was flying over Preffilo. Even from so high in the sky, Johnson could pick out the palace complex at a glance. Flynn said, "Have the Lizards wondered what the *Commodore Perry* is carrying?"

"We haven't had any intercepts indicating that they have,"

Stone said. "Maybe they aren't wondering. Maybe they are, but they're keeping their mouths shut about it."

"Somebody ought to whisper in their hearing diaphragms," Johnson said. "The more they wonder about what'll happen if they get cute, the better off we'll be."

"That's actually a good idea." By the way Stone said it, hearing a good idea from Johnson was a surprise. "We can arrange it, too."

"The ambassador should be able to do it," Johnson said. "If the Lizards will listen to anybody, they'll listen to him."

"They may be the only ones who will," Flynn said. "I understand that that's the purpose of an ambassador and all, but when your own side won't. . . ."

"Healey," Johnson said, in the tones he would have used to talk about a fly in his soup. Walter Stone stirred. He was and always had been in the commandant's corner. He was about as decent a guy as he could be while ending up there, which said a good deal about his strengths and his weaknesses.

Before Stone could rise to Healey's defense, before Johnson could snarl back, and before the inevitable fight could break out, Mickey Flynn went on, "Ah, but it isn't just Healey. There's a difficulty, you might say, with the people from the *Commodore Perry,* too."

"Why, for God's sake?" Johnson asked. "The people on that ship either weren't born or weren't out of diapers when he went into cold sleep."

"Call it institutional memory," Flynn said. "Call it whatever you want, but they don't want to give him a ride back to Earth. He's not like us—he could go home again. He could, except that he can't."

"Where did you hear that?" Johnson asked.

"One of the junior officers who was touring this flying antiquity," Flynn said.

"Only goes to show the brass hats back home haven't changed." The opinion of the powers that be in the United States that Johnson expressed was not only irreverent but anatomically unlikely. He went on, "Yeager saved our bacon back there in the 1960s. He let us come talk with the Lizards now with our hands clean."

"Indianapolis." Stone pronounced the name of the dead

city like a man passing sentence. Anyone who was in Lieutenant General Healey's corner wasn't going to be in Sam Yeager's.

"Yeah, Indianapolis," Johnson said. "How many Lizards in cold sleep did we blow to hell and gone? We say 'pulled a Jap.' The Lizards must say 'pulled an American.' But we were the ones who 'fessed up, too, and they paid us back, and now things are pretty much square."

"Those were Americans," Stone said stubbornly. They'd been round this barn a good many times before.

"Okay. Have it your way. Suppose Yeager kept his mouth shut like a good little German," Johnson said. Stone glared at him, but he plowed ahead: "Suppose he did that, and it's now, and we're here—somebody else is ambassador, natch, because Yeager wouldn't have been anybody special then. We're here, and the *Commodore Perry* gets here, and the Lizards are dithering about whether to make peace or go to war. And suppose they find out just now that we were the ones who fried their colonists all those years ago. What happens then, goddammit? *What happens then?* Four worlds on fire, that's what, sure as hell. You think they could ever hope to trust us after they learned something like that? So I say hooray for Sam Yeager. And if you don't like it, you can stick it up your ass."

Stone started to say something. He stopped with his mouth hanging open. He tried again, failed again, and left the control room very suddenly.

Mickey Flynn eyed Johnson. "Your usual suave, debonair charm is rather hard to see," he remarked.

Johnson was breathing hard. He'd been ready for a brawl, not just an argument. Now that he wasn't going to get one, he needed a minute or two to calm down. "Some people are just a bunch of damn fools," he said.

"A lot of people are fools," Flynn said. "Ask a man's next-door neighbor and you'll find out what kind of fool he is."

"We have to do something to get Yeager aboard the *Commodore Perry* if he wants to go home," Johnson said. "We have to."

Flynn pointed at him. "I advise you to have nothing visible to do with it. You're under the same sort of cloud as he is."

"Ouch," Johnson said. That was altogether too likely. If his name showed up on any kind of petition, Lieutenant General Healey would do his goddamnedest to blacken it. For that matter, Healey would probably do the same for—to—Yeager. The commandant of the *Admiral Peary* was a son of a bitch, all right. Of course, the hotshots on the *Commodore Perry* might not want to pay attention to any of the geezers who'd made the trip before them. They were bound to be sure they had all the answers themselves. Johnson did some finger pointing of his own. "How about you, Mickey? You going to try and give Yeager a hand?"

He asked the question with real curiosity. He knew where Walter Stone stood on Yeager. He'd never been sure about the other pilot. Flynn's deadpan wit made him hard to read.

Flynn didn't answer right away. He didn't seem happy about having to stand up and be counted. At last, he said, "They ought to let the man go home. They owe him that much. I wouldn't leave a half-witted dog—or even a Marine—on Home for the rest of his days."

"And I love you, too," Johnson said sweetly. He was bound to be the longest-serving Marine in the history of the Corps.

"If you do, that proves you've been in space too long." Yes, Flynn kept jabbing and feinting and falling back. Johnson wasn't going to worry about it. However reluctantly, the other man had given him the answer he needed. It also happened to be the answer he'd wanted. *So much the better,* he thought. He hoped Yeager got back to Earth, and wondered what the place was like these days.

Two Lizards walked into the hotel in Sitneff. Sam Yeager sat in a human-style chair waiting for them. He got to his feet when they came in. "I greet you," he called. "I greet both of you. It is good to see you again, Shiplord. And it is also good to see you again, Shuttlecraft Pilot."

"You remember!" Nesseref said in surprise.

Yeager made the affirmative gesture. "I certainly do. You took my hatchling and me up to one of your ships in orbit around Tosev 3."

"Truth—I did. I remembered, because I did not fly Tosevites very often, especially back then. That you should also recall the time—"

"We did not go up there all that often. Each time was interesting and exciting enough for every bit of it to be memorable."

"Touching," Straha said dryly, using the language of the Race. Then he switched to English: "It is very good to see you, old friend. I hope you are well."

"As well as I can be, all things considered," Sam answered.

"Good. I am glad to hear it. And here we are, together again: the two biggest traitors in the history of several worlds."

"No. We did what needed doing." Even though Sam was speaking English, he added an emphatic cough. Straha's mouth dropped open in amusement. Sam went back to the Race's language so Nesseref could follow, too: "And how is Tosev 3 these days? The two of you have seen much more of it than I have lately. That would be a truth even if you had come in cold sleep."

"Since I came out of cold sleep myself, I have watched Tosevite technology change," Nesseref said. "This is astonishing to me. I never would have expected to see the way individuals live change visibly in the course of part of a lifetime."

Straha laughed again. "The change in the years between the coming of the conquest fleet and that of the colonization fleet was in some ways even larger, I think."

"That may well be a truth," Sam said. "We were adapting the Race's technology in those first few years, and—"

"Stealing it, you mean," Straha broke in.

"If you like." Sam didn't argue, not when that held so much truth. "But we did adapt it, too, and use it in ways you never thought of. You also have to remember that our technology had been changing rapidly even before the Race came to Tosev 3. If it had not been, you would have conquered us."

"Well, that is a truth," Straha said. "We should have conquered you, too—that is another truth. Atvar will tell you differently, but it is a truth. Had I been in command, we would have done it. But our officers were afraid of change, and so

they went on doing the same old thing." He laughed again.
"Look how well that worked out."

He'd been saying the same old thing ever since he went into
exile in the United States. Maybe he was right, maybe he was
wrong. Sam suspected he was wrong. To him, the only way
the Race could have conquered Earth was by using enough
nuclear weapons to leave it unfit for anyone to live on. With
the colonization fleet already on its way, the Lizards couldn't
have done that. Sam didn't argue with Straha. What point to
it? All he said was, "No one will ever know now."

"Atvar knows. In his liver, he knows. This is his fault, no
one else's." Straha spoke with a certain dour satisfaction.

Again, what point to arguing? Yeager knew Atvar would
deny everything Straha said. How sincere would the fleetlord
be when he did? That was hard to tell even with people, let
alone with Lizards. Sam said, "Come into the refectory with
me, both of you. We can eat together, and you can tell me
about Tosev 3 these days—and about your trip here on the
Commodore Perry."

"It shall be done, and on your expense account, too," Straha
said. "I shall order something expensive, something I have
not tasted since before I went into cold sleep for the journey
to Tosev 3."

"Go ahead," Sam said. "Be my guests, both of you. As a
matter of fact, the imperial government is picking up the tab
for us for the time being. I suspect that will not last too much
longer. Banking between solar systems will become much
more practical if news of transactions does not require a
good-sized part of someone's lifetime to go from one to another."

"No doubt that is a truth, superior sir," Nesseref said.

"I do not care whether it is a truth," Straha declared. "All I
care about is that I shall eat well—I shall eat delightfully
well—and someone else will pay for it. If this is not the ideal
in such affairs, I do not know what would be."

"Spoken like a male who has spent too much time on the
lecture circuit," Sam said.

"*There* is a truth!" Straha used an emphatic cough. "The
only difference is, meals on the lecture circuit are usually not
worth the savoring. This does not stop me from eating them,

you understand, only from enjoying them as much as I might."
He hadn't been so cheerfully mercenary when Sam first knew
him. Had life in the United States changed him? Or had living as a celebrity rather than a military officer after he returned to the Race done the job? Sam didn't know. He
wondered if Straha did.

"They have made furniture for your shape, I see," Nesseref
said as she walked into the refectory with Yeager and Straha.

"They have tried," Sam agreed. "It is not perfect, but it is
better for us than what you use. Our backs and hips align differently from yours, and our fundaments have a different
shape." Lizards didn't have much in the way of buttocks and
did have tailstumps. Humans could sit in chairs made for
them, but the experience wasn't enjoyable.

A server brought menus. "Ah, plerkappi!" Straha said. "I
have not had plerkappi for a very long time. No Tosevite
seafood comes close to them. Have you tried them, Sam?"

"Once or twice," Sam answered. "The flavor is a little too
strong for my taste." They reminded him of clams that had
started to go bad. If Straha fancied them, he was welcome to
his share and Sam's besides.

Nesseref ordered them, too, so maybe they really were
something travelers coming back after a long time away
would crave. Yeager stuck to azwaca cutlets. Straha sneered.
Sam didn't care. Straha also sneered when he ordered unfla-
vored alcohol. "All you want to do is poison yourself with it,"
the Lizard said. "You should enjoy it."

"I do not enjoy your flavorings," Sam Yeager said. "And
you were not fond of whiskey, either."

"But that is different," Straha said. "Who would want to
drink burnt wood? You might as well drink paint or cabinet
cleaner."

Sam thought the Race's flavorings every bit as nasty as
paint. "No accounting for taste," he said, and let it go at that.

"Well, there is a truth," Straha agreed. The way his mouth
fell open and the way his eye turrets moved were the Race's
equivalent of a sly laugh. "Look at my choices in friends, for
instance."

"I will try not to hold it against you," Yeager said, and

Straha laughed again. Sam tried for the third time: "So how is Tosev 3 these days?"

"It is a very strange place," Straha said. Nesseref made the affirmative gesture. Straha added, "Even those parts of it ruled by the Race are strange these days." Nesseref agreed again.

"This is interesting, but it tells me less than I might like to know," Sam said. "In what ways is Tosev 3 strange?"

"Part of the strangeness is staying the same ourselves while we watch the Big Uglies change all around us," Nesseref said. "This is not only strange, it is frightening."

"She is right," Straha said. "It is as if we are a big pot in water. When we first came to Tosev 3, the water outside was, say, halfway to the top. We had no great trouble holding it out. It has climbed up and up and up ever since. Now it is lapping over the edge, and will flood everything inside. And the Big Uglies know it, too."

"Who was that male from the SSSR some years ago?" Nesseref asked. " 'We will bury you,' he said, and he might well have been right."

"I remember that. It was before I went into cold sleep," Sam said. "His name was Khrushchev, and he was a nasty piece of work."

"No doubt he was," Straha said. "That does not necessarily mean he was wrong. Sometimes I think the nastier a Big Ugly is, the more likely he is to be right. This is not a reassuring thought for a male of the Race to have."

"When I was first revived on Tosev 3, we could do many things you wild Tosevites could not," Nesseref said. "Your military could come close to matching ours, but our civilian life was far richer and more pleasant. One by one, you acquired the things you did not have. Now you have things we do not."

"And, for the most part, we are not acquiring them." Straha made the negative gesture. "No—we are acquiring them by purchase from the Big Uglies. We are not making them ourselves. That is not good."

"And now this," Nesseref said. "Here we are, back on Home, and in days rather than years."

"This, I gather, you decline to sell to us," Straha put in.

"Well . . . yes," Sam said.

"I cannot blame you," Straha said. "If I were a Big Ugly, I would not sell this technology to the Race, either. We tried to conquer you. Thanks to Atvar, we did not quite succeed, but we tried. I would not blame you for returning the favor."

"We do not want to conquer anyone." Sam used an emphatic cough. The refectory was bound to be bugged. "All we want to do is live in peace with our neighbors, both the other independent Tosevites and the Empire."

"Yes, the Empire is your neighbor now—your near neighbor," Straha said. "It is no longer the monster down the hall that stuck a clawed paw into your room. But now, to the Race, *you* are the monster down the hall."

"We are not monsters, any more than you are," Sam insisted.

"Before, we could reach you and you could not reach us. That made us monsters to you," Straha said. "Now you can reach us in a way in which we cannot reach you. Believe me, Sam Yeager, that makes you monsters—large, scary monsters—to us." He added an emphatic cough of his own.

"We are not monsters. We are only neighbors," Sam said.

Straha laughed. "What makes you think there is a difference? We have become your near neighbors. You are still not our near neighbors. That by itself is monstrous, at least as seen through our eye turrets."

He was bound to be right. Even so . . . "Whenever you say these things, you make a war between the Empire and the United States more likely. Is that what you want, Shiplord? If it is, you will find some here who feel the same."

"I will find quite a few, I suspect, even aboard the *Commodore Perry*," Straha said. "Do I hear truly that they wish to exclude you from returning to Tosev 3?"

"Some of them do, yes," Yeager said. "Some of those in power in the United States would like to do the same. Are there none here on Home who would rather you had stayed on Tosev 3?"

"No doubt there are," Straha said. "The American Tosevites did not consult with them, though, and so they are stuck with me."

"That sort of trip is not open to me," Yeager said.

"I know. This is most unfortunate, in my opinion," Straha said. Nesseref made the affirmative gesture. Straha went on, "You should do all you can to get them to change their minds."

"I am," Sam answered. "Just how much good any of that will do, though, I have to tell you I do not know."

Atvar did not enjoy his meeting with the Tosevite officer called Nicole Nichols. The Big Ugly from the *Commodore Perry* spoke the Race's language as well as any of the Americans from the *Admiral Peary*. That did not make her any more accommodating. On the contrary: it only emphasized how different—and how difficult—she was.

When Atvar presumed to speak up for Sam Yeager, Major Nichols just looked at him—looked through him, really—with her small, immobile eyes. "Well, Exalted Fleetlord, I thank you for your opinion, but I am afraid this is the business of the United States, not that of the Race."

"I must say I do not completely agree with you," Atvar replied. "Sam Yeager is your not-empire's ambassador here. What affects him affects us."

The Tosevite looked through him again. *You must be kidding,* was what he thought he saw in her manner. The Big Uglies from the *Admiral Peary* had taken—did take—the Race seriously. They were not sure the United States was the Empire's equal. Atvar hadn't been sure of that, either. Major Nichols assumed the United States was more powerful than the Empire. She might have been right. Even so, the way she acted grated on Atvar. He was used to looking down his snout at Big Uglies. He was *not* used to their doing it to him.

She said, "We have our orders from Little Rock. We may have some discretion, but no one—let me repeat, no one—is going to tell us what to do." She added an emphatic cough.

"You would do well to remember whose world you are on," Atvar said.

"You would do well to remember how we got here," the wild Big Ugly replied. "We can form our own judgments on what needs doing and what does not. We can, and we will. Is there anything else, Exalted Fleetlord?" She sounded polite enough when she used his title, but she didn't take it seriously.

"Only one thing," Atvar said heavily. "You would do well to remember that we can still devastate your planet, even if we cannot do it right away."

"This may be a truth," Major Nichols said. "Then again, it may not. You would do well to remember we can devastate all the planets of the Empire before half a year passes. Whether we could do the same to a fleet moving against us at half of light speed . . . well, I admit I am not certain of that. But the state of the art is bound to improve in the next few years. What we cannot do now, we probably will be able to soon."

She showed that chilling confidence again. What made it all the more chilling was that the Big Uglies had earned the right to use it. Their technology *did* keep getting better and better. The Race's didn't, or hadn't. Now it would have to, or the Empire would go under.

Major Nichols added, "In any case, we can certainly deal with your ships once they decelerate in our solar system."

We can certainly deal with your ships. When the conquest fleet came to Tosev 3, the wild Big Uglies hadn't even been sure its ships were there till the fighting started. They'd thought the scoutcraft were electronic faults in their radar systems. Now . . . Who could say what they could do now?

But Atvar said, "Suppose they do not decelerate?"

"Excuse me?" the American Tosevite replied.

"Suppose they do not decelerate?" Atvar repeated. "A large ship at half light speed is a formidable projectile weapon, would you not agree?"

Nicole Nichols didn't say anything for a little while. When she did, it was one cautious word: "Possibly."

Atvar's mouth fell open. He knew what that meant. It meant the answer was yes, but the American Big Uglies hadn't worried about the question till now. But even though he laughed, he also watched as the wheels began to spin behind Major Nichols' eyes. The Tosevite female was starting to calculate ways by which her not-empire could knock out starships that were also projectiles.

She said, "They still would not arrive for some time. I believe that we would probably be able to intercept them once they got there. And I should also point out that you would have a hard time aiming them precisely. You would be more likely to hit areas on Tosev 3 that you rule than you would be to hit the United States."

"So what?" Atvar answered. "By then, we would be out to destroy all Tosevites. Enough impacts of that sort might well render Tosev 3 uninhabitable, which would be the point of the exercise. For many years, we have considered the possibility that this might become necessary. We never thought it was urgent enough to attempt. If you launch a war against us, though . . ."

He wondered if that would surprise Nicole Nichols. If it did, she didn't show it, not so he could see. She said, "No doubt you would try. Whether you would succeed . . . That is a matter for doubt, Exalted Fleetlord."

"Many things are," Atvar said. "We did not think so, not till we made the acquaintance of you Tosevites. You taught us there are no certainties in matters military. You should remember it, too, especially when a mistake in these matters could lead to the destruction of a world."

"Or of three worlds," Major Nichols said.

"Or of four," Atvar said. "That would be a disaster for four species. The Empire will not go down alone." He used an emphatic cough.

Did the wild Big Ugly finally begin to believe he was serious, believe the Race was serious? Again, he had a harder time judging than he would have for any citizen of the Empire. Tosevites were *alien,* biologically and culturally. Nicole Nichols said, "I will take your words back to my superiors. You may be sure we will treat them with the importance they deserve."

How much importance did the Tosevite female think that was? A little? A lot? She did not say. Atvar almost asked her. The only thing that stopped him was the suspicion that she wouldn't tell him the truth.

After she left, Atvar took notes on their conversation and his impressions of it. He wanted to get those impressions down while they were still fresh in his mind. He was about two-thirds of the way through when the telephone hissed for attention. He hissed, too, in annoyance. He thought about letting whoever was on the other end of the line record a message, but the hissing got under his scales. As much to shut it up as for any other reason, he said, "This is Fleetlord Atvar. I greet you."

Kassquit's image appeared on the screen. She sketched the posture of respect. "And I greet you, Exalted Fleetlord. May I come to see you? There is something of some importance that I would like to discuss with you."

"Give me a little while, Researcher," Atvar answered. "I am finishing up some work. After that, I would be glad to hear what you have to say."

"I thank you. It shall be done." Kassquit broke the connection.

A wild Big Ugly would probably have come to Atvar's room too soon. The Tosevites' notion of a little while was shorter than the Race's. What that said about the two species, Atvar would rather not have contemplated. Kassquit, though, was a citizen of the Empire, and understood its rhythms. A moment after Atvar finished his notes, the door hisser announced that she was there.

When he opened the door, Kassquit came in and gave him the full posture of respect. She rose. They exchanged polite greetings. "What can I do for you?" Atvar asked.

"Exalted Fleetlord, I would like you to speak for Sam Yeager to the American Big Uglies from the *Commodore Perry*," Kassquit replied.

"I have done it," Atvar said. "Much good has it done me. The crewfemale from the *Commodore Perry* is full of her own rightness to the choking point. She becomes offensive to those around her because they do not share in what she reckons her magnificence."

He was going to add that even the name of the American Tosevites' new starship was an affront to the Empire. He was going to, yes, but before he could Kassquit murmured, "How very much like the Race."

Both of Atvar's eye turrets broke off from their usual scan of his surroundings and swung sharply toward her. His voice was also sharp as he snapped, "If that is a joke, Researcher, it is in questionable taste."

"A joke, Exalted Fleetlord?" Kassquit made the negative

gesture. "Not at all. By no means, in fact. Ever since the Race conquered the Rabotevs, it set itself up as the standard of comparison, the standard of emulation. Now the glove is on the other hand, is it not?"

"But we . . ." Atvar's voice trailed away. Again, he didn't get the chance to say what he'd planned to: that the Race, having the most advanced civilization and technology, had earned the right to tell other species what they ought to do and how they ought to live. Somewhere up in the sky, the *Commodore Perry* laughed at his pretensions. The Big Uglies had pretensions of their own. He'd resented those. What had the Rabotevs and Hallessi thought about the Race's pretensions before they were fully assimilated into the Empire? How long had it been since a member of the Race thought to ask the question? Had a member of the Race ever thought to ask it?

His silence told its own story. Quietly, Kassquit said, "Do you see, Exalted Fleetlord? I think perhaps you do."

"I think perhaps I do, too," Atvar answered, also quietly. "Humility is something we have not had to worry much about lately." He laughed, not that it was funny from anyone's point of view except maybe a Tosevite's. "Lately!" Another laugh, this one even more bitter. "We have not had to worry about it since Home was unified. From this, we concluded we did not have to worry about it at all."

"Change has returned to the Race. Change has come to the Empire," Kassquit said. "We had better embrace it, or soon there will be no more Empire."

She was a citizen of the Empire. She was a Big Ugly. If that did not make her a symbol of change, what would? And she was right. Anyone with eye turrets in his head could see that. "It is a truth," Atvar said. "Not a welcome truth, mind you, but a truth nonetheless."

"You spent many years on Tosev 3. You can see this," Kassquit said. "Will those who have lived all their lives on Home and who are not familiar with wild Big Uglies and what they can do?"

"Oh, yes. *Oh,* yes." Atvar made the affirmative gesture. "If the Big Uglies can fly between their sun and ours in a fifth of a year while we take more than forty years to make the same journey, they will see. They will have to see."

"For the Empire's sake, I hope so," Kassquit said, which could only mean she wasn't completely convinced. "And I do thank you for speaking up for Sam Yeager, whether it did all you hoped or not. In his case, the wild Big Uglies should not be allowed to match the Race's high-handedness."

"We agree there," Atvar said. "The American Tosevites from the *Admiral Peary* also agree on it. Whether we and they can persuade the newly hatched Americans from the *Commodore Perry* may be a different question."

"Arrogance lets you think you can do great things," Kassquit said. "To that extent, it is good. But arrogance also makes you think no one else can do anything great. That, I fear, is anything but good."

"Again, we agree," Atvar said. "I do not see how anyone could disagree—anyone who is not very arrogant, I mean." Did that include the crew of the *Commodore Perry*? Did it, for that matter, include most of the Race? Atvar could pose the question. Knowing the answer was something else again. Actually, he feared he did know the answer—but it was not the one he wanted.

Jonathan Yeager and Major Nicole Nichols sat in the refectory in the Americans' hotel in Sitneff. Jonathan was finishing an azwaca cutlet. People said every unfamiliar meat tasted like chicken. As far as he was concerned, azwaca really did. Major Nichols had ordered zisuili ribs. She had enough bones in front of her to make a good start on building a frame house. She wasn't a big woman, and she certainly wasn't fat; she was in the hard good shape the military encouraged. She sure could put it away, though.

A sheet of paper lay on the table between them. Jonathan tapped it with his forefinger. "You see," he said.

Major Nichols nodded. "Yes. So I do. Very impressive." No matter what she said, she did not sound much impressed.

"If you don't take my father home, the rest of us don't want to go, either," Jonathan insisted. How readily he'd got the other Americans to put their signatures on the petition surprised and touched him. It had been much easier than he'd worried it would be when he first thought about taking the step.

She looked at the paper, then up at him. She was a strikingly attractive woman, but she had a sniper's cold eyes. "Forgive me, Mr. Yeager, but you and your wife can't be objective about your father."

That only made Jonathan angry. He did his best not to show it. "I'm sure you're right," he said. "I wouldn't want to try to be objective about him. But you're pretending not to see something. My signature and Karen's aren't the only ones there. Every American on Home has signed it. That includes Major Coffey. Anyone would expect him to be on your side, not ours, if my dad had done anything even the least little bit out of line. And Shiplord Straha and Shuttlecraft Pilot Nesseref signed it, too, and you were the ones who brought them to Home."

"They're Lizards," Major Nichols said. "Of course they'd be happy enough to stay on Home."

"Come on. We both know better than that," Jonathan said. "Nesseref has lived on Earth for the past seventy years. Her friends are there. Friends count with Lizards the way family does with us. And Straha . . . Straha would complain no matter where he was staying."

"In some ways, his situation is a lot like your father's," Nicole Nichols said. She drummed her nails on the white plastic of the tabletop. "He's not particularly welcome no matter where he goes."

"Looks to me as though you're saying being right is the worst thing you can do," Jonathan said tightly.

"Have it your way, Mr. Yeager." Major Nichols folded the petition and put it in her handbag. "Besides, with the Lizards it's academic. They aren't going back to Earth with us, for fear they might pass on a message to the Race's authorities back there. And the choice about your father isn't mine any which way. I will take this document back to the *Commodore Perry* and let my superiors decide."

"Yeah. You do that," Jonathan said. "It wouldn't look so good if you came back to Earth with none of us aboard, would it?"

She only shrugged. She was a cool customer. "We'd handle

it," she said. "We can handle just about anything, Mr. Yeager."
She got to her feet. "No need to show me the way out. I already know." Away she went.

Jonathan muttered under his breath. This younger generation struck him as a mechanical bunch. For a nickel, he would
have kicked Major Nichols in the teeth. He would have tried,
anyway. He suspected she could mop the floor with him, and
probably with any other three people here who weren't Frank
Coffey.

He got up, too, and slowly walked out of the refectory. He'd
done everything he could do. So had everybody else on Home.
He saw that Major Coffey's John Hancock didn't much impress Major Nichols—not that anything much did impress
her. But Coffey's signature sure impressed him. Even if Frank
was going to be a daddy, he didn't want to spend the rest of
his life on Home. He'd signed anyway, to keep an injustice
from being done to Jonathan's father.

A Lizard came skittering up to Jonathan. His body paint
proclaimed him a reporter. Jonathan immediately grew wary.
The Race's reporters were much like those on Earth: too
many of them were sensation-seeking fools. "How does it
feel to travel faster than light?" this one demanded, shoving a
microphone at Jonathan.

"I do not know," Jonathan answered. "I have never done it."
The Race evidently couldn't keep secret any longer what the
Commodore Perry had done.

The reporter gave Jonathan what was obviously intended
as a suspicious stare. "But you are a Big Ugly," he said, as if
challenging Jonathan to deny it. "How could you be here
without having traveled faster than light?"

"Because I am a Tosevite from the *Admiral Peary,* not from
the *Commodore Perry,*" Jonathan said resignedly. "We flew
here in cold sleep slower than light, the same way your ships
travel. You do remember the *Admiral Peary,* do you not?" He
made his interrogative cough as sarcastic as he could.

That might have been lost on the Lizard. After some
thought, the reporter used the affirmative gesture. "I think
perhaps I may. But the *Admiral Peary* is old news. I am sure
of that. I want new news." He hurried away.

"Old news," Jonathan said in English. He sighed. It wasn't

that the Lizard was wrong. In fact, there was the problem: the male was right. The Americans from the *Admiral Peary* were old news, in more ways than one. Had Major Nichols heard the reporter, she would have agreed with him.

Jonathan found himself hoping the none-too-bright Lizard did end up running into Nicole Nichols. He would infuriate her, and she would horrify him. As far as Jonathan was concerned, they deserved each other.

One of the elevators opened up. Tom de la Rosa came out. Jonathan waved to him. Tom came over. Jonathan said, "Beware of idiot Lizard reporters running around loose."

"Sounds like a good thing to beware of," Tom agreed. "And speaking of bewares, have you talked with the gal from the *Commodore Perry*?"

"I sure have—I just finished lunch with her, in fact. I gave her the petition, too." Jonathan set a hand on Tom's shoulder for a moment. "Thanks for signing it."

De la Rosa shrugged. "Hey, what else could I do? Right is right. Those yahoos have no business marooning your old man here."

"You know that, and I know that, but I'll be damned if I'm sure they know that," Jonathan said. "And you know you're taking a chance with that thing. They're liable to call us on it. If they do, none of us goes home from Home."

"Yeah, well . . ." Tom shrugged again. "Linda and I hashed that one out. If they're the kind of stiff-necked bastards who won't bend even when they ought to, I don't think I want to go back to the USA any more. It wouldn't be my country, you know? The company'd be better here."

Tears stung Jonathan's eyes. He blinked several times; he didn't want Tom to see that. *Pride,* he thought, and laughed at himself. "We can be expatriates sitting in the sleazy bars in Sitneff, and all the earnest young American tourists who come here can stare at us and wonder about all the nasty things we've done."

"There you go!" Tom laughed out loud. "The Lost Generation. Hell, we're already the Lost Generation. If you don't believe me, ask anybody from the *Commodore Perry.* Those people are convinced we've got no business being alive any more."

"You'd better believe it!" Jonathan used the catch phrase with sour glee. "Major Nichols told Dad they tried to get here before we did. Wouldn't that have been a kick in the nuts for us?"

"Oh, yeah. Sweet Jesus, yeah." De la Rosa made a horrible face. "We'd've been like the dead atheist decked out in a suit: all dressed up with no place to go."

"As it is, we get into the history books whether our ungrateful grandchildren like it or not," Jonathan said, and Tom nodded. Jonathan's thoughts traveled the light-years far faster than the *Commodore Perry* could hope to. "I do wonder what things are like back on Earth."

"Well, from what I've been able to pick up, the politics are the same old yak-yak-yak," de la Rosa said. "The ecology . . ." He looked revolted. "It's about as bad as we figured it would be. Lots and lots of species from Home crowding out ours wherever it's hot and dry. Earth isn't the place it was when we left."

Jonathan sighed. "Like you say, it's not a hot headline. I don't know how we're going to be able to put that genie back in the bottle again. The place I feel sorry for is Australia." He used an emphatic cough. "It's had its ecology turned upside down twice in two hundred years."

"Isn't that the sad and sorry truth?" Tom said. "You hate to see something like that, because there's just no way in hell to repair the damage. Too many native species have already gone extinct, and more are going all the time. When you add in rabbits and rats and cats and cane toads and cattle and azwaca and zisuili and befflem . . . And plants are just as bad, or maybe worse."

"I know. I don't know the way you do—you're the expert— but I've got the basic idea," Jonathan said, and de la Rosa nodded. "I hope we get to see for ourselves, that's all."

"Me, too." De la Rosa looked fierce. His piratical mustache helped. "If we don't, I'm going to blame you. And I'll have all the time in the world to do it, too, because we'll both be stuck here for the rest of our lives."

"Well, if we start throwing missiles back and forth with the Lizards, that won't be real long," Jonathan said. Tom looked unhappy, not because he was wrong but because he was right.

He went on, "Of course, that's liable to be just as true back on Earth as it is here."

"You think the Lizards can still hurt us back on Earth?" Tom asked. "People from the *Commodore Perry* don't seem to."

"I'm not sure. I'm not sure anybody else is sure, either," Jonathan answered. "I'll tell you this, though, for whatever you think it's worth: the last time Major Nichols came out of a meeting with Atvar, she'd had some of that up-yours knocked out of her. Whatever he told her, it didn't make her very happy. Maybe the Race has figured out how to do something, even if they've got to do it in slow motion."

"I almost wouldn't mind—almost," Tom emphasized. "Where one side figures it can lick the other one easy as pie, that's where your wars come from. If both sides figure they'll get hurt, they're more likely to take it easy on each other."

Jonathan nodded. "That makes more sense than I wish it did." He thought back to Earth again. "Before too long, maybe it won't matter so much. We'll have colonies all over the place. Eggs and baskets, you know what I mean?"

"Oh, hell, yes," Tom de la Rosa said. "We will, and one of these days maybe the Lizards will, too, if we don't kill each other off first. And the Germans will, and the Russians, and the Japanese. . . ."

"Lord!" That took some more contemplating. Jonathan said, "I hope the Nazis and the Reds don't end up with colonies on the same planet. They'd start banging away at each other, same as they were doing when the conquest fleet came."

"Yeah, that'd be fun, wouldn't it?" Tom said.

Jonathan nodded, though fun wasn't what either of them had in mind. He said, "The Nazis owe the Race one, too. If I were a Lizard, I'd worry about that."

"If you were a Lizard, you'd have other things to worry about, like not looking right," Tom pointed out. Jonathan made a face at him. People had much more mobile features than Lizards did. The Race used hand gestures to get across a lot of things humans did with their faces and heads. De la Rosa went on, "I wonder how Kassquit feels about being pregnant now. This isn't the best time to bring a kid into the world—any world."

"She'll do okay, I think," Jonathan said. "There's always been more to her than meets the eye." *And even if she is knocked up, I had nothing to do with it, and Karen can't say I did,* he thought.

Kassquit did not enjoy Dr. Melanie Blanchard's examinations, which was putting it mildly. The wild Big Ugly had warned she would poke and prod, and she did, in Kassquit's most intimate places. For that matter, Kassquit enjoyed next to nothing about being gravid, which was also putting it mildly. She wanted to sleep all the time. Her breasts were constantly sore. And she went on vomiting. Dr. Blanchard called that morning sickness, but it could strike her at any time of the day or night.

Hoping to distract the doctor from her probings and pushings, Kassquit asked, "What possible evolutionary good is there in these disgusting symptoms?"

"I do not know." Dr. Blanchard wasn't distracted a bit. Kassquit hadn't really thought she would be. "I do not believe anyone else does. It is a good question, though."

"I thank you so very much." Kassquit packed as much irony as she could into her voice.

Instead of getting angry, Melanie Blanchard laughed a loud Tosevite laugh. "I am sorry not to be able to give you more help about this," she said. "Some doctors claim that women who have morning sickness are less likely to produce a hatchling that cannot survive than those who do not, but I am not sure this has been proved."

"Produce a hatchling that cannot survive?" The phrase sounded awkward to Kassquit.

"English has a term for this—*miscarry.*" Dr. Blanchard spoke the word in her language. "If you *miscarry,* you discharge the hatchling from your body long before it would come out if everything were normal. *Miscarried* hatchlings usually have something wrong with them that would not let them live."

"I see. They are like eggs that are fertile and laid where conditions are good, but that do not hatch," Kassquit said.

The doctor made the affirmative gesture. "Yes, I think that is a good comparison," she said. "I must tell you, Researcher: I do not know as much as I might about how the Race develops. Keeping track of how Tosevites work is a full-time job in itself."

"I believe that," Kassquit said.

"Good. It is a truth." Dr. Blanchard used an emphatic cough. She peeled off the elastomere glove she'd been wearing and tossed it into a trash can. "For now, I am glad to say, you seem as healthy and normal as any female could."

"This is good to hear," Kassquit said. "Do you have any idea how long the morning sickness will last?"

"It usually ends after the first third of your gravidity—about half of one of Home's years after your egg was fertilized," Dr. Blanchard answered. "Bear in mind, though, that is not a promise. Each female is different. Some never have morning sickness at all. Some have it much more severely than you do, and suffer from it until the hatchling comes out. I am sorry, but you will just have to wait and see."

"I am sorry, too." Kassquit felt like using an emphatic cough of her own. "Have you finished inspecting me for this time?"

"Yes." Dr. Blanchard nodded, then used the affirmative gesture. "As I say, you have earned the stamp of approval." She mimed applying the stamp to Kassquit's left buttock. Kassquit's mouth fell open. That was funny, but not funny enough to make her laugh out loud the way the wild Big Uglies did.

Laughter or no, she was anything but sorry to escape the doctor. Getting examined took her back to the days of her hatchlinghood. Members of the Race had constantly poked and prodded at her then. In a way, she couldn't blame them for that. They were trying to find out as much as they could about Tosevites. In another way . . .

She shrugged. No doubt she would have been addled no matter how the Race raised her. One species simply could not fill all the needs the hatchlings of another had. That was all the more true when the first was imperfectly familiar with the needs of the second.

Part of her wished she could go back to Tosev 3 on the *Commodore Perry.* She would have liked to meet Mickey and

Donald. If anybody on four worlds could understand her and what she'd gone through over the years, the males the Yeagers had raised were the ones. By all accounts, they had done well for themselves in the United States. But they were also surely caught between their biology and their culture. Mickey had said as much in the title of his autobiography.

Had they learned the Race's language, or did they speak only English? If they had learned the Race's tongue, did they speak it with an accent? They would have the right mouth-parts to speak it properly, yes. They wouldn't have the mushy tone Tosevites couldn't help. But they would have grown up using very different sounds: the sounds of English. How much difference would that make?

I should have learned English, she thought. But she had a pretty good idea why the Race had never taught it to her. The males and females in charge of such things must have feared learning a Tosevite language would make her too much like a wild Big Ugly. And maybe they'd even been right. Who could say for sure?

If she did ask to go aboard the *Commodore Perry* and visit Tosev 3, what would the American Tosevites say? Kassquit paused and then made the negative gesture. That was the wrong question. The right question was, how was she worse off even if they said no? If they did, she would be where she was now. If they said yes, she would be better off than she was now. As was true most of the time, asking was the right thing to do here.

But whom could she ask? The formidable female officer named Nichols? Kassquit hadn't seen her around the hotel lately. She hadn't seen anyone from the *Commodore Perry* around the hotel lately. Maybe that meant nothing. Maybe it meant the faster-than-light ship was about to bombard Sit-neff. How could you tell what wild Big Uglies would do next? Kassquit knew she couldn't.

She went to see Ambassador Yeager. He laughed. "You want me to get them to take you?" he said. "I cannot even get them to take me."

"I know that, superior sir. I am sorry for it. I think it is alto-gether unjust." Kassquit added an emphatic cough.

"Now that you mention it, so do I," Sam Yeager said. "I

hope you will not be angry, but I have to tell you that I do not think traveling on the *Commodore Perry* would be good for you, at least not in the near future."

"Why not?" Kassquit demanded. There were times when she thought everyone on four worlds joined together in thwarting her. She knew such thoughts were not true, but that did not always keep her from having them.

"Well, for one thing, you would keep company with many more wild Big Uglies than you ever have before," the American ambassador answered. "You would have a much greater risk of disease than you ever had before. Who can say how you would respond? You have never been exposed to diseases before. And remember, you are gravid. Disease could also affect the hatchling growing inside you. So could traveling faster than light. I do not know that it would. But I do not know that it would not, either. I do know that hatchlings growing inside females are often more sensitive to changes in environment than adults are. If I commanded the *Commodore Perry,* I would not accept you as a passenger simply because you are gravid."

"I . . . see." Kassquit had expected Sam Yeager to argue in terms of politics and statesmanship. Instead, he'd talked about biology. That was harder to refute or get around. Kassquit wasn't sure she should try to get around it, either. She said, "Would Dr. Blanchard confirm what you say?"

"I think so. By all means, ask her," the ambassador replied. "And ask a member of the Race who has studied Tosevites. I am not a physician." He tacked on an emphatic cough to stress the *not.* "All I can tell you is what a reasonably well-educated wild Big Ugly thinks he knows. Experts know better than I do. Talk to them."

"It shall be done." Kassquit pointed accusingly at Yeager. "You make entirely too much sense."

He laughed again, on the same sour note he'd used the first time. "I am glad you think so. I am glad somebody thinks so. There are a good many who think I am nothing but an old fool."

"I have never been one of those," Kassquit said. "The way you think has always interested me, ever since the days when we both pretended to be members of the Race on the computer bulletin-board system back on Tosev 3." She pointed at him again. "You should not have been able to gain access to that system."

Now Sam Yeager's laugh held real amusement. "I know. I had a friend who got the necessary programming for me."

"A friend," Kassquit echoed. She had no trouble figuring out what that meant. "Not another wild Big Ugly, not that long ago. You mean a male of the Race, someone from the conquest fleet."

"Well, what if I do?" Yeager answered. "Even then, plenty of males decided they would rather live in the United States than in the lands the Race ruled. We released all the prisoners of war we held who wanted to go. The rest became what we call naturalized citizens of our not-empire."

"It sounds like treason to me," Kassquit said darkly.

But Sam Yeager made the negative gesture. "No, not at all. You are a citizen of the Empire. You are loyal to the Race and the Emperor. Your species does not matter. When members of the Race become naturalized citizens of the United States, they give it their loyalty. Their species does not matter, either."

"Maybe," Kassquit said. "But I am suspicious of those who change their loyalty after they are adult."

"There is some truth in that, but, I think, only some," Yeager said. "The history of Tosev 3 shows that there can be more reasons for changing one's loyalty than somebody familiar only with the history of the Race might think."

"I would guess the history of Tosev 3 also shows more treason than the history of the Race," Kassquit said.

"And I would guess you are right," the American ambassador said, which surprised her—she'd been trying to make him angry. He went on, "The Race has been politically unified for all these years. That leaves small room for treason. On Tosev 3, we have had and do have all sorts of competing sovereignties. An individual may work for one while loyal to another. We may be barbarous—a lot of the time, we *are* barbarous—but we have more complicated, more sophisticated politics than the Race does."

"More complicated, anyhow." Kassquit was in no mood to praise wild Big Uglies.

Sam Yeager only laughed again. "Have it your way, Researcher. I would like to see you come back to Tosev 3 one of these days. Mickey and Donald would be glad to meet you—you have a lot in common with them."

He could think along with her. She'd seen that before, even when neither of them knew the other was a Big Ugly. She said, "That is one of the reasons I want to go back. I would love to speak with them."

"If the doctor says you should not go yet, you could send them letters," Yeager said. "With the new ships, you ought to have answers before too long."

"That is a truth," Kassquit said thoughtfully; it was one that had not occurred to her. "Would you be kind enough to deliver such letters?"

"You might do better asking my hatchling and his mate," Yeager replied. "They are more sure of a place on the *Commodore Perry* than I am."

"They say they will not go if you do not," Kassquit said. Yeager only shrugged. She left his room wondering what that meant. More complicated Tosevite diplomacy? She wouldn't have been surprised.

☆ 18 ☆

A shuttlecraft from the Empire had brought Karen Yeager and the other Americans down from the *Admiral Peary*. Now another one would take them up to the *Commodore Perry*. That probably suited her father-in-law's taste for irony. The Americans weren't heading back to Earth, not yet. They were traveling as a group to try to persuade their younger countrymen to let Sam Yeager go back.

"Are all you Tosevites strapped in?" asked the shuttlecraft pilot, a dark-skinned Rabotev named Pellakrenk. One by one, the Americans said they were. Pellakrenk made the affirmative gesture. "Good," he—she?—said. "The launch corridor rapidly nears."

Humans would have spoken of a launch window. The image in the Race's language worked just as well. It made Karen think of the shuttlecraft flying along a hallway connecting Sitneff to the *Commodore Perry*.

"I commence countdown," Pellakrenk announced, and did. When the Rabotev got to zero, the shuttlecraft roared away from the field. Karen felt as if several large, unfriendly people were sitting on her chest. Each breath was a struggle.

Through the roar of the rocket motor, Jonathan asked, "You okay, Dad?"

"Yeah," Sam Yeager answered—as much a grunt of effort as a word. After a pause for breath, he asked a question of his own: "How you doing, Melanie?"

"One gravity . . . was bad enough," Melanie Blanchard said. "This . . . is worse."

"Soon no gravity at all," Pellakrenk said in fair English. Unlike the Rabotev who'd brought the first load of Americans down to Home, this one didn't pretend ignorance of the humans' language.

When acceleration cut out, Karen gulped. She sternly told her stomach to behave itself. It did, after a few unpleasant minutes when she wondered whether it would listen. She wouldn't have wanted to go weightless if she had morning sickness. That thought made her sympathize with Kassquit, which wasn't something she did every day.

"Everybody okay?" Dr. Blanchard asked. "I've got airsick bags if you need 'em. Don't be shy. Speak up. We don't want the nice folks who're giving us a ride to have to clean up this shuttlecraft."

"What you mean?" Pellakrenk asked. Maybe Rabotevs didn't suffer from nausea in weightlessness. It troubled the Race much less than it did humans.

Nobody answered the pilot. Nobody asked Dr. Blanchard for an airsick bag, either. Frank Coffey and Jonathan kept gulping for a while after Karen's stomach settled down, but all they did was gulp. Karen turned her head and looked out a window. The sky had turned black. She could see the curve of Home if she craned her neck a little. *Columbus was right,* she thought. *Planets are round.*

"*Commodore Perry* calling the shuttlecraft from Sitneff. Do you read me, shuttlecraft from Sitneff?" The voice, that of a human speaking the language of the Race, crackled from the speaker near Pellakrenk's head.

"This is the shuttlecraft from Sitneff," the pilot answered. "Your signal is loud and clear."

"Good," the human said. "Your trajectory looks fine. Let me speak to Ambassador Yeager, if you would be so kind."

"It shall be done," Pellakrenk said, and passed Sam Yeager the microphone.

"I'm here. We're all here," Karen's father-in-law said in English. "Nice of you to want to talk to me." Pellakrenk probably wouldn't notice the jab there. Karen did. She was sure the other Americans on the shuttlecraft did, too.

If the radioman on the *Commodore Perry* did, it didn't faze him. "Glad to hear it," was all he said. Karen had trouble figuring out what was bothering him. If the shuttlecraft carried explosives instead of passengers, it could get past the starship's defenses, yes. But the little ship could carry explosives *and* passengers without any trouble. If the Empire wanted to start a war, it wouldn't worry about the lives of the diplomats who'd been in Sitneff.

Docking was smooth. The Rabotev's odd hands danced over the controls for the maneuvering jets. The shuttlecraft's docking collar engaged with the air lock on the *Commodore Perry* with a smooth click. "We are here," Pellakrenk announced. "I shall wait for you. If your plans change and you decide not to return with me, I trust you will let me know of this."

"It shall be done, Shuttlecraft Pilot," Karen promised.

The outer airlock door, to which the docking collar was connected, swung inward. One by one, the Americans unstrapped and glided into the air lock. When they'd all left the shuttlecraft, the door closed behind them. Tom de la Rosa said, "My God! The air's the right temperature." And it was. For the first time since going down to Sitneff, Karen wasn't too damn hot.

When the inner airlock door opened, a blond woman in coveralls with a captain's bars on the shoulders floated just inside. "Hello," she said politely. "I'm Captain Benn. Please follow me to Lieutenant General Chesneau's office."

"No guided tour?" Jonathan asked.

Captain Benn just shook her head. "No," she answered.

What Karen saw on the way to the commandant's office were . . . corridors. They looked a lot like the corridors in the *Admiral Peary.* They were painted light green instead of gray, but so what? They had handholds so people could pull themselves along while weightless. They had convex mirrors at intersections to help prevent collisions. They had doors set into them. All the doors were closed. The Americans up from Sitneff saw not another living soul besides Captain Benn.

"Have we got the plague?" Karen asked.

"We're only following orders," Captain Benn answered, which probably meant yes.

An open doorway was a surprise. Stenciled on the door were the words OFFICE OF THE COMMANDANT. "Oh, boy," Sam Yeager said. "We're here."

They went in. Another surprise was the appearance of

Lieutenant General Chesneau. Karen had expected a J. Edgar Hoover–jowled bulldog of a man, stamped from the mold that had produced Lieutenant General Healey. But Chesneau was small and thin-faced and didn't look as if he bit nails in half for fun. His voice was a light tenor, not a bass growl. Mildly enough, he said, "Hello. Pleased to meet all of you. So you're the people who've made my life so much fun since I got here, are you?"

He couldn't have been more disarming if he'd tried—and he no doubt was trying. Sam Yeager said, "Well, General, no offense, but you've made my life a whole lot of fun since you got here, too."

Chesneau looked pained. When he said, "Ambassador, I *am* sorry about that," he sounded as if he meant it. But he went on, "You wore the uniform for a long time, sir. I'm sure you understand the need to follow orders."

"He also understands when not to follow them," Karen said. "Do you?"

"In that sense, I hope so," the commandant answered, not raising his voice at all. Yes, he was trying to be disarming. "Whether that sense applies here may be a different question. And it's because the ambassador chose not to follow them on one particular occasion that I have the orders I do." Something tightened in his jawline. However soft he sounded, steel lay underneath.

"I did it. I'll stand by it," Sam Yeager said. "Here's a question for you, General. Suppose, back in the 1960s, that the Lizards found out we'd done what we'd done to them without finding out any of us gave a damn about it. What do you think they would have done to us? You ask me, the answer is, *whatever they wanted to.* Back then, we weren't strong enough to stop them. Slow them down, maybe, but not stop them."

Will Chesneau believe that? Karen wondered. The commandant was somewhere around fifty, which meant he'd been born in the early 1980s. He'd grown up with the USA pulling ahead of the Race, not struggling desperately to get even. Did he understand what things had been like twenty years after the conquest fleet arrived?

All he said now was, "Maybe." He looked at the people from the *Admiral Peary* one after another, then spoke to Sam

Yeager: "You must inspire tremendous loyalty in those who know you, Ambassador. It's not a small gift."

"Thanks, but I don't think that's what's going on here," Karen's father-in-law answered. "What's going on is, your orders are such a bad mistake, everybody can see it but you."

"No offense, sir, but the ambassador's right," Frank Coffey told Lieutenant General Chesneau. "What he's done here is plenty to earn him a ticket back home all by itself. Those other things a long time ago . . . You can argue about them. I admit that—you can. But for one thing, arguing means there's lots to be said on both sides. And for another, nobody can argue about what he's done here. The Race was thinking hard about a preventive war against us. It might have started by the time you got here if not for him. Meaning no disrespect to the Doctor, but I don't think he could have held it off as long as Sam Yeager did."

Chesneau pursed his lips. "We did not expect that we would find Colonel Yeager holding the position he does," he admitted. Then his jawline tightened again. "So—you say you'll all stay on Home if the ambassador doesn't go back to Earth? I am going to tell you, this is your one and only chance to change your minds. Anybody?"

He waited. He very visibly waited. Karen knew she and Jonathan weren't going to say anything. Coffey? The de la Rosas? Dr. Blanchard? How could you be sure? How could you blame anybody who didn't want to die on Home?

But no one said a word. Chesneau's jaw tightened once more, this time, Karen judged, as a bulwark against astonishment. The commandant inclined his head to Sam Yeager. "What I told you before still holds, Ambassador—double, I'd say."

"Thanks." Yeager's voice was husky. He nodded to his colleagues. "Thanks," he repeated, more huskily still.

"You did the right thing," Karen said. "We should be able to do the same."

"Touching," Lieutenant General Chesneau said dryly. "Last chance, people. Going once . . . Going twice . . . Gone."

"If Dad's not going anywhere, we're not going anywhere, either," Jonathan said. One by one, the men and women who'd come down from the *Admiral Peary* nodded.

Lieutenant General Chesneau eyed them in bemusement. Sam Yeager said, "Just for the record, you ought to know this wasn't my idea."

"Truth," Karen said in the Lizards' language, and added an emphatic cough. Her colleagues made the affirmative gesture. She eyed Chesneau. Plainly, he did understand the word, the cough, and the gesture. That was something, anyhow.

He let out a long sigh. "You are a bunch of obstreperous hooligans."

"Truth," Karen repeated, with another emphatic cough. The rest of the Americans used the affirmative gesture again. By their grins, they took it for a compliment, just as she did.

Chesneau saw that, too. "If you think you can blackmail me . . ." He paused and grimaced and finally started to laugh. "It's possible you're right. If I showed up in the Solar System without any of you, I suspect I would get some fairly sharp questions. So would the administration that sent me out—and unlike you, I can't go into cold sleep and outlast it." Karen's hopes soared. Chesneau eyed her father-in-law. "Well, Ambassador, are you willing to go back to a country where you may not be especially welcome?"

"No, I'm not willing," Sam Yeager answered. Karen stared. But then he went on, "I'm eager, General. What I'm willing to do is take my chances."

"All right, then," Chesneau said. "I'll use altered circumstances here on Home as justification for disregarding my orders—and we'll see which of us ends up in more trouble." He started to add something, but found he couldn't: the old-timers crowding his office were clapping and cheering too loud for anybody to hear another word he said.

As the American Tosevites from the *Admiral Peary* got ready to return to Tosev 3, Ttomalss waited for Kassquit to come wailing to him. She'd done it before, when Jonathan Yeager returned to the United States from her starship orbiting Tosev 3. Now she was losing not only a mate but the sire of the hatchling growing inside her. And Frank Coffey wasn't just traveling down through the atmosphere. He would be light-years away.

But Kassquit did nothing of the sort. She began striking up

acquaintances with the wild Big Uglies the *Commodore
Perry* was leaving behind. The new physician seemed surprised to have a gravid patient, but also seemed confident he
would be able to cope with whatever difficulties arose.

Finally, Ttomalss' curiosity got the better of him. He came
up to Kassquit in the hotel refectory one morning and said,
"May I join you?"

She made the affirmative gesture. "Of course, superior
sir . . . provided my nausea does not make me leave more
quickly than I would like."

A server came up and offered Ttomalss a printout. He declined; after so long, he had the refectory's choices graven on
his liver, and needed no reminders. He ordered. The server
sketched the posture of respect and skittered away. Ttomalss
swung his eye turrets toward Kassquit. "How are you feeling?" he asked.

"About the same as before," she answered. "The wild Big
Uglies assure me these symptoms are nothing out of the ordinary. I have to believe them."

"That is not exactly what I meant," Ttomalss said. "How do
you feel about losing your mating partner?"

"He may come back to Home one day, or I may visit Tosev 3,"
Kassquit said. "With the new ships, such journeys will not be
impossible. I am sad he will go. I am sad, yes, but I am not
devastated. Losing a mating partner was harder the first time I
did it. I had no standard of comparison then, and no prospect
of staying in contact with any other Big Uglies. Things are different now."

"I see." Ttomalss broke off, for the server brought in Kassquit's order just then. After the male left, the psychologist re-
sumed: "You are more mature now than you were then."

"Maybe I am." Kassquit began to eat fried zisuili and fungi.
"This is an excellent breakfast," she said, plainly trying to de-
flect his questions.

"I am glad you like it." Ttomalss wondered what tone to
take with her. No usual one was right, and he knew it. He
could not speak to her as one friend did to another among the
Race. Too much lay between them for that. Except for not
physically siring and bearing her, he had been her parent, in
the full, ghastly Tosevite sense of the word. And yet, as he'd

said himself just now, she was more mature than she had been—too mature to take kindly to his using the sort of authority he'd had when she was a hatchling.

His mouth fell open in a sour laugh. Did Big Uglies ever know these ambiguities? Or did they understand instinctively how such things were supposed to work? He supposed they had to. If they didn't, wouldn't their whole society come tumbling down?

"Is something wrong, superior sir?" Kassquit asked. She must have noticed how unhappy his laugh was. He wouldn't have thought a Big Ugly could. But, as he was the Race's leading student of matters Tosevite, so Kassquit knew the Race more intimately than any other Big Ugly, even Sam Yeager.

"No, nothing is really *wrong*," he replied. "I was thinking about how you respond to stress now, as opposed to how you did when you were younger."

"You said it yourself, superior sir: I am more mature than I used to be," Kassquit replied. "I am also more used to the idea of belonging to two worlds than I was. Before, I desperately wanted to be part of the Race, and if that meant abandoning my biological heritage, well then, it did, and that was all there was to it. But I have discovered that I cannot abandon my biology—and I have also discovered I do not want to."

"You will find your counterpart's autobiography interesting," Ttomalss said. "So will I. I look forward to the day the translation reaches Home."

"Truth." Kassquit used the affirmative gesture. The server brought Ttomalss his food. As he began to eat, she went on, "I would give a great deal to meet Mickey and Donald. I have already told the Tosevites as much. Those two of all people should understand some of what I have experienced—though they at least had each other."

Ttomalss crunched a plump roasted grub between his teeth. He said, "There are times when I feel guilty because of what I have done to you. You are not a normal Tosevite, and you never can be. But you may not be worse off on account of that. The lot of a normal Tosevite, especially at the time when I, ah, found you, all too often proved unfortunate."

"Yes, Frank Coffey has pointed out the same thing to me,"

Kassquit said. Because her room was electronically monitored, Ttomalss knew that. He also knew better than to show he knew. Kassquit went on, "I still think I would rather have been as I would have been, if you take my meaning."

"I think so," Ttomalss said. "Of course, you have not experienced the disease and the hard labor you would have known had I chosen another Tosevite hatchling. You are comparing what you have now against some ideal existence, not against the reality you would have known."

"Perhaps," Kassquit said. "I have certainly learned more of bodily infirmity since becoming gravid than I ever knew before. These are lessons I do not care to expand upon further." She looked at her almost empty plate. "This morning, things seem willing to stay down."

"I am glad to hear it," Ttomalss said. "I gather your gravidity has persuaded you not to travel on the *Commodore Perry*?"

Kassquit made the affirmative gesture. "None of the wild Tosevites seemed to think it was a good idea. No one knows how traveling faster than light affects developing hatchlings, and no one seems to want to find out by experiment. I do not care for this conclusion, but I must say it makes sense."

"I agree." Ttomalss bit down on a ripe ippa fruit. Tart juice and pulp flooded into his mouth. "There will be time enough for such things later."

"I hope so," Kassquit said. "This is one of the occasions, though, when I notice that your likely span is longer than mine." She shrugged. "It cannot be helped. If you will excuse me, superior sir . . ." She rose and left the refectory.

As Ttomalss finished breakfast, he wondered what his likely span was. Kassquit meant that an average member of the Race lived longer than an average Big Ugly. She was right about that, of course. But it held true only in times of peace, of stability. If the missiles started flying, if the hydrogen bombs started bursting, no one of any species was likely to live very long.

The Race and the Big Uglies hadn't blown Tosev 3 sky-high. They'd come close when the Deutsche reached for something they weren't big enough to grab. They'd come close, but they hadn't quite done it. Both sides there had got used to the idea that they were living on the edge of a volcano.

Now all the worlds of the Empire were living by the same crater. Most males and females on Home didn't realize it yet, but it was true. Rabotev 2 and Halless 1 were blissfully unaware of it . . . or were they? Had Tosevite faster-than-light starships appeared out of nowhere in their skies? For that matter, had the Big Uglies bombarded or conquered the other two planets in the Empire? If they had, Home wouldn't find out about it for years—unless more Tosevite starships brought the news.

That thought reminded Ttomalss just what a predicament the Race found itself in. The Big Uglies could know things sooner than his own species could, and could act more quickly on what they knew. For years, the Race had tried to decide whether Tosevites were enough of a menace to be worth destroying, and had never quite made up its mind. Even if it had, doing anything would have taken years and years.

If the American Big Uglies decided the Race was still enough of a menace to be worth destroying, how long would they take to act on their decision? Not long at all, both because they were generally quicker to act than the Race and because they now had the technology to match their speed of thought.

Involuntarily, Ttomalss' eye turrets looked up toward the ceiling. Even if he could have looked up through the ceiling, he couldn't have seen the *Commodore Perry* in orbit around Home, not in daylight. If the starship launched missiles, he would never know about it till too late.

One eye turret swung down to the grubs and fruit he'd been eating. He was glad he'd just about finished his meal before such thoughts occurred to him. They would have robbed him of his appetite.

After he left the refectory, he thought about going out into Sitneff to call Pesskrag and see how her research team was coming. He'd taken several steps toward the door before he stopped and made the negative gesture. What good would that do? She'd said the research would take years. Asking her about it mere days after he'd last spoken to her wouldn't gain him any new information. He would just be tugging at her tailstump, annoying her for no good reason.

But he wanted reassurance. He laughed, not that it was particularly funny. Back when Kassquit was a hatchling, he'd constantly had to reassure her that everything was all right, that he would go on taking care of her, that she was a good little female. Sometimes it had almost driven him mad. Hatchlings of the Race, being more independent from their earliest days, didn't need that constant reinforcement. He'd probably been ill-equipped to give it. Whatever psychological problems Kassquit had were in no small measure of his making.

And now he understood Kassquit in a way he hadn't while he was raising her. In the huge, frightening world of interspecies rivalries and new technologies, what was he but a tiny hatchling calling out for someone, anyone, to help make him feel safe?

He didn't think Pesskrag could do for him what he'd once done for Kassquit. He didn't think anyone could—not Atvar, not even the 37th Emperor Risson himself. He suspected they were all looking for reassurance in the same way he was, and for the same reasons. That didn't make him crave it any less.

Change was here. For millennia, the Race had insulated itself against such misfortunes. Everyone had praised that as wisdom. Countless generations had lived peaceful, secure, happy lives because of it.

Now, though, like it or not, change was hissing at the door. If the Race couldn't change . . . If the Race couldn't change, then in a certain ultimate sense those hundred thousand years of peace and stability might not matter at all.

Ttomalss shivered. Few males or females had ever bumped snouts with the extinction of their species. That was what he saw now. Maybe it was nothing but panic over the arrival of the *Commodore Perry*. On the other hand, maybe panic was what the arrival of the *Commodore Perry* demanded. However much he wished it didn't, the second seemed more likely than the first.

The wild Big Uglies hadn't panicked when the conquest fleet arrived. They'd fought back more ferociously and more ingeniously than the Race dreamt they could. Now the Race had to respond in turn. Could it? Ttomalss shivered again. He just didn't know.

There was Home, spinning by as it had ever since the *Admiral Peary* went into orbit around it. The sight had raised goose bumps in Glen Johnson. Here he was, eyeing the scenery as his spacecraft circled a world circling another sun. The *Admiral Peary* was still doing the same thing it had always done— but the starship had gone from history-maker to historical afterthought in the blink of an eye.

When Johnson said that out loud, Walter Stone shook his head. "Not quite yet," he said. "We still have another few weeks of serious duties to perform. Till the *Commodore Perry* goes to Earth and then comes back here, we're the ones on the spot. Up to us to keep the Lizards from doing something everybody would regret."

He was right. He usually was. And yet, his being right suddenly seemed to matter very little. "Yes, sir," Johnson said. "Sorry about that. We're not a historical afterthought right this minute. But we will be any day now."

Stone gave him a fishy stare. "You never have had the right attitude, have you?"

Johnson shrugged, there in the control room. "The right attitude? I don't know anything about that. All I know is, we're about the most obsolete set of spacemen God ever made. We spent all those years weightless, and now we can't be anything else. And we made a fine, successful crew for a cold-sleep starship—the only problem being that they won't make any more of those. Buggy whips, slide rules—and us. What do the Russians call it? The ash-heap of history, that's what it is. And that's where we're at."

Brigadier General Stone's gaze got fishier yet. "If we are, Johnson, you're still a pain in the ash."

"Aiii!" Johnson looked back reproachfully. "And here I thought you were you, and not Mickey Flynn."

"Is someone taking my name in vain?" Flynn asked from the corridor that led into the interior of the *Admiral Peary.* He came out into the control room a moment later. "How did I get into trouble without even being here?"

"Native talent?" Johnson suggested.

Flynn shook his head. His jowls wobbled. "Can't be that."

"Why not?" Stone asked. "It makes sense to me."

"As if that proved anything," Flynn said with dignity. He pointed to the planet they were circling. "How can I be native talent in this solar system?"

"He's got a point," Johnson said.

Stone shrugged this time. "Well, what if he does?" Without waiting for an answer, he pushed off, slid gracefully past Flynn, and vanished down that corridor.

"Was it something I said?" Flynn wondered.

"Nope. He just doesn't care to be last year's model, but he can't do anything about it," Johnson answered.

"Anybody who can remember when rockets to the Moon were the province of pulp magazines is not going to be right up to date," Flynn observed. "For that matter, neither is anybody who can remember pulp magazines."

"That's true," Johnson said. "I was never on the Moon. Were you? And here we are in orbit around Home. It's pretty peculiar, when you think about it."

"The Moon's not worth going to. This place is," Flynn said.

He wasn't wrong about that, either. The Lizards had been amused when humans flew to the Moon. Since the Race was used to flying between the stars, that first human journey to another world must have seemed like the smallest of baby steps. And when people went to Mars, the Lizards were just plain perplexed. Why bother? The place obviously wasn't worth anything.

"Heck," Johnson said, "they didn't even get all that hot and bothered when we went out to the asteroid belt in the *Lewis and Clark*."

"At least they were curious then," Flynn said. "We had a constant-boost ship. That made them sit up and take notice. And they wondered what the dickens we were up to. Those spy machines of theirs . . ."

Johnson laughed. "Oh, yeah. I remember spoofing one of them when I was in a scooter. I signaled to it just the same way as I had to some of the bases we'd set up on the rocks close by the ship."

"That should have given some Lizard monitoring the signals the spy machine was picking up a case of the hives," Flynn said.

"Well, I hope so. I don't suppose I'll ever know for sure, though," Johnson said. "What I do know for sure is, it gave our dearly beloved commandant a case of the hives. He called me into his lair, uh, office to grill me on the weird signal I'd sent. Somehow, he never appreciated my sense of humor."

"He probably thought it lacked that quality of mirth known as being funny," Flynn said.

"Thanks a hell of a lot, Mickey. I'll remember you in my nightmares." Johnson wished he could have left the control room in a display of at least medium dudgeon, the way Walter Stone had. But it was still his shift. He did everything required of him. He always had. He always would, for as long as he was physically able to. He was damned and double-damned if he would give Lieutenant General Healey the excuse to come down on him for something small like that.

He laughed out loud. "Are you attempting to contradict me?" Flynn inquired in moderately aggrieved tones. "How can I know whether something is funny unless you tell me the joke?"

Johnson explained, finishing, "Of course Healey doesn't come down on me for the small stuff. He comes down on me for big stuff instead."

After grave consideration, Flynn shook his head. "I don't think you'd make Bob Hope quake in his boots, or Jack Benny, either."

"I should say not," Johnson replied. "They're dead."

"I don't even think you'd get them worried enough to start spinning in their graves," Flynn said imperturbably. "Neither would that Lizard called Donald, the one who runs the quiz show."

"How's he going to spin in his grave? He's still alive," Johnson said. "And so is that gal called Rita—oh, yeah." Recordings of *You'd Better Believe It* had made it to the *Admiral Peary*. Some people found Donald funny. Johnson didn't, or not especially. But, like every other male on the ship, he . . . admired the lovely Rita's fashion statements. "One more reason to be sorry I'm not going back to Earth."

"Two more reasons, I'd say." Mickey Flynn paused to let

that sink in, then went on, "However much you might like looking at her, you don't suppose she'd look at you, do you? You were not born yesterday, *mon vieux.*"

Except for the minor detail that gravity would quickly kill him, Johnson was in reasonably good shape for his age, which was about the same as Flynn's. But the other pilot wasn't wrong; neither one of them had been born yesterday, even subtracting cold sleep. After some thought, Johnson said, "I've been accruing pay since the 1960s, and I haven't had a goddamn thing to spend it on. I may not be pretty, but I might do for a sugar daddy."

"Maybe you would—if they still have sugar daddies back on Earth," Flynn said.

"They will. That, I'm not worried about." Johnson spoke with great conviction. "As long as old guys have more money than they know what to do with, pretty girls'll give 'em ideas."

"Hmm. On those grounds, I might even qualify for sugar daddyhood myself," Flynn said. "I've been accruing pay longer than you have, since I joined the crew of the *Lewis and Clark* on the up and up instead of stowing away, and I've been a bird colonel longer than you have. I could outbid you." He seemed to like the idea.

Johnson laughed at him. "If we're back on Earth—or in orbit around it, anyway—there'll be enough girls to go around. You get one, I'll get another one. Hell, get more than one if you want to."

"An embarrassment of riches. And, probably, a richness of embarrassments," Flynn said. "But then, a richness of embarrassments is what sugar daddies are for. I should endeavor to give satisfaction."

How did he mean that? Johnson refused to give him the satisfaction of asking. Instead, he said, "It's pretty good weightless, from what I remember. Of course, it's pretty damn good any which way."

"There, for once, I find I cannot disagree with you." Flynn looked aggrieved. "What an unfortunate development. Who could have imagined it?"

Johnson patted him on the shoulder. "Don't worry. It won't last." Flynn seemed suitably relieved.

When Johnson's shift ended, he went down to the refectory. A couple of doctors were in there, talking while they ate about how they could reacquaint themselves with the state of the art once they got back to Earth. They'd been weightless only since reviving aboard the *Admiral Peary*. Johnson was jealous of them; he couldn't go all the way home again.

He got himself a chopped-meat sandwich and a squeeze bottle full of rhubarb juice. The juice wasn't bad—was damn good, in fact. He wouldn't have been surprised if somebody on the starship were fermenting it. The meat was full of pepper and cumin and other spices. That helped keep people from thinking about what it was: rat or guinea pig. The *Admiral Peary* hadn't brought along any regular domestic animals, and the frozen beef and pork and lamb was long gone. The rodents could live—could thrive—on the vegetable waste from the hydroponic farm. Better just to contemplate them as . . . meat.

In came Lieutenant General Healey. That did more to spoil Johnson's appetite than remembering that he was eating a rat sandwich. How many steaks could you carve off of Healey? Or would he prove inedibly tough? That was Johnson's guess.

The commandant hadn't missed any meals. His face was full. His body was round. If what he ate ever bothered him, he didn't let it show. Johnson eyed him again, in a different way this time. Healey was bound to have even more pay saved up than Mickey Flynn did. But with that scowl on the commandant's face, all the money in the world wouldn't turn him into a sugar daddy.

Johnson quickly looked away when Healey's radar gaze swung toward him. Not quickly enough, though—the commandant got his food and then glided toward a handhold near the one Johnson was using. "Well?" Healey asked. "Why are you staring at me? Is my fly unzipped?"

"No, sir," Johnson said tonelessly. The trousers they wore didn't have flies.

"Well, then? I'm not Lana Turner, either." Healey hopelessly dated himself with that crack. Johnson, also hopelessly dated, got it with no trouble. Did anyone on the *Commodore Perry* even know who Lana Turner was? They leered at the lovely Rita these days—not that she wasn't worth leering at herself.

"No, sir," Johnson said again. Leering at Healey for any reason was a really scary thought.

"Then keep your eyes to yourself," the commandant snapped. "The only other reason you'd stare at me that way is to figure out where to stick the knife." He took a big bite of his sandwich.

But Johnson shook his head. "Oh, no, sir."

"Ha!" Healey jeered. "A likely story."

"It's true, sir," Johnson insisted. "I don't need to figure it out. I've known for a long time." They eyed each other in perfect mutual loathing.

No matter what Kassquit had told Ttomalss about her emotional state, she clung to Frank Coffey now. "I hope you come back!" she said, and used an emphatic cough.

"So do I," he answered, and used one of his own. "I will do everything I can. I want to see you again, and I want to see our hatchling. And if I have trouble coming back for any reason, perhaps you and the hatchling can come to Tosev 3. You and that little male or female are bridges between the Empire and Tosevites."

"Truth," Kassquit said. Tears ran down her cheeks. "I wish you were not going!"

"We both knew I would, sooner or later," Coffey said. "The coming of the *Commodore Perry* has made it sooner, that is all." He shook his head. "I did not think I would be leaving as a sire, though. I will say that. It makes things more difficult. . . . Do something for me?"

"If I can," she said. "What is it?"

"Try not to hate me after I am gone."

"I would not do that!" she said.

"I hope not," he said. "Sometimes, though, after these things end, it happens. It is a way of telling yourself, *He is gone, so he could not have been any good while he was here.*"

Remembering how she'd felt after Jonathan Yeager returned to the surface of Tosev 3, and especially after he formed his permanent mating alliance with Karen, Kassquit made the affirmative gesture. She saw how doing as Frank

Coffey said might make her feel better. In a small voice, she told him, "I will try not to."

"Good," Coffey said. "And one other thing. When the hatchling comes, try to let it get to know both members of the Race and wild Tosevites. There will be a good many males and females from the *Commodore Perry* here. Their physician no doubt did not expect to take care of a hatchling, but I think he will do a good job. He probably knows more than Dr. Blanchard does, just because the state of the art has moved forward since she went into cold sleep."

He said such things as if they were as natural as sunrise or as stars coming out at night. (Even as Kassquit had that thought, she made the negative gesture. She'd grown up in space. There, the stars were always out. She'd had to get used to their being gone during the day.) To the wild Big Uglies, change and technical advances were natural. Were that untrue, they never would have built the *Commodore Perry*. For a whole swarm of reasons, Kassquit wished they hadn't.

"I will do that," she said. "The hatchling will be a citizen of the Empire, but it will know more of its biological heritage than I ever did. And I will do my best to make sure that it does not become an experimental animal, the way I did." She added an emphatic cough to her words.

"Good." Frank Coffey caressed her and kissed her. "Believe me, I like your biological heritage." He had a way of showing enthusiasm without an emphatic cough. They lay down together. *The last time,* Kassquit thought. She did her best to make the most of it.

The next morning, the American Tosevites from the *Admiral Peary* got into the bus that would take them to the shuttlecraft port. Atvar got on the bus, too; he was going to Tosev 3 as final proof that the *Commodore Perry* was what the wild Big Uglies claimed it was. No one on Home really doubted it any more. The Tosevites on the new starship already knew about things speed-of-light transmission from Tosev 3 was just now revealing here. But the Race wanted to see for itself, and the Big Uglies had agreed.

Shiplord Straha and Shuttlecraft Pilot Nesseref also boarded the bus. They would not be going back to Tosev 3. They were colonists no more. The American Tosevites could

not be sure they would not deliver a message ordering Kirel
and Reffet to start a last desperate war.

And Kassquit got on, too. Up till the last moment, she had
not been sure whether she would. But she did. She would
stretch things out to the very end. If that made the hurt that
would follow worse, then it did, that was all.

Much of the talk aboard the bus was in English. Even
Straha spoke the language well. *I should have learned it,*
Kassquit thought once more. *My hatchling will learn it. A To-
sevite should know a Tosevite language.*

After a little while, Frank Coffey told her, "I am sorry. This
must be boring for you."

"I wish it were boring," Kassquit said. "I do not understand
what you are saying, but that is not the same thing. I do
not know how long it will be before I see you again. I do not
know if I will ever see you again. It is hard, but it is not boring."

"I am sorry," he repeated. "This is a chance to go home
again."

"I understand," Kassquit said. "I do understand. But it is
not easy for me whether I understand or not."

Atvar and Straha got into a shouting match, which distracted everyone else. They seemed to be trying to decide
which of them was the bigger idiot. By the way they were behaving, it was a contest they both wanted to lose. Atvar had
made it very plain he did not like Straha. Straha seemed to be
doing his best to show it was mutual.

"Enough!" Nesseref exclaimed after a while. "You will
scandalize the Big Uglies!"

"Truth," Atvar said with such dignity as he could muster.
"It *is* enough, Straha."

Straha only laughed at that—a huge, rude, tongue-wagging
laugh. "You say that because you know you are in the wrong.
There is no other reason. If you thought you were right, you
would tell me so."

"I do think I am right, and in a moment I will put my toeclaws up your cloaca to prove it," Atvar retorted.

"I am not afraid of you," Straha said.

"Enough!" That wasn't Nesseref—it was Sam Yeager.

"Both of you are my friends, and both of you are acting like hatchlings."

The two prominent males hadn't really listened to the shuttlecraft pilot, any more than they'd listened to each other. They did heed the departing American ambassador. Straha said, "Perhaps this is not the ideal time or place."

"Perhaps it is not," Atvar agreed. "After I return . . ."

"After you return, I will be at your service," Straha said. "When you get to Tosev 3, you will also see the other ways the wild Big Uglies have got ahead of us. If we had only done as I wanted—"

"Enough!" This time, all the American Tosevites shouted it together. A volley of emphatic coughs rang out.

When they got to the shuttlecraft port, the row threatened to break out anew. The American Tosevites got between the two angry males of the Race. Jonathan Yeager spoke to Atvar. "I am bigger than you are, Exalted Fleetlord, and my sire is bigger than the shiplord. Between the two of us, I hope we can keep the two of you from disgracing yourselves and the Race."

"I think you have just called us barbarians," Atvar said mournfully.

"What have you been acting like?" Jonathan Yeager asked.

After that, Atvar and Straha really did subside. Embarrassment was a weapon more potent than many. Females and males in the body paint of Security examined everything that would be going up on the shuttlecraft. "We cannot be too careful," they said, over and over.

A dark-scaled Rabotev pilot awaited them, eyestalks turning this way and that. Nesseref went up to him—or perhaps her—and started talking shop. Kassquit turned to Frank Coffey. "Do you see? They still worry that a member of the Race might smuggle ginger."

He found it less funny than she did. "If lots of our ships are going to come from Tosev 3 to Home, they are going to have to worry about it. Either that, or they will have to start to accept ginger, the way the Race has on Tosev 3."

"More changes," Kassquit said sadly.

"More changes," Coffey agreed.

A male whose body paint proclaimed him a security chief

bawled, "Final check! All boarding the shuttlecraft, form a line *here*!" He pointed, reveling in his petty power. Along with Atvar, all the Tosevites except Kassquit formed a line *there*. The security male's eye turrets swung toward her. "What about you?"

"I am not going. I am a citizen of the Empire," she answered. The male started to challenge her, but Atvar spoke quietly to him. He hissed in irritation. Then he shrugged, one of the few gestures the Race and Tosevites shared.

Frank Coffey stepped out of line. The security male hissed again. Coffey ignored him. He came up to Kassquit for one last embrace. "Take care of yourself," he said. "I will be back if I possibly can."

"I know. I believe you," Kassquit said. In a way, she was lucky. She had no idea how many Tosevite males had made that same promise to gravid Tosevite females without the slightest intention of keeping it. Some, of course, did, but not all. She added, "I hope everything goes well for you."

"So do I," he said, and smiled what even she recognized as a tight little smile. Here he was—here all the American Big Uglies were—trusting to a technology that was anything but proved. The Race was more sensible, and would never have allowed anything so risky. That was one reason the Big Uglies now had faster-than-light travel, while the Race had never even looked for it very hard. The rest of the Americans and Atvar started out of the terminal building and toward the shuttlecraft. Frank Coffey let Kassquit go. "I have to leave."

"I know," she said again. *I will not cry in front of him.* That was her last determination. She managed to hold on to it as he let the security male wave a metal-detecting wand around him one more time. Then he hurried after the rest of the wild Big Uglies. The door to the field closed, and Kassquit dissolved in tears. The males and females of the Race in the terminal stared at her. They had no idea what to make of the display, or what to do about it.

She wished for a soft cloth to wipe her snout. It always dripped mucus when she cried; the plumbing between it and her eyes was cross-connected in some strange way. Here, the back of her forearm had to do, as it did for her eyes. When her vision finally cleared, she found Straha standing in front of her. She started to bend into the posture of respect.

Straha made the negative gesture. "No need to bother with that foolishness, not for me," he said. "I am only a writer these days, not a shiplord. I just wanted to tell you that you have turned out better than those who took you have any right to expect."

Kassquit did not feel better. She felt worse. She'd known she would, but knowing didn't help. She tried to think of something that might make her less miserable. To her surprise, she did: "When you were on Tosev 3, superior sir, did you ever meet the males called, uh, Donald and Mickey?" She pronounced the strange names with care.

Now Straha used the affirmative gesture. "I did. I can see why you would want to know. They are also luckier than they might have been, but they make very strange males of the Race. Their mouthparts can form all the sounds our language uses, but they have accents anyway—they are used to speaking English. They know of you, by the way. I have heard them say they would like to meet you."

"I would like to meet them, too," Kassquit said. "That is why I asked." The shuttlecraft took off, riding an almost colorless plume of hydrogen flame. Despite the soundproofing, a dull roar filled the terminal. Misery filled Kassquit's liver. She burst into tears again.

The chamber Sam Yeager got aboard the *Commodore Perry* was cramped but comfortable. The starship accelerated out of Home's solar system at a tenth of a g, so he didn't have to get used to weightlessness again. "We're heading off to where space flattens out," one of the crew, a woman, told him casually. That was evidently supposed to mean something, but it didn't, not to him.

He liked the little bit of weight he had. It was enough to keep his feet on the floor and liquids in glasses, though they'd slop out if he raised or lowered them too suddenly. It also made him feel light and quick, which was something he hadn't felt for years—maybe not since that broken ankle ruined his chances of making the big leagues.

Even better than the low weight was the lower temperature.

He'd spent too long in air that never got below the eighties and was often a lot warmer than that. As Southern Californians were fond of saying, it was a dry heat. That made it more tolerable than its Alabama equivalent would have been. Even so, there was a difference between tolerable and pleasant.

He rediscovered long pants and long sleeves aboard the *Commodore Perry.* He also thanked God that he wasn't a nineteenth-century British diplomat, doomed to wear full Victorian formal finery no matter what tropical hellhole (Washington, D.C., for instance) he found himself in. Those nineteenth-century British diplomats had died like flies. He suspected the Americans on Home would have done the same if they'd gone around in tuxedo jackets and heavy wool trousers.

The most he ever said to any of the crew was, "It could be worse. If you don't believe me, ask your colleagues on Home when you get back there." He didn't even add an emphatic cough.

He reveled in fried chicken and real hen's eggs and orange juice and pineapple and ice cream and string beans and carrots and pork chops and mashed potatoes and coffee and Coca-Cola and all the other familiar things he'd done without for too long. Quite a bit of what he'd eaten on Home had been tolerable. Some of it had been pretty good. But all of it had been exotic—literally so, in that it and he had evolved separately for several billion years. Part of him knew that every time he took a bite.

Little by little, he began to realize he was almost as alien to the crew of the *Commodore Perry* as smoked zisuili ribs were to his taste buds and digestive tract. That wasn't just because of what he'd done in the 1960s and what had happened to Indianapolis, either. Some of them thought he was an ogre for that. Others didn't: like him, they saw Lizards, no less than human beings, as people.

But he remembered the days before the conquest fleet came to Earth. He not only remembered them, he'd been shaped by them. To the crew of the *Commodore Perry,* that made him a Neanderthal. The very language they spoke was subtly different from his. He'd started noticing that with Major Nichols. Oh, the crew understood what he said, but the way he said it often made them smile. And he mostly understood what they said, too—but only because he was also fluent in the Race's language. A lot of it wouldn't have been English when he went into cold sleep.

Such changes had already started before he went on ice. People had begun peppering their sentences with emphatic and interrogative coughs and using them by themselves—something the Lizards always found barbarous. But they'd gone further since. Words and phrases from the Race's language got treated as if they were English. By all the signs, they *were* English now. Even word order occasionally shifted.

The *Commodore Perry*'s crew didn't notice they were doing anything out of the ordinary. "We just talk," one of them said. As far as she was concerned, the emphatic cough she added was as much a part of the language as the words that had gone before it.

Little by little, Sam realized he was the one who was out of the ordinary. Had Shakespeare read Hemingway, the Bard would have felt the same jolt. He would obviously have been reading English. He would have been able to make sense of most of it. Just as obviously, it wouldn't have been the language he was used to using. Most of the time, people didn't notice how language changed around them, because they got the changes one by one, piece by piece. They all fell in Sam's lap at once; he didn't have the time he needed to get used to them.

He wasn't the only one from the *Admiral Peary* to feel the same way. "It's a good thing we didn't have to go back into cold sleep," Dr. Blanchard said at supper one evening. "We'd be like ancient Romans trying to deal with Italian."

Sam suspected they might be like Romans trying to deal with the modern world in other ways, too. He didn't even try to use some of the controls in his room because he couldn't figure out what they were supposed to do. One of Caesar's legionaries behind the wheel of a Chevy could have been no more confused.

When he said as much, Jonathan asked, "Why haven't you asked one of the crew about them?"

"Because I don't want to look like a rube," Sam answered. "Have *you* asked? What *is* that button with the gold star?

What does it do? Does it change the air conditioning, or is it the emergency switch? There's no label on it. You're just supposed to know, and I don't."

His son didn't answer him. Neither did anyone else from the *Admiral Peary*. Sam smiled to himself. Unless he was very much mistaken, none of the other Rip van Winkles knew what that button with the gold star was for, any more than he did. They hadn't wanted to look like rubes, either.

He did eventually find out, but not from the brisk, polite, half-foreign young crewfolk of the *Commodore Perry*. Atvar happened to tell him it controlled the softness of the mattress. The Lizard hadn't been embarrassed to ask; his countrymen hadn't built the ship. He said, "I never have understood why so many Tosevites prefer to sleep on a raised area from which they might fall. That aside, though, the arrangement is comfortable enough."

"I am glad you are satisfied, Fleetlord," Sam said, hoping Atvar hadn't figured out that he hadn't known about the button. "Is the food to your taste?"

"Tolerable," Atvar answered. "Of course, I ate Tosevite food before the colonization fleet brought our own domesticated animals and plants. As long as I add enough salt, it is not too bad."

What the Race thought of as enough salt was too much by human standards. Lizards put salt on bacon. After some meals in Sitneff, Sam had felt like a piece of beef jerky. Dr. Blanchard had clucked about what all that sodium was doing not only to his blood pressure but to everybody else's. If the humans ate local food, though, they had no choice but to eat the salt that went with it.

"This whole starship I find fascinating," Atvar said.

"How do you mean? Because it can go faster than light?" Sam asked.

"No—and yes," the fleetlord replied. "The males and females here have made sure I have nothing to do with that, as is only sensible from their point of view. But our starships are all like your *Admiral Peary*—they are designed to take passengers in cold sleep. This one has passengers and crew who are all fully awake, and has to have facilities for feeding them and bathing them and keeping them entertained. Oh, by the way, I find your showers too weak and puny to do a proper job of cleaning, and what you call soap does not deserve the name."

"Well, Fleetlord, when I was in Sitneff, I always wondered whether your showers or your soap would do a better job of flaying the hide off me," Sam said. "It all depends, I suppose, on whether you have scales."

"Any proper creature—" But Atvar caught himself. "No, that is not so. You Tosevites have taught us otherwise." He aimed an accusing fingerclaw at Sam. "You Tosevites have taught us all sorts of things we had not known. Quite a few of them, we would have been just as glad not to learn, too."

"You cannot always pick and choose about what you would learn and what you would not," Yeager said.

"That too is a truth," Atvar agreed. "Just how bitter a truth it is, we are still in the process of discovering." He skittered down the corridor. His gait was even odder in low gravity than humans' gliding leaps.

Sam was not given access to the *Commodore Perry*'s control room. Neither was anyone else from the *Admiral Peary,* so he didn't have to take that personally. He couldn't look out into space. Instead, he had to make do with what the monitor in his chamber showed him. The image was very fine, but it wasn't the same. Home had rapidly faded behind the starship, lost in the skirts of its sun. Tau Ceti itself went from a sun to no more than the brightest star in the black sky. But Sam could have seen the same kind of thing from the *Admiral Peary* as it left the Solar System if he hadn't been in cold sleep.

When he asked the crew what going faster than light felt like, he got different answers. Most said it didn't feel like anything. One shrugged her shoulders and said, "I'd been on duty till an hour before. I slept through it."

A few, though . . . A few said things like, "It was very strange." When he tried to press them further, he got nowhere. Whatever the experience was, it wasn't something they could put into words.

Two of them said the same thing: "Maybe you'll find out." One spoke matter-of-factly, the other with a certain somber relish. Sam wondered whether he ought to hope he was one of the majority who went through whatever it was without even noticing.

He also wondered whether Lizards might feel the transition differently from humans. When he mentioned that to Atvar, though, the fleetlord said, "Straha and Nesseref made this journey without harm. Neither told me of noting anything unusual at the transition. Had the crew not informed them of it, they would not have known it had taken place."

"I see. I thank you," Sam said. "Well, in that case I do not suppose you have anything to worry about."

Atvar made the negative gesture. "There I must disagree with you, Ambassador. I have a great many things to worry about. It is only that that does not happen to be one of them."

"You are right, of course," Yeager said. "Please forgive me."

"No forgiveness is necessary," Atvar replied. "I thank you for your concern."

"I wonder what the sky will look like when we make the switch," Sam said.

"This has also occurred to me," Atvar said. "I would rather see it for myself than on a monitor. There, it could all too easily prove to be nothing but a special effect. But if we suddenly find ourselves in the neighborhood of Tosev 3, then that concern will fall by the wayside."

"Do you doubt that we will?" Sam asked.

"I cannot doubt that this ship traveled from Tosev 3 to Home in the time described," Atvar answered. "But this is Tosevite technology, which means it is bound to be inadequately tested. Can I doubt that it will work perfectly twice in a row? Oh, yes, Ambassador. I have no trouble doubting that, none at all."

Except for the elevated bed instead of a simple sleeping mat, Atvar found nothing to complain about in the accommodations the Big Uglies had given him. They did a better job of taking care of members of the Race than the Race did for Tosevites. Of course, they'd had more practice than the Race had, too.

How long will that be so? Atvar wondered. He could easily see swarms of Big Uglies coming to Home, either simply as tourists or armed with the get-rich-quick schemes they hatched so effortlessly. If the Race didn't learn how to take care of them, they'd take care of themselves. They probably wouldn't try to colonize Home, not the way the Race had colonized Tosev 3. But, with their furious energy, they might end up taking big bites out of the Race's world anyway.

Or this ship might blow up instead of doing what it is supposed to do. Atvar hadn't been joking when he mentioned the possibility to Sam Yeager. The Big Uglies always took big bites out of things. That was a great part of what made them what they were. Sometimes, though, they bit off more than they could swallow.

Days crawled by, one after another. Then there were only tenths of a day left—or, since this was a Tosevite ship, *hours.* Why the Big Uglies divided days into twenty-four parts, each of those into sixty, and each of *those* into sixty instead of sticking to multiples of ten had always perplexed Atvar, but then, a lot of the other things they did perplexed him much more.

He waited in his cabin for the change. He did not want company, not even Sam Yeager's. Whatever happened would happen. He would deal with the consequences . . . if he lived.

He hadn't been afraid either time he went into cold sleep. He'd been sure he would wake up again. Cold sleep, at least for the Race, had tens of thousands of years of development behind it. Going faster than light . . . How many times had the Big Uglies tried it? It had worked once. That was all Atvar knew.

English came out of the intercom. Someone was announcing something. Atvar hadn't learned much English on Tosev 3, and had forgotten most of that. The American Big Uglies from the *Admiral Peary* spoke the Race's language so well, he hadn't had to worry about English with them. But now he was on an American ship. People on the *Commodore Perry* spoke the Race's tongue, too, but English was the ship's routine language.

And then, apparently for him alone, came a sentence in the language of the Race: "Transition with come in one tenth of a daytenth, so please find somewhere comfortable to sit or lie down."

"It shall be done," Atvar said aloud. He assumed the Big

Uglies monitored his cabin. He noted no one instructed him to strap himself in. That made sense. If something went wrong here, a safety belt around his middle would do him no good.

He waited. A tenth of a daytenth wasn't a long time, but he'd never known what the Big Uglies would have called fifteen minutes to pass so slowly. He kept wondering whether the time had already gone by, but glances at the watch on his wrist kept telling him the answer was no. The watch wasn't his. The Big Uglies had given it to him. They wanted to make sure he had nothing that could signal Reffet and Kirel when he got to Tosev 3.

Here—this really was the zero moment. He felt noth . . . No sooner had the thought started to form in his head than he knew an instant—no more than an instant—of being mentally turned upside down and inside out. He let out a startled hiss, but the moment had passed by the time the sound escaped. It was far and away the most peculiar sensation he'd ever felt. He wondered if it was real, or if he'd just imagined it. Then he wondered if, for something like this, there was any difference.

More English came out of the intercom. Then, again for his benefit, the Big Ugly at the microphone switched to the Race's language: "Transition was successful. We are now shaping course for Tosev 3."

The image of the Big Uglies' home planet appeared in the monitor, its large moon off to one side. Images in monitors proved nothing. No one knew that better than Atvar. But he also knew nothing he'd experienced before was the least bit like the moment the Tosevites called transition. He believed in his belly that the *Commodore Perry* had leaped across the light-years.

Someone knocked on the door to his chamber. To him, that was a Tosevite barbarism; he vastly preferred a hisser. But the Big Uglies had built this ship to please themselves, not him. When he opened the door, he found Sam Yeager standing in the corridor. "I greet you," the white-haired American said. "Did you feel anything?"

"Yes." Atvar made the affirmative gesture. "Not vertigo. What vertigo would feel if it felt vertigo, maybe. Yourself?"

"Something like that, I think," Yeager answered. "You put it better than I could have. What vertigo would feel . . . Yes, that comes as close as anything. The funny thing is, though, I talked to several crewmales and -females as I came over here, and only one of them felt anything at all. I have no idea what that means, or whether it means anything."

"I prefer to think it means you and I are highly superior to those insensitive louts," Atvar said, and Sam Yeager laughed loudly. The fleetlord went on, "I do not know whether that is a truth, but I prefer to think it."

"Fine. I will think the same thing. I do not know whether it is a truth, either, but I like it fine," Yeager said.

"How soon will the ship go into orbit around Tosev 3?" Atvar asked.

"You are asking the wrong male, I fear," Sam Yeager said. "I am only a passenger, and not privileged to know such things. One of the crewfolk would surely have a better idea than I do."

"Perhaps. But I do not care to talk to them," Atvar said.

"Well, Fleetlord, to tell you the truth, neither do I," Sam Yeager said. "Of course, I have no doubt they feel the same way about me. They are three or four generations younger than I am, and our customs and ways of thinking have changed from my time to theirs. I do not believe all the changes are for the better, but they would disagree."

Customs and ways of thinking had changed very little among the Race for millennia. Even something so small as the fad for a Tosevite appearance among the young had taken Atvar by surprise when he came back to Home. He knew Yeager was talking about much more important differences. He'd seen them himself.

One reason Big Uglies changed faster than members of the Race was that they didn't live as long. That made a hundred of their years seem like a long time to them. Hardly anyone hatched at the beginning of such a span would be alive at the end of it, which was far from true among the Race. New To-sevites could quickly come to prominence, and bring new ideas with them. Atvar let free a mental sigh. Shortening the lifespan was not a solution the Empire would embrace.

"I thank you, Ambassador," he said aloud. "I shall just have to wait and see for myself."

Whenever he looked at it in a monitor, Tosev 3 got bigger and closer. After his long absence, he was struck again by how blue and watery the Big Uglies' world looked. He had come to take land outweighing ocean for granted again; that was how things worked on Home and the other two worlds belonging wholly to the Empire. Not so here.

Of course, everything he was seeing could be just some clever special effect. The Race could have produced this. Atvar had no reason to doubt that the Americans could do the same. The only way he could be sure was to go down to the surface of the planet.

The crewmember he had to talk to about that was Major Nicole Nichols. He did not look forward to talking to her about anything. He wondered if she would refuse just for the fun of it. But she did not. She said, "You go right ahead, Exalted Fleetlord." As usual, she sounded sarcastic when she used his title. "We want you to be sure you have come to Tosev 3. We do not want you to think we are trying to trick you in any way, shape, form, color, or size. Then we will send you back to Home, and you can let everyone there know that you made a round trip."

"I thank you." Atvar was not really feeling grateful—on the contrary. He wished the Big Uglies were trying to fool him. Then they would not have this stunning technology. But they all too plainly did.

Except for the pilot, he went down to Tosev 3 alone in the shuttlecraft. The American Tosevites from the *Admiral Peary* stayed behind. Going first was an honor he could have done without, especially when he saw that the shuttlecraft pilot was a Big Ugly. He told himself he'd just come light-years with a Big Ugly at the helm of the starship. Getting down from orbit to the planetary surface should be easy. Telling himself such things helped—some.

"I greet you," the pilot told him. After that, most of what she said on the radio was in incomprehensible English. Every so often, she would use the language of the Race to talk to an orbiting ship or a ground station. The Big Uglies could have faked the responses coming back from those ships and stations—but it wouldn't have been easy.

As the shuttlecraft came down out of orbit, deceleration pressed the fleetlord into his seat. It was made to conform to the contours of a member of the Race, and did the job . . . well enough. Everything seemed routine. The only difference he noted was that he would have understood more of the chatter with someone from his own species piloting. The Tosevite seemed highly capable. Tosevites *were* highly capable. In no small measure, that was what was wrong with them.

He watched the monitor. A large city swelled below him. There was the shuttlecraft port. Rockets fired one more time, killing the shuttlecraft's velocity. The grounding was as smooth as any a pilot from the Race might have made. "Well, Exalted Fleetlord, here we are in Los Angeles," the Big Ugly said.

"Yes," Atvar said in a hollow voice. "Here we are."

The pilot opened the hatch. Cool, moist outside air poured into the shuttlecraft. As it flowed over the scent receptors on Atvar's tongue, he smelled odors both alien from billions of years of separate evolution and familiar because he had smelled such things before. Down deep in his liver, he knew he was on Tosev 3.

"Go on out, Exalted Fleetlord," the pilot said.

"I thank you," Atvar said, meaning anything but. When he poked his head out of the hatch, his eyes confirmed what logic and his scent receptors had already told him. He was on Tosev 3. The color of the sky, the shapes of the buildings and cars—this was not his world.

Big Uglies in wrappings that covered almost their entire bodies ran toward him from all directions. Some of them had guns in their hands. "Come with us, Exalted Fleetlord," one of them called.

"Should I surrender first?" Atvar inquired.

"That will not be necessary," the American Tosevite replied, taking him literally. "We are here for your protection."

"I did not realize I needed so much protecting," Atvar remarked as he came down the ladder.

Instead of answering that, the Big Ugly continued, "We are

also here to make sure you do not communicate with members of the Race here before you go back to Home."

"Do you need so many to do the job?" the fleetlord asked as his toeclaws clicked on concrete. "It seems more as if you are putting me in prison."

"Call it whatever you please." The Tosevite sounded altogether indifferent.

☆ 19 ☆

With the *Commodore Perry* gone from the sky, with Atvar and the Americans from the *Admiral Peary* gone on the astonishing new starship, Home suddenly seemed a backwater to Ttomalss. Even though Big Uglies from the *Commodore Perry* remained behind, this was no longer the place where things happened. In ancientest history, the Race had believed that the sun revolved around Home. Males and females had known better for well over a hundred thousand years.

Even though they knew better, the idea had kept a kind of metaphysical truth ever since. Not only the sun seemed to spin around Home. So did the stars Rabotev and Halless, and the worlds that spun around *them*. And so had the star Tosev and its worlds, most notably Tosev 3.

No more. Now events had literally left the homeworld behind. The most important things that happened for a while wouldn't happen on Home. They would happen on Tosev 3. Even now, not many members of the Race realized that. Most males and females went on with their lives, neither knowing nor caring that events might have passed their whole species by. Mating season was coming soon. If they worried about anything, it was getting ready for the spell of orgiastic chaos ahead.

As for Ttomalss, he did what any academic will do when faced with a stretch of time when nothing else urgently needs doing: he wrote reports and analyses of the dealings between the Race and the diplomats from the *Admiral Peary*. Even as he wrote, he understood that much of what he was recording was already as obsolete as one of the Race's starships. He wrote anyhow. The record would have historical value, if nothing else.

No matter how dedicated an academic he was, he couldn't write all the time. When he went down to the refectory for a snack one afternoon, he found Trir there ahead of him. The tour guide was in a foul temper. "Those Big Uglies!" she said.

A couple of Tosevites sat in the refectory, though some distance away. Trir made not the slightest effort to keep her voice down. "What is the trouble with them?" Ttomalss asked. He spoke quietly, hoping to lead by example.

A forlorn hope—Trir didn't seem to notice the example he set. "What is the trouble?" she echoed at the top of her lung. "They are the most insulting creatures ever hatched!"

"They insulted you?" Ttomalss asked. "I hope you did nothing to cause it."

"No, not me," Trir said impatiently. "They have insulted Home."

"How did they do that? Why did they do that?" Ttomalss asked.

"Why? Because they are barbarous Big Uglies, that is why." Trir still did nothing to keep her voice down. "How? They had the nerve to complain about the lovely weather Sitneff enjoys, and that all the architecture here looks the same. As if it should not! We build buildings the right way, so they look the way they should."

"I have some sympathy, at least in the abstract, for their complaints about the weather. It is warmer here than it is on Tosev 3. What is comfortable for us is less so for them," Ttomalss said.

"I should say so!" Trir exclaimed. "The air conditioners they brought down from this new ship of theirs chill their rooms until I think I am back at the South Pole, or maybe somewhere beyond it."

Ttomalss tried to figure out what on Home might be beyond the South Pole. He gave it up as a bad job. Trir didn't care whether she was logical. Ttomalss said, "You see? You dislike the weather they prefer as much as they dislike ours."

"But ours is proper and normal." Trir was not the sort to think that several billion years of separate evolution could produce different choices. She judged everything from the simplest of perspectives: her own.

"As for architecture, they have more variety than we do," Ttomalss said. "They enjoy change for its own sake."

"I told you they were barbarians." As if sure she'd made a decisive point, Trir got up and stormed out of the refectory.

Ttomalss sighed. Trir came closer to the average member of the Race in the street than any other male or female he knew. Her reaction to the Big Uglies wasn't encouraging. How would the Race react to Tosevite tourists here on Home? Could simple dislike spark trouble where politics didn't?

The tour guide hurried back into the refectory, as angry as when she'd left it. She pointed a clawed forefinger at Ttomalss. "And the horrible creatures had the nerve to say we were backward! Backward!" she added, and stormed out again.

"Did they?" Ttomalss said, but he was talking to Trir's retreating tailstump.

His eye turrets swung to the Big Uglies in their specially made chairs. They'd paid no attention to Trir's outburst. Did that mean they hadn't understood it or hadn't heard it? He didn't think so, not for a moment. It meant they were being diplomatic, which was more than Trir could say. Who was the barbarian, then?

Ttomalss' head started to ache. He hadn't wanted that thought right now. Whether he'd wanted it or not, he'd got it.

So the Big Uglies thought Home was backward? Had the Americans from the *Admiral Peary* presumed to say such a thing, Ttomalss would have been as furious as Trir. The Tosevites from the *Commodore Perry* . . . Hadn't they earned the right? From a Tosevite perspective, Home probably *was* a backward place. But it had proved it could prosper and stay peaceful for tens of millennia. If the Big Uglies dragged their competing not-empires and empires and the Empire into a string of ruinous wars, what price progress?

The psychologist could see what the price of progress would be: higher than anyone in his right mind wanted to pay.

But, now, he could also see what the price of backwardness was. Having moved forward technologically at such a slow pace over the millennia, the Race was vulnerable to a hard-charging species like the Big Uglies. With hindsight, that was obvious. But no one here had imagined a species like the Big Uglies could exist. *We knew ourselves, and we knew the*

Rabotevs and Hallessi, who are like us in most ways, and we extrapolated that all intelligent species would be similar. That was reasonable. Based on the data we had, it was logical.

And oh, how wrong it was!

He glumly finished his food and left the refectory. No histrionics from him. His swiveling eye turrets noted the Big Uglies turning their heads so their eyes could follow him out. Oh, yes, they'd heard what Trir had to say to him, all right.

Escaping the hotel was a relief, as it often was. He walked down the street toward the public telephone he'd used before. Every time he passed a male or female wearing a fuzzy wig or what the Big Uglies called a T-shirt, he wanted to shout. Members of the Race had taken to imitating Tosevites out of amusement. Would they keep on doing it now that the Tosevites were no longer amusing but powerful?

He thought the Race's power was the main reason so many Big Uglies on Tosev 3 had shaved their heads and started wearing body paint that showed ranks to which they were not entitled. Would power attract more males and females here now that the situation was reversing? He wouldn't have been surprised. Monitoring such things would make an interesting experiment—for someone else.

When he got to the phone, he swung his eye turrets in all directions. If that ginger-tasting female and her hoodlum friends were around, he would take himself elsewhere as fast as he could go. He did not see any of them. Feeling safe because he didn't, he telephoned Pesskrag. Impatience and worry overwhelmed the careful logic of a few days before.

The phone hissed several times in his hearing diaphragm. He was afraid he would have to record a message. But then she answered: "This is Pesskrag. I greet you."

"And I greet you. This is Ttomalss," he said.

"Ah. Hello, Senior Researcher," the physicist said. "Let me tell you right out of the eggshell, we have made no dramatic breakthroughs since the last time I talked with you."

"All right." Ttomalss might have been hoping for such a breakthrough, but he hadn't counted on one. He gave himself that much credit, anyhow. Science seldom worked so conveniently. "I hope you have not gone backwards, though."

"Well, no, or I also hope not," Pesskrag answered. "We may

even have taken one or two tiny steps forward. Once we devise some new experiments, we will have a better notion of whether we have. We have opened a door and entered a new room. So far, it is a dark room. We are trying not to trip over the furniture."

"The Big Uglies charged all the way through to the other side," Ttomalss said. "Why can we not do the same?"

"It is less simple than you think," Pesskrag said. "What we have are only the early hints that appeared in the Tosevite literature. I gather the Big Uglies stopped publishing after that. We have to reconstruct what they did after they stopped giving us hints. No matter how provocative the early experiments, this is not an easy matter. We do not want to waste time going down blind alleys."

"And so we waste time being thorough," Ttomalss said.

The physicist let out an angry hiss. "I fear I am wasting time talking to you, Senior Researcher. Good day." She broke the connection.

As Ttomalss was unhappily walking back to the hotel, a male wearing the body paint of a bus repairer accosted him. "Hello, friend," the stranger said, so heartily that Ttomalss' suspicions kindled at once. "Want to buy some ginger?"

"If you do not mind selling to an officer of the police," Ttomalss answered. The repairmale disappeared in a hurry. Ttomalss wished he were a police officer. He would have been glad to arrest the petty criminal.

Kassquit was standing in the hotel lobby when Ttomalss came in. "I greet you, superior sir," she said, sketching the posture of respect.

"And I greet you," he said. "I hope you are feeling well?"

"I am as well as can be expected, anyhow," Kassquit answered. "This new Tosevite physician says the same thing Dr. Blanchard did—my gravidity seems normal to them, however nasty it is for me."

"How are you emotionally?" Ttomalss said. "You do seem less distressed at Frank Coffey's departure than you did when Jonathan Yeager first returned to Tosev 3."

"I am less distressed," she said. "Most of the time I am, anyhow. My moods do swing. The wild Big Uglies say this has to do with hormone shifts during gravidity. But I have experience now that I did not have when Jonathan Yeager left me. And Frank Coffey may come back, where Jonathan Yeager entered into that permanent mating contract. So yes, I remain more hopeful than I was then."

"Good. I am glad to hear it. Whatever you may think, I have done my best to raise you so that you would become a fully independent person," Ttomalss said. "I know I have made mistakes. I think that is inevitable when raising someone of another species. I am sorry for it," Ttomalss said.

"Your biggest mistake might have been to try to raise someone of another species at all," Kassquit said. "I understand why you did it. The wild Big Uglies did the same thing. No doubt you and they learned a great deal. That still does not make it easy for the individuals who have to go through it."

When she'd been angry before, she'd said worse things to him—and about him. "I am afraid it is too late to change that now," Ttomalss said. "For what has happened to you, you have done very well." Kassquit didn't quarrel with that, which left him more relieved than he'd thought it would.

The shuttlecraft's rockets roared. Deceleration shoved up at Karen Yeager. The pilot said, "Final approach now. The rockets are radar-controlled. They fire automatically, and nothing can go wrong . . . go wrong . . . go wrong . . . go wrong. . . ."

On the couch beside Karen's, Jonathan grunted. "Funny," he said. "Funny like a crutch."

Karen nodded. That took effort. After one-tenth g and weightlessness, she felt heavy as lead weighing more than she normally would. The rockets fell silent. Three soft bumps meant the shuttlecraft's landing struts had touched the ground. Earth. One Earth gravity. Normal weight. Karen still felt heavy as lead. She said, "I could use that funny crutch right now."

"You said it," Sam Yeager agreed from beyond Jonathan.

"Are you all right?" she asked him. He was spry, no doubt about it, but he wasn't a young man. What was hard on her and Jonathan had to be worse for him.

"I'll do," he answered. "We had to twist their arms to get them to let me come back here. I'll be darned if I'll give 'em the satisfaction of keeling over the minute I get home."

"There you go, Dad!" Jonathan said.

The pilot undogged the hatch and flipped it open. The air that came into the shuttlecraft was damp and cool and smelled of the sea, the way it usually did around the Los Angeles International Air- and Spaceport. Karen smiled before she even knew she was doing it. To her, this was the feel and smell of home. She and Jonathan had grown up in the South Bay, only a few miles from L.A. International. "All ashore that's going ashore," the pilot said, determined to be a comedian.

"I'm not going first this time," Sam Yeager said. "If I fall off the ladder, I want you youngsters to catch me." Maybe he was trying to be funny, too. More likely, he was kidding on the square.

"Ladies first," Jonathan said, so Karen took the ladder down to the tarmac. Jonathan followed a moment later. "Whew!" he said when he got to the bottom; full gravity was pressing on, and oppressing, him, too. His father descended then. Karen tensed to help Sam if he had any trouble, but he didn't. If anything, he stood more easily than she and Jonathan did.

"Well, well," he said. "We've got a welcoming committee. Only thing I don't see is the brass band."

Karen didn't see a brass band, either. What she did see were cops and soldiers all around, pistols and rifles at the ready. The soldiers' uniforms looked something like the ones she'd known in 1994, but only something. The same applied to their weapons. A captain—her rank badge hadn't changed, anyway—who surely hadn't been born in 1994 came up to the Yeagers. "Please come with me, folks," she said.

"Like we've got a choice," Jonathan said.

She gave him a reproachful look. "Do you really want to stand on the cement for the rest of the day?" She added an interrogative cough.

"Since you put it that way, no," Karen said. "Just don't go too fast. We've been light for a while."

The shuttlecraft terminal was a lot bigger and fancier than Karen remembered. Some of the columns supporting things looked as if they'd fall down in a good-sized earthquake. Karen hoped that meant building techniques had improved, not that people had stopped worrying about quakes.

She and her husband and her father-in-law didn't have

much luggage. Customs officials pounced on what they did have. "We're going to irradiate this," one of them declared.

"For God's sake, why?" Karen asked.

"Who knows what sort of creatures you're bringing back from Home?" the woman answered.

"Isn't that locking the barn door after the horse is gone?" Sam asked.

"We don't think so," the customs inspector replied. "The Lizards have brought in what they wanted here. That's been bad enough. But who knows what sort of fungi or pest eggs you're carrying? We don't want to find out. And so—into the X-ray machine everything goes."

"Do you want us to take off what we're wearing?" Karen inquired.

She intended it for sarcasm, but the inspector turned and started talking with her boss. After a moment, she turned back and nodded. "Yes, I think you had better do that. You come with me, Mrs. Yeager." A couple of male inspectors took charge of Jonathan and Sam.

That'll teach me to ask questions when I don't really want to know the answers, Karen thought. She stripped and sat draped in a towel till they deigned to give her back her clothes. She half expected to see smoke rising from her shoes when she finally did get them back, but they seemed unchanged. The inspector led her out of the waiting room. Her husband and father-in-law emerged from another one five minutes later.

"Boy, that was fun," Jonathan said.

"Wasn't it just?" his father agreed. "Are we all right now?" he asked one of the inspectors riding herd on him.

"We think so, sir," the man answered seriously. "We're going to take the chance, anyhow." He sounded like a judge reluctantly letting some dangerous characters out on parole.

Signs and painted arrows led the Yeagers to the reception area. Waiting there were more cops and soldiers. Some of them were holding reporters at bay, which seemed a worthwhile thing to do. Others kept a wary eye on Karen and Jonathan and Sam. *What do they think we'll do?* Karen wondered. This time, she didn't ask; somebody might have told her.

Also waiting in the reception area were two men about halfway between Jonathan and Sam in age and two Lizards. Karen saw that the Lizards were Mickey and Donald a heart-beat before she realized the two men had to be her sons. She'd known time had marched on for them. She'd known, yes, but she hadn't *known*. Now the knowledge hit her in the belly.

It hit Richard and Bruce at the same time, and just about as hard. They both seemed to go weak in the knees for a moment before they hurried forward. "Mom? Dad? Grandpa?" They sounded disbelieving. Mickey and Donald followed them.

Then they were all embracing, people and Lizards alike. Tears ran down Karen's face, and not hers alone. Everybody kept saying things like, "My God!" and, "I don't believe it!" and, "I never thought I'd see the day!"

"Where are the grandchildren? Where are the great-grandchildren?" Karen asked.

"Add a generation for me, please," Sam said, and every-body laughed.

"They're at my house," Bruce answered. "I'm living in Palos Verdes, south of where your house was."

Sam pointed at Donald. "You have a lot to answer for, buster."

"They drugged me," Donald said. "They held a gun to my head. They waved money under my nose. How was I sup-posed to tell them no?"

"He always was a ham," Mickey said sadly.

"You always were a bore," Donald retorted. "And they al-ways liked you best."

"We did not!" Karen, Jonathan, and Sam all said it at the same time. Karen and Jonathan added emphatic coughs.

Donald's face couldn't show much expression, but his body language did. What it showed was scorn. "I pretend to be human better than you people pretend to be Lizards," he said.

"You've had more practice," Karen said mildly.

Bruce said, "Let's go to the cars, shall we? We can wrangle about this some more when we get back to my house. The kids will want to get in on it and throw rocks, too." He sounded more weary than amused. How often had this argu-ment played itself out—or, more likely, gone round and round without getting anywhere? *It's a family. Of course it has squabbles,* Karen thought.

Two different sets of bodyguards formed up around them as they went to the parking lot. One bunch belonged to Donald. Celebrities had needed protection from their fans in Karen's day, too; she wasn't surprised to see that hadn't changed. The other contingent kept an eye on her father-in-law. That worried her. The two groups of hard-faced men and women affected not to notice each other.

Cars reminded her much more of the ones she'd seen on Home than those she remembered from before she went on ice. The designs were simpler, more sensible, less ornate. "Are any gasoline-burners left?" she asked. Bruce shook his head. Richard held his nose. Karen wasn't surprised. The cleaner air had made her suspect as much. She hadn't been quite sure, though. With its constant sea breeze, the airport had always had some of the best air in the L.A. basin.

The ride down to Palos Verdes was . . . strange. It went through parts of town Karen knew well—or had known well. Some of the buildings were still there. Others had vanished, to be replaced by some that seemed as strange as the shuttle-craft terminal. Karen noticed Sam doing even more muttering than she and Jonathan were. He'd gone into cold sleep seventeen years earlier than they had. The South Bay had to look stranger to him than it did to them.

"It's not even like I've been away since 1977," he said after a while. "I only remember the time since I woke up in orbit around Home, and I keep thinking it couldn't have changed that much since then. And it didn't—but I have to keep reminding myself."

"So do we," Karen said.

Bruce's house impressed her. To her eye, it seemed almost as big as the hotel where the Americans had stayed in Sitneff. She soon realized that was an exaggeration, but her son had done well for himself. So had the other people whose large houses loomed on nearby large lots. Palos Verdes had always been a place where people who'd made it lived.

Both sets of bodyguards piled out of their cars. They formed a defensive perimeter—or was it two? People Karen had never seen came spilling out of the house. Having children calling her grandmother would have been strange enough. Having grownups she'd never seen before, grownups approaching middle age, calling her that felt positively surreal.

Jonathan looked as shellshocked as she felt. "It's a good thing they figured out how to go faster than light," he said. "Otherwise, lots of people would have to try to get used to this, and I think they'd go nuts."

"It gives the Lizards trouble, and they live longer and change slower than we do—and they don't have families the way we do, either," Sam said. "But a lot of their males and females who travel from star to star have their own clique. They understand how strange it is, and nobody who hasn't done it can."

"I know what I understand." Karen turned to her younger son, who seemed to wear more years than she did. "I understand that I could use a drink." She added an emphatic cough.

"Well, that can be arranged," Bruce said. "Come on in, everybody, and have a look around."

Jonathan Yeager felt besieged by relatives. His grandchildren and great-grandchildren seemed to know everything about him up till the minute he and Karen went into cold sleep. But that was almost forty years ago now, and he didn't know anything about these people. To him, they might almost have been so many friendly strangers.

That went even for his sons. Richard and Bruce still had the same basic personalities he remembered—Richard a little more like him, Bruce more outgoing like Karen—but they weren't college kids finding out about the world any more. They'd had all those years to grow into themselves. They seemed to have done a good job of it, but he couldn't say he knew them. The same went for Mickey and Donald—especially Donald.

He walked over to his father, who was sitting with his legs crossed and a drink balanced on his right knee. "Hi, Dad," Jonathan said. "Congratulations."

"Oh, yeah?" Sam Yeager looked up at him. "How come?"

"Because of all the people here, you're the only one who's even more out of it than I am," Jonathan answered.

"Oh." His father thought that over. Then he said, "If it weren't for the honor of the thing, I'd rather walk. Only trouble is, it's a darn long walk back to Home."

"Yeah. That occurred to me, too," Jonathan said. "We're here. We'll just have to make the best of it. They won't throw us in the poorhouse, anyhow. We've got a lot of back pay coming to us."

"Hot diggety." His father made a sour face. "Do you suppose there's anybody else on the face of the Earth who says 'hot diggety' any more? The more I listen to people nowadays, the more I'm convinced I really do belong in a museum. Me and the Neanderthals and the woolly mammoths and all the other things you wouldn't want to see in your driveway at three in the morning."

Bruce's daughter Jessica was sitting a couple of feet away. She smiled. "Don't be silly, Great-grandfather. You can show up in my driveway any time you want."

"Thanks for all of that except the 'Great-grandfather,'" Sam Yeager said. "It makes me feel a million years old, and I'm not—quite."

"What do you want me to call you?" she asked.

"How about Sam? It's my name." Jonathan's father pointed at him. "You can call this guy Gramps, though."

"Thanks a lot, Dad," Jonathan said.

"Any old time, kiddo—and I do mean old," his father answered.

Jessica looked from one of them to the other. Amusement danced in her eyes. She was somewhere in her thirties: a blue-eyed blonde with strong cheekbones. Jonathan tried to see either himself or Karen in her face, and didn't have much luck. Maybe she looked like her mother, the woman Bruce hadn't stayed married to. She said, "You're quite a pair, aren't you?"

"You should see us on TV," Jonathan said. "We're funnier than Donald, and we don't have to paint ourselves into tuxes."

"Nope—just corners," Sam agreed. Jessica made a face at him. He got to his feet. "I need another drink."

"Now that you mention it, so do I." Jonathan followed him over to the bar. His father picked up a bottle of bourbon. He poured some into a glass, then added ice cubes. "Alcohol with flavorings I like, by God. And I don't have to get into a brawl with the Lizards to get ice." He raised his glass. "Mud in your eye."

Jonathan built a drink for himself. "Same to you," he said. They both sipped. Jonathan wasn't so sure he liked bourbon any more. It did taste like home, though: home with a small *h*.

Richard came over to the two of them. He made his own drink—something with rum and fruit juice. Jonathan wouldn't have wanted it anywhere this side of a beachfront hotel at Waikiki. But his son was entitled to his own taste. Richard kept staring now at Jonathan, now at Sam. "This is crazy. You're going to laugh at me," he said, and added an emphatic cough. "You both look just the way I remember you, but it's been a hell of a long time."

"You were a little kid when I went on ice," Sam said accusingly. "How come you're not a little kid any more?"

Richard hadn't been a little kid when Jonathan went into cold sleep. But he hadn't been older than his father by body time, either. They didn't look like father and son these days. They looked like brothers, and Richard was definitely the more weathered of the two. Jonathan knocked back a good slug of bourbon. "I'm not laughing at anything right now," he said. "It's just starting to hit me that the country I grew up in—the country where I lived my whole life—is almost as alien to me as Home. Everything here seems strange to me, so I don't know why I ought to be surprised that I seem strange to you."

"That's . . . fair enough, I suppose," his son said. "I hadn't really thought about what all this must be like from your point of view."

Jonathan put a hand on his father's shoulder. "It's got to be even weirder for Dad. He went into cold sleep quite a while before I did."

"That's only half the problem," Sam said. "The other half is, I was *born* quite a while before you were. All my attitudes are ancient history now. I've tried to outgrow some of the worst ones, but they're still there down underneath. I felt like a geezer in 1977. I'm worse than a geezer now. Christ! It's more than a hundred years since I tore up my ankle and turned into a minor leaguer for good. That was in Birmingham, Alabama, and nobody thought anything of it when they made colored people sit by themselves in the lousy seats."

"Blacks," Jonathan said.

"African Americans," Richard said. Jonathan shook his head, like a man in a bridge game who's been overtrumped.

Three generations of Yeagers. Three men whose births spanned more than sixty years. By body time, fewer than twenty years separated them, and the one who should have been youngest was in the middle. Jonathan shook his head again. Such things shouldn't have been possible. Here they all were, though.

Richard's wife came over to them. Diane Yeager was younger than Jonathan's son—say, about the same age he was himself. She didn't say a whole lot, but Jonathan got the impression she was hard to faze. "Family group," she remarked now, her eyes going from her husband to his father to his grandfather.

"Family group," Jonathan agreed. He suspected his voice sounded ragged. So what, though? By God, hadn't he earned the right to sound a little ragged just now?

"Three generations for the price of one," she said. "You could all be brothers."

By body time, they could have been. Not many sets of brothers were spread as far apart as the three of them, but some were. And yet . . . "You'd have to go some to find three brothers as different as we are," Jonathan said.

"Can't be helped," Richard said. "We are what we are, that's all, and we have to make the best of it."

" 'The fault, dear Brutus, is not in the stars, but in our-selves,' " Sam quoted. "Except that's not true, not this time. If it weren't for Tau Ceti, everything would be normal." He sipped from his drink. "Of course, I wouldn't be here, so I'm not about to complain."

Strictly by the calendar, Jonathan would turn ninety in De-cember, so he wasn't about to complain, either. "Can you imagine how strange it would be if there were thousands and thousands of families trying to sort this out?" He pointed to his father. "How much fun are you going to have trying to renew your driver's license when you tell a clerk—or more likely a computer—you were born in 1907?"

Sam winced. "Hadn't thought of that. Yeah, it ought to make some electronics start chasing their own tail."

"How do the Lizards handle it?" Diane asked, and started to laugh. "I've got three of the world's best experts here to answer my question."

Richard Yeager looked to his father and grandfather. "I defer to the people who've been on the spot, which I haven't."

"You know more about it than we do, son," Jonathan said. "We were either stuck in a hotel trying to be diplomats or we were out being tourists, which isn't exactly a scientist's dream, either."

"That's about the size of it," his father agreed. "Besides, since your wife asked, only fair you should show off in front of her. I'm sure she's never heard you do it before."

Diane Yeager snickered. Richard turned red. He said, "The two big things the Race has going for it are its longer lifespan and its different social structure. It doesn't have families to be disrupted the way we do. We were talking about this in the car on the way down, in fact."

"Truth," Jonathan said in the Race's language. He went on, "Even so, there's a clique of star travelers who stick together because they aren't so connected to the present. I suppose that would have happened with us, too."

"Probably," Richard said. "Better this way, though. Now we don't have to spend some large part of our loved ones' lifetime traveling from star to star."

Before Jonathan or his father could add anything to that, Donald came up to them. He aimed one eye turret at Jonathan, the other at Sam. "Did the two of you have any idea—any idea at all—what you were doing to Mickey and me when you decided to raise us as people?" he demanded.

"No," Jonathan and his father said at the same time. Sam went on, "Do you know of Kassquit, the girl the Race raised?"

"We've heard of her," Donald answered. "We'd like to meet her one of these days. If anybody would understand some of the things we've been through growing up, she's the one."

"She's said the same thing about the two of you," Jonathan said.

"The Race tried to raise a human as much like one of their kind as they could," his father said. "We did the same thing with you. When we met Kassquit, we realized how unfair that was to you, but we were committed to doing it."

"National security," Donald said scornfully. He stuck out his tongue. "This for national security. You ruined our lives for the sake of national security."

"Things could be worse," Jonathan pointed out. "You've made a lot of money. People admire you. Millions of them watch you every night. And Mickey's prosperous, too, even if he's less public about it."

"Yes, we have money. You know that old saying about money and happiness? It's true," Donald said. "All the money in the world can't make up for the simple truth: we're sorry excuses for males of the Race and we're even sorrier excuses for humans. You want to know how sorry? I really do leer at Rita, because that's what a man would do. I can't do anything with her. Even if I smelled pheromones from a female of the Race and got excited, I couldn't do anything with her. But I leer anyway. There they are, hanging out, and I stare at them."

What could you say to something like that? Jonathan looked to his father, who didn't seem to have any idea, either. "I'm sorry," Jonathan said at last. "We did the best we could."

"I know that. I never said you didn't," Donald answered. "But there's a goddamn big difference between that and good enough." He used an emphatic cough. It didn't sound like the one an ordinary Lizard would have made. He had most of the same accent a human English-speaker would have. All by itself, that went a long way toward proving his point.

Jonathan wondered again if coming home had been such a good idea after all.

Of all the things Glen Johnson had looked for while orbiting Home, boredom was the last. He didn't know why that was so. He'd spent a lot of time on the *Lewis and Clark* bored. Maybe he'd thought seeing the Lizards' home planet would make sure he stayed interested. No such luck.

This wasn't entirely bad. He realized as much. He and everybody else on the *Admiral Peary* could have had a very interesting time trying to fight off missiles from however many spaceships the Lizards threw at them. They wouldn't have lasted long, but they wouldn't have had a dull moment.

Still . . . He had to fight not to go to sleep on watch. Back in the Civil War, they would have shot him for that. When he was a kid, he'd known an old man who as a boy had shaken hands with Abraham Lincoln. He wondered if anyone else still breathing a third of the way through the twenty-first century could say that.

When he mentioned it to Mickey Flynn, the other pilot said, "Well, I can't. I had ancestors who fought in it. People were willing to have Irishmen shot to keep the country in one piece, but not to give 'em a job once they'd managed to miss the bullets. American generosity knows no bounds."

"I don't know. Sounds fair to me," Johnson said.

"And what could I expect from a Sassenach?" Flynn didn't put on a brogue, but his speech pattern changed.

"Don't let it worry you," Johnson told him. "As far as the Lizards are concerned, we're all riffraff."

"They are a perceptive species, aren't they?" Flynn said.

"That's one word," Johnson said. "The *Commodore Perry* should be back on Earth by now. I wonder when it'll come here again."

"Sooner than anything else is likely to," Flynn said.

Johnson clapped his hands. "Give the man a cigar!"

"Not necessary," the other pilot said modestly. "A small act of adoration will suffice."

"Adoration, my—" Johnson broke off with a snort. He started a new hare: "I do wonder when the Russians and the Germans and the Japanese will start flying faster than light. The Lizards are probably wondering the same thing."

"I would be, if I were in the shoes they don't wear," Flynn agreed.

Johnson started to reply to that. Then he started trying to work through it. After a few seconds, he gave it up as a bad job. "Right," was all he did say. Mickey Flynn's nod announced anything else was unthinkable.

Home spun past the reflectionless windows. The *Admiral Peary* was coming up on Sitneff. Clouds covered the city, though. The Americans from the *Commodore Perry* were saying it might rain. That didn't happen every day. Johnson hoped the Johnny-come-latelies got wet. It would serve them right. He had little use for the great-grandchildren of his old-time friends and neighbors. They struck him as intolerably arrogant and sure of themselves. Maybe they'd earned the right, but even so. . . .

"No matter how much you influence people, having friends is better," Johnson said.

"And what inspired this burst of profundity?" Flynn's voice was gravely curious.

"The punks downstairs." Johnson pointed to the clouded city where the Americans lived.

"Oh. Them." Mickey Flynn also spoke with noticeable distaste. "They aren't the most charming people God ever made, are they?" He answered his own question: "Of course they aren't. All the people like that are aboard the *Admiral Peary*."

The intercom crackled to life: "Colonel Johnson! Colonel Glen Johnson! Report to the commandant's office immediately! Colonel Johnson! Colonel Glen Johnson! . . ."

Over the noise, Johnson made a wry face. "And some who aren't the most charming, too. Oh, well. See you later, alligator." Out of the control room he went.

As usual, Lieutenant General Healey looked as if he wanted to bite something when Johnson glided into his sanctum. "Took you long enough," the commandant growled.

"Reporting as ordered, sir," Johnson replied blandly. "I would have been here sooner except for the traffic accident on Route 66. I had to wait till they towed away a station wagon and cleaned up the spilled gasoline."

Healey looked more baleful than ever. He probably wasn't thrilled at being stuck in command of the most obsolete starship the United States owned. "Bullshit," he said, and waited for Johnson to deny it. When Johnson just hung silently in midair, Healey scowled and went on, "I need you to fly a scooter to the *Horned Akiss*."

"Sir, the Lizards will search it eight ways from Sunday," Johnson said. "I want your word of honor in writing, in English and the Race's language, that I'm not trying to smuggle ginger."

"There is no ginger on the scooter." Healey spoke in a hard, flat voice that defied Johnson to contradict him. Johnson didn't. He also made no move to leave the commandant's office. He kept waiting. After some dark mutters, Healey grabbed an indelible pencil—much more convenient in weightlessness than pens, which needed pressurized ink to work—and wrote rapidly. He scaled the sheet of paper to Johnson. It flew through the air with the greatest of ease. "There. Are you satisfied?"

To fit his personality, Healey should have had handwriting more illegible than a dentist's. He didn't; instead, it would have done credit to a third-grade teacher. The commandant's script in the language of the Race was just as neat. Johnson carefully read both versions. They said what he wanted them to say. Try as he would, he found no weasel words. "Yes, sir. This should do it. I'll take it with me to the scooter lock."

"When they retire this ship, Colonel, I'll no longer have to deal with the likes of you," Healey said. "Even growing obsolete has its benefits."

"I love you, too, General." Johnson saluted, then brachiated out of the commandant's office.

As usual, he stripped down to T-shirt and shorts so he could put on his spacesuit. When he stuck the folded piece of paper in the waistband of the shorts, the technician on duty at the lock raised an eyebrow. "What's that?" he asked. "Love letter to a Lizard?"

"Oh, yeah," Johnson agreed. "Their eye turrets drive me nuts." He sighed, as if in longing. The tech snickered.

After boarding the scooter, he ran through the checklist. The technician had already cleared everything. Johnson did it anyhow. The technician wasn't going to take the scooter out into hard vacuum, and he was. Everything checked green. He passed the word to the tech, who opened the outer door to the air lock.

Johnson used the scooter's attitude jets to ease the little rocketship away from the *Admiral Peary*. Before firing up the main engine, he called the *Horned Akiss* to make sure he was expected. Healey hadn't said word one about that.

But the answer came back in the language of the Race: "Yes, scooter from the Tosevite starship. We await your arrival. Stop well away from the ship, so that we may inspect you before you enter the air lock."

"It shall be done," Johnson said. That inspection wouldn't be for ginger. The Lizards would be making sure he wasn't bringing them a bomb. The *Admiral Peary* did the same thing when Lizard scooters approached. Nobody really expected trouble now, but nobody took any chances, either.

He aimed the scooter at the *Horned Akiss,* then fired the rear motor. Away the little rocket went. He liked nothing better than flying by the seat of his pants, even if he did have radar to help. A burn from the front motor killed the scooter's velocity and left it hanging in space a couple of miles from the Lizards' ship. One of their scooters came out to inspect it. "All appears to be in order," a spacesuited member of the Race radioed to him when they were done. "You may proceed to the *Horned Akiss.*"

"I thank you," Johnson answered. "Can you tell me what this is all about?"

"Not I," the Lizard replied. "The commandant will attend to it when you have gone aboard."

"Have it your way," Johnson said. They would anyhow.

Once in the *Horned Akiss'* air lock, he had to get out of his spacesuit. With the heat the Lizards preferred, T-shirt and shorts had a good deal going for them as a uniform. Males and females of the Race went over the spacesuit and the scooter. He showed them Healey's pledge. One of them said, "Very nice. We will continue the examination even so." *Not worth the paper it's written on,* he thought. If Healey had lied, though, (maybe) they wouldn't blame the mere pilot so much.

"Everything appears to be as it should," a different Lizard said after more than an hour. "We will escort you to Medium Spaceship Commander Henrep's office."

"I thank you," Johnson said once more. For someone his size, the corridors were narrow, the handholds small and set at awkward intervals. He managed even so.

When he got to the skipper's office, he found another Lizard in there with Henrep. The captain said, "Inspector, this is the Tosevite called Glen Johnson. Colonel Johnson, here we have Police Inspector Second Grade Garanpo."

"I greet you," Johnson said, thinking unkind thoughts about Lieutenant General Healey. Healey hadn't lied to him—oh, no. But even if the scooter didn't have any ginger aboard it this time, he was still in trouble.

"And I greet you," Garanpo said. "I am very glad to make

your acquaintance—I certainly am." He took out a recorder, which escaped from him and floated around till he caught it again. Johnson watched with interest. A clumsy Lizard was out of the ordinary. Having snagged the little gadget, Garanpo went on, "You have flown your scooter to this ship before, is that not a truth?"

"Yes, that is a truth." Johnson wished he could deny it.

"Well, well. So you admit it, then?" the male said.

"Why should I not? I have done nothing wrong," Johnson said.

"Did I say you had?" Inspector Garanpo asked archly. "Now, then—did you ever bring ginger—this herb you Tosevites have—to this ship?"

"No, and I can prove it," Johnson answered. *I never knew I was bringing it, anyway.* He didn't get into that. As far as he was concerned, the best defense was a good offense: "The proof is, your males and females always inspected the scooter, and you never found any ginger."

"Well, that is a truth, just as you say it is," Garanpo said. "But is it a proof? That may be a different question. If the inspectors were corrupt, they would say they found nothing even if they lied. And did they not find traces of ginger on the scooter from this ship after it was returned from its exchange?"

"I do not know anything about that, Inspector, so you may claim whatever you please," Johnson answered. *Oh, my, would I have been set up with that one.* "If you check your records, you will see I did not bring this ship's scooter back here."

"That is also a truth," Henrep said. "It is unusual, in that this Tosevite does most of their scooter flying, but it is a truth."

"Why did you not fly the scooter that time?" Garanpo asked.

"Because my commandant ordered someone else to do it," Johnson answered. Garanpo was welcome to make what he wanted of that.

"Would your commandant—Healey is the name, is it not?—speak to me about this business?" Garanpo asked. He might act like a clumsy buffoon, but that didn't mean he was one. Oh, no—it didn't mean that at all.

"I cannot say, Inspector," Johnson replied. "How can I speak for my superior? You would have to ask him."

"I have seen that you Tosevites are good at hiding behind one another," Garanpo observed.

"Lieutenant General Healey could not hide behind me," Johnson said, which was literally true—Healey was twice as wide as he was.

"Most unsatisfactory. *Most* unsatisfactory. I *will* get to the root of this." Inspector Garanpo used an emphatic cough.

"I wish you luck. Whatever your problems with ginger are, I had nothing to do with them." The first part of that was truth. The second part should have been. As far as Johnson was concerned, that made it effectively true, too. Somehow, he suspected Inspector Garanpo would have a different opinion.

The imperial laver scrubbed off Ttomalss' old body paint. The imperial limner painted on the new. The psychologist absentmindedly made the correct responses to what the two old females said, and to the guards who made as if to bar his path as he approached the Emperor's throne. He hadn't expected this summons to an audience, which made it all the more welcome.

He bent into the special posture of respect before the 37th Emperor Risson, whose gold body paint gleamed in the spotlights that shone on the throne. "Arise, Senior Researcher Ttomalss," the Emperor said.

Ttomalss stayed hunched over. "I thank your Majesty for his kindness and generosity in summoning me into his presence when I am unworthy of the honor." He probably sounded more sincere than most males and females who came before the Emperor, if only because he'd given up hope of ever gaining an audience until the order to come to Preffilo dashed out from behind a sand dune.

"Arise, I say again," Risson told him. This time, Ttomalss did. The Emperor said, "The Race owes you a debt of gratitude for bringing Senior Researcher Felless' alert to the attention of our physicists. We would be much further behind the

Big Uglies than we are—and we would not know where to begin to catch up—if you had not. I thank you."

"Your Majesty, I thought Felless had come upon something important. I turned out to be right, when it might have been better for the Empire had I turned out to be wrong. Felless deserves more credit than I do. She was the one who noticed what the Tosevites were saying—and then, suddenly, what they were not." He didn't much like Felless. He never had, even before her ginger habit made her a whole different sort of nuisance. But he couldn't try to rob her of credit here, not when anyone with an eye turret half turned toward things could tell she deserved it.

"She will have what she deserves," the Emperor said. "Unfortunately, the speed of light still imposes delays for us, so she will not have it right away. I hope she is still living when our signal of congratulations reaches Tosev 3. You being here on Home, I can congratulate you on the spot."

"I thank you for the kindness, your Majesty," Ttomalss said.

"Why thank me for what you have earned and richly deserve?" Risson straightened on the throne, signaling the end of the audience. Ttomalss made a retreat as formal as his advance had been.

Herrep, the protocol master, waited for him in the bend in the corridor just outside the audience chamber proper. "You did pretty well, Senior Researcher, especially on such short notice," Herrep said.

"I thank you, superior sir," Ttomalss said. "This was my first audience with an Emperor. I have long hoped for the honor, and now it is here."

"His Majesty spoke highly of your work, and of what it means for the Race," Herrep said. "You will, of course, be lodged at his expense this evening, and our budget naturally covers the shuttlecraft fare back to Sitneff."

"Everyone at the palace has shown me great kindness," Ttomalss said. That was polite if not altogether true; he doubted whether the imperial laver and limner had ever shown anyone great kindness, or even a little. The two horrid old females got their fingerclaws on him again after he turned away from the protocol master. The laver cleaned off the special body paint suppliants wore before the Emperor; the limner replaced Ttomalss' usual paint. She did it perfectly, without checking any reference books. Ttomalss wondered how many different occupations and ranks she knew. Had she not intimidated him so much, he might have asked.

The hotel put to shame the one in Sitneff in which Ttomalss and the American Big Uglies were staying. The refectory was as fine as any in which Ttomalss had ever eaten. The sleeping mat in his room was almost as soft as a squashy Tosevite bed; it stopped just this side of being *too* soft. The psychologist wouldn't have minded spending much more time there.

He had an excellent breakfast the next morning. The ippafruit juice was as tangy as any he'd ever tasted. A car from the palace waited outside the lobby to whisk him to the shuttlecraft port. As he got out, he remarked to the driver, "I could get used to feeling important."

She laughed. "You are not the first who has had an audience to tell me that."

"No, I do not suppose I would be." Had Ttomalss come to Preffilo just a little earlier, he likely would have mated with her. But the season was over, and he could think clearly again.

Flying back to Sitneff was routine. He wondered how many shuttlecraft he'd flown in over the years. He couldn't begin to guess. A lot—he knew that.

He wondered why he bothered going back to the hotel. Nothing of substance was happening there these days. The wild Big Uglies were just waiting for the *Commodore Perry* to get back so they could finish rubbing the Race's snout in its inferiority. To them, he was just another male. *Just another Lizard,* he thought; the Tosevites had an insulting nickname for his folk, as the Race did for them.

But sitting in the lobby was the shuttlecraft pilot the Americans had brought back to Home from Tosev 3. She got up and came over to him. "I greet you, Senior Researcher," she said.

"And I greet you," Ttomalss answered. "Can I do something for you?"

Nesseref started to make the negative gesture, but checked

herself. "Maybe you can," she said. "Can we talk for a while?"

"I am at your service," Ttomalss said. "Shall we go to the refectory and eat while we talk? I had a snack in the shuttlecraft port, but I could do with a little more."

What he ordered here wouldn't be as good as what he'd had in the hotel in Preffilo. He sighed. He wasn't rich enough to eat there very often. He and Nesseref both chose zisuili cutlets—hard to go wrong with those. The shuttlecraft pilot said, "The American Tosevites do at least try to act civilized. What will become of us if the Deutsche learn to travel faster than light before we do?"

"You are not the only one to whom this unpleasant thought has occurred," Ttomalss said. "I do not believe anyone has a good answer for it."

"This is also my impression," Nesseref said. "And it worries me. The Americans, as I say, do make an effort. When the Deutsche find a group they do not care for, they set about exterminating it. I have seen this at first hand, living as I did in the part of the main continental mass called Poland."

"My memory of Tosevite geography is not all it might be," Ttomalss said.

"The point is that Poland borders the *Reich*," Nesseref said. "It also has a large number of Jews living in it. You are familiar with the Tosevite superstition called Judaism, and with how the Deutsche react to it?"

"Oh, yes." Ttomalss used the affirmative gesture. "That was one of the first great horrors the conquest fleet found on Tosev 3."

"If the Deutsche had it in their power, they would do the same to us," Nesseref insisted. "And if they can travel faster than light, they gain that power. They could appear out of nowhere, bombard one of our worlds, and flee faster than we could follow."

"Our defenses are ready here," Ttomalss said. "We have sent messages to Rabotev 2 and Halless 1, ordering them to prepare themselves. I suppose we could also send ships to help them, though they would take twice as long as the messages to arrive. What we have the technology to do, we are doing."

"I can only hope it will be enough, and done soon enough," Nesseref said, and then paused while the server set cutlets in front of Ttomalss and her. After the male left, she continued, "I had a friend who was a Jew—a Tosevite male named Mordechai Anielewicz. He had been a guerrilla leader when the conquest fleet came, sometimes opposing the Deutsche, sometimes opposing the Race. He eventually decided he could trust us. He never trusted them. Now his grandchildren are fully mature, but they like the Deutsche no better, and I cannot blame them."

"The Jews are unlikely to be objective," Ttomalss pointed out after swallowing a bite of zisuili meat. It was . . . all right. "They have no reason to be."

"Truth—but the behavior of the Deutsche leads me to mistrust them, too." Nesseref also took a bite. She ate with more enthusiasm than Ttomalss felt. "Do you recall the Deutsch pilot who attacked your ship during the war between the *Reich* and the Race? I flew him back down to Tosev 3. His name was Drucker."

"I did not recall the name. I recall the Big Ugly." Ttomalss used an emphatic cough. "What about him?"

"*His* hatchling belonged to one of the bandit groups the Deutsche set up after their defeat to resist the Race covertly," Nesseref said.

"Wait." Ttomalss let out a sharp hiss. "There was a Big Ugly called Drucker who served as the *Reich*'s minister for air and space when the Deutsche began to admit they had such a position again."

"That is the same male," Nesseref said. "He was good at what he did, and cautious about putting his fingerclaws where they did not belong. His hatchling later rose to a high rank in the military of the *Reich*."

"A pity the Deutsche never quite gave us the excuse to suppress them altogether," Ttomalss said.

"A great pity," Nesseref agreed. "But then, one could say the same about the rest of the Tosevites. They were trouble enough when they managed to come to Home by any means at all. Now that their technology has got ahead of ours . . ." She didn't go on. She didn't have to, either.

Ttomalss made the affirmative gesture. He said, "We are

doing what we can to catch up with them." He didn't go on, either. The wild Big Uglies were too likely to monitor what went on in the refectory.

Nesseref might not have realized that. But she did grasp the problem facing the Race, for she asked, "Can we endure until we do?"

"I hope so," Ttomalss answered. "As you say, the Americans do approach civilization, at any rate." He didn't think the Big Uglies would be offended to hear that. They already knew what he and most members of the Race thought of them. But, as Nesseref had pointed out, the Americans were not the only Big Uglies. "As for the Deutsche . . . well, if they attack us here on Home, our colony can strike back at them as soon as it learns of what they have done—and either the Deutsche themselves or the Americans would bring word to Tosev 3 before our signals got there. The *Reich* is not large. It is vulnerable. Its not-emperor must realize this."

" 'Must' is a large word to use when speaking of Big Uglies," Nesseref said. "But I dare hope you are right."

"So do I," Ttomalss said. "So do I."

When the Big Uglies decided it was time for Atvar to return to his own solar system, they didn't fly him back on the *Commodore Perry*. The starship setting out for Home this time was called the *Tom Edison*. That the United States had built more than one ship that traveled faster than light worried him. The Race would have refined the first one till it was exactly the way they wanted it before making more. Tosevites didn't worry about refinement. They just went ahead and did things.

And . . . it worked.

He did ask who Tom Edison was. Learning that the Big Ugly had been an inventor came as a small relief. At least they weren't naming all these ships for warriors. He didn't know how much that said about their intentions, but it did say *something*.

Sam Yeager came to the hotel room where he'd been politely and comfortably imprisoned to say good-bye. "I am surprised they let you in to see me," Atvar said. "Do they not fear you will relay the secret orders I do not have to Reffet and

Kirel, and so touch off our colony's attack on your not-empire?"

"Some of them were afraid of that, yes," the white-haired Big Ugly answered. "I managed to persuade them otherwise. It was not easy, but I managed. We have known each other a long time, you and I. We are not on the same side, but we are not enemies, either. Or I hope we are not."

"Not through my eye turrets," Atvar said. "And who knows? Maybe we shall see each other again. Now that cold sleep is no longer necessary—for your folk, anyhow—it could happen."

"Well, so it could," Yeager said. "If not for cold sleep, though, I would have died a long time ago. Even with it, who knows how much time I have?" He followed the interrogative cough with a shrug. "However long it is, I aim to try to make the most of it. Will you do me a favor when you get back to Home?"

"If it is anything I can do, I will," Atvar replied.

"I thank you. I think you can. Send Kassquit my best, and my hatchling's."

"It shall be done," Atvar said. "Shall I also add a greeting from your hatchling's mate?"

Sam Yeager laughed in the noisy Tosevite way. "If you like," he answered. "But she would not send it, and Kassquit would not believe it if she got it. The two females did not get along as well as they might have."

"This is unfortunate," Atvar said. "Well, I think I will send it. Perhaps being light-years apart can bring peace between them."

"Perhaps it can," Yeager said. "I cannot think of anything else that would."

The fleetlord endured another ride in a Tosevite-made shuttlecraft with a Big Ugly at the controls. The hop up to the orbiting *Tom Edison* was as smooth as it would have been going up to a ship orbiting Home. The pilot seemed perfectly capable. Atvar was nervous even so. Tosevites just didn't take proper care in the things they made.

But they made things the Race couldn't. The looming bulk of the *Tom Edison* as the shuttlecraft approached rubbed Atvar's snout in that. "I greet you, Exalted Fleetlord," a uniformed American Big Ugly said when Atvar came through the air lock. "Let me take you to your room."

"I thank you," Atvar replied.

"It is my pleasure, Exalted Fleetlord," the Tosevite male said. Atvar didn't care for the way his title sounded in the Big Ugly's mouth. Like Nicole Nichols back on Home, the male didn't take it seriously.

Atvar stared as he followed the guide. Not being under acceleration, the ship had no gravity, and they both pulled themselves along by the handholds in the corridors. The *Tom Edison* struck Atvar as being better finished than the *Commodore Perry*. If the Race hadn't been satisfied with the *Commodore Perry,* the ship never would have flown. The Big Uglies let it go out, hoped for the best, and improved the next one. Their way produced more progress—and, every now and then, disasters the Race would not have tolerated.

"Here we are," the Tosevite said. "This room will be yours. Please stay here until we are under acceleration. You can access entertainment in your language through the computer. Food will be brought to you. If you want any special refreshments, you may request them."

"But in the meanwhile, I am a prisoner," Atvar said.

The Big Ugly used the negative gesture. "A guest."

Atvar used it, too. "If I were a guest, I would be able to move freely."

With a shrug, the American Tosevite said, "I am sorry, Exalted Fleetlord, but I have my orders." He sounded not the least bit sorry.

When Atvar tried the door after going inside, he discovered it would open, which surprised him. He wasn't quite a prisoner, then. That made him decide to stay where he was. He would have caused more trouble—as much as he could—if he had been locked up. Not till later did he wonder whether the Big Uglies would anticipate that.

A day and a half later, it stopped mattering. With a deep rumble he felt in his bones, the *Tom Edison* left its place in orbit and began the journey out to where it could leap the gap between Tosev 3's solar system and the one of which Home was a part. Full acceleration took a while to build up. Atvar thought he was a trifle heavier than he had been aboard the *Commodore Perry,* but he could not be sure.

One of the first Big Uglies he saw on emerging from his chamber was Frank Coffey. His dark skin made him easy to recognize. His leaf emblem had changed color, which meant he was a lieutenant colonel now. "So you are returning to Home?" Atvar said.

"That is a truth, Exalted Fleetlord. I am," Coffey said. "I managed to talk my government into sending me back. I would like to be with Kassquit when my hatchling comes forth—and I have more experience on Home than anyone there now."

While the second reason would have influenced the Race, the first was exclusive to the Big Uglies. Atvar did not know who had sired him or who had laid his egg. Except for the Emperor's line and the possibility of inherited diseases, such things mattered little to the Race.

"It will be good, I think, for the American Tosevites on Home to have someone from your generation there with them," Atvar said. "I mean no offense—or not much, anyhow—when I say they make too much of themselves."

"I have no idea whether they will pay any attention to me once I get there." Coffey sounded wryly amused. Atvar thought so, anyhow, though Big Uglies could still confuse him. The American officer went on, "My government says they are supposed to, but even with these new ships my government is a long way away." He shrugged. "Well, we shall see what we shall see. However that works out, I am going back to Home, and I will be there when the hatchling comes forth."

We shall see what we shall see. Atvar thought about that after he went back to his room. It was a truth, but not, for him, a comfortable one. What he feared he would see, if he lived long enough, was the ruination of his species. And he did not know what he could do to stop it.

The journey back to Home was as boring as the one to Tosev 3 had been. Part of him hoped the *Tom Edison* would have a mishap, even if it killed him. Then he wouldn't have to admit to everyone on Home that he'd crossed between stars twice in much less than a year, even counting the time he'd spent on the Big Uglies' native world waiting for them to get ready to send him back.

Was it five and a half weeks till the starship got ready to jump the light-years? Again, Atvar thought not, but he wasn't quite sure. He had to translate the awkward Tosevite term into the Race's rational chronology to have any feel for how long it truly was. He hadn't kept exact track on the journey to Tosev 3, so he couldn't properly compare now. Not keeping track had been a mistake. He realized as much, but he didn't see how he could have avoided it. He'd assumed he would go back on the same starship, not a revised model. As the Race so often was in its dealings with the Big Uglies, he'd been wrong.

When the time for the crossing came, the captain warned everyone in the ship to take a seat: first in English, then in the Race's language. Atvar obeyed. For most of the travelers, it wouldn't matter. Most Tosevites felt nothing. That seemed to be true for the Race, too; at least, neither Straha nor Nesseref had reported anything out of the ordinary.

Then that turned-inside-out feeling interrupted his thoughts. It lasted for a timeless instant that seemed to stretch out longer than the history of the Empire. He was everything and nothing, nowhere and everywhere, all at once. And then it ended—if it had ever really begun—and he was nothing but himself again. He didn't know whether to be sorry or glad.

The captain spoke in English. Atvar waited for the translation: "We are inside Home's solar system. Everything performed the way it should have. We expect a normal approach to the Race's planet."

Two ships. No—at least two ships. How many more did the Big Uglies have? They surely knew. Just as surely, Atvar didn't. Were they visiting Rabotev 2 or Halless 1 even now? If they were, they would outrun news of their coming. They would find the Empire's other two worlds undefended. They could do whatever they wanted. Home wouldn't learn of it for years, not unless the Tosevites themselves chose to talk about it.

We shall see what we shall see, he thought again. Whatever it was, he couldn't do anything about it now.

He knew when the *Tom Edison* went into orbit around

Home, because he went weightless. Before long, a Tosevite female came to escort him to the air lock. "We will take you down to Sitneff now, Exalted Fleetlord," she said.

"I thank you so very much," Atvar replied.

If she heard his sarcasm, she didn't show it. "You are welcome," she said. "I hope you had a pleasant flight." Atvar didn't dignify that with an answer. A hundred thousand years of peace, security, and dominance shattering like glass—and she hoped he had a pleasant flight? Not likely!

His shuttlecraft trip down to the surface of Home was routine in every way, and also less than pleasant. So was the discovery that Straha waited for him in the shuttlecraft terminal. "I greet you, Exalted Fleetlord," Straha said, and bent into a mocking posture of respect. "I trust you enjoyed yourself on Tosev 3?"

"Then you are a trusting fool," Atvar snapped. "I knew you were a fool, but not one of that sort."

Straha only laughed at him. "Still charming as ever, I see. Any residual doubts remaining? The signals arriving from Tosev 3 would kill them, if there are."

"No, no residual doubts," Atvar said. "They can do as they claim."

"And that means?"

Hating him, Atvar said, "It means you are not only a trusting fool but a gloating fool." Straha just laughed again.

Bruce Yeager had settled his parents into a two-bedroom apartment in Torrance, not far from where they'd lived before going into cold sleep. The furniture, or most of it, was even their own; the government had stored it against the off chance they'd come back. The stove and the refrigerator were new, and much more efficient than the ones they replaced.

Jonathan Yeager didn't much care about efficiency. What mattered to him was that Karen should like them. She did.

Also new was the computer. The one that had gone into storage was a hopeless antique. This one . . . This one would do everything but tie Jonathan's shoes. As a matter of fact, it could do that, too, if he fitted it with a waldo attachment. Such things were common and cheap these days. They made life closer to tolerable for handicapped people, and had countless industrial uses besides.

Before very long, Jonathan realized he was a handicapped person in this Los Angeles. He knew exactly what his handicap was, too: he was missing almost forty years. Knowing didn't help. He had no idea how to fix it.

When he complained, Karen said, "It's nothing we have to worry about right away. We may be missing the years, but we're not missing the money from them. We won't miss any meals, either—I promise you that."

"I know," he said. "But I don't want to sit back and twiddle my thumbs the rest of my life. I want to do something useful, and it doesn't look like anything I can do is useful any more."

"We both still know the Race well," Karen said.

He shook his head. "Here, we *knew* the Race well. We know it well on Home. We're up to date there. We're most of a lifetime behind here. Who'd want to pay us to catch up?"

Karen started to say something, but she didn't. Jonathan had a pretty good idea of what she'd swallowed. Yes, their son would doubtless put them on his payroll. That stuck in Jonathan's craw. He didn't think he'd mind working for Bruce. But he would mind getting a sinecure, and anything he would do would only be worth a sinecure.

"I think I'd rather try to write my memoirs," he said. "They'd be up to the minute—well, pretty close, now—and I can tell a story hardly anybody else will ever be able to."

"Can you do it well enough to get people to pay money for it?" Karen said. "I've been asking myself the same question."

"We've both done plenty of writing," Jonathan answered. "We ought to try, anyhow. I think we can do it." He managed a wry grin. "It's our story. What could be more interesting to us than we are?"

"To us, yeah," Karen said. "How about to anyone else?"

"All we can do is give it our best shot." Jonathan laughed out loud. "Maybe we should ask Mickey who his literary agent is."

"Yes, I think we should," Karen said, and she wasn't laughing at all. She sounded bleak, in fact, as she went on, "For one thing, that may help us. For another, Mickey doesn't hate us—or if he does, he's more polite about it than Donald."

"He gives us more credit for doing the best we could." Jonathan wondered how good that best had been. "I think we did better with them than Ttomalss did with Kassquit."

"Not a fair comparison," Karen said. "We knew a lot more about the Race when we started than Ttomalss did about us when *he* started. And Mickey and Donald had each other for company. That had to help, too." Jonathan might have known his wife wouldn't cut Kassquit any slack. But then Karen surprised him by adding, "She'll have her baby before too long."

"So she will," Jonathan said. "I think Frank was smart to go back: over there, he's not behind the times. He helped make the arrangements the new people are dealing with."

"The new people." Karen tasted the phrase. "They really do feel like that, don't they? Like they just started out and everything's ahead of them, I mean. Even when they're our age, they've got that feel to them. I don't know whether to be jealous or to want to pound some sense into their stupid heads."

"They're like the people who went West in covered wagons," Jonathan said. "They can taste the wide open spaces in front of them. And do they ever have them! Jesus! Light-year after light-year of wide open spaces. No wonder they've got that look in their eye and they don't want to pay any attention to us. We're the city slickers who just want to stay back in Philly—and that even though we went traveling."

"Yeah." His wife nodded. "What we did hardly counts these days. It was all the Lizards had for all those thousands of years. It's still all they have. And it's as obsolete as we are."

Jonathan nodded, too. "Melanie will have to go back to school if she wants to keep on being a doctor. They know so much more now than they did when she went on ice. Tom and Linda are as out of date as we are. And Dad's got it even worse. He's older, and he spent all those extra years in cold sleep."

"I think he'll do fine, though, once he gets his feet on the ground," Karen said. "He's had to adapt before. Look how much things changed for him when the Lizards came, but he did okay then. Better than okay, in fact."

"Hope you're right," Jonathan answered. Again, he didn't much feel like arguing with his wife. He didn't have much from which to argue: only the lost look he thought he saw in his father's eyes. He suspected his old man would have indignantly denied it if anyone called him on it. He also suspected the denial would mean nothing, or maybe a little less. Instead of arguing, Jonathan said, "Want to go to a movie tonight?"

"Sure," Karen said, and then, with a wry smile of her own, "This is supposed to help us fit into the here-and-now?"

"Well . . . It depends on which one we pick," Jonathan said. When he and Karen were dating, films showed things they hadn't when his father was a young man. When his sons started taking girls out, films showed things they hadn't in his day. The trend hadn't slowed down while he and Karen went to Home and back. A lot of what ordinary people lined up to see now would have been blue movies in the 1960s.

They didn't have drive-ins any more, either. Jonathan had fond memories of the one on Vermont, but apartment buildings stood where the lot and the big screen had been. Boys and girls these days didn't seem to feel the lack, so they must have had other ways to find privacy when they wanted it.

Karen flipped through the *Los Angeles Times*. Just about all the photos and ads in the paper were in color, which they hadn't been in 1994. "We don't want the sappy kiddy shows," she said. "Those are just as bad as they ever were, maybe worse." Jonathan didn't argue with that, either. She pointed to one movie ad and started to giggle. "Here. *The Curse of Rhodes*. A horror flick. How can they mess that up?"

"Isn't that why we're going?" Jonathan asked. Karen raised an eyebrow. He explained: "To find out how they can mess it up."

"Oh." Karen laughed. "Sure. But we know from the start that this is hokum." She pointed to the ad again. A bronze statue strode across what was presumably the Aegean with a naked girl in its arms. A few wisps of her long blond hair kept things technically decent.

"Works for me," Jonathan said solemnly. Karen made the kind of noise that meant she would clobber him if she weren't such an enlightened, tolerant wife: a noise only a little less effective than a real set of lumps would have been. Jonathan mimed a whiplash injury and pointed out, "You were the one who suggested it."

"Well, let's go," she said. "We can always throw popcorn at the screen if it gets too awful." She paused. "We may pick different times."

"Here's hoping," Jonathan said, and laughed when she made a face at him.

Most of the people buying tickets for the movie were in their teens or twenties. Most of the ones who weren't had ten- or twelve-year-old boys in tow. Jonathan and Karen looked at each other, as if to ask, *What are we getting ourselves into?* They both started to laugh. Maybe a really bad horror movie was just what they needed.

Jonathan bought popcorn and candy and Cokes. The smells of the concession stand hadn't changed a bit since before he went into cold sleep. Prices had, but not too badly. Even back then, theaters had gouged people on snacks.

The slope of the rows of seats was steeper than it had been back in a twentieth-century theater. That let each seat have a proper back without interfering with children's views of the screen. Some unknown genius had thought of putting a cup holder in each armrest. The rows were father apart than they had been; Jonathan could stretch out his feet. He closed his eyes. "Good night."

"If you can't stay awake to leer at the naked girls, don't expect me to shake you," Karen said. He sat up very straight. She poked him.

Down went the lights. There were more ads and fewer coming attractions than Jonathan remembered. Maybe that meant he was turning into a curmudgeon. But, by body time, it hadn't been that long ago, so maybe the folks who ran things were trying harder to squeeze money out of people. The sound was louder than he remembered, too. He had as much trouble enjoying the music as his father had had with what he'd listened to when he was young.

That same pounding, noisy beat suffused *The Curse of Rhodes*. For a while, he hardly noticed it. The special effects were astonishing. A lot of them would have been impossible, or impossibly expensive, in the twentieth century. Computers could do all sorts of things that had been beyond them in those days.

And then Jonathan noticed something that wasn't a special effect. He stared at the elderly archaeologist who was trying to calm the frightened young hero and heroine—and who was bound to come to a Bad End before long. "Look at that guy," he whispered to Karen. "I'll be damned if that's not Matt Damon."

She eyed the actor. "My God! You're right. He used to be just a little older than our kids—and he still is." She squeezed his hand. "We've been away a long time."

The Curse of Rhodes showed that in other ways, too. The violence was one thing. Gore and horror movies went together like pepperoni and pizza. But some of the doings between the hero, the heroine, and the resurrected, bad-tempered Colossus of Rhodes . . . Jonathan wouldn't have taken a ten-year-old to see them in 1994. He wasn't so sure he would have gone himself. The heroine was either a natural blonde or very thorough. She was also limber enough for an

Olympic gymnast, though he didn't think they gave gold medals in *that*.

As the Colossus sank beneath the waves—gone for good or ready to return in a sequel, depending on how *The Curse of Rhodes* did—and the credits rolled, the house lights came up. "What did you think?" Karen asked.

"I know what the curse of Rhodes is now," Jonathan said. "The screenwriter, or maybe the director." Karen stuck out her tongue at him. He went on, "It was really dumb and really gory and really dirty."

She nodded. "That's what we came for."

Was it? Jonathan wasn't so sure. He thought they'd come not least to try to forge some link between the time in which they'd lived and the one in which they found themselves. The movie hadn't done it—not for him, anyhow. Instead, it reminded him over and over what a stranger he was here and now. With a shrug, he started for the parking lot. Maybe time would help. Maybe nothing would. He'd have to find out day by day, that was all.

Some things didn't change. The building in downtown Los Angeles where Sam Yeager faced a colonel who'd been born about the time he left for Tau Ceti was the one where he'd worked a generation before that, before he got saddled with the responsibility for Mickey and Donald. The office furniture hadn't changed much, either. He wondered whether that battered metal desk could possibly date from the 1960s.

Colonel Goldschmidt said, "No, you are not permitted to see any Lizards. You might pass intelligence from Fleetlord Atvar to them."

You bureaucratic idiot. Sam didn't say it. He was ever so tempted, but he didn't. *What a good boy am I,* he thought, even if he didn't have a plum on his thumb. Clinging to shreds of patience, he said, "Colonel, you or somebody gave me permission to see Atvar. I'm sure you or somebody listened to what we said. If I'd wanted to do that, I could have gone to a pay phone the minute I got out of his hotel room."

"But you didn't do that. You didn't telephone any Lizards from your place of residence, either." Goldschmidt had a narrow face with cold blue eyes set too close together. He wore a wedding ring, which proved somebody loved him. Sam wondered why.

"So you've been monitoring me," he said. Goldschmidt nodded. Sam asked, "If you people thought I was that big a menace, why did you let me see him in the first place?"

"There were discussions about that," Goldschmidt replied. He gave no details. Even though the discussions had been about Yeager, the hatchet-faced colonel's view was that they were none of his business. "It was decided that the risk was acceptable."

It was decided. Maybe that meant God had sent down a choir of angels with the answer. More likely, it meant no one wanted to admit he'd done the deciding. No, some things didn't change. Sam said, "Seems to me you people didn't think this through as well as you might have. Now that I *have* seen Atvar, how are you going to keep me away from Lizards for the rest of my life? When I take an elevator down to the lobby and walk out on the street, it's better than even money that I bump into one, or two, or three. We're only a few blocks from the Race's consulate, you know."

Colonel Goldschmidt looked as if his stomach pained him. "I have my orders, Mr. Yeager. You are not permitted to travel to any territory occupied by the Race or to contact any members of the Race."

"Then you can lock me up and throw away the key"—Sam was careful to use the human idiom, not the Lizards'—"because I've already done it."

"What? Where? How?" Now Goldschmidt looked horrified. Had something slipped past him and his stooges?

"My adopted sons—Mickey and Donald," Sam said.

"Oh. Them." Relief made the colonel's voice sound amazingly human for a moment. "They don't count. They're U.S. citizens, and are considered reliable."

"What about other Lizards who are U.S. citizens? There are lots of them." Sam took a certain malicious glee in being difficult.

"As we have not made determinations as to their reliability, they are off-limits for you at this point in time," Colonel Goldschmidt said.

Yeager got to his feet. He gave Goldschmidt his sweetest smile. "No."

"I beg your pardon?"

"It's a technical term meaning, well, no," Sam answered. "I suppose you can keep me from leaving the country if you don't issue me a passport—Lord knows my old one's expired. But if I want to see old friends, I will. Or if I bump into a Lizard on the street, I'll talk to him. You may decide you made a mistake letting me see Atvar, but you went and did it. You can't very well unpoach the egg."

"There will be repercussions from this," Goldschmidt warned.

"That's what I just told you," Sam said. "You people forgot there would be repercussions when you let me see Atvar, and now you're trying to get around them. If you really thought I was a traitor, you shouldn't have let me do it. If you don't think I am, why can't I see other Lizards? You can't have it both ways, you know."

By Goldschmidt's expression, he wanted to. He said, "I am going to have to refer this to my superiors."

"That's nice," Sam said. "Meanwhile, I'm going to do what I think is right." He'd been doing that for a long time. *Yeah, and look at the thanks I've got,* he thought.

He got some more now. "The last time you did what you thought was right"—Goldschmidt all but spat the words at him—"it cost us Indianapolis."

"Fuck you, Colonel," Sam said evenly. "The horse you rode in on, too." He walked out of Goldschmidt's office. As he headed for the elevators, he wondered if the Army man would shout for MPs to head him off. He'd already been held incommunicado once in his life, and hadn't enjoyed it much. The real irony was that he'd told Goldschmidt the exact and literal truth. Atvar hadn't given him any message to pass on to the Lizards here on Earth, and he wouldn't have done it if the fleetlord had. He was and always had been loyal to his country, in spite of what seemed to be his country's best efforts to make him change his mind.

No shouts came from behind him. He stabbed at the elevator's DOWN button with unnecessary violence even so, and clenched his fists while waiting for a car to arrive. Part of him, the part that kept forgetting he wasn't a kid any more, *wanted* a fight. The rest of him knew that was idiotic; one soldier in the prime of youth could clean his clock without breaking a sweat, let alone two or three or four. All the same, the sigh that escaped him when the elevator door opened held disappointment as well as relief.

Sure as hell, Lizards were on the streets when Sam headed for the parking structure a couple of blocks away. They seemed as natural to him as the Hispanic men selling plastic bags of oranges and the British tourists festooned with cameras who exclaimed about how hot it was. That made him want to laugh; after Home, Los Angeles seemed exceedingly temperate to him.

One of the Lizards almost bumped into him. "Excuse me," the Lizard said in hissing English.

"It is all right. You missed me," Yeager answered in the Race's language. He grinned fiercely; he'd taken less than a minute to violate Colonel Goldschmidt's order, and he loved doing it.

The Lizard's mouth fell open in a startled laugh. "You speak well," he said in his own language. "Please excuse me. I am very late." Off he skittered, for all the world like a scaly White Rabbit.

"I thank you," Sam called after him, but he didn't think the Lizard heard. He was tempted to yell something like, *Rosebud!* at the male just in case sitting in Goldschmidt's chair had been enough to plant a listening device on him. That would give the Army conniptions, by God! In the end, though, he kept his mouth shut. He didn't want, or didn't suppose he wanted, to make these moderns any more paranoid than they were already.

His car was a three-year-old Ford. It wasn't enormously different from the ones he'd owned before he went on ice. The styling was plainer—real streamlining had taken a lot of individuality out of design. One year's models nowadays looked like another's, and one company's like another's, too. The engine was smoother. The radio sounded better. But making cars had been a mature technology even in 1977. The changes were refinements, not fundamentals. He had no trouble driving it.

Traffic was worse than he remembered. The Los Angeles area had more than twice as many people as when he'd gone into cold sleep, and it didn't have more than twice as many freeways. Too many cars were trying to use the roads at the same time. But things did thin out as he rode down to the South Bay.

His apartment wasn't far from the one where Karen and Jonathan were living. That was convenient for them in case he got sick. It was also convenient for him: they were two of the very few people he could talk to in any meaningful way. Where cold sleep separated him from the vast majority of mankind, it had brought him closer to his son and daughter-in-law because he'd been in it longer than they had.

"I meant it, Colonel Goldschmidt—you and the horse both," he said when he walked in the door. He assumed the apartment was bugged. What could he do about it? Nothing he could see.

He sat at the computer for a while. Like Jonathan and Karen, he was working on his memoirs. He wondered if anyone would want to read his once he finished. Very few people these days remembered how things had been back in the 1960s. Instead, they knew what they'd learned in school about that time. What they'd learned in school wasn't kind to one Sam Yeager.

He shrugged and typed some more. If he couldn't persuade an American publisher to print the work, he could still sell translation rights to the Race. The Lizards would want to hear what he had to say even if his own people didn't. And faster-than-light travel might mean he could sell the rights not only on Earth but also on Home, Rabotev 2, and Halless 1—and see the money now instead of in the great by and by. That would be nice. He had no guarantee he'd be around for the great by and by. Odds were against it, in fact.

He jumped when the telephone rang. He'd got used to phones on Home that hissed. And he was going well at the keyboard. He said something unkind as he walked over and picked it up. "Hello?"

"Hello, Sam. This is Lacey Nagel." Mickey's literary agent had taken him on, and Jonathan and Karen as well. He hadn't met her in person, but gathered she was about the apparent age of his son and daughter-in-law. She'd been, or at least seemed, more optimistic about the project than he was. Some of that, no doubt, was professional necessity; an agent who wasn't optimistic wouldn't stay in business. But Sam hoped some was real.

"Hi, Lacey," he answered now. "What's up?"

"We have a deal with Random House," she said crisply. Sam's jaw dropped. Then she told him how much it was for. His jaw dropped farther, all the way down onto his chest. "I hope that's satisfactory," she finished.

"My God," he said, and she laughed out loud. He tried to come up with something more coherent. The best he could do was, "How did you manage that?"

"Well, I didn't do anything to the acquiring editor that left a mark," she said, which made him laugh in turn. She went on, "They're excited about it, in fact. They must be, or they wouldn't have made that offer. They said it was high time you told your own story."

He couldn't very well have told it before this unless he'd done it before he went into cold sleep. That hadn't even occurred to him back then. Now the book would feel like history to everybody who read it. "My God," he repeated.

"I hope that means you're pleased," Lacey Nagel said.

"I'm more than pleased—I'm flabbergasted," Sam told her.

"Now there's a word I haven't heard in a while," she said.

"I'm not surprised," Sam said without rancor. "I know the way I talk is old-fashioned as all get-out these days." Saying *all get-out* was old-fashioned these days, too.

"Don't worry about it," Lacey said. "No matter how you say it, what you have to say will be right up to the minute."

"I hope so." He still felt a little—more than a little—dizzy. "I was working on it when you called."

"Oh-oh!" she said. "That means you want to wring my neck for interrupting you."

He shook his head. Lacey Nagel couldn't see that; his phone didn't have a video attachment, which only proved how old-fashioned he was. "Oh, no," he said. "If you've got news like that, you can call me any old time. Thank you. I don't think I said that before. Thank you!" He added an emphatic cough. When he walked back to the computer, his feet didn't touch the carpet once.

Karen Yeager walked softly around Jonathan. The two of them and Sam Yeager all had book deals now, but Jonathan's dad had got his more than a month before either one of them. That didn't bother her much. But she could see how it got under her husband's skin. She laughed at herself. She'd almost thought of it as getting under Jonathan's scales—proof, as if she needed proof, she'd spent too much time around the Race.

Jonathan hadn't said much about the way he felt, but he didn't need to. Spells of alternating gloom and bad temper said it for him. He'd come in second to his old man again, and he didn't like it one damn bit.

Hearing the doorbell came as a relief. "Who's that? What does he want?" Jonathan said, grumpy still.

"One easy way to find out." Karen opened the door. "Oh, hello, Mickey! Come in."

"Thanks," Mickey said. Karen waved him to a chair. They'd bought a couple adapted to a Lizard's shape. But Mickey sat down in an ordinary armchair. "I'm more used to these damn things." He swung one eye turret toward Karen, the other toward Jonathan. "And whose fault is that?"

"Well, we could blame the federal government," Karen said. "It's a handy target—and it is where Jonathan's dad got your eggs."

Mickey shook his head. He did that as naturally as most Lizards shaped the negative gesture. "Too big a target. I need to blame *people,* not a thing."

"We've already apologized," Jonathan said. "There's not much else we can do about it now. And you'll have the last laugh—even with our cold sleep, odds are you'll outlive us by plenty."

"Your father already told me the same thing," Mickey said. Most of the time, that would have been fine. Now . . . Now, Jonathan made a noise down deep in his throat. He didn't want to hear that his father had got there ahead of him one more time. Mickey went on, "Yeah, I'll live a long time. But what will I live *as*? A curiosity? Hell, I'm a curiosity even to myself."

"Would you like to be a curiosity with a drink?" Karen asked.

"Sure. Rum and Coke," Mickey said. As she went to the kitchen, he added, "You Yeagers, all of you, you're my family—all the family I've got, except for Donald. The only problem with that is, I shouldn't have *any* family, and if I did have a family, it shouldn't be full of humans."

Karen brought him the drink, and scotch for her and Jonathan. "Well, we'll try not to hold it against you," she said.

Both his eye turrets turned sharply toward her. Then he realized she was joking, and chuckled—a rusty imitation of the noise a human would make. "Donald would have bitten you for that," he said, sipping.

"Donald may resent people, but he's piled up a hell of a lot of money making them laugh," Jonathan said.

Mickey shrugged. "I've piled up a hell of a lot of money, too. I've got nothing against money—don't get me wrong. Life's better with it than without it. But Donald was right about what he told you the day you came down from the *Commodore Perry*—the fellow who said it can't buy happiness knew what he was talking about. That makes Donald angrier than it does me. Instead of biting them, he makes them laugh—and then he laughs at them for laughing at him."

Jonathan caught Karen's eye. He nodded slightly. So did she. That made more sense than she wished it did. It also went a long way towards explaining the urgency of Donald's performance on *You'd Better Believe It*. Something not far from desperation surely fueled it.

"Do you laugh at us, too?" Karen asked.

"Sometimes. Not quite so often. I still want to be one of you more than Donald does," Mickey answered. "Yeah, I know that's silly, but it's how I was raised. I speak English as well as I can with this mouth, but I have an accent when I use the Race's language. Ain't that a kick in the head?"

"Kassquit speaks the Race's language as well as she can with her mouth," Jonathan said. "It's the only one she knows. She never learned any of ours."

"That's a damn shame." Mickey added an emphatic cough,

but a lot of human English-speakers these days would have done the same thing. "You could have done worse. I've never said anything different. Donald may have—but Donald doesn't always even take himself seriously, so why should you?"

Before either Karen or Jonathan could answer, the doorbell rang again. "Grand Central Station around here," Karen said. When she opened the door, she found Donald out there on the walkway. "Well! What can I do for you?" .

"May I come in?" he asked. "Please?" Mockery danced in his voice.

"Of course." Karen stepped aside. "You're always welcome here. We're not angry at you. We never have been, no matter what you've decided to think about us."

"How . . . Christian of you." That was more mockery, now flaying rather than dancing. But Donald started slightly when he saw Mickey. "Ah, my Siamese twin. The only Lizard on four planets as screwed up as I am—except he won't admit it."

"Oh, I admit it," Mickey said. "How could I do anything else? It's true, for Christ's sake. The difference is, I don't think we can do anything about it now, and I don't think there's much point to getting upset about the way it happened."

"Why not? They're to blame." Donald pointed to Karen and Jonathan. "Them and old Sam."

"We'll take some of the blame for the way you turned out—some, but not all," Jonathan said. "You have to blame yourself, too."

"Don't hold your breath," Mickey said. Donald let out an angry hiss. Like some of the purely human noises Kassquit made when she was furious or surprised, that one seemed instinctive in the Race.

"Can I fix you a drink to go with everyone else's?" Karen asked Donald. She gave him her sweetest smile. "No need to check it for rat poison, I promise."

"Meow," he said. "Most of the time, I get paid for being rude—though there are some people for whom I'd do it for nothing. I'd love one, thanks. Whatever he's having." He pointed to Mickey's rum and Coke. "You Yeagers made damn sure our tastes would be the same, didn't you?"

"In a word, no," Karen answered over her shoulder as she

went back into the kitchen. "It did work out that way a lot of the time, but not always. It often does with two brothers, especially when they're the same age."

"Brothers? How do you know we're brothers?" Donald said. "All we were when you got us was a couple of eggs. They could have come from anywhere—from two different anywheres. For all you know, they did."

Now Karen and Jonathan looked at each other in consternation. They and Jonathan's father had always assumed the eggs they'd got from the government came from the same female. Karen realized Donald was right: they had exactly zero proof of that. She wondered if the people who'd got the eggs from the Lizards had any idea whether they belonged together. After seventy years, she couldn't very well ask. Odds were none of those people was still alive.

"If you want to know bad enough, there's genetic testing," Jonathan said.

"I've talked about it. The Race thinks I'm some kind of a pervert for caring one way or the other," Donald answered. "But I *do* care—and there's one more thing that's your fault. I'm a goddamn human being with scales, that's what I am. I already told you I watch Rita's tits, didn't I? Yeah, I thought so. I shouldn't give a damn. I know I shouldn't give a damn. But I do. I can't help it. It's how I was raised. Thanks a lot, both of you." He raised his glass in a scornful salute, then gulped the drink.

"I watch women, too," Mickey confessed. "I keep thinking they're what I ought to want even though I can't really want anything unless I smell a female's pheromones. Even then, half of me thinks I ought to be mating with a pretty girl, not with a Lizard."

Oh, Lord. They're even more screwed up than Kassquit is, Karen thought miserably. As far as she knew, Kassquit had never wanted to lie down with a Lizard. But then, the Race didn't parade sex out in front of everybody and use it to sell everything from soap to station wagons the way people did. Except during mating season, Lizards were indifferent—and after mating season, they tried to pretend it hadn't happened. With humans, the titillation was always out there. Mickey and

Donald had responded to it even if they couldn't respond to it . . . and if that wasn't screwed up, what the devil would be?

Donald thrust his glass out to her. "May I have a refill, please?" Now he didn't even give her the excuse of rudeness to say no.

"All right." She wasn't all that sorry for a chance to retreat.

"We do have a lot to answer for. I know that," Jonathan said. "We went ahead even after we knew what Kassquit was like. That should have warned us—it *did* warn us. But we went ahead anyway."

Mickey slid a sly eye turret in Donald's direction. "Don't beat yourselves up about it too much. For all you know, he would have been crazy if the Lizards raised him, too."

Donald used a negative gesture that didn't come from the Race but that nobody in the USA was likely to misunderstand. "You just give them excuses," he snarled.

"Enough!" Karen said suddenly. "Enough with all of this. We did what we did. It wasn't perfect. It couldn't have been, by the nature of things. But it was the best we knew how to do. And it's over. We can't take it back. If you want to hate us for what we did, Donald, go right ahead. We can't do anything about that, either."

"Well, well." If anything ever fazed Donald, he didn't let it show. "And I thought I was the one with the sharp teeth." Letting his lower jaw drop, he showed off a mouthful of them. "Aren't you afraid I'll make nasty jokes about you on the show?"

"Go ahead, if that's what you want to do," Karen answered. "They'll make you look worse than they do us, and you'll just give me more juicy bits for my book. Or would you rather I put you over my knee and paddled you?"

She hadn't done that since Donald was *much* smaller. Sometimes, as with human children, it had been the only way to get his attention. He rose now with what might have been anger or dignity. "No, thanks," he said. "However messed up I am, I don't take pain for pleasure."

"Take it, no," Karen said. "Give it . . . ?"

Donald spun and sped out of the apartment. He didn't even slam the door behind him. "Congratulations, I think," Mickey said. "I've never seen anybody do that to him before."

Karen got herself another scotch. As she put ice cubes into the whiskey, she said, "I don't want congratulations. I want to go back into the bedroom and cry. Rip van Winkle didn't know what to do when he woke up, either, and we were asleep a lot longer than he was."

"O brave new world, that has such difficult people in't!" Jonathan misquoted.

"Now that you mention it, yes." Karen turned to Mickey. "Nothing personal."

He shook his head. "It's all personal. If it weren't, you wouldn't be so upset."

He was right, of course, and Karen knew it. She'd thought they could come back to America and fit in better than they'd managed in the few months since they'd come down from the *Commodore Perry*. Maybe things would improve as time went by. She hoped so. It wasn't the country she'd left close to forty years earlier. She hadn't changed, and it had, and she had trouble getting used to it. Who was right? Was she, for thinking things had been fine the way they were? Was the rest of the country, for going on about its business without her? Was it even a question of right and wrong, or just one of differences? She knew she'd be looking for answers the rest of her life.

The refectory was the only chamber in the *Admiral Peary* big enough to gather most of the crew together. Even Lieutenant General Healey came to hear the presentation by the officer from the *Tom Edison*. Seeing Healey's bulky form did nothing to delight Glen Johnson, but he stayed as far away from the commandant as he could.

Lieutenant Colonel Katherine Wiedemann carried a mike the size of a finger that let her voice fill up the hall. They hadn't had gadgets like that when Johnson went into cold sleep. "I want to thank you for your interest and attention," she said, and tacked on an emphatic cough. "Ever since the *Commodore Perry* got here and found you'd arrived safely, we've had to work out what would be best for you. This was especially challenging because so many of you are restricted to weightlessness. But now we have the answer for you."

"Not 'we think we have the answer.' Not 'we have an answer,' either," Mickey Flynn murmured. "Oh, no. 'We have *the* answer.' "

"Hush," Johnson said. But he took Flynn's point. These twenty-first-century Americans were a damned overbearing lot. They thought they could lord it over the twentieth-century crew of the *Admiral Peary* by virtue of owning forty more years of history. The evidence—and the power—were on their side, too.

"You will have a choice," Lieutenant Colonel Wiedemann said. She was blond and stern-looking—if anyone argued with her, she was liable to send him to the woodshed. "You may stay here aboard the *Admiral Peary* if you like. Or you may return to the Solar System in the *Tom Edison*."

No matter how stern she was, she had to pause there because everybody in the refectory started talking at once. Three people shouted the question that was also uppermost in Johnson's mind: "How? How do we do that?"

With the help of her strong little wireless mike, Lieutenant Colonel Wiedemann answered, "If you'll listen to me—*if you'll listen to me*—ladies and gentlemen, I'll tell you." She waited. The hubbub didn't stop, but it did diminish. At last, she nodded. "Thank you for your attention." She would have made a hell of a sixth-grade teacher. "We intend to send the *Tom Edison* off to the transition point at a lower acceleration than normal—just .05 g. Our medical experts are confident that this will not be dangerous even to those of you who have been weightless the longest. The journey will take longer because of the lower acceleration, but it will be safe." Again, she left no possible room for doubt.

This time, Johnson was one of the people calling questions: "What do we do when we get there?"

Maybe he was very loud. Or maybe she was going to answer that question next anyhow. "When you arrive in Earth orbit, you will have another choice," she declared. "You may stay in orbit, in weightlessness, on one of the U.S. space stations, for the rest of your lives. The stronger of you may also choose to settle at Moon Base Alpha or Moon Base Beta. The gravity on the Moon is .16 g. Permission to settle there will be granted only with the approval of physicians at the space stations."

Johnson tried to imagine himself with weight again. The trip back on the *Tom Edison* didn't worry him so much; his effective weight there would be about eight pounds. He exercised regularly, and was sure he could deal with that. But if he tried to go live on the Moon, he'd weigh about twenty-five pounds. That was enough to notice. Some people—Flynn, Stone, and Lieutenant General Healey, too—had been weightless even longer than he had, because they'd gone into cold sleep later. But it had still been close to twenty years by his body clock since he'd felt gravity.

"What do we do if we stay?" someone asked.

"In that case, you will remain aboard the *Admiral Peary,*" Lieutenant Colonel Wiedemann replied. "We will send replacements across from the *Tom Edison* to handle the jobs of those who elect to return to the Solar System. We want to continue to have an armed presence in the Tau Ceti system—and a monitoring presence, too. This ship is the only choice available for that until we have more FTL craft in service. That day is coming, but it is not yet here."

More questions followed, but those were the ones that mattered most. "What do you think?" Johnson asked Flynn as the gathering broke up.

"Interesting choice," the other pilot answered. "We can be obsolescent here or obsolete there."

That was about the size of it. Johnson said, "New faces back there."

Flynn twisted his not-so-new face into a not-so-happy expression. "By what I've seen from the *Commodore Perry* and the *Tom Edison,* new faces are overrated. They're an improvement on yours, sure, but that's not saying much."

"Gee, thanks a bunch," Johnson said. Mickey Flynn regally inclined his head.

Lieutenant General Healey zoomed past, as usual a bull in a china shop. "No, I'm not going anywhere," he said to anyone who would listen. "My assignment is commandant of the *Admiral Peary,* and I aim to carry it out. When I leave this ship, I'll leave feet first."

Johnson hadn't been in much doubt about what he would do. Hearing that removed the last traces of it. Going back to Earth would be strange. Seeing it and not being able to land on it would be frustrating. Spending the rest of his life with Lieutenant General Healey would be like going to hell before he died.

He didn't know how much that particular worry bothered other people, but a majority of the crew on the *Admiral Peary,* Mickey Flynn among them, applied to go back to the Solar System. Johnson wondered if Healey would try to hold him back, but the commandant didn't. Healey probably wanted to be rid of him as much as he wanted to be rid of Healey.

When a shuttlecraft took Johnson to the *Tom Edison,* his first thought was that the new starship felt much more finished than the *Admiral Peary* did. The *Admiral Peary* was a military ship first, last, and always, and had no frills or fanciness of any sort. The *Tom Edison*'s accommodations, though cramped, were far more comfortable. And computers had come a long way since the *Admiral Peary* left the Solar System. Johnson discovered he had access to an enormous library of films and television programs, including a whole great swarm that were new to him because they'd been made since he went on ice. He hoped that meant he wouldn't be bored on the way back to Earth.

No matter what Lieutenant Colonel Wiedemann said, he had worried about what owning any sort of weight again would do to him. But the tough-looking officer turned out to have known what she was talking about. The only time he really noticed he had weight was when he missed a handhold as he brachiated through the starship. Then he'd slowly glide to the floor instead of just floating along to the next one. His legs proved plenty strong to push him on to the next gripping point.

Mickey Flynn weighed more than eight pounds, but he also seemed to be coping well enough. "Nice to eat new meals," he remarked in the galley one day, then raised his hand in self-correction. "I should say, new styles of meal. We didn't eat the same supper over and over on the *Admiral Peary,* after all."

"No, it only seemed that way," Johnson agreed. "Of course, these ships don't have to recycle as much as we did. They can get resupplied whenever they come back to the Solar System. We were out there for the long haul."

"It certainly seemed like a long haul," Flynn said, and Johnson couldn't very well argue with that.

He dutifully lay down on his bunk when the ship neared the transition point. The warning announcement said that some people felt what it described as "unusually intense vertigo." That didn't sound like a whole lot of fun. What he felt when the *Tom Edison* leaped the light-years was . . . exactly nothing. He shrugged. Anyone who suffered from vertigo wasn't going to make it as a pilot.

That evening in the refectory, he asked Flynn whether *he'd* felt anything. "Not me," the other pilot replied. "I'm normal."

"God help us all, in that case," Johnson said. Flynn looked aggrieved. He did it very well. Johnson wondered if he practiced in front of a mirror.

Seeing Earth again, even if only on a video screen, brought a lump to Johnson's throat. He'd got occasional glimpses of the home planet when he was out in the asteroid belt on the *Lewis and Clark*. But a blue star near a shrunken sun wasn't the same as seeing oceans and clouds and continents—and there, by God, there was the United States. Clouds covered most of the eastern half of the country, but he didn't care. He knew it was there.

When the *Tom Edison*'s shuttlecraft took him to a space station, he found a tall mound of paperwork to remind him in another way that he'd come home. He formally retired from the Marine Corps and discovered just how much money he had to draw on. "This doesn't include the living allowance you'll have here," said the functionary handling his case. "This is accumulated pay and interest."

"It's mighty interesting," Johnson allowed. He really could be a sugar daddy down below—if it weren't for gravity. Up here? He wasn't so sure about that. Finding out could also be mighty interesting, though.

The functionary looked pained. "Do all you Rip van Winkles make bad puns?"

"Ah, you've been dealing with Mickey Flynn," Johnson said, and surprised the man all over again.

"Will you want to stay here in weightlessness, or would you rather settle in one of the bases on the Moon?" the modern asked.

"I don't know yet. Do I have to decide right away?" Johnson replied.

Reluctantly, the other man shook his head. "No, not yet. But the longer you stay weightless, the harder it will be for your body to get used to the Moon's gravity—if it can at all."

"I've been weightless for years and years," Johnson answered. "I don't think a few days to make up my mind will kill me or my chances."

The longer he stayed at the space station, the less inclined he was to leave. It was a much busier operation than any he'd known in space before leaving Earth's orbit. Of course, that was almost seventy years ago now. In those days, space travel had been almost exclusively military. Nowadays, this place was a tourist trap.

He shopped. He spent money in stores and bars. That felt strange, after doing without cash and credit cards for so long. In one of those bars, he met a woman from Cincinnati who hadn't been born when he went into cold sleep. Donna thought he talked a little funny (he thought everybody these days talked a little funny), but she thought he was interesting, too. One thing most enjoyably led to another.

"I've never done it weightless before," she said in his chamber. "It's different."

"Yeah." It had been a hell of a long time since Johnson had done it any other way. It had, in his opinion, been too damn long since he'd done it at all.

"What do you think about being back after all the things you did and all the places you went to?" she asked.

"Well, right this minute I like it fine," he answered. That made her laugh, though he was kidding on the square. In an odd way, the encounter—which lasted only a day—made up his mind. This wasn't Earth, but it was the next best thing. He'd stay here.

Kassquit stared down at the little female hatchling in her arms. She'd already known that Tosevite hatchlings were much less able to fend for themselves than those of the Race. In the twenty days since hers came forth, she'd seen that again and again for herself.

But the hatchling did know how to feed itself, and sucked

greedily now. Kassquit's breasts were still tender, but she was getting used to nursing. It wasn't anything the Race would do—it wasn't anything the Race *could* do—but it had a satisfaction of its own. And she was convinced it helped forge the emotional attachment between mother and hatchling that formed such an important part of Tosevite society.

Along with things like that, she was finally learning some English. Having a word to describe *nursing* instead of the long circumlocution she would have needed in the Race's language came in handy. And, since the hatchling hadn't exactly hatched, *baby* seemed more precise. Because it was female, it was a *daughter.* Had it been male, it would have been a *son.* That puzzled her, because she thought *son* was also the word for a star. Sooner or later, she hoped it would make sense. As with a lot of things that had to do with wild Big Uglies, though, she recognized that it might not.

Someone knocked on the door. That had to be a Tosevite; a member of the Race would have used the hisser. "Come in," Kassquit called. "It is not locked."

She'd hoped it would be Frank Coffey, and it was. "I greet you," he said, and then, to the baby, "and I greet you, too, Julia."

"And I greet you," Kassquit answered, "and so does Yendys, even if she cannot tell you so because her mouth is full." That wasn't the only reason the baby couldn't talk, of course. Coffey's chuckle showed he knew she'd made a joke. They both agreed the baby should have two names, since it had two heritages.

"How are you feeling?" asked Julia Yendys' *father*— another English word Kassquit had come to know.

"Day by day, I get stronger," Kassquit answered. She would much rather have laid an egg than gone through what Tosevite females did to produce an offspring. Unfortunately, she hadn't had the choice. The Tosevite physician had seemed capable enough, but he couldn't make the process any too delightful. And afterwards, as soon as it was finally over, she'd felt as if a herd of zisuili had trampled her. Little by little, that crushing exhaustion faded, but only little by little.

The baby swallowed wrong, choked, and started to *cry.* Having one word for the horrible noises a baby made was useful, too—not pleasant, but useful. Kassquit put a cloth on her shoulder and raised Julia Yendys to it. She patted the baby's back till it expelled the air it had swallowed—and some sour milk. That was what the cloth was for. Bare skin didn't do the job.

She'd got the cloth from the American Big Uglies. They used such materials much more than the Race did and were better at manufacturing them, just as the Race knew things about paint that the Tosevites hadn't imagined. She patted Julia Yendys' face with the cloth. "Are you done now?" she asked. As usual, the baby gave not a clue.

"Let me hold her," Coffey said. Kassquit passed him the baby. He was bigger than she was, and could comfortably hold his daughter in the crook of his arm. He had had no off-spring till this one, but he still seemed more practiced with her than Kassquit did. He crooned vaguely musical nonsense to the baby.

"What is that song?" Kassquit asked.

"We call it a *lullaby*," he answered. "Sometimes, it helps make a baby go to sleep. Since she has just had some food and she is still dry—I stuck a finger in there to check—maybe this will be one of those times."

And Julia Yendys' eyes did sag shut. Coffey also had an easier time than Kassquit at getting her to go to sleep. Kassquit sometimes resented that. Right now, it came as a relief. The baby stirred when Coffey eased her down into the crib—which had made the trip from Tosev 3 on the *Tom Edison*—but did not wake.

Kassquit stared down at her. "She is halfway between the two of us in color," she said.

"Not surprising," Coffey said. "We both have something to do with her, you know."

Kassquit made the affirmative gesture. "Truth. But I am used to the Race. All the subspecies that used to exist here have mixed together till it is practically uniform. I know that is not true for Tosevites, but here I see a beginning of such blending."

Frank Coffey shrugged. "Our subspecies were mostly iso-lated till much more recently than those of the Race. And we are also more particular about whom we mate with than the

Race is. Males and females of one Tosevite subspecies often prefer a partner from that same group."

"Not always." Kassquit set a hand on his arm.

He covered it with his own hand. "I did not say 'always.' I said 'often.' I know the difference between the two. But that also helps make mixing slower with us."

"I understand," Kassquit said. "Do you suppose Tosevites will ever become as blended as the Race is now?"

"Before the *Commodore Perry* came to Home, I would have said yes," Coffey replied. "Now I am not so sure. Some of the groups that form colonies will all come from one kind of Tosevite or another. On their new worlds, they will breed only with themselves. Colonies are much easier to start now, which also means that isolation of subspecies is easier to preserve."

"That is not good, especially when members of some of your subspecies think they are better than others," Kassquit observed.

The wild Big Ugly laughed, though he did not seem amused. "Members of *all* our subspecies think they are better than others," he said, and added an emphatic cough. "I think that is too bad, but I have no idea what to do about it."

"How will it affect the Empire?" Kassquit asked.

"I have no idea about that, either," he told her. "Anyone who says he knows now is lying. We can only wait and see. It depends on many things."

"How soon the Race learns to travel that way," Kassquit said. "How soon the Deutsche do, too. Whether you Americans decide on a preventive war against us."

"And whether the Race decides to try to destroy Tosev 3," Coffey added. Kassquit made the affirmative gesture; that did also enter in. The American went on, "Too many variables, not enough data. We have to find out. I already said that."

Kassquit wanted certainty. She'd learned that from the Race. She couldn't have it. Every time Tosevites touched her life, certainty exploded. Every time the wild Big Uglies touched the Race, its certainties from millennia past exploded.

She looked down at Julia Yendys, who'd exploded the certainty that she would never breed. She still didn't know what to think about that. Raising a Tosevite hatchling was an astonishing amount of work. She began to understand why family groupings loomed so large among the wild Big Uglies. Without them, hatchlings—*babies*—would die. It was as simple as that.

"Wait until the baby begins to *smile*," Frank Coffey said. "It will not be too much longer. That is a day to remember."

"Maybe. But I cannot return the smile. I never learned how." Kassquit imagined herself as a hatchling, trying again and again to bond with Ttomalss through facial expressions. But Ttomalss wasn't biologically programmed to respond, and so her own ability to form those expressions had atrophied. She didn't want that to happen to Julia Yendys. Her own baby should be a citizen of the Empire, yes, but should also be a complete and perfect Tosevite.

"Do not worry too much," Coffey said. "I promise I will smile lots and lots for my daughter." After an emphatic cough, he pulled back his lips and showed his teeth in a big grin. "And there will be plenty of other wild Big Uglies to show her how to make funny faces." He made a very funny one, crossing his eyes and sticking out his tongue.

It startled Kassquit into a laugh. "That is good," she said. "I was just thinking the baby should have more of its Tosevite heritage than I do."

That made the American Big Ugly serious again. "Well, you were raised to be as much like a member of the Race as possible. I would not want that for Julia Yendys, and I am glad you do not, either."

"What I want for her is the chance to grow up and live out her life in peace and happiness. How likely do you think that is?"

Frank Coffey sighed and shrugged. "Kassquit, I already told you—I have no better way to judge that than you do. I just do not know. All we can do is go on and hope and do all we can to make that happen, even if we know it may not. If we do not try—if the United States and the Race do not try— then we are much too likely to fail."

"What would you do if there were a war?" Kassquit asked.

"Probably die," he answered. She gave back an exasperated hiss, one that might have sprung from the throat of either a

Tosevite or a member of the Race. He shrugged again. "I do not know what else to say. It would depend on what happened, on where I was, on a thousand other things. I cannot know ahead of time."

That was reasonable. Kassquit had hoped for a ringing declaration that he would never fight no matter what, but a little thought told her that was too much to expect. He served the United States with as much dedication as she served the Empire, and he was a military male. If his not-empire required him to fight, fight he would.

He said, "You should have the baby immunized against as many of our diseases as you can. She will meet many more wild Tosevites at an earlier age than you did."

"I have already talked about this with the new doctor," Kassquit said. "He agrees with you that this would be good. I will follow his advice. He also urges me to get more immunizations, for the reason you mentioned. Faster-than-light travel will mean more Tosevites coming to Home, which will mean more chances for disease to spread."

"Good. Not good that disease may spread—good that you and the doctor have thought about it," Coffey said. "He does seem to know what he is doing. Call me old-fashioned—I cannot help it, considering when I was hatched—but a lot of the moderns get under my scales and make me itch." He had no scales to get under, but used the Race's phrase all the same.

Kassquit made the affirmative gesture. "This doctor knows much more than Melanie Blanchard did. I am sure of that. But I liked her, while when I see him it is all business."

"He is a better technician, but a poorer person," Coffey said.

"Truth! That is what I was trying to say."

"You do what you can with what you have. I do not know what else there is to do," Coffey said. "The other choice is not doing what you can with what you have, and that is worse. If you do not make the most of what you have, why live?"

"Truth," Kassquit said once more.

Have I made the most of what I have? she wondered. Looking back, she didn't see how she could have done much more. Some things she did not have, and never would. She could rail at Ttomalss for that, but what was the point? Her upbringing was what it was. She couldn't change it now. She remained bright. Even by Tosevite standards, she remained within hissing distance of sanity. And she'd had—she'd really had—an audience with the Emperor!

She looked down at Julia Yendys once more. Now she also had a chance to make her baby's life better than hers had been. That was a chance members of the Race didn't get, not in the same way. She intended to make the most of it.

When the telephone rang, Sam Yeager jumped like a startled cat. He'd been deep in work—deeper than he'd thought, obviously. Well, it wasn't going anywhere. He walked over to the phone. "Hello?"

"Hi, Dad. What are you up to?"

"Oh, hello, Jonathan. I was reading the galleys for *Safe at Home,* as a matter of fact. They've got a tight deadline, and I want to make sure I get 'em done on time."

"Good for you," his son said. "Catch any juicy mistakes?"

"I think the best one was when 'American helmet' came out as 'American Hamlet.' That would have spread confusion far and wide if it got through."

Jonathan laughed. "You're not kidding. Are you too busy to come over for dinner tonight? I hope not—Karen's got some mighty nice steaks."

"Twist my arm," Sam said, and then, "What time?"

"About six," Jonathan answered.

"See you then." Sam hung up. He looked at his watch. It was a quarter past four. He worked on the galleys for a little while longer, spotting nothing more entertaining than "form" for "from." Like the one he'd told Jonathan about, that passed muster on a computerized spelling program. Most of the errors he found were of that sort. The rest came on words and place names from the Lizards' language: terms that weren't in spelling programs to being with. With those, typesetters could inflict butchery as they had in years gone by.

He set down the red pen, put on a pair of slacks instead of the ratty jeans he'd been wearing, and went down to his car. On the way to Jonathan and Karen's place, he stopped in a liquor store for a six-pack of beer. He remembered being disappointed with Budweiser ninety years ago, when it started reousting local beers after the first round of fighting between humans and Lizards ended. Things hadn't got better up till he went into cold sleep. Bud and Miller and Schlitz and a couple of others had swept all before them. They were available, they were standardized, they were cheap . . . and they weren't very interesting.

But while he'd been on ice, beer had had a renaissance. Oh, the national brands were still around. Even their packaging hadn't changed much. But, to make up for it, swarms of little breweries turned out beer that cost more but made up for it by not only tasting good but by tasting good in a bunch of different ways. Who wanted to drink fizzy water with a little alcohol in it when porter and steam beer and barley wine were out there, too?

Jonathan laughed when Sam handed him the mix-and-match six-pack. "It'll go with what I went out and bought," he said.

"Fine. If I get smashed, you can put me on the couch tonight," Sam said.

"If *I* get smashed, Karen'll put me on the couch tonight," his son said. "You can sleep on the floor."

"If I'm smashed enough, I won't care." Sam sniffed. "Besides, I'll be full of good food." He pitched his voice to carry into the kitchen.

"You're a nice man," Karen called from that direction.

The steaks were as good as promised, butter-tender and rare enough to moo. "What we had on Home wasn't bad," Sam said after doing some serious damage to the slab of cow in front of him. "It wasn't bad at all. We didn't have any trouble living on it. But this tastes *right* in a way that never could."

"I've heard Lizards say the same thing, but with the opposite twist," Jonathan said. "They don't mind what they get here, but to them the good stuff is back on Home."

"I'm not convinced," Karen said. "Put us in Japan and we'll think Japanese food is weird, too. Japanese people feel the same way about what we eat. A lot of it has to do with cooking styles and spices, not with the basic meat and vegetables. A lot more has to do with whether we're used to eating what's in front of us. Sometimes different is just different, not better or worse or right or wrong."

Sam thought about that. After a few seconds, he nodded. "I've been used to eating my words for years, so they don't taste bad at all. You're right. I'm sure of it."

No matter what he'd said to Jonathan, he didn't get drunk. Back when he was a kid, he'd thought tying one on was fun. He wondered why. Part of it, he supposed, was coming to manhood during Prohibition. He was one of the last men alive who remembered it, and wondered if they even bothered teaching about it in U.S. history these days. It would be ancient history to kids growing up now, the way the presidency of John Quincy Adams had been for him.

But he'd gone right on getting smashed after drinking became legal again. A lot of his teammates had been hard drinkers. That wasn't enough of an excuse for him, though, and he knew it. He'd enjoyed getting loaded. He hadn't enjoyed it so much the morning after, but that was later. He wondered why he'd enjoyed it. Because it gave him an excuse to get stupid? That didn't seem reason enough, not looking back on it.

Jonathan and Karen also held it to a couple of beers. He knew they'd done their share of drinking before he went on ice and stopped being able to keep an eye on them. He laughed at himself. No doubt they'd missed that a lot—just the way a frog missed a saxophone. They'd done fine without him, which was, of course, the way things were supposed to work.

He drove home with no trouble at all. His head was clear enough to work on the manuscript for a while before he went to bed. When he got up the next morning, he didn't have a headache. He didn't have any memories of stupidity or, worse, holes where he needed to find memories.

Aren't I smug and superior? he thought as he sipped his morning coffee the next day. He was more sober than he had been once upon a time. So what? All over the world, people by the millions needed no excuse at all to drink as much as they could hold, or a little more than that.

He'd just come out of the shower when the phone rang.

That made him smile: whoever'd tried to catch him in there had missed. "Hello?"

"Yes. Is this Sam Yeager that I have the honor to be addressing?"

Alertness tingled through Sam. Though speaking English, that was a Lizard on the other end of the line. "Yes, this is Sam Yeager. Who's calling, please?" Talking to members of the Race, once one of Sam's greatest pleasures, was fraught with risk these days. They still hoped he might have a message from Home for them. The American government still feared he did. He didn't, and wouldn't have delivered it if he had. Nobody—not Lizards, not American officials—wanted to believe him when he said so.

"I am Tsaisanx, the Race's consul in Los Angeles."

Sam whistled softly. Tsaisanx should have known better. He'd been consul here for a human lifetime, and was a veteran of the conquest fleet. If he didn't know better than to call here . . . maybe it was a mark of desperation. "I greet you, Consul," Sam said, using the Race's formula but sticking to English. "You do know, I hope, that anything we say will be monitored? You had better tell me very plainly what you want."

Tsaisanx let out a hissing sigh. "I would rather talk in greater privacy. . . ."

"I wouldn't." Sam used an emphatic cough. "I have nothing to say that others can't hear. Nothing—do you understand me?"

"I cannot believe that," Tsaisanx said. "You aided us before. Why not now?"

"I helped you when I thought we were wrong," Sam said. "I'm not going to help you when I think we're right. So we know something the Race doesn't? All I have to say is, good for us. We didn't do anything we shouldn't have to learn it. All we did was make experiments and see where they led. If you want to do the same thing, okay, fine. Go right ahead."

"You are not showing a cooperative attitude," the Race's consul complained.

"Tough." Sam used another emphatic cough. "I'm very sorry, but I don't feel like cooperating here. Not only that, I damn well can't. Am I plain enough, or shall I draw you a picture?" He was about to hang up on the Lizard, a bit of rudeness he couldn't have imagined before coming back to Earth on the *Commodore Perry.*

"You are painfully plain." Tragedy trembled in Tsaisanx's voice. "What is also plain is that my civilization—indeed, my entire species—trembles on the brink of extinction. And you—you do not feel like cooperating."

"I'm afraid I can't be polite about this, so I won't bother trying," Sam said. "When the conquest fleet came, you intended to do to us what you did to the Rabotevs and the Hallessi. You were going to turn us into imitations of the Race and rule us forever. If we didn't like it, too bad. You were ready to kill as many of us as you needed to get the message across. I was there, too. I remember. If you think I'm going to waste a hell of a lot of sympathy on you now, you'd better think again. That's all I've got to tell you."

"Rabotev 2 and Halless 1 are both better, happier, healthier worlds than they were before they became part of the Empire," Tsaisanx said. "Tosev 3 also would have been. We would have made sure of it."

Take up the white man's burden, Sam thought. He didn't doubt that Tsaisanx meant it; the Lizard was nothing if not sincere. All the same, he said, "The United States is a better, happier, healthier place than it was before you got here, and we did it all by ourselves."

"How much of our technology did you steal?" Acid filled Tsaisanx's voice.

"A good bit," Sam admitted. "But we would have done it without that, too. If you'd never come, we'd be better and healthier and happier than we were ninety years ago. We wouldn't be the same as we are now, but we wouldn't be the same as we were back then, either. You think progress is something to squash. We think it's something to build on. And we would have, with you or without you."

"We really have nothing to say to each other, do we?" Tsaisanx said sadly. "And here all this time, I thought you understood."

"I do—or I think I do, anyhow," Sam replied. "I just don't agree. There's a difference."

"Farewell." Tsaisanx hung up.

"So long," Sam said, though the Lizard couldn't hear him. He put the handset back in the cradle. Shaking his head, he returned to the galleys of *Safe at Home.*

A minute later, he stood up again. He couldn't concentrate on the words in front of him. All these years, all these upheavals, and what did it mean? His own people thought he'd betrayed them, and now the Lizards thought he'd betrayed them, too? He wondered if he should have called the book *A Moderate's Story.* What was a moderate but somebody both sides could shoot at?

But he still thought he'd had it right with Tsaisanx. Even if the Race hadn't come, the United States would be a better place now than it was in 1942. The rest of the world might be better, too, in ways it had never had a chance to show with the Lizards sitting on half of it.

He shrugged and returned to the galleys. He'd already seen so much happen, more than almost any man alive. He'd gone from horse and buggy to spanning the light-years one way in cold sleep, the other in the wink of an eye.

And what would the next chapter be? He could hardly wait to find out.